young pushkin

Yury Tynyanov

Young Pushkin

A NOVEL

TRANSLATED FROM THE RUSSIAN BY
ANNA KURKINA RUSH AND CHRISTOPHER RUSH

OVERLOOK/ROOKERY
NEW YORK, NEW YORK

YOUNG PUSHKIN

This edition first published in The United States of America in 2008 by
The Rookery Press, Tracy Carns Ltd.
in association with The Overlook Press
141 Wooster Street
New York, NY 10012
www.therookerypress.com

Translation, introduction, and notes copyright © Anna Kurkina Rush and Christopher Rush
First published in Great Britain by Angel Books

Cataloging-in-Publication Data is on file at the Library of Congress

Printed in the United States of America
FIRST EDITION

ISBN 978-1-58567-962-1
1 3 5 7 9 8 6 4 2

Contents

All the characters in this novel
existed in real life

Introduction

WHAT Pushkin means to Russians was memorably described by the poet Aleksandr Blok in his speech delivered at a celebration of the 84th anniversary of Pushkin's death on 11 February (29 January Old Style) 1921 at the House of Literature, St Petersburg:

> From early childhood we have had one cheering name in our minds: Pushkin. This sound, this name has filled many of the days of our lives. There are the gloomy names of emperors, generals, inventors of instruments of death, torturers and martyrs. And beside these stands one bright name: Pushkin.

It is hardly surprising that Yury Tynyanov, one of the most compelling and original of twentieth-century Russian writers, should have devoted the final part of his planned trilogy on nineteenth-century Russian literary figures to the (eventual) author of *Eugene Onegin, Boris Godunov, Mozart and Salieri, The Bronze Horseman, The Queen of Spades, The Captain's Daughter, The Tale of the Golden Cockerel* and lyrics such as 'I remember the wonderful moment' and 'I loved you'.

Pushkin's period had striking similarities to Tynyanov's own. It was a time of restlessness, foreign invasion, and rapid political change veering from a heady breaking of shackles to sombre repression. Progressive ideas and individuals emerged, only to be dropped and abandoned. The unique school attended by Pushkin for six years, the Lycée established by the Tsar in a wing of the palace in Tsarskoye Selo, symbolised the early part of the new era. It was a product of the Enlightenment sweeping through Russia following the reign of the harsh tyrant Paul I. It was staffed by specialists from the best European universities, there was no corporal punishment, and education took place in a spirit of equality and free intellectual enquiry (though a respect for religion was maintained). The aim of the school was to produce enlightened graduates who would take up high posts; they were sorely needed in a Russia mired in corruption and the excesses of slavery. When the Lycée was opened in 1811, with Pushkin in the first intake, the abolition of serfdom and the creation of a parliament were in the air. Six years later the whole political atmosphere had changed. Alexander I, previously known as 'the tsar-liberator', was now advised by reactionary conservatives and religious obscurantists, and it was not long before the uncontrollable pen of the twenty-one-year-old Pushkin, already a famous poet, earned him exile: here *Young Pushkin* ends.

Yury Tynyanov was born in 1894 in Vitebsk province in what is now Latvia, the younger son of a doctor. He was educated at a grammar school in Pskov and St Petersburg/Petrograd University. From an early age, literature was what he lived for. By the age of seventeen he had read virtually the whole of Russian literature as well as the Greek and Roman poets. He referred to the great Russian authors by their first names and patronymics, as if they were members of his family. Pushkin was the writer he most worshipped, identifying with him at one time to the point of growing sideburns to look like him.

Graduating from Petrograd University in 1918 in history and literature, Tynyanov proceeded to pursue a stellar career as a prolific literary historian and a highly respected and popular lecturer. A professor of literature at the Petrograd Institute of History of the Arts, by the mid-1920s, alongside Roman Jakobson, Viktor Shklovksy and Boris Eikhenbaum, he had become a leading figure of Russian Formalism, the most important of the non-Marxist literary groups that flourished after the Revolution. For several years he was head of the scenario department of Sevzapkino (later Lenfilm). An intellectual and a visionary, Tynyanov never lived in an academic ivory tower; the other side of his personality embraced a talent for impersonation, caricature and word play.

In 1925 he surprised his friends and colleagues by producing a novel, *Küchlya*, about the poet Wilhelm Küchelbecker, a Lycée friend of Pushkin's. This made Tynyanov the founding father of the Soviet historical novel – an ironical definition considering that he was a product of the tsarist system of education and therefore liable to be branded a fellow traveller. But like many Russian intellectuals, Tynyanov welcomed the Bolshevik Revolution and worked to the best of his ability to implement its ideals. 'If there had been no revolution, I should never have understood literature', he said on one occasion. Undoubtedly, witnessing one of the greatest civil upheavals of the twentieth century gave him a keen understanding of history in the making.

By the late 1920s the new regime showed itself to be more restrictive towards freedom of speech than its predecessor. Tynyanov's novels reflect his personal intellectual odyssey as well as the general disillusionment of the intelligentsia, who had walked trustingly and willingly into a fatal historical trap. Whereas his first, highly acclaimed novel dealt with the Decembrist Uprising of 1825, in which Küchelbecker took part, prepared to sacrifice his life for the higher cause, Tynyanov's next, published three years later, had a different tonality: disappointment, betrayal, unrealised potential, wasted talent, and death by savage murder. *The Death of Vazir Mukhtar** dealt with the tragic last year in the life of the dramatist-diplomat Aleksandr Griboyedov, another of Pushkin's contemporaries, author of the celebrated verse comedy *Woe from Wit*. Bolshevik reviewers of the novel deprecated the dark mood and accused Tynyanov of 'vulgar sociology'; the wider public, however, loved it, as it did all his fiction.

In 1930 Tynyanov resigned his post at the Institute when it changed its orientation. Multiple sclerosis had already been diagnosed, but he kept on working incessantly, living fast and hard, only too well aware of the brevity of life. From 1928, when *Küchlya* was published, until 1935, when his crowning achievement, the novel *Pushkin*, began to be serialised, he also wrote three historical novellas, a number of film scripts and essays on film and film criticism, essays on the history of Russian literature, reviews of contemporary poetry, and did much editorial work – all with brilliance and apparently effortlessly. By 1940, however, Tynyanov had become almost entirely immobilised. In 1943 he was terminally ill; his sight was failing him and he was drifting in and out of consciousness. Even in this extremity, the very mention of the name of Pushkin would revive him somewhat and cause his lips to move. Somewhere in the darkness inside him he was reciting his hero's poems.

He died at the early age of forty-nine at the end of 1943, leaving a number of projects unrealised. Both his fiction and his scholarly work remained out of print after his death until after the 'Thaw' of 1956, but thereafter *Pushkin* and his other novels and stories achieved classic status in Russia and have been avidly read ever since.

The first two parts of *Pushkin* were serialised in the literary journal *Literaturnyy sovremennik* ('Contemporary Literature') in 1935–37, and the third part, unrevised and unchecked by the author, in *Znamya* ('Banner') in 1943.

It was Tynyanov's mission, his destiny, to write this novel. He wrote it partly to address and explore what he considered to be the burning issues of the day, the personal freedom of the individual in society and his relation to that society, partly to dispel the existing myths about the untouchable god that Pushkin had become to Russians in the early decades of the twentieth century, and partly to examine and portray the character of the poet both from within and without, and to do so not merely by an effort of the imagination but also by meticulous research. No one consulted documents or

* Translated (abridged) by A. Brown with the title *Death and Diplomacy in Persia*, London, 1938.

examined archives as Tynyanov did, and no one knew more about Pushkin. His methods were encyclopedic, and he was scrupulously honest in his efforts to uncover the truth as he saw it. He succeeds in dismantling the Russian cult of Pushkin as a god. The poet is portrayed for 'what he was', not as his unthinking admirers would have him, a porcelain poet, prettified on a pedestal. In doing so Tynyanov also addresses some large themes – truth, evil, the nature of poetry and of genius.

'I conceived the novel,' he said in an interview, 'not as a fictionalised biography, but as an epic on the origins, development and death of our national poet. I don't distinguish in the novel between the hero's life and his work, and I don't distinguish between his work and his country's history.' *Young Pushkin* is a unique blend of scholarship and art. Tynyanov thinks cinematographically, uses montage and stream of consciousness, *becomes* his character, disappears authorially from time to time. The force and humanity of his work as well as its deep psychological insights into a wide variety of characters appeal to a reader who might know nothing about Pushkin. Further themes are explored arising from but outside the central concern of the main character: East and West; Slavophiles and Francophiles; the destiny of Russia; how its past affects its future; tyranny and freedom; the problem of the isolation and vulnerability of the intellectual in Russia. While under Stalin the novel's subject-matter protected Tynyanov from persecution, it also allowed him the secret licence to comment on the present under the camouflage of the past, in much the same way that Shakespeare commented on the politics of his time from under a Roman toga or a Greek helmet.

Tynyanov's intention was to cover Pushkin's entire life. His premature death robbed us of a work that might have taken on Proustian proportions. But fortunately, this first volume of the planned scheme, covering Pushkin's childhood and youth, is a complete novel in itself, and we feel justified in titling our translation accordingly.

Pushkin's emotional life, the growth of his mind and personality, and also the life of the society of the time, the first two decades of the nineteenth century, are opened up on an intimate, everyday level in a dazzling panorama of the human, social and political forces that played their part in the development of Russia's greatest poet. Dealing with a period of Pushkin's life much less well documented than his later years, Tynyanov presents a panoply of characters who do not come in for anything approaching such space, concentrated attention, psychological fascination or vividness of portrayal in even the best biographies. Given the scarcity of known biographical facts, Tynyanov's creation of Pushkin's childhood and schooldays is taken by Russians for the real thing.

The extraordinary degree to which Pushkin comes to life springs largely from Tynyanov's ability to recreate the whole world in which he lives and everyone in it, from his nanny to the Tsar. For much of the novel we don't see Pushkin at all: we are with his father and uncle at their literary soirées, his mother taking possession of an inherited estate, the Lycée staff and their preoccupations, the Tsar and his ministers. When we do see him, Tynyanov has the genius not to give us too much: as in life, we get glimpses and moments face to face, but what happens and what we see in those moments can be unforgettable. Details such as Pushkin's sudden high-pitched scream of a laugh, the way he turns pale when hearing poetry that impresses him, or runs out of a room when moved, or is roused to fury by any kind of prying into his activities – here is the electricity of a living person. His own mindset is both shared with the world around him and totally, jealously his own, and we seem to get the full force of his innermost thoughts, feelings and impressions.

Tynyanov's presentation of Pushkin's parents is characteristic of his approach. Sergey Lvovich, his father, has been written off by biographers as 'a colossal lump of egotism ... [with] a measure of self-pity altogether offensive' (Simmons); 'an overgrown, selfish, spoiled, sentimental, sensual baby' (Troyat); 'at his best in some salon ... inscribing elegant sentiments in ... ladies' albums' (Binyon). According to Tynyanov, none of this is true, and all such simplifications falsify and distort history. The truth as Tynyanov sees it is that Sergey Lvovich, though a drifter and dreamer and a work-shy little fop, left his son a greater legacy even than the freedom of his library. Sergey Lvovich was a restless fantasist whose imaginative streak went into his son – equipped by genius to harness and utilise what we might risk calling the inherited imagination. Tynyanov does not proceed to judgement on Sergey Lvovich, he understands him and humanises him instead.

If Sergey Lvovich has had a bad biographical press, the poet's mother, Nadezhda Osipovna, has been virtually vilified. We learn little about her from her son's biographers beyond her vanity, bad house-keeping, irascibility and tendency to sulk for days on end; and of course her neglect of Aleksandr and the punishments she invented to cure his awkwardness and bad habits. But Tynyanov's treatment of this woman, so physically attractive and yet so apparently undesirable, is revealing in its sympathetic insights and, once again, its suggestion of just how much Pushkin took from his parents. Tynyanov introduces her as 'an extraordinary creature', encouraging admiration rather than criticism, and hinting at her exotic ancestry – she was a granddaughter of Peter the Great's favourite brought from Africa, Abram Hannibal – and often instinctual actions, the psychological springs that help explain, if not excuse, both her behavioural problems and her son's 'African' anger. Pushkin's passions, like his poetic power, sprang from a deep source, and whatever the flighty characteristics he may have inherited from his father, there seems little doubt that the primitive fury of which he was capable must have come in large measure from *la belle Créole*.

Tynyanov's ability to convince us of 'reality' owes much to his deliberate adoption of a linguistic strategy. He used his enormous knowledge to study the idiom of Pushkin's time and fuse it with the idiom of his own, thus recreating the authentic voice and pulse of the Alexandrine era. In our translation we have not attempted anything similar in English terms, but have simply done our best to avoid both archaisms and the extremes of modern idiom and vocabulary.

Tynyanov's very distinctive style, however, and his 'mosaic technique', can come through in translation. *Young Pushkin* is made up of condensed episodes and short scenes from multiple viewpoints, including a section from a diary; epigrams and other snatches of verse, Pushkin's and other poets', run through the whole. The elliptic, stabbing style, abounding in short, sometimes verbless sentences, seems to give us the characters' unmediated thoughts and emotions. It is a style redolent of cinema.

Young Pushkin cannot be classified as a straightforward historical novel; it sits more subtly and secretively among the genres – fictionalized biography, historical fiction, psychological novel. The reader seems to see old negatives from the archives suddenly developing and becoming moving images of life, startling us by their individuality and immediacy. Sergey Lvovich and Nadezhda Osipovna are only two of an extensive gallery of the people who left their impression on Pushkin or significantly impinged on his life: leading figures of state, peasants, educationists and teachers, writers. His grandfather, the lecherous Osip Hannibal, and great-uncle, the alcoholic social disaster Pyotr Hannibal, leap to life, as do his uncle Vasily Lvovich who achieved notoriety as a scurrilous poet of some talent, the famous old poet Derzhavin, the contradictory Tsar Alexander I, the visionary reforming minister Speransky (who conceived the idea of the Lycée) and less sympathetic advisers and ministers of state – Count Arakcheyev, the architect of Russia's slide back from reform, the idle Count Razumovsky, and the rake turned religious bigot Prince Golitsyn, the last two being successive education ministers. Two key characters are the influential writer, moderniser of the Russian language and imperial historiographer Karamzin, a family friend of the Pushkins, and his lovely, lonely second wife, Katerina Andreyevna. Pushkin himself is portrayed from a variety of perspectives.

For some individuals – and Pushkin is an example – history is one of the pressures moulding the individual life. Thus Tynyanov turns the famous family story of the hat into an illustration of how close Pushkin came to history, even as an infant. Tsar Paul I is supposed to have passed by with his military entourage when he saw the one-year-old Pushkin out with his nurse Arina, and reprimanded her for failing to take off the infant's cap in the presence of royalty, ordering her to rectify the insult to his person immediately. Tynyanov relates this episode partly through the eyes of the panic-stricken Sergey Lvovich, who milks it for all it is worth. True, false or exaggerated, it is a dramatically memorable image: the mounted Emperor not only threatening the nanny but sawing at the reins so that the horse's prancing hooves tread the air inches above the infant's bared head. You can't get much closer to history than that.

Twelve years later, in 1812, Pushkin stands outside the Lycée watching the Russian troops on the move and cheering them on, wishing he could go to war. Tynyanov had Tolstoy's genius for humanizing history, though his treatment is more subtle and understated than Tolstoy's and he never hectors the reader. He takes us through the entire 1812 campaign, from Napoleon's invasion to the Grande Armée's wretched retreat from Moscow, seen from the touchlines by schoolboys; the result is sometimes amusing, sometimes poignant, always startlingly dramatic and revealing of the growth of Pushkin the poet.

We see Pushkin fully and freshly revealed in settings and situations that have hitherto been nothing more than passing references in indexes of biographies: lost in the Usupov garden in Moscow, sampling the erotica in his father's library, strangely unaffected at his brother Nikolay's funeral, developing his fiercely independent character at the Lycée as well as forming life-long bonds with his classmates,* seeing off oppressive staff – and of course perpetually scratching out poems completely oblivious of what is going on around him; beginning his adult life by visiting the hussars, the theatres, the brothels of the capital; and finally, en route to the Caucasus and the Crimea to begin his exile for over-daring liberal verse and sharp lampoons on high-placed figures.

Tynyanov was a dying man as he worked on the third and last part of the novel, the shortest. It is pressurised prose, and you can hear the ticking clock and perhaps even something of the panic it inspired. But this seems only to heighten the sense of breathless excitement and yearning that pervades these last pages.

As the novel hastens towards its conclusion, there is one thing about which Tynyanov has no doubt: the identity of the love of Pushkin's life, over which many have puzzled ... The book brims with Pushkin's responses to women – girl servants, sisters of his fellow Lycéeists, his uncle's mistress, a 'nymph'

---

* Some of whom had notable later lives: the rebel poet Küchelbecker, subject of Tynyanov's first novel, who was to spend ten years in solitary confinement followed by life exile in Siberia; the poet and journal editor Baron Anton Delvig, who published Pushkin; Prince Aleksandr Gorchakov, Russian Foreign Minister for 26 years from the conclusion of the Crimean War. These three feature prominently in Tynyanov's novel.

seen bathing in the river, a lady-in-waiting's maid, an actress and a relative of the Principal of the Lycée – the last two being not the only relationships during Lycée days and later in St Petersburg that Tynyanov, unlike Binyon and other biographers, treats as far from platonic. As the novel ends with the poet speeding into exile on the nimble frigate *Mermaid*, however, the all-consuming object of his thoughts as he writes an elegy is none of these. Tynyanov's version of events has good circumstantial historical grounding, and the eloquent testimony to the love of a lifetime in the final passage is a most moving conclusion.

While working on his novel Tynyanov drafted the basis of an introduction, in which he noted:

This book will not be a biography. The reader will not find in it exact facts, precise chronology, or a retelling of the findings of scholarly studies. That is not the task of a novelist but the duty of a Pushkin scholar. In a novel, surmise often takes the place of a chronicle of events […] What I want to do in this book is *to get as near as possible to artistic truth about the past*, which is always the goal of the historical novelist. [Emphasis – A. K. R.]

He goes on to observe that in a novel, conjecture has to take over where chronicle leaves off; 'I begin where a document ends,' he writes. In another fragment he further delineates his task and his goal:

Literature differs from history not by 'invention' but by a greater, more intimate understanding of people and events, by deeper concern about them [...] 'Invention' is a chance thing that depends not on the essence of the matter but on the artist. It is when there is nothing of chance, only necessity, that the novel begins. But the perception must be much deeper, the intuition and the daring much greater, and then comes the ultimate in art – the sense of discovered truth: this is how it could have been, this, perhaps, is how it was.

I believe this passage contains the key to *Young Pushkin*. The conventional labels so casually tagged to it – 'historical novel', 'fictionalised biography', 'psychological novel' – simply do not apply. They are over-simplistic. One thinks of Aristotle's distinction between 'history' and 'poetry', the former describing what has been and the latter what might be, 'particulars' against 'universals'. *Young Pushkin* is universal rather than particular. And at the same time, to read it is to experience the full flow of Tynyanov's 'sense of discovered truth', the firm conviction that this is indeed how it was.

Anna Kurkina Rush
Fife Ness
October 2006

The Characters

Family and household

(See also family trees, pages xxii–xxiii)

Abram Petrovich Hannibal (c.1696–1781), *an engineer general, Aleksandr's maternal great-grandfather.*

Aleksandr Petrovich Pushkin (d. 1726), *Aleksandr's paternal great-grandfather, after whom the poet was named.*

Aleksandr Sergeyevich Pushkin (Sashka, Sasha, Cricket; 1799–1837).

Aleksey Mikhaylovich Pushkin ('the other Pushkin'; 1771–1825), *a major-general, a distant relative of the Pushkins; translator of Molière.*

Anna Lvovna Sontseva (Annette; 1765–1824*), Aleksandr's aunt, sister of Sergey Lvovich.*

Annushka (Anna Nikolayevna, Anka, Anyuta), *Vasily Lvovich's common-law wife, previously his wife's serf-maid.*

Arina Rodionovna (Arishka, Irina, Irishka; 1758–1828), *a former serf from Marya Alekseyevna's estate Kobrino, Olga and Aleksandr's nanny.*

Ivan Abramovich Hannibal (1735–1801), *retired general, a great-uncle of Aleksandr, eldest son of Abram Petrovich Hannibal.*

Kapitolina Mikhaylovna (Circe; 1779–1847), *Vasily Lvovich's first wife.*

Lev Aleksandrovich Pushkin (1723–90), *Aleksandr's paternal grandfather, who caused the death of his first wife and later married Olga Vasilyevna.*

Lev Sergeyevich Pushkin (Lyovushka, Lolka; 1805–52), *Aleksandr's younger brother.*

Margarita (1810–89), *Vasily Lvovich's daughter by his second wife Annushka.*

Marya Alekseyevna Pushkina (1745–1818), *Aleksandr's maternal grandmother, wife of Osip Hannibal.*

Montfort, comte de, *Aleksandr's tutor, an impoverished aristocrat who has fled France during the Revolution.*

Nadezhda Osipovna (Nadine, *la belle Créole*; 1775–1836), *Aleksandr's mother, wife of Sergey Lvovich.*

Nikita Timofeyevich Kozlov (Nikishka), *a serf from Sergey Lvovich's estate at Boldino, who looks after Aleksandr as a child; later his valet.*

Nikolay Petrovich (Nikolashka), *the Pushkins' cook.*

Nikolay Sergeyevich Pushkin (Nikolinka; 1801–07), *Aleksandr's younger brother.*

Olga Sergeyevna Pushkina (Olka; 1797–1868), *Aleksandr's elder sister.*

Olga Vasilyevna Pushkina (1737–1802), *Aleksandr's paternal grandmother, second wife of Lev Aleksandrovich Pushkin.*

Osip Abramovich Hannibal (1744–1806), *retired naval gunnery officer, Aleksandr's maternal grandfather, husband of Marya Alekseyevna Pushkina.*

Palashka, *Osip Abramovich's housekeeper at Mikhaylovskoye.*

Petka (Pyotr), *servant of the Pushkin family.*

Pyotr Abramovich Hannibal (1742–1826), *retired general, Aleksandr's great-uncle, Osip's brother.*

Roussleau, Monsieur, *Aleksandr's tutor at home.*

Sergey Lvovich Pushkin (1767–1848), *Aleksandr's father.*

Sontsev, Matvey Mikhaylovich (1779–1847), *husband of Aleksandr's aunt Yelizaveta Lvovna Pushkina.*

Tatyana (Tanka, Tatyanka), *a maid of the Pushkin family.*

Ustinya Yermolayevna Tolstaya, *a widow whom Osip Hannibal has married bigamously in Pskov, abandoning Marya Alekseyevna with Nadezhda as a small child.*

Vasily Lvovich Pushkin (Basile; 1760–1830), *Aleksandr's uncle, brother of Sergey Lvovich.*

Vlas (Blaise), *Vasily Lvovich's cook.*

Yelizaveta Lvovna Pushkina (Lizette, Liza, Lizka; 1776–1848), *Aleksandr's aunt, sister of Sergey Lvovich.*

Zateplensky, *newly appointed bailiff of Nadezhda Osipovna's inherited estate of Mikhaylovskoye.*

General

Alexander I, Tsar (1777–1825), *reigns 1801–25.*

Arakcheyev, Aleksey Andreyevich, Count (1769–1834), *virtual ruler of Russia for ten years after being appointed deputy chairman of the Committee of Ministers; a brutal martinet.*

Batyushkov, Konstantin Nikolayevich (1787–1855), *a major early nineteenth-century poet; will become insane in 1821.*

Bludov, Dmitry Nikolayevich, Count (1785–1864), *diplomat and a co-founder of the Arzamas Society; later, holding various governmental posts, a reactionary.*

Chaadayev, Pyotr Yakovlevich (1794–1856), *hussar and philosopher.*

Dashkov, Dmitry Vasilyevich (1788–1839), *an Arzamasian, subsequently Minister for Justice.*

Derzhavin, Gavriil Romanovich (1743–1816), *the major Russian poet of the eighteenth century.*

Derzhavina, Darya Alekseyevna (Milena), *Derzhavin's second wife.*

Dmitriyev, Ivan Ivanovich (1760–1837), *poet and fabulist, Minister of Justice, 1810–14, unsuccessful suitor for the hand of Sergey Lvovich's sister Anna.*

Dowager Empress (Mariya Fyodorovna; 1759–1828), *widow of Tsar Paul I.*

Franz Ivanovich, *personal secretary to Minister Speransky.*

Gnedich, Nikolay Ivanovich (1784–1833), *poet, translator of the* Iliad, *and publisher of* Pushkin's narrative poem Ruslan and Lyudmila.

Golitsyn, Aleksandr Nikolayevich, Prince (1773–1844), *President of the Bible Society in Russia and Minister for Education, 1816–24; a conservative reactionary.*

Golitsyna, Avdotya (Yevdokiya Ivanovna, *la princesse nocturne;* 1780–1850), *wife of Prince Sergey Golitsyn, enlightened hostess of a St Petersburg salon.*

Illichevsky, Damian Vasilyevich (b. c.1779), *former seminary student with Speransky, who appoints him Governor of Tomsk.*

Karamzin, Nikolay Mikhaylovich (1766–1826), *prominent writer and linguistic reformer, Imperial Historiographer, author of* The History of the Russian State *(1818–24); a friend of the Pushkin family.*

Karamzina, Yekaterina Andreyevna (Katerina; 1780–1831), *illegitimate daughter of Prince Vyazemsky; Karamzin's second wife.*

Katenin, Pavel Aleksandrovich (1792–1853), *poet, playwright and critic, a close literary associate of Pushkin after he leaves the Lycée.*

Kaverin, Pyotr Pavlovich (1794–1855), *a hussar who takes part in the 1812 campaign.*

Kheraskov, Mikhail Matveyevich (1733–1807), *poet, playwright and novelist.*

Khvostov, Dmitry Ivanovich, Count (1757–1835), *Senator and prolific, ambitious but giftless poet.*

Lavrov, Ivan Pavlovich, *Director of the Executive Department of the Ministry of Police.*

Maistre, Joseph de, Comte (1753–1821), *political philosopher, diplomat and writer, Sardinian ambassador to St Petersburg, 1803–17, staunch monarchist and zealous Catholic.*

Masson, Olga, a *St Petersburg prostitute.*

Michael, Grand Duke (1798–1849), *younger brother of Tsar Alexander I.*

Molostov, Pamfamir Khristoforovich (1793–1828), *officer of the Guards hussar regiment frequented by the Lycéeists.*

Natalya, *a serf singer in Count Varfolomey Tolstoy's theatre.*

Natasha, *maid to Princess Varvara Volkonskaya.*

Neledinsky-Meletsky, Yury Aleksandrovich, Prince (1752–1828), *director of entertainments and poet at the court of the Dowager Empress at Pavlovsk.*

Nicholas, Grand Duke (b. 1796), *younger brother of Tsar Alexander I; to reign as Nicholas I, 1825–55.*

Orlova-Chesmenskaya, Anna Alekseyevna, Countess (1785–1848), *daughter of Catherine the Great's lover Count Aleksey Orlov; heiress to a multi-million fortune, most of which she has donated to churches and monasteries.*

Osipova-Vulf, Praskovya Aleksandrovna (1781–1859), *country neighbour of the Pushkin family.*

Pankratyevna, *a famous Moscow madam.*

Paul I, Tsar (reigns 1796–1801); *assassinated in 1801.*

Pengeau, Monsieur, *popular Moscow dance-master to children of the nobility.*

Photius (Pyotr Nikitich Spassky; 1792–1838), *Archimandrite, a zealous fanatic who fights Golitsyn for the preservation of the supremacy of the Orthodox Church.*

Rayevsky, Nikolay Nikolayevich, General (1771–1829), *hero of 1812, father of Nikolay, Aleksandr, Yekaterina, Yelena, Mariya and Sofya.*

Rayevsky, Nikolay Nikolayevich (1801–43), *General Rayevsky's son, who as a boy fights in the 1812 campaign.*

Razumovsky, Aleksey Kirillovich, Count (1748–1822), *Minister for Education, 1810–16.*

Saburov, Yakov Ivanovich (1798–1858), *a hussar with whom Pushkin becomes acquainted in his final year at the Lycée.*

Samborsky, Andrey Afanasyevich (1732–1815), *Lycée Principal Malinovsky's father-in-law; Court Chaplain and Confessor to the boy Prince Alexander; Speransky's patron since childhood.*

Shakhovskoy, Aleksandr Aleksandrovich, Prince (1777–1846), *poet and playwright (mostly of comedies), the first professional Russian stage director; member of the Symposium of Amateurs of the Russian Word.*

Shalikov, Pyotr Ivanovich, Prince (1768–1852), *sentimentalist poet and imitator of Karamzin.*

Shikhmatov, Sergey Aleksandrovich, Prince (1783–1837), *poet, member of the Russian Academy and the Symposium of Amateurs of the Russian Word.*

Shishkov, Aleksandr Ardalionovich (Shishkov Junior; 1799–1832), *nephew of Admiral Shishkov, cuirassier, poet, translator, imitator of Pushkin.*

Shishkov, Aleksandr Semyonovich, Admiral (1754–1841), *poet, translator, founder of the Symposium of Amateurs of the Russian Word; President of the Russian Academy, 1813–41; Minister for Education, 1824–28.*

Speransky, Mikhail Mikhaylovich (1772–1839), *reforming minister of state under Tsar Alexander I in the years preceding 1812; creator of the Lycée.*

Steingel, Lisa, *a St Petersburg prostitute.*

Tolstoy, Fyodor Ivanovich, Count ('the American'; 1782–1846), *a card-sharp and duellist who spreads rumours about Pushkin.*

Tolstoy, Varfolomey Vasilyevich (1754–1838), *owner of a serf theatre near the Lycée.*

Trubetskaya, Anyuta, *daughter of Old Trubetskoy-Chest-of-Drawers, aunt of Nikolay Trubetskoy.*

Trubetskoy, Nicholas/Nikolay/Nikolinka Ivanovich (1797–1874), *one of the 'Trubetskoys-Chest-of-Drawers' family; Pushkin's childhood friend.*

Turgenev, Aleksandr Ivanovich (1784–1845), *man of letters and historian, a close friend of the Pushkins; Cabinet Minister, 1810–24.*

Volkonskaya, Varvara Mikhaylovna, Princess (1781–1865), *lady-in-waiting to Empress Yelizaveta Alekseyevna (Tsar Alexander I's wife); her maid Natasha is much admired by the Lycéeists.*

von Fock, Maksim Yakovlevich (1777–1831*), Chief of the Secret Police.*

Vsevolozhsky, Nikita Vsevolodovich (1799–1862), *wealthy nobleman with an interest in theatre and music.*

Vyazemsky, Pyotr Andreyevich, Prince (1792–1878), *poet and critic, an active Arzamasian and friend of the Pushkins.*

Vyndomsky, Aleksandr Maksimovich (d. 1813), *father of Praskovya Osipova.*

Yekaterina Pavlovna, Grand Duchess (1788–1819), *a sister of Alexander I; favourite granddaughter of Catherine the Great.*

Yelizaveta Alekseyevna, Empress (1779–1826), *wife of Tsar Alexander I.*

Yusupov, Nikolay Borisovich, Prince (1750–1831), *a fabulously rich Moscow aristocrat on whose property the Pushkins live in 1802–03.*

Zakharzhevsky, *Commandant of Tsarskoye Selo.*

Zhukovsky, Vasily Andreyevich (1783–1852), *the leading Russian Romantic poet, with whom Aleksandr becomes acquainted through his uncle Vasily.*

Lycée staff and students

Bakunin, Aleksandr Pavlovich (1799–1862), *student, brother of Yekaterina.*

Bakunina, Yekaterina Pavlovna (1795–1869), *Bakunin's sister, with whom Pushkin falls in love in the first months of 1816.*

Boudri, David de (David Ivanovich), *teacher of French and brother of the notorious French Revolutionary figure Jean-Paul Marat, the name change concealing his identity.*

Broglio, Silvery Frantsevich, Count (1799–early 1820s), *student; after graduation will be killed in the Greek War of Independence.*

Chirikov, Sergey Gavrilovich (1776–1853), *tutor, drawing instructor and amateur dramatist; the first published likeness of Pushkin, a drawing of c. 1815, is attributed to him.*

Danzas, Konstantin Karlovich (1800–70), *student; after graduation to become an army officer; Pushkin's second in the fatal duel with D'Anthès.*

Delvig, Anton Antonovich, Baron (1798–1831), *student; poet and close friend of Pushkin; to become a literary journal publisher.*

Engelhardt, Yegor Antonovich (1775–1862), *Principal of the Lycée from 1816.*

Foma, *usher.*

Frolov, *tutor with military background who introduces a regime of military discipline at the Lycée.*

Galich, Aleksandr Ivanovich (1783–1848), *teacher of Russian and Latin, 1814–15.*

Gauenschield, Friedrich Leopold August von (Fridrikh Matveyevich; 1780–1830), *teacher of German; an Austrian secret agent.*

Gorchakov, Aleksandr Mikhaylovich, Prince (1798–1883), *student, to become a diplomat; Foreign Minister, 1856–82.*

Grevenits, Pavel Fyodorovich, Baron (1798–1847), *student; to serve in the Ministry for Foreign Affairs.*

Guryev, Konstantin Vasilyevich (1800–after 1833), *student, expelled from the Lycée for homosexuality.*

Ikonnikov, Aleksey Nikolayevich (1789–1819), *tutor, 1811–12; ousted from the Lycée by Inspector Piletsky for alcoholism.*

Illichevsky, Aleksey Damianovich (Olosya; 1798–1837), *student, son of Damian*

Illichevsky; to become a civil servant and writer.

Ilya, *see* Piletsky, Ilya.

Kalinich, Foty Petrovich (1788–1855), *teacher of calligraphy.*

Kartsov, Yakov Ivanovich (1784–1836), *teacher of physics and mathematics.*

Kaydanov, Ivan Kozmich (1782–1843), *teacher of history.*

Kemersky, Leonty, *Lycée servant who sets up a tuckshop.*

Komovsky, Sergey Dmitriyevich (1798–1880), *student; to become a civil servant, eventually Deputy Secretary to the State Council.*

Korff, Modest Andreyevich, Baron (1800–76), *student; to serve in the Ministry for Justice; author of hostile reminiscences of Pushkin and the Lycée.*

Korsakov, Nikolay Aleksandrovich (1800–20), *student; to serve in the Ministry for Foreign Affairs.*

Koshansky, Nikolay Fyodorovich (1781–1831), *teacher of Russian and Latin.*

Kostensky, Konstantin Dmitriyevich (1797–1830), *student; to serve in the Ministry for Finances.*

Küchelbecker, Wilhelm Karlovich (Küchlya, Don Quixote, Willie, Willinka, Wilmushka; 1797–1846), *student and poet, a close friend of Pushkin; as a Decembrist rebel, will be imprisoned for ten years and then exiled to Siberia for the rest of his life.*

Kunitsyn, Aleksandr Petrovich (1783–1841), *teacher of moral philosophy; will be sacked from the Lycée in 1821 for free-thinking.*

Kunitsyn, Mikhail, *brother of Aleksandr Kunitsky.*

Lomonosov, Sergey Grigoryevich (1799–1857), *student; to serve in the Ministry for Foreign Affairs (no relation to the literary reformer and scientist Mikhail Lomonosov).*

Malinovsky, Ivan Vasilyevich (1796–1873), *student; son of the first Principal of the Lycée; to serve in the Guards.*

Malinovsky, Vasily Fyodorovich (1765–1814), *first Principal of the Lycée.*

Matvey, *usher.*

Matyushkin, Fyodor Fyodorovich (1799–1872), *student; to become a scholar and maritime adventurer, and in 1867 an Admiral.*

Myasoyedov, Pavel Nikolayevich (1799–1869), *student; to join the army and later serve in the Ministry for Justice.*

Païssy, *priest at the Lycée chapel.*

Peshel (Peschl, Franz Osipovich; 1784–1842), *doctor who treats Pushkin in 1817.*

Piletsky, Ilya, *tutor; brother of Martin Piletsky.*

Piletsky, Martin Stepanovich (1780–1859), *Inspector, academic and moral supervisor at the Lycée, 1811–12.*

Pushchin, Ivan Ivanovich (Jeannot; 1798–1859), *student, Pushkin's dormitory neighbour and close friend.*

Sazonov, Konstantin (b. c.1796), *Pushkin's valet at the Lycée.*

Steven, Fyodor Khristianovich (1797–1851), *student; to become a civil servant in Finland and Governor of Vyborg.*

Tyrkov, Aleksandr Dmitriyevich (1799–1843), *student; to become an army officer.*

Valkhovsky, Vladimir Dmitriyevich (1798–1841), *student; to become an army officer; will be brought to trial in connection with the Decembrist Revolt but acquitted.*

Yakovlev, Mikhail Lukyanovich (1798–1868), *student; amateur composer and talented impersonator; to become a civil servant, member of the Privy Council and Senator.*
Yesakov, Semyon Semyonovich (1798–1831), *student; to become an army officer.*
Yudin, Pavel Mikhaylovich (1798–1852), *student; to serve in the Ministry for Foreign Affairs.*

The Hannibals

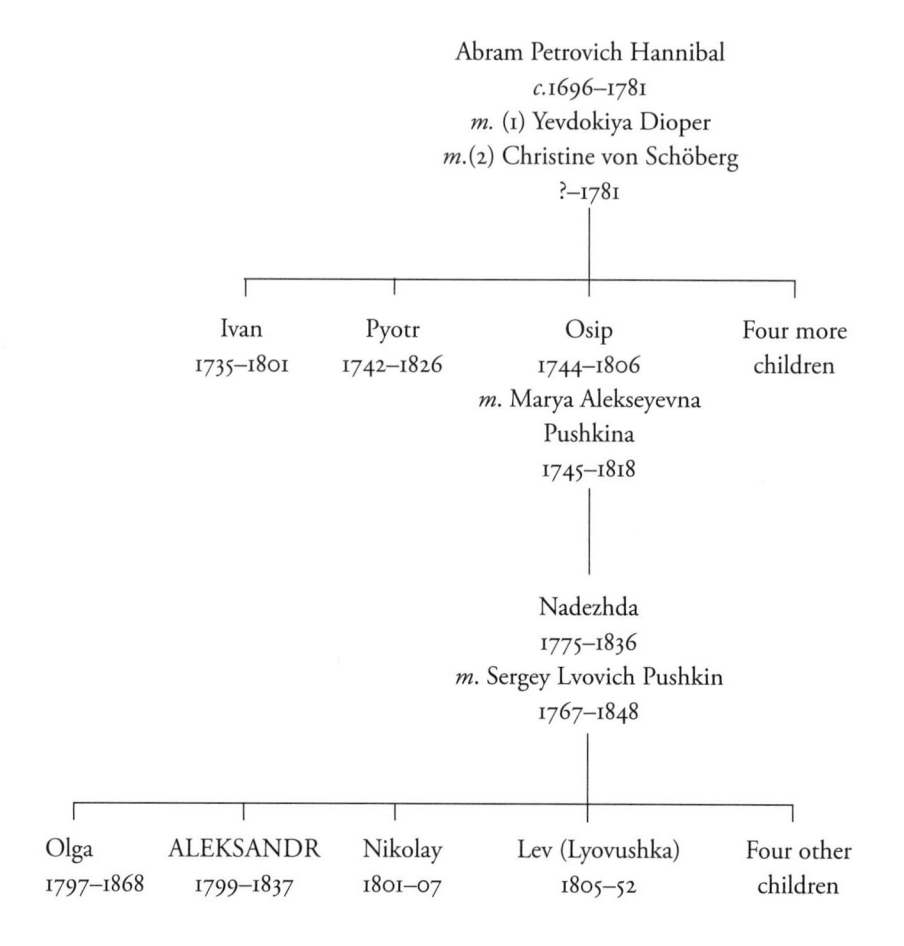

Abram Petrovich Hannibal
*c.*1696–1781
m. (1) Yevdokiya Dioper
m.(2) Christine von Schöberg
?–1781

| Ivan | Pyotr | Osip | Four more |
| 1735–1801 | 1742–1826 | 1744–1806 | children |

m. Marya Alekseyevna
Pushkina
1745–1818

Nadezhda
1775–1836
m. Sergey Lvovich Pushkin
1767–1848

| Olga | ALEKSANDR | Nikolay | Lev (Lyovushka) | Four other |
| 1797–1868 | 1799–1837 | 1801–07 | 1805–52 | children |

The Pushkins

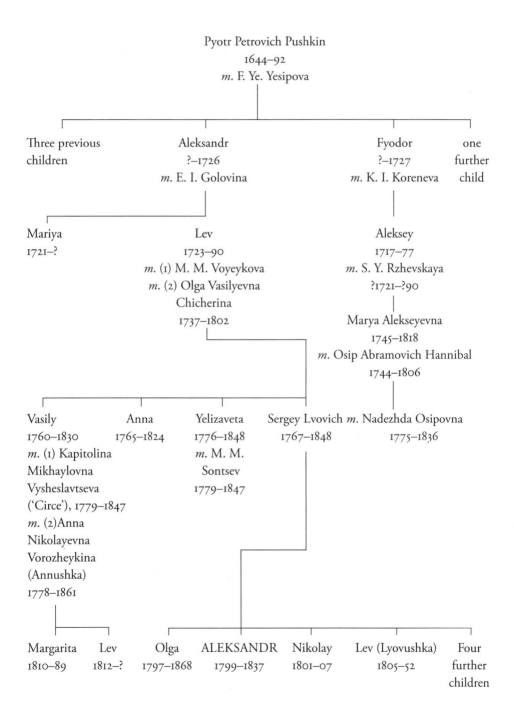

Pyotr Petrovich Pushkin
1644–92
m. F. Ye. Yesipova

| Three previous children | Aleksandr ?–1726 *m.* E. I. Golovina | Fyodor ?–1727 *m.* K. I. Koreneva | one further child |

Mariya
1721–?

Lev
1723–90
m. (1) M. M. Voyeykova
m. (2) Olga Vasilyevna
Chicherina
1737–1802

Aleksey
1717–77
m. S. Y. Rzhevskaya
?1721–?90

Marya Alekseyevna
1745–1818
m. Osip Abramovich Hannibal
1744–1806

Vasily
1760–1830
m. (1) Kapitolina
Mikhaylovna
Vysheslavtseva
('Circe'), 1779–1847
m. (2)Anna
Nikolayevna
Vorozheykina
(Annushka)
1778–1861

Anna
1765–1824

Yelizaveta
1776–1848
m. M. M.
Sontsev
1779–1847

Sergey Lvovich *m.* Nadezhda Osipovna
1767–1848   1775–1836

Margarita
1810–89

Lev
1812–?

Olga
1797–1868

ALEKSANDR
1799–1837

Nikolay
1801–07

Lev (Lyovushka)
1805–52

Four
further
children

young pushkin

PART ONE

Childhood

One

THE Major was tight-fisted. He locked himself in his room, sighed and surreptitiously re-counted his money.

He recalled a former fellow-officer who had owed him a certain sum ever since they had served in the Guards – and got upset. He hushed the canary that had started up its chirping at the worst possible moment, changed, preened himself in front of the mirror for a while, took a cane, hurried to the hall and told his boy-servant drily:

'Get ready – and change into something clean!'

Then he crept stealthily to the side-door, set it ajar, and said gently:

'I'm just off, sweetheart.'

There was no answer. The Major tiptoed to the front door and opened it gingerly, making sure it didn't creak. The lad followed him carrying a carpet bag.

The house had a yard and a back garden with flower-beds, lime-trees and gravel paths. The boy had been instructed to chase away the neighbours' hens.

The watch-dog heard their footsteps and grumbled in its sleep. The Major slipped silently through the gate. He was moving quite nonchalantly now, though it was obvious that he was afraid he might be called back.

He sauntered down the street. The German street he lived in was rather dull: a long fence silvered by many years of rain, a faded little icon on the gate, and dirt. It had not rained for ages, but the street was still muddy and in poor condition – clods, rubble, ruts. Some German workmen were passing by and a woman was carrying a goose; he didn't look at them. Walking along the lanes he reached Razgulyay, the district that was named after a famous tavern. There, after bargaining with a coachman, when his face became uncharacteristically hard, he hired a cab, but only as far as the Pokrovsky Gate. The mare trotted slowly and the boy raced after it. At the Gate the Major got out onto the boulevard.

As soon as he did so he seemed to become another person.

His blue necktie matched his eyes, he leaned on his light cane and glanced around as he strolled along, fanning himself slowly with his silk handkerchief as if catching the coolness of the boulevard with half-open mouth. Then he bought a bunch of wild flowers from a country-girl. It was July, and the sun was scorching. The boy followed him at a distance.

In this manner he paraded as far as the Myasnitsky Gate and reached Okhotny Ryad. He walked jauntily, looking around, eyeing up the passing women. The boy was struggling, wiping away the sweat. The Major went down the steps to the wine-shop. In spite of the early hour two connoisseurs had already turned up and were busy arguing about the relative merits of Burgundy and Lafite. He took his time in choosing the wine, trying to find the best bargain. He bought three bottles, one Saint-Péray and two Lafite, offered the payment casually, pointed to the wine and asked the boy quietly but loud enough for those standing by to hear:

'Do you remember the address, idiot? Of course you don't. Repeat after me: next to the Countess Golovkina's house, the house of Guards Major Pu-ush-kin. Anyone will tell you. But I know you, you dunce, you won't remember. I'll write it down for you. Or you can ask the sentry.'

And with a chuckle he jotted it down.

The boy glanced at him blankly and thrust the note into a pocket full of holes.

2

The Guards Major, in actual fact Captain-Lieutenant, had already been retired for a year and now served as a clerk at the War Commissariat. His uniform was not that of the Guards, but he still introduced himself as Guards Major Pushkin. These were difficult times. 'Chill winds' were blowing for the time-honoured families, as was often said to avoid direct mention of the Emperor Paul and his reforms.

By calling himself a Guards officer and wearing the Commissariat frock-coat the Major was hinting at noble-minded reasons for a resignation which would actually be only temporary. In reality, both his brother Vasily Lvovich and he had had to resign because the Guards lifestyle was quite beyond their means, while his post at the Commissariat at least brought him in a salary.

Together with his mother, brother and sisters he owned some land in Nizhny Novgorod Region: a village called Boldino which was a rather old-fashioned estate of three thousand souls. The trouble was that nine years earlier it had been unfairly divided and his half-brother from his father's first marriage had lopped off the major part of it for himself and his mother.

Since then, deep in his heart Sergey Lvovich had always had a certain wariness of relatives and had blotted his half-brother from his mind once and for all.

Sergey Lvovich had never been to the estate and winced every time his mother hinted, not without venom, that it wouldn't hurt to call in. He knew that the estate had at least a thousand souls, that there was a mill on the river, a tavern and thick surrounding forest. He had absolutely no idea what might be in this forest – berries, wolves, that was all he could imagine. But he always enjoyed receiving the income from the estate, a windfall which would make him feel suddenly rich. When the money was late in coming, he became vaguely uneasy and depressed. In this Guards officer's household money disappeared fast through pockets full of holes.

As a Guardsman, on the other hand, and a refined young man and a *bel esprit*, as the young ladies called him, Sergey Lvovich enjoyed invariable success.

He spoke French so well that even his Russian was an explosion of sibilants and nasal noises. He knew all the latest French romances and had an interest in Russian literature too. He loved the society of men of letters and the privileges of that society. Where else could one be completely in one's element? He never missed an opportunity to call on Nikolay Mikhaylovich Karamzin who lived in the neighbourhood. He was the prophet of the fine arts. Nowadays he was rather burned-out, a star that had lost its lustre – but he was tolerant as ever, courteous, discerning, and as far as Sergey Lvovich was concerned, remained a shining light. He was still living in Pleshcheyev's house in Tverskaya Street.

Sergey Lvovich had been married for two and a half years. His wife, Nadezhda Osipovna, was an extraordinary creature. The St Petersburg Guardsmen called her 'the beautiful Creole' or 'the beautiful African', but her servants, tired of her moods, called her a 'negress' behind her back.

She was the granddaughter of an African, the famous Abram Petrovich Hannibal, General-in-Chief, who before that had been a protégé and valet of Peter the Great. Her scoundrel of a father had abandoned her mother, Marya Alekseyevna, when she was a baby and she had grown up something of an orphan. Some concern for her, however, was shown by her uncles: Quartermaster-General Hannibal (Ivan Abramovich), who had inherited his father's choice estate of Suida outside St Petersburg, and Major-General Hannibal (Pyotr Abramovich), who lived in Pskov Region. The Pushkin brothers used to stay at the Quartermaster-General's, and Sergey Lvovich's brother Vasily had even extolled Suida and its owner in verse. And her black grandfather had been a friend rather than a mere valet of the Emperor Peter, and even if he had been a servant, he nevertheless enjoyed the rank of General-in-Chief. Hannibal was a distinguished name. Nadezhda Osipovna, furthermore, was extremely beautiful. Falling head over heels in love with her, Sergey Lvovich had courted her according to the rules of the best society but had entertained little hope of marrying her. Very soon, however, he proposed, still not believing she would even look at him, and to his great surprise, the beauty accepted him.

In spite of Nadezhda's entangled family circumstances she brought the Major a small village in Pskov Region. He was also led to believe that after her father's death she would inherit quite a substantial village nearby. Her father, Osip Abramovich (the third son of Abram Petrovich), though not really a scoundrel, was thoroughly irresponsible. Although married already, he wedded a woman from Pskov, Ustinya Yermolayevna Tolstoy, then in the full bloom of her charms, who bewitched him and fleeced him, and not only him but the entire family, even his brother Pyotr. His spending was unbelievable. He and money could never co-exist, and he spent it as if it were going out of fashion. Whenever he came into money, he would immediately use it on gold and silver dinner-sets for his charmer. A situation of bigamy, in which each wife considered the other and the husband the villains of the piece, occupied the major part of his life; the lawsuit with the second wife still continued. One moment the old enchantress would be moving in with Osip Abramovich, the next she'd be leaving him, and in either case she demanded money. Now he lived in his village, Mikhaylovskoye, spending his days, as rumour had it, in an absolutely scandalous situation for an old man. Next to Mikhaylovskoye was a tiny village, Kobrino, the dowry of his daughter, the young African.

And then the Empress Catherine passed away. The young African and her Guards Major had a daughter, Olga, and her mother Marya Alekseyevna came from St Petersburg for a visit. Now that he was married Sergey Lvovich resigned from his post. He was twenty-nine. The Major imagined his family house would be an ivy-coloured affair with white columns (even if made of wood). And this was the start of his vague discontent with life: he seemed to understand nothing about choosing and managing a house. Nothing in the couple's life was permanent; the house they rented at random in a Moscow suburb was no mansion but just an outbuilding that had been slung up by English merchants as an office. The new Tsar had a quick temper and disliked the English. So they sold the house to the Major and left the country. Sergey Lvovich hated any kind of effort. The price was cheap and the Pushkins moved in at once.

All that was left of Sergey Lvovich's bachelor days were two cages, one with a parrot and the other with a canary. His life-style now changed completely. A month earlier his son had been born and he called him after his grandfather, Aleksandr.

And now, after the christening, he was going to throw what the Guards called a *courtage*, or, as he liked to describe it, a little gathering of 'those dear to our hearts'.

3

Marya Alekseyevna had been bustling about since morning. She was expecting the guests and her son-in-law's relations and was worried she might slip up. They were fashionable people from the capital and she was not terribly sophisticated. The hall had been tidied up, the family candlesticks rubbed with chalk, the rubbish – and there was a lot of it – swept out of the vestibule.

Deep in her heart she felt that the best and most important place in her life was a town called Lipetsk, not far from which was her father's estate where she had lived as a girl. The town was clean and the main streets were lined with oak and lime saplings. There were cherries and pears by the cartload. The peasant girls wore embroidered blouses. And at this time of year the limes were in blossom and gave off a thick and pleasant fragrance. In summer the highest society came from the capitals to bathe in the Lipetsk mud-baths. The most refined of the superior artillery officers were sent to the Lipetsk iron-foundries on assignments from the capital. When she had been preparing to get married everybody had been envious, though they pretended not to care and even laughed up their sleeves at her marrying a negro. Her fiancé was a naval gunner, eminently courteous, zealous, passionate and ready to do everything for his bride. But he turned out to be a scoundrel.

Outrageously abandoned by him with a baby on her hands and without any support, she had gone to her parents who lived in the country. But her father being well on in years, the negro's intrusion into the family had cast a gloom over his life and he had died of a stroke. The negro became a double villain.

After her father's death, Marya Alekseyevna had lived with her mother and young daughter in grinding poverty. Quite often there was not even a crust of stale bread in the house. The servants left them, afraid of starving to death.

And later, as neither a wife nor a widow and with a young daughter, living on the estate of her father-in-law Abram Petrovich at Suida, then in St Petersburg itself, and now in Moscow, Marya Alekseyevna had never felt at home. She considered all these places temporary and shifting and grew used to a life of unmitigated poverty. At her father-in-law's at Suida she lived in an attic. In St Petersburg she had her own cottage in the grounds of the Preobrazhensky Regiment. Then she sold it and moved with little Nadezhda to the Izmaylovsky Regiment. Her brothers were officers; her husband, though a scoundrel, did at least have a position in the Navy and she felt she belonged to the services. She and her daughter led a military life: drums beating reveille – time to get up; the bugle – time for lunch. The sabres rattled, the spurs jingled past their windows. They rose late and sat by the windows watching the passers-by.

Nadezhda grew up. There, in the precincts of the Izmaylovsky Regiment, Guards Captain-Lieutenant Pushkin wooed her. He was a relative by marriage. Marya Alekseyevna was a Pushkin by birth and Sergey Lvovich was her second cousin once removed. Inquiries were made – and he proved solvent. The proposal was naturally accepted. The newly married couple moved to Moscow and now she was visiting them, as was the custom, and again she found herself in an attic, just as it used to be at her negro father-in-law's, this time with her granddaughter Olga.

Marya Alekseyevna had seen all sorts of people. She knew how to butter up or snub the bureaucrats she had to deal with in the case against her bigamist husband, and how to appreciate people who offered her shelter and kindness. And she hated to be judged or called poor. Now everything had changed; education and fair skin were in fashion.

Only Lipetsk had kept its dear old ways.

Presently she was managing all her son-in-law's household, not huge but difficult enough. There were not too many servants but for want of discipline they had got quite out of hand. Nikolashka, the cook, was a drunkard, and he really was a scoundrel. The rest were lazy loafers, all fingers and thumbs, and told lies. Fortunately, she had taken an experienced nurse with her, a peasant woman, Irishka. Against all expectations money was not easy to come by. Marya Alekseyevna did not conceal her disappointment: it was practically impossible to understand whether Sergey Lvovich was rich or poor. A thousand souls – it couldn't be denied. And yet there was not a lump of sugar in the house and they were in debt to the shopkeeper. She alone was in charge of everything. Sergey Lvovich's only wish was to scuttle away from the house. She didn't like the way Nadezhda went about things and she put no trust in her daughter's ability to put her life in order. Marya Alekseyevna couldn't help being aware of her daughter's alien features; her face was like her negro father's, her palms were dark yellow. And there was a certain aloofness about her, an indifference and laziness foreign to Lipetsk. For days she would walk about in a dressing-gown biting her nails and then, all of a sudden, as if a horsefly had bitten her, the house would go mad. The furniture would be shifted, the servants lectured, the pictures rehung and the dishes smashed.

Only in Lipetsk did the clock stand still.

4

The Pushkins were the first to arrive: Sergey Lvovich's sisters Anna Lvovna (known as Annette) and Yelizaveta Lvovna (Liza). Marya Alekseyevna disliked them both; she couldn't bear the sisters' chatter. As far as she was concerned Liza was a shallow thing. Her husband was a good deal younger than she was. Marya Alekseyevna couldn't help drawing comparisons between Matvey Matveyevch Sontsev and Sergey Lvovich – and Sontsev never failed to stand up better. On the corpulent side, he was kinder and gentler than the Major and not one to be skipping away from home all the time. Not a dandy exactly, but rather sweet, and his hair was curled in the latest Paris fashion modelled on portrayals of Marcus Aurelius. As for sister Annette, Marya Alekseyevna disliked her because she was so affected. Anna Lvovna was already in her thirties (*well* into her thirties, Marya Alekseyevna would stress), but she was still awaiting suitors, and she dolled herself up and spoke in a silvery, languorous sort of way. She drooled over Sergey Lvovich, was concerned about his pallor and begged him to look after himself. To Nadezhda Osipovna she gave souvenirs – mere knick-knacks in Marya Alekseyevna's opinion; trifling little feathers and buckles.

Lately however, Anna Lvovna seemed to have succeeded in her search for a husband. Sergey Lvovich had just announced to the family circle that she had received a proposal from Ivan Ivanovich Dmitriyev, a St Petersburg poet, an eminent person and a Full Councillor of State. Marya Alekseyevna congratulated her but deep down didn't believe a word of what she had heard. When the sisters came she would often leave the room as if to check the stove – in reality to take a deep breath.

'Nonsense!' she would mutter and come back in.

Vasily Lvovich and his wife arrived in a fine patent-leather carriage which jingled like a bell. Marya Alekseyevna livened up – she liked the couple. Vasily Lvovich, breezy and always ready for a gossip or a joke, presented himself today in all his glory: coiffured à la Duroc, the style made popular by Napoleon's general, and in spite of the uncertain times a fairly thick jabot, which, however, he had the sense to hide underneath his coat, which in turn concealed his figure. Vasily Lvovich was well aware of his thin-leggedness and lop-sidedness. Next to him sat a woman he was very proud of, even prouder than of his fame as a poet, or of his pedigree or his carriage. This irresistible creature was his wife, Kapitolina Mikhaylovna. People in the street would gaze at the couple when they saw them.

Vasily Lvovich knew it and assumed his aloof and mysterious air to the very end of the main street, and only when the houses became shabbier and there were fewer people in sight did he allow himself to look about him – only to discover that all the attention was being paid to his wife and not to himself at all.

'*Mon ange, mon ange*,' he babbled admiringly and anxiously, 'cover your shoulders, will you, in this wind ...'

And he threw a shawl over those shoulders.

Marya Alekseyevna always smiled to Kapitolina Mikhaylovna and screwed up her eyes in the way people had done in St Petersburg thirty years earlier when wanting to show their approval.

Kapitolina Mikhaylovna was the subject of great gossip. The Guardsmen called her 'Circe'. As for Marya Alekseyevna, she firmly believed all men to be scoundrels or at least potential scoundrels and she was not one to disapprove of female inconstancy.

'She has a lot to learn still. Meanwhile let her enjoy herself,' she would say, pursing her lips.

Marya Alekseyevna and Sergey Lvovich met the guests in the hall.

'Nadezhda is coming,' said Marya Alekseyevena.

The sisters' faces turned sulky. One of them was holding presents. The brothers started their gossip, each murmuring to the other exactly the same story: Madame Schnü, the owner of a famous coffee-house and celebrated for her ugliness, had lost the sight in her right eye the previous week. Some verses had been composed about her, amusing enough but not to be recited in the presence of ladies. They raised their voices. At Count Saltykov's estate, Marfino, Nikolay Mikhaylovich Karamzin had sung in his own vaudeville – in the interlude, the prologue and the play itself – and very well indeed. The Count had followed his wishes closely and changed the sets at the last moment. The plot, however, had been quite trivial: rustic love, *rivalité*, the kind-hearted husband comes home from the army (the Count himself – everybody applauded when he appeared) and joins the lovers. But what style! The poems, the tunes! The news had already reached St Petersburg. The peasant girls, in their flimsy clothes, had danced superbly. The entire undertaking had cost about ten thousand.

One brother waited impatiently for the other to stop and as if helping him to finish sooner, copied his lip movements.

Sergey Lvovich was obviously stealing his brother's thunder. Vasily Lvovich had been to Marfino himself and therefore knew every minute detail of the performance a good deal better than his brother. He wanted to drop into the chatter the title Karamzin had given the play, but Sergey Lvovich interrupted him. The title was 'Only for Marfino'. Irritated, Vasily Lvovich nodded impatiently at Sergey Lvovich, then looked around and relaxed, remembering that it was only the family looking on. He yawned.

Nadezhda Osipovna made a graceful entrance and exchanged kisses with the women. She was crumpling her handkerchief. Her palms and fingers were covered with 'birth-marks' and yellow as if singed – traces of her African ancestry. She smiled at Vasily Lvovich and that smile changed everything.

The poet Vasily Lvovich narrowed his eyes, and his expert glance slid from the white shoulders of his beautiful wife to the swarthy ones of his sister-in-law.

He wanted to pay her a compliment. In his poetry he aspired to truth and avoided depictions of nature. He believed easy jocularity to be his forte; but no sooner did he see a beauty than he melted and recalled somebody else's verses, some anonymous madrigal, perhaps even a few scraps of his own composition. He was a creature of the moment both in his poetry and in his life.

Meanwhile the table was being laid under a slender lime tree in the garden.

Two important guests were expected: Nikolay Mikhaylovich Karamzin and a Frenchman, Montfort, or Count Montfort as he called himself, an artist and musician, still young and invariably good-humoured. He had been born in Bordeaux and had recently arrived in Moscow in the retinue of the Duke of Bordeaux, who had been staying with the brother of the executed King Louis in Mitava. Exiled from Paris and France, the party now lived in Russia enjoying Emperor Paul's hospitality or, as the military liked to put it, 'boarding'.

As soon as the Frenchman came in with his jaunty step and ironic glance, both sisters fluffed up their hair and smiled. Anna Lvovna was smiling in the current fashion, with her eyes half-closed and her lips moving as if she were whispering or chewing sweets. Later she told Marya Alekseyevna that she had been terribly shy in 'these Frenchmen's' presence. One didn't know how to behave with them and might easily commit some *bêtise*. Marya Alekseyevna thought her smile obscene. She went out and hissed:

'Ridiculous!'

And came back.

Nikolay Mikhaylovich Karamzin was simply dressed and in sombre mood.

'Since dandyism is not in favour nowadays,' he said quietly. 'I've come to you informally.'

As soon as Nikolay Mikhaylovich arrived, the guests proceeded to the garden in pairs. Sergey Lvovich was nowhere to be seen. He had returned to his study, where he opened a small casket, took out the last wad of bank-notes and, not counting them, summoned the valet Nikita.

'Nikishka,' he said hastily, 'there isn't enough wine. Run to the tavern, you know which, and buy one ... two ... three bottles of claret, Burgundy, whatever you can find. Hurry up! Make sure you don't stain your frock-coat!'

He adjusted Nikita's lace cuffs anxiously. The valet Nikita wore a smart dark-blue frock-coat.

'Can you remember your ballad? The whole thing?'

'I can, sir,' replied the valet Nikita, 'after all, it's my own poem, not someone else's.'

The valet Nikita was an author. Recently Sergey Lvovich had found out that he had written a long verse tale. His new hair-style and frock-coat, however, did not suit him. He was of average height, pock-marked and fair-haired. But his composure was remarkable, and today Sergey Lvovich was going to show him off. Nikita's poem about Yeruslan Lazarevich and Nightingale the Robber, which Sergey Lvovich called a ballad, was certainly amusing, but the Major was clearly worried about whether or not Nikita would be able to remember his own lines.

5

Everything was provided for and they could now enjoy the homely atmosphere and the pleasant chatter. It was as easy to relax and unwind under this lime tree as it would have been in the seclusion of the countryside.

The garden was tiny, and that is what made it so charming. Vastness precluded simplicity and formal gardens no longer fired the imagination. A vase of wild flowers stood on a round table, which would have been impossible a decade before.

The times were unsettled. Everybody craved for pastoral tranquillity in an intimate circle, because no one could be trusted in a wider social circle. A kitchen-garden, always with fresh radishes, goats, rowan clusters and fragrant raspberries; a jug of thick cream; rain-washed rustic scenes – all these seemed to awaken memories of lost childhood, and people behaved as if nature had just been discovered. Even the lot of a petty bourgeois or a workman suddenly seemed a happy one. One's own patch of earth, an orchard near the house, pink flowers in a window-box – strange how the poets of old failed to notice the delights of such an existence! They went in for wars, extremes of nature and universal upheavals. These little houses looked like clean bird cages. But what did it matter – as long as the people living in them were happy?

Pastels were coming into fashion, the soft shimmer was gaining ground in female attire; loud colours reminded everybody of things to be avoided. Luxury seemed repellent, its insubstantial pageant all too familiar. Only melancholy brought pleasure. A corner of the garden in summer, like a place in front of the fire in winter, was the most satisfying spot, completely ousting the wider world from the imagination. *Jeux de société* were in vogue, amusements that helped to beguile the time. People played *bouts rimés*, charades, acrostics, activities that developed one's poetic talents; spoke about court affairs in a low voice and about their own with a sigh.

Sergey Lvovich suddenly became anxious about things not being prepared properly, or not having been bought at all. Marya Alekseyevna could not be relied on and Nadine left much to be desired as a hostess. He became so taken up with these thoughts that he didn't notice the silver had not been cleaned and of the two decanters it was the cracked one that had been put on the table.

But Nadezhda Osipovna smiled calmly at everyone, showing her white teeth.

He relaxed.

'And a row of pearly teeth,' thought Vasily Lvovich, echoing somebody's verses. 'But Kapitolina's are finer and the peasant girl Annushka's are finest of all.'

Vasily Lvovich was talking to the Frenchman. Freedom from formality, spontaneity and free expression in conversation – all this and adoration for women, it was all close to his heart, something he could relate to. Twenty years before, Moscow and St Petersburg had been full of Frenchmen, but what Frenchmen they had been! Fashionable shopkeepers, valets and tutors, a few of them quite amusing, really. More recently, after the Revolution the real aristocracy had been arriving – in straitened circumstances and looking for refuge. After seven years they had become a familiar sight and were treated without ceremony; even princes of pedigree could be lured to dinner. Now when the war with the Sansculottes was on they had become fashionable again.

The Count's jacket, however, was rather frayed. His clothes were as threadbare as his affairs were muddled. The Tsar had recently grown stubborn and stingy. The French royal retinue and even the future King himself were impoverished. But purely for entertainment's sake the Count was going to offer French lessons, if necessary lessons in painting, and perhaps music. Sergey Lvovich became convinced at this point that the Count was going to ask for a loan – and mentally apologised in advance for having nothing to spare.

But of course it was not the Count who was the chief guest here. Nikolay Mikhaylovich was the oldest of the gathering. He was thirty-four – the age of dying down.

The day of love has turned to dark,
And isn't it a sad affair
To be ensnared but not ensnare –
To be on fire but not to spark?

His long white face was still unwrinkled, but it had grown cold. In spite of his humour, in spite of his fondness for 'the ticklers' as he called young ladies, it was obvious that he had been much worn down by life. The world was falling to pieces. In Russia there was so much ugliness, even worse than the atrocities in France. So much for dreams of the happiness of man! His heart had been broken by a beautiful woman. After his journey to Europe he grew even icier towards his friends. *Letters of a Russian Traveller* had become a handbook for educated speakers and hearts. Ladies wept over it.

Now he was publishing a literary miscellany, which had been given a woman's name as a title, *Aglaya*. Women loved it and it had started to bring him in some money. But it was just a trifle (though the barbarous censor came down even on trifles). Emperor Paul now, he had failed to live up to the expectations that had been placed on him by all the 'friends of goodness'. He was self-willed and irascible, and surrounded himself not with philosophers but Gatchina corporals who knew nothing of the fine arts.

His sadness calmed and chastened those he met; and he was in great demand as a friend, so soothing was his company.

He called the Pushkins 'my Nizhny Novgorod friends' – he had estates near Nizhny Novgorod. Provincial or country estate life brought people living in the capitals closer together.

Now his thoughts were wandering. Looking at the hostess, he remarked to Sontsev that beautiful ladies could make simple things graceful and even in imitation remain very much themselves. Nadezhda Osipovna was dressed in the latest fashion, in a flimsy white dress with a high waist-line, with ribbons gathered in a knot. French fashions were forbidden; quite recently round Jacobin-style hats had been ripped off their wearers in the streets, and so had tail-coats. But women's fashion seemed to have survived without check and high waist-lines had been copied from the liberated Frenchwomen. This dubious trend was more fashionable than the heavy little frock-coat dresses encouraged by the Emperor and worn by court ladies. Nadezhda Osipovna blushed with pleasure.

And he told them about what he had been planning and hoping for recently – a journey to Karlsbad and Bad Pyrmont, though he did not specifically refer to either place. He was unwell and the authorities were unlikely to hinder his travelling for treatment. The Moscow climate was now bad for him.

'Lord,' he said, 'just imagine the favourable climates of Chile, Peru, St Helena, Ile Bourbon, the Philippines, all those ever-blossoming, ever-fruit-bearing trees – the Moscow heat can stifle you to death.'

And everyone sighed ecstatically over what they had just heard, as if sharing this universally pleasant and meaningful melancholy. Marya Alekseyevna immediately told Petka to bring chilled drinks.

Nikolay Mikhaylovich smiled at this old-fashioned simple-heartedness and seemed to cheer up. Dinner proceeded without a hitch. Sergey Lvovich indulged himself in the food. The game pâté was as piquant as it should have been. This rogue Nikolashka was a better cook than the ones at the English Club. Even if they offered ten or fifteen thousand for him, Sergey Lvovich would not sell him, and if he ever did, he would regret it. He was eating slowly, enthusiastically, like a connoisseur.

After dinner, pleasantly relaxed, they proceeded to the drawing-room to pass the time till evening tea. The semi-dark hall felt slightly musty, but Nikolay Mikhaylovich looked around with pleasure and commented that every visit to their house reminded him of London.

Sergey Lvovich, who could not get used to the house, suddenly felt conscious of all its advantages.

Petits jeux were organised. *Bouts rimés* were played; the rhymes were: *nouveauté – répété, avis – esprit.*

Nikolay Mikhaylovich, of course, composed more gracefully and skilfully than Vasily Lvovich and much more wittily than Montfort.

Everyone spontaneously applauded his quatrain.

Montfort did some fairly successful drawings of curly-haired Cupids (looking like Sontsev) with bows and arrows. Asked to demonstrate some more of his art, he quickly drew in Nadezhda Osipovna's album a blind Cupid with chubby arms and legs, finely curled hair and prominent dimples on his cheeks.

It was not by chance that Vasily Lvovich had asked him to draw the Cupid. He had heard about Karamzin's inscriptions: when he was the guest of a certain beautiful lady, Nikolay Mikhaylovich, with the hostess's permission, had written all over a marble Cupid from head to toe. With a faint smile he agreed to recall these verses, and inscribed them on Montfort's Cupid in various places. On the head –

> *Where the head is employed*
> *The heart has no work;*
> *No trace of love there –*
> *No love where words lurk.*

On the blindfold –

> *Love is blind to the world,*
> *One precious subject*
> *Is all that it sees,*
> *And to all else is cold.*

And finally, on the admonitory finger –

> *Discretion is its own reward:*
> *So have your fling – but not a word!*

Vasily Lvovich gave a huge sigh of delight. He admired and prized social refinement. Just a glance at his circle made him utterly ecstatic, though that didn't prevent him from having flings with serf-girls or any other paramours on the side through the notorious procuress Pankratyevna – he liked simplicity in love. However, he tried to keep everything strictly confidential and was discreet. He was indignant with his brother for not having a marble Cupid. He remembered a few more verses for the Cupid's hand, wing, foot and back, but the album page had been written all over.

Sister Annette, fiancée of the poet Dmitriyev, was made to sing his song about a cooing grey dove, which was on everybody's lips.

Anna Lvovna had a very shrill, high-pitched voice; shrill voices were in vogue. Marya Alekseyevna left the room to see to the tea and said behind the door:

'That's a squeaky one!'

They made Nadezhda Osipovna sing too and she sang *Float, thou sylph, in ether of spring*. Her voice was deep, sultry and throaty, with rolling *r*s. Sergey Lvovich listened with screwed-up eyes, gently crazed with melancholy and inspiration. His sister-in-law's shoulders were right in front of him, and repeating the words with his lips only he seemed to be kissing those shoulders so famous among the Guardsmen. Nadezhda Osipovna's singing reminded Vasily Lvovich of the husky songs of gypsies and swarthy pharaohesses, not the songs of fair ladies, and pleased him greatly.

> *Float, thou sylph, in ether of spring,*
> *From rose to rose fly revelling!*

Nikolay Mikhaylovich was moved to tears. The words of the song were highly evocative for him.

'She might have become a musician – with a little more self-discipline,' said Marya Alekseyevna.

They were in the agreeable mood of people meeting by choice and not by chance, able to appreciate and enjoy each other's company.

A deep crimson sunset looked in through the window, promising fine weather. 'Pure Ossian, isn't it?' said sister Annette.

And Nikolay Mikhaylovich smiled at her indulgently as if she were a child.

Wine was offered – and now, feeling warmth, mist and moisture about the eyes, a sign of inspiration with him, Nikolay Mikhaylovich made a speech, not in the English manner, but from the heart. He proposed a toast to his native region, that of Simbirsk where he had been born and spent his years of innocence; and to his friends, the Simbirsk poets. That meant Dmitriyev. Nikolay Mikhaylovich had received a letter from the poet, who was going to resign from his post and abandon damp St Petersburg to settle down in Moscow. He already had his eye on a small house with a little back garden near the Red Gate. All was ready for Philemon's happiness; only Baucis was missing.

As if by universal agreement everyone started to clink glasses with Annette – and Annette blushed to the roots of her hair.

'My dear friends,' said Nikolay Mikhaylovich, 'Horace glorified Tivoli! Permit me to drink to the Red Gate and Samara Hill!'

He particularly liked Samara Hill, not far from Moscow on the bank of the Pererva River, opposite the village of Kolomenskoye, because he had written *Poor Liza* and *Natalya* there. He had firmly decided that if he were not allowed abroad, then this would be his sanctuary, open to all friends of mankind, all the truly enlightened, rather like the refuge of the great Jean-Jacques.

It was the right moment to produce Nikita, the homespun poet, and to listen to his amusing ballad. Nikita was a complete success. Nikolay Mikhaylovich laughed wholeheartedly, then changed mood and spoke quite seriously about the new Lomonosovs. In accordance with the Emperor's order, Lomonosov's family had been freed from the poll-tax, and the forgotten poet was remembered once more, with complete respect, his primitive taste forgiven, which of course everybody had shared in those distant times. The younger people in the company became more talkative. Everything old-fashioned seemed so ridiculous. Derzhavin was mentioned.

Nikolay Mikhaylovich had a sort of diplomatic friendship with Derzhavin – the old poet had sent him his poems for publication. Karamzin had chuckled and published them, reluctantly. Vasily Lvovich quoted a couple of lines from Derzhavin's ode on Betsky, who had died four years previously:

> *You died and spread around*
> *A pleasant fragrance …*

Derzhavin was comparing old Betsky with the fragrant fire of an icon-lamp, but since it wasn't clear that the aroma referred to the icon-lamp rather than the man, the lines became ambiguous and rather distasteful. Vasily Lvovich prattled all this out mischievously and everyone smiled, though the ladies simply couldn't or wouldn't understand the point of the joke.

'So this is why our Derzhavin likes icon-lamp smoke,' Nikolay Mikhaylovich said subtly, smiling at how bold Vasily Lvovich had grown in the presence of ladies. He shook his finger at him.

'You are an old *brigand*, a pirate from a galley,' he told him.

Vasiliy Lvovich grew even more impressive from sheer pleasure. The Galley was a fun-loving, even too fun-loving society in St Petersburg. Wonders were told of it and the escapades of its members. Vasily Lvovich was one of its leading members and that St Petersburg reputation of his was highly rated in Moscow; he was suspected of pranks that he was not even capable of. But it was for that reputation that the beautiful Kapitolina Mikhaylovna had mainly fallen.

Nikolay Mikhaylovich reproached him for his indolence – the sweetest reproach for a poet. He reminded him that he was preparing the next issue of his literary magazine. Vasily Lvovich choked and started to splutter: he had nothing worthy ... however, he had lots of ... well, various ... trifles.

Sergey Lvovich wanted to shine too but lacked the confidence. He had manuscript copies of works of scatological verse in his bookcase (naturally kept only for their rarity); these were not the coarse or obscene effusions of some petty clerk, but scatological light verse par excellence, in which everything was described hazily and under veils and the most erotic moments were rendered by groans ('Ah!' or occasionally 'Oh!'). In other verses not only Eros and women were satirised, but some very important persons too. Sergey Lvovich fretted: I mustn't, I mustn't ... Nowadays even the sinless were turned into the sinful; that is, simply speaking, even an innocent sheep could be brought before Christ and fleeced.

But when Nikita and Petka lit the candles and everyone sat down to tea, he felt calmer and completely contented.

Nikolay Mikhaylovich praised the cherry jam:

'I am really enjoying this jam.'

At that moment they heard the rattling of a heavy carriage, bells tinkled and it stopped directly in front of the gate.

Sergey Lvovich turned noticeably pale.

At night-time the sound of an approaching carriage, even for those innocently drinking tea, was an unpleasant one. This was how special messengers arrived. Somebody was heard talking hoarsely and abusively in the hall. A pale Nikita opened the door and announced, looking apprehensively into Sergey Lvovich's eyes:

'His Excellency Major-General Pyotr Abramovich Hannibal.'

6

He was short, small-headed, with yellow hands and a thin waist, a bulging forehead and grey shaggy hair. He wore an antediluvian dark-green military frock-coat and moved lightly, his heels not touching the floor. He took a couple of hurried steps and halted.

Then he bowed and spoke in stops and starts:

'I heard from my dear brother ... from Ivan Abramovich ... about the happy event ...' He flung a glance at the guests. 'And since I was passing by, I considered it my duty' (he bowed to Marya Alekseyevna) 'to congratulate you, madam, my dear sister, and you, sir' (he addressed Sergey Lvovich indifferently) 'and to see ... my grandson ... and ... there's a little cross for him from his grandfather ...'

He paused and inquired:

'Where is he now? My grandson, eh?'

Nadezhda Osipovna's uncle Pyotr Abramovich was an artillerist like all the Hannibals. When his brother, Nadezhda's father Osip Abramovich, had taken up with the Pskov adulteress and abandoned the family, Pyotr Abramovich had had no choice but to accept the thankless burden of guardianship. But in spite of his concern for his niece and her fate, he had proved to be quite useless in that role, of which he had a weird notion: he made journeys to see his criminal brother to reproach him, occasionally wrote long letters to Marya Alekseyevna, addressing her as 'madam' and 'dear sister', but kept silent about monetary matters. The truth of the matter was that he himself was financially insecure and had actually spent half his life under investigation for the embezzlement of artillery shells, until his brother Ivan Abramovich had somehow managed to scotch the scandalous case. By that time Pyotr Abramovich had already resigned from the army, divorced his wife and gone off with some flighty girl from Pskov, where he was living at the time, to settle in his own village, Yeltsy, and from there informed his wife that for his own peace of mind he could no longer live with her. When he went to his criminal brother to admonish him for his behaviour he found instead a certain affinity between them and it was clear they were birds of a feather.

These visits would end up in brotherly drinking-bouts lasting for a week or more. Soon the old adulteress had involved Pyotr Abramovich in the pair's money affairs. On his brother's acknowledgement of his debts, Pyotr made over a mint of money to her and very nearly went bankrupt himself. Soon afterwards, retired but still hale and hearty, he finally went to live nearer his brother, lured by the dissipated luxury which Osip Abramovich enjoyed. Now he lived with his dazzler in the small village of Petrovskoye, next to his bigamist brother's estate of Mikhaylovskoye. Rumour had it that he lived there in great style, neither paying nor receiving calls. He went out mainly to see to the thorny lawsuit concerning his separation from his spouse and son Veniamin. That was how he happened to be in Moscow.

Everyone was astounded.

The encounter was particularly unpleasant for Sergey Lvovich because of the presence of Karamzin. The Hannibals to whom he had become related were a family not without significance owing to their extraordinary and celebrated origins, and were even respectable in a way. That at least was the impression he liked to create in conversation, away from the physical presence of the old negroes. Out of sight of them nobody could imagine how black and yellow their faces actually were. Therefore, while treating Osip Abramovich, like all young St Petersburg Guardsmen, with a deferential grin and a condescending curiosity, he was never eager to set eyes on his prodigal father-in-law and certainly had no desire to meet his wife's relatives in the presence of people whose opinions he cared so much about. *La belle Créole* was pretty, her story was fascinating, but her negro uncle's arrival was quite inappropriate. His face was uncompromisingly negroid and the sudden interest shown in him by those outside the family was unseemly. Everyone was embarrassed by the curiosity the old negro paid to the baby in whose honour Sergey Lvovich was actually throwing today's *courtage*. Busy with each other, with recent events, games, remembered affairs of the heart and poetry, the guests had had neither time nor occasion to think of the baby, which had not made its presence known by the slightest sound all this time. Indeed, where was it? Probably asleep in the attic.

The negro was hesitant too. He had not expected to meet guests. His tiny face was wrinkled and screwed up, the lively little brown eyes were coffee-coloured, with dark-yellow whites like those of a hepatitis sufferer – and there were those wide nostrils. The Frenchman looked at him curiously. The old man suddenly fixed his little monkey's eyes upon Sergey Lvovich and asked hoarsely:

'Perhaps my visit is unwelcome?'

Marya Alekseyevna replied quickly, put out but still polite:

'Now Pyotr Abramovich, sit down, will you?'

The negro smiled. He bared his white teeth and instantly his wrinkled baked apple face became child-like.

'Thank you, madam, my dear sister,' he said gently, and the women realised that the negro was really a courteous and rather nice old man.

Nadezhda Osipovna went up to her uncle.

'So, this is how you've turned out,' he said, paying her a compliment by deliberately miscalculating her age, and kissed her forehead. 'Your father-in-law is asking you to call this summer, dear sir, with your wife' (now addressing Sergey Lvovich), 'to taste our berries.'

Sergey Lvovich accepted the invitation amiably. Everything was turning out much more agreeably and decorously than he had supposed. The old negro had simply come to give them his father-in-law's invitation.

A talk with his father-in-law lay ahead, perhaps about the dowry. And nature in summer time was marvellous. The thought of eating berries at his father-in-law's suddenly appealed to him. Sergey Lvovich liked berries. Marya Alekseyevna could stay at home with the children.

Marya Alekseyevna left the room and said behind the door:

'Just look at this messenger!' – and came back.

Pyotr Abramovich refused to take any wine and straightaway asked for vodka. Marya Alekseyevna produced a bottle of an ancient absinthe liqueur.

He took a first sip and gave the company a serious look, moving his tongue and lips slowly.

'I, dear sister,' he told Marya Alekseyevna, 'don't take liqueurs. I distil them and bring them to a certain degree of strength so that the taste of the garden and the bitterness of cherries lingers in the mouth.'

He noticed Kapitolina Mikhaylovna and cheered up to see a number of young women at the table. He drank a glass in their honour.

The beauty, Kapitolina Mikhaylovna, nodded to him politely. She was flattered by the old negro's attention. She simpered.

Suddenly he scanned the room narrowly.

'Is it warm enough in this outhouse?' he asked, and without waiting for an answer forgot his question and remembered the baby.

'What have you called him?'

He switched topics rather abruptly.

Sergey Lvovich frowned – the negro uncle had called their house an outhouse. It was indeed an outbuilding, but a completely refurbished one, in the English fashion.

When he learnt that the baby was called Aleksandr the uncle clasped his hands:

'What a splendid name,' he said. 'The two greatest military leaders in history, madam, were the unsurpassed Hannibal and Alexander the Great. Aleksandr Vasilyevich Suvorov too of course. Congratulations, dear sister, on choosing such an illustrious name.'

'The name has been chosen in memory of a member of the family,' said Sergey Lvovich reluctantly, 'after his great-grandfather Aleksandr Petrovich, the founder of the family's prosperity. Not after Suvorov,' he added as delicately as he could, and squinted at Karamzin.

Suvorov was in favour only with very old men. Nowadays he was senile, everybody knew that. That was why the war with the Sansculottes was going so badly.

Pyotr Abramovich glanced at him sullenly and took another glass of liqueur.

'I don't recall him, sir,' he said, 'No, I don't think I knew your grandfather.'

He spoke to the men abruptly and churlishly, quite differently from the way he spoke to the women. 'On second thoughts, yes,' he said suddenly and hoarsely, 'I do remember your grandfather. My father used to mention him – Aleksandr Petrovich. My dear sister, wasn't his wife stabbed to death?'

Sergey Lvovich threw back his head and screwed up his eyes. Vasily Lvovich readjusted his jabot.

If their uncle had not been so eccentric and had not spoken so disconnectedly and incoherently, this would have been an obvious insult.

Their grandmother, Aleksandr Petrovich's wife, really had been stabbed to death while in labour. Her husband, Aleksandr Petrovich, after whom the baby had been named, had stabbed her in a jealous frenzy and spent the rest of his life on trial. It was entirely tactless to mention all this just at that moment; it was also discourteous.

On the other hand, judging from his abrupt manner, the old negro might just be responding to a sudden flash of memory. It was rather obvious that before the liqueur the Major-General had already been drinking vodka.

Karamzin decided to put a word in.

He had been scrutinizing the negro for some time and now, in his calm, deliberate way, asked if the Major-General had had a chance to travel.

With his bright coffee-coloured little eyes, his briskness and agility, the old man looked more like a widely-travelled African out of some English novel than a Pskov landowner.

He felt quite comfortable under the curious stares – he was obviously used to them.

'I, my dear sir, have spent my whole life in the artillery, in the service of the Tsar.' He spoke with dignity. 'I've made many journeys, but a traveller I have never been. Now, when there's a war abroad, by all means, I'll ask the authorities to send me there. The army can do with old men like myself.'

As the author of *Letters of a Russian Traveller* Karamzin might have felt offended. Had the Major-General remotely resembled a reader of literature, his remark would have sounded impertinent. But the sophisticated Nikolay Mikhaylovich realised that the old negro had taken offence at the very word 'traveller'. He was amused.

Marya Alekseyevna glanced suspiciously at her husband's brother.

'Why, may I ask, this sudden hankering after foreign parts ...? So you'll be leaving home? Will you be allowed to go?'

Marya Alekseyevna had in mind the Pskov beauty who had taken the Major-General from the family. She had never seen her but hated her even more than if she had been her own rival.

'Because, dear sister,' the Major-General suddenly said softly and tenderly, 'I would like to find father's principality. That's all.'

He spoke to Marya Alekseyevna respectfully and patiently, but without flattery. He had spoken to her in the same manner when she had been young.

'What principality might that be?' asked Marya Alekseyevna, again with obvious scepticism.

'Arabia,' answered the Major-General calmly and flung a glance at Karamzin, 'in the Kingdom of Ethiopia or Abyssinia. The province of Arabia was father's principality for sure. My father's father, my grandfather, was an African prince.'

Karamzin gave him a slight pale smile.

'Never heard,' Marya Alekseyevna said, 'anything about a prince. Why is it then that neither you, dear Pyotr, nor your brothers, in all your lives, have ever found that principality?'

'I have been busy, dear sister,' Pyotr Abramovich continued in the same tone, gentle but firm. 'I have been busy in the service of the State,' he repeated, listening to his own words, as if convincing himself, 'I've had no time to look for father's principality. And my brothers haven't either.'

Marya Alekseyevna shook her head, but at this moment Karamzin intervened again. The man of letters suddenly manifested himself. The negro's lot fascinated him.

'Isn't your father Abram Petrovich's life most unusual?' he remarked courteously. 'Has he left any papers, letters and so on? These would be precious for the historian.'

The old man bristled. The mention of papers made him instantly suspicious.

'I have none, sir,' he said apprehensively. 'Father didn't like them either. Some papers might have been left with my brother, Ivan Abramovich.'

The embezzlement affair and the ongoing lawsuit had taught the Major-General to fear papers.

Karamzin decided to leave the old man in peace. He asked Sontsev, who had the reputation of a newsmonger:

'Is it true that Kutaysov is leaving?'

At this time 'to leave' meant to fall out of favour.

Kutaysov was a captured Turk turned barber, who had been given to the Emperor as a gift and was now in charge of all the country's horses – a Count, a cavalier and the talk of the town.

'On the contrary,' Sontsev answered with obvious delight, 'he's been awarded the Aleksandr Nevsky Cross!'

He had friends in the Heraldry Office where the decoration had been prepared.

The Major-General fixed his eye on Karamzin. His nostrils flared.

'Kutaysov,' he said hoarsely, 'is a valet and got his decoration simply because he was close to the Emperor. He shines people's boots. My father became famous for his great services. He named me after Peter the Great.'

That was exactly Karamzin's train of thought. He was aware that the renowned negro had been Emperor Peter's valet or orderly and that had reminded him of Kutaysov.

He hesitated.

'My father was a prince,' the old man continued aggressively. 'Doesn't matter that he was an African one. He was brought to Russia as an example, to study fortifications. The fact that he was black meant that his face stood out so that you could remember all the better what a great man he developed into. Have a look here, sir. You see this owl.'

He bent his finger and showed them a black signet-ring on it.

The intervals between his sips had grown shorter. He emptied glass after glass and the liqueur bottle had been going down fast.

'There's a document to prove it, a trustworthy document, in German. But I won't give it to you, sir.'

He was beginning to get drunk.

'How mean!' declared Marya Alekseyevna.

And again the old man was deferential to her.

'Believe me, I am always and forever yours, madam,' he told his sister-in-law. 'What if my father's face wasn't handsome? His heart was the heart of a real Hannibal. You have the word of a Hannibal for it.'

Marya Alekseyevna sighed as she came out with the sudden retort:

'His heart was evil and his face was ugly but he had more courtesy than you, Pyotr … He had a nice smile,' she said significantly.

Pyotr Abramovich was lost in admiration for his sister-in-law.

'Ah, a heart of gold,' he said and suddenly showed his white teeth in a smile.

'He was better than you and his teeth were whiter.'

Marya Alekseyevna waved her hand.

Sergey Lvovich was afraid that Nikolay Mikhaylovich might feel offended. His heart froze. Unsure what to do, he told Nikita to repeat his ballad. The valet started but lost the place.

Nikolay Mikhaylovich had begun to look somewhat bored, to say the least. He had not understood much of the old man's edgy speech, though Pyotr Abramovich had tried his best. The negro was perspiring and wiping his head with a handkerchief.

He really had seen the document he had referred to, in his brother Ivan's house. His father, after being mocked for the blackness of his face by German officers in Reval, had charged a trustworthy German to record his pedigree. The old man had summoned his sons, and with the help of a German pharmacist of their acquaintance they had read it and learnt it by heart.

Abram Petrovich had needed this pedigree in order to acquire noble rank. Peter the Great's time had been a busy one and the old negro had remembered about his title only when Elizabeth came to power and everybody was eager to authenticate his noble origins. Then, together with noble rank, he had been granted the coat of arms Pyotr Abramovich was boasting about now: banners crossed above a naval telescope and above them an owl, symbol of learning and intelligence. This coat of arms was carved on Pyotr Abramovich's signet-ring.

The document stated that Emperor Peter intended to give an example to the nobility, and had taken pains to acquire a negro child with good abilities. Negroes, also known as 'Niggers' and 'Moors', were in widespread use as serfs, the German wrote, and Peter wished to prove that they could be educated by learning and diligence. The example he wished to present to the nobility would be best remembered, the Emperor believed, if his skin were black, since the nobility were lazy and resisted him. The principality of Arabia was not mentioned in the document, but according to the testimony of Abram Petrovich himself, he had been an Abyssinian, from a princely family ruling over three towns. Pyotr Abramovich was sure that the German had summed it all up properly.

Karamzin was greatly disappointed.

The famous negro, the Emperor's favourite, had been a celebrated and precious feature of Peter's all too impetuous reign.

Legend had it that the Emperor had shown particular curiosity about giants, dwarves and negroes. His wild notions of human nature seemed to Karamzin, disciple of the Swiss theologian Lavater, rather amusing.

Now the Major-General was absolutely drunk.

'What's your name?' he asked Nikita abruptly.

'Nikita, sir.'

'You, Nikishka, are no good,' said the Major-General. 'My serf Grishka sings to me and plays his psaltery, and he sings straight to my soul – it makes me shiver, it reduces me to tears! A heart of gold! You speak through your nose. You are no good.'

Nikolay Mikhaylovich started to take his leave. The evening was spoilt for him.

Samara Hill, refuge of the friends of the heart, the Moscow home in English style, pastoral seclusion – all had vanished at once.

The negro's arrival, his rudeness and his toadying to Marya Alekseyevna – like the behaviour of an African seafarer or a drunken landowner – had shattered Karamzin's pleasant illusions.

Sergey Lvovich had spoken of a Boldino he knew nothing about. Montfort was the courtier of a non-existent court. Karamzin's future was obscure.

The Frenchman left with Karamzin. He had managed to persuade sister Annette to wear a high coiffure but had had no time to ask for money.

Sergey Lvovich saw the guests out and came back in gloom. The money spent had been wasted. Karamzin had left dissatisfied, and without him the rooms seemed dark and empty. All his life he had tried but failed to be and to act like everybody else. The droll tone of the old uncle, which had been too much for Karamzin, exasperated him too, but he found it difficult to put his indignation into words.

The old negro got up and headed towards the staircase to the attic.

'I want to see my grandson,' he murmured. 'That's all. Where is my grandson, eh?'

Marya Alekseyevna barred his way.

'I won't let you,' she said, angry and alarmed. 'The baby is asleep and it's untidy in there.'

The negro stepped back.

His little eyes looked bleakly at his sister-in-law.

'His grandfather?' he wheezed, 'Your own brother-in-law? Here's a little cross … from his grandfather.'

He pulled a little gold cross out of his pocket, clutched it and shook his fist.

Unusually calm, Nadezhda Osipovna had been staring at her uncle. She had seen her father only twice in her life before, in her childhood – and she had remembered him better after the first time than after the second. She remembered the little flowers and glass buttons on his waistcoat, his chequered necktie, his moist kiss and astonishingly light way of walking – he had bounced away from her like a ball. All her life, all her twenty-three years she had remembered and known that this was the man who had made her and her mother unhappy. And now she was gazing with wide-open eyes at his brother, her uncle.

He stretched his neck muscles and with frightening determination tottered drunkenly on his short light legs up the stairs to the attic. His greying hair stood on end.

Nadezhda Osipovna stood up and followed her uncle. Marya Alekseyevna stepped back, sat down by the fire-place and turned away.

'He wants to see his grandson!' she said. 'Some grandfather!'

She swallowed her tears silently, tear after tear – as she had done in her youth when tyrannised by her monster of a husband.

7

The remaining guests were not sure whether to stay or go.

Vasily Lvovich was blinking and breathing heavily as he always did in adverse circumstances. The sisters screwed up their eyes and furtively pressed each other's hands seeing the changes in Marya Alekseyevna's face.

Sontsev was truly upset. He had had a good meal and now the unintelligible new turn of events was interfering with his digestion. Distressed, he chewed the remnants of fish pie in his mouth.

Only Kapitolina Mikhaylovna, conscious of her beauty, had not gone to the trouble of either worrying about or being angry with the negro. The old negro did not seem indifferent to her charms.

There had in fact been neither argument nor quarrel, and as far as could be seen no reason for any. Marya Alekseyevna could never understand the noise, commotion and irritation that had always arisen around the Hannibals like a skein of hot steam around someone in a bath-house.

Following the others, Sergey Lvovich climbed the staircase with short angry steps.

'Don't worry, Marya Alekseyevna,' Yelizaveta Lvovna said. 'Is it worth it, my darling?'

Marya Alekseyevna wiped her eyes and without looking at the sisters went up to the attic.

Annette squeezed her sister's hand furtively. They both listened avidly to what was going on upstairs.

8

A tallow candle was flickering and sinking; nobody had removed the drips. There were no curtains on the windows and the moon was gaping in. The walls were bare. Linen was piled in the corner, nappies were drying on a washing-line near the stove, a steaming tub stood in the centre of the room, and the negro stumbled over it. The disorder was unbelievable. The flickering fire lent the nursery the atmosphere of a gypsy camp. This room was not meant for the eyes of outsiders. The Pushkins were used to the minimal conveniences.

A small girl curtsied before the negro.

'Who is this?' he asked in amazement.

'Olga Sergeyevna, sir,' the nurse answered, bowing. 'Good evening, sir, Pyotr Abramovich.'

She had young eyes, and she was sharp and sprightly-looking.

'Hello,' the negro said, 'what's your name?'

He had become calmer in the nursery; the intoxication was clearing away.

'Arishka, sir, from Kobrino, the Hannibals'.'

Arina spoke in a singsong. She had been given to Marya Alekseyevna as a young girl. She bowed to Pyotr Abramovich. On the Hannibals' estate the serfs were trained to dance attendance.

'What an awful smell in here, Arishka. You take care of the little master.'

Sergey Lvovich came into the room at this moment.

The negro leaned over the baby.

'Please, be quiet, *mon oncle*,' Nadezhda Osipovna said in a muffled voice, 'he's asleep.'

'No he isn't,' the negro said.

Indeed, the baby was not asleep. He was staring calmly with the unthinking eyes of an infant – eyes of that indeterminate, ultramarine colour. The negro took a close look at him.

'Tow-haired,' he said.

He looked again.

'He's a very fair colour.'

The baby stirred, looking past everyone.

'Let me smother him with kisses!' shouted the negro, 'The word of a Hannibal – he's a lion cub, a real little negro! My precious! Hannibal the Magnificent! The spitting image of his grandfather! The very expression! Our breed! Bring the wine!'

Sergey Lvovich stepped forward. The drunken negro was issuing orders in his house, as if he were on his own estate. In spite of his feelings towards his wife he had always believed that he had somewhat elevated the Hannibals by allying himself with them and raising them to his level. From childhood he had always remembered the progress of some grandee through St Petersburg, the mist, the street lamp, the cry: 'Stand aside!' and a Kalmuck with a negro in red livery on the footboard of the carriage. Now Moscow bent its knee to the old nobility. Everybody loathed the Turk Kutaysov.

The old negro had frightened away the guests and was addressing his son as a Hannibal and a negro.

'My dear sir,' Sergey Lvovich sighed, speaking with exceptional dignity, 'Aren't you tired after your long journey? Wouldn't you like to take a rest? And, now … as for the blood in my son's veins … I dare believe that he isn't a … lion cub … and he isn't a little negro, but a Pushkin as I am. I like and respect your family – when they are civilised,' he added severely, 'but you must agree that my son … that a father as I am …'

With surprising agility the negro suddenly lifted the baby, ran with him to the candle and gave him a loud, slobbering kiss.

Holding the child in one hand, he thrust the little cross into his swaddling-clothes.

Marya Alekseyevna, outraged, took the boy away.

'You'll drop him,' she said, pushing the old man aside. 'Hands off, Herod!'

She began to rock the baby, which had burst into tears.

The negro turned to Sergey Lvovich. He made a short movement as if grasping at his sabre on his belt. There was no sabre there, the old man had been long retired.

'How can I … how could you!' he spluttered, and it was surprising how many deep, bubbling, guttural sounds there could be in a human throat. 'Who are you? You, sir, are a nobody and I am a Hannibal. And this is my breed!'

His eyes were watery and hazy. He was befuddled.

Sergey Lvovich grew pale.

'Don't shout, *mon oncle*,' said Nadezhda Osipovna indistinctly, and her face had broken out in blotches, 'the baby is sleeping. I won't allow shouting in here.'

'Shout at your own wench,' Marya Alekseyevna drawled in a sing-song voice.

The negro moved backwards.

His lips were trembling and he could not find words.

'I renounce … the Pushkins!' he yelled, clutching his little fists. 'I am shaking their dust from my feet!' He kicked a chair with his foot and tore off down the stairs. He could be heard clattering through the room below and running out into the hall.

Marya Alekseyevna laid the baby in the cradle and suddenly shrank into a little thing, dry, old, sharp-nosed. She sniffed and staggered off shaking her head.

Sergey Lvovich, still pale, paced the room, sticking out his chest. He was blinded and deafened by shame. All the guests had now left.

Marya Alekseyevna sat down by the window.

'What an ambassador,' she murmured, 'Grandfather indeed!'

She was breathing with difficulty. Her head was swaying.

The Major-General was strutting through the yard with impetuous but uncertain steps.

The carriage was waiting for him.

'Just look at that grandfather,' Marya Alekseyevna said. 'He can hardly keep upright. Good grief!'

Sergey Lvovich swaggered about for a long time. He was still striding up and down the nursery, kicking away the linen scattered on the floor. He tried to understand how this absurd argument had started, where it had come from and where it had led.

'I am ready to sacrifice anything for the sake of peace,' he said more than once, his hand on his heart, 'ready to bear everything, and it isn't in my character, my love ... But if I am cut to the quick, and what's more – in my own house! I have no wish, my love, to see that ... old horseradish ever again!'

He cast a look at Nadezhda Osipovna and froze.

She was sitting on Arishka's bed, swinging the cradle with her foot, oblivious of his presence. Her eyes were wide-open and she was crying without blinking – big, muddy tears were rolling down from her eyes. She was unaware of them. She glanced at the baby as if it were a stranger. Suddenly she looked at Sergey Lvovich, saw him pacing about, his shoulders jerking, all his noble indignation, and stirred herself.

'Off you go!' she said almost voicelessly.

Bewildered, Sergey Lvovich drew his head into his shoulders and left the room. This was the first time she had banished him. He couldn't understand why she had done so.

'The uncle has been shown the door,' Arina reported in a whisper in the servants' hall. 'He's never to come again. He kept shouting: "We, the Hannibals!" He recognised me. Hasn't seen me for twenty years, but he remembered me. What terribly sharp eyes those Hannibals have!'

'He came here drunk,' Nikita said, 'His manners are insufferable. He's a boor, he speaks the language of the gutter. A General, is he? Huh!'

Two

Soon afterwards and quite unexpectedly, the family ship weighed anchor from Moscow: the roof had started to leak in the attic and there was nowhere to move to. Marya Alekseyevna was going to St Petersburg to sell her cottage in the precincts of the Izmaylovsky barracks ('or else the servants will bring it to rack and ruin – I know them'). Sergey Lvovich wanted to look around. He had a great faculty for moving from one place to another. He loved to break free from all the burdens of life at a stroke by getting into a spring carriage or a large family coach, and then he forgot all his problems. A general decisiveness appeared in his face at the sight of clouds and fields – he loved travelling.

Many happy flying thoughts had been born to the creaking of cartwheels and to chance encounters on the road, and in their absence he enjoyed the sweetness of sleep.

Without a second thought the Pushkins moved to St Petersburg and Sergey Lvovich, remembering his father-in-law's invitation, made for Mikhaylovskoye, leaving it to his wife and mother-in-law to settle into the new abode.

The meeting with his father-in-law disturbed him. He had expected family hugs, tears, remorse and reminiscences, and had mentally pictured a scene of forgiveness. He would forgive his father-in-law on behalf of his wife, Marya Alekseyevna and himself.

Nothing of the kind occurred.

The old negro's indifference was profound. He shook his son-in-law's hand indifferently, inquired about his health mechanically – and a moment later gave him a pale lingering smile. After that they sat on a bench blackened by rains, yellow leaves covered the garden paths, and the negro said not a word. His purple cheeks bulged out over his collar and the eyes were bloodshot – he had been helping himself to vodka since morning.

His lips moved but he remained silent, gazing at the road, the leaves and the trees. He looked more like a derelict building charred by fire than a man. Where was the celebrated lightness, 'as if he were on springs', that

Marya Alekseyevna, Arishka and everybody remembered? He seemed to have forgotten about his companion, oblivious of everything, working his sunken mouth. And only when some peasant girls in coloured sarafans, with baskets in their hands, appeared at the turn of the road and sailed on to the nearest grove to pick mushrooms, did the negro stop chewing. He followed them with his eyes and addressed his son-in-law. His eyes had cleared up.

'Pretty, aren't they?' he said and smiled like all the Hannibals – with his teeth.

Then he started to doze again. He nodded off with his eyes open and steady, his mouth moving and his belly heaving rhythmically. His expensive silk waistcoat with the sparkly glass buttons was soiled.

On the last day of the visit he took his son-in-law for a walk. Leaning on a thick stick, he showed him the forest and the boundaries of his property – three young pine trees on a hillock formed, as it were, a gateway to the estate. Traces of decay and desolation were everywhere: a rotten bench, a crooked arbour, ploughed fields overgrown with charlock. They walked down the hill and stopped. On their right and left were blue lakes, on the surfaces of which ripples appeared like the wrinkles on an old woman's face; when they disappeared, the water grew younger again. Sergey Lvovich was distressed by the general decay and yet strangely soothed by the tranquillity of his father-in-law's estate.

'Like the sea,' he told him, gazing at the lake.

He had never seen the sea. The negro looked at him uncomprehendingly. He stood leaning on his stick for a long time and his son-in-law did not disturb him. Then the old man looked at him and, as if reading his thoughts, pointed with his stick to the lake, the pines and the forest.

'All this I leave to you.'

His father-in-law's estate remained something of an enigma to Sergey Lvovich. The manor-house, which Marya Alekseyevna had described as rather grand, in fact had a thatched roof; it was an elongated, barn-like structure with shingled walls. There was a small bath-house nearby, there were outbuildings to the right, a flower-bed in front of the house – and that thatched roof! But the old negro's gesture had been generous, the lakes were deep, and Sergey Lvovich left in a quandary, with his father-in-law's moist and dispassionate kiss on his cheek. Lush pale flax fields stretched away along both sides of the road, and as he drove along he convinced himself that they were wheat fields.

'Good harvest this year,' he said contentedly to Hannibal's one-eyed cabman, Fomka.

On the way home he recovered somewhat. At the next post-station he chatted to a couple of local landowners, and when he reached home he praised the hearty welcome his father-in-law had given him, telling his wife and mother-in-law meaningfully that the old man had grown frail and seemed to be fading and that the estate was run down.

Winter came and still they stayed on in St Petersburg, not daring either to settle down or to move. Everybody was in a haze, nobody wanted to do anything decisive or to make plans for more than a month ahead. The Emperor's condition was such that things changed every day. Sergey Lvovich decided to keep his head down and see how the land lay, but not to settle in St Petersburg. The further from the capital they were the better.

They lived with the Izmaylovsky Regiment, taking care to avoid the park and the main streets, where the Emperor's presence was strongly felt.

Marya Alekseyevna was now back in the bosom of the army, and her acquaintances among the officers called on her as of old and passed on the latest gossip.

2

The nurse Arina wrapped the little master up, pulled a fur-cap with ear-flaps down over his head and sailed along past the First Company and the Second, singing to the baby as only nurses and nomads do – about everything they see around them.

'There's a soldier marching along. Look at him, dear sir, Aleksandr Sergeyevich, look at the soldier … In a bronze hat … glittering in the sun … and under the badge there's a gleaming cross. A good little hat he has on. When you grow up, you'll wear one exactly the same.'

There were soldiers everywhere. The brass hat with the Maltese Cross was worn by a passing soldier from the Preobrazhensky Regiment.

'And look, Aleksandr Sergeyevich, dear sir, those are cannons. Listen to them! How they boom and roar! All the time, like church bells. Pull the cap down over your ears, it's frosty, you mustn't get cold. Yes. Those are cannons.'

Arina was passing the artillery barracks. The gates were open, and the soldiers were wheeling out cannon. Two of them squatted down to clean them.

'Hey, ma,' said one of them in a low voice, as the nurse was passing, 'Taking the little master to pick mushrooms? Would you care to give the gun a rub?'

'I don't need any of your impudence!' Arina replied calmly.

She sailed on past them to the broad main thoroughfare, Izmaylovsky Street, holding the boy by the hand. He watched everything intently and steadily.

'Ah, look at those little horses – those tassels on the saddles, those red caftans and blue breeches!' Arina was singing. 'They're wearing Bokhara hats. Look at the beards on those men!'

These were Cossacks of the Urals Squadron, which the Emperor kept in St Petersburg. They were moving slowly along Izmaylovsky Street, on which there was no other traffic.

'Now, just look at this general coming! Yes, my dear sir. Just look at the little man in his blue uniform with white breeches! Listen to the little bells ringing, and see how he's tugging the bridle.'

And the diminutive general was indeed hauling at the reins and the horse under him was snorting as it settled down.

'The gentleman's blood is up, you see. Look how angry he is.'

And she stopped as if rooted to the ground. Yanking the reins angrily, the general turned his horse on her and nearly trampled them. He stared straight at the nurse with mad grey eyes, breathing heavily in the frost. His broad face and his hands clutching the reins were red with cold.

'Hat off!' he said hoarsely, flapping his little hand.

More generals rode up, even more splendidly attired.

'Make way!'

'On your knees!'

'The hat, you fool!'

Only then did Arina fall on her knees and rip the cap off the little master's head.

The little general looked at the curly flaxen head of the child. Suddenly, abruptly, he laughed. The cavalcade passed.

The child looked after them, imitating the sound of the galloping horses.

Sergey Lvovich was mortified when he found out what had happened.

'Foo-ool!' he said, pressing both hands to his chest. 'It was the Emperor! You fool!'

'Good Lord!' Arina said. 'So it was.'

The event worried Sergey Lvovich sick. At first he thought they would be summoned, and he wanted to flee to Moscow without delay. By the evening he had calmed down. He visited a friend of his, Baron Bode, and cautiously described what had happened. The baron was highly entertained and Sergey Lvovich grew bolder.

In strict confidence he went over the details and described how the Emperor had shouted:

'Take off that hat! Or I'll …' – jerked his horse's reins over Aleksandr's very head – and galloped off towards the artillery barracks.

'My son's first meeting with His Majesty,' he said with a bow, spreading his hands.

A week later he finally decided that it was unsafe to stay in St Petersburg and that they should move to Moscow. In his view there were only two cities in Russia in which it was possible to live: St Petersburg and Moscow.

3

A month after Sergey Lvovich and his family had escaped back to Moscow and he had been creeping into the office with just one wish – to keep his head down – Emperor Paul died.

The news of his death reached Moscow unusually quickly – within twenty-four hours, faster than the fastest mail. When the details came, there was much excitement. The Emperor had in fact been assassinated, and the nobles regained their liberties. French round hats and breeches were once again permitted. Sergey Lvovich feared the Court to the very core of his soul and therefore imagined himself in conflict with the powers that be. Together with everybody else he was happy to hear about Kutaysov's amusing fall and his escape on foot along the streets in his underwear. Only to think of it! He used to be an equerry! Within a few days Moscow was eager to make up for Paul's Lenten fast. That year people's tongues grew looser on the street and at home than in three of the previous years together. The succession of balls was never-ending.

Whenever Nadezhda Osipovna was preparing to go out, the house was turned upside-down. She was slow and never got dressed in time. Up to the very moment of her departure the maids constantly darted about the house, spilling hot water from the tubs, producing clouds of steam and rustling the ironed silks. In her room Nadezhda Osipovna would yell at the servants; poured water was splashed everywhere and faces were slapped. The maids dashed about with red swollen cheeks and had no time to cry. Half-naked, Nadezhda Osipovna would rush to the next room and fly back like a whirlwind. Sergey Lvovich would narrow his eyes, not without pleasure, while Marya Alekseyevna shrugged her shoulders and retired to her room in high dudgeon.

'You don't feed the hounds before the hunt starts!'

Then, slowly and gracefully, with great dignity, Nadezhda Osipovna would emerge from her room. Sergey Lvovich would screw up his eyes and look her up and down as if seeing her for the first time. They would go out leaving pandemonium behind them.

At balls people let their hair down. Even older folk felt younger and more cheerful.

Sometimes the Pushkin children woke up at night and heard their mother and father quarrelling. Next day their parents would sleep deep into the afternoon.

For those two months everybody felt the hero of the hour, always in the public eye. All distinctions became blurred – between old aristocracy and small fry. Everybody had hopes. A female French artist, Vigée-Lebrun, appeared and churned out daily portraits of fashionable beauties. It took her just two sittings to paint a miniature portrait of Nadezhda Osipovna – very appealing, with ringlets. Sergey Lvovich was displeased that the nose in the picture was hooked but was afraid to say so and praised the portrait.

He believed that the nobles' resumption of their privileges had freed him from work and stopped going to the office. The days were too full anyway; he had no time to see to everything. He briefly patted his children's cheeks and made for Okhotny Ryad. Renowned connoisseurs crowded round the stalls and big-bellied shop-keepers in blue caftans made low bows to them. Everybody spoke in an undertone. Fish, still alive, lay in quivering piles; the experts scrutinised them, their gills and their eyes – whether they were floppy, whether the fins were pale or red, sniffed them, exchanged opinions and gossip. Footmen stood waiting. Sergey Lvovich did not always buy fish and often had no intention of doing so. These visits to the stalls were more a kind of social gathering, a meeting of friends; nothing in the world was sweeter – except perhaps his secret escapades. What were brilliant but precarious careers by comparison with these? Sergey Lvovich had no yearning for them whatsoever.

That was how he spent his days. And life went on like this for two or three months. Then Moscow calmed down somewhat, everybody found his bearings and took up his place. Sergey Lvovich felt some distress from time to time: how could he have made such a blunder? – to move with the whole family (not without difficulty – their carriage had broken down on the road) a month before it had all happened, and the new era, the reign of Alexander I, had begun? In St Petersburg titles and positions were being granted to the really clever people. However, in Moscow too, within days, Nikolay Mikhaylovich Karamzin had acquired an extraordinary importance and had received two diamond rings. But for some reason the new reign had nothing to offer Sergey Lvovich, he remained at the Commissariat, even if not putting in the hours, and his wife was expecting again.

Nadezhda Osipovna was near her time indeed, and soon another son was born. They named him Nikolay.

Sergey Lvovich was bewildered to see himself the father of a growing family. He had no clear thoughts about it and the future began to look uncertain. One event followed another – and he was unprepared. In fact everything in his life happened too quickly and he never seemed to have time to make sense of it all. Everyone, for example, forgot that sister Annette was engaged. Her fiancé Ivan Ivanovich Dmitriyev, the poet, had bought a little house with a little garden in Moscow, but was in no hurry to marry. When nobody was listening Marya Alekseyevna would say:

'He never intended to. She dreamed it all up.'

Sister Annette's complexion turned sallow and she started to wear dark clothes. She fluffed her hair up as usual but became a zealous church-goer. She felt that both she and her brothers had been victimised – neither Nadezhda Osipovna nor Kapitolina Mikhaylovna could make a man happy. Sergey Lvovich secretly had the same belief. His wife was 'the beautiful Creole', much admired by everyone. He would turn pale with rage when she danced at a ball with some tall Guardsman: it brought home to him his own small stature. Meanwhile, since she had become pregnant, a house arrest had been imposed on him, which was becoming more and more irksome. Nadezhda Osipovna was anxious not to lose sight of him. He was not even allowed to pinch a housemaid's cheek, an absolutely innocent piece of play.

In this uncertain state he was dying to get out of the house, to pay visits – from the Buturlins to the Sushkovs, from the Sushkovs to the Dashkovs – even smaller fry would do. On Tuesdays he went to the Nobles' Club. He desperately needed diversion, as if pursuing lost time or searching for something forgotten. His worst fear now was that the new order might estrange his friends and acquaintances or that they might grow snooty. Dashkov's casual bow on one occasion had made him tremble. Looking at him stealing away from the house, Marya Alekseyevna softly hummed an old folksong:

> *I am young, I am pretty,*
> *I shall never find a place.*

By lunch-time or by evening, if he had had a lunch out – lunch at home was rather cheese-paring – he would feel a pleasant tiredness and yawningly remember the *bons mots* and events of the day. Nadezhda Osipovna would look at him closely and suspiciously; Sergey Lvovich would sense her distrust and tell her lies. She did not entirely believe him, and with good reason. Having been brought up on Marya Alekseyevna's tales of the schemes and stratagems of men, she suspected Sergey Lvovich of having some vile attachment on the side. Life with such a husband was insecure. And the truth was that Sergey Lvovich didn't spend all his time shining in the best circles. Recently he had taken to the company of his young colleagues from that cursed Commissariat staff, still essentially children but mentally in tune with him. He had been secretly gambling with them. Fashionable games were organised: boston, vingt-et-un, macao, and the very latest – shtoss and 'three-and-three'. Sergey Lvovich would fairly throw himself into the game and experience a passionate thrill when showing his card. When he won, he felt like embracing the whole world. The one thing he was afraid of was that his opponent might forget to pay up. He made sure of concealing these entertainments from his family. When he won, however, he found it difficult to resist the temptation to reveal it all to Nadezhda Osipovna. He would jingle the coins in his pocket, bite his lip, and then sigh – he was not understood in his own home.

4

Once a month Sergey Lvovich assumed a businesslike air and went out to Ogorodnaya Suburb to pay a visit to his mother, Olga Vasilyevna. Her house was large and cold. She never went out. After a life of passion she now ruled a bunch of old women and three half-blind servants. To rule the lives of her sons was already beyond her power and she just grumbled about them occasionally. Her daughters were completely under her control.

There was a room in the house that she never entered. It was crammed with all sorts of lumber and had been turned into a storeroom. When her sons visited her, they would cast sidelong glances at the locked door with the usual childish cowardice – this was where their father had spent his last years. By tacit consent neither Olga Vasilyevna nor her sons ever mentioned Lev Aleksandrovich. Only the dim-eyed servants talked about him sometimes, in the evenings or at night when they could not sleep. He had been a hot-blooded and ruthless man and had caused the death of his first wife. Growing jealous of the Italian tutor in service with them, he had imprisoned his wife in the cellar, and she had died there in chains on the straw. As for the Italian, he had given him such a beating that he fell dead on the spot.

Olga Vasilyevna was his second wife; she had survived. By the end of his life her spouse had gone mad. He had been put in a side room and Olga Vasilyevna had managed the house and the children. It was high time. Lev Aleksandrovich had retired at the age of forty, immediately after Peter III's death. He had refused to recognise Catherine the Great and been incarcerated for two years. After his release, he had squandered his fortune in bouts of rage and rancour, directed either at himself or others. He liked fast horses and in the course of his life had ridden whole stables of expensive mounts to death. People approaching from the opposite direction would take refuge in the roadside ditch on hearing Pushkin coming. When Olga Vasilyevna had started to sort out the bills and the pawn-tickets, she had felt the earth open up under her: the family fortune had been crumbling on all sides. She had brought order to it, placated the creditors, gathered together everything that was left, and given her children a start in life. Lev Aleksandrovich had died ten years previously. Olga Vasilyevna had waited for this event for a long time, but after his death she had suddenly felt bored and empty. She stopped going out, realising that no matter what she did, she could neither help her children nor prevent them from doing as they pleased. Since her husband's fall Olga Vasilyevna had never stopped condemning Catherine the Great and the Empress's favourites, the Orlovs in particular.

'They call themselves Counts? They're nothing but grooms! The only things they're good at are breeding mares and brawling.'

She considered Peter III the rightful Tsar and grumbled when people zealously called Catherine 'mother' in her presence.

'Mother – and father too!'

She had previously lived in constant fear of her husband's fits and foibles but now she was sorry to see that her sons were so unlike their father, quite lacking in his fibre. She was harshly critical of them, and would probably have been strangely pleased had they indulged in colossal drinking-bouts, riotous behaviour, or gone to some other extreme. But they did nothing of the sort. Her sons were *idlers*.

The old woman would give Sergey Lvovich her flat waxen hand to be kissed and peer at her unreliable son with her sharp little eyes. She suspected both him and his brother to be spineless wastrels. She had changed her will twice. But she respected Vasily since he was the elder and she made excuses for his failure to advance, putting it down to bad luck. She believed that Sergey Lvovich would squander his entire fortune in no time at all. She looked upon her daughter-in-law with suspicion, convinced that she was the reason why 'Sergey's career was unsatisfactory'. Nervously she patted her grandchildren's cheeks, looked into their eyes and, suppressing a sigh, sent them outside for a walk:

'Why should they make a noise in here?'

Sergey Lvovich transformed himself in his mother's presence, just as he did when he went to the Commissariat. He tried to look dignified, told the old lady about St Petersburg, passed on the latest Court gossip and frightened her with an account of events abroad. He spoke of French victories, Bonaparte, the Consul's wife Josephine, the Creole. His mother looked at him askance – he dropped into the conversation the names of the most important persons in St Petersburg, as if he had just been with them. Sometimes he berated them:

'*Ce coquin de* Kochubey ...,' he would say.

Once he gave his mother a fright by tearing Prince Adam Czartoryski to shreds when he came to power.

'His claims to nobility are fake,' he said, 'he is a bastard, and we know his menial's pride. His mother is a scheming, dissipated Pole, she's been in the pay of the French – that's all.'

Olga Vasilyevna was alarmed. Her son was heading for the fortress like

his father before him. But those French rebels! She changed her opinion of
her son as an idler. In Moscow everyone knew how precarious things were.
The Tsar was young. Old men were now falling out of favour and the young
taking their place. With that quiff over his forehead and that negress of his,
her son might be in favour any moment now.

The old lady screwed up her eyes irritably. She was defeated.

At night, in a bed warmed up by the fattest serf-girl, Olga Vasilyevna told
her half-blind confidante Ulyashka:

'Negroes are in power now. In Paris, their most important man – what's his
name? – he has a negro wife.'

Ulyashka agreed:

'Men are always after novelty.'

5

At the moment the Pushkins lived in a neat wooden house belonging to Prince
Yusupov, a man of consequence. He himself lived in the manor-house nearby.
Sergey Lvovich was very pleased by that proximity, though the Prince rarely
appeared in Moscow. Only once had Sergey Lvovich witnessed his arrival, in
summer: the valet had been fussing about, the serfs opening the windows and
carrying the trunks – and then a stout man with thick lips and sad un-Russian
eyes had gone straight into the house. On another occasion the Prince had
caught sight of Nadezhda Osipovna and had given her a sweeping bow, in
either the Asian or the latest European manner. Afterwards he had sent his
housekeeper to tell the Pushkins that their children could play in his garden
whenever they wished. The Prince was a notorious womaniser and Nadezhda
Osipovna was flattered by his attention. He went away soon afterwards.

The bailiff was in despair about the tenants.

'Major Pushkin,' he wrote in a report to the Prince, 'who lives in the middle
part of the house, paid a month's rent in May and since then there have been
no payments for over six months. I called upon him three times demanding
the rent, but he ordered the servants to say he was out. Would Your Excellency
instruct your obedient servant in detail as to how to deal with Major Pushkin
and whether he should be evicted?'

Meanwhile Sergey Lvovich suffered bereavement – his mother Olga
Vasilyevna passed away. She had fallen ill, summoned her sons, given them a
long stare, wagged her finger at them, and died.

After his mother's funeral, Sergey Lvovich moved into a better and more
spacious house in the same area.

Nadezhda Osipovna's eyes shone: she loved changing houses. The bailiff
personally helped the cabmen to pack the furniture and household things.

Taking advantage of the Prince's permission, the children, accompanied by the nurse, continued to have walks in Yusupov's garden.

6

It was a magnificent one. Yusupov had a Tatar fondness for climbing plants, plenty of shade and fountains, and a Parisian's affection for regular-shaped paths, passages and ponds. He had long served as an envoy in Venice and Naples and had brought home some ancient statues with ample bottoms and blackened knees. A close-fisted oriental, he did not, however, begrudge money on art. This garden that he had developed on the outskirts of Moscow spread over more than three acres.

The Prince allowed his friends and those he wanted to favour to walk in the garden; he let children in very rarely and reluctantly. Certainly the garden would have been better preserved without visitors, but there is nothing more mournful for a superstitious person than a deserted garden, and the Prince's acquaintances, unaware of their role, livened up the landscape. A Muscovite, an enthusiast for all things Western, climbed the stairway in the Versailles style he had read about or heard of, and his Moscow gait changed completely. The statues seemed to greet him like sentinels. He walked on and, fascinated by the regular avenues, started to promenade about a circular pond in an exaggeratedly elegant manner; the pond was so round that the very surface of the water seemed to him to curve. When an hour later he left the garden and returned to his home neighbourhood still walking in this way, he kept imagining himself to be greatly refined. Only when he heard the cries of a pie-vendor or ran into an acquaintance did it dawn on him that something was not quite right, that this was not Versailles and that he was not French.

The nurse and the children remained welcome in the garden.

Arina climbed the steps bravely, and took great care that the little masters and Miss Olga Sergeyevna had not dropped their toys or broken a baluster. She had a worried look. Trying not to look at the statues, she concentrated all her attention on the pond.

'They're not moving,' she said. 'The fish must be bored in water like this, little master. Look how fat they are!'

The master had no interest in the fish. He was scowling at the statue of Diana. He remembered something. The bailiff had once told him that the statue was of Diana, and on another occasion that it was a nymph. At home he had asked his father who Diana was. Sergey Lvovich had laughed a lot and then said meaningfully that the girl was one of the Olympian virgin goddesses. The goddess, her head carelessly thrown back, was warming her pointed nipples and slender knees in the sun. The big toe on one foot was broken off.

'Ugh!' – Arina was upset and secretly spat. 'Would you like to run around the pond, master?'

They passed on to open ground, a glade with lush grass. The path was sprinkled with damp yellow sand. At the very centre of the glade stood a Roman fountain, with the water falling like glass into a stone bowl.

'It's like a mill,' said Arina with a smile. She liked this spot. She found the fountain entertaining.

'Wealthy Tatars, master Aleksandr Sergeyevich,' she said mysteriously, 'always like running water in a garden.'

The nurse busied herself with Olga Sergeyevna who was pottering about in the sand, and wiped Nikolay Sergeyevich's nose.

He ran off far beyond the regular path, walked along the side paths past the white faces and stone bellies, and then got lost. He could hear voices in the distance, his nurse calling, but paid no attention.

They searched for him but he ran deeper and deeper into the garden. It was real Tatar wilderness here, the new cultivated garden ended and the old overgrown one took over. The tree trunks were covered with moss as if with ashes. Brushwood grew around the statues. He liked their blank, unseeing eyes, their open mouths, their indolent poses. Indistinct, mysterious words came to his mind as in a dream. For a long time he stood still, smiling unconsciously and aimlessly and touching the dirty white knees. They were disgustingly cold. Then, slowly and sullenly, he wandered towards the pond and back to Arina.

The summer was stiflingly hot. Moscow, like Samarkand, was burning in the heat. The leaves on the trees hung lifeless and dusty. The Boldino village headman reported to Sergey Lvovich that the corn had burnt away to nothing. Nadezhda Osipovna roamed about the half-dark rooms in a night-dress – the shutters were kept closed during the day.

In the autumn the earth still would not cool down and the children spent a lot of time in Yusupov's garden, where the symmetrical lawns and the water moderated everything, even the heat.

It was two in the afternoon – the hour to drowse and dream. Arina was dozing off on the bench, her mouth half-open. Suddenly a faint wind sprang up, the leaves on the trees stirred. He saw a slender stone body rock twice towards him, as if about to fall on him. His heart skipped a beat. Nikolay and Olga burst into tears. Arina woke up. With the pointless artfulness of a child, he pretended to have been looking all this time at the pond.

They went home. Only by the end of the day did the gossips spread the news that there had been an earthquake in Moscow. In the evening a thick fog came down. That night he couldn't sleep and pricked up his ears. Arina's breathing came deep and slow as if she were singing. He heard the sounds of heavy barefoot steps, like some beast's, coming from behind the door: his mother was still roaming about the house. A glass tinkled, she drank water and breathed heavily. Father said something or called to her from a distance and she laughed in reply. The solid barefoot steps resounded throughout the rooms again. He fell asleep.

The dense fog lingered in Moscow for five days and people stumbled into each other. Everywhere there was talk of the earthquake. Cracks were found in the walls of a cellar and people went to inspect them as if they were a famous attraction. In another place a crevice appeared nearly a metre wide. Grandmother Marya Alekseyevna claimed that she had felt the earth shaking.

'I told Nikolashka to start cooking a pie, and I'd just sat down when I saw the table rocking like a jelly,' she said, doubting it herself.

The only conviction the Pushkins held was their firm faith in signs and fortune-telling. If on leaving home Marya Alekseyevna came across a woman with empty buckets, she would go back at once. Nadezhda Osipovna was afraid of the evil eye. As a young girl she had always dripped wax into water at Christmas-time and had predicted that her betrothed would be sharp-nosed. Even Sergey Lvovich, meeting a priest, would quietly cock a snook at him in his pocket. In the evenings grandmother Marya Alekseyevna would talk at length about amazing coincidences.

The whole household looked grave. The earthquake was a bad omen. Karamzin wrote an article explaining to his fellow citizens that earthquakes are merely a physical phenomenon. But his equanimity had been ruffled too and he had failed to persuade the Muscovites to enjoy life like the Antilleans, the Filipinos, the Indonesians, the Sicilians and particularly the Japanese, for whom daily earthquakes are like summer thunderstorms in Moscow. He mentioned, somewhat inopportunely, the earthquake that had occurred in Moscow under Tsar Vasily the Dark, when the city had burnt to the ground.

Karamzin's physical explanation had frightened Marya Alekseyevna and Nadezhda Osipovna all the more: that fire constricts air masses shackled and incarcerated deep in the earth, which, with incredible energy, seek a way out; that the Moscow earthquake had been an echo of another one; that earthquakes always have an epicentre; that there are interconnected hollows in the earth where the inflamed air rages, and two opposite points on the earth can shake at the same time! Any city on earth could be one of these – including Moscow, with its streets and rivers. The good news – maintained Nikolay Mikhaylovich – was that another three and a half centuries could pass until the next earthquake, the same span of time as had elapsed since Vasily the Dark's reign. So time was on their side.

At night Nadezhda Osipovna dreamed of fire passing through empty passages like the corridors in their house, and dug Sergey Lvovich in the ribs. She was convinced all this meant that the servants wanted to set the house on fire, that today Nikolashka had had the look of a pirate, and whimpered that weak gentry always had unruly serfs. Such conversations were common now in Moscow. Sergey Lvovich would breathe fiercely and noisily and go back to sleep.

Three days later the cook Nikolashka got drunk and proposed a toast to Consul Napoleon in the servants' hall. Sergey Lvovich ordered him to be flogged and personally saw to it that the punishment was duly carried out in the stables.

Then the fog cleared away, everything returned to normal, and the earthquake was forgotten.

Three

Sister Annette had not got married, their mother had passed away, there had been the earthquake and very soon afterwards, that same year, Vasily Lvovich's life had turned upside-down. His wife moved out of the house and left him.

Sister Annette found her vocation. Together with Yelizaveta Lvovna she was forever going excitedly from Vasily Lvovich's to Sergey Lvovich's house and even paid a visit to a Moscow sorceress to have their fortunes told.

Vasily Lvovich was dismayed and kept rubbing his forehead.

Twice, in the presence of strangers, he broke down in tears. They tried to soothe him; he took long desperate gulps of water and waved his hand in bewilderment and despair.

Everything was falling apart.

'Nothing like this has ever happened to me before,' he said naively.

Sergey Lvovich and sister Annette turned out to be the strictest defenders of their elder brother's honour. Kapitolina Mikhaylovna's name was consigned to oblivion and banned from use; she was always referred to as the 'villain'. Whenever the conversation came round to her, Anna Lvovna hushed the children and sent them out of the room, and Sergey Lvovich narrowed his eyes meaningfully.

Vasily Lvovich's explanations, his ahs and ohs, his hand-clasping, his babbling and exclamations, were completely incomprehensible. In other respects, however, he remained as he had previously been – he ate a lot, wore his hair curled and in between floods of tears would recite a verse or two.

'Dear heart, *Basile,* darling, try to think how it might have begun,' his sister Anna Lvovna begged him.

And Vasily Lvovich did so. Horse Guardsman Prince W.'s visits had become more frequent – this was how Vasily Lvovich pronounced his name – 'Prince Double-U'. He had become suspicious, given her warnings – and at last had found her gone. He could not, he spluttered, put down her flight from home to anything else but adultery. In his opinion, his wife was going to marry another man. It was unprecedented! A wife going to marry another man! With her husband still alive!

Abruptly, Sergey Lvovich demanded:

'His name?'

He insisted on knowing the name of the seducer.

When asked why he needed the name, Sergey Lvovich gave the icy reply: 'To call him out.'

Avoiding looking into his brother's eyes, Vasily Lvovich refused to name him.

He was not sure if it was really Prince W., he said. Perhaps Prince W. was being used just as a blind, a figurehead. He had certainly been seen to pay her attention on one occasion, using the familiar form of address, but who could really say for certain?

'He flirted with her …' Anna Lvovna asked slowly, 'in your presence?'

'Yes, but he's a cousin,' Vasily Lvovich replied evasively.

'*Le cousinage est un dangereux voisinage,*' Anna Lvovna chanted in her thin voice, compressing her lips. Her face at that moment looked just like a Catholic prelate's.

'*He* may have been just flirting with her, but she – try to remember, darling – maybe *she* took it seriously?'

In Vasily Lvovich's presence, taking pity on him, Anna Lvovna never called her sister-in-law 'the villain' but simply referred to her as 'she'.

All in all, there was some mystery about the matter. The maid Annushka, or as Anna Lvovna called her, Anka, walked around quietly, with tear-stained eyes and an elegant new brooch. She was as pretty as usual, buxom and fresh-faced. Anna Lvovna told her to leave the room, at which Vasily Lvovich gave a blink and a snort.

All of a sudden, without looking anyone in the face, but quite emphatically, Vasily Lvovich announced that he had no grudge against his wife. He did not know the ins and outs of the matter but had only one desire – for his wife to come back; he was not going to divorce her, on the contrary, in future he wanted to live with her inseparably – he was her husband and a Christian and he was prepared for anything.

Sergey Lvovich was deeply moved.

'Angel,' Annette said.

Vasily Lvovich repeated in a firm voice that first and foremost he was a husband and a Christian. He cheered up noticeably and at once put on his new dark-blue tail-coat, sprayed himself with scent, and for the first time after what had happened he went out to take a walk along the boulevards.

Sergey Lvovich changed his mind about the duel. It was decided that they should discuss matters with the wayward wife. Nadezhda Osipovna was authorised to go to see the sinner and talk to her.

Against all expectations Nadezhda Osipovna came back stone-faced and reported drily, even gloatingly, that Kapitolina Mikhaylovna had said she would never return and 'was ready to die in a monastery, on a pile of straw, and live on focusts and wild honey …'

'*Locusts*,' Sergey Lvovich corrected her.

' … rather than return to that house.'

Then Nadezhda Osipovna conversed in whispers with sister Annette, and sister Annette clasped her hands.

'Beware, Nadine!' she said. 'How can you trust that villain!'

Brother and sister went off at once to Vasily Lvovich's house.

That evening they found a remarkable difference in him. He lost all control and flung himself groaning around the room. Fearing for his life, Anna Lvovna put him to bed; it looked as if a fever was starting. In a weak voice he asked for Annushka. In spite of Sergey Lvovich's protestations, Annushka was brought in; Anna Lvovna even sat her down by the bed as a nurse. The doctor was sent for.

The doctor pronounced Vasily Lvovich's life out of danger. There was no fever, but in the evening Vasily Lvovich told his sister that his life was over.

He said that a messenger from either Kapitolina Mikhaylovna or Prince W. – he did not wish to know which exactly – had turned up at his house and extorted a letter from him. When he mentioned the letter, Vasily Lvovich started to toss about the bed. Anna Lvovna sprinkled him with water. Somewhat recovered, he confessed that in the letter he had monstrously slandered himself and authenticated those wrongful accusations with his signature.

'Annushka, leave the room,' said Anna Lvovna sharply. 'But darling *Basile,* how could you have written such a thing?'

'I was delirious,' Vasily Lvovich said, spreading his hands helplessly.

He jumped from his bed and told his sister with extraordinary animation:

'I am not giving her a divorce and never will – as a punishment. I am not afraid of legal proceedings, madam. We'll see!'

2

Sontsev was sent to talk to Kapitolina Mikhaylovna. He came back puffing and panting and said that he could not believe his eyes when shown the letter in Vasily Lvovich's own hand confirming that since for two years and one month he had been having an illicit relationship with a certain serf-girl of his, he could not, in all conscience, oppose his wife's demand for separation and gave her complete freedom to do as she pleased and to marry whoever she wanted.

Wincing, Vasily Lvovich said:

'I don't remember this, it's a complete blank in my mind. It's completely untrue. I remember nothing of the kind.'

He began to resume his moaning, but in lower tones than before, and soon nature took its course – next day he went out for a walk and from then on began to go to the theatre as if nothing had happened.

General curiosity, however, was aroused. The rumour spread that indeed Vasily Lvovich had been having an affair with his maid Anka.

One evening even the portly Sontsev, sitting in the family circle beside sister Annette, when the conversation turned towards Vasily Lvovich, narrowed his eyes, heaved his belly and announced that his brother-in-law had always had in him that Russian folk fibre that was attracted by female earthiness. Sister Annette immediately asked him to say no more.

At least five times a day Vasily Lvovich had to swear to his friends that he was not to blame, but his friends fed his vanity, smilingly nicknaming him after such prodigious heroes from popular French novels as Céladon and the chevalier de Faublas.

But he sensed with some alarm that the reputation he had enjoyed hitherto, of a poet and an independent personality, a man of some consequence, was tottering. People were now starting to treat him condescendingly, using the familiar form of address with him, even those he was not close to.

The renown of a St Petersburg *brigand* had been pleasant in Moscow, when it had related to the past and been attached to him from a distance, so to speak. Now, however, this renown was quite inappropriate. Vasily Lvovich had sometimes dreamt of the rank of chamberlain. He did not want to have the reputation of a notorious womaniser, and especially, as he would point out, since it was not so much he himself as unfortunate circumstances that were to blame.

He certainly had no wish to be on familiar terms with all those callow youths, a familiarity that had been threatening him since the scandal broke. He was gossiped about, he was pointed at in the street.

Intending to bring this dubious situation to an end, Vasily Lvovich, though inwardly seething with indignation at his wife, decided to appeal to his father-in-law, an old translator, a respectable man in his own way, but a slow-witted nobody to whom he had done a favour: a year earlier Vasily Lvovich had composed for his deaf father-in-law's magazine, *The Gift of Religion*, two thoroughly fitting poems, *Oh Thou, Who Bore me in Thy Womb* and one about *a wife burdened with her sins*. The second poem was most moving, beginning with a description of the prodigal wife:

> *A wife, heavy with her sinful bale,*
> *Goes to her master, ashamed and pale …*

and ending with her complete absolution.

Vasily Lvovich now planned, when he saw his father-in-law, to apply this poem to Kapitolina Mikhaylovna.

But the old fool refused to see him.

All his attempts to assume a solemn tone and fend off the morbid curiosity of the callow youths were of no use. Vasily Lvovich himself could not bear a solemn tone for more than half an hour, and the youths continued to impose themselves on him as 'friends'.

Eventually he found himself the talk of the city.

Meanwhile Kapitolina Mikhaylovna had officially applied to the court for divorce.

Vasily Lvovich had not expected this. Somehow he managed to buy her off and to hush the matter up, but with every passing day it was becoming more and more difficult for him to remain in Moscow. Even sister Annette, a spinster, though indignant with his villainous wife, started to grumble about Vasily Lvovich on the quiet, and Sergey Lvovich too came to distance himself clearly from him, shrugging his shoulders and falling silent when asked about his brother, feigning ignorance, and speaking to him only when necessary.

Once Vasily Lvovich came home from the theatre to find in his pocket a slip of paper bearing a famous poem by Grécourt written out in neat childish handwriting. It was a poem about a servant girl in an unknown translation:

> *Let those who wish to faire la cour*
> *To all those beauties nobly bred.*
> *Such is my nature, my amour,*
> *That from dawn to midnight hour*
> *I must kiss my pretty serving maid.*

Vasily Lvovich was stupefied.

It was definitely a poor translation – meaningless and unmetrical. Undoubtedly it was a prank of the young rascals who thrust themselves on him these days, and they must have got a child to copy the verses to throw him off their trail. In spite of his indignation Vasily Lvovich corrected the illiterate last line into a much better one: *I must embrace my amorous maid* – and only then tore the slip into small pieces.

The worst thing was that a close friend of his youth, a boon companion from the St Petersburg Galley, a relative and namesake, Aleksey Mikhaylovich Pushkin, had joined the Moscow youths. He was quite a character. Both his father and uncle had been found guilty of forgery and deported to Siberia and it was later decreed that they should be called 'the former Pushkins'. The former Pushkins' son had been brought up by strangers, but his unstable character made him a chip off the old block. Moreover, he built up this instability into a law of life. He was a drawing-room preacher of atheism, of the idea that the universe contains nothing but the swirling mists of imagination. He had been a success in Moscow and soon became indispensable in games and dramatic performances. He was waspish and spiteful, though there was something amusing in his malice.

Meeting Vasily Lvovich at the theatre and in society, he made a point of tormenting him with insinuations and witticisms, together with an exaggerated demonstration of his friendship and affection. He would hug him, press him to his bosom, kiss him firmly, then look strictly into the eye of the dazed Vasily Lvovich and explain with a shudder: 'Oh, you never change! You loafer! Ladies' man!', and immediately push him away as if he were afraid to touch him.

Vasily Lvovich's religious poems composed for his father-in-law provided Aleksey Mikhaylovch with the most indecent amusement. At a crowded ball at the Buturlins', standing next to Vasily Lvovich, he warmly praised his poems and then suddenly hissed the unexpectedly loud aside: 'Tartuffe!'

Vasily Lvovich did his best to avoid meeting his cousin, but after the divorce had been announced, his atheist relative made his life impossible. Seeing Vasily Lvovich in society, he would sigh loudly and sternly wag an admonitory finger at him. Vasily Lvovich began to suspect that his cousin had had a hand in the verses he had received.

He grew tired of his scandalous fame. His pride was more than satiated, he had no more appetite for it.

3

Vasily Lvovich told everybody that he was leaving for Paris.

Some of his friends believed it, others didn't, but their curiosity was aroused. Deep in his heart Sergey Lvovich didn't believe it. Moscow talk was of nothing else but Vasily Lvovich's trip. His idle young friends bet big money – would he leave or stay?

Vasily Lvovich overheard old Prince Dolgorukov asking his companion at a ball:

'Could you show me, my good fellow, where Pushkin is, the one who is leaving for Paris?'

Vasily Lvovich pretended not to hear but his heart skipped a beat with delight. He grinned – he couldn't deny it – this was fame!

'Not much to look at,' the Prince said. 'What's this obsession with Paris?'

It turned out that it was necessary for Vasily Lvovich to ask permission to visit Paris for the purpose of getting medical treatment from famous physicians. Surprisingly, the permission was granted.

Vasily Lvovich was transfigured. Suddenly he became dignified as never before, as if he were strolling not on the Kuznetsky Bridge but along the Champs-Elysées. So that he would be able to keep up with the Parisians, every day he bought something at the French shops on the Kuznetsky Bridge, and eventually accumulated a hoard of handkerchiefs, canes, and charms on steel chains. On seeing him his friends would ask him with respect and envy:

'Are you still here? We thought you were in Paris!'

Now not only the young idlers but even his old friends took an interest in him. Karamzin commissioned him to write letters as soon as he arrived in Paris and not to delay in sending them to him for publication.

'I'll be writing about absolutely everything in the world,' Vasily Lvovich promised firmly.

At last the date of departure was fixed. The general attention he had enjoyed during his preparations rewarded Vasily Lvovich for a month of painful seizures.

Three days before his departure, Ivan Ivanovich Dmitriyev, who had been stung to the quick by Vasily Lvovich's forthcoming trip, had written a narrative poem: *N. N.'s Journey to Paris and London*:

My friends! Dear ladies! I'm in Paris!

The poem went round from hand to hand, faster than news in newspapers. It was better than anything that Dmitriyev had ever written seriously; it was of an absolutely new, lively and gossipy kind. So poetry was enriched not only by Vasily Lvovich's verses but by his actual adventures.

One of the young idlers managed to slip the new poem to Vasily Lvovich, saying that it was, well, just a trifle.

In his haste Vasily Lvovich forgot about it. In the evening, seated by the window and looking out onto the familiar street, he wanted to compose an elegy, but it wouldn't come to him. He became sad. And he never wrote elegies when he was sad.

At that moment he remembered the trifle given to him by his friend that morning. From the first lines it was obvious that the poem was about Vasily Lvovich's visit to Paris. N. N. was Vasily Lvovich! He chuckled. Yes, this was fame.

I know every street and boulevard,
All the fashionable shops ...

The second section pained him somewhat: here Vasily Lvovich was staying on the fifth floor of a Paris hotel.

'This betrays the fact that he has never been to Paris,' said Vasily Lvovich with a grin. 'There are hardly any five-storey buildings there – and lodging in attics is not for me, thank you!'

The poem went on outlining, rather pleasantly, his weaknesses:

> *For instance, I enjoy assailing*
> *My audience with lyrics and failing*
> *To see when they're no longer listening …*

'I don't write lyrics,' said Vasily Lvovich softly with a pale smile, 'only elegies and fables, as you do, Ivan Ivanovich.'

> *I like to stroll about the squares*
> *Dressed as the latest mode declares …*

'Like the French,' he whispered.

> *Tail-coat, jabot, waistcoat, shirt*
> *All outfit of the latest sort …*

'That rhyme … rather impure,' said Vasily Lvovich, narrowing his eyes. The more his fame grew, the more it smacked of bragging; there was nothing honourable about it.

Looking around feeling wounded, he caught sight of Annushka: she gave him her usual affecting glances – pretty, ruddy and buxom as ever. He consoled himself by embracing her.

'A poet is always in the public eye!' he said.

Annushka was near her time.

On the day of his departure Vasily Lvovich felt some anxiety. He was going to travel further than he ever had before. Sergey Lvovich, sister Annette and all the family saw him off and cheered him up.

Sergey Lvovich looked at his luggage with jealous regret. Annushka wept big, peasant girl's tears and planted a secret kiss on her master's shoulder, while Vasily Lvovich, exercising the right of a traveller bound for foreign countries, kissed her loudly and for the first time called her Anna Nikolayevna. All his friends accompanied Vasily Lvovich to the Moscow gate. There they drank a bottle of wine in his honour, Vasily Lvovich embraced them all, gave a sob, made himself comfortable in the coach, waved his handkerchief, then his cane – and off he went to Paris.

Four

BY the age of six he had become heavy and awkward. His flaxen curls started to darken. He had a vaguely fixed look and moved awkwardly. All the games he was forced to play by his mother or his nurse seemed totally alien to him. He would drop his toys with complete indifference. He didn't remember other children, his play-mates; at least, he gave no sign of being glad to see them or sad to leave them. He seemed to be preoccupied with some serious, taxing business which he did not or could not communicate to those around him. He was taciturn. Sometimes he was caught unawares at what seemed like a private game: he would measure objects and assess the space between them, lifting his fingers to his narrowed eye. It might have been a mathematician's pastime, but not one for a young gentleman. When called, he responded reluctantly and petulantly. He acquired bad habits – he dropped handkerchiefs and several times his mother caught him biting his nails, though this was a vice he had undoubtedly picked up from her.

His mother would give him long stares. When he noticed them, she would look away. Her uncle Pyotr Abramovich had been absolutely right: he definitely took after his grandfather, Osip Abramovich. She didn't remember her father and since childhood had been afraid of the mere mention of his name. She had never asked Marya Alekseyevna but she felt instinctively and with absolute certainty that her son took after him – no one else. She would pin to his clothes the handkerchiefs that the boy kept dropping, but this was embarrassing and he learned to do without a handkerchief. She tied his hands with a belt to prevent him from biting his nails. She had no idea what to expect next, what unpleasant and unnatural features might reveal themselves in this boy, so similar to his grandfather. The child did not cry; his thick lips trembled; he studied his mother.

In general, he promised to be unsociable. His aunt Anna Lvovna sensed it with some preternatural instinct. She was never away from their household – brother Vasily had been temporarily rescued and safely placed in Paris, and now brother Sergey had to be saved. She said not a word to Nadine but spotted anything and everything out of order. If a cracked glass was brought to table, she would say:

'Look, that glass is cracked!'

When Nikita forgot to bring a vinegar-cruet for Sergey Lvovich, she told him icily:

'Bring the vinegar, the mustard and everything that's needed.'

In her presence Nadezhda Osipovna dropped cups deliberately, purely to relieve the anger that was boiling up inside her.

But both Annette and Nadine shared the same conviction: Aleksandr was not growing up the way he should. There was no civility in him. His aunt believed it was his upbringing that was to blame.

'Aleksandr, stand up,' she would say.

'Sashka, say thank-you to your father and mother.'

His mother and father called him Sashka when they spoke affectionately, but his aunt pronounced the name maliciously and he couldn't bear it.

Aleksandr would stand up. He would say thank-you to his father and mother. Once he looked at his aunt and suddenly smiled. She was stupefied: the child's smile was abrupt, improper and impertinent.

'What are you laughing at? Why are you showing your teeth?' she asked, alarmed. 'What's so funny?'

'Sashka, off you go,' ordered Sergey Lvovich. Aleksandr got up from the table and went off.

At the door he stumbled into Arina. Looking at him tenderly, Arina thrust a honey-cake into his hand and in passing pressed him to her broad warm bosom.

He would steal through his parents' house like a wolf-cub – sidling among the secretly hostile objects. He was clumsy and broke an incredible amount of crockery, at least so it seemed to the anguished Sergey Lvovich, who felt the value of each glass that fell from this child's hands. Not normally aware of the household objects surrounding him and unappreciative of them, he felt their irreplaceability with unusual clarity at the moment of breakage. This was the Pushkins' greatest fear – loss, the wear and tear of things. Sergey Lvovich would become desperate over a missing handkerchief. He would grow faint with anxiety when he did not find some new French book in its usual place; life without it seemed miserable and incomplete. He blamed his children. When the book was found he would fling it aside indifferently. Objects really did seem irreplaceable: nothing could compensate for their destruction. Every glass was in danger.

Nadezhda Osipovna would slap the cheeks of the maladroit boy exactly as she did her servants' faces. She struck with a swinging stroke, resoundingly, like all the Hannibals. His parents would bend over the fragments of glass.

Sergey Lvovich would try to put them together again and wave his hand hopelessly: impossible! Aleksandr smashed things to smithereens. Nadezhda Osipovna would carry her rage into the maids' quarters, to return breathing heavily and speaking abruptly, but appeased. A subdued sobbing would be heard issuing faintly from the maids' room – a beaten girl was whimpering.

Gradually, and each independently of the other, his parents started to grow vaguely irritated if they had to look at their son for too long. He was anything but a loved child; he had betrayed their hopes; he had not filled their house with chattering as Sergey Lvovich had supposed he would.

Soon the third son was born. He was named Lev.

Lev was curly-haired, joyful and round. For the first time Sergey Lvovich felt like a father. He was moved and gave Nadezhda Osipovna a hearty kiss. Tears rolled down his face. Nadezhda Osipovna too, unexpectedly, at once fell madly in love with her son; the other children ceased to exist for her. It was a week before everything settled down.

Sometimes, preoccupied with his thoughts, Sergey Lvovich suddenly caught sight of his elder son and was amazed. He was puzzled and upset. Other people's children were children in all the pleasant meanings of the word: his son was like the son of a savage, a son of Chateaubriand's Natchez. He liked Chateaubriand and it flattered his pride that his marriage to Nadezhda Osipovna was generally remarked on. But a mistress, even a wife, was one thing and a son quite another. He craved so hungrily to have everything just as all respectable people did, but encountered such cruel misunderstanding on all sides! Secretly, Sergey Lvovich had reached an impasse in his domestic life. Once installed in new quarters – and he and his wife changed their home almost every year – he would first of all choose a room for his study and a spot by the fire. His desk would occupy nearly half the study and there was always a clean sheet of paper on it. This was where Sergey Lvovich wrote his letters. He would look out of the window and stop servants hurrying to the kitchen or the servants' hall, enquiring who had sent them and where they were going. As a matter of fact he didn't write many letters and the same clean sheet would lie on his desk for weeks. His eyes became hazy, his lips moved and smiled. He would lose himself in a dreamy witticism. He nonplussed imaginary opponents with his unexpected epigrams. Vulgar reality did not invade his study and his family respected his absorption. Sometimes he would unlock a desk drawer with its special little key and take out certain hidden notebooks in green stamped bindings with gold-blocked spines. He would open them and read slowly, narrowing one eye. His hand would shake slightly. The pictures were drawn in pink or red Indian or sometimes ordinary ink by an experienced and bold hand. There was all of Piron, selected extracts from Dorat, and the anonymous work of the riff-raff of Parnassus, some of it so spicy that Sergey Lvovich's eyes became glazed. There were some Russian authors as well, but Barkov was too coarse, too far removed from the spirit of the French. The French could make nudity itself amusing.

Nadezhda Osipovna, who migrated like a gypsy from room to room and kept rearranging the furniture and changing everything in her path, did not dare to interfere with his occupations. Her life was centred on her bedroom: she sat there for days on end, unkempt and unwashed while there were no visitors, and bit her nails. Then she would be seized by a sudden desire to educate her children. Next month, the exhausted Sergey Lvovich had to take her out every night. Then she would sink back into the desolation of her room.

In the presence of guests Sergey Lvovich shrugged off a dozen years, because it was only guests who could fully appreciate him. In company he lived and breathed. Pacing in front of the mirrors in the drawing-room in the morning he would even occasionally briefly rehearse the first moment of a guest's arrival: bowing lightly, almost imperceptibly, and immediately tossing his head back. Aleksandr would see his father's lips moving and smiling and his expression growing amiable and intelligent. Catching sight of Aleksandr, Sergey Lvovich would wince and assume his bored air. The boy distracted him.

Aleksandr liked it when guests came. The candles were lit, his mother's voice became melodious, her laughter was guttural, like the cooing of pigeons in a dovecote in spring. His father sat in his chair confidently, not on the edge as usual. He looked the head of the family and led the conversation. It was as if they were a different family, unfamiliar strangers, younger and finer people. His mother listened to her husband submissively and never volunteered an objection. In their guests' presence his mother smiled at him in the way she occasionally smiled at Lyovushka. Long stories about the children were told, to which he listened in bewilderment. He and his sister were referred to as 'mon Sashka' and 'mon Lolka' with a tenderness that frightened him.

Particularly often this happened when Karamzin – ironic, measured and serene – came to see them. Aleksandr was aware that Karamzin was different from other guests. When he came, his parents forgot to tell their son to go to bed.

On one occasion Sergey Lvovich had a real field day when a neighbour from their Nizhny Novgorod estate paid a visit to him. He had never been there even once but he spoke with aplomb, met all questions on the management of the estate with a meaningful silence – remarking that his main estates were in Pskov Region – and presented himself as a far-sighted landowner. Twice, with a sigh and a quick glance at his guest, he mentioned his grandfather,

Aleksandr Petrovich.* The awkward guest was spellbound by it all, and gazed at Nadezhda Osipovna as at a wonder of nature. Afterwards the pair had a long chuckle, remembering the simpleton's manners.

After the departure of guests, his mother would give an ugly yawn and unbutton her belt that had been too tight for too long. The furniture seemed old and grey again.

But guests came less and less often. In spite of all Marya Alekseyevna's efforts, butter was rancid at the Pushkins' and the eggs were rotten. Karamzin was absorbed in important concerns and projects, and Sergey Lvovich was no longer interesting to him.

2

When Sergey Lvovich for some reason stayed in, he would immediately look around to see if he could steal away. Then he accepted the situation, put on his dressing-gown, and took his place by the fire. On evenings like these he liked to leaf through the newspapers searching for news of promotions of his fellow-officers in the Guards. One was a general, another a regimental commander, a third was serving under the minister Golitsyn. In the new reign many of his friends had succeeded in making a career. The very thought of service made him feel sick; for him the only worthwhile things were the privileges of the gentry and enjoying the life of pleasure. This was what he always asserted – but could not help being upset.

The fireplace attracted him with its play of light and warmth. It was not for nothing that his brother Vasily had written a successful epistle 'To a Fireplace'. Now Vasily was in Paris and enjoying not only fireplaces and the play of light. Karamzin was publishing his letters from Paris in his journal. Parisian theatres! Dear God! It was amazing how misfortunes could lead to happiness. Sergey Lvovich envied his brother secretly and profoundly, especially his aberrations. He was often asked about his brother, and it always both flattered and upset him; Vasily Lvovich had not written a single letter to him. But Moscow did not forget Vasily Lvovich – he was often and eagerly caricatured on the Champs-Elysées, next to Bonaparte or Madame Genlis. Montfort drew Vasily Lvovich standing open-mouthed in front of a sharp-nosed Bonaparte, his hat fallen to the ground.

And here was Sergey Lvovich in Moscow, sitting by the fire! He would recite Molière. He read with nobility, without any of that nasty shouting of the new, vulgar school. He was especially good at the parts of Harpagon and Tartuffe, rendering particularly well Harpagon's speech on his lost treasure-

* See page 24.

box and conveying Tartuffe's noble baseness with great subtlety.

Nadezhda Osipovna disliked his recitations. Perhaps it was her husband's actorly self-esteem that seemed to her ridiculous; anyway, his recitations wearied her. She liked everything about the theatre but the stage. Or perhaps in a strange way she found that his performances revealed his weaknesses, the absurdity of his character.

He found an audience, however, in his son. He studied Aleksandr anxiously when the boy appeared at the fireplace. Then he would sigh indifferently and start to hum some nonsense or other.

Aleksandr would listen. His father would seem unaware of his presence until the boy came out with a sudden request for him to read Molière. Sergey Lvovich would be genuinely amazed.

'Are you sure you want me to?' he would say reluctantly. 'I haven't much time. Very well then, here you are.'

The only thing that wounded his pride was that his son never voiced either approval or admiration, though his attention was flattering.

Sergey Lvovich was an excellent reader, and he knew it. He had an instinctive feeling for Molière's verses and always observed the caesuras. He was best of all with the innuendoes and pregnant pauses, and performed these incomparably in *The School for Husbands*:

> *Il me semble …*
> *Ma foi …*

He was oblivious of his listener, only bowing when necessary to the imaginary Elmire. The words, the space in front of the fire and even his frock-coat acquired extraordinary dignity. When somebody entered the room he would fall silent, deeply offended. In particular he could not bear Marya Alekseyevna's presence, and when she entered the room he turned cold and sardonic, speaking through set teeth.

When he finished a scene, he looked at his listener closely and stood there feeling pleased with himself.

'Molière had a superb understanding of things,' he would say in a superior tone.

Taking another furtive look at his son's face, he would clap his hands: 'Petrushka! Take the drip off the candles!'

He would forget about Molière and his son, and return to reality.

3

He had never set foot in the nursery of their present house, considering it unnecessary, absurd and embarrassing for him to do so. Only once did he spend an hour or so there. His children watched him with interest; he appeared to be hiding. He hushed them to silence and listened attentively to what their mother was saying in the living-room. Now and again he knitted his brow and once he even pulled the door handle as if about to leave the room, but quickly restrained himself. At last the living-room fell silent. Paying no attention to the children and snorting weirdly, their father rushed out of the nursery. In all that time he had not said a word, as if they had not been there.

Sergey Lvovich had been hiding from a creditor.

He was fastidious in the extreme. Whenever he found a forgotten children's thing anywhere, he took it between two fingers and deposited it in a distant corner. He never reprimanded Nadezhda Osipovna, this he hadn't done for a long time; nor did he call Arishka, he simply dropped the object to the floor. And there seemed to be more and more of these children's things.

Soon Sergey Lvovich had an irritating and unforeseen experience: his elder son asked him for money. Aleksandr wanted to buy some wretched children's trifles. He stood in front of his son for some time, and having firmly decided not to give him a kopeck, he suddenly pictured those childish trifles – a ball and so forth, and handed over the money at once, and it upset him. He had made a discovery – his son was growing up. Sergey Lvovich understood with a secret unease that his sons' upbringing had become an important matter, and that this son would need money on more than one occasion in the future.

One evening, passing by the nursery, Sergey Lvovich overheard a conversation and halted. Arishka was talking. He listened at the door.

Arishka was telling master Aleksandr a folk-tale. She spoke unhurriedly, interrupting her story with an occasional yawn and it was obvious that she was busy knitting. Sergey Lvovich smiled and listened again. Soon he frowned: the nanny's tale was pointless and in poor taste. He half-opened the door. The nurse was knitting a sock and Sashka sat on a footstool gazing at her fixedly, his mouth half-open. Sergey Lvovich felt stung, as a father and as a reciter of Molière. Without saying a word, he retreated. Here was this boy, who spoke nothing but French, who seemed to understand the language of Racine, listening spellbound to menials!

That night he told Nadezhda Osipovna, in a thin squeaky voice, that if they did not want to see him turning into a boor, Sashka should not be entrusted to Arishka any longer. They needed a *Madame* to look after him. A

Madame was essential; he had had enough of these slovenly nurses with their absurd speech.

He spoke in such a way that Nadezhda Osipovna preferred to keep silent rather than object as usual. Nowadays, the ability to imitate French sophistication was the main social asset. Nadezhda Osipovna was one of the first in St Petersburg to kiss women on both cheeks like a genuine Frenchwoman instead of making a greeting with an old-fashioned bow. Sergey Lvovich admired that promptitude. Their house could really be entirely French: French books, news, language – and Vasily Lvovich in Paris. Sergey Lvovich was delighted to note that sometimes he did not utter a single Russian word from one week to the next, except for the orders he gave to the servant-boy: 'Take the drip off the candles' or 'Serve dinner'. He spoke Russian only to the servants or when he was particularly irritated. Sergey Lvovich even started to teach Nikita to read and write French, but nothing came of it. In other words, a *Madame* was an absolute imperative. But they were difficult to obtain and besides, were beyond their means. Real *Mesdames* were very costly and in great demand.

4

Sergey Lvovich had always been quick at making up his mind because he had a vivid imagination. He hoped to get his children off his hands to the *Madame* and she would teach them French language and finesse. Following sister Annette's advice they hired an old woman, Anna Ivanovna, a poor but noble lady with fluent French who could pass for French in front of guests even though she was not a proper *Madame*. This sharp-nosed old woman appeared in the house and started to educate the children, to scold them for their pranks, babble in French and take them for walks. Marya Alekseyevna hated her at once. Arina and she conspired against her and began to spy on the poor woman. Soon she was found guilty of certain misdemeanours: furtively eating sweets she squirrelled away from the dinner table, getting lost on a walk with the children, and then shifting the blame onto them for allegedly having left her.

'Now then, my good lady,' said Marya Alekseyevna.

Finally, realising that she was besieged on all sides, the old woman grew embittered and started to grumble in Russian. Arina even heard her saying that till now she had never lived with negroes. The same day she was dishonourably dismissed from the house.

Madame Lorges who took her place lasted more than a year. She was a genuine *Madame* – with curls, a cheerful voice, a robust constitution, and she could even make hats in the latest fashion, which won over Nadezhda Osipovna. She filled the house with herself, and all complaints stopped.

She had strong hands, rapidity of movement and a thoroughly French insouciance. She constantly hummed songs, rustled her skirts and laughed as only Frenchwomen can. She paid almost no attention to the children. Sergey Lvovich was delighted and chatted to the governess with obvious enjoyment.

She was dismissed summarily and without warning by Nadezhda Osipovna personally. Sergey Lvovich was the cause; he had started to glance too freely at the French governess's shapely shoulders. Just one glance of that kind was enough: Madame Lorges was sent packing.

Governesses did not take root in this house.

5

Vasily Lvovich returned home with a thousand Parisian trifles, in high boots à la Suvorov, with lightly scented handkerchiefs and with a sharp quiff; pomaded and preoccupied. He had developed an even bigger squint, did not recognise old friends and laughed a lot. People were curious. Rumour had it that Circe was going to return to her husband. The gossip, however, proved false: Circe was getting married again – a fact that did not dishearten Vasily Lvovich. He had brought Annushka a tall lace cap of the latest cut to make her look like a French *soubrette*. He spoke of Mme Récamier casually:

'Graceful figure, but not good-looking.'

He praised her palace, however.

'Glass, glass and more glass. Glass everywhere.'

Bonaparte had attracted his interest most of all, and he was asked to describe what he looked like. No one would believe that Bonaparte was of such small stature.

Vasily Lvovich squatted a little and lifted his palm to his forehead, forming the shape of a cap peak to show the Consul's height. Then, with every reason to be pleased with himself, he let the women smell his hair.

Like Bonaparte, he had studied the art of oral delivery with Talma in Paris, and with noble classical simplicity, he gave a half-turn and recited Racine to everybody who would listen. His protruding belly somewhat hindered his recitation.

He had a very high opinion of Parisian ballet and spoke favourably of Parisian opera.

'*The Barber of Seville* was superb.'

He had much to relate of the rivalry between Mademoiselle George and Mademoiselle Duchenois.

'George has such gestures – such hands!' he said, and stretched out his own.

'But Duchenois has the legs,' he said, raising a trouser leg, 'My God! What legs!'

In the absence of ladies – children were not taken into account (nobody noticed them and they listened to everything) – he talked, breathlessly, about coffee-houses and their female habituées. Then he took a breath and fanned himself with a handkerchief still smelling of Paris.

In the mornings he strolled along the Tverskoy Boulevard specially dressed for the morning. His gait had changed; he kept hitching up his trousers. Women looked round at him. He had previously disliked Okhotny Ryad,* but now he went there regularly. He talked about Chevette's shop in the Palais-Royal. Chevette sold chilled pâté, duck liver from Toulouse and fat juicy oysters. Connoisseurs' lips moved responsively and Vasily Lvovich was reputed to be a gourmet. Now he devised recipes in his kitchen intended to represent French dishes, and invited experts to taste them. Some dishes were praised but the experts declined any further invitations. Now he took to calling Vlas, his cook, by the name of Blaise. Vasily Lvovich's favourite dish, in actual fact, was buckwheat kasha.

Karamzin, who had nearly forgotten the Pushkins, was again favourably disposed to them. And once more Vasily Lvovich was on the list of those in vogue: Karamzin, Dmitriyev, Pushkin. He was the hero of the hour – *l'homme du jour*. When in conversation Karamzin expressed his indignation at the destructive ambition of Bonaparte, whose only wish was to wage wars, Vasily Lvovich sighed deeply:

'Bonaparte is dangerous! Very dangerous!' and immediately reported that the most delicious cakes in Paris were called 'nuns' – *nonnettes*.

An old general at a ball wanted to know details of the war Bonaparte was waging and called him a rascal. Vasily Lvovich frowned and became angry:

'My God! Nobody in Paris is talking about the war! Paris is Paris!'

For he had become liberated. He even ordered a sofa, exactly like Récamier's. She entertained guests and visitors half-reclining on her sofa; he would rest on his after dinner.

His cousin Aleksey Mikhaylovich asserted that Vasily Lvovich had been expelled from Paris for dissolute behaviour – and that while there he had bought a poetry-producing machine which contained a large number of separate lines. Just grasp the handle, give it a turn – and there was a madrigal. Prince Shalikov, a musician, took down the latest Parisian songs straight from Vasily Lvovich's lips.

---

* 'Hunters' Row', where hunters once sold their game; later a row of foodshops, the centre of a busy market-place popular with Muscovites.

6

Soon Vasily Lvovich suffered a stroke of fate such as any other, more positive person would never have survived. Either the rumour about his free-thinking had reached the ecclesiastical authorities or his devout father-in-law had pulled strings, but the ecclesiastical authorities had set about the matter of his divorce with a new will. Circe was proclaimed innocent and Vasily Lvovich a sinner, which of course he was. The Synod resolved to give his wife a divorce and allow her to marry again. As for the other spouse, he was to be given a seven-year penance, six months of which were to be spent in a monastery, and the rest of the period under the supervision of a spiritual director. Against all expectation, Vasily Lvovich endured the blow cheerfully enough. He performed the part of the innocent victim with great ease. Kind-hearted women sent him flowers and Vasily Lvovich sniffed them, pondering the reverses of fortune. His cousin Aleksey, however, immediately made fun of the penance, emphasising that its main feature was Vasily Lvovich's transition from Blaise's cuisine to the monastery's, and claiming that on the first day of his penance Vasily Lvovich gorged himself on sturgeon. The location of the monastery chosen for the penance was as lucky as could be, and Vasily Lvovich spent spring and summer in the monastery inn. In Aleksey's words, it was as if he were renting a room at a holiday inn from God Almighty. Once more, Moscow had been given something to gossip about. When his sisters told him the news, Vasily Lvovich realised that he was a celebrity again, although at times he felt his joy to be soured. There was nothing honourable about the Pushkins' fame; society was interested in them purely for scandal's sake.

Sergey Lvovich, who seemed to live in the reflection of his brother's and cousin's fame, was concerned for Vasily's future. Aleksandr understood very well his father's sighs and innuendoes and grimaces, now proud, now pleased, now humble, whenever he talked about his uncle. It was a matter of fame, fame in the *beau monde*. His father was gratified by his uncle's sudden eminence and at the same time envied him. The children knew all Aleksey's farcical stories about their uncle, and Sergey Lvovich almost believed them. The priest who was their uncle's spiritual director was a secret gourmet, and that was why he came to exhort his spiritual son so often. He was lured by Blaise's cuisine – such was the fable fabricated by Aleksey, son of a 'former Pushkin', just for fun. Sergey Lvovich, however, took it less playfully and grew angry. These priests irritated him. They were bringing *Basile* to ruin, eating and drinking at his expense. Oh, these *vieux renards de Synode!*

He made no attempt to hide his feelings. Sister Anna Lvovna, overhearing her brother's blasphemous complaints, plugged her ears and shouted at him, wide-eyed:

'Brother!'

And she told the children to get out of the room.

7

He had two brothers and a sister. The baby Lyovushka was the family favourite. Sister Olga, a sharp-nosed but nice-looking little shrew, complained about her brother Sashka in her thin voice. Their aunt Anna Lvovna would bring presents for her – little dolls, little fans – which she would hoard in her own corner. Brother Nikolay was sickly and fair-haired.

He treated them like glass that should not be dropped, otherwise he would be punished. His aunt Anna Lvovna would tell him that since Nikolinka and Lyovushka were his brothers, he should give Lyovushka his ball and let Nikolinka have what he wanted because he was younger. He was unwilling to do this, and tried his best to avoid catching her eye.

His home and his parents had two different faces – one public and in company, and another for when there were no strangers present. There were also two languages – French and Russian. French gave everything value and dignity, as if there were guests in the house. When his mother was addressed as *Nadine,* she was a completely different person from the one his grandmother called Nadezhda. *Nadine* sounded similar to *Diana,* the nymph in the Yusupov garden. That was the world his parents talked about at the dinner table and from which they returned in the small hours. His aunts Anna Lvovna and Yelizaveta Lvovna pronounced Russian words nasally, like French ones. His father snapped his fingers – he was short of Russian words – and French ones turned up. When his parents were being tender to one another they spoke French together; when they quarrelled they always shouted in Russian.

He liked to hear women's talk, with its incorrectness, its amusing sighs, babbling and muttering. For some reason their grimaces seemed sweet. Female guests spoke quickly, interspersing their Russian with French phrases like fine round peas, burring and vying with each other. In general, when guests spoke, it was as if they were not serious, as if they were changing into elegant, un-Russian masquerade costumes, and only the sidelong glances they cast at one another were of an absolutely different, Russian sort. Their sighs were feigned, French and charming. But it was male speech that brought him real joy, the French phrases at meeting or parting. People exchanged them with friends like presents – but when talking to strangers, it was as if they were duelling with intricate antique weapons.

It was in French that guests spoke of the war with the French, calling them *les freluquets,* pipsqueaks; of the Tsar who issued edicts written in a fine style and evidently was fighting or was going to fight these *freluquets*; and even of the archimandrite who conducted public prayers. But as soon as anybody in the conversation was taken by surprise, he or she switched to Russian, the language of nannies and old women; and then their jabbering mouths opened wider and more simply, not like the narrow chinks that characterised their spoken French. Sontsev, who spoke exquisite French, suddenly said in Russian:

'And while we are chatting, those French thrash the life out of us!'

Aleksandr always noticed these sudden shifts, after which people spoke much more softly and unhurriedly, mostly about their servants, their mail, their villages and their losses.

When his parents were out, he would steal into his father's study. There were portraits on the walls: Karamzin, with long hair drooping down his temples, very true to life but much younger and more handsome; a pink and squinting Ivan Ivanovich Dmitriyev with a gristly nose which the boy for some reason disliked; and a dark-eyed, broad-hipped girl in airy, lilac attire. There were French books on the shelves. On the bottom shelf there were huge volumes covered with dust that made him sneeze: the pages were porous, the letters spacious, there were banners and heroes in the pictures. He felt them with his fingers – they were embossed. Next to these was the volume he particularly liked, also illustrated – with pictures of tall, serene women in long tunics with bare feet and eyes without pupils, all similar-looking garden nymphs and goddesses, each of them, like living persons, having her own name.

8

'Turn to the wall, my love, and try not to look around, or you'll never get to sleep. You're too young not to sleep. If you live as long as I have, you might have reason not to sleep. I'm not telling you another story, I've told you enough already. And don't look out of the window – you'll find it harder to sleep. It's the city that keeps you awake, it's so much better in the country, in summer a maple sticks its paw through the window and gives you sweet dreams; and there are trees in winter too. There's nothing but street lamps here. They just stand and blink. Go to sleep. Everyone's asleep, Lyovushka and Nikolinka are asleep, you're the only one who isn't.

'... On and on we drove – and all of a sudden our large coach overturned, a bolt had come off. Your grandfather said: "We'll have to walk." I said: "I'm not used to it. I haven't travelled all this way to come to the house for the first time on foot." Somehow or other the bolt was put back on. Right at the gate your grandfather got nervous:

"'If he shouts at you, I beg you, sweetheart, kneel down in front of him just as I'll do. Then he'll forgive us."

'He was so afraid of his father – he had married me without permission. I said: "I am not the kind of person to be shouted at. I won't kneel." And he says that in Africa everyone does it and it's not considered a disgrace. Maybe it's all right in Africa but not here, in Pskov. Your grandfather even burst into tears, he was so distressed. The tears rolled down his cheeks. At that time men didn't cry as they do now. I was very frightened and we got out of the coach. We changed in Arina's room, your grandfather got into his uniform and I put on my mother's pearls – I had to pawn them later. We sent word to the old man to ask if he could see us. We waited for the maid for an hour or two – she didn't come back. By evening we were trembling. We were sitting in the peasants' house, in the larder, ashamed to be seen. They gave us bread and water as if we were prisoners. Then the maid finally came back in tears: she'd been flogged. All that night, my love, I was awake, just as you are now. Next day I said I didn't know what was going on and that I was going back to my parents. Your grandfather begged me to stay and led me to the house. I don't remember how we got in. On the threshold, your grandfather – in his uniform and with his sabre – knelt down. But I kept standing, looking down. When I looked up I saw the old man sitting in a chair, with a cane in his hand, his uniform unbuttoned. His face was black, not exactly black – yellow; his nostrils were flared. He looked at your grandfather and said nothing. Then he looked at me and still said nothing. Suddenly he lifted his cane. I was so frightened I screamed and fainted … When I came to my face was damp. The old man was bent over me and sprinkling me with water. I looked at him again and screamed and he burst out laughing, but it was false laughter.

"'Do I, madam, really seem so frightening to you? I have never scared women so much before."

'He was courteous. But he kept ignoring your grandfather. And his eyes were flashing.

' … What happened next? Not much. There's nothing more to tell you about … What about your grandfather? He died, he's no more. Go to sleep! And don't roll your eyes like that. Well, I can't cope with you. Arina will tell you a story or sing your favourite song. I'm tired, I can't stay any longer.'

9

Arina entered the room noiselessly and sat down at the foot of his bed. Not looking at him, slowly groaning, yawning and nodding, she told him about evil spirits. There was a great number of them. Woodsprites lived in the woods. A watersprite lived in the lake behind his grandfather Osip Abramovich's manor, near the Mikhaylovskoye mill, the serf girls had seen him. In Trigorskoye there was a woodsprite too; that one was a simpleton – everyone had seen him and heard his great halloo. At the house of Osip Abramovich there had been a girl who used to go to the forest to pick foxberries. Her name didn't matter – was it worth remembering? The sprite had hallooed to her and tickled her to death. Her soul had come out of her with laughter.

'If you, Aleksandr Sergeyevich, don't go to sleep, he'll tickle you to death too. If not a woodsprite then a housesprite. But he might come out of the woods. There now, listen, something is singing softly in the chimney: Sleep, it says, Aleksandr Sergeyevich, sir, fall asleep, it says, as fast as you can – you're a real torture at night – for your grandmother, for your nanny and me, your housesprite at Mikhaylovskoye.'

10

They were all taken for a walk together, 'the whole camp', as Marya Alekseyevna called them – Olinka, Aleksandr, Lyovushka and Nikolinka. Aleksandr usually lagged behind. Other boys mocked him, calling him 'Little Negro!' and running away. Each time he suddenly boiled with an anger that frightened Arina. He bared his teeth and rolled his eyes. To Arina's surprise, his anger subsided as quickly as it had started, without a trace. He never talked to anyone at home about these incidents.

That day he had fallen behind on purpose and sat down on a bench by the fence. He thought that Arina wouldn't notice and they would keep walking. Across the road a fat man in a dressing-gown was observing the street through an open window. At that hour the street was not particularly interesting. Next to the fat man a young woman was feeding a bird in a cage. The fat man caught sight of Aleksandr and grinned. He peered at him in amusement and pulled the young woman by the sleeve. She too stared out of the window. Aleksandr knew that they were calling him 'a little negro'. He muttered like his aunt Anna Lvovna:

'Why are you showing your teeth?'

And he went off to catch up with the others.

Aleksandr never spoke to anyone about his negro grandfather and never asked why other boys mocked him by calling him 'Little Negro'. When he asked his father if his grandfather had died a long time ago, Sergey Lvovich did not understand at first and thought that Aleksandr was asking him about *his* father, Lev Aleksandrovich. He replied with a sigh that it had been a long time ago and that his grandfather had been a person of rare spirit:

'The darling of society!'

Having realised that Aleksandr was asking him about his grandfather Hannibal, Sergey Lvovich was shocked at first and then said that *that* grandfather had never even thought about dying; then he frowned, summoned up his courage – they were in Marya Alekseyevna's presence – and announced that Aleksandr should forget about that grandfather, because he was a Pushkin, and no one else.

'And both your grandmother and your mother are Pushkins!'

Marya Alekseyevna said nothing.

Afterwards, for over an hour, Sergey Lvovich rummaged among the papers in his study and suddenly rushed out of the study as white as a sheet:

'They've disappeared!'

It turned out that his pedigree had vanished, the whole roll of documents that Vasily Lvovich had entrusted him with when leaving for Paris. Wringing his hands, Sergey Lvovich said that he had sealed the envelope with the family seal and locked the drawer of his desk with a special key, but now it contained only an album, some verses and an old landscape of Suida, and no pedigree roll. Sergey Lvovich ransacked the drawers of his desk with shaking fingers. Pale and alarmed, his family helped him. He hesitated and left a couple of secret drawers unopened.

'There are some secret papers in here,' he blustered, frowning. 'Masonic papers.'

Marya Alekseyevna waved her hands and closed her eyes. She was afraid of Masons.

In the end the documents were found, the rolls were completely safe. Sergey Lvovich had simply forgotten that he had locked them not in his desk but in a special case where he kept rare books. He was ecstatic.

Slowly he untied the ribbon on a big parcel, broke a big red seal and showed the old documents to Aleksandr.

'Have a look here, will you? Can you see the seal? This big seal. The letter is a very old one, but I was told that it's a letter of complaint from the serfs on your grandfather's estate – two hundred and twenty souls or so – about the increased taxation during the war with the Turks in the Crimea. And these are records of a court case, not important.'

Lowering his voice, Sergey Lvovich told his son:

'And this is the document that retired your grandfather from the service, due to ill health. It was really a matter of government intrigue.'

II

When he turned seven, his home suddenly and unexpectedly collapsed.

Marya Alekseyevna had given up her son-in-law and daughter as a bad job. She had been holding out too long, and at last she made up her mind: she scraped together her widow's money, took some mortgage deeds and contracts out of her casket, went off to do some business and came back in a transport of delight – she had bought an estate near Moscow. The estate was in the Zvenigorod district; it had poplars, gardens and a church, all that it should. The name sounded alien: Zakharovo, but what was in a name? The outbuildings and the house were of stone, the road was not dusty; there were flower-beds, a grove, a village at the foot of a hill, a prosperous village full of peasant-girls and oats. Her daughter and son-in-law and the children would be heartily welcome in summer. Moscow's dust, stench and noise were driving her mad. She was leaving Arishka to look after the children – she herself had had enough.

Nobody held her back.

In autumn the long-awaited news arrived: Osip Abramovich had died and bequeathed the village of Mikhaylovskoye to Nadezhda Osipovna.

Five

IN his last few years the old negro had grown monstrously fat. His step, however, was lighter; he walked as if he were dancing, waltzing around with his belly. But in the final months, he could no longer walk and just sat by the window in a large soft striped armchair, his head lolling backwards and his breathing laboured because of his corpulence, ill health and old age. He slept there too. He had quarrelled with his brother Pyotr Abramovich about money. Everybody had abandoned him.

The master's favourite, Palashka, managed the house. It was said that from time to time she still brought peasant-girls to sing and dance for the old man. But now he was quietening down, and for hours he would follow the flight of a fly or listen even more listlessly to the creaking of a cart behind the woods, echoing the creaking in his chest.

It was autumn. Maples, red as if on fire, and yellow waxen birches were shedding their leaves in front of the window. The rains had stopped. It was very dry.

He grew worse overnight, and moaned in such an eerie voice and shook so violently that next morning Palashka sent into town for the doctor.

The doctor examined the patient, prohibited hare-meat as it excited lust, and prescribed a medicine to clear his throat in the evenings.

'Try to avoid all emotional stress,' he told him.

The old man lay back in the chair, his face sallow, staring vaguely, dimly into space. And suddenly, spontaneously, as if it were coming from somewhere else, a wheezing, whistling, gurgling sound came out of his chest, and his belly started to quake. His breath came hoarsely, and with that grating sound rusty bolts make when they are being tried.

When he recovered his breath he asked the doctor:

'How long have I got?'

The doctor replied:

'You have a couple of days, yet, Your Excellency.'

The old negro suddenly sprang up from his chair. The wheezing stopped.

'Liar!' he shouted at the doctor and shook his fist at him.

Then, turning to Palashka, he ordered:

'Get him out of here and don't pay him! Out with him!'

He lay for half an hour absolutely motionless, his breath coming short. Then he fixed his eyes on his father's portrait. In the picture Abram Petrovich had an ill-natured face the colour of clay. He was wearing a General-in-Chief's full-dress uniform with the ribbon of the order of St Anne across his shoulder.

He ordered the portrait to be taken to the attic. Then he gave orders for the bath-house to be heated up and for himself to be carried there. His servants carried him across the estate in the high striped chair on their shoulders. When they reached a small hillock he ordered them to stop, surveyed the scene and then withdrew into his own world. It took five men to carry him, such was his obesity. Palashka followed them. He didn't want to steam, just to lie for a while in the bath-house dressing-room.

'Sweat me out, would you?' he asked Palashka.

Palashka lashed him with the hot birch-besom about his black shoulders and he snorted and coughed. It was getting dark.

Then he ordered them to carry him to the stables. It was cold and quiet out there. Three stallions stood in their stalls, snuffling heavily and shifting their legs. One of them, a fiery one which had given the groom a bad bite, was chained like a criminal. The mare drank water, snorting rhythmically. He gave her some oats which she took from his hand, her soft lips sighing quietly.

'Two days!' he said to her. 'Imbecile!'

Once back in the house, he ordered every candlestick to be brought and all the candles to be lit; then he ordered some leafy twigs to be picked from the grove and brought to the living-room.

'They're restful to the eye and they help me to breathe.'

Palashka offered him a glass of wine but he took only a sip. Suddenly remembering the stock of wine in the cellar, he ordered all of it to be brought to the room.

'Girls!' he commanded Palashka.

The manor-house was brightly lit up and could be seen from a distance.

'Living it up again,' they said in the village.

'The old devil is not afraid of death itself!'

The Hannibals' older serfs all believed that old Abram Petrovich and Osip Abramovich and his brother Pyotr Abramovich were devils. One old peasant woman claimed that Abram Petrovich had claws in the shape of hoofs.

The serf girls formed a shameless dancing troupe at Osip Abramovich's. They always performed for him when he was carousing. He had his musicians too: one serf played the guitar, two others sang, and a servant-boy beat the tambourine. He had Palashka give each of them a glass of wine and motioned the musicians to begin. They immediately broke into his favourite song.

'Mashka, out here!' he wheezed.

Masha was the best dancer.

The negro sat still with his eyes half-closed.

'Nothing on!' he said.

Masha danced for him without a stitch on. He wanted to get up but couldn't move. Only his lips and fingers twitched and trembled like Masha's gyrating hips. The musicians performed his favourite song more and more loudly and rapidly, the servant-boy beat the tambourine without stopping. Masha's feet moved faster and faster.

'Ah, white swan!' the old man groaned.

He waved his hand, grasped a big fistful of air, closed his fingers tightly and burst into tears. His hand fell down, his head dangled. The tears were rolling down his face onto his thick lower lip and he swallowed them slowly.

When the dancing was over, he first ordered all the wine to be given to the serfs, then had second thoughts and told them to leave half of it.

'Bring a tub and some oats in here!' he ordered.

The tub was filled with wine in front of him and then the oats were soaked in the wine.

'Feed the horses! ... Open the windows!'

The horses were fed in the stables with the intoxicating oats.

'Set the fiery stallion free! I'm letting the horses go!'

The wind was blowing into the living-room. He sat by the open window and took in the chill night air through his open mouth. It was dark outside.

Tossing their manes with loud neighs, throwing up clods of earth with their stamping hoofs, the drunken horses galloped past the windows.

He answered them with silent laughter:

'All ours, all the Hannibals'! My father's, Peter the Great's! Farewell to it all!'

2

When Pyotr Abramovich was told that his brother Osip Abramovich was unwell and unable to speak, he failed to come to see him. He had seen the brightly lit windows in Mikhaylovskoye the previous night, had assumed that his brother was on a spree again, and was angry that he had not been invited to take part. He assumed that Osip Abramovich was suffering from a hangover and said that he wouldn't be visiting him and that his brother would be fine without him. He was in a different mould from his brother – sprightly and lean. And he kept up his grudges.

Palashka had not lost her head, and immediately after the doctor's visit, by force of habit, she sent a messenger to Ustinya Yermolayevna Tolstaya's country house near Pskov where she spent each summer and autumn.

All that day and the following night Osip Abramovich lay unconscious, like a black hulk, and only his whistling and wheezing assured Palashka that he was still alive. The next day, against all expectations, Ustinya arrived.

She had aged and become leaner, but she still had the same way of walking as twenty years before. Even her enemies had to admit that Ustinya had a fine gait.

She stepped lightly out of the carriage, went straight into the house – and backed out at once from the scene of the recent orgy. Heaps of maple leaves lay about the floor.

'Sweep that rubbish out of here!' she ordered Palashka angrily. 'Look at the mould that's growing! And just look how much mud has been brought in!'

Only when the room had been cleaned up did she sit down by the window. She looked at the dying man apprehensively. There were huge drops and streaks of sweat on his purple forehead. She wiped it with a handkerchief and frowned.

Since their official divorce more than twenty years before, Ustinya had lived neither as a widow nor as a wife. She had made every effort to get her hands on 'everything she should'. From the very start of their relationship she had transferred all Osip Abramovich's money into her account. He had built her a house with an apple orchard in a peaceful quarter of Pskov, and had bought her a country house outside Pskov, at Devil's Brook, also with an orchard, conservatories and a flower-garden. He had given her a carriage and horses. She loved gold, apples and plums most of all. She had a gold dinner-set, and her apples were as sweet as honey.

'No one grows apples like mine. Those lazy idiots are good for nothing but stupid gossip!' She was speaking of her enemies, the Pskov landowners and their wives who refused to receive her.

She considered herself to be the victim of slander. If she were married to the negro and if he had still been in love with her, she would have triumphed over the Pskov gentry – 'all those Tatars', Karamyshevs and Nazimovs, who shunned her as 'a bad character'. But the affair had ended in nothing and her liaison with the negro had become a scandal, like a fling with some valet or itinerant clown. As an injured party, therefore, she believed she was entitled to his money, and indeed to rob him of everything he had.

Ustinya had moved in and out of the negro's household many times. The last time she had moved in had been five years before, and she had moved out again a month later. She had suddenly begun to miss her garden and the old man bored her to death.

When she was told that the negro was dying, she did not hesitate for a moment. There was unfinished business between them. For years the settlement of the village of Mikhaylovskoye, drawn up according to all the legalities by her scrivener, had been gathering dust in her bureau; it remained only to write the date at the bottom of the page and to have the negro sign it. But he had always been firmly against the settlement and whenever the conversation turned to Mikhaylovskoye he had simply refused to discuss it. Ustinya had brought the document with her.

Since their last separation he had also kept her shawl, which he wouldn't give back, saying that it was something to remember her by.

For breakfast Palashka served up baked potatoes with cream and a glass of foxberry water. There was nothing else in the house.

While breakfasting Ustinya looked around. Everything here was so dismal, the unpainted floors, the low ceilings – the shabbiness appalled her. How had all her wealth managed to come out of this poor cabin, her gardens, the dinner-sets and the horses? The negro was dying in dreadful squalor in much the same way as his grandfather had probably expired, somewhere in Africa. She spoke to Palashka about the shawl.

Palashka rummaged through all the drawers – there was no shawl. Looking at the shambles that surrounded the dying man, Ustinya said with disgust:

'How can you find a shawl in all this? You could lose yourself in here!'

She finished her breakfast but did not touch the foxberry water.

'It's bitter. Don't you know how to souse foxberries?'

She sat for a while by the chairs where the old negro was lying stretched out.

'Why have you sent for me? What am I to him? Not even a relative.'

'Well, hardly a stranger either,' Palashka said.

She sent Palashka away.

Ustinya gazed resentfully around the half-bare room that she had been ravaging for a decade. On the chest of drawers there used to be a clock with a figure of Cronus devouring a baby; it was in her house now. There used to be a porcelain piece on the bureau – a faun and a nymph – now hers as well. Only the big elk antlers, a hunting trophy, were still hanging above the table.

The negro was fumbling at something with his fingers, his lips were moving and his eyes were half-open.

'Well now, what do you want?' She addressed the dying man sternly, pulling his fingers away from his face.

His nails were blue, as they had always been. He had long fingers; there was a ring with a beautiful yellow stone on his left hand, like a widower's ring, carved in the shape of an arbour by a jeweller of the old school; she knew about precious stones. Palashka still hadn't found the shawl. A Turkish one too, with a fringe. A great pity. She looked at the ring again, admiring it. Then she took him by the hand and, gently at first, tried to pull the ring off his finger. The negro's fingers were swollen and the ring refused to budge. At last she managed to tug it off and put it on her thumb. And suddenly she froze: the negro's big dimmed eyes were calmly staring at her and the ring. He had regained full consciousness. Then a shadow seemed to pass across his face – he gave a faint smile and grasped her hand.

'You fool,' the dying man spoke distinctly, 'give me a kiss, you fool!'

He never regained consciousness.

Pyotr Abramovich arrived in the evening, and Ustinya immediately left for Pskov. She put the unsigned settlement back into her casket. That night Osip Abramovich Hannibal, retired officer and naval gunner, passed away.

Pyotr Abramovich put on his full dress uniform to bury his brother.

The negro lay in the coffin, black as coal, in his naval uniform of Catherine the Great's time. The priest gave the peasants a sermon about Saint Moses the Moor who had also been an Ethiopian, and a robber in his youth. The next day an assessor from town arrived for the funeral feast of wine and pies. He sent Nadezhda Osipovna and Marya Alekseyevna notification to present themselves in order to enter into possession of what was now their village, Mikhaylovskoye, since the father of the one and the spouse of the other, Osip Abramovich, in accordance with the will of God, had passed away.

3

On receiving the news of his father-in-law's death, Sergey Lvovich assumed a grave and sober look and accepted condolences as if they were congratulations.

'*Que la volonté du ciel soit faite!*' he said solemnly.

At the funeral sevice he crossed himself quickly and cursorily and gave a couple of deep and distinct sighs. Sister Anna Lvovna embraced Nadezhda Osipovna and gave a little sob, but it was received in the coldest possible manner.

The late negro's estate with its contents, as well as the money, if there was any, now belonged to his wife and daughter. Marya Alekseyevna, who now had her own estate, did not want to return to her old hearth, from which her husband had fled leaving her in the lurch, and she let Nadezhda Osipovna take it over. A man's help was needed. Sergey Lvovich, however, showed no desire to go to Pskov and take possession of his father-in-law's estate, excusing himself on account of the war and his superior's reluctance to let him go. Taking leave now could damage his career.

Nadezhda Osipovna, an absolute tyrant at home, was an unusually helpless person outside it and easily frightened. Later in the month, nevertheless, she went to Mikhaylovskoye and Sergey Lvovich stayed at home, promising to follow her as soon as circumstances allowed.

Only when the door shut behind her did Sergey Lvovich enjoy his feeling of good fortune. He had inherited an estate and suddenly found himself free for at least a month. That same evening he sneaked away from the house.

It was a time of war and upheaval. Moscow was full of unrest, everything was uncertain. According to the communiqués the Tsar was prevailing over the French, yet the newsmongers reported that the French were 'lambasting us'. The staff of the Commissariat was frantic, forever travelling about, drinking and gambling. Everybody was worked up. People visited the Commander-in-Chief's to hear the latest imperial rescript. Suddenly the public's views had changed: Bonaparte was a madman. Vasily Lvovich forbade Blaise to cook French dishes. There was universal shock in the air.

Pale and frowning, Sergey Lvovich sat at the green table at two in the morning losing a second hundred roubles at rocambole. His hands were shaking; a gloomy future loomed in front of him.

Sergey Lvovich had no doubt that the truth would be out and Nadezhda Osipovna would learn it, but he was banishing the thought. At first he had simply intended to spend some time with old friends, then the rocambole had started, and from the very beginning, trembling with agitation, he kept losing. Unlucky hands of cards followed one after another.

At four in the morning, a complete bankrupt, he wrote out promissory notes. 'I undertake to pay a hundred … two hundred … five hundred roubles. Day. Month. Year. Sergey Pushkin.' He was so terrified that he was on the point of bursting into tears. At five o'clock he won everything back and was even in profit. He went completely limp and took a drink of water, utterly exhausted. His entire past life, the life of a head of the family and an obedient husband, had vanished in a moment. All that previous life had been loss, only now was he really winning. Within an hour his spirits revived considerably. He decided to stop gambling, but if he ever lost again, to volunteer for the battlefield. Nadezhda Osipovna was not so much of a threat to a military man.

Next morning, still enjoying his new freedom, after a short hesitation he let his friends take him to the notorious house in the suburbs, Pankratyevna's, 'to warm up'. Pankratyevna, a stout old woman, kept a house across the River Moskva, offering well-built girls and rich cabbage soups, and she was famous for her earthy simplicity.

'Sweet as honey!' the connoisseurs would say about her protégées, screwing up their eyes.

With his civility, Sergey Lvovich produced the most favourable impression on Pankratyevna, and ate the celebrated cabbage soup with real appetite.

He stayed until noon, and rediscovered himself. He realised that he had actually been born for the good life, not for business or for the family. There was even some money left over from his win. He recounted it and put it into his purse for luck, having made up his mind not to spend it. He came home with an unusual feeling of dignity and calm. He tried not to think about the promise he had given to Nadezhda Osipovna; he had the most profound aversion to anything concerning inventories, the bureaucratic procedures of coming into possession and the like. Arina was looking after the children, so in that respect he had nothing to worry about.

At Pankratyevna's he took a particular liking to a girl called Grushka. He paid her visits in the mornings and was made very welcome. If he wasn't admitted on Povarskaya Street, he went immediately to Tverskaya. He had lunch where everyone did – at the houses of male and female acquaintances of the older generation, and in the evenings the young rogues appeared and took him along to Pankratyevna's. No one could hold him back now.

4

His mother was far away. She was at his black grandfather's estate, which his parents never mentioned but the existence of which was often indistinctly felt. He got used to the curiosity of his playmates and passers-by who stared at his swarthy complexion and his fair curls.

He had been told that his grandfather was dead. Now he had died again. He was fascinated by that black grandfather's fate. Now they had an estate and his father said there was a beautiful lake there. His mother had had a gloomy look. She had kissed the younger children on both cheeks and himself on the top of the head and left. He was free.

In the mornings he sometimes saw his father's guilty figure returning from whatever he had been up to and scuttling quickly into his study. He knew that gait very well – it was how he behaved when he was afraid of his wife. In the evenings his father would disappear again. Sometimes his study happened to be vacant for a whole day or two. He learned to command the study like a conquered enemy camp. He read the piles of books that cluttered the window-sills; he read brief anecdotal works, tales of treachery, the eloquent utterances of kings, tales of Roman military leaders and glorious women who were good at hiding their lovers. He turned the pages of a dictionary of Roman courtesans; he liked the cunning Lais, the fat Aristippus' paramour, best of all. He read about people who were capable of witty sallies on the executioner's block.

He read quickly, sporadically, indiscriminately. He was very amused when he first saw Voltaire's portrait: the old man's head was like a monkey's and he had big, curved protruding lips and wore a white night-cap. He was a philosopher, a poet and a mischief-maker. He had ridiculed King Frederick and played tricks throughout his life.

He took a particular liking to a poem about two pious old ladies who came home, went to bed, found a strapping young man in it and fought over him. These pious old ladies, hypocritical spinsters, reminded him of his aunt Anna Lvovna. And his mother spoke to guests in the same affected way as Mme Deshoulières.

But what he adored most of all was poetry. Rhyme was a kind of proof that the events described had really happened. He read hastily, catching the ends of the lines with his eyes and biting the tips of his swarthy fingers in sheer ecstasy. Hearing a sound, he would put the book neatly in its place and, craning his neck, prepare himself for the unexpected. A sudden change had come over him that autumn. The plodding stride of the bumpkin had disappeared, the slow, inquisitive look in his eyes become sharp and bright. He had turned seven.

Eventually, with the help of the ladder, he reached the top shelf in the study, where pocket-size books in leather bindings were kept. He started to read them and a new world opened for him. Every woman had her sweet secrets; everybody was betraying everyone else in various ways; maidens banished shepherd-boys with mock modesty; grandees gave their witty ripostes; fauns pursued nymphs with some mysterious purpose; riders broke in fiery mares to the point of exhaustion; hunters slew their mysterious quarry; a gardener planted a rose in Annette's basket. When the night's conquests were calculated, one, two or three were ludicrous, they were supposed to be countless. Meanwhile, all males were overwhelmed with desire, it was a continuous, endless battle; they spoke of a woman as of an unknown country which was about to be discovered – with all its woods, mountains, hills, grottoes and cool shades. It was breathtaking. He could only guess at the mysteries behind it all.

Now, with his mother out of the way, he found a new freedom of movement and suddenly felt full of brightness and energy.

He could easily, from a standing position, jump onto a table, or leap over a chair without turning it over. He just couldn't keep still. Taking himself by surprise, he would jump out of his chair, dropping his book, and sit down somewhere else. He played ball with other boys in the yard; his aim was precise and he had perfect coordination between his eye and every muscle of his body.

He spent most of the day in the maids' hall. Arina grumbled at him at first but soon gave up. The girls grew accustomed to him. They greeted him naturally, in their sing-song peasant voices; they laughed and snorted in his presence, talking about Nikita and the cook Nikolashka. They sang their long-drawn-out songs and their faces turned grave. They saw how he loved their songs and they sang one every time he appeared – about white snow, a birch tree or a blue tit.

Once when Arina was out, the liveliest of them all, Tatyana, ran up to him, put her arms around him, and started to romp about with him. The girls laughed and squealed, but when Arina entered the room they immediately fell quiet. Tatyanka flushed. Arina gave her a sharp telling-off:

'Just you wait! I shall tell the Mistress, Tanka!'

One night he couldn't sleep and asked Arina to bring Tatyana to sing to him. Arina felt hurt that he liked Tanka's songs better than her folk-tales; nevertheless, peeved and grumbling, she fetched the sleepy, barefoot, loose-haired Tatyana. She leant over him and sang slowly, wordlessly. He stared at the sleepy girl, at her billowing, half-bare bosom and her yawning mouth, then shut his eyes and fell asleep.

All of a sudden his life was full.

The spoilt Lyovushka whimpered without their mother; Olinka, who was very like their aunt Anna Lvovna, peeped into their father's study a few times a day to check if he was there. The sharp-nosed Nikolinka clung to Arina and buried his nose in her skirts.

But he enjoyed the freedom.

Lying in bed before going to sleep, he would laugh softly into his pillows. Arina would look at him anxiously, thinking that he'd been playing pranks again. These days he got away with his escapades. He had accidentally chipped off the lip of the crystal decanter when nobody was about. He had hurled his ball against his grandfather Lev Aleksandrovich's portrait in the drawing-room; the canvas had been torn and some paint had flaked off. Arina was terrified, but it turned out to be all right. Sergey Lvovich hardly ever so much as glanced at his father's picture and he noticed nothing.

'Good grief! Your grandfather almost blinked on the wall!' Arina said.

She would make the sign of the cross over him and become angry. She stopped telling him stories because he found it even more difficult to fall asleep afterwards, so she told him stories in the afternoon instead. He never interrupted her and never asked any questions. Once, when Lyovushka interrupted, he lashed out at him.

At night he would laugh ecstatically and fall asleep.

5

The 'Trubetskoys-Chest-of-Drawers' lived nearby. They took their nickname from the architectural form of their house. The Trubetskoys' heavy square house with its bare yard was indeed somewhat reminiscent of a chest-of-drawers. Moscow had its caricature ready for everyone; and so the Trubetskoys became 'the Trubetskoys-Chest-of-Drawers' and old Trubetskoy was referred to simply as 'Chest-of-Drawers'. That nickname distinguished him from another Trubetskoy who was known as Tarare after his favourite opera, and a third one who was called Vasilisa Petrovna. Three generations of Trubetskoys-Chest-of-Drawers lived in their chest-of-drawers. The old gentleman, big-nosed and lean, was now frail and stone-deaf. His daughter Anyuta, a forty-year-old spinster, managed the house. On his walks Aleksandr often ran into Nikolinka Trubetskoy and his governess. The boys became acquainted, Anyuta sent Sergey Lvovich a nice letter, and Aleksandr started to frequent the Trubetskoys'.

Nikolinka Trubetskoy was small, lazy, fat and yellow as a lemon. His old grandfather, eking out his days, was very sensitive to cold so the house was generously heated in winter and never aired in summer. Their servants crawled about like autumn flies. Life was quiet, stuffy and boring in the Chest-of-Drawers. Even the young seemed to be just living out the rest of their days together with the old gentleman. Nikolinka never played ball or chased about with other boys. He had a sweet tooth, he was a glutton and his gentle aunt overfed him.

The old gentleman spent his days in the fireplace. Autumn had just begun but he was feeling the cold already. Despite his deafness and frailty, he was garrulous and demanded that his daughter should give him a full account of everything that was going on. He caught sight of Aleksandr and asked his daughter loudly:

'Who is that?'

Having heard the name of Pushkin, the old man just as loudly started to enquire:

'Musin-? Bobrishchev-? Bruce-?'

His daughter answered the deaf man with some exasperation:

'No, *mon père*, Pushkin.'

The old man thought for a while. Then, in the same muffled, cracked bass, he asked:

'The *former* Pushkin's son?'

His daughter sighed and said he was the son of their neighbour, Sergey Lvovich.

Then the old man thought again and finally remembered:

'Ah, the poet!'

The tone of the aged voice implied that the recollection was amusing. Apparently he had no recollection of Sergey Lvovich but remembered something about his brother.

When a few minutes later the gentle aunt entered the nursery to see what the children were doing, Aleksandr was straddling Nikolinka and giving a faithful impression of a horseman riding at full speed, and Nikolinka, on all fours, was patiently representing an obedient horse.

The gentle aunt did not approve of the game.

That evening Aleksandr asked his father who 'the former Pushkins' were. Sergey Lvovich was stupefied and loftily demanded to know who had told him about 'the former Pushkins'. All these Nikolashkas, Grushkas and Tatyankas who dared talk through their hat – he would have them flogged. There were no 'former Pushkins', there never had been and never would be; he forbade mention of any 'former Pushkins'. When he learned that it was old Trubetskoy who had said this, Sergey Lvovich muttered condescendingly through gritted teeth:

'Ah, poor Chest-of-Drawers! He's so old now, poor old fellow!' – and he touched his brow with his finger.

Then in the same tone, disdainfully and through clenched teeth, he asked his son what he thought of his new playmate. Aleksandr snorted and replied:

'*C'est un fainéant*, he's a lazybones.'

Sergey Lvovich was astonished at the contempt in his voice. He looked at his son not entirely displeased.

6

Nadezhda Osipovna had come into possession. The serfs, all dressed up, bowed low to her and did not look up.

She had never been a landowner. She had spent her youth in the capital with her mother. Living in the little house in the grounds of the Preobrazhensky Regiment, she had only occasionally gone out to a Guardsmen's ball. She had lived in bitter, carefully concealed poverty, every outing costing both daughter and mother many a pang and a great deal of trouble. She did not remember Suida where she had spent her infancy, and knew nothing of country life. She entered her alienated father's house, therefore, with some apprehension. The grey thatched building scared her. She looked at the serfs grimly and gloomily. The old negro's harem hid themselves from the new mistress.

The house looked like a barn; not only were there no traces of luxury, the rooms were bare. Nadezhda Osipovna was amazed – since childhood she had always believed her father to be well-off. Where possible the signs of havoc had been smoothed away by Palashka. But in the room where her father had died, by the chairs, there still lay, neatly and disquietingly, an untouched phial of medicine, an unfinished flask of wine and a plate; and thrown in a heap were a pipe, a bag of tobacco, a silk neck-tie like the ones fashionable forty years before, and some scraps of paper covered in rust-coloured faded ink. Next to all this was a large withered, dust-covered flower tied up with a silk ribbon; it smelt of musty old hay. Palashka zealously took out all the odds and ends from the bedside table.

She read through her father's papers: bills and letters.

To silver tea-spoons, diamond ring and cat's-eye ring: the sum of 370 roubles …

*

My Dear Sir, Osip Abramovich,
Since I failed to obtain the Court's decision last Tuesday and the Secretary instructed me to come myself next Thursday, I doubt whether a decision has been reached and therefore I humbly beg Your Excellency to come to see to the conduct of your case in person, and may I inform you that the sum you advanced has been defrayed on food and in disbursements to the Secretary, this pursuant to your orders in full. But he has neither said anything about formal divorce, nor given me a decision …

*

My Dear Heart, My Precious Devil,
I could not sleep last night without you, my body is burning for you and my arms are aching for you, I am all on fire …

*

But such an act exposes you as the lowest of the low! I, sir, have already realised and now know for sure what a monster of cruelty, what a coward and a scoundrel you are! The most weak-willed child would not have done this! …

She tossed all the things she had found on the bed-table into the stove. The flower crackled and crumbled into ash. Then she called for Palashka and instructed her to rearrange the rooms – her father's study was to become a drawing-room and the drawing-room was to be turned into her bedroom. The servant-girls stuffed a fresh hay mattress and brought in a trestle-bed – she had no wish to sleep in her father's bed. His wardrobe was dragged out of the room, leaving the marks of its heavy feet imprinted on the floor, which disturbed her like tracks of bygone times.

Next morning, hardly had she opened her eyes when harness bells jingled outside the windows. The district council assessor and a clerk had arrived. The whole day they roamed about the estate, measuring the bathhouse and various shrubs with a long yard-stick, while Nadezhda Osipovna anxiously watched from the window. The clerk drew up an inventory of all the movable and non-movable property of Naval Artillery Captain Osip Hannibal. A witness for the gentry arrived and signed the document in an unsteady hand. He was blind in one eye and had brought a huge dog which he tied up to the porch. He introduced himself to Nadezhda Osipovna as Ensign Zateplensky, retired, her neighbour, always at her service. Afterwards they sat, as was the custom, at table and Palashka offered them some vodka. By the end of the evening the assessor had become incapable and had slid under the table. The witness for the gentry threw some water into his face and told Palashka and the girls to take him to the bathhouse to be sobered up. The following morning the assessor and the clerk drove off. The witness untethered the dog, bowed to Nadezhda Osipovna, kissed her hand and left too.

'Blood-suckers! Leeches!' Palashka hissed after them, almost the very words that the late Osip Abramovich had habitually used.

She had good reason to complain about the assessor's hard drinking. He had regularly tasted Pyotr Abramovich's fruit liqueurs and home-made cognacs.

While waiting for Sergey Lvovich to come, Nadezhda Osipovna started her life as a landowner. It did not prove difficult. As in town, her maid would bring her morning tea in bed. She would sleep well after midday and then discuss the dinner menu with Palashka. Next she would take a walk, hoping to run into her neighbours. Then she had dinner, criticised it, and afterwards took some rest. Her uncle Pyotr Abramovich, who lived not far off, at Petrovskoye, still remembered the quarrel with the Pushkins and did not visit. Neither did she.

Soon she made the acquaintance of her neighbours. The Rokotovs and Vyndomskys had sent invitations to dinner. The Rokotovs lived five versts away. They turned out to be misers. The wife was a pompous lady who pronounced Russian nasally like French and her husband was a squeaky-voiced wretch. They served a poor dinner. Old Vyndomsky, a widower, lived nearby in the village of Trigorskoye. His young daughter Praskovya Aleksandrovna, who was married to a landowner in Tver called Vulf, was visiting him at that time; she amazed Nadezhda Osipovna by her masculine daring, which in the capitals was not in vogue. In the mornings she lunged horses, rode, and supervised the field work, paying little attention to her children, six-year-old Annette and one-year-old Aleksey. She was sturdily built, talkative, with curls on her temples. In the evenings she sat down by the fire and began to read Sallust in French; tired out, she would fall asleep straight away. The old man and his daughter were related to Nadezhda Osipovna: her cousin on her father's side,

Yakov Ivanovich, a junior officer in the Navy, was married to Vyndomsky's second daughter. Nadezhda Osipovna, however, was acquainted with neither her cousin nor his wife.

Mikhaylovskoye was boring and eerie in the evenings. The rooms were bare; everywhere there still lingered the faint reek of stale tobacco and wine, and of the old owner of the house – her father whom she had not known and had been frightened of and with whom it was over now and for ever. She would wake up in the middle of the night, the rain drumming against the windows, something rustling in the thatched roof as if somebody was tripping over, and then there would be the sudden screech of birds and the howl of a mighty wind, as if some giant bellows were being blown above her. When she lit the candle, the windows would be weeping. By dawn the night birds had flown away, and she would shudder to think how close they had been.

But Trigorskoye was merry and bright. The Vyndomskys' substantial house, with its shingled walls, stood on the high bank of the Sorot river. The children played, the candles sputtered and the crickets chirped. Praskovya Aleksandrovna strummed spiritedly on the not entirely out-of-tune harpsichord and sang the most doleful songs. The children danced and played pranks. Nadezhda Osipovna was asked to stay for the night. Nothing reminded her here of the inhospitable Mikhaylovskoye, and even the birds that flew over the house seemed different.

Praskovya Aleksandrovna looked her straight in the eye and had a firm voice, and her judgement was sound. She talked frankly with Nadezhda Osipovna. Without beating about the bush she told her at once and in plain terms that Ustinya Tolstaya had fleeced the old man, but dissuaded her from initiating a scandalous lawsuit against the old skinflint, considering the case hopeless. Nor did she speak highly of Palashka – a pimp and a thief.

Very soon Praskovya Aleksandrovna had got to know all the latest fashions from the capital, and her simple-hearted amazement flattered Nadezhda Osipovna.

It was she who helped Nadezhda Osipovna to manage the estate until Sergey Lvovich arrived.

She accompanied her to Pskov where Nadezhda Osipovna slipped some money to the clerk for a drink and he assigned the patrimony of Mikhaylovskoye to Hannibal's wife and daughter. The patrimony also included Ustye with the villages of Kossokhnovaya, Repshchino, Vashkovo, Morozovo, Loktevo, Voronovo, Luntsovo, Lezhnevo, Tsyblevo, Grechnevo, Makhnino, Bryukhovo and Proshugovo – over three hundred acres altogether comprising ploughlands, meadows, woods and a lake, farmsteads, villages, streams and kitchen-gardens, with about a hundred and eighty male and about a hundred female souls. The clerk issued her with an official deed of inheritance with a big red seal, for which he demanded an extra payment for vodka.

Nadezhda Osipovna was very pleased with the number of her and her mother's villages. But when she went to inspect them on the way home, all she found were four tiny little blackened hamlets of five or six dwellings each, with high slanting porches on piles, miserable and bare. Old peasants in coarse heavy clothes greeted her along the road, bowed from the waist and complained about their poverty. An old peasantwoman offered her a big black Pskov carrot pie on a wooden platter; Nadezhda Osipovna took a nibble and went on. The other villages could not be found: apparently they featured on the deed just for old time's sake. The ploughland was poor, but as mentioned in the inventory, the streams really did babble between sandy banks, though they were slightly frozen in some places and covered with thin ice in others.

Frightened by the intangibility of her possessions, Nadezhda Osipovna started to count her serfs but gave up in despair after the thirteenth girl. She didn't say a word about it to anybody, not even Praskovya Aleksandrovna, afraid to ask what had become of her villages. She decided that Tolstaya was to blame and together with fury against that plunderer of a woman, her father's ruin, she felt bewildered anger against her father, who had sacrificed everything for the sake of his passion. Accompanied by Praskovya Vulf, she went to the Holy Hills where her father was buried. On his grave stood a wooden cross, down which a huge resin tear had ploughed. Pyotr Abramovich had made an inscription on it in pencil: 'Navy Captain, 2nd rank, God's slave, 62 years old, Hannibal'. Pyotr Abramovich had absent-mindedly written his brother's name in old-fashioned style, with a flourish. Nadezhda Osipovna stood for a moment by the cross that still gave off an odour of pine. She could see the entire surrounding landscape from the hill. She made up her mind to place a black tombstone over her father with a more appropriate inscription.

Sergey Lvovich still hadn't made it to cold and bare Mikhaylovskoye, and Nadezhda Osipovna grew sick of it all. She could no longer be bothered even to go over to Trigorskoye. She couldn't accustom herself to either her house or her possessions; she had a constant feeling that she was in the wrong place and that the estate would soon be taken away from her – by the same villainous Tolstoy woman in Pskov, just as she had taken her other villages, now vanished. She was indignant with Sergey Lvovich who had never come and left her helpless in this desolate place. She grew sick with the harsh black boredom hanging over her, alienated and remote from Pskov. In the evenings she sat in her bedroom with her eyes half-closed, bit her nails and fingertips and wept huge turbid tears. The house hushed down like a hen-house under threat from a goshawk. The old man's harem still waited to know their fate and kept quiet.

When a holy day came along, the enterprising Palashka made up her mind. All the serf-girls dressed up and came to congratulate their mistress. The bored Nadezhda Osipovna came out and looked at them through a lorgnette. The girls bowed and began to dance. Nadezhda Osipovna ordered the striped armchair to be brought out and sat down. A tall, slender girl suddenly sprang into motion and started to dance with a rhythmic step and moving her shoulders. She was followed by others – a second and a third … not dancing to their full capacity, but moving gently as they used to when the old master was sober and bored. As in the old days the household servants gathered in a circle and watched from a distance; they kept silent, for the old man had not encouraged talking. Nadezhda Osipovna watched it all through her lorgnette. Gradually she livened up, her nostrils started to flare and her face flushed. The girls, who had been taught to understand their masters' expressions, picked up the tempo. The weather was fine and clear, and all was quiet. Nadezhda Osipovna, looking through her lorgnette, sat fixed in her chair, but her entire body danced – her eyes, lips, shoulders and nostrils quivered. She ordered the girls to be given a pie. Her boredom had vanished.

After a council of war with Vyndomsky, she gave her orders: Palashka was banished to the poultry-yard and the harem was dismissed. Following the old gentleman's advice she appointed Ensign Zateplensky, the witness for the gentry, as bailiff. He was a firm and capable manager. He showed up promptly together with his dog, as if rising out of the earth, and temporarily occupied the bath-house to stay in since it was the warmest place.

The servants saw Nadezhda Osipovna off as far as the boundary of Mikhaylovskoye. Two girls nearly lifted their aprons to their eyes, but quickly regained their composure. Nadezhda Osipovna departed with relief, scarcely believing that in a week's time she would be dancing at the Buturlins'.

7

The cook Nikolashka, whom Marya Alekseyevna had left with the Pushkins until spring, had run away.

He had been a distinguished figure among the Pushkins' servants. Clean-shaven and taciturn, he had spoken seldom and reluctantly; no one had ever shouted at him. Once Marya Alekseyevna had nearly slapped his face – the goose had been burnt, but he gave her one look of his eyes, blank and colourless like glass beads, and she didn't dare. The girls respected him and addressed him as Nikolay Petrovich.

Unlike Nikita who drank little but much too often and was always merry, Nikolay Petrovich had never touched spirits.

Shortly before Nadezhda Osipovna's return, Sergey Lvovich had counted his losses and decided to whitewash himself in front of her. He had no doubt that the losses would be found out; so he started to look for a thief. And he soon found one – Nikolashka had spent excessive amounts in shopping. The culprit maintained that their butter was rancid and the beef and game slightly off, therefore he had had to buy food in the shops, and so on.

Sergey Lvovich summoned him and, spluttering and trying to work himself up into a fury, called him a thief. Nikolashka did not reply. That day Sergey Lvovich left the house even earlier than usual.

In the evening, making for the maids' room, Aleksandr heard singing in the servants' hall. He set the door ajar. Nikolay, pale-faced, was sitting at the table in a new frock-coat. An empty litre bottle stood in front of him. He was singing a long, monotonous song without words, which sounded like a low, long-drawn-out wail.

He glanced at Aleksandr with his blank bright eyes and grinned. He gave him a wink and whistled.

'You Pushkins,' he said slowly, 'you're all bankrupts! And you'll be beggared too! Just you wait!'

Slowly he started to get to his feet. Scared, Aleksandr backed away.

Two days later Nikolay left the house and did not come back. The servants went about in silence. Sergey Lvovich reported him to the police and became extremely agitated. He told everybody about the robbery and escape. His aunt Anna Lvovna came to see him in the evening, and kept crossing herself, and Sergey Lvovich too, when she heard about it. Nikolashka might have stabbed them all!

In the evening Aleksandr asked Arina where Nikolay had gone.

For some time he had done his best to be fearless, but Nikolashka's fixed, piercing stare and the long low wail of the Russian song had affected him in an inexplicable way.

Arina shrugged her shoulders: Poland. Where else should he go? All robbers fled to Poland. They stuck a knife down one of their top-boots and to follow them would have been a wild goose chase. And later, they turned up dressed like lords!

And soon Nadezhda Osipovna was back.

8

Nadezhda Osipovna had had a foreboding from the very beginning. She was amazed and stunned by the fact that everyone could so easily do without her. She had almost forgotten her home and could not recognise it.

It was clear that Nikolashka had fled because of Sergey Lvovich. She could see in Sergey Lvovich's eyes that he was guilty of many things. There was no money at all in the house. Sergey Lvovich placed the blame on the shoulders of 'that scoundrel Nikolashka' – *ce faquin de Nicolachka*, 'those thieving maids' – *ces friponnes de Grouchka et de Tatianka*, 'that rogue Nikishka' – *ce coquin de Niquichka*. Soon, however, the truth was out. He received a humorous note from one of his disreputable young friends with an invitation to visit Pankratyevna's sanctuary. By ill luck the note got into Nadezhda Osipovna's hands.

That day was a frightful one. The children hid themselves, the servants were nowhere to be seen. Nadezhda Osipovna sat at the table face to face with Sergey Lvovich and silently smashed crockery. She was awesome in her anger; her face was motionless – not just pale but almost white, completely colourless, her eyes were hazy, her half-open lips curled in an ugly grimace. She hurled plate after plate to the ground. When Sergey Lvovich's decanter smashed on the floor, spilling wine all over the place, he trembled with fear, resentment and anger, but suddenly grew furious, and flicked a little wine glass from the table. Nadezhda Osipovna was taken by surprise.

'Ah, now you're breaking the crockery?' she said, pale, calm and terrifying. 'Go and break dishes *chez votre Pankratievna*!' Her eyes started to roll and became bloodshot.

Sergey Lvovich slowly stood up and then threw back his head. His whole stance expressed extraordinary dignity. Nadezhda Osipovna stared at him with a face of stone.

'*Mon ange*', he said in a thin voice, without pausing for breath but already triumphant, 'I am leaving for the war, for the battlefields!'

Nadezhda Osipovna grew confused. She looked at the broken dishes. Her spouse's conduct left her nonplussed. She feared the very thought of Sergey Lvovich's becoming a soldier – then she would lose her power and he would no longer be awaited for dinner. The thought of being left a widow with a litter of children terrified her. Furthermore, if Sergey Lvovich was really going to the war, it partially justified his going to Pankratyevna's. All soldiers behaved disreputably. Sergey Lvovich took a deep breath. With a brisk step he made for the vestibule, loudly ordered the servant-boy to give him his overcoat, and left the house – no doubt to seek enrolment in some regiment.

Nadezhda Osipovna did not know whether to believe her husband or not. She was furious with him for putting on such a despicable act in front of her, with herself for having driven him to the field; and most of all over the fact that in spite of being the one in the wrong, he had emerged the winner and she had been outmanoeuvred.

As if blown by the wind, Nadezhda Osipovna dashed off to the maids' room. The girls sat holding their breaths. In the corner she was astounded to see Aleksandr. It seemed that in her absence both her husband and her son had acquired new habits. She grasped him by the collar and almost carried him out to her room.

In the doorway of her bedroom she ran into Arina. Arina's face was pale and still, and her eyes suddenly looked faded and sunken.

Nadezhda Osipovna shouldered her way past her. Arina moaned and leaned against the door-post.

'Bitch!' Nadezhda Osipovna said, not daring to look at her.

Arina stepped aside from the door and let the mother with her son pass by.

After the door had shut behind them, she continued to stand there for a while.

'Birchrods!' yelled Nadezhda Osipovna.

Arina crossed herself and went to the servants' hall. There she sat bolt upright on the bench and put her hands on her knees. The servant-boy was already hurrying to respond to his mistress's call. Arina turned even paler and pressed her hand to her heart.

Nadezhda Osipovna gave her son a prolonged beating, until she grew tired. Her son kept silence. When she had recovered her breath, she threw herself on the pillows and fell asleep, exhausted. Arina remained sitting in the dark servants' hall for some time. Then she rummaged in her chest, found a little phial, took a sip from it, and felt better. She sipped a little more, and drank it to the dregs. Only then, intoxicated and rocking from side to side, did she burst into tiny tight little tears.

Six

SERGEY Lvovich never went to war, neither in autumn nor in winter. War was now being waged with both the French and the Turks. The old Moscow nobles did not speak highly of it. Napoleon was winning; rumour had it that the Tsar was in tears. The Commander-in-Chief, the elderly General Kamensky, sent requests to be discharged, and soon, in fact, deserted from the army.

Odes were written and published every day. They were mostly dedicated to the Governor-General of Moscow and eventually the public wearied of them. Sergey Lvovich cooled down like everyone else.

Meanwhile, masquerades were thrown all over Moscow, and at one of them Sergey Lvovich and Nadezhda Osipovna witnessed a highly amusing fight that occurred between two friends over the beautiful Mme Kafka; they seized each other by the hair. But the Pushkins could not laugh together because they were not on speaking terms.

In winter they hired a tutor for Aleksandr. They had been hesitating over the choice for a long time, and eventually the person who undertook to educate their son turned out to be none other than the comte de Montfort. This was not, however, the Montfort of old: his nose had sharpened and reddened, his breeches were permanently soiled, a frayed jabot hung loosely on his chest. He was still courteous but nearly always too cheerful and garrulous. In the evening he played the flute. He shared a room with Aleksandr and the boy became friendly with his tutor; the Frenchman readily forgave his pranks.

While they took long walks along the Moscow streets and gardens, Montfort chattered away ceaselessly. Soon the boy had learned all the amusing scandal of the French court since the times of the marquis de Dangeau.

As soon as he got up in the morning the Frenchman would take some balm, after which he brightened up; he took it at night as well if he did not play the flute. He greatly enjoyed drawing everything that entered his mind on scraps of paper, most frequently the pretty heads and little feet of his Parisian paramours; the profiles were always the same, but the feet differed.

Once he told the boy about all the celebrated duels of the latest two reigns. He placed him three paces off and taught him to defend himself. They had no sabres, but Montfort grew so heated that he once yelled to Aleksandr:

'You're dead!'

He quite often told Aleksandr about the Parisian *beau monde* and theatre and once, taking his balm after such a conversation, he hung his head and burst into tears.

2

In spring the whole family went to Zakharovo to see Grandmother Marya Alekseyevna. Mikhaylovskoye was too far away, it was a shambles and in any case there was no one to welcome them there.

It was his first journey and first taste of country life. The coachman overhead was singing over and over a song without beginning or end and whipped up the horses, and he saw the striped milestones, the occasional wooden houses of peasants with their chimneyless stoves, the hills, ploughlands and little surrounding groves, their trees still bare and drenched by the latest rains. He listened avidly to the unfamiliar music of the wheels and the coachman, and inhaled the new smells of tar, smoke and wind. Black, shaggy dogs barked furiously after them, baring their teeth.

This was the highroad that had been sometimes cursed by his uncle and his father – up-and-down, muddy, and lined with empty sentinels' boxes. The houses of the country gentry gleamed like white lace on the slopes.

No one pestered Aleksandr with orders on the journey. Under the influence of the road, or the balm, the Frenchman dozed off.

Aleksandr enjoyed the trip – he would gladly have spent eternity in this carriage, shaken and tossed on the ruts.

Nadezhda Osipovna had kept silent the whole winter.

Knowing that he would get no reply, but still hoping, Sergey Lvovich had once asked her quickly in a pleasant voice:

'Dearest, where is that book by Lebrun? Do you remember it, the little one I was reading yesterday? Can't find it! Has Aleksandr taken it?'

But he was met by a disaffected glance and complete silence. Nadezhda Osipovna was not concerned in the least that Aleksandr might have taken the book. She was good at keeping up a hostile silence. Sergey Lvovich languished and melted, he gave her little presents, once he even bought her a necklace with the last money he had. Or he tried to attract her attention in another way – once at dinner he said that the game was putrid and pushed the plate aside with a sigh, refusing to eat it. The game was from their own estate, had been frozen and really had gone off, but Nadezhda Osipovna did not respond.

Sergey Lvovich spoke to her exclusively in sighs and moans, sometimes soft and deep and with a lisp, sometimes loud and vigorous.

On the trip to Zakkharovo they became noticeably more affectionate to one another. But a few miles before journey's end Nadezhda Osipovna grew sulky again. When they passed Zvenigorod, Sergey Lvovich seemed moved by the singing of a young girl sitting on a balcony. She sang in a very thin voice:

If you killed the hope
In my passionate heart …

Nadezhda Osipovna's face suddenly broke out in blotches, her eyes dimmed and her bosom started to heave. She stared long and hungrily into Sergey Lvovich's eyes. He noticed her stare, shrank and turned away, and shouted to the coachman nonchalantly:

'Hurry, hurry! Have you fallen asleep?'

When jealous his wife was frightening. She had a heavy hand.

Seeing that Sergey Lvovich had been beguiled by the singing, Nadezhda Osipovna said through clenched teeth:

'What an old hag! And whined like a mosquito.'

In Zakharovo the family dispersed in different directions. Sergey Lvovich took walks in the little grove with a French book in his hands. The grove was tiny, but serf-girls went there to pick berries. Nadezhda Osipovna spent hours sitting on the high bank of the pond looking down at the water; the servants could not understand what was so interesting about it. Aleksandr and his tutor wandered along the roads. Marya Alekseyevna shrugged her shoulders:

'They all go their separate ways!'

The children stayed in a dilapidated outhouse set apart from the manor. Olinka and the younger children occupied the biggest room, Aleksandr and the tutor shared another one.

Sharp-nosed, sallow-skinned, pretty Olinka was a canting hypocrite. Her aunt Anna Lvovna had taught her to pray before going to bed and in the morning – for dear *papa*, dear *maman*, little brother Nikolinka, little brother Lyovushka, and Sashka. Olinka was very friendly with Nikolinka. In the morning she would hurry to the big house to snuggle up to her mother and granny and would take Nikolinka with her. She walked about with an impatient mincing step until they noticed her, and immediately dropped a curtsy. Her grandmother was not impressed by this or by her prayers performed solely to earn praise.

'All this is Annette and Lizka's godliness! Damn these do-gooders!'

Nikolinka was his father's favourite. He had the Pushkins' sharp nose, which he turned up in his father's manner when he got excited. He was short-tempered but physically weak. Occasionally he had a fight with Aleksandr and then ran to his father to complain about it, who in turn complained to his wife.

His parents' quarrel had played into Aleksandr's hands – for the time being they forgot about him and Montfort. Only his granny would take him by his chin, lift it, tousle his hair, and give a perplexed sigh.

Out of his window he could see the pond, lined with wilted birches. A dark fir-wood grew on the opposite side, which Nadezhda Osipovna enjoyed for its gloominess – it was in harmony with the new sombre elegies – but which Sergey Lvovich hated. The manor-house and the outbuilding were on top of a hill. The garden was lined with old maples. Everything in Zakharovo bore the traces of its previous owners – the maples and poplars were planted in two rows, remnants of the old forgotten alley. In the grove Sergey Lvovich read other people's names cut on the treetrunks, blackened long ago. On the trees he often came across the old emblem of a heart pierced with an arrow and three little circles – drops of blood trickling down from the tip. The names were in pairs, referring to lovers' trysts in bygone days.

Zakharovo had changed hands many times. It was a newish property, lacking roots and warmth. No one had settled there for long – the owners felt like guests too.

Sergey Lvovich gave way to despair in all this family gloom and dreamt of escape.

Only the homeless Montfort was at ease. He whistled like a bird, and carelessly and mechanically sketched the sights of Zakharovo – always the same: a jagged forest, the pond that looked like any other pond, and instead of the manor-house – a castle with a tall spire. He often took Aleksandr to Vyazyomy, a prosperous village nearby, where he renewed his supplies of the balm. Talkative peasantwomen greeted the little master; they had seen many of Zakharovo's owners in the village. There was a lop-sided belfry in Vyazyomy – rumoured to date from Godunov's times – and a little church next to it, but even the elderly did not know who the builders had been and what things had been like in Vyazyomy in the old days.

Heartily sick of idleness, Sergey Lvovich suggested that all the family should make an excursion to Vyazyomy and attend midday service.

Threatening to fall apart, the ancient, decrepit and unwieldy carriage that had brought the Pushkins to Zakharovo rumbled along the road. The bewildered peasantwomen looked up at the masters and bowed low.

'That carriage clangs like a bell!' they said as the Pushkins passed by.

The bell in Vyazyomy was cracked.

During mass Sergey Lvovich caught the eye of a pale young lady, their neighbour's daughter, and cast a furtive glance at her. But the young lady was easily frightened and quietly stole away. Sergey Lvovich left, displeased by the aged half-blind village priest who had not paid enough attention to the Zakharovo gentry.

That evening he had a conversation with Montfort. Montfort believed that faith was essential for common people. His knowledge of spiritual books was limited to just one, *The Deeds of the Saints in the Elysian Fields*, and the chapter about masquerades in particular. After the visit to the Vyazyomy church, Montfort's opinions were congenial to Sergey Lvovich. Decidedly, he felt like a French marquis. The evening was concluded with Montfort's recital of Scarron's poem about the life hereafter.

> *Tout près de l'ombre d'un rocher*
> *J'aperçus l'ombre d'un cocher,*
> *Qui, tenant l'ombre d'une brosse,*
> *En frottait l'ombre d'un carrosse.**

Sergey Lvovich was ecstatic and patted the head of Aleksandr who was sitting next to him.

The fairs in Vyazyomy were so noisy that the sound of drunken songs reached Zakharovo and irritated Marya Alekseyevna:

'Just like a coaching inn! No respect for the nobles!'

She spoke in a low voice, secretly disappointed with her new estate. The neighbouring peasants paid little attention to the Zakharovo gentry.

Aleksandr and Nikolinka swam in the river, listened to the singing of orioles in the bushes and accompanied Montfort to Vyazyomy to renew his stock of balm. Once Aleksandr lagged behind and witnessed a miraculous apparition – a big-bosomed nymph with her hair loose was bathing in the river. She rose and fell in the water. His heart beat fast. Somebody called the nymph:

'Natalya!'

Raising her palms to her lips, she replied in a ringing voice: 'Halloo!' and resumed her rising and sinking.

That night, as he fell asleep, somebody kissed his forehead.

When two days later in the grove he ran into a young lady in a white dress with flowers in her hands, he was captivated and felt that he could not live without her and would soon die. Montfort made a bow – it was the young lady from the neighbouring estate. He could not remember her name – Shishkova? Sushkova? Yushkova? *Quelque chose* ending in *-ova*.

---

*Near the shade of a rock
I saw the shade of a coachman,
Who, holding the shade of a brush,
Was brushing the shade of a coach.

Aleksandr began to visit the grove on purpose but never saw her again. Eventually he realised that she came there at night. Once he overcame Montfort's vigilance and headed for the grove along the familiar moonlit path. She was sitting on the bench, sighing and gazing at the moon. A thin kerchief rose and fell on her breast. Here was the transparent kerchief, the pale bosom and the moon he had read about in some poem or other.

She was listening. When she heard the sound of an approach, she screened her face with her fan and started to breathe excitedly. She was amazed to see that it was Aleksandr and burst out laughing. She seemed to be waiting for someone else. Her cheeks were aglow, her dress was flimsy. She spoke to him. He wanted to reply but couldn't find his voice and ran away, confused.

3

Sergey Lvovich was fed up with the peaceful life of Zakharovo and with the place itself. He had not been born for rustic tranquillity. Once at dinner he mentioned that he really had to get back to Moscow – his career would be ruined if he lingered in Zakharovo. He did not make it to Moscow, however: on the very day of his departure Nikolinka fell ill, and died three days later. It was a bolt from the blue.

At his brother's funeral, Aleksandr fidgeted and turned around. It was a warm morning. His faint-hearted father was supported by the arm on each side behind the coffin. Nadezhda Osipovna walked to the church silently, without any assistance. Looking at her father, Olinka cried a lot. When there were no tears left, she would start to sob in a plaintive manner that was feigned – but in fact she felt the loss of her dear brother deeply. Little Lyovushka was carried into the church; sleeping now, he did not disturb the mournful business. Only Aleksandr was indifferent to the proceedings. Like everyone else he pressed his lips to his brother's pale forehead and could not recognise the brother he had teased just a week earlier. He was struck by the strange calm of the dead boy. It was the first time he had seen death.

A very old man in a coarse caftan sat at the church-porch leaning on his walking-stick. He made low zealous bows and copper coins were dropped at his feet.

The birdsong and the white stone church wall seemed new to Aleksandr that morning. The medieval belfry stood aslant, threatening to collapse at any moment. There was pristine peace and tranquillity all round; the Vyazyomy peasants stood in a crowd, silent. Nikolinka was buried next to the church. His mother pressed little Lyovushka to her breast and held him until she left for home.

From then on the only child whom Nadezhda Osipovna paid any attention to was Lyovushka. She ignored Aleksandr completely. It was Sergey Lvovich who decided to take him in hand.

Being a superficial person, Sergey Lvovich had been unprepared for grief. He felt nothing but fear and behaved with extraordinary faint-heartedness. One moment he would prattle as if nothing had happened, then at dinner he would suddenly laugh and then burst into tears. Sorrow made him sleep a lot.

'*Que la volonté du ciel soit faite!*' he would say with a loud sigh, with a shrug of his shoulders.

Alarmed and vexed with Aleksandr who did not cry, and with himself for feeling no enduring grief either, Sergey Lvovich reproached his son for being callous and heartless. Nadezhda Osipovna listened, oblivious of everything around her. After their son's death the couple made it up and came to share the same view of Aleksandr and his behaviour. He was unfeeling, ungrateful, a cold fish. Montfort, who was supposed to have 'influence' over him, had none.

The Pushkins departed before autumn began. On the last morning Aleksandr was especially disturbed, and before the departure he suddenly disappeared. He was found in the grove – sitting on the ground pressing his cheek to the bench.

The Pushkins' sorry, heavy carriage lumbered along. Unoiled, its wheels whining, it was practically falling apart, like a pile of old dry sticks.

The uprooted Frenchman refreshed himself with his balm and babbled to Aleksandr with whom he shared the cart:

> *Oh! l'ombre d'un cocher!*
> *Oh! l'ombre d'une brosse!*
> *Oh! l'ombre d'un carrosse!*

Seven

Day was breaking. He was waking up. A dim uncertain light filled the room. The bed sheets seemed startlingly white. Lyovushka was breathing gently, Montfort's breath came in subdued little snorts. He was listening hard, his hearing sharp and alert like a game bird's roused by a hunter. A cart was creaking slowly along the street – it was the water-carrier. Then silence: it was still early morning.

He crawled out of bed and slipped out of his room noiselessly, passing by the half-open doors to his father's study. Barefoot, wearing only a night-shirt, he threw himself into the leather-covered chair, seated himself on one bent foot and, unconscious of the cold, began to read. The little books in pale blue covers had been much thumbed over and perused. He was already conversant with Piron. In a tiny frayed book there was an engraving showing a fat old man with a heavy chin, roguish eyes and the lips of a glutton. He had composed his own epitaph: 'Here lies Piron. He was nobody in his lifetime, not even an Academician.' He admired the old man's reckless free spirit, and his amusing fairy-tales whose meaning he already understood more than the mischievous and wily Voltaire. His favourite character was the devil, at the very mention of whom his aunt Anna Lvovna always spat superstitiously. Piron's devil, however, was a jolly fellow, and good at tricking nuns and saints. He reflected sadly that in Moscow there was nobody quite like that fleshy poet.

He liked the travel literature too, the precise descriptions, the exact names of the towns, the numbers of miles – the more miles there were, the farther away from home.

On the desk there were usually a few issues of the *Moscow Messenger* that Sergey Lvovich received twice a week. He read the advertisements. The names in those from the wine shops – Clicquot, Moët, Aix – sounded like music to him; the ring of the words themselves gave him immense pleasure.

He found no Russian books in his father's study; although Sergey Lvovich did read Karamzin's journal, he never actually bought it. Only an abandoned volume of Derzhavin, borrowed from somebody and never returned, was lying on the window-sill. He read a page and put it aside.

Once the forbidden bookcase caught his fancy. One of its drawers was unlocked and pulled out – his father had forgotten to lock it. He peered inside and saw a thick green, morocco-bound manuscript volume, five or six leather-bound notebooks and a few letters. The contents of the notebooks and the morocco volume turned out to be hand-written; the letters were in verse and prose. He listened to make sure nobody was about and dipped into the notebooks.

All the writing was in Russian, in various hands, starting with the old-fashioned square script like Nikita's, and finishing in his father's brisk hand. The notebooks had been given to Sergey Lvovich when he had been in the Guards Regiment by his distant relative, his cousin, the Guards Lieutenant who had then vanished, and later Sergey Lvovich had finished them himself. They still retained the strong reek of Guardsmen's tobacco.

The morocco-bound volume was entitled *The Virgin's Toy*, a composition by Ivan Barkov.* He put it aside with the firm resolution to read all of it later, and leafed through one of the notebooks. He read a few pages and stopped in amazement. It was a hundred times more entertaining than the subtle puns of the Marquis de Bièvre's *Almanac des calembours*. On the first page he read a short poem dedicated to the late Emperor Paul:

> *To great wise Paul we owe such thanks*
> *As shown by the poor from the Neva banks.*

And to his bust:

> *Oh, wisest mother of the Russian nation!*
> *How did you bear this malformation?*

Then followed a poem about 'the characters of the Ministers of State':

> *You'll kill me if I truly pen*
> *The qualities of these great men:*
> *Kochubèy's the brainiest by a mile,*
> *Lopukhin's head is full of guile,*
> *Chartoryski's best with the knout,*
> *Chichagov's the champion lout,*
> *Zavadovsky will grudge a loaf –*
> *Rumyantsev is the leading oaf.*

On the same page there was also a very simple poem in reply.

---

* A poet of the mid-eighteenth century whose priapic verse was not published in Russia until the twentieth century.

The directness of these poems, their everyday diction, was a revelation to him. They made reference to the names of people his father and Vasily Lvovich spoke about in their boring conversations, the shop talk that made Sergey Lvovich so discontented.

Epistle to Kutaysov

It's time to part, my dearest fellow,
O Count so arrogant and shallow.
Soon we'll have to leave the spot
Where you and I made such a pot,
Where we trod on human trash
And turned it into heaps of cash
And everything except the gold
Left us absolutely cold.

He enjoyed the deft insinuations, though there were some he couldn't fathom:

Yours might not have been such joy
If you'd not been rescued by Lanskoy.

He was struck by the caustic satire on the governing Senate.

The Senate lay in darkness, then it came to pass,
The Tsar commanded it to rise – and saw its arse.

Most of all he admired a long poem about Tverskoy Boulevard. First it ran on about some fops he knew nothing of, then suddenly he came across the name of Trubetskoy. Undoubtedly it had been written about the Trubetskoys-Chest-of-Drawers – Nikolinka's grandfather and aunt. To read a poem written about people he actually knew seemed to him extraordinary. On another page his father had hastily scribbled out an elegy in which Aleksandr recognised his uncle Vasily Lvovich's work, which had been written only the previous year. All this was pure magic.

Almost everything the books contained was anonymous, except for the name Barkov on the morocco-bound one. Some of the poems were followed by a few mysterious letters, quite unlike the signatures at the ends of letters or documents.

A sleepy maid had already come out of the servants' room. She yawned and splashed some water over her hands. Montfort's grunting – he was about to take his balm – sounded as from a distance. Barefoot, in a night-shirt, he was reading *The Nightingale*.

> *It sang, the rogue, the whole night through.*
> *'Ah, how I love this bird, I do!'*
> *Katyusha spoke between the sheets –*
> *'See the love-flush on my cheeks!'*
> *Meanwhile, Aurora has arisen*
> *And gently from the far horizon*
> *She begins to pluck the sun.*
> *It's time, my friend, that you were gone!*

It really was time.

He was quite oblivious to the chill of his father's unheated room, his eyes were glinting, his heart pounding. Russian poetry was a secret that had to be hidden like a sacred mystery, in poetry things were written about Tsars and love; things normally undiscussed and never mentioned in the journals. It was a secret he had now discovered.

It contained veiled taboos, unexpected perils.

The early-morning church-bell chimed. He heard footsteps. The key was sticking out of the folding bookcase door. He shut it quickly, and clasping the key in his hand, sped like a shadow to his room. He had just enough time to throw himself on his bed and pretend to be asleep. His heart was hammering, he was triumphant. Montfort, having taken his balm, waved an admonitory finger at him.

2

He read the treasured bookcase within a week. Barkov was the boldest and the brightest of its gems.

He learned the miraculous mechanism of love from the French books. The mysteries turned out to be more down-to-earth than he could have guessed. Love was an endless delightful war with its stratagems and deceptions. According to a certain epigram it even had its own casualties who passed over to the service of Bacchus. But love in Barkov's poems was a mad tavern brawl, filled with shouts and screams, where no holds were barred, where people got exhausted, covered with lather and foam, like spent horses. By the age of ten he had learned expressions of which the Frenchman Montfort was wholly ignorant. He read Barkov and took huge delight in the knowledge that he was reading forbidden verses. He laughed and flashed his white teeth at his aunt Anna Lvovna every time she sent him away from the table, and flushed when Sergey Lvovich dropped a hint about some Muscovite's escapades. From these readings he gained the benefit of understanding his father better, although he had accepted the declaration of war made on him by his parents and Aunt Anna Lvovna.

Sergey Lvovich had not noticed that the treasured bookcase was unlocked. The house had increasingly been falling into neglect. Nothing actually disappeared, everything was still in place, but at times he had a sudden feeling that his servants were thieves, that somebody had stained his new coloured tail-coat, and knitting his brows, he started endless and futile arguments and complaints that ended in loud sighs and wails. Since he did not dare shout at Nadezhda Osipovna he yelled at Nikita, who had got used to it. The stained tail-coat was actually his old one and it had been stained by Sergey Lvovich himself.

Aleksandr was already ten years old and Olga was twelve; so their parents had to hire a tutor because there was a limit to what Montfort could cope with. The tutor cost them good money and on holidays he was even asked to share the family table, yet the children made dubious progress. The priest from the neighbouring parish, who had been recommended by Anna Lvovna, said that Aleksandr Sergeyevich had no knowledge of the Scriptures and was a stranger to the catechism. Both Nadezhda Osipovna and Sergey Lvovich, who had a similarly faint idea of the catechism, looked at Sashka in no little despair.

The children, moreover, had to be properly dressed, and this was the bane of their lives for both Sergey Lvovich and Nadezhda Osipovna. No question of buying fabric from the French shop for Sashka and Olka! Instead the children wore old clothes. Arina cut out some rags for Olga, and Nikita, who had some knowledge of clothes-making, stitched together some garments for Aleksandr out of cast-off tail-coats. A foppish passer-by who found himself in Kharitonyev Lane laughed till he cried at the sight of a curly-headed boy in the street wearing a pair of ancient frayed grey trousers.

3

Vasily Lvovich had gone up in the world and was leading the high life. His trip to Paris placed him in the front rank of the literati. The young and famous Batyushkov who occasionally visited Moscow had befriended him. The name of Pushkin was sometimes linked with his, or their names were even put together with those of Karamzin and Dmitriyev. Soirées at his house had come into vogue. Blaise the cook baked *pirozhki* and Vasily Lvovich prepared a stock of charades and *bouts rimés*. His guests would laugh and eat heartily. Sergey Lvovich, tired of his drab life, found at his brother's everything that his life could and should have been. At these evenings Vasily Lvovich kissed Annushka and worked at impromptus. Annushka went on blossoming, and gave birth to a girl whom Vasily Lvovich named Margarita; his friends cheerfully clinked their glasses and drank a toast to her. Circe was forgotten. Coiffured in curls, in his Parisian narrow tail-coat, with impromptus in the pockets of his straw-coloured trousers, Vasily Lvovich threw himself into the Moscow *beau monde*, rolled his *r*s in the style of the Palais-Royal, and at night fell into the warm arms of his Annette – Annushka.

The times were right for all this. Now the French held very strong sway, when only yesterday they had been the hated enemy. The Tsar went to Tilsit and Erfurt for a conference with Napoleon ('cap in hand' it was said in Moscow, and the older generation even added venomously: 'to the master'). Everyone joined a particular group. The flighty youths were very happy with this state of affairs, while their elders were indignant. An old general who had dared refer to Napoleon as 'Buonaparte' in the company of young men was abandoned on the spot; everyone melted away from him and the venerable old man, leaning on his walking-stick, was left to hail his lackey for himself.

Vasily Lvovich enjoyed a tremendous success with the Moscow ladies.

'*Oh, ce volage de Vasily Lvovich!*' they would say, wagging their fingers at him, a gesture that made him breathe noisily with sheer pleasure, simper and ruffle his scented head.

Both the old and the new aristocracy had given up all things Russian for lost a long time ago. They were always going off abroad, for travel in foreign countries was considered the only worthy occupation for the noble-born. In the boarding-schools of St Petersburg Jesuits taught Latin prayers and French religious philosophy to the young princes Gagarin, Golitsyn, Rostopchin, Shuvalov, Stroganov and Novosiltsev. Old ladies hastily embraced Catholicism; the abbés Jourdain and Surugue were their preceptors. The Pushkins' neighbours' son Nikolinka Trubetskoy had already been taken to the Jesuit College in St Petersburg.

Sergey Lvovich enjoyed listening to his son speaking French. Vasily Lvovich made a point of having long conversations with him. While talking to him he felt as if he were on the Boulevard des Capucines again.

The older generation of Moscow were reconciliatory; while in St Petersburg they were now a spent force, retired, out of favour, in opposition. They were very soon obliged to pay attention to the new genius.

For Vasily Lvovich was very close to fame and revelled in it. He was invited to Kheraskov's, the Moscow Homer, now retired. In an old-fashioned drawing-room, amid total silence, Vasily Lvovich recited his imitation of Horace – an address to the amateurs of the Muses. The master of the house, named Virgil in the poem, was already familiar with the verses and had approved them.

… Where's the gold goblet? Let's sit by the fire!
Let the gods rule the world as they desire! …

The older generation admired his free-thinking – let the St Petersburg set do as they liked! Where's the gold goblet? Vasily Lvovich recited with a soft whistling sound and, like Talma, with strong shifts of feeling.

Where are the lyres? Phoebus is burning,
The Russian Virgil is among us
And inspires us all to learning!

This was no poetic licence: the host had been curator of Moscow University.

Kheraskov was noticeably thrilled, his grey hair stirred. As one the ladies turned their faces to Vasily Lvovich.

And I'll be famous throughout the world!

he proclaimed enthusiastically.

Oh joy, oh rapture! I too am a bard!

He was utterly exhausted and wiped his brow with a handkerchief. Virgil was rising from his chair. The ladies knew: now, with a kiss, he would pass his lyre to Vasily Lvovich.

But at that moment Vasily Lvovich felt an impromptu in his palm, probably pulled out of his pocket together with his handkerchief, an impromptu that had come to him the previous night, a once-in-a-lifetime inspiration. He felt he had done his best to pay tribute to Homer and Virgil, and at the same time he wanted to read something light and pleasant, to make the ladies smile – an appeal to the lovers of the Muses might have been somewhat too elevated for them. Not noticing the rising Kheraskov, he stretched out his hand and made a sign. Everyone fell silent. The poet began to recite. The crucial moment had been missed and Kheraskov resumed his seat. However, having heard the title, he nodded approvingly. Poetic rapture – he knew it when he saw it. The poet was reciting a *Discourse About Life, Death and Love*.

From the first lines the audience was thrown into confusion.

Where shall I start? I can see that 'ram'
Will never do here when the right rhyme is 'ham'.
Well you know, my friends, a jackdaw's no emu:
I love you so much, I'll not deceive you.

Vasily Lvovich felt that in a moment the fair ladies and Kheraskov-Homer would break into smiles, and went on reading his *bouts rimés*:

... What is our life? – A book, pure paper.
What is our death? – A haze, pure vapour.
What's best of all? – salt cod and roast beef.
And when I die, the raven's beak
Will tear my corpse ...

The venerable old Kheraskov, the Moscow Virgil, who had invited the new
genius to his house to give his recitation, sat sulkily, his eyes wide-open.

... Death is a boar – a ferocious beast ...
... The grave is no couch, but still, at least,
Better than a suit-case ...!

At this point the sensitive literary Moscow ladies who were habituées of
Kheraskov's *soirées* all burst out laughing at once. The reader was ecstatic.
Slowly, leaning on his cane, his crosier, with trembling hand, the old poet
rose indignantly. His cheeks were flushed like a child's. He took a glass of cold
water in a gulp and left the room, not only forgetting to pass on his lyre but
even without taking his leave.

Next day the old poet said coldly of Vasily Lvovich:

'His head is filled with dew.'

And he suddenly added:

'And curly as a ewe.'

4

That was the end of the brothers' rivalry. One was covered with glory and
fame, an acknowledged poet and a Moscow madcap: another one was going
to pieces in obscurity, according to the young a henpecked 'slave of Hymen'.

Vasily Lvovich usually made social appearances in the company of two
notorious cranks – his cousin Aleksey Mikhaylovich Pushkin and Prince
Pyotr Ivanovich Shalikov. The former was a Voltairian and a scoffer of the
most caustic kind; the latter, with his shaggy eyebrows, was a melancholy,
delicate but choleric person who easily lost his temper. The first dressed carelessly, the second was a dandy and always wore a flower in his buttonhole.
Both were great eccentrics. When the trio turned up in people's drawing-
rooms they caused a furore. Vasily Lvovich had become particularly close
to his cousin, who ribbed him constantly; the two were often referred to as
'the two Pushkins'. Sergey Lvovich was made distinctly *de trop* by this duo;
if he was present, he was called 'Pushkin's brother'. He lost both his own
name and his own existence. He could feel it in everything – in the way he
was scrutinised through lorgnettes, in the way he was introduced. Gradually

he started to avoid 'the two Pushkins' and made every effort to be invited to the sort of evening or children's party where they would not be present. But Nadezhda Osipovna was once again in the spotlight, the old ladies of Moscow whispered about her, indicating her with their eyes, and for a while Sergey Lvovich recovered his former independent air. 'Pushkin's brother' envied his brother's fame and secretly and painfully vied with him for the attention of Aleksey Mikhaylovich. He had soured, was losing his good nature, and the *beau monde* did not forgive that.

Vasily Lvovich was very absent-minded, like all the Moscow poets. He was the last person to see the most obvious things. His status as the elder brother flattered him. But it worried him that Sergey Lvovich had ceased to appear at the houses that he used to frequent. Only then did he really appreciate the expression 'Hymen's slave' and feel his brother's degradation in the eyes of society. Being less than keen-eyed and indeed having something of a cast, he paid little attention to all the Sashkas and Lolkas frisking about in his brother's house. Once he saw one of them dressed in strange attire, the work of a domestic tailor, which gave the youngster the look of a clown, of a *bouffon*. He burst out laughing:

'*Oh, c'est un franc original!*'

Now he suddenly became pensive. Till then Sergey's fate had never bothered him, but the Pushkins had to be accepted, they had to shine everywhere. A trivial failure at old man Kheraskov's had not daunted him – it was in vogue to be half-French, half-anything, and he didn't give a damn about the opinions of old fossils. He started to visit his brother more often and made himself pay attention to Sashka and Lolka; till then he had always mixed them up. Lolka, only a toddler, seemed to possess an exceptional memory. Once Vasily Lvovich recited one of his impromptus in his presence and Lolka repeated it at once:

> *Life is a merry round of charades,*
> *Day and night we play at cards,*
> *Fall silent, or we slander friends –*
> *What a heaven that never ends!*

Such a sharp memory was unprecedented in one so young! Here were the makings of a poet. Who knows – the two Pushkins might become a trio, with the addition of the youngster. Vasily Lvovich was reminded of the flattering remark made to 'the two Pushkins' by a Frenchman at old Arkharova's ball:

'In your country the name Pushkin favours wit – *esprit* – and a passion for literature.'

Lolka was mischievous; Sashka was obstinate and wild, his sister Annette seemed far too strict with him. His brother Sergey had also been insufferable in his childhood; this one might turn out all right after all – sometimes he did show some common sense.

5

His parents drifted about other people's drawing-rooms. Here at home they lived out mere scraps of their existence. For them home was just a coaching inn where they could doze off, yawn, quarrel, yell at the maids, the children, and settle themselves to sleep. They had no sense that this house and this existence was the hub of their children's and servants' lives.

Aleksandr loved the hour before their parents' outings. He would watch his father's evening toilette. Sergey Lvovich got dressed in his study. A glorious fop of former days awoke in him. He would clean his nails quickly with a file and a little brush and watch Nikita curl his hair à la Duroc, directing his movements and making witty and pointed remarks. Afterwards he would spruce up his new tail-coat and pace the room, assuming various expressions and uttering brief individual words through his teeth. He would fluff up his hair as he passed in front of the mirror, and catching sight of Aleksandr say condescendingly, in a deliberately astonished voice and seeming to refer to somebody else:

'Ah! You here!'

And he would click his heels and swiftly leave the study.

Suddenly it would grow quiet. His mother would come out of her bedroom quickly and lightly, her eyes glistening. His father, dressed in his finest, would treat her respectfully and gallantly, as if she were a stranger. Once, through the half-open door Aleksandr watched his father, already smartly dressed, scented, and his hair curled, waiting for his mother and humming a tune in his thin voice. Unaware of being watched, he suddenly started to bend his knees and rotate slowly, prattling and smiling. He danced. His mother came in, breathing quickly, with shining eyes, as was her wont before a night out. His father kept waltzing slowly, and held her, and she glided next to him readily and obediently on her quick short legs, her heavy bosom heaving strongly. Then she stopped and they left.

From the maids' room came a long-drawn-out song. Arina sighed and grumbled softly. The rooms were chilly – the house was rarely heated because they were sparing with logs, so expensive in Moscow.

Sometimes he asked his father where they were going. His father replied reluctantly, through his teeth:

'To old Beloselsky's.'

Everybody went to old Beloselsky's. He had been living out his days loudly and eventfully and had long been bankrupt.

'To Buturlin's.'

Buturlin was an old friend.

At such moments his son's voice seemed unpleasant to him – harsh and abrupt, and this questioning was embarrassing. He carefully kept the secrets of society from his son. But his son knew already: society was miraculous, inscrutable.

6

But even in this bleak house and nomadic family there came a time when everything changed and acquired its own odour, colour and meaning – winter.

The first snow always impressed him irresistibly.

Arina would enter the room with a meaningful look.

'The snow has taken the sleepers unawares,' she would say sombrely.

It had snowed on the previous night, when everyone had been asleep.

'What do you mean exactly?' Nadezhda Osipovna would say uncertainly. She was scared out of her wits by all these signs and superstitions and believed in them unconditionally. Arina had always had a reputation as a dancer and singer, and latterly as the leading fortune-teller in the Hannibal household.

'It's going to be a hard winter,' Arina would say in a low voice.

The children would fall quiet, and Sergey Lvovich retort uneasily:

'How so, in what way will it be hard?'

'It will snow heavily,' Arina would say reluctantly.

'Nonsense,' and Sergey Lvovich would turn pale.

'Yes indeed, nonsense,' Nadezhda Osipovna would repeat desperately, sensing that Arina was keeping something back.

By lunch-time the ice would be hard, not breaking at the edges, and the year would be pronounced a good one. Snow that took the sleeping unawares was simply a sign that heavy snowfalls were to follow – that was all. And everybody would cheer up.

Nurse Arina understood lots of things that were beyond his parents' experience and in her presence they quailed somewhat. A superstitious cheerfulness fell on the house. Aleksandr secretly wished his nanny was right; he wanted the winter to be hard.

White flakes would cover the black little garden, abandoned since autumn. The street was white, the lights were lit early, the fire crackled in the stove in dozens of voices. The candles burned with a special brightness. The sighing, crackling and snapping of flaming logs filled the rooms. Blue-grey cinders smouldered in the fireplace.

And then the Christmas season would begin. Blizzards danced along the streets, harness-bells rang, troikas tore along, hussars flew by on low, wide sleighs, laughing and singing. It was the time of fortune-telling.

Nadezhda Osipovna always slept poorly and lightly. Sergey Lvovich usually slept like a baby, whistling the same endless and pitiful melody through his nose. In winter dreams came more often. Nadezhda Osipovna had dreams every night. There was a dog-eared volume in Church Slavonic in the house, with a black Solomon circle on its cover, and Aleksandr had a superstitious fear of it. It was an interpretation of dreams by the sage Martin Zadok. Every dream had its meaning. Nadezhda Osipovna's dreams were lengthy and muddled, and if the beginning of a dream promised deception and bankruptcy, its end boded unexpected wealth. Sergey Lvovich had dreams too but no matter how hard he tried to recall them he never could. Only once did he manage to remember one: it was a dream about Admiral Argamakov's old wife. Nadezhda Osipovna opened the prophetic book. An old woman betokened troubles and betrayal by friends. Then she looked up 'Admiral's wife' – and the clue to the dream was found. 'To dream about an admiral's wife' was interpreted in the book as a sign of love. Sergey Lvovich's dream proved true.

Generally, his dreams were less rich and strange than Nadezhda Osipovna's. Sometimes their meaning was obscure. Once in his sleep he called Nadezhda Osipovna by another woman's name and sounded particularly tender towards her. He claimed that he had dreamt of the admiral's wife again but she did not believe him. He had to swear several times to Nadezhda Osipovna that her hearing had played tricks on her and he had called her *Nadine* as he always did, but she was unconvinced. For a fortnight he was out of favour, and only an evening invitation could dispel Nadezhda Osipovna's anger.

Nadezhda Osipovna believed her dreams. Once she dreamt of a rendez-vous with a former lover, of tears, an oath, a quick departure and a long journey. She spent the whole day crying and could not sleep the next night. Sergey Lvovich kept sighing and never dared ask who the former lover was. Nadezhda Osipovna was uncertain herself – maybe it was the Guardsman she had had a secret tryst with a long time before Sergey Lvovich, the one that had nearly ended in catastrophe. However, this was highly unlikely. He had long been married and was a hard drinker, and Nadezhda Osipovna had never given him a moment's thought. She had no idea who the lover might be and kept on crying. A month, two months passed and the old lover never showed up. But he still might appear – dreams never lied; they were interchangeable, and their meanings could be shuffled.

That was how they altered and supplemented their lives – with dreams.

Sometimes after dreams like these Nadezhda Osipovna burned with incomprehensible excitement, the maids shifted the tables, the repositioned wardrobes screeched and rattled, the rooms were changed around as if the family were moving to another house and another city.

But their lives were unchanged and they did not move anywhere.

Arina took a stack of cards to tell fortunes. The sight of the cards gave Sergey Lvovich a pleasant thrill – he had pledged not to play. The honours of whist all appeared in sequence before his mind's eye.

'For the house, for the heart, what will happen, what will not, what will calm your heart.'

It turned out that there would be a journey and that troubles would calm the heart. If a black ace had its spike upwards, Nadezhda Osipovna shuffled the cards at once and Arina dealt again. For the heart there was a king of diamonds, a very young one, and the heart was calmed by money and an official letter. Perhaps a legacy? That was how they determined their destiny and how they tried to thwart it.

Montfort put on a melancholy expression and asked Arina politely to tell his fortune too. Arina warned the Monsieur of danger and of a fight with a king of hearts.

Montfort was furious when her words were translated for him and never again asked Arina about his future.

Aleksandr sat in the corner holding his breath and watched his nanny's nimble hands. His parents' expressions constantly changed – one minute they were pale, then they were smiling. Such was the power of fate.

The maids' way of telling fortunes was more frightening, sombre and fatalistic.

Once he saw how they did it. His parents had gone out, and Arina had seen them off. Montfort took some of his balm and offered a little to Arina.

'You are tottering a bit, Monsieur,' Arina said and thanked him. 'All on account of your balm!'

All was quiet that night. His brother Lolka and sister Olga were in bed. Arina whispered into Aleksandr's ear that there would be a fortune-telling that night, but there was no need for him to worry and he could sleep soundly. When she had left the room and shut the door, he waited a little until his brother and sister had fallen asleep, then quickly dressed and stole out of the room. In the vestibule he threw on his fur-coat and pulled on his cap. He went out into the yard and hid behind the door; there Montfort caught up with him. He was no less curious than Aleksandr and they both waited behind the door. Aleksandr's heart was pounding.

Arina crossed the yard across the crunching snow. He stole behind her. She set the door to the maids' room ajar and said in a low stern voice:

'Out you come, girls!'

Warm steam was issuing from the servants' hall. One after another Tanka, Grushka and Katka ran out into the frost holding their boots in their hands. The girls ran barefoot over the fresh snow. They went as far as the gate and each hurled a boot over it.*

'You crazy girls!' said Arina sharply, 'So this is how you tell fortunes here in town! Who's going to crush your boots? We're in Moscow, you know. They're more likely to be stolen and that will be the end of your fortune-telling. Who'll be to blame then if you lose them? Bring your boots in out of the snow, you fools! In town it's better to tell fortunes by voices.'

Only then did she notice Aleksandr and groaned. He clasped his nanny's skirt and she made him promise not to tell his parents about it.

'Otherwise I'm done for, old fool that I am! Lev Sergeich might wake up any moment and you, sir, you're another problem!'

The girls were embarrassed and unwilling to tell fortunes in the presence of the young master and his tutor.

'Aleksandr Sergeyevich is just a child,' said Arina. 'Don't you worry about him. And the Monsieur, he's a strange one, and not one of us. Don't you worry about them!'

And the girls ran into the lanes.

Katka was the first to guess her fortune. All was quiet until suddenly the fine, clear, sharp sound of a harness-bell rang out – a sleigh flashed by and was out of sight.

All the girls panted with excitement. Katka burst into tears and then into laughter.

'You'll leave the house,' said Arina with approval. 'The bell had a clear sound – it was for happiness, but it was a distant one – your happiness will take some time to come.'

Then Grushka guessed, and soon they heard talking and laughing in the lane. Three young men were walking and laughing, half-inebriated. One of them said: 'Don't be afraid!' when he saw the girls and the three burst into laughter. One of them started a song and all of a sudden – distinctly, somewhat sadly but good-humouredly – let out a curse.

Grushka stood her ground, looking dumbly at Arina.

'It's all right, the talk was good-natured, there was no spite in it,' Arina said. 'It must mean an important discussion – an arrangement. The voice was a kind one. It doesn't matter if he swore, it wasn't out of malice.'

Grushka sobbed softly.

Then Tatyana guessed – and quite nearby, from the neighbour's house, a black shaggy dog ran out and began to bark furiously in the frosty air.

The girls giggled, and Arina hushed them. They respected her and stopped laughing.

---

* In accordance with a folk fortune-telling custom, girls would throw a boot onto a highway and the owner of the first to be crushed by a passing vehicle would be the first to be married.

'A cross husband,' said Arina weightily. 'Look how shaggy and huge the dog is! I've never seen it here before!'

Tatyana howled in a half-tone, burying her face in her sleeve. Montfort stroked her head.

'Don't cry!' said Arina, 'You'll get used to him. Look, even Montfort is feeling sorry for you.'

'I've always been unlucky,' said Tatyana, choking and trembling. She quickly cheered up and gave Montfort a loud kiss. The girls giggled.

'Ah, the devil take it!'

She put her arms around Montfort's neck. Montfort was laughing with the rest of the girls.

Arina became angry and spat in disgust.

'That'll do, you mischief-makers,' she said crossly, and took Aleksandr to his room. 'It won't do, your mother will be back soon, she'll be angry and we, sir, Aleksandr Sergeyevich, shall be called to account.'

He asked his nanny quickly why Tatyana had cried.

'I've foretold her a cross husband. Yesterday the girls were burning wood chips and hers burned miserably. That's why she cried. You'd better go to bed, my dear sir, or Monsieur will scold you.'

Aleksandr could not sleep. Montfort did not come back. Eventually he appeared, in a merry mood, laughing softly in the dark. He called to Aleksandr in a low voice. Aleksandr pretended to be asleep and the Frenchman started to undress, softly whistling a tune. He took a sip of his balm. Taking care not to wake the children, he hummed his absurd little song:

Oh, l'ombre d'une brosse …

And with a protracted, happy yawn the Frenchman was asleep.

But Aleksandr was still awake.

The frost, the girls' bare feet on the crunching snow, the sound of the harness bell, the barking of the dog, other people's happiness and sorrows were miraculously mixed up in his head. The Moscow moon, bald like his uncle Sontsev, was peering through the windows. The coal was languishing to embers in the stove. Arina peeped into the room through the half-open door, came in and squatted in front of the stove to poke the ashes.

He fell asleep.

He spoke, read and thought in French. His face was like his negro grand-father's. But his dreams were Russian, the same as those of Arina or Tatyana who was sobbing in her sleep that night. It was snowing and snowing, the wind was blasting, and the house sprite was pottering about the corners of the house.

Eight

H E was ten. He was an unloved son who shared his room with Montfort, learned the things all ten-year-olds learn, and came alive only when reading. He had long walks with his tutor and knew Moscow better than Montfort. He knew the lanes with their dingy little houses, as sand-blind as the old folk sitting on the benches in front of them, the magnificent Kuznetsky Bridge, broad Tverskaya Street with its huge spacious two-storey mansions. Droshkies and carriages waited by front entrances. Street vendors traded briskly in *pirozhki*; the French shop on Kuznetsky Bridge shimmered with colourful silks.

Walks were always adventures for him. Once he witnessed a strange equipage. An old gentleman surrounded by his luxurious retinue was riding a splendid horse, which was covered with an embroidered gold saddle-cloth; the entire harness was made of gold and silver chains. The retinue rode silently on horseback. The old gentleman was smoking a pipe; his face was wrinkled. Montfort, stunned, bowed hastily, thinking this was the Turkish Ambassador arriving in Moscow. It turned out to be old Prince Novosiltsev taking a ride before lunch. The retinue were his servants. Another time he saw a carriage of wrought silver moving slowly along Tverskaya, followed by a throng of onlookers. Old Prince Gagarin was driving to Maryina Grove.

The Moscow noblesse passed by in dandified carriages pulled by tandems, with negroes on the rear footboards. A great number of carriages was gathered outside the Nobles' Club in Tverskaya Street: they belonged to the Moscow cranks, the grandees who were out of favour and were living out their lives without any hopes for a precarious future.

Montfort glanced at the passers-by through his lorgnette. He walked shakily and his hands trembled; he was falling to pieces. Arina protected him and covered up his weaknesses. Sneaking into the maids' room one evening, his face flushed by his balm, he ran into Nadezhda Osipovna, but Arina diverted her attention with housekeeping matters. Quite often the Frenchman would pour some balm into her cup as well and without turning a hair she would drink it to the dregs, to the Monsieur's and Aleksandr Sergeyevich's health.

Montfort had influential connections: he was patronised by the comte de Maistre, for instance, a Petersburg philosopher and a Jesuit. Even when Tatyana, all in tears, confessed her illicit desires towards Montfort, the matter was hushed up, mainly because of her employers' laziness. Tatyana was exiled to Mikhaylovskoye to look after the cattle. Montfort got away with another crime too: the Frenchman had treated his pupil to his balm. Aleksandr's mouth was pleasantly burning and his head was spinning; strange words, poems and laughter were escaping his lips. Tutor and tutee, both dead drunk, had fallen into a deep and pleasant sleep.

Montfort was ruined by a quite different affair: he dared to play donkey with Nikita in the vestibule and was caught red-handed by Nadezhda Osipovna. This was his undoing – playing cards in the vestibule, and with a lackey! Even his title could not save him. Sergey Lvovich shrugged his shoulders and said contemptuously:

'You start by playing donkey, then it's conkers, then piggy-back and who knows what comes next! Is this how you want things to be?'

It was his way of picturing Montfort's gradual degradation. An experienced card player spoke in him.

Next day the Frenchman bundled up his possessions, drew a farewell picture of a borzoi for Aleksandr, wrote beneath it in French: 'Honour before happiness', signed the inscription with his full name and title, and took his leave.

There was one more circumstance that had been Montfort's undoing. Nikolinka Trubetskoy, a pupil of the Jesuits, had come to see his parents on a short leave and had been visiting his neighbours. He was dressed in a black velvet jacket with lace cuffs. He spoke in a monotonous, soporific voice which neither rose nor fell even for a moment, and listening to this even and formal manner of speech, Sergey Lvovich suddenly felt distressed. His son spoke French hoarsely, abruptly, laconically and, as he thought, vulgarly. For both boys French was virtually a mother tongue, but Nikolinka talked like a priest and Sashka like a street urchin. Nikolinka pronounced 'Povarskaya' like a Frenchman, *Povarskaia,* and instead of 'Kharitonyev Lane' said *Au Saint-Chariton.* When taking his leave he would say *vale* to his friend in Latin. Sashka was far behind him. Montfort was a failure as a tutor.

The new tutor was very different. His name was Roussleau.

He had wide nostrils and a thin moustache, was arrogant and had a very high opinion of himself. Arina hated him from the very outset.

'That Monsieur was open-hearted,' she kept sighing, 'God bless him! He must be drinking himself senseless right now. This one is a bull.'

Nadezhda Osipovna and Sergey Lvovich, however, held a different opinion of him. Nowadays Nadezhda Osipovna did not go out very often and when once Roussleau saw her wearing a morning cap and a dressing-gown, the sleeve of which had slipped down and bared her arm, the Frenchman was unable or unwilling to conceal his admiration. She smiled: his attention was flattering. Roussleau began to strut about like some prince or sultan. He spoke to Aleksandr sharply and abruptly. Acting the part of the old soldier, he issued assignments as if they were orders. He found out about Aleksandr's incursions into his father's study and punished him by putting a stop to them. There were no more long walks. Roussleau set him French vocabulary and arithmetic to learn. Roussleau was an author, a poet, and he made his dignified presence felt every time Sergey Lvovich read Racine (he would still permit himself recitations from time to time). Roussleau would recite his own poems, which Nadezhda Osipovna admired greatly. All of them without exception were devoted to a proud lady whose beauty had driven the poet mad, but who was inaccessible; one of the elegies ended with the sigh of the poet dying of love:

Ah, je meurs! je meurs!

At dinner Nadezhda Osipovna would surreptitiously put the most succulent pieces on his plate. Monsieur Roussleau grew noticeably ruddier and more portly.

One day a small black carriage pulled up at the Pushkins' gate. A gentleman in black, with a sallow, aged face, yellowish-grey hair but youthful eyes, looked out of the carriage. His elderly French servant in frayed livery jumped off the footboard and asked if Montfort was at home. The comte de Maistre wished to see him.

Sergey Lvovich became agitated. The comte de Maistre was a permanent Envoy of the King of Sardinia, though now deprived of his estates; a philosopher, a Jesuit and, rumour had it, a prominent and mysterious personage in St Petersburg.

Sergey Lvovich asked the comte de Maistre in. The old man spent just five minutes with him. Having heard that Montfort had left some time ago, after glancing at Monsieur Roussleau, who bowed low to him, the old man looked at Sergey Lvovich with his lively piercing little eyes. Sergey Lvovich was astounded: his gaze was acutely intelligent, exactly as he had imagined the eyes of a Jesuit to be. He started to mutter that unfortunately Montfort had moved out and that nowadays it was hard to get children a good education. Gradually Sergey Lvovich warmed to his theme. He liked Montfort very much but could not but deplore his weaknesses, forgivable but absolutely intolerable in a teacher. Life demanded a wider and larger knowledge; his head swam when he thought about his children's education.

The old man turned his intent, experienced gaze on the boy and, with a distracted smile, once more scrutinised Roussleau.

'It is not only the mind that should be educated,' he said, staring at Roussleau, who assumed a dignified air, 'and what's more, it's not at all easy. What ought to be educated is not what is normally called the mind.' Roussleau looked aside. 'One should not burden a child with unnecessary knowledge. One should foster quite different qualities in a child. You are familiar with the consequences of education in Paris, aren't you?'

Then he huddled himself up against the cold, wrapping a black kerchief round his scrawny neck, and was gone, leaving everyone perplexed.

A few moments later de Maistre's carriage disappeared down Kharitonyev Lane.

Sergey Lvovich told everyone about the comte de Maistre's visit. Taking no notice of Sashka and Lolka and scarcely aware of Olga's existence, he kept repeating that education nowadays was an extremely difficult matter and that the Jesuits were absolutely right to assert that the main thing was not the mind but taste. Hang them, those sciences! The comte de Maistre was right three times over!

This opinion and particularly the news of the comte de Maistre's visit were taken seriously.

'The last time the comte de Maistre was at my house ...' Sergey Lvovich grew fond of repeating.

2

All of a sudden the atmosphere in Moscow changed and the very air seemed to have grown warmer. The elderly forgot their pride: they threw open their doors, smiled to all, renewed old connections and remembered their kinship. Sergey Lvovich suddenly recalled that the Pushkins' noble status was six hundred years old if not almost a thousand, and undid his roll of documents again. Soon his heart was warmed by a visit from Karamzin whom he had not seen for a very long time.

The reason was official business from St Petersburg.

Moscow was a backwater; it was living out its time. Its elderly grumbled loudly, like the deaf do in other people's presence without realising that they can be heard. When anyone resigned, he did his best to move to Moscow in order to have an opportunity to grumble. Moscow was ruled by old ladies; it was a matriarchal realm. They sat like frogs in the chairs of the Club of the Nobility and looked sternly about them. Each of them had her court and its enemies, remembered everything and knew everybody. Ofrosimova's opinions and stories about Khitrovo were the Moscow equivalent of newspapers, which were read only in time of war. Winter was the time of the brides' fair. In autumn these precious commodities had been put into carriages, carefully tucked in on all sides, and driven along the main roads to Moscow. At the city gates the carriages stopped: the gold domes of the churches shone brightly, the gardens were green and the brides' hearts fluttered. They were shown to the old ladies of Moscow, who scrutinised them and took them under their patronage. And soon, at one ball or another, a girl's fate was decided. The old ladies delivered their judgement, settled destinies, divided families and brought them together again. The slaves of Hymen – henpecked husbands, ruined gamblers or people whose careers had never taken off – comprised middle-aged Moscow. Sergey Lvovich felt at home in Moscow and scorned St Petersburg. To grumble and spread gossip was his passion, the passion of the middle-aged genteel poor of Moscow.

Moscow youths were fops, babblers, scatterbrains. They spoke delicately, avoided harsh sounds and lisped.

The Court and the Government were in St Petersburg. Even literature was different in St Petersburg: the Land Admiral Shishkov,* who scorned the Moscow gallants, was a Petersburger, and he made fun of the effete Muscovites, not sparing even Karamzin. He armed himself against French tutors and clothes shops and recommended reading the Lives of the Saints. On the Fontanka Derzhavin was still grunting out his life and addressing posterity with his lengthy treatises on the ode.

But it wasn't just a question of the St Petersburgers, the young and the elderly. The trouble was that while Moscow sighed, gorged itself on Shrovetide pancakes and marvelled over Blaise's *pirozhki* at Vasily Lvovich's, 'the Clerk' had sneaked through the corridors of power and taken a firm grip of it.

'The Clerk' was the nickname the older generation gave to the Minister Speransky. His name had first come to general attention when it was rumoured that the Tsar was going to take the Clerk with him in his 'cap in hand' trip to Bonaparte, and the rumour had proved true. Another rumour had it that Bonaparte himself had spoken to the Clerk and had been extremely courteous to him. Having heard that, the older generation, who cursed Napoleon in their various ways, felt passed over and came to the conclusion that Napoleon and the Clerk had managed to find a common language. When one edict followed another, the older generation realised that this was the beginning of the Napoleonic era. The first edict concerned Court titles, the second civil

* Leader of the literary conservatives and champion of the Greek-Slavonic linguistic tradition; the natural enemy of the innovative Karamzin and the francophile Vasily Pushkin in the Russian internal literary war waged alongside the military one in the Napoleonic era.

ranks. Higher society had been established in Catherine's time. Men of higher society had spent their lives in higher occupations; they had been granted the title of Kammerjunker and the rank of fifth class when still in the cradle. Babies smiled at their burly wet-nurses, passed into their nannies' hands, and became Kammerherrs with the rank of fourth class. They had plenty of leisure time to refine their tastes; later they might catch the eye of the Empress's lady-in-waiting who chose her favourites, and even if this did not happen, they eventually attained high rank in the civil service. Such were the rights of the nobility.

On the third of April 1809 the Clerk, now firmly established in St Petersburg, issued an edict and put an end to all this. From now on the titles of Kammerjunker and Kammerherr did not entitle their bearer to a place in the Table of Ranks and were considered only nominal distinctions. Within two months everyone had to apply for a civil service post; those unwilling to apply were to be considered retired. Many nobles who had not changed their lifestyle and views suddenly found themselves in retirement. Three generations of Trubetskoys, all of whom had titles and had been reckoned to be in service even though they had spent their lives in the Chest of Drawers, found themselves dismissed. There was agitation in every household. The old general who had called Napoleon 'Buonaparte' kept threatening to go to St Petersburg to beat up the Clerk. But what embittered the noblesse most of all were the taxes that piled up with every day that passed.

'He obviously feeds well!' they would say, meaning either Speransky or the Tsar himself. 'Things are even worse than in Paul's reign!'

In summer, when taxes were the talk of the city and the older generation threatened to die rather than pay, the Clerk issued another edict. Henceforth no one could be promoted to the rank of collegiate assessor without passing examinations and obtaining a certificate. The whole civil service class was ordered to forget all its old habits and aims and instead of having potential employers to dinner, to prepare for examinations in natural law and elementary mathematics.

The whole bureaucracy was up in arms.

It was said that in one office a certain secretary cried publicly, wiping his tears with a big red handkerchief and attracting everyone's attention. Meanwhile, petty clerks seeing nothing to aim for in future and losing any hope of passing examinations and obtaining the rank of collegiate assessor, gave way to despair and began to demand such huge bribes as could shake the very foundations of the state. All this had important consequences.

The Moscow noblesse, who had heaped blame on the officials after the first edict, now called Speransky 'the son of a priest' and 'an unfrocked monk'.

In the face of this universal problem differences in tastes and inclinations were forgotten. The traffic on the streets of Moscow had grown heavier – everyone went out in the mornings to gauge social opinion. Sergey Lvovich resumed his attendance at the Commissariat in the mornings too. Now the entire office was busy copying new epigrams about Speransky; every day Sergey Lvovich brought home fresh ones, read them, and locked them in his secret drawer.

They were quite pointed. One of them, about weeping bureaucrats, was entitled *Elegy*:

> *Weep, petty clerk, and tremble, scribbler!*

It had a caustic line that soon became a catchphrase:

> *Assessor's rank, so eagerly desired!*

This poem, however, had been written rather as a satire on officialdom in general and apparently in defence of the edict, but at first the officials could not tell this and made copies of everything they came across about the edicts, considering it 'counter-revolutionary'.

Sergey Lvovich liked *Thoughts of a Despondent Nobleman* best of all. It was poor poetry but made a strong emotional impact:

> *From Ryurik's days the nobles have been free*
> *And Russia known for her supremacy.*

It concerned 'the son of a priest' who 'soared like a soap bubble' and, further, 'got Russia into trouble' and 'brought chaotic muddle'.

An epigram on Speransky was of a different kind – it was brief. It had been written by the brother of the general who had called Napoleon 'Buonaparte':

> *The son of a priest has shown us great things –*
> *With knowledge and science the nobles he stings.*

Learning frightened people. Doctors studied medicine, the clergy divinity. Among the gentry too there were eccentrics or patrons of the arts who could read Latin. But to study the sciences as doctors were duty-bound to do was beneath the dignity of nobles. A nobleman acquired rank through moral qualities and through services rendered. There was no connection between learning, nobility and rank. The seminarian Speransky had brought chaos and turned things upside-down.

For some reason Sergey Lvovich felt even more indignant than others. The thought that Kammerjunker and Kammerherr would be not ranks but titles was particularly unbearable for him, though neither he nor any relative of his was either. He searched for words to express his indignation but could find none.

'This secretary, *cette canaille de* Speransky ...' He spoke of Speransky as if the Minister had previously served under his command, and pronounced his surname through his nose.

This was in fact highly typical of Sergey Lvovich. He was always eager to dabble in any sort of opposition. He would grumble at the fire-place exactly as his mother Olga Vasilyevna had once done; on one occasion he even echoed her word for word. Snorting, he said that all the present troubles had started with the Orlovs; the muddle had begun when they had managed to make their way into the upper ranks of the nobility. It could not be denied that good breeding confers good manners, and good manners, as his dear mother used to say, were the most important thing! They meant civility, the ability to shine, and quick wit. Anyone unable to understand this was not worth talking to. It must be said that although Sergey Lvovich's knowledge of history was vague in the extreme, his feelings were strong.

Many quills screeched all over Moscow in these months. Clerks copied poems, nobles wrote to the Tsar. Even Sergey Lvovich, sitting at his desk over a clean sheet of paper, once wrote with a thin quill: *Your Gracious Majesty!* but after that his inspiration left him.

Everybody was anxious to hear what Karamzin would say.

3

Old friends said he had become haughty and withdrawn. Feeling that he was losing touch with everyone and that important work lay ahead of him, he left Moscow for long periods of time. At last, like Rousseau, he had managed to find his own Hermitage on his father-in-law's estate, Ostafyevo. A spacious garden, a pond fed by springs, and spreading lindens took the place of his friends. A young, tender-hearted wife had become his Clio, his Muse of History. Muscovites began to treat him apprehensively. He would occasionally pay visits just to say a few meaningful words, pass a remark or give a smile; nowadays tolerance of human vice had become his main characteristic. The amiable Sontsev, sister Lizette's husband, nevertheless remained particularly afraid of him. The prevailing confusion in Moscow had summoned Karamzin out of his seclusion for a few weeks.

Sergey Lvovich was anxious to see him. They had not seen each other for some time. Wondering how best to time his visit and afraid that he might be interrupting, he had chosen the period between lunch and dinner. After a short deliberation he stuck the Moscow poems into his pockets, put on his new tail-coat, gave a sigh and set off.

He met with a cordial reception. There was no one else, just the two of them. They sat in plain chairs in a half-dark room with unlit candles. Nikolay

Mikhaylovich spoke very little; he even seemed to doze off, reclining in the depths of his easy-chair. But Sergey Lvovich was garrulous. He chatted away about everything: first of all about the vicious attacks of Admiral Shishkov, who had lashed Karamzin publicly and recently called Sergey Lvovich's brother Vasily Lvovich an atheist, a libertine and an enemy of the throne.

Nikolay Mikhaylovich smiled, expressing his faint approval. He had nothing to do with the Francophiles: the juxtaposition of Vasily Lvovich's name with Karamzin's seemed ludicrous.

He asked Sergey Lvovich about his dear wife's health. Sergey Lvovich thanked him heartily and complained about the difficulties of educating children. Now, when a nobleman was supposed to study the academic disciplines and pass examinations, he shuddered to think about his children's future. The comte de Maistre, who had been to his house lately, was probably right: the most important thing was the education of taste and respect for parents, and the rest – hang it! As the father of a rising son, he realised this very well.

Nikolay Mikhaylovich now cautioned him gently that it was no good mixing up two different concepts – examinations were one thing and enlightenment was another. Without enlightenment there would be neither Shakespeares nor Bonnets. A refined mind was closer to nature than ignorance, and the noblesse should be made to understand this truth once and for all. Of the comte de Maistre he said with some coldness that he had no idea the comte was in Moscow. But the examinations – alas! – one wondered how long they would harm learning itself!

Sergey Lvovich could restrain himself no longer and began to recite to Nikolay Mikhaylovich his copy of *Thoughts of a Despondent Nobleman*.

Nikolay Mikhaylovich seemed to liven. He listened to the verses closely and asked for a copy to reread later. His cheeks flushed. Then, in a low voice, gently and patiently, he explained to Sergey Lvovich the meaning of current events.

Sergey Lvovich did not stir in the semi-darkness. He listened avidly to everything Nikolay Mikhaylovich had to say and it seemed to elevate and strengthen him. He sat importantly, his cheeks resting upon his white collar, and completely forgot about Nadezhda Osipovna, Sashka and Lolka, his debts and his home. Once again he was what he was supposed to be – a nobleman with a six-century pedigree, a man of the world, one of those whose company was sought and who was spoken to. The idea was so pleasing that he missed half of what Nikolay Mikhaylovich said. He laughed whole-heartedly at the subtle mockery of the Clerk.

In the semi-darkness without candlelight, Nikolay Mikhaylovich was saying that nowadays the Head of the Civil Service was supposed to know Homer and Theocritus, the Senate Secretary had to learn the characteristics of oxygen and all other gases, and the Vice-Governor had to have some understanding of Pythagoras' theorem ...

Sergey Lvovich giggled softly.

... and the madhouse warden had to know his Roman law ...

Sergey Lvovich made a mental note of it.

'Oxygen, Pythagoras, warden,' he repeated with his lips.

But nobody seemed to have noticed that the edict itself and the commentary on it were written ungrammatically, in a flowery, almost servile style.

Sergey Lvovich recalled the fresh sheet of paper on which he had written: *Your Gracious Majesty!* He confessed his audacity to Nikolay Mikhaylovich and flushed like a schoolboy admitting mischief, but happy and sure that it would be approved of. He had been going to write to His Majesty ... from the heart! Good God! But almost everybody in Moscow was going to write to the Sovereign these days!

Nikolay Mikhaylovich fell silent. And he remained silent, responding to Sergey Lvovich's babbling and laughter only with a delicate cough.

It had grown almost completely dark. Nikolay Mikhaylovich did not stir in his chair. Was he dozing off? Only when Sergey Lvovich was taking his leave did Nikolay Mikhaylovich ask him in a weak, completely cold voice to give his regards to his dear wife.

Sergey Lvovich left wondering why, having favoured him with such a friendly chat at first, Karamzin had lost interest in him in the end. The fact was that for many weeks during his Ostafyevo seclusion Karamzin had also been pondering over sheets of paper. He had actually been writing to His Majesty about the spirit the Clerk was introducing into the course of history of the Russian state.

4

On his return home Sergey Lvovich ran into Aleksandr in the vestibule. The sight of his son perplexed him.

Immediately and decisively, in spluttering haste, he told Nadezhda Osipovna about his conversation with Karamzin and passed on his compliments.

'One should educate refined taste,' he said resolutely. 'It forms a person.'

Nadezhda Osipovna never objected to her husband's opinions on important matters. She was taken aback by his strange resolve. It had never been easy for Sergey Lvovich to bring himself to act, but if he made up his mind, he could not stand procrastination. He burned and crackled like a rocket. That very day they ordered a new suit for Aleksandr to be made out of Sergey Lvovich's old tail-coat by the tailor in German Street. Nadezhda Osipovna bought some new lace garments in a French shop. She spent a long time dressing in front of the mirror and went out shopping at day-break. Everybody cheered up. From now on the children were to be educated in a new fashion. At last the suit was ready: Nadezhda Osipovna scrutinised Aleksandr through her lorgnette and argued with the German tailor. For a week Sergey Lvovich calmed down. But having paid visits to the Buturlins, Sushkovs and others, he found out that the children of the nobility were taught dancing at Iogel's.

Iogel was the dancing-master in vogue. The German was the first in Moscow to teach children to dance in the correct way. He organised children's masquerades on his premises; the noblesse took their sons and daughters to him. Costumes were made following his advice: an English admiral, a Turk; wigs, cocked hats – every detail was taken care of in advance by loving mothers and children's tailors.

Iogel's dancing hall was brightly lit. Iogel himself, a tall hunchbacked old man in a black tail-coat, stepped forward and played a tiny pocket-size fiddle. The children bounced around in regular dances with the indifference characteristic of their age, surrounded by a circle of Moscow crones who censured their parents, called to the children and gave them spice-cakes which they produced from their handbags. Iogel's evenings became more and more fashionable. The old ladies scolded the German because he was a poor teacher: the boys knocked about and the girls rushed around like things possessed. The mothers cursed him for his exorbitant fees and put a beauty-spot on their cheeks to attend his evenings.

Sergey Lvovich told Nadezhda Osipovna that they should take Aleksandr and Olga to Iogel. She agreed enthusiastically. It was decided to dress up Aleksandr as a Turk and Olga as a Greek girl. Nadezhda Osipovna spent three days shopping in the clothes shops. The silk that she bought for the children's masquerade dress was extremely expensive; she admired it for a couple of days and finally made up her mind to keep it for herself. Sergey Lvovich bit his lip. He was dying to visit Iogel's. One day at lunch, he announced that the celebrated dance-master Pengeau had agreed to teach their children dancing.

'He's much better than Iogel,' he said uncertainly. 'Iogel is just an old rogue, that's all.'

Anna Lvovna was astounded by her brother's extravagance in the matter of the children's education.

'Ah, Sergey, Sergey, you'll regret it!' she would say.

Sergey Lvovich himself was a little bewildered by his decision to engage Pengeau.

He paced the room impatiently while Anna Lvovna scrutinised the children, who seemed unable to appreciate their parents' concern for them.

Nikita lit the candles in the drawing-room and soon the renowned Pengeau appeared. He was short and lean, with finely-moulded little legs; he wore silk stockings and tiny shoes with minute buckles. He was very old but tried to keep his spirits up even though his head shook.

Nadezhda Osipovna took Olga and Aleksandr by their hands and brought them to the centre of the room. Anna Lvovna sat down at the piano and the lesson began.

'*Glissez, glissez!*' the celebrated Pengeau commanded in a jaded voice and clicked his heels. His feet were unstable, he looked like a grasshopper who would like to jump but was unable to.

With a strange feeling of revulsion Aleksandr led the frightened Olga, who was painstakingly bending her knees and babbling voicelessly: '*Un, deux, trois … un, deux, trois …*'

Sergey Lvovich looked at the celebrated Pengeau, paying no attention to his daughter and son. Anna Lvovna strummed the old piano diligently.

'*Tour sur place! Tour sur place!*'

Pengeau stopped the children. They had been plodding along out of time and out of step and were unable to make a proper turn. He lifted the tail of his coat slightly and fixed a smile on his face. Olinka was supposed to imitate this smile. An icy glittering in his wrinkled eyes, he strutted aloof, with the light step of a cockerel, his aged head shaking constantly. This was how Aleksandr was supposed to step. Then he started to make a slow turn. Sullen and bored, glancing angrily at his parents from under his brow, clumsy and distracted, Aleksandr got muddled up and danced out of time.

His aunt kept playing and bending at every bar, stubbornly stamping her heels on the floor.

'*En avant! En avant!*'

Pengeau grew tired and wiped his brow with his white lace handkerchief. He sat down in a chair.

At that moment Nadezhda Osipovna stood up. She had already been biting on her handkerchief for a long time and her face had broken out in blotches. She looked at the children hazily through tears. She had not been feeling well all day – so they said later to Pengeau. She was staring at her children, confused and outraged. She had always been, or at least thought herself to be, a beauty; dandies called her *la belle Créole*. The boy with the eyes of a monkey, swarthy skin and awkward gestures, almost ugly – was *her* son. The thin, sharp-nosed girl with a stooped back, shifty little eyes and straight colourless hair was *her* daughter. Feeling inexplicable disdain, anger and bitter self-pity, she rose, grasped her son firmly by the ear and her daughter by the scruff of her neck, and hurled them both behind the door like kittens.

'Freaks!' she said, not hearing herself.

Pengeau stood up.

'Children may be capable or incapable of dancing. But you can't tell a dancer from the first minuet. The famous Duport was also awkward at a tender age.'

Pengeau spoke as he danced – mechanically. He had been teaching the same thing for twenty years and had grown used to everything.

Anna Lvovna forced herself to smile at the Frenchman. She was outraged by her sister-in-law's bizarre behaviour: she should not have behaved like this in the Frenchman's presence.

Sergey Lvovich rushed to Nadezhda Osipovna, having no idea what was going on, as usual. She had already calmed down.

The celebrated Pengeau was never invited to come again. Olinka whimpered a little but soon calmed down too; she was used to her mother's temper. In bed before falling asleep, Aleksandr suddenly sighed loudly – as children never do.

His mother disliked looking at him, and sometimes averted her glance as if embarrassed. He always avoided her touch. He had not thought about this before, but suddenly it all became clear to him: he was ugly, he was a freak. He was deeply hurt. He remembered how he had danced to the music with his sister and burst into tears of humiliation. This time no one came up to his bed; Arina was somewhere far away. The Frenchman was sitting at the table cleaning his nails with a little knife and brush in sullen concentration.

5

Vasily Lvovich invited his brother to dinner. Nadezhda Osipovna was ill and Sergey Lvovich took his son with him. He did not want to but Nadezhda Osipovna had insisted. If Sergey Lvovich had refused, she would have thought that she was being deceived and that the dinner was with ballet-dancers or French actresses. He took Aleksandr grudgingly. In fact, the dinner at Vasily Lvovich's was without ladies. His new friends had the reputation of not caring for women; they were known as misogynists.

They were a most fashionable set. All of them had the title of Archive Junker, and were known simply as 'Archivists'. This post was in vogue: they served or were reckoned to serve in the Foreign Affairs Archives, nowadays the training-ground for young men of the nobility. All of them had been educated at Göttingen University and were therefore called 'Göttingenians' or simply 'Germans'. One by one they were being won over from Moscow to St Petersburg by the poet Ivan Dmitriyev, who was the Minister in the Department of 'Jurisprudence' as the older generation called it. They made forays on Moscow. Everything about them was novel – their manners, habits and tastes. They had a polite manner and spoke German among themselves volubly and softly, as if cooing. Their outlook inclined to the melancholic.

They looked up to each other and looked down at others.

When first in their company Vasily Lvovich had been indignant, and then bewildered, but soon he realised that these people belonged to the newest, the latest fashion, and that his tail-coats and Palais-Royal phrases were obsolete. At heart he was a man of fashion, and he accepted the new luminaries. Besides, everyone found them polite and genial, not like the young Moscow club scoundrels whom he had had a hard time ridding himself of. They were known in Moscow as 'Turgenev's litter' and 'Dmitriyev's brood', and he, like everybody else, respected both Turgenev and Dmitriyev. He was friendliest with Aleksandr Turgenev to whom he felt very close. Young Turgenev was inclined to gluttony and was fidgety, bustling and congenial, with pendulous cheeks and a vast belly. He rushed about spreading gossip. He was accommodating and sentimental by nature – huge tears were ever-ready to roll from his eyes. After a meal he would often doze off at the dinner table. Göttingen and the Germans were forever on his lips. Vasily Lvovich readily identified with these qualities – he was gluttonous, forgetful and flighty himself.

Other Göttingenians were not so pleasant: Bludov was a chatterbox but a sly one; Uvarov was icily good-hearted and bitter-sweet; Dashkov was chubbily serene, with a lethargic dignity. Vasily Lvovich made friends with all of them. He could not entirely fathom them at times. They had secrets, they exchanged sidelong glances and innuendoes. He hated their chuckles – soft, venomous and somehow devious. Sometimes they assumed a pompous air as if they were aware of something beyond his comprehension, and it made him uneasy. Suddenly, in between jokes they would start talking in half-tones and Vasily Lvovich knew that it was about affairs of state. For a moment they would become oblivious of his presence and ignore his questions. He would grow apprehensive and start to ingratiate himself with them, whereupon they would flatter his vanity by praising his poems. He always responded to that praise with all his being, accepting it eagerly like a fish swallowing the bait.

In general they puzzled and confused him. These youngsters were much more self-assured, more *solid,* than the previous generation. They seemed to have matured early in their lives and become precociously sophisticated. One of them, Uvarov, a mere youth, had been abroad on important missions and had struck up a close friendship with Stein himself. Stein! The Prussian leader! His name was on everybody's lips. Exiled by Napoleon, he had spent some time in hiding in Vienna; he loved his fatherland ardently and under Napoleon's very nose had established his own *Landwehr* and *Landsturm*. The exile was openly dreaming of the liberation of mankind – liberation from Napoleon. But according to *Le Moniteur* which Vasily Lvovich occasionally read, Napoleon himself was dreaming of the liberation of humanity, beginning with liberation from Stein. All this was double Dutch to Vasily Lvovich, and he felt even more respect for his new friends.

Their work excited his superstitious fear. Uvarov busied himself with Greek affairs and wrote fluently in Greek. Dashkov could even speak Turkish, whereas the only Greek Vasily Lvovich was familiar with was Anacreontic and even that in translation, while the only thing he knew about the Turks was that they kept harems. The archpriest with whom Vasily Lvovich had happened to have lunch from time to time while doing his church penance had always brought up this fact as an example of disgrace and dissipation, but Vasily Lvovich took another view of it altogether. He could not grasp what made these young old men take such trouble over the Greeks and Turks, and decipher their scrawls and scribbles which meant so little to him. It was not part of the education of the noblesse. The newcomers were professional men, but seemed to be no use to him, just a waste of time. Only when war with the Turks had broken out did he understand these young men's foresight; their scribbles had come in handy after all. They had become diplomats. Vasily Lvovich was afraid of diplomats.

He was depressed and frightened by the Göttingenians' erudition. Generally speaking, they had many quirks – they almost never spoke of women and did not seem to like their company, admitted only friendship and wrote a lot about melancholy. Their friend the inspired and prolific poet Zhukovsky avowed platonic love. It was the latest and especially German fashion – young people plunged themselves into gloom and spoke of suicide. Uvarov had written poems in French about the advantages of dying young, and everybody copied them and read them to others. Ladies wept while reading them: the advantages seemed to be indisputable. Dashkov had published an article about suicide, gently refuting his friend. These young men, ardent to die, advanced swiftly in service.

New kinds of posts had arisen. Vasily Lvovich had never suspected that, for example, alien confessions could be conducted – with Jesuits, Shamans, Mohammedans and Jewish tribes. It seemed to him a mysterious business. This, however, was what Aleksandr Turgenev was doing under Prince Golitsyn's command – Golitsyn who used to be a famous prankster and debauchee, devotee of beautiful youths, and now had the most solemn of appointments – he was the Synod Chief Prosecution Counsel! Life seemed to be full of posts of the most diverse descriptions. And his new friends, the melancholics, had been able to find their way through this labyrinth and turned out to be the most professional and indispensable of fellows.

Very soon, despite the differences in temperaments, Vasily Lvovich found himself their accomplice and associate in the literary war that had long been in full swing in the capitals. Far from stopping, it seemed to flare up more and more. In Moscow there seemed to be no other taste but the true one, no other aspiration than refinement, and there was no other literary prophet but Karamzin. In St Petersburg Admiral Shishkov had suddenly led a fierce assault against 'the friends of beauty and humanity'. Karamzin, Dmitriyev and then Vasily Lvovich had been attacked.

Shishkov had declared a crusade against the French. It would have been a different matter if it had been a campaign against the disastrous French Revolution and the Jacobins. In such a case Vasily Lvovich would have joined it eagerly. But the old man had armed himself against the former French *marquis*, as he called the society poets. If he had flown in the face of the French tutors only, who would have argued with him? Hang them! – Vasily Lvovich did not give a damn how his Annette was going to educate the fruit of her master's love. But Shishkov had been up in arms against French fashion shops too! And the language of the emotions! And the elegy!

He was a real barbarian. He had written a savage piece of doggerel in a sweet lady's album beside her friends' poems:

> *Lass, you are fair without white powder,*
> *Nature's own blush could not be louder,*
> *Pale skin, rose cheeks, a priceless treasure,*
> *And every parent's pride and pleasure.*

That 'lass' particularly enraged everyone.

'*Cette noble* "lass" …' Vasily Lvovich kept repeating indignantly.

The Göttingenians were friends of Dmitriyev; Bludov was even related to him. They treated Karamzin with respect and scoffed at the Admiral and his 'lass', and Vasily Lvovich shared these opinions. He had opened his heart to his new friends and to Prince Shalikov as well. Only Aleksey Pushkin called them 'cry-babies'; but he was a renowned grumbler and cynic.

Vasily Lvovich had been waiting for his new friends with some trepidation. Only Turgenev, Bludov and Dashkov had promised to come. Zhukovsky was on holiday in the country, in Mishenskoye, and was preoccupied with nature and platonic love. He was not to be expected. Maybe it was for the better: Vasily Lvovich quailed in his presence. Uvarov was getting ready for his trip to St Petersburg and would not come either. Never mind – he ate little and knew nothing of good food. Of his old friends, he expected only his cousin Aleksey Pushkin and Shalikov. That was all. Yes, and his brother Sergey with his fledgling Sashka, imposed on him by his mulatta *Nadine*. Vasily Lvovich felt all the advantages of his family state. He strutted like a sultan or a cockerel about the house, and Annushka, like a faithful slave, obeyed his every wish. She took care of things, looked after her master and kept house. When the guests arrived she retreated into a back room.

The guests patted young Aleksandr on the shoulder and Turgenev even gave him a hug.

This gathering of clever young men and older wits was a most enjoyable prospect. The clever young men, like all active people, enjoyed leisure. All of them were inveterate wags. The especially clever Bludov had written a 'tailor's declaration of love':

Oh you who patched my heart …

Vasily Lvovich already had the poem in his bureau. Everyone was crazy about it. Almost immediately the confessions of love of a clerk, a priest, a doctor, a police-officer and other professional people appeared.

Classes and professions, their language, degree of education – Speransky had talked his head off about it all and it was on everybody's mind. That was why love was declared in different ways. It was amusing and sophisticated.

Vasily Lvovich's new friends' idleness was not, it had to be said, like his. Their style was luxuriantly oriental – Bludov and Dashkov were wealthy, with annual incomes of around fifty thousand. Their sense of humour was different too. It was not the wit – the *esprit* – of Voltaire or Piron, but German jest – clumsy, physical, elaborate – *Witz*. Vasily Lvovich forced himself to grin when they joked. He had prepared a nice treat for them: the latest edition of the complete works of Count Khvostov.

Count Khvostov was a notable personality in the literary war. Among Karamzin's friends, particularly the young ones, there were those who seemed to spend their whole lives obsessed with Khvostov, moving from one drawing-room to another to spread news of him.

Everything about this poet was in accordance with the atheist Aleksey Pushkin's theory of the imaginary. Starting with his title – he was a Sardinian Count, a title that had been solicited for him by Suvorov from the King of Sardinia. Khvostov was married to Suvorov's niece and the Generalissimo, with his taste for reading rubbish, patronised him. The Count's poems were not merely talentless, but ambitious beyond all measure. He was confident that he was the only talented poet in Russia, and that all the rest were misguided. He called himself 'the bard of the Kubra' after the name of the river that flowed through his estate, and pointing out the diversity of genres he worked in, he eagerly drew comparisons between Horace and himself: he wrote fables, odes, eclogues, epistles, epigrams and translated prolifically. He was a scholar too – he collected and recorded all the information he could find on early literature. He had one passion above all else – vanity, and he served it faithfully, to the point of ruining himself. Rumour had it that while waiting for horses at post-stations, he would read his poems to post-stage masters and they would give him horses without delay. Leaving their friends' houses when Khvostov had been there, many would find the Count's works stuck into their pockets either by Khvostov himself or by his manservant. He paid handsomely for complimentary articles about himself. He showered the journals and almanacs with his poems and the editors developed their own language in order to communicate with him, not exactly Aesopian but plain Khvostovian – politeness bordering on insult. Every month Khvostov sent his poems to Karamzin's journal. He never published them and replied politely: 'Your Excellency! I have received your letter with the enclosed ...' and so on. 'The enclosed' was what he called the Count's poems.

The Naval Officers' Club in St Petersburg had a bust of the Count. It was somewhat embellished: the Count had a long face and a fleshy nose, whereas the bust had pronounced classical features. His fame had spread to the provinces too. Cheap popular prints with caricatures of the poet reciting his verses to the devil, trying to flee from the author but being detained, were pasted up at many post-stations. In the town of Tver he was believed to be a Jacobin. The Count's works were printed continuously at his own expense. Recently a new collection of his parables had been brought out, and Vasily Lvovich had eagerly bought this: the Count was at his most ambitious in the genre of fables and parables.

They started to play a game: each person opened the new complete edition of Khvostov and without looking placed his finger on a passage and read it aloud. Bludov was first; he opened the book and lit upon the line:

Suvorov is my kin and I write verses.

Bludov said:
'A complete biography in a few words.'
Even Vasily Lvovich could not have expected a better beginning. Everyone beamed and the hunt for literary game began.

The book passed to Aleksey Pushkin. He poked his finger at the page and declaimed:

*If you crawl
You can't fall.*

Sergey Lvovich came across the fable *A Snake and a Saw*. The title itself was ambitious. The Count was keen on bringing together unrelated objects. Sergey Lvovich particularly liked the opening lines:

*On the locksmith's table lay a saw.
A snake came there – I don't know what for.*

Sergey Lvovich spontaneously repeated a phrase he had heard recently but hadn't quite understood at first:
'There is something elevated about stupidity.'

The phrase was a success; it was accepted favourably and Dashkov was visibly surprised that Sergey Lvovich could have expressed the idea so well.

Pleased with himself, Sergey Lvovich wanted to continue with his turn, but Vasily Lvovich was impatient. He started to fidget in his chair and bent over the book so low that his nose prevented Sergey Lvovich from leafing through it. Not without indignation and a short struggle, Sergey Lvovich let his brother have the book. He was about to hold it back when Vasily Lvovich pulled it towards himself, risking tearing it apart, and in this way Khvostov came into his hands.

The short struggle between the brothers was noticed. Aleksandr seemed to catch sight of Bludov giving the wink to Dashkov.

Vasily Lvovich's turn was a happy one – a fable. Choking and spluttering, he started to read … but was unable to get very far:

> *A pike had swallowed hook and line*
> *And therefore it began to whine,*
> *To pull and panic, peak and pine.*

A paroxysm of laughter took hold of him. The words came out of him like bullets from a gun, together with hiccups and saliva:

> *'Myself … I … blame!'*
> *The pike … did exclaim …*

Everyone was roaring with laughter. Aleksandr bared his white teeth too. But soon he noticed that it was not the fable or Khvostov but his uncle everyone was laughing at. Vasily Lvovich became soft and flabby with laughter; he sneezed loudly and incessantly, tried to say something and in between sneezes and hiccups babbled some gibberish. He was pathetic. They gave him a glass of water. He sighed, gave a final hiccup and came to himself. Dashkov did not read. He had his reasons – he stuttered.

Now it was Prince Shalikov's turn. He opened the book, scrutinised it, and to everyone's surprise read a poem that was not just serious but even tolerable. It was the epigraph to the Parables:

> *Here is a rare book. It babbles*
> *Of morality dressed up as fables.*
> *It is a comedy with a most amusing cast,*
> *About the universe so vast.*

Everyone exchanged doubtful glances.

Turgenev asked the book to be given to him, opened it, turned a page and read:

> *Here we see a bumpkin thick,*
> *Who with his enormous stick*
> *Makes a mighty lion sick!*

He leafed the book through and read again at random:

> *The dogs break –*
> *Neck and neck.*

He passed the book back to Shalikov and as if by magic the poems turned out to be reasonable. Turgenev humorously screwed up his eyes and gave a sigh. Bludov and Dashkov exchanged glances. The game stopped because it was not turning out so well for Vasily Lvovich: Shalikov was already at war with his young friends.

The fact was that Prince Shalikov, associate and follower of Karamzin, had recently opened up secret relations with none other than Count Khvostov himself. The clever young men had no time for the Prince. Rumour had reached him that they sneered at him just as they did at Khvostov. In the album of one gentle lady whom the know-alls visited he had come across a caricature: a black-browed dandy on short thin legs with a huge nose and a flower in his button-hole. It was himself. He had lost his temper, cursed and immediately fallen out of the gentle lady's favour. He had previously been followed by respectful and envious stares on the boulevards; he had heard people whispering: 'Shalikov, Shalikov,' but now when he appeared, the dandies chuckled. He was getting old. When the Prince sent his poems to Karamzin they were never published, just like Count Khvostov's.

Prince Shalikov was against all the scoffers. He sensed that in the literary war 'the friends of the beautiful', Karamzin's friends, would sell him out for a penny and abandon him to the enemy. And so he had written a letter to the ridiculed Count and concluded a secret alliance with him.

The literary war, with its treasons and strategies, was running high in front of Aleksandr.

Vasily Lvovich sensed something wrong and changed tactics at once – he showed his friends his library. He collected only rare books and scorned ordinary ones. He showed them a very rare book that he had brought from Paris. It contained such lewd drawings that Shalikov, having at first leered at them, then screened his eyes with his handkerchief. Everyone (including Aleksandr) looked at the pictures in amazement.

The 'former Pushkin' spoiled the moment.

'How many pictures are there, old fellow?' he asked.

Vasily Lvovich glanced at a page in the notebook where, as a bibliophile, he put down the details of every book in his possession, and replied:

'Thirty.'

'There are forty of them in my copy,' his cousin said impassively. 'They swindled you in Paris, old boy.'

Vasily Lvovich grew pale. Books were his passion and if somebody had the same book, it lost its value in his eyes.

'Yours is different,' he said with indignation.

'No, the same, only without the marks and slobber stains,' objected his cousin.

Dashkov, Bludov and Turgenev were increasingly enjoying the society of 'the two Pushkins'. Vasily Lvovich muttered something, hurried off and led the guests to the table.

The dinner was of high quality, and the table was meticulously laid – Annushka had been bustling about all day. It was the first time Blaise's fish *à la française,* with all its refinements, had turned out a success. Vasily Lvovich himself had instructed Blaise since first thing in the morning. The Parisian recipes were written down in his notebook. The fish stew tasted exactly like the dish he had had at the Gros-Caillou; the restaurateur had told him the secret of its preparation personally. Only the fish itself had been different – it had been a sea-fish, not fresh-water burbot like this one. But it made no appreciable difference. The secret was in the dressing – the pepper, salt, vinegar, mustard and their proportions.

The guests ate a lot and eagerly – all but Dashkov.

Vasily Lvovich asked him if he was enjoying the fish stew that was exactly the same as he had had at the Gros-Caillou.

Dashkov replied slowly and apathetically:

'N-no.'

Dashkov the stutterer was pompous and arrogant. Vasily Lvovich felt hurt.

His cousin Aleksey wore an air of indifference and detachment and was frowning as usual. He said that the fish stew lacked something, and muttered about English cuisine. Vasily Lvovich pricked up his ears: it was the first time that his cousin had approved of English taste. Vasily Lvovich had been to England but in his opinion, besides damp, beef and innumerable egg-dishes there was nothing of any interest there. Bludov smiled and quietly mentioned beefsteak. In the same bored, cracked voice Aleksey asked Vasily Lvovich if he had been to England at the time when the new machine had been invented …

'Wasn't it you who told me about it?' he said suddenly, staring at Vasily Lvovich sharply and impatiently and making an effort to remember. 'Of course it was you! And now you disapprove of the English!'

'What exactly did I tell you?' asked Vasily Lvovich, perplexed.

'About the machine you saw in London …'

All around him were experienced travellers. The pride of the traveller who has been the first to describe a novelty spoke in Vasily Lvovich.

'I don't seem to recall, perhaps I did see it,' he said off-handedly.

Everyone asked Aleksey Pushkin to tell them about the machine. But he had a mouthful of stew and nodded towards Vasily Lvovich, who in turn shrugged his shoulders to let his cousin tell the story. He had absolutely no memory of the machine he had supposedly told his cousin about, and with the pride of an author was waiting to listen to his own creation.

The guests were waiting too.

Finally, reluctantly and abruptly, with meaningful glances at Vasily Lvovich, Aleksey Pushkin told them about it. A very simple-looking machine had been invented in England, in London – a kind of wagon with iron bars and steps leading up to it. Vasily Lvovich had some vague recollection of this. A bull was led up the steps into the wagon … This seemed to be one of Vasily Lvovich's memories of the London Zoo.

' … a live bull. So they lead the bull into the wagon …'

Vasily Lvovich had indeed told them about the transportation of animals that he had witnessed. He nodded to his cousin.

' … and lock the door. That's the entrance, and from the exit, an hour and a half later, out of the machine come dried leather, hot beefsteaks ready for eating, horn-handled combs, knee-high boots and all the rest of it …'

Vasily Lvovich sat with his mouth wide open. The story made him sit up.

Apparently Aleksey Pushkin was absolutely serious. He might have mixed up Vasily Lvovich with somebody else, though machines in England were invented almost every day, and weirder and weirder ones. Sergey Lvovich, whose attention was distracted and who had heard only the last phrase about horn-handled combs and boots, seemed to recall reading about the machine.

'I think I remember an article about it in the *European Messenger*', he said.

Turgenev tore himself away from his plate with a kind of a moan, and quickly finishing a mouthful, burst out laughing. Suddenly the table was in uproar.

Vasily Lvovich was laughing too but for some reason broke out in a sweat and wiped his brow with his handkerchief.

'No,' he responded weakly, 'I didn't see this machine, and I should confess, I'm not very keen on machinery. But I did see a freak woman in a coffee-house, they showed her for money.' And Vasily Lvovich, choking and blowing bubbles, told them about the freak Englishwoman. In his confusion he embroidered his story.

'Where did you see her?' asked his cousin harshly.

'In London,' replied Vasily Lvovich.

'What was the price of the show?' asked his cousin.

'One pound sterling,' said Vasily Lvovich reluctantly and glared at his cousin fiercely.

But Aleksey Pushkin seemed to take no notice of his expression.

'Would you like to see a woman like that for nothing?'

'I would,' said Vasily Lvovich fiercely.

'In that case, old chum, go to Marosseyka Street, Kucherov's house, on the right. It's much nearer than London.'

And once again, as when his uncle and his father had had their struggle over Khvostov's *Parables*, it seemed to Aleksandr that Vasily Lvovich was being made fun of. He thought he saw Bludov screwing up his eyes and giving Dashkov a wink. But Dashkov looked unruffled, and just for a moment let a smile crack the corners of his mouth.

His uncle, Vasily Lvovich, was amusing indeed. Aleksandr couldn't restrain himself and gave a sudden brief laugh when everyone was silent, then bit his tongue. The guests looked at the white-toothed mischief-maker with a certain attention. His eyes were bright and lively. To judge by his expression, he understood much more than he had been expected to and, perhaps, more than he should.

Sergey Lvovich immediately started to complain about the difficulties of educating children. You needed an army of teachers! But no single person could combine a knowledge of all those oxygens and Pythagoras theorems which nowadays even madhouse or prison wardens had to be familiar with (for such was the will of *Monsieur de Speransky*), French literature – which in spite of *ce diacre de Speransky* was essential in educating the emotions – and dancing, which, whatever you said about it, developed a child's refinement. Oh, the comte de Maistre, who had paid him a visit last time he had been to Moscow, was right three times over: hang them, all those sciences and gases! Even Karamzin found dancing very helpful for the young – and no wonder! But every teacher was competent in something, either in oxygens or in dancing. In order to give his son a proper education he had gone to extremes; an army of teachers swarmed about the house! Pengeau taught him dancing, the priest initiated him into the Scriptures, Monsieur Roussleau tutored him in French literature – from early morning till late at night, with no let-up. It seemed that only the Jesuits could give one's child a really decent education.

'That old bumpkin Pengeau teaches children minuets which goats used to dance with Noah,' Aleksey Pushkin said indifferently.

The former Pushkin's gratuitous spitefulness was well-known throughout Moscow, as natural as mustard and vinegar at dinner. But Sergey Lvovich could not bear his retorts and as always took offence.

'Pengeau is the former pupil of Vestris the Elder,' he said drily.

Dinner was over. The guests had coffee and subsided into easy-chairs, in as equable a mood as it was possible for them to be. Turgenev and Bludov unbuttoned their waistcoats. They might have been interested in the issue of education had they not been so full.

'Why haven't you enrolled him at the University boarding-school?' asked Bludov dispassionately.

Sergey Lvovich was confused. Indeed, Sashka was growing up. The other boys of his age had been sent off to various places and only his son knocked about like a bumpkin. The University boarding-school for children of the nobility was not far off, a stone's throw away, and it would have been easiest to enrol Sashka there. But Nadine couldn't be bothered with the matter, which fell upon his shoulders entirely. He paused and gave Bludov a shrewd look. No, this boarding-school … hang it! He preferred … St Petersburg.

'Are you going to send him to the Jesuit College?' asked Bludov.

Sergey Lvovich replied with a certain irritation. Neither his *bon mot* about Speransky nor his friendship with de Maistre had been noticed.

'Yes, I am,' he said with a sigh. 'Of course, to the College! Where else can one send one's child?'

Sergey Lvovich was not going to send Aleksandr to any college, nor was he planning to send him to St Petersburg. He was displeased with himself for initiating the discussion about education.

Turgenev was being tormented by the hidden hiccupping he was obviously struggling with, now suppressing it, now giving way to nature. Resting his hand on his belly, he turned to Sergey Lvovich and, gazing dimly at Aleksandr, said hastily:

'Petersburg, Petersburg …'

At this point, imperturbable and motionless as a statue, Dashkov focused his attention on Vasily Lvovich's nephew. Then, letting his glance pass indirectly across Sergey Lvovich, he said:

'The Jesuits are expensive.'

Sergey Lvovich felt stung. Leaning back slightly in his chair, he turned quickly to Dashkov and asked in a matter-of-fact tone:

'How much do the reverend fathers, *ces révérends pères*, charge for an education?'

Dashkov again gave him an unconcerned glance and an even shorter answer:

'No idea.'

Turgenev, who was supposed to know such things because of his post, had also forgotten.

'A thousand and a half – two thousand,' he said.

Suddenly Aleksandr saw a complete change in his father. A light smile was playing on his lips, he was slightly screwing up his eyes; all his being expressed dignity – the desperate pride of a liar and an envier. In genuine amazement, Sergey Lvovich, not abandoning his even tone, asked Turgenev:

'Altogether?'

'Yes,' said Turgenev, 'altogether.'

'So it isn't much then,' said Sergey Lvovich slowly and calmly.

Dashkov stared at him. A thousand and a half or two thousand roubles was an exorbitant fee, and the St Petersburg Jesuits had fixed it with the express purpose of attracting only élite youths into their boarding school and preventing destitute noble small-fry from butting in. But at this moment Sergey Lvovich forgot all the figures in the world – how much Nadine owed to the French shop, how much they owed for butter, vinegar and eggs. In any case, he soon expected a new stock of food supplies from Boldino.

Shalikov, who had been patiently biding his time, decided that it had come, and in a husky voice started to recite the words of a romance;* there was no guitarist, and unfortunately he could not sing it. The guests were half-listening to him. Stony indifference was expressed on Dashkov's broad face; Bludov's little eyes were closed; Turgenev was breathing deeply, losing his battle with hiccups. Immensely contented with his answer to Dashkov, Sergey Lvovich was the only person listening to the poet.

No one took any notice of Aleksandr. He left the room and roamed about the house. In a back-room that he had always thought uninhabited, he ran into a young woman working at an embroidery frame. Catching sight of him, she hastily stood up and bowed. They started to talk. Her broad face was kind, her tender white hands slid about the frame swiftly and adroitly. From the adults' conversations Aleksandr vaguely knew that this woman, Anna Nikolayevna, was living at Vasily Lvovich's. His aunt sometimes called her Anka for old time's sake. Suddenly he realised what it meant.

She asked him about the dinner and flushed with pleasure when she heard that it had been most delicious. He helped her to unreel the silk threads. Then she told him to go.

'They might scold you,' she said apprehensively, 'your uncle will scold you,' and suddenly stroked his head nervously and smiled.

'Go, go, Aleksandr Sergeyevich,' she jabbered quickly, waving her hands at him.

He did not want to go. He did not like the guests and their conceit. He had

---

* Original: *romans*, a setting of lyric verse for solo voice with piano or guitar accompaniment, the Russian equivalent of the German *Lied*.

a particular dislike of Dashkov. It was warm in this room, Annushka's eyes were full of joy, and being here and talking to the humble recluse suddenly made him feel immensely happy. His uncle Vasily Lvovich, who was now in the drawing-room being sneered at by Dashkov, had suddenly raised himself in his estimation. He stubbornly refused to leave. Then Annushka put her arms around him and, restraining his arms, with an unexpected strength and deftness pushed him out through the door.

The evening was at an end. He was being called, the guests were taking their leave and dressing noisily in the vestibule. Shalikov, red-faced and dissatisfied, was trying to stick his arms into the sleeves of his fur-coat. His romance had not been a success; everyone had roared with laughter during the most touching stanza because of the sound of belching: Turgenev had failed to subdue nature. The new friends seemed to laugh at everyone alike, at the older generation of St Petersburg and at Karamzin's circle. Shalikov had made up his mind to write to Count Khvostov immediately – he was the only person who could value friends, unlike these novices.

The street-lamps were already lit as everyone returned home. Moscow was falling asleep.

When his son asked him what Bludov's occupation was, Sergey Lvovich paused and then replied reluctantly, sighing and wincing with a peevish grimace:

'They're all diplomats.'

Aleksandr did not ask about Annushka. He felt that he should not, must not ask questions about this joyful recluse.

Nine

His parents had aged noticeably in their pleasurable pursuits. Sergey Lvovich's hair, soft as flax, was receding and thinning on the temples, and there was a pink bald patch on the crown of his head. Nadezhda Osipovna had grown more portly and her face had become coarser. Another son, Paul, had been born but died in infancy.

They led a superficial life, secretly believing that servants, teachers and children were the cross they had to bear. If somebody asked Sergey Lvovich whether he was rich, noble or what he thought of himself, he could have given two answers. In his heart of hearts he believed he was wealthy and that the reason for his stinginess was prudence. He also believed he was a distinguished person – by birth, for his title and rank was only Provisions Staff Commissioner, seventh class. This was the blunt reality he preferred to turn away from. Occasionally giving his ten-year-old son half a rouble for his entertainments, he worried that it might be lost and sometimes checked that the money was safe. As soon as he got some money, he would have a fashionable tail-coat made and buy his wife a ring – a souvenir of the heart.

But soon they were brought to the brink of ruin.

The source of the trouble, as always, was the Hannibals.

His uncle, Pyotr Abramovich, had not forgotten his grudge and all of a sudden had perpetrated a genuinely villainous deed.

Marya Alekseyevna was hoping to spend the rest of her days on her own estate, and was eager to forget her bitter youth. She had even refused to go to Mikhaylovskoye to take over her inheritance. The very memory of the Hannibals seemed unbearable to her.

And now her estate and peace of mind, just as in the days of her youth, had turned to dust and ashes and she was left without a roof. To make matters worse, Mikhaylovskoye was also under threat.

The African seemed to have calmed down and to be spending his last days peacefully in his hamlet, Petrovskoye, as a connoisseur of fruit liqueurs and cognacs, when unexpectedly he decided to recover the debts still due to him and submitted his late brother Osip's letters of acknowledgement to the local court. These letters had been written by the deceased at the time of his frenzied passion for Tolstaya and both brothers seemed to have forgotten them. According to the letters, large sums were due to Pyotr Abramovich since his late brother had thought no sacrifice was to be spared for the sake of female beauty: one letter stipulated three thousand roubles (for a gold dinner-set and a garden for Ustinya), and another eight hundred and forty-two roubles (for dappled bay horses and crystal vases).

Pyotr Abramovich seemed to be taking revenge for all the insults that had ever been inflicted on the Hannibals. Soon the same assessor and a clerk as before (the ones whom Palashka called leeches) drove into Mikhaylovskoye, and despite the one-eyed Ensign's resistance – he announced that there was not a kopeck in the house and unleashed the dog – made an inventory and valuation of the estate.

Simultaneously, a suit was brought against Marya Alekseyevna, and soon Zakharovo was sold by auction. Sergey Lvovich and Nadezhda Osipovna would not believe their eyes when they received and read the Ensign's letter. And only when they looked out of the window and saw the carriage and Marya Alekseyevna herself did they realise what was going on. Sergey Lvovich waved his hands, stamped his feet and burst into tears like a child. Twice that day he started to wring his hands and to crack his knuckles, and then flew into spluttering rages and yelled that Ivan Ivanovich Dmitriyev would not let this matter rest, threatening the old negro with Siberia and a monastery. By the evening he had quietened down and let Nikita take himself off to rest.

Next morning they started the day by rereading the Ensign's letter. The part where the Ensign mentioned his dog and described the battle with the assessor aroused everyone's approval.

'Well done,' said Marya Alekseyevna. 'You can see an honest man at a glance.'

She couldn't believe the amount of the debts and shrugged her shoulders helplessly.

'I know him only too well. He was paid back more than two thousand. The damned drunkard wants more for vodka!'

Sergey Lvovich immediately sat down to write a letter to Dmitriyev, the Minister of Jurisprudence. The first two pages, in which he expressed his indignation with dishonest, cold-hearted and cruel people and his hope for friendly protection, were powerfully written, dignified, and altogether magnificent. Then he went on to set out the circumstances of his case. He wrote about the ridiculous financial demands that the dissipated old Major-General had made on innocent people indebted to no one but God Almighty. He had demanded the sum of three thousand eight hundred and forty roubles, whereas by due accounting it was clear that almost everything – over two thousand roubles – had already been paid back, and here he quoted Marya Alekseyevna. He almost believed this himself, and his hurt dignity prompted him to express it. So the debt was just a thousand roubles. And because of this petty thousand the vast property had been villainously distrained.

Furthermore, he found it necessary to cite the number of his villages and serfs distrained by the villains.

He asked Nadezhda Osipovna how many villages they had near Mikhaylovskoye.

Nadezhda Osipovna remembered the document issued by the clerk, the wax seal, the peasants' black carrot pie and, unwilling to acknowledge the non-existence of the villages, replied:

'Twenty.'

Sergey Lvovich put it down.

'And how many serfs are there, my angel?'

Nadezhda Osipovna thought a little again. She remembered a bunch of servants and peasants in coarse caftans.

'Two hundred,' she said.

Sergey Lvovich mentioned these details too to the poet Dmitriyev: the ancestral estate of Mikhaylovskoye, twenty villages and two hundred serfs, had been distrained for the sake of a thousand roubles. This had been done against the law – shamelessly and unscrupulously. He also mentioned the case of Marya Alekseyevna's estate to the Minister but did not plead for it as it was a hopeless cause. Actually, she had never asked him to.

Once again Marya Alekseyevna was living in the attic. She roamed about the house like a shadow, quiet, thin and nervous, and did not know how to keep herself busy. She sighed, stroked the children's heads and looked at them in amazement:

'How they have grown up!'

'She's melting away like a candle!' Arina told the children surreptitiously, and waved her hand in despair.

Sergey Lvovich enclosed the letter and sealed it long and carefully with his signet ring. When he had finished he gave a sigh of relief.

He sent Nikita with the message about the unfortunate event to Vasily Lvovich, and soon his sisters arrived.

Annette pressed her lips to her brother's head and gave him a kiss on his pink bald patch. Sergey Lvovich was moved to tears and only at that moment realised the depths of his unhappiness. Under the stress of emotion he clasped his hands and froze.

Informed of the news by Nikita, Vasily Lvovich too arrived. In great agitation he threw his fur-coat off onto the floor and hastened to his brother, kissing his sister-in-law's hand in passing.

Sergey Lvovich laid his head on his brother's shoulder.

'Oh, *mon frère*,' he said, remembering Racine, and his voice trailed off.

Then he embraced Sashka and Lolka who stared at him attentively, pressed them to his chest as if protecting them from an assault and, acting the part of Laocoön with his sons, exclaimed to his brother:

'It's not myself I have worries about!'

His sons' noses were tightly pressed into their father's waistcoat, which gave off a mixed odour of scents and tobacco. They were gasping for breath.

'Brother! Brother!' babbled Anna Lvovna.

Vasily Lvovich felt the noble envy of the actor. The spirit of Talma awoke in him. He had expected this to be his role – the heartfelt gestures, the groans and embraces. But his brother had forestalled him.

Suddenly Vasily Lvovich said, screwing up his eyes icily and speaking through his teeth:

'*Cela ne vaut pas un clou à soufflet*. All this is not worth a brass farthing. Look here!'

The sons felt their father's embrace growing weaker. They looked at their uncle askance. Everyone was staring at him, Sergey Lvovich with his mouth half-open, sister Liza with fear.

With his chin raised Vasily Lvovich paced the room.

'*Pas un clou à soufflet*,' he repeated again slowly. He could not understand how these words had escaped his lips. On his way to his brother, he had considered him ruined. Now he was thinking what to do or say to him and how to explain his words.

'Oh, brother, brother,' said Anna Lvovna, trembling.

'I'll write to Dmitriyev,' said Vasily Lvovich still screwing up his eyes, 'and tomorrow the court decision will be overruled. Rest assured,' he went on, 'they are in our hands!'

And Sergey Lvovich consoled himself. His elder brother had revealed such a firm resolve, he seemed more forceful and confident than he had intended to be himself. Sergey Lvovich's gullibility was incredible. But he could not pull himself out of his state of depression. He pointed to Aleksandr with his finger and gave a loud sigh:

'College? Ah!'

He recalled his dreams of the Jesuits and his proud reply to the wealthy. Now everything was collapsing. This was what his exclamation meant. Meanwhile Vasily, seeing his sisters' admiring eyes and the mistrustful eyes of his sister-in-law on him, said in a calm voice, surprising himself:

'I'll personally take him to St Petersburg, to the Jesuits!'

He looked around. Nadezhda Osipovna sat hushed like a little girl, staring at him, her mouth half-open.

'Rest assured, my dear ones,' jabbered Vasily Lvovich. 'I'll take charge of all this, and everything … but all this – *pas un clou à soufflet.*'

He responded coolly to the kisses of his sisters, who clung to him, fanned himself with his handkerchief, and was gone, leaving everyone rooted to the spot. He got into his droshki and, bewildered, squinted at the street on either side. Reaching Tverskaya Street, he rubbed his forehead and spread his hands helplessly. He could not understand how it had happened. His magnanimity had carried him away. He pouted like a schoolboy caught in a prank. Passing along Tverskaya he told the coachman to stop by the coffee-shop, where he met a few genial and good-humoured acquaintances and informed them that he was taking his nephew to St Petersburg to the Jesuit College. His friends looked at him with some interest and seemed delighted. Prince Shalikov appeared too. As usual he held a snow-white handkerchief in his hands and pulled at it, smiling at everyone amiably; and as usual he wore a pair of close-fitting, fashionably tailored trousers. At times Vasily Lvovich envied him his new trousers. Having learned that Vasily Lvovich was taking his young nephew to St Petersburg to the Jesuits, the Prince put his cup of hot chocolate on the table and gave Vasily Lvovich a hug and a firm triple kiss on the cheeks. He summoned the *garçon*, who brought them a bottle of chilled claret. They drank to Vasily Lvovich's health and kissed him with all their heart.

The Prince asked him to send a heartfelt kiss to 'the nonpareil'. Everyone clinked glasses to the health of 'the nonpareil', fully conscious that they were drinking to Ivan Ivanovich Dmitriyev.

They asked Vasily Lvovich if he would be in St Petersburg for long.

'Oh, for a long time,' answered Vasily Lvovich melancholically, the words full of sorrow and significance. They ordered Burgundy, Aix, and then lunch.

Returning home replete with food and drink, Vasily Lvovich felt resolute and happy, and took a nap on the couch that resembled Récamier's. He woke up in the evening and slapped his brow, and Annushka seemed to hear her sultan exclaim:

'What the devil have I done!'

He turned to her, gave a sigh and told her to pack – he was going to St Petersburg.

Annushka asked him if it was to be a long visit, and looking at her gloomily and enigmatically, Vasily Lvovich replied:

'Yes, a long visit.'

Frightened, Annushka was about to start packing but Vasily Lvovich waved his hand and said that he would be leaving in a month's time.

He was displeased with himself all evening, and tossed in bed for a long time.

Next morning, still lying in bed, he pictured St Petersburg life in detail, and carried away by his imagination, went into raptures at the thought that he would soon be walking along Nevsky Prospect. He recited his latest poem by heart, already imagining himself in Dmitriyev's drawing-room, and, imitating the imagined responses of some beautiful female listeners, babbled: 'Bravo! Bravo!'

Then he got up, threw on his dressing-gown, took a cup of tea and wondered: should he take his entire household – Annushka included – to St Petersburg?

He liked the idea very much. He had many acquaintances in St Petersburg, and, no matter what people said, it was the capital of the country. Vasily Lvovich, a born and bred Muscovite, suddenly felt that nowadays Moscow could not compete with St Petersburg. It was too old-fashioned.

As with all the Pushkins, his changes of mind were sudden and whimsical.

2

Very often Aleksandr wandered about the rooms oblivious of sounds and people, biting his nails and gazing at everything and everyone around him, Monsieur Roussleau, Arina, his parents, household objects, with a withdrawn and blank expression. Certain sounds, fragments of shadowy and unreal poems from somewhere, tormented him; he scribbled them down unthinkingly, unaltered, just as they came to him. They were in French, mechanical and meagre, the rhymes coming to him before the lines themselves. He repeated them in his mind, sometimes forgetting a word or two and substituting others; going to sleep at night he voluptuously remembered the half-forgotten rhymes. These verses were not entirely his and not entirely anyone else's.

It was not without reason that Sergey Lvovich boasted about Roussleau. He was a pedagogue in all senses of the word. He was strict and demanded that his pupil should learn arithmetic and the rules of grammar, and above all punctuality. He permitted games and nonsense only after homework had been done. He put up with chasing games, as long as Aleksandr did not choose servants' children as his playmates, as had already happened twice, holding that boys should take exercise so that their bodies developed properly. He did not, however, relish Aleksandr's leaps and bounces over chairs and stools, and he utterly disapproved of the pandemonium when his pupil, as if possessed, threw things about and upset everything in his way, howling or chanting some wild, discordant gibberish.

But what really made him lose his temper was the absent-mindedness, the silence and numbness of the boy when he did not respond to calls, occupied instead with some strange contemplation, though he had no real thoughts – the flickering expressions on his face betrayed this. And in any case he should not have had thoughts at his age. Monsieur Roussleau started to watch him carefully: the boy was writing something, looking around apprehensively, apparently afraid that he might be caught.

Soon the matter was cleared up: Roussleau found a few scraps of paper hidden away under the mattress. They turned out to be verses in French, and slight irregularities in the lines drew the Frenchman to the conclusion that these were Aleksandr's own poems. He read them with a smile, but without pleasure. Roussleau was an author himself. He had tried to find his way into print and had sent his poems to the *Almanac des Muses* three times. Each time he had been turned down, and he had become embittered. He suspected intrigues and plots on the part of the poets who were published, many of whom, in his opinion, wrote worse verse than his. That was why he read the poems of the diabolical boy sourly – he was just a child but already dared to scribble on paper, to dabble in composition. He was particularly stung by the overall coherence of the poems, although they contained numerous spelling mistakes, which Roussleau corrected, marking the worst blunders with double lines. Finally, he put a big question mark in pencil in the margin to express his doubt about the propriety of the poems.

Nadezhda Osipovna especially relied on the Frenchman's services, and he led a free and easy life at the Pushkins'. Sergey Lvovich skilfully used the Frenchman's influence to facilitate his affairs; he deliberately encouraged him to gossip when he wanted to slip away from the house. Nadezhda Osipovna was very fond of Roussleau's stories and did not notice her husband's absence. In this way Monsieur Roussleau had become an indispensable member of the family and even acted as mediator during the spouses' quarrels. Nadezhda Osipovna would follow his advice on the making of a new dress; the Frenchman's compliments delighted her; his remarks revealed the complete understanding of the shrewd boulevardier – they were always about how high the waist and how low the neck-line of a dress should be.

After lunch on the day of his discovery of the poems, Roussleau got down to business. In an expressionless tone he said that as an honest man he would soon have to relinquish his duties, feeling one too many in the house. Nadezhda Osipovna and Sergey Lvovich were stunned: there had been no previous indication of this; Roussleau had seemed rather cheerful in the morning and had even been whistling to himself. At lunch he had indeed seemed pensive and preoccupied, but his appetite had been unspoiled and he had eaten so much that Sergey Lvovich had been distinctly concerned.

At first Roussleau was unwilling to answer the questions put to him, but then reluctantly, weighing his words and expressions, he complained about Aleksandr, about his laziness and idleness, which he said he was unable to redress. Aleksandr knitted his brows and suddenly said abruptly and rudely:

'Lies!'

Nadezhda Osipovna was about to usher him from the table when the Frenchman restrained her.

He pulled the carefully folded sheets of paper out of his pocket and started to read the poems loudly, slowly, emphatically, imitating some tragic actor and jerking up his eyebrows at the end of every stanza. It was a triumph – Nadezhda Osipovna burst into peals of laughter and Sergey Lvovich, who all too seldom got a chance to laugh, expressed his delight that Roussleau was staying and that all this had turned out to be just a joke.

At this point they looked at the author, Sashka, not without gratitude for the entertainment he had provided. The boy sat at the end of the table crumpling the edge of the tablecloth in his hands. His mother tapped her hand on the table as she always did to call the children to order. He did not listen and went on twisting the tablecloth around his finger. She spoke to him. Then he stood up and gazed at them all without seeing them or understanding anything. His face grew white and dull, his mouth twitched, his eyes turned bloodshot. With a soft and sudden spring and the fierce grace of a young tiger he threw himself upon Roussleau, snatched the poems from his hands and with a growl shot out of the room.

Everyone was stupefied. Roussleau, insulted both professionally and personally, waited silently for the parents to react. Nadezhda Osipovna remained subdued, Sergey Lvovich held his peace. Almost every day he either had to be involved in quarrels or to pacify quarrellers. He couldn't even have his lunch in peace! He was indignant with them all – every day brought some absurdity or other. It was like living on top of a volcano.

But Roussleau remembered his duties and set off to talk to his pupil. Nadezhda Osipovna, bored and too full after lunch, sat passively. As for Sergey Lvovich, he longingly recalled those days when he had enjoyed Pankratyevna's renowned cabbage-soup and Grushka had served him with all her artless adroitness. Was she alive, and above all, was she well? Once again he felt the pull of that carefree life, the company of bachelors, cuckolds and loose girls. Meanwhile here he was sitting at the lunch table, bored out of his mind and waiting for the end of another quarrel. At this moment they heard a thin plaintive cry from the nursery, and dashed there at once. The cry was Roussleau's call for help.

The stove was lit in the nursery. A pile of logs was lying next to it, and on the cinders burning paper was curling and turning from white to black.

Roussleau stood by the stove, boxed into a corner, stretching out both hands for protection and calling for help. In front of him, like a little devil, stood Aleksandr with a hefty log lifted above his head, baring his teeth in a triumphant smile. The Frenchman's predicament was pitiful. Nadezhda Osipovna dashed to Aleksandr to retrieve the log from him, but quite unexpectedly she could not tackle her son, who turned out to be surprisingly strong. He stood taut as an uncoiled spring, firmly clutching his weapon, and his mother could not unclench his fingers.

Finally he tossed the log into a corner and ran out of the room.

Roussleau recovered his breath. He was cut to the quick. He told them what had happened. Entering the room, he had noticed Aleksandr squatting before the furnace and burning those scraps of paper of his. He had asked him to get up but the boy had failed to obey. He had touched his shoulder and repeated his order. But instead of obeying him, the boy had grabbed a log and attacked him, allowing him no time to defend himself. Thanks to his agility, sheer luck and the habit of an old soldier, Roussleau had managed to dodge the blow. He begged them to free him from the duty of educating this little monster.

The parents sighed in unison and begged him to stay. The Frenchman was unbending. Finally Nadezhda Osipovna mentioned a rise in his salary and the tutor's obstinacy was shaken. Sergey Lvovich grudgingly brought the negotiations to an end, afraid that his wife might add too much. At last the teacher gave a dignified bow and declared that he was staying only because of the noble feelings shown by the parents.

Aleksandr was searched for and found in Arina's room.

To his surprise he was not punished.

But henceforth he often woke up at nights with his heart hammering and hatred dimming his eyes. He would scrutinise the sleeping tutor's face with icy fury. Since he had stuck his sheets of paper, defamed by the Frenchman's hand, into the furnace, he had never ceased to wish him dead, stubbornly and passionately. If he had been older he would have challenged him to a duel: Montfort's tales about duels and his demonstrations of quart and tierce might have proved useful. But they had no swords, and it was all too ridiculous for words.

Little by little his imagination carried him away. He imagined he had fled his home, escaped from Moscow and roamed the roads. Or had covered himself with glory. He pictured Roussleau's stupid face when one morning he would wake up and find he was gone. Once he got up early, waited behind the door for the tutor to stir, and enjoyed the argus's sleepy expression through a chink in the door. But the Frenchman seemed to have identified and understood something important in the little monster: he calmed down and started to treat him as an adult, which flattered the boy's self-esteem. The teacher shifted his bed to the door, saying that it was too draughty by the window, brought over his pillow and slept on the very threshold, like Cerberus.

3

At the age of twelve, in the clothes made by the homespun tailor and with his sharp elbows, he seemed a stranger in his own family. Like a hunted wolf-cub, his eyes glittering, he would come down for breakfast and awkwardly kiss his mother's hand. He derived real pleasure from misinterpreting the sense of his parents' conversations. At the age of twelve he brought his parents to trial, the cold and merciless trial of youth, and condemned them. They suspected nothing. But they too began to be weighed down by him and waited impatiently for Vasily Lvovich to remember his promise. For some reason nothing was going very well this year; the house was cold and empty.

4

Sergey Lvovich had one invaluable quality, which sustained him and was a guarantee of his happiness: he was incapable of being depressed for very long. Having shed a tear, he cheered up as soon as he remembered a *bon mot* or anecdote he had heard the previous day. Moscow was full of anecdotes. On a visit to Moscow the Tsar was said to have danced the first pair with old Arkharova at the Nobles' Assembly ball, and at that very moment the old lady felt that she was losing her underwear. Like a matron of ancient Rome she had kept her composure, stepped over the fallen article, and with a proud bearing sat down next to the Tsar. The older generation of Moscow were delighted; they bragged about it and claimed that none of the beauties of the day was capable of carrying off such a stunt:

'And she didn't turn a hair!'

The day after the loss of Mikhaylovskoye, Sergey Lvovich was gossiping about all this.

The letter to Dmitriyev had been sent, and thus the necessary measures had been taken; the only thing to do was to wait. In the evenings Sergey Lvovich recalled his visit to his father-in-law and in those memories Mikhaylovskoye seemed a vast property, surrounded with thick forests; the size of the lake reminded him of a sea ('a sealet', he would say); the house was huge, cosy and warm in the old style; the outbuildings were conveniently situated. There were vast surrounding woods. Nadezhda Osipovna listened without contradicting him. Marya Alekseyevna grieved for her Zakharovo, wiping her tears with a handkerchief, and applied all these details to her estate. Eventually she suggested that her son-in-law and daughter should write personally to the villain.

'Perhaps something just came over him and by now he has already changed his mind. All the Hannibals are like that – it depends on their mood. Perhaps he has come to his senses and regrets it now.'

Sergey Lvovich frowned and refused point-blank.

'Oh no,' he said with menacing calm. 'I'll make him regret it! No, I am not going to write to him.'

The same evening, though it made him tremble with revulsion, he wrote a letter to the Major-General, asking him to suspend the penalty and to stop the proceedings. If it were possible, would His Excellency have the kindness to wait for a short time – on account of a lack of cash? Hoping for his magnanimity as a nobleman and an uncle, he looked forward to hearing from His Excellency, remained his devoted servant, and so on. Nadezhda Osipovna added a few short lines to the letter.

Neither Dmitriyev nor the negro answered him.

Sergey Lvovich began to grumble. The loss so vividly took hold of his imagination that he no longer expected salvation. He grumbled at Dmitriyev for becoming so arrogant that he could not even write back to his old friends; he grumbled at the government. Eventually he went so far as to announce that the only just reign had been the brief one of Peter III.*

'If he had ruled just three years longer,' he said once, '*I* should not be asking for Dmitriyev's protection: *he* would be asking for *mine*.'

In the same way as the distrained Mikhaylovskoye had turned into a vast estate in his memory, his father's lost influence had become the Pushkins' past power.

'And later *tous ces coquins*, all these grooms and rogues appeared, all shouting *à gorge déployée*, at the tops of their voices – and what about? God knows! Is it worth one's while talking to them? *Chute complète!*'

Sergey Lvovich did not approve of all these appointments, offices and courts:

'A complaint is a complaint, and a clerk will always be just a bureaucrat and nothing more.'

And suddenly, when they had ceased to expect anything, they received a letter from Dmitriyev sealed with a thick wax seal.

Sergey Lvovich tore the letter open. His hands were shaking as on that memorable night when he had been losing and suddenly had good fortune

---

* During his six-month reign in 1762, ended by the palace revolution that brought his death and his wife Catherine the Great to the throne, Peter III freed the nobility from obligatory military and other forms of state service.

– a stack of lucky cards.

Dmitriyev had sent Sergey Lvovich a copy of the Pskov Provincial Prosecutor's report. Sergey Lvovich read it, threw it on the floor and trampled on it. He was white in the face.

The Magistrate was apparently a lover of the old negro's liqueurs and cognacs. His report was uncouth and contemptible. First of all, there was something wrong with the figures. The Magistrate had counted ('obviously when drunk', Sergey Lvovich said) the servants at Mikhaylovskoye and the serfs in the villages, and claimed that there were altogether only twenty-three males and twenty-five females, not two hundred as Sergey Lvovich and Nadezhda Osipovna said. Mr Pushkin's complaint was absolutely unfounded, the rascal went on, *ce faquin de sécrétaire*, since there was no record of the payment of the two thousand roubles.

'No record of the payment!' said Sergey Lvovich, growing even paler and grinning. 'That's a good one! No record indeed!'

Major-General Hannibal had presented in court the letter from his niece Nadezhda Osipovna and her husband Pushkin, who had asked him, Hannibal, because of a lack of cash …

Sergey Lvovich skipped two lines … but he, Hannibal, could not agree to this. What the said Pushkins had written had involved the court in completely unnecessary correspondence and was a sheer waste of everyone's time.

'I'm going to the Tsar!' said Sergey Lvovich and shouted to Nikita: 'Prepare my wardrobe!'

Only afterwards did he read Dmitriyev's letter. The poet wrote politely that he had instructed the Provincial Prosecutor to postpone the case and not to execute the judgement against the Pushkins, and he enclosed a copy of the Prosecutor's report. Unfortunately, he could not see any grounds for retrying the case. At the end of the letter he asked Sergey Lvovich to pass on his compliments to his dear sisters. He would write to Vasily Lvovich under separate cover.

Sergey Lvovich calmed down immediately. He picked up the wretched Prosecutor's report off the floor with the tongs, threw it into the fire and obliterated even the ashes.

Next morning nobody could tell that Sergey Lvovich had been about to go to the Tsar and had cursed the government. The case had been postponed – that was the main thing. Five or ten years could pass before the case was wound up and then – who knew? – with God's help, the uncle could die. And even after Peter III's reign one could just about live, though maybe not so well. Of course, Dmitriyev could have put an end to the case, but never mind. However, it had been quite unnecessary to send him copies of the reports of all those rascals under his command. One could be a high-placed person without being a man of the world, and a poet could be totally ignorant of good manners. Sergey Lvovich even started to believe that Dmitriyev's poems were not so good after all and contained strained passages.

Mikhaylovskoye belonged to them again, but was no longer the huge estate that it had seemed when they had been deprived of it. The house might indeed be comfortable, but the roof was thatched.

Now they no longer had to bother about Sashka and arranging his future. Everything was turning out perfectly well: brother *Basile* would take him to St Petersburg, to the Jesuits, and Sashka would be educated with all those young idlers, the Golitsyns, Gagarins and *tutti quanti. Ces révérends pères* would form his character, which in all honesty was unbearable as yet. The constant noise in the house, the fights with Lolka and quarrels with Roussleau – it was all enough to get on anyone's nerves.

5

Olinka walked about the house diffidently, feeling and knowing with all her being that she was unloved. She was so afraid of her mother that her knees trembled and she grew pale when her mother looked at her sharply. She used cunning, kept things back and always told lies even when it was unnecessary.

'*Parole d'honneur!*' she would babble when they didn't believe her.

Were it not for her mincing walk, the gait of a little girl who knew that she had been naughty and was afraid of punishment, were it not for the wandering expression that made her lies obvious, and her colourless eyelashes, one might, perhaps, have called her pretty. She was the spitting image of Sergey Lvovich, and only in a certain coarseness about her nose and the area around her mouth did she take after her mother. Her hair curled on the temples. A couple of short-term governesses, one of whom had stayed in the house for a month and the other for a week, then to vanish without trace, had made the only contributions to her upbringing. Montfort had taken no notice of her. Roussleau, as an assiduous member of the family, occasionally taught her French grammar and the rules of arithmetic. A German dance-master, invariably drunk, came to the house for a short time and also instructed her in strumming on the clavichord. He played very badly but was cheap. Olinka would fail to keep time, he would slap her rather painfully on the hands with a ruler and she would whimper. Nadezhda Osipovna grew tired of this music and so Olinka's musical education came to an end. On weekdays the clavichord was used as a stand for dishes with leftovers; when guests were expected, the dishes and other objects were removed and the clavichord was dusted, but nobody ever touched its keys. It stood like a coffin in the drawing-room.

Olinka loved Sashka's escapades: his quarrels with their mother and Roussleau were a feast for her; she hid herself behind the door and listened voluptuously to Roussleau's reprimands, her mother's screams and that strange abrupt snorting in reply – Sashka's answers.

She had been the silent witness of Sashka's assault on Roussleau. Pulling her head into her shoulders, her eyes glistening and her mouth open, holding her breath, she had spied on them through the key-hole. Their rooms were adjacent. Since then, and especially because Sashka had escaped punishment, she had nurtured a fearful respect for him.

Suddenly, overnight, it turned out that she was no longer a child, there was something new in her step, in the evenings guests took notice of her and exclaimed how she had grown up! She'd be a bride soon! And Nadezhda Osipovna grew frightened. Was she really thirty-six, was her daughter a young girl, perhaps soon to be a bride? She sat undressed in front of the mirror till noon, staring closely at her reflection. Apart from the eyes and teeth there was nothing young about her face. But her neck, her bosom, the heavy torso that had attracted Sergey Lvovich – was she really an old woman yet? Her sons were growing up but this fact did not make her any older; she did not think too much or too often about them. Sashka had a bad character, but soon he would be taken to the Jesuits; Lyovushka was chubby and charming. But she did not wish to be told that her daughter was a bride. Her life had flown past and was sinking into oblivion – uneventful, without passions or betrayals. She regretted that that catastrophe, before Sergey Lvovich, with the Guardsman who was now a drunk, had not been fully played out. Anyway, he had not been a drunk then. How sick she was of her husband's declamations in front of the fireplace, his witticisms, his dressing-gown, his very gait!

She became stricter with Olga; the children were ruining them – clothes alone cost a fortune! Olga was made to wear only old clothes. Arina darned her stockings, mended the holes and kept silent. Olga complained to her in a quick whisper, but Arina grew used to her complaints and kept her mouth shut.

Once Olga had no one to complain to – it was evening; their parents had gone out and so had Roussleau. She found Sashka in their father's study reading, and in her usual rapid whisper started to complain about their mother and papa and their brother Lolka who was given the best bits at dinner, and then told Sashka sincerely that she admired him and the things he got up to and that Roussleau was a swine.

Thus a friendship was struck up.

Olga's confession and the almost superstitious fear in her eyes had flattered him. But he despised her rapid whispering and her cowardice, he disliked the way she complained about everyone to everyone and looked ingratiatingly at their mother, hoping to earn her sympathy.

He felt sorry for her and angry with her at the same time.

'You're a cry-baby and I'm a hooligan. But I'm not afraid of them!' he told her curtly.

Ten

H E knew he was leaving soon. Everyone at home looked at him differently; they did not find fault with him any longer and he was left to his own devices. He himself looked at this house as if from a distance, at this room, at this corner between the stove and the wardrobe where he had read books, bitten his nails and once had nearly killed his tutor. All these places seemed poorer now, smaller, more pathetic. His father, whom he had always considered tall, turned out to be of small stature. He thought little about all this, however. In his thoughts he was already dashing along the highways, leaving all the other travellers behind, and soon was in the wondrous city of St Petersburg, which his father, envious of his son, never ceased to sigh about but which was scorned by the older generation of their acquaintance.

Imperceptibly his step had become brisker.

He had a peculiar flowing step, with body leaning forward and lengthy stride. He walked endlessly about Moscow; the proud Roussleau kept reminding him of the forthcoming interview in vain. The interview seemed to frighten Roussleau more than his pupil.

He looked at Moscow, its streets, houses and people in a different way too – with a new sweeping gaze. Endless strings of carts stretched across the city, creaking their way slowly through the streets, accompanied by plodding peasants bringing country tribute. And suddenly there would come a ringing of laughter from a side-street and some hearty Moscow fellows on troikas with jingling bells would dash nonchalantly by. The houses either hid themselves in their gardens or here and there crawled with their stone steps up to the side of the road, like ill-tempered deaf old men stepping on the feet of passers-by.

The broad Moscow streets seemed to him ugly and clumsy now.

Here were the houses of eminent persons, hidden in their dense gardens as thick as forests, the Moscow castles whose owners scoffed at St Petersburg with its dandies, and grew old among hosts of old ladies and detachments of house servants, negroes and pug-dogs. Sometimes, at an untimely hour, horn music could be heard from one of these: old Novosiltsev was having tea.

Some footmen had run by him shouting: 'Look out!' and a strange carriage rattled heavily along. And with amazement Aleksandr looked at this equipage too as if from a distance: there were five negroes on the footboard of the carriage and in front of it ran the footmen in weird dress, with white plumage on their hats, gasping for breath and shouting: 'Look out!'

Then he passed by the main streets where the houses seemed to compete in eccentricity. In Neglinnaya Street there was a Chinese palace, gold and green like a peacock. Dragons opened their jaws at the passing Muscovites; in secluded niches stood yellow-faced idols with umbrellas – mandarins. Luxury, somnolence and coolness were reflected in the dim windows of this house in which no one seemed to live. But slowly, with a Moscow wheeze, the gate opened – old Demidov was setting off for a walk.

He went along Tverskaya Street.

Knitting his brows and without noticing him Prince Shalikov drove by, in the direction of the coffee-house. And there, mincing along the street with a carefree smile and pale-blue rolling eyes, was the flabby though as yet unaged figure of his father, who presently screwed up his eyes to turn his lorgnette on an old lady driving by. There was a pug-dog in the old lady's lap. Sergey Lvovich made a bow and the old lady ordered her coachman to stop. Like lightning Aleksandr turned into a side-street.

His departure was set for a month's time. He would be leaving for St Petersburg with his uncle Vasily Lvovich.

2

It was spring, the time for birds to return. In the bushes lining the boulevard and in the garden trees there appeared lively little piping creatures, of whose names, being a city-dweller, Vasily Lvovich was unaware. He had twice listened to the nightingale at Count Saltykov's outside Moscow, and had enjoyed its garrulous trills as much as he enjoyed an imitation of the real thing: at the Pozdnyakovs' balls a servant, hidden in the shade of the Seville orange trees, had trilled like a nightingale.

The birds had arrived, and Vasily Lvovich got ready for his journey to St Petersburg.

He had written to his St Petersburg friends and they had booked comfortable and not particularly expensive rooms for him at Demouth's on the Moyka river. Vasily Lvovich intended to spend a few months in St Petersburg, appear in society, renew the friendly ties with Dmitriyev that had already begun to slacken, and finally, enrol his nephew at the Jesuit College. There was much to do.

The time for departure was drawing near. Vasily Lvovich had already ordered a comfortable carriage from the post-stage for himself and his nephew and a cart for the luggage and servants.

Sergey Lvovich roused himself as the moment of his son's departure approached. Meanwhile, as bad luck would have it, this business with the old negro had occurred. They had to pay up in order to stop the greedy African's gullet for a while; Marya Alekseyevna now called him an outright villain. And how much they had had to pay in bribes! This had been yet one more example of the callousness and cupidity of the red-tape army, which he had always hated.

Re-examining his coffers, Sergey Lvovich found them depleted. He decided to make a sacrifice: a green high-waisted flecked tail-coat which he had intended to have ready by summer had not yet been made. A fashionable cut had already been chosen and Sergey Lvovich had been imagining himself attired in this tail-coat; all he had to do was to stick a flower in its button-hole. And they started to think about selling the serf-girl Grushka who had become lazy and in general was not needed in the house. Frugality was necessary. The Pushkins' dinners grew more and more meagre. The Boldino yield was no help: it was June. Then one day Sergey Lvovich made a drastic change of plan: he pawned the Boldino serfs, and felt rich and easier in his mind. He ordered the tail-coat to be made at once. And Aleksandr could be educated with the Jesuits.

Having raised the money, however, Sergey Lvovich, as always, got carried away and became devil-may-care. Sometimes he glanced at Nadezhda Osipovna enigmatically and she turned cold with fear: Sergey Lvovich's undertakings had always seemed doubtful and even dangerous to her. One day he read about the foundation of the Lycée in Tsarskoye Selo and was immediately filled with excitement. He had only a very faint notion of what the Lycée might be like, but it suddenly took hold of his mind. He talked to his friends. Rumour had it that the Tsar's younger brothers, the Grand Dukes, would be educated there.

Chance, which had ruled people's lives and had brought some unexpected happiness during the previous two reigns, had struck again. Their son might become the future Tsar's playmate or run into the Emperor and the Empress while having a walk in the gardens; one way or another his fate would be decided. They recalled the well-known anecdotes of the previous reigns. Sergey Lvovich imagined Sashka being educated in Tsarskoye Selo, almost in the Palace itself, and realised that an opportunity like this could occur only once in a lifetime. The Jesuits no longer seemed so appealing to him. At the same time, deep in his heart he was almost sure he would not succeed in enrolling Aleksandr at the new institution. Even so, his ambitions were stirred. He quivered. On the quiet and without consulting his wife he decided to try his luck. His rank and title were insufficient; he was aware that many applications would be submitted, and feared refusal. Without telling Nadezhda Osipovna he sent an application for his son's admission to the new establishment. Though frightened, he had made up his mind not to give up: either the Jesuit College or Tsarskoye Selo. The application was well written, but that in itself was not enough.

The certificate of pedigree had turned out to be not so easy to obtain. He had to resort to the powerful patronage of Dmitriyev. The necessary certificate was sent to him. The poet's patronage, however, had convinced Sergey Lvovich once again that the poet and the minister was a pedant. The signatures of both Dmitriyev, the Minister of Justice, and Count Saltykov appeared on the certificate, which was meaningless and even ambiguous. These two exalted persons certified that the minor Aleksandr Pushkin really was the legitimate son of Sergey Lvovich Pushkin, an official of the seventh class on the staff of the Commissariat. Such a document, no doubt, could have been acquired from the parish registry.

The old-fashioned word 'minor', scoffed at even by Fonvizin in his famous play titled with the term and now applied to his son, not only offended Sergey Lvovich, it also made him slightly afraid.

'Legitimate or not, in all the senses of this word, is none of your business, dear sirs,' he whispered.

However, the signatures and the authority of the Minister spoke for themselves.

Grudgingly, Sergey Lvovich divulged his plans to his brother Vasily Lvovich, leaving it to him to choose between the Jesuits and the Lycée. He had also written a brief and extremely courteous letter to Aleksandr Ivanovich Turgenev. Talking to Aleksandr, Sergey Lvovich twice vaguely mentioned Tsarskoye Selo where the new Lycée was to be opened, but was sidetracked into descriptions of nature and fell silent.

The Jesuits were a surer bet: to enter their college required fewer formalities, though this too was no certainty. Vasily Lvovich would have to make a decision on the spot. As an experienced gambler Sergey Lvovich believed in luck, but even in advance his pride was stung.

He looked at his son with mild irritation. Did he deserve such care? Was he worth all this trouble? His son was the fruit of his early passion but he was growing up heartless. Sometimes, in the evenings, he gave him detailed instructions with the worldly wisdom of a person who had experienced many things. He remembered more and more of St Petersburg, with all its subtleties and trivialities, Nevsky Prospect, his youth as a Guardsman, his lost career, and he suddenly developed a burning desire to go there himself instead of this callow youth. What could Sashka find in St Petersburg? Why did he need St Petersburg? He could be perfectly well educated in Moscow. The trouble it caused, one's children's education!

It was too late, however, to change anything.

He admonished his son bitterly, with a sigh:

'Don't buy rolls and pies at the arcade. The vendors will be all around you shouting: "Rolls, hot rolls!" Those rolls are poison. Once I nearly died of them.

'Remember, you might run into His Majesty on Nevsky Prospect. They say he walks there every day. If you see him, stand like this – and bow like this.'

Sergey Lvovich showed Sashka how to bow, but remained dissatisfied.

'Like this, not like that!'

He had been to the Heraldry Office and there his fat brother-in-law Sontsev had issued Aleksandr with a certificate stating that he was descended from the ancient noble stock of the Pushkins whose coat of arms was included in the public armorial. Aleksandr's fate had been decided. Sergey Lvovich had done all he could for his son and now forgot all about him for a while.

His sisters Anna and Lizette took an active part in all this. Anna Lvovna enjoyed *The Reader for the Fair Sex* and it had become her manual. It was very handy: at the end of the book there were a few blank pages with ruled columns: one section for visits and balls, another for cards – losses and gains, and the third one, the biggest – for anecdotes and *bons mots*. Anna Lvovna kept regular notes on the pages. In the 'anecdotes' section she recorded the Moscow gossip about female infidelities; under '*bons mots*' her brothers' sentiments. The first part of the book, called 'Famous Women', was her favourite reading. She was familiar with the terrible morals of Poppea, Fulvia and Cleopatra. She had always felt sorry for Melonia whom the insolent Caligula showed to his retainers disguised as Venus – naked and crowned with a wreath of roses. The same part of the book also contained a survey of gentler heroines, among them Empress Catherine I who had sacrificed all her jewellery for her husband's ransom from Turkish captivity. Anna Lvovna strove to play exactly the same role among her relatives – the role of saviour.

3

May passed, then June, but Vasily Lvovich was still not ready to depart. Sergey Lvovich was afraid to remind him – what if he had changed his mind? Aleksandr pined and often woke up in the middle of the night in a cold sweat. Intending to show off his tutee's knowledge, the Frenchman exhausted him with French vocabulary and the rules of arithmetic. Aleksandr was forgetful and unsociable. Time crawled by.

At last, at the beginning of August, Vasily Lvovich announced that he was leaving. The day of departure was fixed.

That day Arina woke up a little earlier; all mending, darning and packing had long since been completed. She put the school books that Aleksandr Sergeyevich was taking with him in even piles to prevent them from tumbling down during the jolting of the carriage; she found a forgotten little volume on the window-sill and after a short consideration stuck it into his suit-case too – Voltaire's *Madrigals*. Then she carefully took the smallest leather-bound books off Sergey Lvovich's shelves, the ones Aleksandr Sergeyevich had spent most of his time with. Sergey Lvovich had not been to these shelves for a long time. She quietly put the tiny volumes into the suitcase too, at least twenty of them.

'Who needs them here?' she muttered sharply, but not without some apprehension.

The books were of the most entertaining kind: Piron, Grécourt, Gresset, the latest anecdotes. Aleksandr Sergeyevich had always chuckled while reading them.

'They might cheer him up,' she decided. She was restless. She rushed to the kitchen where veal was being fried for meals on the journey; she brushed his clothes again.

She found nothing else to do and became sad. She peeped secretly into his room: Aleksandr Sergeyevich was sleeping calmly and evenly. She was struck by his serenity.

'He's so young, still a child,' she said to Nikita, 'who's going to look after him?'

Nikita disliked talking to her, considering all women stupid.

'It's for his education,' he said reluctantly.

'Education!' she echoed, 'from strangers! What was wrong with Monsieur?'

Montfort had impressed Arina most favourably as a tutor.

Nikita did not think this worth a reply.

'Everybody will hurt him,' said Arina, lifting her apron to her eyes.

'Doesn't Monsieur hurt him?' Nikita responded.

The servants hated Roussleau.

'At least he's at home,' said Arina.

Nikita waved his hand irritably and went off.

It was a hot morning, the sun was scorching. His mother, father and aunts, formally seated and subdued, cast sidelong glances at the departing traveller. Arina stood deathly pale. On the threshold she made the sign of the cross over him and whispered something, but he did not hear. His heart tensed.

They were leaving by the Tver road.

The family saw them off to the city barriers.

Vasily Lvovich examined the carriage, was not pleased with it and scolded the post-master, as was the custom of all travellers.

At the moment of parting Anna Lvovna, looking not at her nephew but at her brothers, handed him over a sealed envelope.

'Here is a hundred roubles, it's for you to buy nuts,' she said meaningfully. 'Make sure you don't lose it!'

Sergey Lvovich clasped his hands and gently reproached his sister. She was too generous. Vasily Lvovich was astounded. He said he would take charge of the money; he took the envelope Aleksandr held in his hands and, not knowing what to do with it, stuck it into his pocket.

Anna Lvovna was satisfied with the impression she had made on her brothers. Sashka thanked her but did not seem either grateful or surprised. She had hardly expected anything else.

The coachman climbed into his seat, the bells clanged, and he was gone.

At the corner of the road Vasily Lvovich turned his dignified gaze on the young fledgling who was leaving his hearth and home for the first time. He froze: the youngster's eyes were burning, his mouth was half-open with a strange expression that Vasily Lvovich could not understand. The fledgling appeared to be laughing.

PART TWO

The Lycée

One

T
HE Minister's day was coming to an end.
Today he had gone neither to the State Council nor to the Palace for a meeting with His Majesty. In the afternoon he had had a few visitors, the last an inconspicuous clerk from the Secret Department who hadn't said a word, had stayed just long enough to hand in a parcel and gone. This particular visitor was one who never lingered.

Peeping silently through the door, his German secretary could see the Minister's huge stooped back. He sat motionless as he wrote, and by studying his back the secretary could tell whom he was writing to – His Majesty. An hour passed, then another. Without halt or hesitation, like an automaton, he covered page after page with his rounded regular handwriting. Not a sound was to be heard – the Minister demanded absolute uninterrupted silence. A large English clock ticked monotonously. His old housekeeper, Miss Stephens, moved irritably about the house in her slippers. Ten years before, when he had served as an insignificant clerk in a dispatch office, his English wife had died in labour. He left home without taking a look at the baby and didn't come back for a fortnight. He did not attend his wife's funeral and was generally assumed to be dead. He had returned in a torment, dirty and soaked, his eyes rolling. Of all living creatures he responded to none but his daughter. For a month he uttered not a single word; then he resumed work. He never entered his dead wife's room – his heart had been broken and his life seemed to be over. It turned out that it was just beginning.

Now he was forty, a Minister and Secretary of State. In fact, with the sole exception of military affairs he shouldered the responsibility for the entire state. His power was enormous and its boundaries were blurred. He had numerous enemies: the nobility damned him, his subordinates cursed and feared him, the courtiers despised him. After his wife's death he had moved into a modest two-storeyed house in Sergiyevskaya Street where he now lived. It was a cosy house, with English furniture. He had a small study upstairs where he slept on a leather sofa. The windows of this room faced the desolate frozen Tauride Gardens, and he could see Prince Potyomkin's squat palace behind the trees; its windows were barred, it had been uninhabited for a quarter of a century. Occasionally, on Alexander's, Constantine's or Elizabeth's name-days, the palace suddenly livened up and shone brightly. On these days the garden paths were swept and smartly dressed people strolled along them once again, looking with mixed feelings at the Minister's residence in Sergiyevskaya Street. When the name-days passed, the windows would be nailed up again and Potyomkin's Palace snowed up, like an empty theatre after the performance is over and the travelling actors have left.

He avoided high society and its bustle and did not entertain guests. Occasionally his closest friends visited the Minister: the mine-owner Lazarev and the tax-farmer Perets. Lazarev was an enterprising and powerful Armenian who had settled with his entire clan and intimate circle in Moscow, and hence the lane where he lived had been named Armenian Lane. Recently he had been thinking of founding a large eastern-style college for his compatriots and often sought the Minister's advice. Perets was resourceful and bold in financial matters and often enchanted the Minister with his startling ideas.

At last the Minister stopped writing and rose in one movement.

He was tall, long-armed and big-boned. He had a pale face, a receding forehead and half-shut, oriental eyes. After carefully placing the papers before him in order, he locked them away in the bureau and rang the bell summoning his personal secretary.

Franz Ivanovich entered the room.

'Has Illichevsky arrived?'

'He arrived two days ago. He's here today to see you. It would seem he is leaving tomorrow.'

'I would rather not see him today.'

'I don't think it will be possible to cancel the appointment without hurting his feelings.'

'Franz Ivanovich, my dear friend,' said the Minister, 'see to the wine. I need decent port, nothing too fancy. The port Bergin sent me last time was far too good. I can do without subtlety of that sort. I don't find it particularly wonderful. We're all tired of Château Margaux too. I've no idea why his tastes have become so refined.'

The Minister smiled his wet smile, baring gums with firm yellow teeth.

He was expecting guests that night. Illichevsky, his former seminary class-mate, had been appointed Governor of Tomsk and was leaving to take up his post.

The Minister put his huge hand on a remaining pile of sheets.

'Have a think and choose another informer with a more literate style. Look at what I've had to do with this.'

The narrow sheets were folded in two. Every line written in the clerk's hand, before the fold, had been crossed out and opposite it, on the other half of the page, everything had been completely rewritten by the Minister.

'We've been looking for a year and we can't find a better man. Anyway, it's not the style we have to think about but the content.'

'How extraordinary!' said the Minister with regret.

'May I humbly suggest that you change your people?' Franz Ivanovich said suddenly in a softer voice.

Both were silent for a while.

'Go on,' said the Minister in a different voice.

'It has been discovered that yesterday Lavrenty offered a hundred roubles to Count Kochubey's valet to find out where the Count goes in the evenings. He's a spy.'

The Minister and the secretary fell silent again.

'I would have sacked him,' said the Minister flatly, 'but who can take his place? There aren't very many loyal people around.'

He was left alone once more. The mail had arrived, the most important moment of the day.

He opened the parcel just brought by the clerk and began to peruse its contents – copies of letters intercepted on the Minister's specific request. There was bad news. A letter from Austria to a French émigré about the war as if it were a foregone conclusion, as if it were already happening. Another letter, from Tver, confirmed what he already knew: the nobles had issued another petition to the Tsar, an extensive one, and this time he was expected to act.

The Grand Duchess Yekaterina Pavlovna, the Emperor's favourite sister, had been trying to guide her brother through this situation, and she had passed on to him the documents from the oppressed nobles, which the Minister called 'bleats'. Karamzin was the presumed author of the latest bleat. He hurled the sheet into the fire, then took the tongs and poked the ashes. Apart from Karamzin's name there was nothing new in the letter. Karamzin was a frightening enemy. The Minister had managed to protect himself from him once: it was he who had insisted that Karamzin should not be appointed Minister for Education, though Razumovsky, who had got the post, was hardly any better. As for the war, this was still an unknown quantity, and he knew that better than the author of the letter.

He sat by the fireplace staring into the flames for a while, poking and rearranging the coals and watching them slowly turn to ashes. He hated the chaos of war; it was like some vast accident with unforeseen consequences. War thwarted men's plans and arrangements. He was a civilian, and if war broke out his established power would turn to cinders and ashes. War was imminent and would be decisive, and undoubtedly Russia would be defeated and collapse. He had realised a long time ago that in politics as in life, it was undesirable and unnecessary to take everything into consideration at once and to attempt to think everything through to the end. This was the rule he had established for himself, and he obeyed it like a schoolboy.

He suddenly stopped thinking about the war – it had been looming for nearly a year and had become almost an accepted part of everyday life. Karamzin was a bigger and more urgent problem than anything else the Minister had in front of him at that moment.

He took *Don Quixote* off the shelf, opened it at random and started to read. His favourite book had its usual soothing effect on him. The friendship between the portly Sancho Panza and the spindly aristocrat was more elevated and poetic than anything he had ever known. His loneliness vanished, he felt pleasantly in control. He read for half an hour, put the book aside and wrote in his neat round handwriting on a fresh sheet of paper: 'A special lycée for *all* classes.'

The upbringing of the Grand Dukes, one of whom would surely succeed to the throne, was a new and extremely important matter. During their last meeting, as if in passing, the Emperor had personally charged him with the task, and had done so in his characteristic manner: as if it were not a mission binding upon him but merely an optional detail.

2

It had been noticed that several times this year the Emperor had suddenly started a conversation about his brothers. Not that he had any brotherly feelings. It would soon be ten years since his father, Emperor Paul, had died and in all this time he had seen his brothers only twice. They were entirely in the care of their mother, at either Gatchina or Pavlovsk, and occupied themselves with military games. He had never visited Gatchina. He might have conducted himself differently towards them if on one occasion, when he was talking to his mother about them, he hadn't noticed a familiar expression of fear and disgust on her face. He had promptly put an end to the conversation.

He found politeness burdensome. He had harboured feelings of guilt since childhood. He had felt guilty in the eyes of the Empress for insinuating himself with his father – he could not have helped it, because he had been afraid of his father more than anyone else in the world. He had also felt guilty towards his father – at first without any reason and then with very good reason. He had known about the plot to assassinate him and so had been a passive accomplice to his murder – a parricide. For the last ten years he had had an uneasy relationship with his mother, who considered herself the legal heir of her murdered husband and believed her son to be a criminal. He felt guilty about his wife too. He had been made to marry when he was a boy. He had always treated his wife, a frigid and melancholy Baden princess, with mild aversion. She had been the Russian Empress for years but she was still uncomfortable with her role and in her heart remained a Baden princess. It infuriated him that he had to appear in her society. He preferred his Polish mistress, Mme Naryshkina. He also found some consolation in the company of his beloved sister Catherine, who was as unbridled and unstoppable as their brother Constantine. Now she was married and lived in Tver.

He had a husky voice and his father's violent temper, but since he was a child he had learned to control himself and to smile at his tutor, the courtiers and foreigners. Later he had developed a love of reading, some subtlety in conversation and, when alone, the art of day-dreaming. He could sit for hours with the same smile on his lips and his features motionless, ruminating and staring blankly into space. Seeing him at these times the ladies-in-waiting called his smile angelic. His eyes were pale blue, his broad face was as fresh as a girl's, the fat-lipped silent smile beatific. He had the distracted and peculiarly enigmatic expression of the short-sighted, while the lop-sided smile lent him a capricious look that in no way contradicted his established nickname – Angel.

His one genuine love was for himself: his walk, his figure which had grown heavier, his delicate hands. Court life had taught him a subtle, almost feminine coquetry and a mild, almost imperceptible foppishness. He was very fond of black military frockcoats, which set off the fine paleness of his complexion. Nowadays he was an ageing dandy, and like a woman he regretfully watched the appearance of wrinkles on his face. His hair was receding. At first he had worn a wig, but then had taken a fancy to the white shining skin of his skull. Early baldness had come into fashion. His step was unstable, his legs were unsteady, but he had convinced himself this was due to his desire to seem – and to be – agile.

His father had taught him military drill from childhood and he still enjoyed the soothing effect of its precision and the absence of any conscious thought during parades. He was considered to be treacherous: he could break his word easily and unexpectedly and for no obvious reason. The real reason was that he simply failed to think things through – he opened his mouth, gave assurances and denials automatically, and thought about it later. Abroad, where he had realised for the first time that he owned and ruled half the world, he was reputed to be inscrutable. He liked foreign countries and foreigners best because there and with them he felt like a real sovereign. Apart from his palaces, only some of which were comfortable, and the towns, mostly small and chaotic, he found nothing memorable about Russia except the roads – barbarous, bumpy and muddy, and reeking revoltingly of dung. The villagers had a bestial look. But he appreciated the impressiveness of sheer space in terms of the miles shown on the map in his study, and the size of the population – fifty million. At home that figure and that space frightened him. In Europe he liked to talk about it – and to frighten others.

His reading and education, and his experience of the Court and the feud between his grandmother and father, had developed in him the qualities of subtlety, evasiveness, an understanding of human nature, and personal opportunism. He had a keen awareness of everything that either threatened or furthered his power. He had little understanding of politics and, finding himself at the centre of European affairs, had more or less leased the government of the state to Speransky. The time he had been obliged to devote to Europe had brought up many questions new to him. He felt that any worthy administration, or at least one that wished to be or to appear so, had to deal with these questions. Speransky was the perfect man for the post: he had learning, unusual for the son of a priest, was capable of thinking logically and introducing innovations, and he was a born communicator.

The Emperor liked Speransky's modesty, his fluent speech, his profound deference and incredible powers of work, though lately he had received many proofs to the contrary. Presented by Speransky's enemies, these had nevertheless been highly plausible. Besides, Speransky seemed too capable by far. Napoleon had given him his portrait as a gift – a sign of excessive familiarity, insulting to the monarch. This son of a priest had been selected and accorded distinction because of his intellect and his humility. He had signed the two edicts drawn up by Speransky directed against the ignorance of the aristocracy. Remembering the advice of his lifelong friend Stroganov, the Emperor had also unhesitatingly signed the edict for increased taxation of the nobility.

When the edicts were made public the general outrage had frightened him, though Speransky had forewarned him about this. The Tilsit peace had angered the nobility and taxation embittered them. War with Napoleon was drawing near. He was not particularly brave; although he had spent the last five years in the wars he could not get used to the sight of fighting – the blood, the corpses and the stench of the battlefields – and he had cried like a woman. He had no doubts that if war broke out, Russia would lose and his power would inevitably collapse. He started to question the State Secretary's loyalty; he might betray him, using the war to his advantage if he wanted a new political order. The Minister's friendship with Napoleon and his idolisation of the Frenchman were common knowledge; reports made it clear that he often exceeded his powers. These were ominous signs. For six months Speransky's house had been under surveillance by de Sanglin of the Secret Department of Police. The Emperor had elevated his father's faithful servant, Arakcheyev, a common, ignorant petty nobleman who called himself nothing but 'your humble slave'; his old-fashioned loyalty was touching. Speransky spoke to him like a European, creating the impression that every edict he signed would be praised in the next day's issue of *Le Moniteur*. This was fame, but the situation was dangerous, exhausting and, in his estimation, unnecessary and potentially harmful. Sometimes Speransky surprised him by his unexpectedly penetrating opinions and he felt suspicious, envious and upset.

Count Arakcheyev did not speak French, but he had a knowledge of artillery matters and drill – and in the latter he and the Emperor were keen rivals. Alexander was surrounded by people who had either known about the murder of his father – as he himself had – or had plotted it. Arakcheyev had been his father's only faithful servant, and his father's friendship with him justified the son and freed him from the sin of parricide. Talking to Arakcheyev was like talking to an old valet of his father's, and made him feel younger.

It would soon be ten years since the assassination and the beginning of his own reign. His torso had grown heavier, his belly sagged and he had to wear a corset; his face had grown even paler. He was German by origin but his face had lost its character in constant travelling like a world-famous actor's. Only the smile and the white plump face remained German.

He watched his younger brothers with a gloomy eye. He knew the Moscow gossip. Everybody was waiting for a chance to replace him with one of them. Two of his daughters had died in infancy. The court doctor, an Englishman, tried to comfort him: the Emperor was still young; he would have heirs. The monarch looked at the Englishman and became pensive:

'No, my friend,' he told him, 'God does not like my children.'

The old diplomat de Maistre, hearing of this exchange, maintained that the Emperor did not want children because he did not want premature heirs, he himself having been one.

His brothers worried him. He realised it might be just his imagination but he had a vague sense of danger. His mother's behaviour in the last two winters had been particularly bizarre: she had moved with her sons from nearby Pavlovsk to forsaken Gatchina. The lady-in-waiting Volkonskaya had recently told him that the Empress had withdrawn her sons from their playmates, who were supposed to have been too great a distraction for them, the young Benckendorff, for example, her friend's son. The Emperor knew nothing of the people surrounding his brothers and found it impossible to keep an eye on them. His mother guarded her sons like a tigress guarding her cubs. The only way to tear or loosen this bond was to move them into his Palace, away from Gatchina – the place he was afraid of because of childhood memories. He had already thought of a suitable location for them. The new wing of the Palace where his sisters had stayed before they got married and moved out was vacant. A suitable pretext had to be found or his mother would never agree to it. At that time an incident occurred which gave rise to much gossip: the fourteen-year-old Grand Duke Nicholas had a tutor, Adelung, who taught him Latin and morals. The Emperor had been informed that, tired of morals, the Grand Duke had gone up to his tutor and, pretending to be giving him a hug, had suddenly bitten him in the shoulder and trodden painfully on his toes. The pretext had been found – education. His brothers' wildness was intolerable. He had told Speransky in passing that there was now a need for a new *special* educational establishment.

3

By the time the guests arrived the Minister had changed his clothes. He knew how to dress well and enjoyed doing so, having been a dandy in his youth. He wore a smoke-coloured tail-coat and white stockings in the English fashion.

He went downstairs to the drawing-room through the women's half of the house – spacious and adorned with potted plants by the windows and along the walls.

It did not look like a government official's residence. The faint odour of a tea-plant in blossom filled the room. The bureau had been locked for two years and contained the plan of a huge project the Minister had kept secret from anyone, intending to devote himself to it whole-heartedly when he was free of various minor matters. It was the plan of a philosophical and moral novel, *The Father of a Family*. But minor matters kept multiplying and the project was still awaiting its realisation. It was the secret hope of his heart. Deep within himself he believed he had been born for creative writing.

Illichevsky was the first to arrive. The Minister had shared a desk with him at the Aleksandr Nevsky Seminary. Recently he had remembered his old friend and appointed him Governor of Tomsk. His former classmate, summoned from the Ukraine where he had been teaching rhetoric in a seminary in Poltava, had come to thank him.

He was a tall man, narrow-shouldered, with fair hair and a pale face, and had cunning little pewter-coloured eyes. At college he had been nicknamed The Candle, or sometimes *Pater Damianus*. The Minister had not seen him for five years.

His old comrade was obviously nervous; his little eyes glittered.

'Gracious Father.' He addressed Speransky with his seminary accent, and with a sly, deferential glance as if asking how he should conduct himself towards the Minister.

'Hello, Damian,' Speransky answered, his tone indicating that he had not forgotten the seminary and remembered old friends. Both had been top students – Illichevsky had been first in poetry and rhetoric, Speransky in oratory and philosophy. Both were rivals in the arts of good manners, courtesy and persuasiveness, and the old Rector had called them 'eels', saying that they 'slipped through one's fingers'.

But now Illichevsky's obvious weakness was his greed. Through half-lowered eyelashes he had already scrutinised the room. The unassuming furniture had apparently surprised him, though the silver candlesticks on the round table had not escaped his attention. His friend had evidently advanced much farther in life than he had.

'Are your mother and your brother Kozma well?' he asked the Minister. 'How are they?'

'They are well, thank you,' replied Speransky.

Speransky's brother was a provincial priest, his old mother made communion bread and now lived in the country in peace and quiet.

In accordance with his rule of dispersing the individuals he knew personally about the Empire with the aim of acquiring information that could be of some future use, the Minister had appointed Illichevsky Governor of Tomsk in spite of his cupidity, and was going to talk to him tonight about his appointed task of eradicating bribery and corruption in Siberia.

Soon two more guests arrived – old Samborsky and his son-in-law Malinovsky. The Minister greeted the old man with a quick low bow. The old Court Chaplain Samborsky had been the Minister's patron since childhood. It was he who had brought the Minister's wife and her mother from London where he had served as the Mission priest. He had been Alexander's confessor when he was a boy, and had then served his sister in Hungary. He had travelled a lot and was now retired and enjoying his influence at Court.

He did not look like a Russian priest – he was shaven and had good English. His son-in-law Malinovsky was lean, upright and tightly buttoned. His ruddy face, grey hair and clear eyes made him look English. London, his favourite city, where he had spent a long time, had left its imprint on him. He led his elderly father-in-law by the arm.

Speransky rang the bell for tea to be served. They were having tea *à l'anglaise* – in the drawing-room, at the round table. The secretary Franz Ivanovich joined them.

They struck up the kind of conversation the Minister, a master of rhetoric and dialectic, was so fond of, moving freely between the professional and the informal. Samborsky had heard everything that was going on at Court. Without asking direct questions or demanding direct answers, Speransky was able to find out from him everything he needed to know. Malinovsky was a person who could be trusted, but Illichevsky was superfluous today. The Minister led the conversation. Smiling, he remembered how Illichevsky had beaten him at cards at the seminary.

Malinovsky burst out laughing. Illichevsky cheered up.

'I gave up gambling a long time ago,' Speransky said. 'I've noticed that I fly into a temper easily and make enemies with the person who has beaten me. In my position that is dangerous. It's a shame though. The old Adam is strong in me.'

And with the same smile, without pausing, he said to Samborsky:

'Well, I think we'll soon have secular education.'

Making use of various people in various ways, Speransky was trying to ensure that the Grand Dukes' school education would be a civilian, not a military one, and that they would then enter university, setting an example for the nobility. In this case his 'examinations edict' which had caused so much fuss and anger would become indisputable and indispensable. Samborsky knew about his intentions and approved of them.

In order to prepare for university the Grand Dukes would first have to go to a college. This would not only be useful to them but would also remove them from the uncertainties of the Court, its bustle and its gossip. A special college would be exactly the right place for them.

Illichevsky listened to him meekly – he might know these men well, but they were too powerful for him, above the league of a mere teacher of poetry from Poltava. His little eyes were shining. Unconsciously his fingers stroked the base of a silver candlestick. Speransky noticed it and smiled, changing the subject to Siberia, the corruption and bribery that had taken root there. The Governor in charge of the area lived in the capital and ruled from a distance, while the strangest things happened in the remote provinces. One fine day they would not be able to find Siberia in its place, it would all be looted out of existence.

'You are the only hope, Damian. You must bring order to Tomsk first, and then …'

Illichevsky took his hand off the candlestick.

'We haven't enough honest, loyal people, just a handful, that's all,' Speransky said to Samborsky. 'The older ones are wallowing in corruption; the young – those who are honest – keep quiet. In the beginning was the Word, but our civil servants still can't put two words together!'

It was his favourite topic and complaint. A structure was needed to embrace, comprehend and bring Russia to order. The laws should be impeccably drawn up and strictly implemented. The generals who had extended the Empire had not only been unable to create the balance which was the focus of government, but even opposed the concept of order, because they did not understand it. The country needed efficient civil servants from the humblest level. He needed people who would share his views and assist him.

'The people are not bound together by any belief,' Malinovsky said suddenly.

Speransky looked at him obviously pleased. He knew what Malinovsky meant.

The Minister talked and his oriental eyes were half-closed, as if unseeing; his retreating forehead lost its frown. He spoke without pause, softly and suavely, and his friends looked at him spellbound. At the end of every speech he made, always greeted with absolute silence, a new idea about the reform of some branch of the law or the creation of some new institution would always cross his mind, though it usually seemed to have no obvious connection with the subject of the conversation. In his youth he had given sermons and now, as in former days, he relished the perfection of the words he conceived.

The study was his accustomed place. He looked at the English grandfather clock, and its big pendulum which swung slowly behind the glass door according to mechanical principles he knew nothing of was as necessary to him as the silent audience.

When the Minister spoke he knew that nobody would interrupt him. He was aware of his oratorical power and he had tested it in the Palace. The Emperor had never interrupted him and by the end of every conversation seemed persuaded and agreeable. But as soon as the Minister had left the imperial presence, his logic would crumble to ashes and the Tsar would grow bored and forgetful.

The Minister spoke of the sort of people he needed. Talking of people's characters, he considered the Emperor. What sort of people were in greater demand: those with sense or those with sensibility? A kind heart seemed to count for much. But when you heard the words 'a sensitive person' you thought of a person without sense. A 'sensitive person' was like a machine that did not comprehend its own workings, a machine that kept on behaving according to blind habit. Such a person was a spring wound up by a particular upbringing.

Karamzin's female readers were unable to understand this.

It was quiet outside. This was the place where twenty years before, the Empress's favourite, Prince Gregory Potyomkin, used to come to rest and dispel his depression, to bite his nails and smash expensive vases. It was quiet inside the Minister's house – his daughter and her grumbling grandmother were in the back rooms. Franz Ivanovich, the Minister's most frequent and most taciturn companion, sat next to him. The muffled tones of the clock slowly struck eleven and cut the speaker short.

He had finished sooner than he had expected. He needed people with humane principles; reason should prevail over emotion and control it. Without this there could be no order. The mind should be educated in the same way as habits were formed by upbringing. But upbringing by itself could not educate the mind. The nobility lived in dissipation, the clergy in ignorance.

Illichevsky's little eyes were shining; the former philosopher and teacher of rhetoric had recalled the seminary rector's sermons and the disputes they used to have. Stroking his narrow beard, he said, in the manner of the seminary:

'Merciful father! The mind can be aware of the parts but only virtue can comprehend the whole.'

'Yes,' said his former fellow student, 'yes, Damian, you have understood me perfectly – *la vertu est un élément, peut-être, le plus rare*,' and the seminary word 'virtue' had suddenly assumed a Jacobin sound in the French translation.

Illichevsky complained to Speransky: his son Olosya was growing up – a bright boy with a vivid imagination who wrote fluently and composed the most marvellous and faultless poems. But he was too young for the university and was unsuitable for the seminary because his inclinations were secular, not ecclesiastic. To take him to Tomsk would mean to extinguish his gift.

The complaint was well-timed.

Speransky answered eagerly and without hesitation:

'There are a number of very good schools here: the English one – Collins', the French ones – Muralte, Deboir. If you don't want him to be taught by the French – wait. We'll find a place for your Olosya, Damian.'

The new Governor of Tomsk left shortly after this. Just as he had done in the old days he spoke to Speransky in Latin:

'*Pax tecum. Ave.*'

The Minister asked Malinovsky and old Samborsky to stay on. And as soon as the door had shut, he told them what he had been thinking about and what had now taken shape in his mind.

If the Grand Dukes were to go to university, they should be adequately prepared beforehand. In order to take them away from military drill and the habits of the Court, and to rescue them from the hands of the sycophants in charge of their upbringing who were only anxious to please the imperial family, a special college should be established, a Russian one. He had already thought of a name, and reading Plutarch, he had come across an appropriate one – the Lyceum, or *Lykeion*. The Grand Dukes would attend the college just like any other students. In due course those students would develop into the Minister's assistants and would take up important posts in the service of the state.

It was a bold new project.

Samborsky doubted if the Tsar would like it, or, more importantly, whether his sister would approve of it. But Malinovsky warmed to the idea. His face glowed. In the last five years he, like many others, had been considering Russia's need for a new breed of people and how they should be educated.

He was six years older than Speransky, and having devoted thirty years to the civil service he had always had a feel for innovations and those who made them. He himself was the founder of the Moscow Philanthropic Committee and Director of Workhouses. He had been a 'new man' in his youth too – he had spent three years in the Russian Mission in England, where he had married Samborsky's daughter. His time in London deeply influenced him, and he preserved his English habits for the rest of his life – he spoke in a calm, measured tone as English people spoke. When he grew excited, however, it became obvious that he was a priest. In England he had studied a business new to Russia – manufacturing – and had become convinced of its effectiveness. Then he had gone to Turkey in the diplomatic service; he could speak Turkish and had translated the Hebrew Bible. He had been preparing himself for the career of a politician. When he had stayed in England, he had come to the firm conclusion that Russia was governed by aristocratic despots, by the master-grandees, and that its people lived in a degraded situation, suppressed by superstitions, ignorance, slavery and drunkenness. Slavery corrupted both the slaves and the masters. Russia needed a parliament and deputies who would draw up new laws and abolish serfdom forever, and then the public spirit that Russia so lacked would emerge. Now the dreams of his youth were close to their realisation, unless the rapacious Bonaparte were to interfere. There was one more hindrance: the old officials were all corrupt, secretaries took bribes, heads of departments were lazy and fond of luxury. These bureaucrats should be removed and new blood educated. But how could all these new ideas be implemented by young blood? It wasn't only the worthy ones who would be selected, because of the same old Russian trouble – nepotism and opportunism. A virtuous person would be able to find his way, but the problem was that nowadays their places were being occupied by the unworthy.

Speransky had no answers to these questions. How and out of whom was the new breed to be created? But he smiled like a person who had long resolved such doubts.

The Minister picked up a sheet of paper and a pencil; the taciturn Franz Ivanovich had sharpened the pencil well. He quickly outlined a plan for a *special Lycée*. The new institution of learning would bear the name of the Ancient Greek *Lykeion* in Athens where Aristotle had walked and talked with his students. The new generation of leaders of the state was to start with their complete separation from their families. The youths would be taken from different social classes and tested in morals and general knowledge. They would form a group of boys clothed and fed in the same way. They would address each other and live as equals just as they had done at the original *Lykeion* in Ancient Greece. They would be taught in Russian. Thus the public spirit that Malinovsky had talked about would be created. The boys would not be allowed access to the Court, although the Emperor wanted the college to be in the Palace. But the college was to be a place of learning, and the sycophantic habits of the Court would corrupt the new students and ruin everything. If the boys appeared at Court, it would be only after classes – to spend their leisure time with the Grand Dukes. True camaraderie would be sacred. The number of students? The fewer the better – ten? The number would be in inverse proportion to standards. No more than fifteen, the same age as the Grand Dukes Nicholas and Michael. They would study Literature, History, Geography, Logic and Oratory, Mathematics, Physics and Chemistry, Philosophy, Natural and Public Law, Moral Sciences, gradually passing on from one subject to another, doing their best to master each in turn. They would be taught informally; their capacities would be stimulated by discussion. Inspired by the example of their classmates, the Grand Dukes would in time become virtuous, though scarcely gifted, for talent was the voice of Nature and the Minister considered it impossible to produce it where none already existed. Thus the future of the state would be provided for. The younger Duke, in whom undesirable qualities had been observed, would no doubt improve, and rid himself of those bouts of anger that were common to all three brothers – they took after their father. Nor would he be hypocritical and perfidious like the present Tsar.

With clear-thinking and open minds, free from the stagnant habits of their fathers, the young men would graduate from the Lycée ready to serve their fatherland and state, honest and intelligent and sharing the ageing Minister's views. They would be the figures he would surround himself with, and would earn the major appointments.

'Will there be any corporal punishment?' Malinovsky asked softly.

His practicality appealed to Speransky.

'No, Vasily Fyodorovich,' the Minister said tersely, 'not because of any aristocratic privilege, but simply because it is humiliating and offensive and leaves lifelong marks. We shall be fortunate in putting the rod aside – for the Grand Dukes' sake.'

The main problem lay in the selection of teachers.

Where to find the men capable of educating the new breed? Foreigners were detached and disinterested, they would be unsuitable – and why indeed should Russian children be in the care of foreigners? The new school could easily do without them, especially since the teaching would be in Russian. Would Malinovsky himself like to teach, the man standing at the baptismal font of this new breed and their new school? The Minister had not thought of it before, but the idea had suddenly sprung to mind.

'I'll speak to Minister Martynov about you and we'll come to a decision.'

Malinovsky thanked him gratefully. But wasn't the young Kunitsyn worthier and better qualified?

Kunitsyn was a seminarian from Tver and Speransky had been showing increasing interest in his future. Kunitsyn had studied for three years in Heidelberg and Göttingen, where his attainments were said to have been brilliant. He had read Law and Philosophy and had only recently returned from his studies.

'Yes, Kunitsyn, of course.'

The Minister wrote down the name of Kunitsyn.

Little Samborsky sat like a statue, sunk into the leather easy-chair. His sunken face was serene – he was asleep.

The clock struck midnight. Malinovsky took the old man carefully out of the chair as babies are taken out of the cradle. They wrapped him up in his big thick fur-coat and deposited him carefully in his covered sleigh. The Minister saw his old mentor to the gate.

A shadow darted across the road near the Tauride Gardens and disappeared. Was it a nocturnal reveller coming home, or a robber sneaking about, or a spy? The gate was sound and the locks were heavy.

He returned to his room. He had sent the secretary to bed. In the next room the being most precious to him, his daughter, was asleep, and so was her spiteful and grumbling grandmother whom Providence had sent him as an example of female wretchedness. He paced the thick soft carpets with his great soundless steps. Everyone was asleep and he was alone in the study, the only person awake. His inspiration had gradually subsided. He added one more paragraph, concerning ushers – one per four students: lack of discipline could ruin the new institution. The ushers would keep order and report any violations to the director. Privileges would be granted on grounds of academic progress in order not to cultivate favourites and informers, as had happened at his seminary. One such, Illichevsky, had just sat at this table. Speransky hoped his friend would not be caught embezzling in Siberia; Damian had been greedy from his youth. His son would be welcome at the Lycée – he might be an improvement on his father. The most important thing was that he shouldn't let this whole project fall into the hands of the Minister of Education, Razumovsky, Speransky's worst enemy. He would speak frankly to His Majesty about it.

He put the outline into the folder for most urgent business and started to read and correct the pages that he had written the previous morning – the memorandum to His Majesty. His face changed. The only kind of flattery that had any effect on Alexander was absolute, unqualified obsequiousness, when his interlocutor seemed to dissolve, melt, cease to exist as a personality. With a pale smile on his face Speransky modified his tone: needlessly, but in appropriate places, he inserted little addresses to the Emperor – 'Your

Majesty' and 'Most Gracious Sire'. He called them compliments. Making the final copy, he admired his handwriting – simple and clear. It was his hand that had brought him so far.

He finished and gave a sigh, cracked his knuckles and went up to the window. Showing dimly through the dead trees he could see the deserted palace of Grigory Potyomkin, the former Moscow student expelled for laziness and truancy, inordinate in both talent and vice.

He stood by the window, deep in thought. Then he bared his gums in a sudden slow smile.

'Just like you I have to do it all alone, Prince Grigory,' he murmured, barely audibly. 'All over again. Don't be offended.'

4

They were standing by the window in his study and the Emperor, with his palm raised to his ear – the pose indicating that he wished to seem attentive – was listening.

The Grand Dukes would be educated exactly like the other boys and would then enter university. Speransky suggested the appointment of the experienced Malinovsky as Principal, and also recommended a young and learned Göttingenian, Kunitsyn, whom he knew personally, as one of the masters.

The Emperor had not yet formed any personal view of all this but he could very well picture the anger and amazement of the Dowager Empress. His rooms in Catherine the Great's spacious palace were decorated in delicate tones. He had wanted them to look unassuming, somewhat languorous, without all that variegated Asian brightness that Catherine had so admired. There was no mixture of Chinese silks, Dutch stoves and Indian vases here, a minimum of gilding and only the most essential furnishing. Unlike Napoleon's excessively grand court, the Emperor craved simplicity of line, plenty of empty space, and the colour blue. He dressed simply: in preference to all his military uniforms he had chosen a black frock-coat with silver buttons as his daily attire. His grandmother had built a special palace for him but he disliked it because of certain memories and preferred the huge older palace which made him feel younger.

He thought he had seen the Commandant's daughter passing along the alley. She was an attractive creature. Whistling, he listened to the Minister and cast rapid glances out of the window, screwing up his eyes. He had always exaggerated his short-sightedness and showed it off. His expression became mysterious. He was slightly deaf and might quite easily have missed most of the presentation even if he had not been so distracted that day. The idea of sending his brothers to university, away from the army, vaguely appealed to him, but at the same time seemed absurd.

Speransky particularly insisted on not letting the new Lycée pass into the hands of the Ministry of Education, since it was a special institution, which needed special supervision. Razumovsky and Speransky were sworn enemies. The Emperor promised not to let Razumovsky see the memorandum. Talking to Speransky about family life or children, he had always felt his superiority over him and treated him condescendingly. The Minister spoke about these subjects with emotion; such sentimentality was now in fashion. Speransky's family life interested the Emperor and he had received precise information about it. Speransky was a widower, lived in a small house, worshipped his daughter, and so on. Alexander enjoyed the innocence of it all, which at the same time enhanced his feeling of superiority. The only aspect of the Minister's life that drew any respect from him was his rumoured closeness to his dead wife's sister.

From the windows he could see the distant perspective of the old park. The Commandant's very young, rosy-cheeked daughter was out of sight. He suggested that Speransky should accompany him to see the new wing and suddenly screwed up his eyes again, this time without affectation. A smile seemed to him to hover over the Minister's expressionless oriental face. He frowned, looked closer and saw no smile. Speransky's face had its usual inscrutable expression, inclined to suggest obsequiousness. The valet helped the Emperor to put on his thick-wadded frock-coat.

It had already started to thaw. The lion muzzles on the palace walls were opening their jaws – the taste of the previous century, which seemed absurd now. Catching sight of the Emperor's black frock-coat and the Minister's fur-coat, the sentries along the walls stood silently to attention. The Emperor looked at them and involuntarily appraised their posture. It was chilly, and he shivered.

They were satisfied with the condition of the wing, though some refurbishing was needed.

The wing was right under his nose so that the students could be easily observed. The question of his brothers' education had been solved.

The Emperor could only vaguely imagine what the future Lycée would be like. He assumed that his brothers' classmates might be able to go to St Petersburg once or twice a week. But a cab from Tsarskoye Selo to Petersburg cost twenty-five roubles. He might have believed that people of all classes had horses, or perhaps he had no idea of the cost of a cab. But the Minister had no objection – he always tried not to weary the Emperor with petty details.

Meanwhile the Ladies-in-Waiting Wing was in a state of excitement – the ladies' heads appeared for a moment at the window and immediately disappeared. When the Emperor and his Minister were returning to the Palace, they encountered old Volkonskaya and her young niece. Both ladies curtsied. He heard the usual whisper behind his back: '*Notre ange!*' He hated this whispering, but did not know what he would do without the sound in his ears. He let Speransky go and went into his rooms upstairs. He would go for a walk later – he hoped to run into the Commandant with his young daughter.

A footman proffered him a letter on a tray. He perused it – it was from his mother. She always referred to herself in the third person, as had been the rule for inferior persons at the Prussian court. A week later would bring the anniversary of his father's death. His mother was reminding him importunately of the fact, not for the first time – as if he had forgotten or could forget this day. It had always been the day of her triumph and was unbearable for him, and not only because of its memories. There would be a day-long service at the Peter and Paul Fortress. His mother would stand by the grave on a special platform, and he and the rest of the congregation would be below. It was the kind of occasion he found intolerable, as if it were a public humiliation.

His mother's reminder was crude.

The idea of a walk in the park and an encounter with the Commandant suddenly seemed impossible. He went white with fury and his big chin started to tremble. When his tears fell, they were like a natural phenomenon: they bounced onto his chest like hail and he felt immediately relieved. But he restrained himself and turned even paler. The footman stood waiting for orders.

Alexander was breathing loudly. In a husky trembling voice, he asked:

'Have you been sniffing tobacco again?'

He pinched the footman cruelly, and stamping loudly with his boots, which suddenly felt heavy, took a few paces and collapsed into a chair.

Tears welled up in his eyes.

The footmen hurried to take his boots off and loosen his corset; his heavy white belly relaxed and he started to breathe more freely. He stared at the white skin covered with golden hairs and gradually felt calmer.

Five minutes later the moment had passed. He had regained his composure. He summoned Volkonsky and calmly gave him his orders. Then he ordered the memorandum on the special Lycée to be delivered to Minister Razumovsky. Speransky must be watched. The phrase 'from all social classes' and indeed the whole concept of the Lycée was so daring that it might actually make sense.

5

When old Razumovsky received the plan for the new educational institution – another one! – at first he paid it no attention. He was feeling depressed – the state that made his servants, his daughter and subordinates particularly afraid of him.

He had been summoned from Moscow the previous year in order to perform the tedious duties of Minister of Education. From then on he had not seen visitors, busy with refurbishing his home, and missed his Moscow life. A house had been built for him in Gorokhovy Court: it looked like a boyar's palace; it was constructed of solid oak beams; the garden, with ponds in which rare fish swam, stretched for four versts. He had lived there among his paintings, books and flowers, getting rid of his wife and confining his son in the Schlüsselburg Fortress, not allowing anyone to get close to him, in a proud solitude that frightened the bustling city; the count's cruelty was Moscow gossip.

The son of a herdsman who had later become one of the first grandees of Moscow, Razumovsky did not treat his servants, subordinates or ordinary noblemen as human beings. He loved plants, and cultivated them on his countryside estate near Moscow. His foreign gardeners had grown a new species which they called *Razumovskia*. It was a bluish, thin-leafed, astonishingly prickly juniper. Its heavy red berries ripened in autumn. It was for this plant bearing his name, rather than his daughter, that Razumovsky nurtured fatherly feelings. In his conservatory *Razumovskia* shrubs stood in serried rows on both sides of the path, so that the prickles caught visitors' clothes. The old man smiled with amusement. When the Emperor had stayed in Moscow, Razumovsky had introduced himself to him. The Emperor had been allured by the old man's French – his pronunciation, that of an old aristocrat, his almost carnivorous grin, his delicate hands fumbling with his lorgnon, his stooped frail body which reminded one who had never seen Ukrainian choristers of a French aristocrat. That was how Razumovsky had come to be appointed Minister.

Having moved to St Petersburg, he had bought some land, and had been building and rebuilding his palace with a huge garden on the Fontanka river, between the Obukhovsky and Semyonovsky bridges. He had never been seen in the Ministry. He had been missing his Moscow estate and now only the creation of his new palace and garden was of any interest to him. The only person who had access to him was Joseph de Maistre, the envoy of the now powerless King of Sardinia. The two old men would shut themselves up in the Minister's library, which contained not a single Russian book, and he would listen to the fervent Frenchman for hours, occasionally interrupting him in a low voice. The old footman would serve black coffee in the library – the Minister scorned the hot chocolate which was fashionable among the upstarts. *Razumovskia*, his pride and joy, was here too, growing in a Chinese porcelain pot.

Only after a few days did he return to the file from the Emperor, the memorandum on the special Lycée. The very word 'special' in the heading stunned him. He recalled that the matter concerned the young Grand Dukes, and sent for de Maistre. They locked themselves in the library. The Count was still feeling low, longing for the countryside and lamenting the absence of his favourite volumes, not all of which had yet been brought from Moscow. The hated St Petersburg hung unpleasantly over his thoughts. The Lycée project, however, aroused his interest; he had himself been educated in a special mini-ature 'Academy' on the Tenth Line on Vasilyevsky Island, St Petersburg, with only a few other boys. The court of the time had taken a great interest in this 'Academy of the Tenth Line'.

He liked the term 'Lycée'. It reminded him of his youth which had so suddenly ended and been followed immediately by old age. In those days the Parisian Lycée had been the talk of the city. This had been an academy for women patronised by the King and the comte d'Artois where Marmontel and La Harpe taught literature and Condorcet mathematics, and where the most charming ladies arranged rendezvous. The Revolution had put an end to it all. The heads of most of the teachers and their pretty students had rolled.

Bewildered, de Maistre fell silent. He smiled when the Count remembered a Parisian song about the Lycée and sang softly:

> *Là tout le beau sexe s'amuse*
> *Du carré de l'hypothénuse*
> *Et de Newton.*

That was why he liked Razumovsky. When they sat like this in his conserva-tory or library, the *ancien régime* was alive in the Russian grandee's rooms: as if there had never been a revolution or that villain Bonaparte. He was aware of Razumovsky's doubtful pedigree but he admitted that the Minister behaved like a real aristocrat – childishly cruel, learned and frivolous.

De Maistre prompted the Minister:

> *Voulez-vous savoir la chimie,*
> *Approfondir l'astronomie?*

They talked. De Maistre was the poet of court gossip; he and Razumovsky referred to people by their nicknames. Naryshkin, whose wife was the Emperor's mistress, was 'the happy spouse'. The Frenchman called Speransky 'your Jacobin', and following him the Minister called him 'our Jacobin'. Gradually the Minister's face hardened. Even the mention of Speransky's name filled him with hatred.

'There is something tree-like about all these seminarians,' he said. 'The only quality of trees that they lack is the capacity for silence.'

When de Maistre was taking his leave, the *Razumovskia* caught his sleeve with its prickles. They burst out laughing again – though this time the Frenchman's was forced. Count de Maistre valued his attire.

Two weeks later the plan for the special Lycée was revised. Razumovsky returned Speransky's memorandum to the Emperor with a brief memorandum of his own and a lengthy note by de Maistre composed in a form he had mastered better than any contemporary authors – the informal epistle.

The Emperor read the papers as soon as he received them. He was fond of reading and appreciated fine literature. He disapproved of popular novels – he read them from cover to cover and then reread some passages, especially those of a dubious kind, marking them in pencil. In the same way certain philosophers took his fancy. The fashion of the time obliged him to be polite; he spoke of Enlightenment and Virtue like many other European kings. The proclamations that he signed always made reference to the Russian people, the army of the Orthodox, the virtue of the citizens and Russia's exalted destiny. He signed them without reading them. That was why he liked the philosophers, who sought to refute everything that, by virtue of his status, he had to affirm over and over again – Russia's greatness, love of everything Russian, and so forth.

De Maistre, whose views were similar to Razumovsky's, professed himself against reason and knowledge, his arguments, however, appearing extensively buttressed by reason and knowledge. Were the Russians created for learning? They had not yet proved it. The Romans had been profoundly ignorant; they had produced neither great artists or sculptors, nor any mathematicians, but they had been great warriors. Cicero had called Archimedes a nonentity. In general, reason and knowledge made a man absolutely incapable of great undertakings; he became incapable of making any allowance for other people's opinions or being critical of authority, incapable of innovation. Russia did not need knowledge; the building of schools which now stood empty had brought the state to financial ruin. Its schools were fine hostelries in a country where no one travelled. In them the heads of the young were stuffed with superfluous rubbish and habits of thought most harmful for youthful minds: systematisation and abstract ideas.

The French system was an introduction to materialism. The only thing the young should know was that God, who had created man, had made government absolutely necessary in society and that obedience was crucial. All other teachings that stirred up philosophical thoughts in young minds, even if they were taught by well-meaning people, were dangerous. The fatal consequences of such doctrines in France were well-known.

Natural history was useless. A young man from a noble family should rather agree to take part in three campaigns and fight in six battles than study chemistry; it was an idle science. For a warlike nation such as Russia, learning was not only useless but harmful. It destroyed courage. The best teachers were the clergy, but not the half-literate Russian clergy. New institutions of learning should be modelled on the Jesuit system. Students should have no dealings with the outside world: they should live in isolation, as if on an island. The young should be versatile and obedient. They should be constantly supervised. A strict rule of silence should be kept. At night students should sleep in separate rooms, in order to avoid any communication. The doors to the dormitories should be of glass and the dormitory floor should be lit at both ends. An approved person should walk the corridor all night long and watch over the youths' repose as over the sick. Every fortnight those who made the greatest progress should be encouraged by the award of a cross like that, say, of St Vladimir or St Anne.

The Emperor leafed through Razumovsky's note and read about the aim of the Lycée – the preparation of boys 'from the most illustrious families' for the most prestigious appointments of state. Speransky's memorandum was attached to this paper. The first paragraph concerned the occupancy of the most important posts and the selection of students 'from all social classes'. On a separate page was the order for the appointments of Malinovsky and Kunitsyn.

He read the pages written in de Maistre's clear hand. He underlined in pencil the paragraph he liked most of all – about the students' sleeping arrangements, the glass doors and the night vigils. The gallery in the wing was wholly suited for this purpose. Under no circumstances was any dissipation to be countenanced. He was disgusted by the coarse literature his brother Constantine revelled in, chuckling and rubbing his hands as he read. The Emperor favoured the veil of suggestion, the decency of ambiguity; sometimes he would reread the state laws that concerned moral misdemeanours. What he enjoyed reading was not only the descriptions of the situations that were the subjects of the laws, but also the thoroughness with which every imaginable misdemeanour was catered for by its particular law, which he found exquisite pleasure in studying. Such intellectual pleasures were, it seemed, appreciated only by a select few. His brother Constantine was too coarse and simple-minded. With a smile the Emperor crossed out the paragraph that mentioned crosses. The Frenchman was not familiar with Russian customs: there would be a great fuss from all holders of St Vladimir and St Anne crosses, the young men would start to turn up their noses and discipline would be undermined. He finished with the first two papers, walked about his study, went out to the white hall, returned, and in order to protract the pleasure, put the reading aside. With the same purpose he went downstairs and took a walk in the park with his hands folded behind his back. His adjutant accompanied him, but the Emperor was unwilling to talk. He made only abrupt remarks to which the young man replied respectfully with longer sentences.

'Rather fresh.'

'Yes, Your Majesty, spring is long overdue but it hasn't arrived yet.'

'Windy.'

'Yes, Sire, the wind has been blowing since early in the morning; it might become warmer in the evening.'

The Emperor enjoyed such pointless conversations.

Abruptly, in military fashion, he turned round and brought the walk to an end. Arakcheyev was waiting for him.

The General stood upright. Seeing the Emperor, he moved towards him with his whole body, and, as was his habit at their meetings, the Emperor embraced him. They began the kind of conversation both were keen on: full of sighs, sudden smiles and meaningful silences. Arakcheyev's features were impassive; he did not take his eyes off the Tsar. His eyes were dull, his wrinkled face sorrowful. Some secret sorrow permanently weighed upon this simple, stern, efficient and impeccably reliable artillery commander. Was it the same sorrow that sometimes caused the Emperor's tears and anger? He found it particularly pleasant to comfort the General. Gaps in their conversations opened up more and more often – a sign of the Emperor's emotional fatigue, when for long periods he would stare into space. At such moments Arakcheyev kept a meaningful silence, aware of the significance of the Emperor's behaviour. After the pause they would both smile.

The Emperor translated a few phrases from de Maistre's note for the General. The Frenchman's opinion of mathematics alarmed Arakcheyev.

'No, dear Sire, Your Majesty,' he said after a moment's thought, his thin but sonorous voice echoing with deep meaning. 'Teaching fortification is impossible without geometry; and without drawing it is impossible to master artillery. Only civilians can do without mathematics.'

The General believed that civilians should not be allowed to meddle in or upset the smooth running of military matters. He realised however the importance of educating civilians.

But he agreed that both natural and human history were unnecessary subjects.

'The less one thinks about nature, the sounder one sleeps. As for history – God bless it! ...'

They burst out laughing.

'Dear sir, Your Majesty,' said Arakcheyev in a softer, lilting voice. 'I myself did not enjoy an expensive education, and I wonder, if we prepare young men for the main posts in the state, who is to be chosen? The true servant is the one who is loyal to his benefactor – poor but faithful, as I understand it.'

The Emperor nodded. In his conversations with Arakcheyev the vast state which, when talking to Speransky, he imagined as an unwieldy chunk of Europe turned into a huge patrimony inhabited by faithful and unfaithful servants.

'There should be no corporal punishment, I think.'

At this point Arakcheyev scratched his forehead.

'I believe there should,' he said slyly. 'The Grand Dukes are still very young; they might benefit from seeing others punished.'

But the Emperor did not give in, shook his head and seemed to cheer up.

Shortly afterwards, confident in their knowledge of the subject, they began to choose the school uniform. They went through the colours that would please the eye and would not be confused with the colours of the regiments. Their choice fell on the former uniform of the Tatar-Lithuanian Regiment, long out of use: a single-breasted dark-blue jacket, with red stand-up collar and cuffs of the same colour. There would be two tabs on the collar: junior – embroidered in silver, senior – in gold.

The Emperor crossed out the sentence containing the phrase 'the most illustrious families' in Razumovsky's document, and in Speransky's note the words 'from all social classes', and signed the paper in one flourish, omitting his first name, indicating that he had read and approved it.

The Grand Dukes' education would be confined to the Lycée, which would be equal in status to a university. Their classmates would be of noble background. The number of students at the school would be between twenty and fifty. Every student would have his own room with his own number on it.

Civil Councillor Malinovsky was to be appointed Principal. The Lycée premises were to be renovated as soon as possible. Now only the consent of the Dowager Empress was needed.

6

That summer the Dowager Empress was staying in Pavlovsk, which unlike Tsarskoye Selo was small, regular and could be taken in at a glance. It was in his father's taste – diametrically opposed in the minutest detail to his grandmother's.

The Emperor lowered his head and presented his cheek for his brothers' kisses. Nicholas, lean and slim in his tightly-strapped uniform, greeted him in

a voice that had broken. The Emperor gave him a surprised glance – Nicholas
had grown up. As usual his mother met him surrounded by her retinue of
elderly German ladies; old Lieven and Benckendorff were always at her side,
like bodyguards. She was dressed as she had always been when his father had
been alive and carried herself on her thick high heels as erect as a sentry. She
wore a toque with an ostrich feather, a necklace round her bare neck and
a black bow with a white Maltese cross on her left shoulder. Her dress was
rather short for her age, with a high waistline and puffed sleeves; her long
kid gloves reached up to the elbows of her plump arms. She was tightly laced
up and was out of breath immediately after giving her hasty, indistinct and
burring salutation.

The old court was the enemy of the new. The Emperor knew that it lived
on hearsay from Tsarskoye Selo and vague rumours of change.

They spent an hour walking in the park having their usual meaningless
conversation. Everything here reminded him of his father. At first his brothers
cast apprehensive glances but soon grew bolder. At the lake they separated
from the adults and talked loudly among themselves. They were accompanied
by their tutor, Lamsdorf, a decrepit German with a wrinkled face like a statue
of an old woman in the Hermitage. They paid no attention to him. Another
tutor, Glinka, a rather feeble-looking man, seemed, however, firmer and more
intelligent.

The Dowager Empress and the old ladies tried to engage Alexander in
conversation, but he was busy listening to his brothers. Being slightly deaf, he
could not hear what they were saying – only their voices.

Nicholas had interrupted his brother Michael a few times in his harsh
voice; forgetting himself, he laughed crudely and loudly. Michael sounded
hurt and spoke in a pathetic tone, on the verge of tears. Old Lieven suddenly
flushed and rushed towards them, short of breath, and cut him short. The
Emperor heard her talking German to his brothers, apparently forgetting that
etiquette demanded French. They replied roughly and capriciously.

They were ill-bred and rude.

His mother walked with the little slow steps she had used on ceremonial
occasions when his father had been alive.

A page followed her at a distance carrying a plain wicker chair – the
Empress used only that chair, a habit she had kept up since the days of her
reign, when such ingenuous simplicity had been in fashion. The Empress had
grown corpulent and was accustomed to the seat. At the pond they sat down,
the Emperor on the bench and the Empress on her chair. They admired the
crimson-coloured water – the sun had set. Sensitive to particular associations
of feeling, the Empress had grown used to watching sunsets and sunrises at
Pavlovsk as she had once done when living here; whereas at Gatchina, which

reminded her of the rough and pugnacious temper of her husband, she would shoot rabbits driven towards her by the hunters.

The tallow candles in high pewter candlesticks were lit in the round hall and the youngest lady-in-waiting sat down at the harpsichord. The pages waited upon the gathering. Without turning her head, the Empress lowered her hand and stretched her fingers behind her shoulder; a page gave her a fan. It was his father's gesture. The tallow candles hissed, smoked and spluttered. As a sign of favour the Emperor suggested a game of billiards to Nicholas. The billiard table was not a full-size one, and had been custom-made for the Grand Dukes. The Empress had made the balls with her own hands; she was fond of bone carving and good at it. Old Lieven flattered her, saying that there were only two Russian monarchs who had understood this art – Peter the Great and she herself. Both courts knew about the Emperor's weakness: whatever game he played he liked to win. Lamsdorf bent towards the Grand Duke to warn him about this. But roughly and impatiently Nicholas thrust the old man aside.

The game started. Nicholas had a good eye. The Emperor, as if on purpose, lost one shot after another. The retinue watched them and gradually fell quiet. Engrossed in the game, Nicholas moved quickly round the billiard table taking aim, laughing loudly when pocketing the balls, his cheeks flushed; he was clearly carried away by the game. The Empress particularly feared this hereditary feature: like his father, he was easily excited. After a lucky shot Nicholas exclaimed:

'Hurrah!'

The Emperor's face stiffened. He put the cue down and the game was over.

The Empress, accustomed to these battles of wills since her husband had been alive, became worried. Meanwhile the conversation went on. The Emperor asked Lamsdorf about his brothers' academic progress and what they had been studying recently. The Empress cast a sidelong glance at the tutor. He replied that their progress showed a turn for the better, and that the latest essay had been on the advantages of peace over war. The Emperor nodded approvingly. Looking at a now chastened-looking Nicholas, he asked the tutor what his brother had written on this important subject. The Empress was listening to the conversation unsmilingly, with visible displeasure, and not taking part in it.

Old Lamsdorf paused and replied:

'Nothing.'

The Emperor looked first at him and then at his brother and turned around abruptly as if he had never asked the question. The Empress blushed deeply and dismissed both her sons and their teacher.

Indeed, out of adolescent unruliness the Grand Duke, set the task of writing the essay, had not written a single line in his exercise-book. The Emperor was obviously displeased.

The others left him alone with his mother.

Looking down, the Emperor asked her if she had ever considered any changes in her sons' education and upbringing. He would like to direct her attention to a special institution of learning, called the Lycée, that would shortly be opened in Catherine's Palace and that would be under his personal patronage. He wanted Glinka, his brothers' tutor, to be appointed Principal. What was her opinion of him? This last thought had occurred to the Emperor during the walk. He added that it was wise to be prepared, one could not foresee the future and nobody knew who would next ascend the throne.

He added the last phrase without believing it. He had always avoided the question of succession. His brother Constantine, who was just two years younger than himself, was an unfettered spirit, but was fond of Alexander. As for his mother, she hated him and showed affection towards him with one purpose only – that he would declare Nicholas his successor. He also knew that his mother secretly hoped to survive him. A mere hint that he might make Nicholas his successor would be sufficient. In reality he intended to do nothing of the sort, at least not in the near future.

He looked up: his mother's face and shoulders were crimson; she was glaring at him with narrowed eyes and breathing heavily. She wore her familiar expression of greed, irresolution and fear of her son.

Panting for breath, she replied that she knew Glinka and could only speak highly of him as a learned and modest man. But she did not consider it possible to interrupt the Grand Dukes' course of education along the lines she had planned.

A few minutes later the Emperor left Pavlovsk.

The Lycée, established as a boarding-school for the Grand Dukes, was to open soon, but the Grand Dukes were to stay with the Empress.

In January 1811 the decree on the foundation of the Lycée was promulgated.

7

Just as daughters were taken to Moscow for the bridal market, so sons were now to be brought to St Petersburg for their education.

The times were changing. Fathers suddenly realised that their sons would be passed over and forgotten without a St Petersburg education. To keep them at home in adolescence had become impossible and even dangerous. Without education they would have no career, though it was generally unclear and unimportant to most what their sons were actually to learn at school. It became rare now to find an old-fashioned grandee educating his sons in the time-honoured way – abroad.

The opening of the Lycée had suddenly stirred up the hopes and pride of parents.

Fathers whose own careers had been unsuccessful or had ended abruptly were particularly enthusiastic about the project.

An officer who after honourable service had achieved the rank of major despite being the son of a captain from Holstein who had fallen into obscurity after the death of Peter III; a collegiate councillor; a former clergyman now the Governor of Tomsk; a prince descended from Ryurik whose ancestral estates had been sold by auction before he was born; a former Commandant of Pavlovsk whom Tsar Paul had elevated on the eve of his death and had had no time to rise – all these were now striving to obtain their sons' enrolments at the new college. From their own bitter experience they knew that patronage was essential and that without influential support nothing could be achieved. Kinship and connections had come back into play.

Two

A s soon as he woke up, still in his night-shirt, he rushed to the window. A deep black canal stretched below in a narrow stone channel. Stone and walls were everywhere. Vasily Lvovich's friends had rented three small, rather sombre rooms for him, in Demouth's hotel in Moyka Street. He occupied the largest room, next to which was Aleksandr's room, and behind these was a tiny dark closet with a partition for Annushka; behind the partition Blaise the cook and Vasily Lvovich's valet were accommodated. The beds were massive, the curtains on the windows thick.

After taking tea in Annushka's back room he went out into the street, not hearing her farewell admonition:

'Don't lose your way, dear sir, Aleksandr Sergeyevich!'

His uncle was still asleep. Drowsy servants and maids, some with uncovered heads, others properly dressed and with their caps on, hurried up and down the corridor. The place was crowded.

He went down to the stone slabs of the embankment not knowing the names of the streets, only the Moyka where they were staying. He was struck by the unfamiliar aspect of the city – it was so different from Moscow. There were no wide boulevards, no manor-houses screened by foliage, no spring lanes brimming with lilac blossom, none of the gates that made the Moscow streets look like passageways or private roads, none of the multitude of churches large and small, the latter with their surrounding mounds swarming with beggars in torn overcoats. In the endless street he came across a couple of Roman churches looking like ordinary houses. This was Nevsky Prospect, which Sergey Lvovich had told him about. Sentries with glistening halberds walked along the street. He turned about, crossed a square and saw a deserted river – it was in a granite bed like the canal. He walked along the embankment, majestic and quiet at this hour, farther and farther, and finally crossed a bridge to find himself in a street lined with small houses. Even poverty seemed different here – starker and more frightening than in Moscow. A man in tattered rags stood by the bridge, his bare flesh visible through holes of sack-cloth. His bony feet were bare, his face emotionless.

He went a fair distance but did not lose his way. He came back along the same route without asking directions. There were no Moscow cul-de-sacs here; straight streets, gardens, stone, the river. Light carriages drove along Nevsky Prospect. The streets grew noticeably crowded.

His uncle had been up and about for quite some time and was cross at Aleksandr for taking off into the unknown. He was starting to feel for Sergey Lvovich, unable to cope with his wayward family. He grumbled and explained the layout of St Petersburg to his nephew.

'If you walk to the left, you'll find yourself in a street very similar to Bond Street in London, perhaps longer. So if you're in a street and you can't see where it begins or ends, then you'll know, my boy, that it's Nevsky Prospect. Oh, and the Summer Gardens, they're the Summer Gardens. You'll recognise them when you see them. When you've finished your revision, you can have a walk for another half hour or so. But no longer than that and not at noon – the Emperor takes his walks at that time. Don't go too far or you'll get lost. If you lose your way, ask a policeman the way to Demouth's Inn. Everybody knows it.'

Vasily Lvovich was talking about streets Aleksandr had already explored and perhaps knew better than he did.

His uncle slept well into the afternoon and then disappeared from the house. He returned late at night when Aleksandr was asleep. During the day Aleksandr wandered about the city and came home only when he felt hungry. So in the first few days they hardly saw one another. Vasily Lvovich renewed his old fellowships, calling on Dashkov and Bludov; his friends were eager to invite him for lunch or dinner. The literary war between linguistic reformers and conservatives was in full swing, and he was as busy as a bee. His nephew had to revise all his arithmetic and grammar in preparation for the Jesuit Fathers' questions. Rumour had it that they were quite demanding. At dinner he would complain to his friends about the Jesuits:

'If they want their students to know everything before they enter college, as *ces révérends pères* do, what the devil are they going to teach them then? The poor boys will be exhausted from learning. I've brought my nephew with me. He's a clever and inquisitive lad. But instead of satisfying his curiosity he has to master a lot of boring rules. The devil take them, all these reverend fathers!'

Vasily Lvovich was glad to use the occasion to refurbish his reputation as a St Petersburg *brigand* and a free-thinker. He had neither the time nor the energy to oversee his nephew's activities. Once he found some madrigals by Voltaire and poems by Piron on his nephew's desk. At first he was surprised, then he became engrossed in reading, took them to his room and forgot to reprimand the boy.

Two days later no one could have recognised the rooms occupied by Vasily Lvovich – books were scattered everywhere, all over the window-sills and the floor. Vasily Lvovich cut the books of his enemies not with a paper-knife but with a fork, as if ripping their bellies open, and Aleksandr could spot them at once. These were the books that were strewn carelessly across the floor. Vasily Lvovich was living and breathing the literary war. Shishkov and his Slavophiles had cut him to the quick: he was raring for the fray.

Once Aleksandr woke up in the middle of the night to hear low snorting, growling and moaning sounds from the next room. He stole up to the door. His uncle, in a night-gown, was sitting on a stool in the middle of the room. A lighted candle stood on the floor. There was a book in his drooping hand. His lop-sided belly was heaving. He glanced at the amazed Aleksandr and went on laughing. At last he wiped his brow with a handkerchief, gave a sigh, and said to Aleksandr:

'A twosome!'

And he recited:

> *But who is it riding to war*
> *On a twosome fast and far?*

'A "twosome" means a pair,' he explained at once. 'In their old Russian language it's a pair. So writes their bard, that Prince Shikhmatov, the damned clown. It's a madhouse! It's a tavern, my dear chap! "The dawn of midnight!" Ha!'

His uncle was spluttering all over the place.

He read the whole poem to Aleksandr.

To his disappointment, apart from the 'twosome' he had failed to find anything worth comment in the poem.

'Boring,' he said, 'how utterly boring! Some bard! Bards like that should be locked away in attics. That's where they should be!'

To Aleksandr's surprise, his uncle turned out to be a fine swearer. Curses were pouring from his lips. He picked up another book from the floor; it was Shishkov's Slavonic dictionary.

'To belch,' his uncle read and suddenly flew into a temper. 'Here, look, he drags a vulgar word, a public bar word into poetry! And it is encouraged! And published! The old buffer has gathered together a gang of lackeys and clerks. He's a priest in a tavern! That's what the Symposium* is! Everybody should know it! What is going to happen to true taste! I shudder to think!'

'You, dear sir, call me a "taste warrior",' he yelled, 'Yes, I *am* a taste warrior!

---

* The Symposium of Amateurs of the Russian Word, founded in 1811 by Admiral Shishkov with the aim of upholding 'classical' Russian against foreign infiltration.

Your term is absurd and mean, it's a clerk's term. But from now on, I accept it. I *am* a taste warrior! I was born one and I shall die one!'

Literary passion transformed him. It was the first time Aleksandr had seen him so worked up.

'*FETLOCK – see FEET; FETISH – see FEET*,' his uncle read from Shishkov's new *Dictionary of Word Formation*, '*FEATHER – see FEET*. Nothing but 'feet'! *MISTRESS – see MIST*. Why on earth should I look up "mist" for "mistress"!'

In the next room there were also signs of awakening. A few brusque words and the jingling of coins made it clear that there was gambling going on behind the wall.

'*TO SNORE* – see *TO SNORT*,' his uncle read, shrugging his shoulders in bewilderment.

'It's one thing to snore in one's sleep,' he told Aleksandr, 'and another to snort in society. The first is just an unhappy habit, the second is bad manners. Just because I happen to snore at night does not mean that I snort in the presence of ladies. Mr Shishkov's manners are so vile that he makes no distinction between snoring and snorting.'

Then, in the same book from which he had quoted the lines with the 'twosome', he read out a new fable by Krylov – in his opinion, equally coarse and graceless:

> *With a long long switch*
> *A peasant drove geese*
> *To sell and get rich.*

'How do you like that? What sounds! -itch-eese-ich!' muttered Vasily Lvovich.

The new fable also stirred up strong indignation in him from a moral point of view.

'Yes, our ancestors saved Rome! Yes, yes, yes!' his uncle screamed. 'They did! And your ancestors, gracious sir, apparently grazed geese! One can tell the difference at once! You and your fables are so very inferior to Dmitriyev's.'

His uncle was in excellent form. He no longer called his enemies by their names: Shishkov was an Old Fogey or an Old Fossil, someone else was given the title of a Dauber or Scribbler.

'Sodom and Bedlam!' he pronounced, amazed by his own felicity.

He jumped off his stool and wrote down the sudden phrase. In his defence of subtle taste he was using some strong language.

In the adjacent room a card game finished – somebody whistled through his teeth and then hummed quietly:

> *Time, that grey old man,*
> *Never stops his caravan.*

His uncle suddenly grew calm.

He listened for a minute and then looked triumphantly at his nephew, pointing to the wall:

'Those are my friend Shalikov's words. Nobody would want to sing Shikhmatov!'

Aleksandr was in raptures. He was thoroughly enjoying it all – the night outside, his uncle's rage, the song behind the wall and the literary war in which Vasily Lvovich was a warrior. His uncle's literary opinions seemed to him incontrovertible; he was on his side with all his heart. At last his uncle collapsed into bed, sent Aleksandr back to his room, and a minute later they were both fast asleep.

2

He was very curious about everything around him: Demouth's rooms facing three streets, their various occupants, the maids hurrying along the corridors, the sombre valets, the clinking sound of glasses coming from open doors. His eyes suddenly opened. He could tell a tryst by the quick glimpse of a slender heel in the corridor and a hastily donned shawl. The taciturn foreigner in a corner room turned out to be a violin-player who practised monotonously in the mornings. It was a new world very different from Moscow and Kharitonyev Lane. Nothing here faintly resembled their entrance-hall, with Nikita dozing off, his father's study and his corner by the stove. One night among his things he found a stale spice cake put there by Arina. He thought of Arina, reflected for a bit, and ate it.

Vasily Lvovich was discontented with the capital. He couldn't bear the heat. In the mornings he sat down by the window and sipped lemonade, wiping off his sweat. As a reminder that the country was on a war footing, regiments constantly marched along Nevsky Prospect; the campaign against the Turks went on without victories or defeats. He read the *Northern Bee* with a feeling of indignation. Only in Paris were masquerades thrown and carousels put up in honour of the new-born King of Rome. Everywhere else there were fires and more fires. Vesuvius was threatening another eruption. In the *European Museum,* which Vasily Lvovich had bought hoping to find out the latest news on poetry and fashion, there was an article about the preparation of dried cabbage soup for soldiers in the field, and another philosophical one, *Should Suicides Be Considered Insane?*

'Of course they should.' Vasily Lvovich grew irritated as he sipped his lemonade.

Demouth fleeced them unmercifully. In the morning, when Vasily Lvovich ordered a waiter to bring a glass, he was brought a glass of hot chocolate. The proprietor did not allow empty dishes to be supplied. The rogue was eager to cash in on everything.

His uncle called the waiter a fool and shouted after him:

'Robbers!'

In St Petersburg Vasily Lvovich, as a renowned dandy, had hoped to renew his stock of English pen-knives, curling-irons and nail-files, but soon real-ised that here there were none of these things. Ships did not arrive because of the continental blockade and he had to use curling-paper. The sight of their master going to bed in paper-curlers made Annushka laugh and the servants scuttle away. Being a slave of fashion, Vasily Lvovich had bought a round hat with a flat crown and narrow brim, which made his face look perfectly round. Going out for a walk he disgustedly pulled on tight trousers and hussars' knee-high boots. The new-fangled fashion did not become the thin-legged and big-bellied Vasily Lvovich, but everyone in St Petersburg was dressed like that. He was without rose-water and dye for his moustache, and his valet Aleksey was run off his feet. Even Vasily Lvovich's cuisine seemed to be behind the times. Soufflé and cheese that gave off an amazing stink were currently in vogue. Roast beef had to be rare, as eaten by those blood-thirsty savages whose adventures were described in novels. Lots of dishes quite outside Blaise's repertoire were popular in the capital.

In the mornings, at breakfast, Vasily Lvovich would order his lunch, and Blaise would grumble:

'Yes, sir. As you like, sir. I can whip it up and keep it out of doors for a time – it will be a proper soufflé. They say there are no oranges in this city. Of course, the roast beef can easily be underdone, that's no trouble.'

And he would look away, hurt and angry.

His master made great demands of Blaise's cuisine, always his secret pride, which had now been deeply wounded. He had brought Blaise to St Petersburg on purpose, now that their most dangerous rival had been eliminated. That rival had been the renowned cook Tardiffe, who had made the French ambas-sador Colencourt's cuisine the talk of the city. Rumour had it that two years previously Tardiffe had bought seven fabulous pears from the Tsar's hot-house for the amazing sum of seven hundred roubles. The Tsar had sent Colencourt ten pears, but they had been stolen in transit and taken to Moscow. The thief had been found and drafted into the army as a punishment, and later the pears had been found too. Three of them had rotted and the rest had been bought by Tardiffe in St Petersburg. Vasily Lvovich shrugged his shoulders and said that Colencourt had made up the story himself – he was a notorious trickster, and that his Blaise was not a jot worse than Tardiffe. Now, after Colencourt's recall, which Vasily Lvovich thoroughly approved of, unimpressed by Tardiffe's fame, he wanted to surprise his St Petersburg friends with Blaise's humble talent. Vasily Lvovich was the creator of that talent but he seemed to have exaggerated the virtues of his cuisine. It had become outdated, whereas Vasily Lvovich had always kept abreast of things. Once he even declined his home-made dinner and Anna Nikolayevna had to order one from the inn. He groaned at nights – the new dishes did not agree with him, his stomach hurt, everything was too peppery, crispy or flaky. But such was the new taste and he did not dare argue with it.

Soon Blaise panicked him with the news that there were no oysters in the city because ships were not allowed to dock in the harbour. On their way to St Petersburg Vasily Lvovich had told Aleksandr about the foreign oysters and explained how to eat them – that they should be sprinkled with lemon juice before being swallowed. His mouth had grown distorted at the memory. He had been relishing the prospect of a visit to an oyster cellar here in St Petersburg, and now he was told that no oysters were available. Vasily Lvovich lost his temper.

'The Neva is bare, *comme mon cul*,' he told Aleksandr in despair one morning. 'No oysters. The French won't let the English ships through and the French ships aren't allowed to dock. This is the result of the continental blockade. I knew the Emperor Napoleon personally and will admit that he used to have admirable qualities. But this is the last straw!'

3

One day he told Aleksandr with a special expression that the boy knew well on his father's face too:

'Today we're going to see Ivan Ivanovich Dmitriyev. He said he'd be at home between six and seven.'

He looked at his nephew uneasily.

'Aleksandr, be sure to be polite to him. Remember, this is the man your fate depends on.'

Aleksandr glowered narrowly at his uncle. There was nothing polite in his nephew's expression.

Vasily Lvovich was seized with momentary fury and despair – the youngster was a thoughtless fellow and had no idea how to behave. He had difficulties enough already. Rumour had it that Abbé Nicole was closing his boarding-school down. His friend Aleksandr Ivanovich Turgenev, who now held a senior post in the Directorate of Foreign Confessions, was in such a turmoil, so harassed and beleaguered, that it was almost impossible to get hold of him. People in St Petersburg tended to be so self-centred they didn't want anything to do with other people's problems, unlike the Muscovites. The Lycée was beyond their reach, there was no chance of entry without an influential patron. Ivan Ivanovich Dmitriyev was a long-standing patron of the family. Their literary connections, the marriage to sister Anna that had been in prospect – everything seemed to bring him close to Vasily Lvovich. He explained the state of affairs to his nephew and emphasised that he should be particularly polite. It would be nice if Aleksandr could, as if by chance, recite one of Dmitriyev's poems as a kind of tribute, and gave it a thought: *As Others Understand It* was too long, *The Fashionable Wife* was too suggestive, the apologias were too short. In the end he chose two of Dmitriyev's latest fables, *The Ox and the Cow* and *The Elephant and the Mouse*, suggested that his nephew should recite them, and sat back to listen. But continuing to scour at his uncle, Aleksandr seemed in no hurry to read the fables. His uncle waited a little longer and then read them himself.

At six sharp they were at Dmitriyev's.

He met them with a smile. He was ruddy-faced and grey-haired, cross-eyed and with a suspicious look. He apologised – he could spare his friend no longer than an hour.

'I don't feel at home here: my home is in Moscow,' he said – and began to complain, obviously not for the first time. 'I waste my time in trivial correspondence, dealing with odds and ends, paying courtesy visits to the Court, handing out visiting cards and all this takes up the time I could have spent, if not usefully, then at least enjoying myself. If only you knew how much nonsense there is in court life!'

He was dressed simply, and remarked on it immediately.

'How dare Zhukovsky publish my full-dress portrait with the star? For my public I am not a minister but a man of letters.'

'A poet,' Vasily Lvovich corrected him.

'Poetry requires time,' remarked Dmitriyev. 'I wonder how my little garden is doing, the one by the Red Gate?' he asked, visibly saddened, and inquired after Karamzin: was he in good health, why did he not write letters, and why had he given up poetry?

'What evenings we used to spend in Moscow!' he said to Vasily Lvovich, shaking his head.

In all this time he had paid no attention to Aleksandr.

He spoke with deliberate plainness; he cultivated this simplicity which was his hallmark – he was his own man. His study was simply furnished too: the Emperor's bust by a long desk; under a glass dome a statue of Themis blindfold; a simple wall clock; a bookcase, and large pots with balsam and a rubber plant by the windows – the Minister liked flowers. But at the same time the study was too spacious, the damask wall-paper and big easy-chairs were over-luxurious. The house Dmitriyev lived in was paid for by the government. Huge paintings hung on the walls; one of them was a picture of a night feast in a dim and dusky grove, another a battle scene.

'At times I find myself thinking I can live only in Moscow and nowhere else. Here I feel like an alien abroad.'

Vasily Lvovich immediately started to complain about life in St Petersburg: it was impossible to buy oysters or toiletries, all those small but absolutely indispensable things, and all because foreign ships were not allowed to dock.

Dmitriyev squinted at him intently and ignored his last words.

'Yes, Moscow, Moscow …' he repeated, and this time Vasily Lvovich was aware that his former friend was a Minister, preoccupied with his own thoughts, and disinclined to discuss important matters.

'Where else can you get oysters if not in St Petersburg?' Vasily Lvovich said, confused.

There was a short silence. Then Dmitriyev spoke reproachfully:

'My dear friend, if only you could taste sturgeon in my native town, Syzran, you wouldn't give a thought to oysters.'

He had not been to Syzran for many years and liked to lapse into after-dinner reminiscences. But here in St Petersburg Vasily Lvovich could not bring himself to think about Syzran. He prepared to start a conversation about the Symposium and produced a few preliminary snorts, but they had no success. Dmitriyev opposed the Symposium in every respect. Rumour had reached him that the Slavophiles had privately ridiculed the title of his collection *My Bagatelles Too*. The title was a heartfelt reference to Karamzin's *My Bagatelles*, which had recently been published. Giving a similar title to his book, Dmitriyev was expressing his complete solidarity with Karamzin and authorial humility. The rumour, however, needed to be checked; one had to admit that so far the Symposium had been courteous, and had even elected Dmitriyev to the board, together with the cabinet ministers Zavadovsky, Mordvinov and Razumovsky.

'Even if they make mistakes,' he said to Vasily Lvovich, 'in a way, their aim is respectable enough. They have elected Karamzin an honorary member of the board.'

Dmitriyev was superior to the rest in age and rank; he was a friend of Karamzin and had been a close friend of Derzhavin. He stood for peace in literature.

Vasily Lvovich mentioned in that connection that Dmitriyev's latest fables *The Three Travellers* and *The Elephant and the Mouse* had aroused interest in Moscow, where they had been particularly enjoyed, especially *The Three*

Travellers – it had been received as no mere fable, but a real poem.

Aleksandr saw a sudden change in Dmitriyev: his cross eyes sparkled.

'The fable is an unforgiving genre and they don't come easily,' he said with a smile. 'Our language is too unyielding.'

'But what about your *Ox and Cow*? And *The Three Travellers*?' Vasily Lvovich objected, almost reproachfully.

'Well, yes indeed, this fable or, as you say, poem, is one of my best,' Dmitriyev said casually. 'So, they still remember me in Moscow, do they?'

Vasily Lvovich then commented on Krylov's fables, saying that one could not get one's tongue around them, to say nothing of their moral message – they were clerks' pieces.

'*A peasant drove geese to sell in town*! … Cackle-cackle-cackle!'

Dmitriyev burst out laughing.

'A good imitation! The sound of the Symposium – cackle!'

Vasily Lvovich grew bolder and said that it was too bad of Shishkov to trouble Derzhavin's old age. It was hard to imagine how much trouble the meetings of the Symposium caused him! Everyone said the Fontanka was crowded on those days. Sessions of the Symposium took place at the old poet's house, where the great hall was made available. Members of the Symposium called it a sacrifice on the altar of Russian literature; their opponents said that the old man had gone mad.

Gradually Dmitriyev relaxed. He was obviously susceptible to praise.

He shook his head sorrowfully and said about his great friend:

'Now he is back on his estate, having a rest. He has aged. Only occasionally does he write poems as in the old days. But he's quite cheerful, attends Court and goes about on foot visiting. He's busy with criticism, he keeps writing about the Ode.' The last remark was made with a sigh.

And casting cross-eyed glances around the room, Dmitriyev whispered:

'God forbid that one should survive oneself!'

Finally the uncle remembered the aim of his visit. He had a young nephew with a sharp memory. He was Ivan Ivanovich's admirer and had already started to write verses.

Dmitriyev for the first time looked at Aleksandr with a stern expression. He seemed to be displeased that the boy had already started to write verses.

'You'd better wait for a while before you start writing yourself,' he said. 'It's better for the young to read other people's verses than to write their own.'

Vasily Lvovich said hastily that he had brought his nephew to put him down for the Lycée.

'I highly approve of that institution,' said Dmitriyev, glancing at the clock. 'At last they are going to teach boys in their native language! We find ourselves in a situation where we have no one capable of writing memos!'

Waiting for the clock to strike, the trembling Vasily Lvovich did not dare interrupt his friend.

'Both Speransky and Count Razumovsky agree,' said Dmitriyev. 'In due course I would like to establish fully equipped law schools throughout this country. I won't tolerate court clerks without proper certificates. Away with ignorance and incompetence!'

His literary air had suddenly vanished. No one would have said that just half an hour ago they had been discussing poetry.

Vasily Lvovich asked Dmitriyev outright to take his nephew under his wing.

The clock struck seven.

The cross-eyed Minister gave the youngster a condescending look. The boy was curly-haired, bright-eyed but rather gloomy-looking. There was nothing civilised about him.

'I'll have a word,' the Minister said, getting up, 'with Count Razumovsky next time I see him. But he has grown so reclusive and unsociable that I've no idea when the next meeting will take place.'

He smiled at his visitors, patted Aleksandr on the head with a hand as hard as a block of wood, and saw them out.

Outside, Vasily Lvovich looked around and commented on the street the Minister lived in:

'A gloomy place.'

St Petersburg seemed huge, alien and unfathomable. Vasily Lvovich was cross with Aleksandr. His nephew had been unsociable and shy. He had expected this meeting with Dmitriyev to have taken a different course.

It had gone well, but the parting had been chilly.

Aleksandr suddenly asked where Derzhavin lived.

'Over there,' his uncle answered with a wave of his hand, 'on the Fontanka, next to Garnovsky. A fine house, though they say the old master has gone to pot. He roams about in an old lady's cap and a striped dressing-gown. Like some Tatar prince! And he wails psalms into his beard, like a priest.'

They kept silent for some time. Then Vasily Lvovich cheered up and said to his nephew:

'God bless it, the Lycée! If you don't get in, you'll go to the Jesuits'. Have you seen their school? It's a marvellous building … And whatever they say, *The Three Travellers* is just a fable, not a poem.'

4

Aleksandr Turgenev came to visit them. He was flustered. Fanning himself with a handkerchief and brushing off the flies, he threw himself into a chair and informed them that he had arranged a meeting with the Abbé Nicole at his house so that they could make each other's acquaintance and he could introduce the prospective student – but suddenly everything had changed: the Abbé was closing the Jesuit College down. A mysterious epidemic had broken out at the school and had carried off most of the students. The Abbé was displeased with St Petersburg and St Petersburg with the Abbé. Speransky was strongly opposed to him; Razumovsky supported him; the principal teacher at his school, the Jesuit Father Septaveau, had died. Nicole was leaving St Petersburg in despair to stay with his friend Richelieu in Odessa, where the Jesuits had taken the place of the Capuchins, the Franciscans and the Carmelites. Turgenev's superior, Prince Golitsyn, believed this was good news, unlike Turgenev, who saw no advantage in the sidelining of the Carmelites, maintaining that they could have played a useful part in the administration of the Crimea. In order to vex the authorities of the new Lycée, Abbé Nicole was intending to use the name 'Lycée' for his new boarding-school in Odessa. It was expected that measures would be taken against the Jesuit College in St Petersburg. Overall, it was the most inconvenient possible time for Aleksandr's application: if they could just wait for a year, everything would be clearer. And to crown it all, it was unbearably hot.

Vasily Lvovich was stunned. He couldn't tell the difference between Capuchins and Jesuits and he didn't care a damn about the Crimea. The new Lycée and the Odessa Lycée – all this just boggled his brain. The only thing he knew for sure was that Nicole's school, to which he had hoped to send Aleksandr, no longer existed. Things changed quickly in St Petersburg. He regretted following the ties of blood so impulsively that he had undertaken to see to his nephew's enrolment at a boarding-school that had now closed down. Now he could truly appreciate the meaning of the saying that other people's children should be none of one's concern. He studied Aleksandr closely, wondering what was to be done with him.

The boy looked confused as they talked about his future. He had felt completely settled in his mind that he would be with the Jesuits. The novelty of the prospect appealed to him. He had imagined the high vaults of the Jesuit buildings, the silence of his despondent classmates, the Latin speech, the austere monastic rules which deep in his heart he was ready to break at the slightest opportunity. Now it all had fallen through. The very thought of going back to his parents went against the grain and he had already made up his mind to do anything rather than return home. He scowled gloomily at his uncle and at Turgenev, who noticed his confusion.

'You should send him to the Lycée,' he said. 'Boys are going to be educated there in the latest way. The Grand Dukes might be going there too. Speransky is behind it and so is the Emperor, they say. The Jesuits are furious.'

He promised to put in a word to Golitsyn. He just needed to find the right moment; at the moment the Prince was depressed and liable to be edgy.

'The Lycée at Tsarskoye Selo is going to be very good,' Turgenev explained, 'It's not exactly a boarding-school, nor is it a college or university – it's all of these. A boarding-school because they will stay at the Palace, a college because they are all fairly young, and a university because they will be taught by university teachers. My brother Nikolay's friend Kunitsyn has just come back from Göttingen and has already been appointed.'

Vasily Lvovich cheered up; Prince Golitsyn was much more powerful than Razumovsky or Dmitriyev. He embraced Aleksandr heartily and shook his friend's hand as if handing his nephew over into his care. Aleksandr's destiny was decided in a flash.

Vasily Lvovich revealed that he had had his suspicions about the Jesuits for some time. He had heard, for example, that in order to develop blind obedience in their students they made them plant walking sticks in garden beds – walking sticks with handles! And then what? They made the poor fellows water the sticks every day as if their handles would sprout. The brutes! To be honest, everybody was sick and tired of the Society of Jesus. And the happy-go-lucky, easy-going Vasily Lvovich immediately remembered Boileau's *bon mot*. After Boileau had quarrelled with the Jesuit Fathers they had sent round two of their members to have a word with him. Boileau asked them who they were. They replied that they were from the Society of Jesus. Boileau then enquired whether the society was for the newly-born or the dying Jesus? Jesus had, after all, been born in a shed among cattle and had died between two robbers.

Vasily Lvovich was ecstatic. The thought of his nephew being educated in the palace tickled him pink. He could not help looking proudly at Aleksandr, who just a minute ago had been a millstone round his neck. He was staggered by the easiness and suddenness of this St Petersburg play of fortune. He could not stop chattering.

Aleksandr Turgenev was laughing too. This was what he liked about the Pushkins. To be busy with St Petersburg affairs and people, to be the first to learn the news, to feel the pulse of St Petersburg life, and to follow German or Italian philosophy – all on the same day – was no easy matter. Turgenev felt and adored the Moscow soul with his whole being. The way Vasily Lvovich had changed his mind about the Jesuits before his very eyes was enchanting.

Though he had laughed, Turgenev did not share Vasily Lvovich's opinion; in his view the Jesuits had their uses. In the German community of Saratov, among the people of the Caucasus, on the Mozdok steppe, on the borders of China, their activities were far from superfluous: no others would voluntarily go to such places, but the Jesuits were prepared to face anything.

Vasily Lvovich waved his hand. The Jesuits no longer concerned him. The Lycée or Lykea – that was where his nephew was going to study. By the way, what was the correct pronunciation?

Turgenev was not entirely sure. They decided on Lycée – it sounded more masculine.

His uncle sent out for wine and made Aleksandr drink his glass to the dregs. St Petersburg seemed the city of happiness. At this point Turgenev suddenly remembered what he had been so eager to share with Vasily Lvovich – he had brought Batyushkov's latest poems.

Batyushkov was a bone of contention between his St Petersburg and Moscow friends; Zhukovsky and Vyazemsky would not let him leave Moscow, and his friends in St Petersburg were furious and jealous. Recently more tender ties had kept him in Moscow. Aleksey Pushkin's wife, Yelizaveta, a clever and beautiful woman, had befriended him. But the poet that St Petersburg and Moscow had been arguing about had grown tired of all this. Sometimes he would escape to his estate exactly half-way between the two capitals. The latest poem Turgenev had managed to get hold of before the Muscovites was the poet's epistle to his Moscow friends Zhukovsky and Vyazemsky. Turgenev was sure that Vasily Lvovich had not yet heard of it, but he had left his copy at home. The epistle was called *My Penates* and was more than two hundred lines long. Vasily Lvovich clasped his hands:

'Two hundred lines! Well, well, well …'

Turgenev could recall only the first two stanzas:

> *While the god of time*
> *Runs hoary and blithe*
> *And mows the grasses*
> *With his heartless scythe,*

> *Let us take what life offers,*
> *My friend, in full measure,*
> *Let us outdo death*
> *And live for pleasure!*

'Splendid!' Aleksandr suddenly cried out.

'Splendid!' repeated his uncle, astonished, 'he has surpassed us all!'

They made Turgenev recite the lines again:

...
Let us outdo death
And live for pleasure!

Vasily Lvovich was taken aback.

'They're ignoramuses in Moscow!' he said, indignant with his young friends who had not showed the poem to him.

Aleksandr's eyes were shining. In Moscow he had never experienced this St Petersburg poetic fever. The wine and Batyushkov's poetry mixed in his mind. In a transport he asked Turgenev to recite the poem again, and Turgenev did so. The candles burned, the moon shone through the open windows. The air gradually cooled. All three of them sat on under the spell of St Petersburg's latest feat.

He woke up in the middle of the night. His head was going round. The night was as bright as day. Batyushkov's poems seemed to fill the room.

5

Vasily Lvovich suddenly changed beyond recognition. He had previously luxuriated in bed, yawned unhurriedly and melodiously, clapped his hands summoning either a servant or the cook, and generally indulged in indolent oblivion until eventually it was time to go out. For an hour or two he'd slip back into slumber, accompanied by such loud and sudden snores that Anna Nikolayevna would jump every time she heard them. Now everything changed. At nights he was wide-awake. His quill screeched, the ink splattered, his belly heaved: he roared with laughter. The frightened Anna Nikolayevna would peer through the door and every time she would see the same picture: Vasily Lvovich, a dressing-gown thrown over his frame so negligently that it spilled onto the floor and hardly covered his lop-sided belly, sat at the table and wrote page after page, with peals of laughter. His sparse hair stood on end. Anna Nikolayevna would quietly cross herself and go back to bed. At such moments Aleksandr would observe his uncle with curious admiration. Once he happened to break in on him and immediately drew back, gazing at him blankly. Vasily Lvovich was making a mooing sound. He would often hear hissing and soft whistling from the other side of the wall – his uncle was reading poems. He would rub his hands, laugh and then abruptly stop. Then silence – and soon the screeching of the quill was heard again. His uncle spent a fortnight in this way, never out of his dressing-gown, oblivious of everything on earth. And then he transformed himself. He had his hair curled and pomaded, sprinkled himself with scent, and disappeared from the inn. An old scribe turned up in his room with a bundle of pens. Anna

Nikolayevna, who couldn't bear clerks, was full of indignation. But the clerk sharpened his quills and started to copy the papers assiduously, his tongue sticking out slightly, and this pacified her: sometimes she would even order a glass of vodka to be given to him. The only worrying thing was that while copying the pages, the scribe would be giggling. Anna Nikolayevna was not happy and stopped the vodka. As he went out next day, Vasily Lvovich could not conceal his joy. He stuck his papers into the pockets of his trousers with a triumphant air and looked at Aleksandr. Screwing up his eyes, he revealed that a poem in an extraordinary new genre had been produced – both satirical and heroic. Aleksandr could not understand some things yet; so unfortunately his uncle could not read it to him. But it meant the end of all these sons of priests, lackeys, grey-haired old Father Shishkov and his gang. Unfortunately the poem was anonymous.

It was obvious that the author was his uncle.

Thus unexpectedly he'd found inspiration here in St Petersburg, where he had come to send his nephew to the Jesuit school, the Lycée or God knows what other educational institution. He had no idea in what fortuitous way it had happened. He felt such passionate scorn for Shishkov's supporters, all those lackeys and sons of priests who had rebelled against refined taste; he had so often compared the Symposium's meetings to a tavern or a brothel that the poem had just come out by itself. He seemed to have been possessed by some demonic muse. It had come about in the following way. He had sat down at his desk in his usual indolent pose to scribble out a few thoughts that had crossed his mind – about Shishkov – and instead had jotted down a few verses. He had read them through, amazed, choking and spluttering with delight – they were good. And they had just poured out of him. He had written them down open-mouthed. That was it. Polishing them had actually taken him longer than the composition itself. The setting of the poem was a sanctuary very similar to Pankratyevna's, which he and his brother knew so well. The poem ended with a fight among the patrons of the house, a genuinely Homeric contest. One of them was a parish priest – he had come in for it most of all. Vasily Lvovich had fairly given it to the clergy for all the insults he had suffered at their hands at the time of his notorious divorce from Circe. The clergy had not let up even now, and Shishkov was vilifying him as a godless person. Very well then!

As for the madam, she and two hefty female guests were admirers of the comedies of Shakhovskoy. The playwright was a member of the Symposium, a friend of Shishkov and an enemy of Zhukovsky and Karamzin. Vasily Lvovich described the appearance and build of the ladies in graphic terms. He had entitled the poem *The Dangerous Neighbour*. Now Vasily Lvovich went about St Petersburg reading his poem.

Its success was incredible. All the red-tape army, the clerks in all the departments were in a frenzy copying out the poem. Real fame had come to Vasily Lvovich at last. When he drove by in a cab, all eyes turned on him. Only one thing dispirited him – publishing the poem was out of the question. He started a rather mysterious conversation with Aleksandr, trying to prove that the best works of literature had not been created for print; even Homer hadn't written to be printed, because there had been no printing at the time. Neither had been there any censors, he added with a touch of venom. Vasily Lvovich was dying to read his poem to his nephew – it had to be admitted, the boy understood poetry. He had taste – that feature, in his uncle's opinion, which was highly characteristic of the Pushkins. At the same time he was hesitant to initiate the young boy into what he called the gist of the poem. He tested it out on Anna Nikolayevna the first evening he stayed in and Aleksandr was at the Pushchins'. The effect was entirely unexpected; she burst into tears. The rudeness of some of the expressions did not seem to embarrass her, nor did she understand the literary innuendoes, but she took the fictitious hero of the poem – a device adopted by Vasily Lvovich to carry the narrative – to be Vasily Lvovich himself. Since this hero took part in a fight, the tender-hearted woman was afraid for Vasily Lvovich's safety. He was somewhat surprised: this imaginary person who was supposed to have visited forbidden places and experienced all these adventures was the mirror image of himself, with his heartfelt repentance in the poem for yielding to temptation:

The candle died, the mattress on the trunk was there …

When he read the scene in which a policeman came into the place, Anna Nikolayevna started to sob.

'Ah, my dear,' said Vasily Lvovich, vexed, 'but it didn't really happen!'

'How have you come to write all this then?' Annushka said, wiping her tears.

Vasily Lvovich waved his hand impatiently and swore never to read any poems to her again. As if by chance he left a copy of the poem on his desk. Aleksandr read it. *The Dangerous Neighbour* was wonderful indeed, and extraordinarily amusing. Now Aleksandr couldn't conceal his respect for his uncle and gazed at him with admiration.

Vasily Lvovich was not insensitive to these admiring glances. He felt it with all his being, he knew it for sure: here was fame. He couldn't help screwing up his eyes and breathing heavily.

'Logical progression, my boy!' he exclaimed. 'It's hard to achieve perfection! I read the whole of Dumarcet, Buffon, Rousseau, Pope, Hume, Fontenelle – until I became … what I am now reckoned to be!'

6

He explored St Petersburg with a new awareness. He knew, he was sure, that he would never return to Moscow. Everything in this city struck him as unusual, especially its vast spaces. Looking at the tall houses he felt as if he too were taller. His gait became more decisive.

He was on his own.

At a corner he bought a few *pirozhki* from a busy little vendor, forgetting his father's admonitions, and once even drank a mug of milk that he bought from a taciturn Finn. Soon after their arrival in St Petersburg, his uncle had given him three roubles and the same warning as his aunt, Anna Lvovna, who had given him the hundred roubles:

'Make sure you don't lose it.'

But his father's and aunt's admonitions and even the aunt herself had been instantly erased from his memory. With great difficulty Vasily Lvovich managed to make him write a letter home.

There was not one whiff of Moscow in this new city or in Vasily Lvovich's temporary lodgings here. His childhood vanished, dropped off his shoulders as if it had never been. He had forgotten his sister's and brother's existence within the first week, as if he had never walked or played games with them just a week before.

One day, strolling along Nevsky Prospect he suddenly heard somebody saying:

'His Majesty ...'

Ignoring Sergey Lvovich's exhortations, he rushed forward at once, curious, but could not see anything.

In front of him were two men wearing plumed helmets, farther ahead another two in black military caps, and almost abreast of him – a fat pink fop fanning himself with a handkerchief. All around him people were bowing to one another.

'No,' the pink fop said to somebody, 'he's on Kamenny Island at the moment.'

Usually he turned to the right and walked along the canal. To the left was the Winter Palace with its black statues on the roof that looked like sentries. He would walk along the river Moyka with walls on both sides of him as if it were a continuation of the corridor in Demouth's inn. Once he found himself in the Tsaritsa's Meadow. This was a wasteland. It was the first time he had perceived and instinctively understood that cities were built on empty spaces and surrounded by wilderness. His head swam. In front of him, across a monotonous field, was the Neva with its embankments of stone, slow-flowing and just as desolate. Everything was monotonous and methodical in this city of space.

The Summer Gardens were surrounded by cast-iron railings. The foliage was damp: the presence of the Neva, obstructed by the trees, could be felt here. With total absence of interest his eyes registered some strolling children, and a number of statues. He was approaching the Swan Bridge. And indeed there were two swans swimming in the canal, stretching their necks, old and dirty. A deserted castle like an impregnable fortress rose from an island in the canal; it gave no signs of life. An old man passing by told him it was St Michael's Castle, where Emperor Paul had lived and passed away ten years before. He knew that the Emperor had been murdered. According to his father, the Emperor had met Aleksandr when he had been a baby and had scolded him.

'You, young sir, were not even born then,' the old man said, noticing his absorption.

'Yes I was,' he said obstinately and walked on.

In Moscow everything was so far away. Here everything was close, much closer than he had ever imagined it would be.

That night he went to bed early, unwilling to talk to his uncle. When he addressed him, he shut his eyes pretending to be asleep.

At night he listened to the St Petersburg sounds; there was no rattle of night-watches, there were no late-night voices. Some footsteps reverberated on the slabs of the pavement below. He looked out of the window: the night was light; a belated reveller was making his way home and the pavement rang under his feet. In the next room his uncle tossed in bed and groaned, not like his father but much louder and more complainingly. Suddenly he was glad his uncle was so close.

7

Soon his uncle introduced him to two of his future fellow-students, Lomonosov and Guryev.

'Here, my young chap, are your Lycée classmates!' he said and flitted away, leaving the boys to their own devices.

They looked at each other.

Lomonosov was fair-haired, courteous and sharp-witted. His bow to Vasily Lvovich was relaxed. He smiled easily. Guryev was languid and overweight. The two stared at Aleksandr in amazement and he looked back at them sullenly. They began speaking French to each other and he joined in. Lomonosov was one of seven boys transferred to the Lycée from the Moscow University boarding-school and he referred to his classmates as 'Muscovites'. They had known each other for some time, and talking to Guryev Lomonosov deliberately made remarks that would be properly understood only by the two of them.

'You remember what I told you about Danzas?' and they both laughed.

Guryev asked Aleksandr on whose recommendation he was applying for the Lycée.

Aleksandr was somewhat confused. He understood why they had visited Dmitriyev and what his uncle had said about Golitsyn and Razumovsky but he had no idea who his patron might be and preferred not to think about it. His father's pride spoke in him. He remembered Sergey Lvovich's sidelong glances when he had talked to him about Dmitriyev.

'No one,' he said.

Both boys fell silent, amazed.

'My patron is my godfather, Grand Duke Constantine,' Guryev said.

Then they jumped over the chairs and chased each other, ignoring him. They rushed into Anna Nikolayevna's room, completely taken up with themselves, hastily took their leave and were gone.

Aleksandr had imagined his prospective classmates otherwise. Suddenly he missed the despondent novices in monastic garb whom he had been ready to live with at the Jesuits' College. The aloofness, indifference and flightiness of his new fellows had taken him aback. Deep inside he felt hurt, though nobody had actually hurt him.

8

It was unmistakably the end of summer. The foliage of the Summer Gardens had already turned dull and dusty. Occasional withered yellow leaves showed here and there. August had come. The summer that year was showery, with frequent thunderstorms. The carriageway turned white with hail in a moment, as if covered with snow. In the morning Turgenev brought the news: Aleksandr had been named as one of the candidates for the Lycée. His uncle turned to Aleksandr and told him briefly:

'You're a candidate.'

They were to be introduced to the Minister and the interviews were set for the eighth of August. The candidates who had not arrived yet were to turn up on the twelfth, or by the eighteenth of August at the latest.

As soon as Turgenev had gone, over a cup of hot chocolate Vasily Lvovich decided to test his nephew's knowledge. He asked him questions on Russian grammar and logic, using Shishkov's writings as reference.

'My dear boy, are a swap and a swoop the same?' he asked.

Aleksandr was stunned. He knew what a swap was. His uncle was delighted with the reply.

'Very well. But Shishkov, my boy, believes their origins are the same. What blasted nonsense!

'And what, dear boy, can you tell me about the common features of bodies?' his uncle asked, looking at the syllabus in consternation.

His nephew's answer satisfied him with its brevity and precision. Bodies were solid, liquid and gaseous. Vasily Lvovich was surprised to see that he took an entirely original interpretation of the qualities of bodies.

Testing Aleksandr's knowledge of basic geography, his uncle asked him what was the most famous river in France, whether the Volga's source was as obscure as it was said to be, and out of which district of Tver Region it flowed. Vasily Lvovich remembered the place since he had spent some time there as a Guardsman. On the subject of history he asked him about Alexander the Great, but decided not to test Aleksandr's mathematics. He was satisfied by the boy's assertion that he knew the basic rules. Like all middle-aged people he remembered no arithmetical rules. The division of receipts from trading transactions and calculations of volume concerning the emptying and filling of reservoirs repelled him. Instead he dictated to Aleksandr, in Russian and French, two quatrains from his poems just to see how literate the boy was. Aleksandr wrote out the two quatrains lightly and easily, his hand free from clerical flourishes and thickenings; his quill flew and the handwriting was regular if careless. But he made a number of spelling mistakes. Both these errors and the handwriting betrayed the pupil of Montfort.

His uncle decided that it would be better if he pretended to be late and presented himself on the twelfth of August. The new kind of interviews introduced by Speransky seemed to take an alarmingly indefinite form.

9

On the day of their introduction to the Minister, Vasily Lvovich woke at dawn. Waiting for him with curling-irons was a hefty valet who wrapped him, as in a toga, in a powder-mantle and began to curl his hair. Finally Vasily Lvovich sprinkled his jabot with perfume, fluffed it up, scrutinised his nephew as if he were seeing him for the first time and ordered the valet to curl his hair too. The valet was sullen and tight-lipped. He held aloof, telling Aleksandr:

'Your hair doesn't need curling-irons. It curls naturally.'

He brushed his shoulders in slapdash style and gave his waistcoat a tug.

Aleksandr glanced at himself curiously in the mirror and they were off. On the threshold his uncle suddenly stopped him.

'Aleksandr,' he said, 'the main thing for you is not to be clumsy.'

Aleksandr, proud of what he imagined as his upright posture and easy gait, immediately stumbled.

His uncle was displeased.

'In the *beau monde*, my dear friend, the way you walk means a great deal if not everything. Thousands of eyes follow you, your career may be a success or a flop, you must remember to walk lightly and freely. Otherwise you are lost.'

And the ungainly Vasily Lvovich suddenly walked nimbly and naturally out through the door.

On the way to their destination he gave Aleksandr one more piece of advice: not to squeak – Aleksandr's voice was breaking.

The introduction to the Minister lasted only for a moment, but together with the crowd of other candidates accompanied by their relatives and tutors, they had been waiting for the Minister in his reception hall for over two hours: Razumovsky got up late. Aleksandr was in a haze: the early hour, the long hall and the great number of other boys of his age all struck him forcibly. Meanwhile his uncle introduced him to another potential new classmate who seemed confused too, looked at Aleksandr vaguely and held his hand lingeringly in his own.

The crucial moment finally came; an official called his name and Aleksandr presented himself to the Minister, who barely glanced at him. Afterwards everything happened in a flash, everyone went downstairs to be seen out by a corpulent porter with a mace – and his destiny was determined.

It all seemed to have taken no more than ten minutes. But they were late for their lunch.

His uncle grumbled:

'The *beau monde*, my dear boy, hasn't changed a jot. He must have gambled all night and is still asleep in the morning, while respectable people are waiting for him. Let's drop in at the coffee-shop, dear boy. I'm faint with hunger. At least for a cup of hot chocolate. They're all of them like this; he had his son arrested and put in the fortress and your grandfather ended up in the fortress because of his father too. It's in their blood. Your grandfather, however, was a man of duty, not a choirboy!'

After a cup of hot chocolate his uncle calmed down.

'The burden is off my shoulders,' he said. 'I believe the interview will be a pure formality. You should write home and tell your parents that you've got into the Lycée.'

10

And indeed his interview on the twelfth of August lasted only a few minutes; everything had already been decided.

There were three other boys who came late for their interview: Yesakov, swarthy and feeble, muttering something under his breath, apparently memor-

ising what he had been studying; the white chubby Korff; and Guryev whom
Aleksandr already knew. One by one a clerk called them into a small room
where the Minister and a few officials sat at a table – the masters perhaps. This
time Razumovsky's palace seemed to Aleksandr a damp unfinished building, not magnificent at all, and the Minister himself elderly and boring. A
tightly buttoned official glided about the room like a soundless shadow and,
arching his back, whispered something into the Minister's ear; the Minister
gave no reply, examining his polished nails, and only once lifted his lorgnette
to his eyes and smiled. Aleksandr was told to recite something. A little old
Frenchman who was sitting at the table asked him eagerly which French poet
he knew best, and hearing the reply 'Voltaire' gave a disapproving smile.

Two days later the Minister's messenger delivered an official letter informing them that Aleksandr Pushkin had been accepted into the Imperial Lycée
as entrant number fourteen. He was to come to the Principal's premises to be
fitted for his uniform.

His uncle was delighted.

'I know the brother of your Principal pretty well; he helps Karamzin in his
work with all those documents, chronicles and genealogies – the devil's own
job. I've met him. He's a quiet chap but very efficient. Send your Principal
my kindest regards.'

At the Principal's he met the classmates he had caught a hazy glimpse of
during the reception at Razumovsky's and on the day of the interviews. The
Principal's son, a boy of his age, also entering the Lycée, acted as host, greeting
the boys, introducing them and showing them round.

He was struck by the bareness of the spacious room. There was only the
most essential furniture and not a single portrait or etching on the walls. The
Principal's apartment was formal and austere. A bearded peasant-like man in
a smock stood at a high English desk and took down their measurements.
Three or four candidates stood in the middle of the room in their underwear.
Aleksandr stopped indecisively, ashamed of his undergarments darned by
Arina. But his classmates were hardly better off and he relaxed. Pushchin,
introduced to him by his uncle at the Minister's, was there too. All the boys
sized each other up like army recruits. The bearded man was discussing the
lining of the uniforms with a steward. He seemed dissatisfied with the size of
one of the boys.

'It's going to take a lot of lining!' he complained to the steward, wincing.

In general, nothing at the Principal's put him in mind of the Lycée as he
had imagined it at Razumovsky's reception. The procedure for the making of
the uniforms got underway in the most homely manner; the pock-marked
steward entreated the tailor to obtain material without delay and to make sure
it was thick enough.

'Rest assured,' the tailor said, 'the material is from the Palace and for the waistcoats I'll use white piqué. What we measure, we make. Their Honours will wear their uniforms for twenty years.'

'As long as they last for six …' said the steward.

These estimates amazed them. The bearded tailor stood with dignity and looked down his nose at the steward. He had a deep voice. Aleksandr had never come across anyone like him before. After he had gone, Gorchakov asked the steward:

'Who was that peasant?'

The steward looked around and whispered:

'Exactly, he is a peasant and he looks every inch a peasant. He is His Majesty's chief tailor, Mr Malgin, he's an important person.'

Aleksandr kept close to Pushchin; he was out of his element in this group of boys his own age and was easily embarrassed. They all came back for the fitting and at last their uniforms were ready. Fascinated, they looked at each other, trying on their round fur winter hats, flesh-coloured trousers, summer jackets and boots. They looked different now. The Principal showed them their ceremonial cocked hats and told them to try them on and then their everyday cloth peak-caps, and afterwards the steward locked everything up in the storeroom. Many of the boys kept their distance, arriving timidly and leaving inconspicuously. New friendships were struck up. Aleksandr made friends with Gorchakov.

Gorchakov was more of a dandy than the rest, and tried to be amiable with everybody. He screwed up his eyes – from either short-sightedness or pride. Aleksandr remembered the notebook in his father's secret bookcase containing *The Nightingale* with Gorchakov's signature to it, and other frequent occurrences of the name attached to the most risqué pieces. Still feeling self-conscious, Aleksandr asked his new friend what relation the poet was to him:

'Uncle,' Gorchakov said carelessly.

Aleksandr understood this to be untrue.

Malinovsky, the Principal's son, was inseparable from a short, lean, freckled Lycéeist called Valkhovsky, who was extremely quiet and never smiled. When they tried on their cocked hats, he put the toes of his boots together and held himself upright like a military man. He looked a forthright character, and he and Malinovsky seemed to act in concert.

The tallest boy, whose height had taken the tailor aback, was older than Aleksandr and the others. He was very thin and fidgety, and had an uneasy air. His name was Küchelbecker.

It was easy to pick out the pranksters. Their impassive faces and dragging gait betrayed them. Such was Danzas – fair-haired, sombre, with raised eyebrows, turned-up nose and a tuft sticking out at the back of his head. He was sharp-eyed and obviously biding his time. And Broglio – a fat, swarthy, black-haired French youth with an aquiline nose. It was clear that they would come into their own at the Lycée. The boys were called for tea. They sat down casting sidelong glances at one another: the future lay equally before them all. Küchelbecker was clumsy; he spilled his tea, turned pale and twitched. The pranksters exchanged quick silent glances. Aleksandr realised that the tall boy's fate was decided. To his surprise many looked with the same expression at him, but he ignored them and sat down with his leg bent under him as he had been accustomed to sit at home. In vain had Nadezhda Osipovna tried to break him of this wretched habit. He felt his leg growing numb but he sat like this to the very end and managed to endure everyone's stares. He had made up his mind not to be put down.

II

Vasily Lvovich wrote to his brother that he had secured Aleksandr's entry into the Lycée and that his future gave no cause for further worry; the classes were starting in October and everyone was delighted. Turgenev had helped a lot. Dmitriyev had played his part, as had been expected. Vasily Lvovich had attended a performance at Yusupov's where the Prince had asked after Nadezhda Osipovna's health and had sent his regards. They had performed a very old show, in which the dancing was so-so; nobody in Moscow would believe this but at one point, as if with the wave of a magic wand, the fairies' clothes had dropped off. The effect had been indescribable, a tremendous success. Not a word more. Details to follow on his return to Moscow. Dmitriyev's latest fables were much inferior to his previous ones. The Symposium was producing a lot of threats and noise. Nevsky Prospect had gone up considerably in his estimation; the houses had been painted and many trees planted, but against all expectations it was impossible to find oysters in St Petersburg – foreign ships were simply not docking. The theatre could not stand comparison with Moscow's. Shakhovskoy was stirring things up shamelessly and ruling the theatre like a tyrant, with his splutter and burr. Vasily Lvovich had heard an acclaimed opera-singer, Semyonova's younger sister. She was as pretty as her elder sister, if slightly but pleasantly plump. Bobrov in the role of King Pirithous had rubbed his hands like their servant Nikita, which had been scarcely appropriate for the hero. Batyushkov's latest poems contained some felicitous ideas; his epistle to Zhukovsky and Vyazemsky was two hundred lines long.

Now Vasily Lvovich would come home before nightfall. St Petersburg cheered him up and reminded him of his youth. He rose late. In a new dressing-gown with long tassels he sat at his desk noting down ideas. More than once Aleksandr witnessed the appearance of his uncle's muse.

'My dear boy, you are not troubling me at all,' his uncle would say, writing on a fresh page: 'Nothing can prevent the flow of true poetry.' Then he would tuck in his napkin, enjoy his breakfast, get dressed and leave the house.

One morning at breakfast he screwed up his eyes and bit his lips for a while, obviously keeping something from his nephew. It was the morning after the performance at Yusupov's.

'It's amazing, in dancing, how much depends on clothes!' he said with a sigh.

He was overwhelmed with the need to share what was on his mind. He hesitated and added:

'And the flimsier they are the better!'

Strangely enough, Aleksandr looked at him slyly as if he guessed or knew just what it was all about. Vasily Lvovich, astounded, made a note in his note-book and went out earlier than usual. On the threshold he ran into Pushchin and embraced him ceremoniously.

12

Aleksandr's solitude had ended. Pushchin lived not far away, on the Moyka, in a dark old ancestral house, and came to see him every morning. Plump, round-faced, with clear grey eyes, he was very different from Aleksandr. Once, when Vasily Lvovich was putting the finishing touches to his toilette in front of the mirror, as usual oblivious of their presence, the two exchanged smug glances and his new friend's eyes twinkled – he looked every inch a rogue. They both avoided talking about their families, and their replies were as terse as their questions. When asked where his father served, Pushchin replied briefly: 'In the Senate.' They knew each other's parents' names. Pushchin's father was Ivan Petrovich and his mother Aleksandra Mikhaylovna. They stared into each other's eyes and Pushchin was the first to look away. They asked nothing more about their parents. Instead they spoke eagerly about their uncles, the one about his uncle the Admiral, the other about his uncle the poet. Aleksandr read *The Dangerous Neighbour* to Pushchin, who very much admired the poem. They shared the view that it was unsuitable for print because of its uninhibited nature, but that that didn't spoil it. Pushchin's grandfather was also an extraordinary man: obstinate, quirky and morose. It was he who had brought his grandson to be introduced to the Minister and, it was learned later, had scolded an official for the Minister's making them wait so long. Pushchin said that if it hadn't been for his grandfather, Razumovsky would have let them languish there till night. He didn't want to talk about his sisters, saying they gave him too hard a time.

Pushchin's parents were unable to spend much time with their children. His father, a passionate but stern man, was Naval Quartermaster and had recently been appointed a Senator, but unfortunate impulses had ruined him: love for a lower-class woman had led to alienation from the rest of the family. His mother had gone mad and was permanently locked up in her room. The sisters ruled the household and their brothers loathed them.

The two new school friends now roamed St Petersburg together, at times surprising each other with their knowledge. There was, for example, their experience of love. Up till now each boy had believed that he was the only one who knew about such strange matters, and that no other boy of his age was aware of or could ever be aware of them. Aleksandr was astonished to learn that Pushchin knew as much as he did. They felt respect for one another.

When they were hungry they went back to Demouth's and Anna Nikolayevna fed them.

She couldn't settle in St Petersburg and was overcome with the heat and idleness. From an itinerant French *modiste* who was staying in a neighbouring room she had acquired a fashionable Anne d'Autriche hairstyle, and from early morning busied herself in front of the mirror adjusting the hair on her temples and curling it. She had very long braids which she styled in five thick coils on top of her head like a crown. Vasily Lvovich approved of her efforts. With this heavy coiffure, Anna Nikolayevna waddled about the rooms like a swan out of its element. Missing her little girl whom she had left in Moscow, she took care of Aleksandr and Pushchin instead. She gave them cups of tea with cloudberry jam, and they tucked into everything she served them; it flattered her pride.

'Go on, help yourselves,' she would say.

She would sigh as she looked at them, continuing her knitting. Vasily Lvovich had ordered her not to let Aleksandr Sergeyevich and Ivan Ivanovich get too mischievous. In fact they turned out to be a lively pair. In the evenings, as soon as they came back from their walk they would start wrestling, romping about, twisting each other's hands and trying to knock each other down. They wrestled long and doggedly, panting heavily, not looking at one another, each absolutely preoccupied with the thought of winning, of throwing his rival down and then sitting astride him or pinning him to the floor by his shoulders. Pushchin was a slow but persistent learner at this sport, Aleksandr quick and as slippery as an eel. Eventually Pushchin started to get the upper hand and a well-executed trip was all that he needed to win. Anna Nikolayevna remembered Vasily Lvovich's order and rushed to separate the two friends. A moment later she was lying on the floor, one boy twisting her hands, the other embracing her and pressing her down, making it impossible for her to resist. Then they both flushed, something went dim in their eyes, and suddenly, sheepishly they went out to take a walk. Embarrassed, Anna Nikolayevna adjusted her coiffure and muttered softly and uncertainly, as she sometimes did to Vasily Lvovich:

'Totally mad …'

Three

Aleksandr Kunitsyn's Journal

My landlady said that at the market she heard an explanation of the meaning of the comet which can now been seen in Ursa Major, and that its appearance is by no means accidental.

Wasn't worth explaining to her that a comet is a physical phenomenon, it only made the old woman angry.

Rumours and fearful expectations of imminent war on everybody's lips. I still can't believe it, though last time I was in Paris they were already refusing to exchange Russian money.

Went to see Koshansky today. He rents a squalid flat which he shares with his fat female cook. He only dresses up to go out – at home our dandy wears a dressing-gown to spare his clothes. He's full of gloom, looks down on everyone and seems to think he is the best poet in Russia. He firmly disapproves of Batyushkov's latest poems, which in his opinion contain many serious breaches of the rules. I think he is simply jealous.

'It looks as if I'll have to write a book on the principles of poetry,' he said to me.

I am afraid Göttingen has increased his pride but not his intellect or talent.

Koshansky wearied me reciting his latest poem. His philosophy is very simple – he glorifies silence, as of course, Lomonosov did. The last five stanzas are devoted to Speransky.

Eventually schnapps (not from Göttingen) appeared on the table, the cook served radishes, the poet started his libation to Bacchus and I made for home. It's Sunday tomorrow and I am going to see my brother.

It feels only yesterday that I left Göttingen; it seems only an hour ago that Turgenev, Galich and Kartsov saw me and Kaydanov as far as the city gates and we spent the last night with heavy hearts but still carousing. It was a moonlit night. With his usual sang-froid Turgenev woke up the inn-keeper and ordered a supply of red wine. What a shame Kaverin was away in Jena – we might have marked that night with some of our escapades! The moon, the thick lime-trees, the memories of the years spent there even made Nikolay Turgenev forget his pipe and his arrogance. And all this has suddenly gone like a dream.

Where am I now? What are my friends doing? We're all unrecognisable now. We've all been thrown out of our tidy dreams into the mire of reality.

Also visited Aleksandr Turgenev, and discovered that all Göttingenians, *tous les vieux étudiants*, as Kaydanov says, will be interviewed and the whole flock will be appointed masters at the Lycée. What is this Lycée? Turgenev answered my question by saying it was easier to tell me what it isn't: not a college, not a university, not a military school but all of those, at the moment only God knows what it is; it will become clear later. On that note we parted.

Aleksandr is quite different from his brother Nikolay; he has none of that righteousness, aloofness, that detached omniscience and supreme disdain of his poor unenlightened fellows. On the contrary, he is business-like, communicative, generous and hospitable. He was right to point out that Nikolay and I have no proper knowledge of the Russian language. Our letters are awkward and strained; they should be briefer and simpler. Now I try to speak without flourishes.

I shall be in debt to him as long as I live. How and when shall I be able to pay him back? Can't afford to owe anything to anyone because I've nothing to repay them with. My brother Mikhail still shudders and his teeth chatter when he talks of the detention cell where he was shut up recently. He gets five or ten roubles a month from Aleksandr Turgenev, who also gives him clothes off his own back. Thanked my friend as best I could, gave him a book by Flasson which is quite rare in Paris, and talked to him about Paris and Göttingen. Aleksandr said: 'You should be grateful not to me but to Count Arakcheyev. Write him a nice letter of thanks and then introduce yourself.' He seemed to be blushing with embarrassment. Nearly cried when writing the letter, but not out of gratitude. Mikhail is a soldier attached to the Count's office and consequently on the same footing as his servant. But the main thing is – they gave me a pretty clear hint that a certain merry nymph called Pukalova, the Count's comforter and confidante, lives in Petersburg, and that it might be a good idea to show respect by presenting her with some foreign novelty. I bought a shawl for my mother in Heidelberg by scrimping and virtually denying myself food. Found out this Pukalova's address and sent the charmer this shawl with a polite note.

The Count refused to see me, but what does it matter? My brother is a non-commissioned officer with a salary of sixty roubles.

I've no idea what lies ahead of me. Asked Malinovsky – he seems to have ambitious plans: creating public spirit, education without flattery and servility; in short, bringing up a generation of true worth.

'But when this new breed of men become officials, what use is their education going to be? Won't our efforts be in vain?'

'I wouldn't have accepted this post if I hadn't been confident. Any idiot can write a memorandum to the Emperor or a Governor.'

'Whom exactly are we going to educate, and to what end?'

'We shall educate the legislators. Sooner or later this will have to be done to raise the Russian people, to demonstrate their intellect to the world and to make them believe in themselves. According to the Lycée's founding statute, the young men are to be prepared for important state posts. I believe that soon the most important post will be a deputy in an elected chamber.'

Malinovsky confessed he hasn't published a line in the last eight years. He has been more interested in the civil service and has been working on a plan for an elected body. Russian agriculture is inefficient, much land is wasted. The root of the problem is that it is the higher classes who possess the land. Those who work on the land should own it. Slavery corrupts and devastates. It is insulting to the Russian people to be considered unable to draw up their own laws. Had a discussion on the social contract and the theory of citizenship.

'Russians will benefit more by basing their laws on the understanding of their *own* minds, not foreigners',' and so on.

Some of it I agreed with, some not.

Eight years of silence! Malinovsky let me read the speech he is going to make at the opening of the Lycée. I was stunned – it was all about the salutary atmosphere of Tsarskoye Selo and not a word about what he'd just talked about. His caution seems unnecessary. He suggested I too write a speech and I agreed.

Kartsov angry as the devil, Galich a good soul but drinks a lot, Kaverin, the amiable madman, still in Göttingen.

Ran into Kaydanov the other day; he looked busy and said his book was being published. What is it about, I wonder? His speech is full of French words which he distorts mercilessly, pronouncing all the letters. Either learn good French or don't speak it at all! What's the point of provoking ridicule you can't defend yourself against? Ignorance and bragging are the characteristics of our seminary education.

Wandered about St Petersburg. Is it always like this? The houses, streets and passers-by seem strange to me. It's sombre and quiet and everyone is in a hurry. Autumn has suddenly come. Is my landlady right – will war break out?

I remember Paris, the Latin Quarter, the friendly students who greeted me like a brother, the rosy-cheeked Mary who gave me a bunch of wild flowers – and I can't believe it.

Told Malinovsky about Paris and mentioned the huge lamps that light up its streets. Samborsky was present during our conversation. He seized his head with both hands: 'How can we fight against them?' I objected: first, lamps are not cannon, you can't shoot with them; secondly, it's not guns that bring victory, it's the spirit of the troops; and thirdly, perhaps war can be avoided. Malinovsky just sighed.

Wrote my speech in one night. I've no idea how it will be received. Wrote it by candlelight, in tears. Handed it in to Malinovsky, who was unenthusiastic about the reckless daring with which I contrast real valour with noble families who owe their status entirely to their ancestors.

'Very good. But keep in mind that the Tsar, the State Council and high-ranking officials will be present at the opening ceremony. You'd better be cautious. These are troubled times.'

Regretted the heartache I wasted on the paper.

Couldn't get an appointment with Speransky for a long time. Was told he was extraordinarily busy and wasn't admitting anyone. Eventually he saw me. He has become paler, thinner, icier. But his smile is as warm as ever. I've studied the paintings of the old Italian masters and I know the power of a smile. Nothing will ever take away my respect for this man – neither experience nor time – even though I know how slippery he is. He has to be, in a state like ours. Our talk lasted over half an hour. It's a pity a certain Gauenschield was there too. He's a gloomy-looking Austrian who can hardly speak Russian. Speransky introduced him as Minister Uvarov's friend and a member of the Vienna Academy. What is this Vienna Academy? He raised his little finger, looking at me sternly. I knew this Masonic greeting but didn't consider it worthwhile to reply to the Viennese Academician. We spoke a good deal in German. However, I told him in Russian what I was going to say in my speech at the opening of the Lycée, and then Speransky livened up. He liked the speech, and indeed it does seem to be a success, especially the bit where I say it isn't famous ancestors who give a person his worth, and that a thinking person should be free to choose the predecessors he admires. He asked me to add something else. Here you are, then, Vasily Fyodorovich.* He took a pencil, underlined the passage that appealed to him most of all, and said to me with a smile:

'True! And we have to remember that we are Russians!'

* Malinovsky.

He said what he particularly liked was that I spoke about the *Fatherland*, which accepts the responsibility to look after and to educate its people, and not about the generosity of the Government, His Majesty, and so on.

The fact that Gauenschield was present during our conversation but did not understand a word in Russian seemed to amuse Speransky, and he added that he took personal comfort from the thought.

'Haven't we got enough Russians, rather than Germans? And what people we have!'

At this point he glanced derisively at the portraits around the walls – one of them was by a fairly decent master and portrayed Emperor Alexander in his youth – plump, effeminate, coral-lipped and grinning (Liesl from the Göttingen tavern The Golden Deer could have been a model for it, were it not for the grin). To the right of the desk hung a small portrait of Lomonosov. There seemed not enough space for the two portraits on the same wall. Speransky nodded, seeing that I understood him, and waved a finger at me. Then, still casting sidelong glances at the portraits, he told me about the playful kind of education that had been in fashion at Catherine the Great's court, where children were believed to be an amusement. Our present Minister, Count Razumovsky, turned out to have been educated in one of these academies in St Petersburg, on the Tenth Line on Vasilyevsky Island – called 'L'Académie de la Dixième Ligne'. Very young children, almost toddlers, were taught by the Jesuit Academicians and by the age of fifteen they had forgotten the Russian language and been stuffed with half-knowledge. The courtiers had amused themselves with the Academy of the Tenth Line, as if the boys were their lap-dogs. Speransky warned me that in certain hands the Lycée could also become a toy; nurturing infantilism was the most harmful thing.

The Viennese Academician strained the muscles of his face and chewed much liquorice trying to grasp the gist of the conversation that partially concerned him as well. He did understand, though, the meaning of Speransky's glance at the portrait of the Tsar. I am surprised by the childish indiscretion shown by the great man. Besides, a suspicious-looking footman was hovering about the room. Finally, Speransky encouraged me to carry on fulfilling my plan – to educate intellect, not blind feeling, which is nothing more than a mechanical habit, 'and perhaps our numbers will grow – the necessary people will begin to emerge!'

Gauenschield was a nuisance: such a gloomy face can't possibly belong to a decent person. He was a hindrance at our meeting.

Speransky said that the timing of the speech was particularly good. Perhaps he meant the war that was on everybody's mind if not on everyone's lips?

At the end of our meeting he said:

'I'll need a few new people before the Lycée course ends. I'll need you personally quite soon. A new political magazine along the lines of *Le Moniteur* is to be published soon and I want you to edit it.'

His praise encouraged me. When I got home I sketched out a plan for the magazine. I'm not young any more, in two years I'll have turned thirty. In Göttingen, when I couldn't sleep at nights, I'll admit I dreamt secretly not about education but about statesmanship. If only it were not for this blind senseless war!

The expressions that Speransky underlined in my speech, and thought were the best, seem to coincide with his own ideas:

> *... Not the ability to show off superficial knowledge, but true education of the mind and heart ... If citizens forget their duties and prefer self-interest to society's benefit, society will collapse and the well-being of its citizens will be destroyed ... The Fatherland will entrust you with a sacred duty to protect the welfare of society ... Those of you who pitifully rely on your ancestors' renown ... The Fatherland blesses the memory of her great men and relegates their unworthy descendants to oblivion ... What is the use of being proud of titles obtained not by your own deserts when you can see scorn, hatred and damnation in the eyes of those around you? ... Early Russians who won centuries of fame ... <u>In these desolate forests</u> that once witnessed the glory of victorious Russian arms you will be told of the deeds of heroes who conquered hostile lands ... You will not want to be the least of your kin, to mingle with a crowd of mediocrities, to languish in obscurity ... Love of glory and your Fatherland ...*

He underlined the words 'in these desolate forests' twice. Perhaps it's an exaggeration to refer to Tsarskoye Selo in this way, but it will be important to stir the boys' imaginations: indeed, until recently these parks were wasteland. To urge them to reject their vain pride in their ancestors and to challenge them to compete with them seems the only way to make these innocents try to achieve something. The second and the hardest way is poverty. But that is out of the hands of teachers.

Had a strange visitor today. Somebody knocked at my door. I thought my landlady had come to talk about the comet. A man I'd never seen before came in. Had my dressing-gown on but he gave me no time to change – I was embarrassed. He was an extraordinary figure: a skeleton of a man, with sunken eyes and wearing a black frock-coat, a very long one, reaching down to his heels. He told me in a soft, pleasant voice that he was to be a supervisor, that is to say inspector, at the Lycée and since he had learned that I, like a number of my Göttingen friends, was going to be a master, he had come to make my acquaintance. His name is Martin Piletsky. He was at Göttingen too, he graduated five years ago.

Expected questions about the town and the teachers. Asked him where he had lived in Göttingen. He smiled pleasantly and said that he had no right to tax my patience but if, however, I would be so kind as to talk to him about Göttingen, he would like to know if Professor Heren was still alive. To my reply that Heren was alive and still lecturing, my guest broke into soft laughter and said that in his whole life he had never come across a bigger fool and windbag.

Didn't know what to make of this. But now my visitor got down to business. He asked me if I knew the boys I was going to teach. I had to confess that I did not.

My visitor pulled out of his pocket a fistful of paper scraps, painstakingly folded, and suggested that I should read this list of students and their parents and the brief information about each of them.

Thanked him and started to read, but soon saw that the information was of a strictly police nature, detailing not only the age of each student but also gossip concerning his parents and their unlawful relationships, or simply reading: 'father – a gambler', 'father – an extortioner', and so on.

I was indignant and refused to read on. The visitor didn't seem surprised. Then he put the lists away and told me drily that classes would start in a month and since he was in charge of the students' morality and academic progress, 'we should waste no time.' He said with a grin that he understood my displeasure, but how could we achieve our goal if we were ignorant of our students' age, character and family? (This made sense in spite of its meanness of spirit.) He went on with his main idea: more than half of the students were from dissipated or impoverished backgrounds, and so on. In order to develop into perfect citizens they should eradicate all memory of their families from their minds.

'But not of themselves, I believe?' I asked him at length.

'And of themselves as well,' he said firmly. 'Each should be cleansed of the outside world, and become a *tabula rasa.*' Growing gradually more animated, he said that any thought of any attachment, except to God, should be obliterated.

His cheeks glowed. He seemed self-oblivious. Not once raising his voice, he expounded to me his conception of *moral supervision*. He was not going to harass the students but they would always feel his moral presence. While going off on their own, holding secret chats, conversing in whispers, even while tacitly expressing their thoughts, they would be aware of being seen and heard. And this would save them from the vice and temptation that would otherwise be inevitable. Day and night, this invisible – that was to say moral – presence, or supervision, would prevent them from succumbing to dissipation. During classes they would be supervised by tutors.

'What exactly do you call dissipation?' I asked.

'The same thing as you do,' he retorted caustically. His face was crimson.

'Half of them are dissipated, you said' (I interrupted him as calmly as I could), 'but why should the other half suffer – the virtuous half?'

He seemed to come to his senses, and after a pause reluctantly replied that in the Lycée there would be neither dissipated nor virtuous students, just as there would be neither rich nor poor. Everyone would resign himself to the higher authority.

It remained unclear to me whom he meant by 'the higher authority' – himself, the kind-hearted Malinovsky, or God Almighty? I told him that if he wanted to prepare his charges to be monks, he would be right, but as for myself, I'd never have dreamt of undertaking the education of a holy monk, and intended to lecture my students on moral philosophy in order to develop the young men's intellect. And this task was not an easy one.

My visitor spotted a pocket edition of Rousseau's *Émile* on my desk, took it into his long, veritably inhuman fingers with a smile, pressed it between his palms, and put it down.

'And who is *your* saint – Father Jean-Jacques?' he asked with an impish grin.

As soon as he had gone, I opened the window to let in some cold air, and the fresh air soon dispelled the shadow of his visit. The moral absence of this person produced a reviving effect on me. Messrs Gauenschield and Piletsky – what wonderful colleagues. Logic by itself won't be enough to prevail against *them*.

Spent the most enjoyable evening at Turgenev's. The poet Pushkin with his nephew, my future student, was there too. We talked a lot about the gossip and rumour of the city. I was made to tell Pushkin a few Göttingen stories about Kaverin, his duel, and so on. Neither Turgenev nor Pushkin believes there will be war.

Told them about the political magazine Speransky was launching and regretted it at once. Turgenev got very interested in the idea. I assume he himself would like to be its editor. Pushkin yawned, hiccupped and asked if they were going to publish poetry in the magazine and what it was going to be called.

Pushkin doesn't look like a poet at all! Just an aged fop, gluttonous and slovenly. Speaking of Shishkov and Derzhavin he twice used strong language, quite inappropriate in the presence of his young nephew. He was angry about the expulsion of proprietors of fashion shops from St Petersburg. They might be French, but in his opinion they are definitely needed.

'For pity's sake!' he said. 'Where are our beauties going to buy their clothes?

They'll soon be wearing peasants' sarafans! And besides, any decent fellow wanting a rendezvous with his charmer could get a room with a couch and a glass of lemonade at an affordable price in those shops, provided with politeness and guaranteed comfort. Believe me, they have nothing to do with Napoleon …' and so on.

And all this in his nephew's presence! But everyone, including, it seems, his nephew himself, is well accustomed to it. If Piletsky had seen it, that would have been the end of us! Things are discussed quite openly in families nowadays in the presence of children, without any attempt at discretion. In complete contrast to his uncle, the nephew is shy and unsociable. He didn't say a word. I chatted to him a little and that seemed to cheer him up. I hadn't thought about what my magazine was going to be called – the poet was right at least about that.

Meanwhile I've finished the dissertation I started in Göttingen, *Ithaca: or The Science of Morals*. The chapter about passions and indifference, intellect and superstition is good. I don't know if I'll get it published.

Met a number of people at Malinovsky's today: a tutor, Ikonnikov; a Frenchman, de Boudri; and Kalinich. Ikonnikov a nice chap but looks frightened and smells of vodka. Kalinich is a calligraphy teacher but his hands shake. He's big and taciturn. Monsieur de Boudri is fat and dignified and wears a curled wig. He invited me to his home.

My brother Mikhail took a day's leave to see me. Having seen me dressed in a tail-coat and ready to go out, he felt so timid he started to address me in the formal second person. I made him sit down, and could hardly suppress my tears. What have they done to Misha! He looks as if he was actually born a soldier – standing to attention with an expression of dejection on his face. I don't know if education can turn an animal into a man, but I am sure that it can easily turn a man into an animal.

To David de Boudri's, and I still can't get over it. His greased and powdered wig, velvet coat and that proud 'de' before his surname simply aren't to my taste. I've seen so many impoverished French grandees, these birds driven from their home habitats by frosts, who teach our young gentlemen manners as well as the French language – how to hold a fork, how to bow, and so on. Destitution makes them even more puffed up, though they know almost nothing.

When I came to old de Boudri's house I saw his head at the ground floor window: he was sitting without his wig, with his glasses on, smoking his pipe and reading a book.

He didn't recognise me at first and received me haughtily – I had obviously interrupted him. When I reminded him who I was, the old man livened up at once and no longer stood on ceremony.

The conversation turned to my travels in Germany. I recalled my arrival in Dresden and was gauche enough to mention the statue of Gustav II that had struck me as so funny – of solid German workmanship with the King wearing a huge wig resembling a horse's mane. At this point de Boudri looked at me rather fiercely. Since I make a rule of admitting to gaucheries, I told him it was not the wig I had laughed at but the statue.

Monsieur de Boudri calmed down but stayed silent for a long time.

Told him I was not planning to stay at the Lycée for long, since my main aim was to edit a magazine. He replied rather sternly that neither in his youth nor at any later stage had he thought of being a teacher. He used to have a galloon factory in Russia, but Emperor Paul changed the fashion and brought him to ruin.

De Boudri had heard from Malinovsky about my prepared speech. He asked me what kind of moral philosophy I intended to teach, he'd heard it was the same as Holy Scripture. I replied that Holy Scripture gives no interpretation of the passions or reason or of the social contract, all of which I discuss in the first part of my thesis. Here de Boudri suddenly jumped up and started to pace the room silently, with his hands behind his back. Then he stopped in front of me and began to speak so quickly that I had to ask him to slow down because I'm not fluent in French. He told me the philosophy of a mathematician friend of his. According to him, a person's development was like a butterfly's, and the most dangerous thing at the youthful stage was the immobility and inertia of the pupa. The major task of education was to enable the butterfly to break out of the cocoon. I liked the image but said that sometimes a pupa developed into the wrong kind of butterfly, and he agreed. His friend's name was Gilbert Romme.* His portrait hung on the wall – a gloomy face, sunken eyes. De Boudri explained that he had met Romme in St Petersburg almost thirty years previously, when they had both been tutors, de Boudri in the house of Count Saltykov and his friend at Stroganov's. Shortly afterwards Romme and his charge left for Paris. He never saw Romme again before he died.

De Boudri gave me to understand with a gesture that the reason for Romme's death was his predilection for drink. He then told me, with complete composure, that soon after his arrival in Paris Romme became President of the Convention.

At this moment his young wife, who is German, came in and we sat down to table.

At table David Ivanovich became noticeably more cheerful, and after a few

* See end note.

glasses of wine confessed that he was anxious to visit Switzerland, his native country, which he had not seen for thirty years. He was born and bred in the town of Boudri, then studied philosophy in Geneva and once even saw Jean-Jacques himself, but didn't dare to approach him. The only thing he remembered was the thinker's stooped back and his grey frock-coat. I looked at him in admiration.

The old man sipped his wine with a connoisseur's air; it was the favourite wine of his youth, Frontignan, which he had not tasted for two decades. Gradually he seemed to grow younger. He began to reminisce about his family: his father had been a Sardinian and his mother a Swiss. He didn't know what had become of his beloved sister Albertine. A miniature portrait of her by an inexperienced hand hung on the wall.

'I painted her from memory,' de Boudri told me.

His sister's face was thin, with huge black eyes. De Boudri was not a terribly good artist, but he had framed the portrait himself, beautifully. Next to it was a portrait in similar style of a man in middle years with close-cut hair, coal-black eyes and a fleeting smile.

'My brother,' de Boudri said. 'He was a great man.'

He told me that his brother had been a famous physicist who had published a treatise on the dreadful disease of syphilis. He had opposed the profit motive and doctors hated him because he had demanded that they publish the secrets they had concealed from their patients in order to make fortunes out of their miseries. This was a novel idea to me. Asked David Ivanovich about his brother's work. The old man had melted by now; he was obviously proud of his brother and his powerful intellect. His research into electricity might have been of great use if only the French Academy had not rejected him. He said his brother had been a victim of scholars who had attacked him unmercifully at a conference. Voltaire reviled him but Diderot acknowledged his talents. He said his brother's life had been full of storms and misfortunes.

During Catherine's reign he had been invited to serve in Russia in an educative role, but he had declined, and David Ivanovich very much regretted this.

'We might have been living in the same city, under the same skies,' he said, sipping his wine.

Surprised I'd never come across the name of this brother de Boudri spoke so highly of. Also surprised by the similarity between the name of his native town and his surname, and asked him about this. He stared at me, astonished, and asked me if I took him for a nobleman with a title, which of course I did, though not so much from his surname as from his wig. Noticing my curiosity the old man explained that the name de Boudri meant simply 'from Boudri'. I was more intrigued still. Seeing this, David confessed, rather unwillingly, that his real name is Marat, which is awkward to mention here. In confusion I asked him rather awkwardly when he had seen his brother last and immediately realised how stupid my question was. Marat replied with the same reluctance that he had last seen his brother in his youth and had had no opportunity to see him again before he died.

Couldn't help glancing at a vacant chair at the round table next to the comely hostess, imagining Marat sitting here in St Petersburg, at his brother's, and gave a start. The old man looked at me askance and kept silent, as if regretting he had allowed himself to lapse into untimely reminiscences. He had evidently not expected his stories to produce such a strong effect, and frowned. Not a word was uttered at dinner, and barely waiting for it to end I finally took myself off, on numb feet.

Wandered about St Petersburg today and didn't recognise the city. Cannon dash along Liteynaya Street and turn into Artillery Square, and the gunners, with fuses in their hands, wedge the cannon into line. All the main roads are clattering.

They said it was an artillery inspection by Arakcheyev, but it looks like real war – in which I don't believe.

Strolled about the city lost in thought and suddenly saw Gauenschield. Was about to make a bow but he didn't notice me, turned his collar right up to his ears, looked around and hurried past. Thought his behaviour strange. Glanced at the house he had just left and saw the coat of arms of the Austrian Embassy on the door. Metternich's building has a sinister air. Didn't think about this at the time but when I came home, over a cup of tea a sudden silly thought struck me: Gauenschield was an Austrian spy. Remembered the Viennese Academician's behaviour at Speransky's and became almost convinced of it. Imagine!

Couldn't sleep last night: the wind was howling down the chimney. Tried to think rationally but could not.

The possibility of war seemed more and more real to me. The Lycée hasn't opened yet. The teachers are a Jesuit, a Jacobin, a spy and myself, Aleksandr Kunitsyn. Remembered Göttingen and still couldn't believe that only six months ago I was drinking wine under the green oak at the Göttingen gate, and only ten months ago, in Paris, in the Latin Quarter, I was raising my glass to sweet Marie!

Thought of a few possible titles for the magazine: *The Spirit of Enlightenment, Athenaeum,* and others.

The Lycée opened a week ago. The initial chaos has subsided though the students are still unsettled. Classes have started but the students pay no attention.

The event, by the way, has been reported by the *Northern Mail* and some journals, and my speech was mentioned. It will stand me in good stead when I start my editing.

Malinovsky summoned me two days before the opening but didn't tell me how to get to Tsarskoye Selo. Had to hire a cab, and the fee is exorbitant – twenty-five roubles. It won't be easy for parents to pay that to see their beloved offspring! Surely the best way of keeping families at bay and ensuring the students' isolation as the programme prescribes. I could have waited for the palace cab – everybody seems to have forgotten about us. But my pride doesn't permit me to travel with footmen, and I'm intimidated by the arrogance of the palace lackeys.

Hired a cheap silent Finn as a cabman and went incognito wrapped in my overcoat.

Awful jolting, but none of the rattling or the ringing of the cabs in Göttingen, because there's no carriageway here. When it's scorchingly hot it's all dust around you, when it's rainy – nothing but mud. The milestones looked like graveyard monuments, perhaps more fitting for a memorial. A reminder that I was going to Catherine's famous abode. Soon we caught up with a string of carts that stretched for more than a verst. Pigs' carcasses, butter tubs and clinking wine-carts obstructed the highway. The Finn kept meekly behind the last cart and ignored my requests and even orders to drive faster and overtake the carts. Finally, outraged, I gave up and asked him what all that food was meant for. The automaton replied: 'To be eaten.' An answer worthy of Diogenes.

Arrived at Tsarskoye Selo on Tuesday night in the dark. Only on the day of the opening did I get to know that the cursed load that had detained me was food sent as a present by Count Razumovsky: carcasses to be served at breakfast for the guests of honour, which is being so much written about in the journals at the moment and being compared to Potyomkin's feast. The carcasses I saw were in imitation of Potyomkin's roasted oxen. Razumovsky is said to have spent eleven thousand roubles on the two-hour breakfast and made the parents, the teachers and all those dedicated to the cause of education blind drunk. Such was the commotion in the kitchen that you would have thought it was a new restaurant, not a school that was being opened.

Have to admit I was excited too, and reprimanded myself for it. Malinovsky was taciturn, formal and shy. Looked at him and cheered up.

The carriages started to arrive early in the morning, and the uniforms were really dazzling. At half past twelve the old Empress came from Gatchina with her ladies-in-waiting and her daughter, the Grand Duchess, and was annoyed to learn that her son hadn't yet arrived. She was about to go back, unwilling to wait, and this caused confusion among the courtiers. With great difficulty they managed to dissuade her.

Eventually, the Emperor and his retinue arrived and after a public prayer the Lycée was declared opened. Malinovsky made his speech. He was pale, stuttering and almost inaudible. The list of the students was read aloud and it was my turn.

Before I started a heard a whisper, and couldn't believe my ears: Count Arakcheyev was expected to arrive, and his name flew along the rows.

Began my speech feeling vaguely uneasy. Spoke loudly, since, as Malinovsky had warned me, His Majesty is slightly deaf. And indeed, at first there was an absent-minded expression on his face; he glanced here and there through his lorgnette, then said something to his brother Constantine sitting next to him, who replied rather loudly, which was most impolite. Both Empresses seemed to listen attentively, probably because they don't understand a word of Russian – despite Empress Elizabeth's studies in Russian literature with Professor Glinka. She prefers Catherine the Great above all Russian writers, rumour has it. The Baden Princess Amalia, her sister, sat next to her. They look very alike, but Amalia is fatter and simpler; no matter how she tried, she still nodded off. Of all the faces I remember Count Varfolomey Tolstoy's best of all – completely expressionless, pale like a woman's, with sad eyes and voluptuous lips. Malinovsky told me afterwards that the Count keeps a whole harem of serf actresses. My speech must have seemed alien to him.

The young students stood still and set a good example to others. But they stared at His Majesty. On a few faces I spotted a glimmer of attention; since my speech was addressed primarily to them, it was these faces I was looking at, unlike Malinovsky, who while saying 'Dear students!' couldn't take his eyes off His Majesty.

Gradually my inhibitions vanished. Suddenly there was dead silence. I assumed Arakcheyev had arrived. Piletsky squeezed quietly through the crowd towards the door, and all faces turned towards it. Even His Majesty raised his lorgnette and cast a glance. I was at a loss and paused. His name, the mystery he surrounded himself with, and the rumours about him made me dry up. However, from the affair of the shawl I know more about him than most. Pulled myself together and dismissed him from my thoughts. When I had attacked the aristocracy which spends its time being so proud of its ancestors, I looked up again. Some guests were frowning, Count Razumovsky was looking at me through his lorgnette, not concealing his displeasure, but His Majesty was listening closely with his palm raised to his ear. Constantine was dozing off and so were the two Empresses. Arakcheyev hadn't, in fact, shown up. When I finished, the general response was silence but His Majesty clapped his hands and the rest of the audience followed suit. Count Razumovsky gently tapped two fingers of each hand together. Took this as a sign of displeasure and expect no good from him.

In the corridor Malinovsky shook my hand full of admiration that I hadn't mentioned His Majesty even once – an unprecedented thing! – and said I was lucky everything had ended well. On the contrary, I think it was just this that appealed to people; everyone is sick and tired of flattery.

Then we had the breakfast that held me up on the road to Tsarskoye Selo. The students ate in the classrooms and the Dowager Empress personally tasted their soup. I noticed a pale man trembling as if in a fever – it was the steward. But the soup turned out to be good. The famous *Frühstück* lasted till evening: Razumovsky's food was served by footmen in the palace and hired waiters in the Lycée. We, the teachers, were served, not so luxuriously, with what looked like the remains of the glorious *Frühstück*.

After the meal, quoting the servile language of the *Northern Mail*, those present said farewell to one another in the inner chambers of the Palace and departed for Gatchina and St Petersburg. Finally we masters were left alone. Malinovsky and I left the Lycée together and went to his quarters – he had offered to put me up for the night.

The air was fresh, the snow had thawed slightly. Almost everyone had gone. Only a couple of important persons in their uniforms and star-decorations remained, waiting for their carriages and talking in half-tones. Suddenly one of them, apparently tired of waiting, clapped his hands loudly and shouted almost into my ear:

'Lackey! Lackey!'

This was how he spoke to cabmen and this was how my day ended.

Don't remember how I fell asleep.

I've since learned that yesterday some old Senator was mistaken for Arakcheyev, and seeing that he was late, immediately vanished like smoke.

Today Malinovsky congratulated me on being awarded the Vladimir Cross *for my speech*.

Another incident that took place on the day of the opening.

On the eighteenth of October the Neva had frozen and it suddenly started to snow heavily. The snow, soft and fine as fluff, covered all the trees. On the nineteenth the students arrived in sleighs – those who were accompanied by their parents. Those who could not afford it took the palace wagonette specially provided for this occasion.

One of these was Valkhovsky, the boy Malinovsky talked to me about. He has been accepted for the Lycée on Malinovsky's *personal* recommendation. As soon as he arrived he went up to Malinovsky and talked to him so frankly and naturally that the Principal was touched.

The students changed into their uniforms, and at once, in spite of the ushers' ban, ran outside to throw snowballs. Piletsky turned up and hissed at them to stop the game. Somebody threw a snowball at him. Piletsky demanded the discipline book to register the culprit but his request was disregarded because the Lycée had not yet opened.

January 1812.
It's been a long time since I made that last entry.

I'd not expected that I would be lecturing to mere children, but nevertheless I decided not to change my plans and to deliver my lectures as I had originally intended.

They've inherited a lot of nonsense from their upbringing. They've learned things by hearsay and have the same idea of moral philosophy as most people do.

The first problem I came across was the complete indifference of my audience, who are wholly unprepared to listen. I am determined to overcome this. Ran into Kaydanov the other day; he was in a black mood. He said that he scolded the students, 'tore them to pieces', and called those who didn't listen 'animals'.

'I really do. I say: "Mr Yakovlev, Mr Animal." So far they tolerate it. Somebody has to teach them a lesson.'

He has become just like his seminary tutor, whom he likes to imitate. I don't like his rudeness. The students dislike him and Kartsov most of all. I've made up my mind to treat these youths like real students and not allow any familiarity. I am convinced that this flatters their boyish pride. I make them listen, these pupae, as Boudri calls them, who pull faces and doze at lectures; perhaps some butterflies will emerge.

Told them today about Aristippus and Zeno the Stoic.

The quills screeched. Some made notes on the teacher of pleasure, others on Zeno who taught how to conquer the passions. Didn't tell them that I for one have failed to learn how to achieve this. Asked Myasoyedov to leave the classroom – he's not merely stupid but rude as well. Some students were simply not interested. After classes Valkhovsky asked if he could borrow a book to read about Zeno the Stoic, and Pushkin asked about Aristippus. I promised to bring them Lévêque's *Apophthegms.*

I believe that philosophy is impossible without logic. So I've gone over the rules of logic with them and explained syllogisms. This has been met with indifference. Asked them a few questions and realised that they had not understood me.

They seem to find syllogisms amusing. For instance: 'All men are mortal. Mr N is a man, consequently, Mr N is mortal.' The too obvious truth that Mr N is a man made Pushkin smile and when I asked him why, he replied:

'I must admit I don't understand logic, along with many others, cleverer than myself. Logical syllogisms are weird and impossible to understand.'

But at the same time they enthusiastically declaim the enumeration of the types of syllogisms. Perhaps they think it's some new Virgil:

> *Barbara, Celarent, Darii, Ferioque, prioris*
> *Caesare, Camestres, Festino, Baroco, secundae.*

It is as difficult to prove that syllogisms do make sense as that these lines are nonsense, just names strung together to make them easy to remember. The names of Darius and Caesar seem to fascinate them.

Spoke of the Golden Age of natural freedom today, and again managed to rouse my students from their sleep.

Normally, it is not those who really understand who seem to be attentive. I already knew from our seminary in Tver what ostentatious diligence is: disgusting hypocrisy. Nothing but the craving for praise can be read in the eyes of students who show it. So I won't say anything about Savrasov, Tyrkov, Myasoyedov (an absolute clodhopper), Kostensky and others. But those who understand or could understand normally don't listen.

Gorchakov is intelligent but he's a Narcissus. Valkhovsky is impeccable, Matyushkin is quiet. Küchelbecker is obviously a laughing-stock to his classmates: he is extreme in everything he does – if he writes, he breaks his quills out of sheer enthusiasm; if he talks to you, he asks you to repeat yourself very loudly since he is slightly deaf. Broglio is like Danzas, incorrigible: he pulls faces and doesn't care about anything, or at least he doesn't appear to. Pushkin gnaws his quills and sketches on paper, totally absorbed, as if there were no one else in the classroom.

Delvig goes to sleep – literally. Korff is the most decent of them all.

Told them about primeval freedom, the natural state of mankind in its infancy when no social contract had yet been arrived at or profaned by tyrants. This time they listened attentively and some of them seemed amazed. Küchelbecker and Valkhovsky made notes. Pushkin, who never asks any questions, asked me after the classes if there were any peoples still living in that state. I replied that some savages still retained their original innocence but they are rare; education has penetrated even remote huts, bringing with it widespread vice. Chateaubriand's Indians are noble savages, wild and innocent. I was taken aback by this question; they can not only think, but also apply their thoughts to the present time.

Growing more and more friendly with Ikonnikov. He's very poor – to put it bluntly, destitute. You couldn't imagine a weirder tutor, but at the same time he influences the youngsters in a good way. He's a Candide, and always tells the truth and nothing but the truth. I once overheard a conversation he had with Gorchakov. The boy started speaking French to him to make him feel uneasy, and spoke derisively. Ikonnikov listened to him for a while and suddenly retorted in French that if Gorchakov didn't immediately apologise to him, he would consider him a boor. Gorchakov was embarrassed. Now Ikonnikov is everybody's favourite. They read their writings to him and value his frankness and fine taste. By the way, they say Illichevsky writes marvellous poems, and Yakovlev, Pushkin and two or three other students are also writers. Another tutor told me that Ikonnikov gave one of them (Yakovlev or Pushkin) a hug and a kiss for his translation of Anacreon's *Rose* from the French.

If Koshansky were to find out, he would ruin Ikonnikov. Ikonnikov has had a most bizzare life. He's the grandson of a famous actor and he used to perform on stage himself; then he served as an interpreter in the Foreign Office; after that he was an orderly officer in the Mines Corps and taught geography, history and French there – but he never lasted long in any of those posts. He's so poorly dressed that it has often occurred to me to offer him some help, but I don't want to wound his pride.

Ikonnikov and I went out for a walk today. I don't like these parks – you can unexpectedly come upon a statue or a sentry among the trees, or feel somebody watching you. The vigil here is close and relentless; a perpetual moral presence. The streets of the settlement itself, the houses in Tsarskoye Selo and its small shops are much more friendly. There's deep snow now but the streets are regularly cleared. Ikonnikov read me a few of his poems and took me by surprise. They were short elegies written with genuine passion, not like our Koshansky's. But they all seem unfinished and unpolished. I asked him why he did not send them to the press.

'So as not to get a rejection.'

Too proud and too poor.

Eventually he confessed that he was writing a long poem and his future depended on its success. But he refused to read me a single extract from it. He'd confided in me, he said, only because I 'seem more honest than the others.' This confession of Candide's made me burst out laughing; he took offence and tried to walk away but I caught up with him and made it up, though I couldn't squeeze another word out of him. Today I had a conversation with Malinovsky about him. Having extracted my word of honour that I wouldn't tell anyone, he read me Piletsky's denunciation of Ikonnikov. The letter said that Ikonnikov had not taken communion for two years, that he was a blasphemer devoted to everything French, and a drunk. I persuaded Malinovsky to hold it back. Perhaps there's a grain of truth in our inquisitor's letter about Ikonnikov's drinking. Sometimes Ikonnikov does seem to smell of wine.

What I said about Zeno, who taught the subjugation of the passions to the intellect, fired the imagination of all my students. They asked me to talk about the passions again. I remembered my walk with Ikonnikov and said I was going to talk about pride. There were other requests: Küchelbecker wanted me to talk about justice, Gorchakov about cowardice and Pushkin about miserliness. Somebody laughed but I said I found that of these three subjects only miserliness is a passion in the true sense, and promised to talk about it next time.

Küchelbecker objected with ardour that justice is a passion. Valkhovsky supported him, and said that kindness is a passion too. Delvig broke into sophistry and tried to prove that the most powerful passion was impassiveness, and he made everyone laugh.

I told them that *good* means conformity of a thing with its function, neither more nor less than that. Things are *good* when they serve a means to attain an end. Good is a striving for happiness. They seemed to be struck by such a simple explanation. Malinovsky would have called it cynical. But my aim was achieved – not one of them was left uninspired. In the meanwhile I expounded my understanding of pride and started by quoting Weiss: limit your expenditure according to your pride – be a Spartan if you can't afford to be a king.

Speaking of pride, I said that false pride is based on imagination that for no reason denigrates other people and elevates the arrogant. I took the ancient Roman Emperor Constantine as an example: he was short and feeble. Driving his horse under a huge arch during his triumph, he lowered his head as if to prevent himself from coming into contact with it. At this point I noticed some agitation in the classroom. Gorchakov had involuntarily lowered his head, and Malinovsky was pointing his finger at him and Myasoyedov and exclaiming loudly: 'Look at them!'

Hadn't expected my words to have such a strong effect and to be applied so soon. To make it worse, tutor Ilya, the Jesuit Piletsky's brother, began to reprimand Malinovsky for shouting in class and, following his brother's instructions, forced a 'repentance' out of him. Must talk to the Principal and try to put an end to this. Gorchakov is very proud of his title and his excellent memory, and Myasoyedov of his father who is a Senator.

A rumpus at the Lycée today. Piletsky found books of madrigals by Voltaire and poems by Piron, with other (as he put it) 'foul books', in the possession of one of the students, Pushkin. He was for removing and even burning them. Malinovsky was distressed and said that wouldn't do, especially since this particular student is no lamb. First of all there is no library at the Lycée yet, and secondly, madrigals by Voltaire are permitted reading. They're not, after all, epigrams! God forbid! This makes me think of our sexton Father Païssy, who believes Voltaire to be the Devil.

The new rules are even sillier than the previous ones: the students are forbidden to write poetry because it distracts them from their studies. The idea must have come from Ilya and Koshansky; or perhaps Kalinich has grown tired of sharpening quills? No one would recognise the students now, especially Pushkin – at lectures he gnaws quills and writes ceaselessly. Asked Malinovsky to restrain Ilya. I hear that Piletsky (who made this rule) is going to issue a journal with the students instead.

Rumours of war. The gossip in Tsarskoye Selo is that the Empress has summoned astronomers – it isn't just my landlady who is showing an interest in the comet. Soon my teaching career will come to an end: I've already got the first issue of my magazine in draft. Next week I'll try for an appointment with Speransky.

Nobody knows for sure if war has started or not. The *Northern Mail* doesn't mention it, nobody dares talk about it and apparently not without reason. His Majesty is travelling. Napoleon is travelling. The uncertainty of the situation tortures people, just as an imminent storm troubles sheep and makes them huddle together. Koshansky has been revising the end of his poem *Our Time*: at first he had it as a sapphic stanza, now it's in the form of an ode. The students, or as Kaydanov calls them, 'the lads', feel everything as acutely as we do, but so far everything is as usual during walks and classes.

Piletsky is very busy. Thanks to him, informing has pervaded the Lycée, it really is a revolting business. I've noticed that nobody bothers to conceal his hatred for him any more. Only Boudri is as calm as ever. I asked him (having looked around first – what it has come to!) what his thoughts about the war were. He said there'll be no war.

'But everybody talks about it!' I objected.

'*On dit – c'est un menteur*,' he replied.

'But what if it does break out?' I asked.

'If it breaks out, there'll be a great upheaval, but no greater than the one there's already been.'

The old man has lived such an eventful life that nothing can ruffle his calm. '"They say" – it's a lie.'

There *should* be no war. No one seems to question our inevitable defeat – the faces of the Tsarskoye Selo courtiers have fallen; some of them are rumoured to be packing their things. What cowardice!

Speransky doesn't talk of the journal any more. I've got the first issue ready. There'll be an editorial – articles on current events, philosophy, education, history of ancient Russian law, aphorisms – a whole range of topics.

Suddenly the frost has set in.

Speransky was arrested last night, and taken as a common criminal to an unknown destination. No one knows anything about it.

Gauenschield flaps the tails of his frock-coat like a crow waving its wings. Piletsky keeps making notes during breaks between classes. Everything is quiet at the Palace – the footmen beat the carpets indifferently. In general, footmen are the last to respond to the upheavals of history. Are Speransky's innovations to be suspended? Stopped? It seems so. Does virtue – the only thing that gives one strength to live, to think and to act – really exist? Like Speransky, like Malinovsky, like all of us Göttingenians, I am of the clergy. But I have cultivated my reason, I've come to believe in its beneficial power, in the sanctity of the social contract, I want to see a new breed of people – How can I turn back to the primal state of goalless savagery? I've made rather a confused tally of how things have turned out for me this year. The civil service is closed to me now, just as the poetic field is closed to Koshansky. So I give lectures with double zeal. Boudri's example spurs me on. The old man seems to understand the whole significance of the changes but is in no way confused. He has witnessed too many great events, he says. There has been a commotion in the Palace today, with some strangers darting about the gardens.

The window is open now, the park is dark but for the lights of the Lycée and the Ladies-in-Waiting Wing. All is quiet, the moon is shining as it did a year ago. Am staying the night with someone in Tsarskoye Selo, because Malinovsky's wife has fallen ill. My host has a simple-hearted look, the house is small but comfortable, the coals are crackling in the fire-place. I like this pleasant routine existence.

I'm not quite sure why I'm writing this, because I'll think I'll burn it in a moment. Isn't it just a social thirst, a craving for immortality?

Went to see Aleksandr Turgenev. The reason for Speransky's fall isn't clear. Razumovsky maintains that the Minister is a Jacobin who aspires to ascend the throne, not noticing a striking contradiction here – he's either a Jacobin or a monarchist. Many people call Speransky a republican. The mother of a

Lycée student, Mme Bakunina, told her son when she last saw him that she'd always seemed to smell the reek of sulphur coming from Speransky and seen blue infernal flames in his eyes. His fall is celebrated like the first victory over the French, and like the death of the cruellest tyrant. But there's great despondency too.

What a time has passed since Göttingen, and where are we now? Like a stone thrown into a pond, within a year I've witnessed a man's rise and fall, hopes and hopelessness. War is looming. I'm thinking about the charges put into my care by Speransky. They too have experienced more than other children usually experience in five years: leaving their homes, and now this approaching war that will shake everything.

When we parted, Aleksandr Turgenev asked me in particular about Pushkin, in whose future he takes an interest. He asked me to be considerate towards him because he had a joyless childhood. Knowing how neglectful his parents are, Turgenev asked me not to abandon the boy. I was moved and gave my promise but told him quite openly that he needed a more understanding person. I am just a teacher – I form our students' *intellect.* Our tutors are useless, what I count on most of all is the boys' friendship, but differences of upbringing and their experience of life so far drive them apart. Turgenev's protégé Pushkin also bears the unhappy traces of his upbringing. He is bright but shy; stubborn, mercurial, frenetically short-tempered yet full of fun. I can say nothing more about him so far.

After the catastrophe of Speransky's fall I don't believe I shall aspire to any post other than that of a teacher of juveniles. I'd like to give them a lecture on the fatherland and civil duties. Reading Karamzin. He is certainly the most eloquent of our writers. But I don't like his separation of love for the Fatherland into three kinds: physical, moral and political – much too rational. The first is common and natural; the second comes with a certain age, and the third is a matter of conviction and is attainable only by the educated. Love itself is divided into three loves. The false note offends the ear, and the false logic insults the mind.

In the same despondent state went to see my brother Mikhail. He is ill in hospital. The rules are strict nowadays: they were unwilling to let me in and the meeting was brief. The poor fellow was delighted to see me. He livened up and recalled our childhood of long ago in that far-away village near Tver; how our mother used to put loaves into the oven – and how that aroma seemed to us then the most wonderful smell in the world. I'd almost forgotten about it all. Though the high command keeps all information about the military situation secret, the preparations are obvious to everyone. Mikhail isn't frightened by the rumours of war. He has asked to be accepted into the army and I believe he will be. He spoke quite convincingly of the disadvantages for the

French of waging the war on the enemy's territory. He told me that whenever he's sad or hurt, he tells himself: 'Don't fret, Mikhail!' and it works. So now too he'll be telling himself: 'Don't fret, Mikhail', and he'll put on his pack, take a sabre in his hand and march.

What kind of Karamzinian love is felt by a poor soldier like Mikhail? Do only educated people possess that reason without which love for one's country is impossible? And what is education? True education is as far from worldly, superficial education as the sky from the earth.

As Jean-Jacques says about education: 'What is it that inspires hearts to love their country and its laws? Shall I tell you? Children's games – an idle thing in the eyes of shallow people, but precisely what forms precious habits and invincible bonds.'

And again: 'Education should so shape people's hearts and direct their opinions and tastes that it becomes their natural inclination to be a patriot, their passion, their need. A real republican sucks in love for his country, its laws and its freedom, with his mother's milk. If he is alone, he is nothing; if he has no Fatherland, he is non-existent; and if he is still alive, he is worse than dead.'

Thought about Speransky and the sort of half-playful education he talked to me about. Children should be treated without a shade of condescension; they will understand all the better exactly what one thinks of them. Bad habits like Gorchakov's – the languorous glances, mimicking of senility, dandyish irresolution that are in fashion nowadays – should not be indulged.

Haven't burnt my notes yet. I've reread them, and the hopes I entertained six months ago, in the glorious complacency of youth, now seem ridiculous to me. Time to calm down. Went to Malinovsky's and we had a long and frank talk. He is still depressed and frightened; he has burnt his paper on the 'Convocation of Deputies', the fruit of eight years of work. If war breaks out he would like to fight as a private soldier, like Mikhail. He's terrified to see Gauenschield stay on at the Lycée; he won't be able to cope with him. It seems as if yet another innovatory initiative is going to founder. We talked about Speransky, and Malinovsky told me that when he was young he wrote a novel, *The Father of the Family* – judging by the title an imitation of Diderot.

Today passed on Turgenev's best regards to Pushkin, and keeping my promise had a talk with him. He is extremely unsociable, but without a shadow of malice. He is considered a 'prankster' by the tutors and indeed, he is one and seems proud of it. He asked Turgenev to send him a book by Gresset.

'How did you come to know Gresset?'

'I read him in my uncle's and my father's libraries.'
'And what did you enjoy most of all?'
'*The Lectern.*'

But the poem is indecent! It must have been his uncle who gave it to him to read. They've kept *nothing* from him, he's been treated like an equal. He is a complex and witty character, he knows Voltaire, Gresset, Piron and, it seems, all the French satirists. He doesn't share Koshansky's tastes (nor do I). To my amazement he likes classical thinkers too. Gave him a book about Stoics and Cynics called *Philosophical Apophthegms*. These anecdotes are more useful for a young man than the usual textbooks. He asked me why in my speech I'd called the Tsarskoye Selo gardens 'desolate forests'. I said that till recently there had been forests and wasteland all around and that even now the gardens preserved some of this primeval grandeur. He didn't reply but seemed pleased with the explanation. During their walks the boys wander deep into the forest and come out onto desolate roadways. I was surprised that he remembered so well the precise expression I used in my speech at the Lycée opening more than six months ago. Finally asked him if he wanted to send a message to his parents through Turgenev. He thought a little and said no. He's obviously not homesick. Koshansky is mistaken – the boy is not malicious, he must have laughed at his teacher's style of declamation and Koshansky felt stung. Pushkin has a child's smile.

Spoke to Valkhovsky too. He's a more practical fellow. After classes he came up to me and asked me ...

Four

I

O N the first day at the Lycée, just a few paces away, he saw what Sergey Lvovich had talked about, biting his lip and with anxious eyes – the Court. Right in front of him was the stooped plump back of the Emperor, closely outlined through soft cloth. There were also a few old ladies, several young women with monograms on their shoulders and men in uniforms and frock-coats, all sitting in a small hall. He could see his uncle Vasily Lvovich among them, and he seemed every inch what he really was – a short, squint-eyed and ridiculously dressed figure.

A stocky, decisive-looking man, in a tail-coat and with narrow sideburns, read a speech from sheets of paper. He was the first and only person who paid any attention to them that day. He looked into their eyes while address-ing them. They were behind the rest of the gathering. When he finished, the audience turned round and looked at them in amazement, as if seeing them for the first time. The speaker was a master, Kunitsyn. Aleksandr later remembered a sound of low voices that had risen and fallen away; in the evening Gorchakov told him that Arakcheyev had been expected but had never arrived. Aleksandr asked him who Arakcheyev was, but Gorchakov just scrutinised him, screwing up his eyes slyly, shrugged his shoulders and gave a complacent chuckle. Gorchakov knew everything.

From next day they were forgotten. They rose at six o'clock. The tutor Ilya assembled them in files and took them to the first floor dining-hall where they had a glass of weak tea. Piletsky instructed his brother Ilya to see to it that there were strictly no games before classes upstairs or in the dormitory, or on the first floor where they had tea, because games were a needless distrac-tion. They had lectures from seven till nine, then went out for a walk, had lunch, did their homework, had three more lectures, took a second walk, had an afternoon snack, dinner, a third walk, and at ten they once again went 'in files', which after a short time ceased to be regularly observed at that hour, upstairs to their third floor and dispersed to their cells, each of which had its own number. Aleksandr's number was fourteen. Next door, behind a partition of planks, number fifteen, Pushchin would breathe heavily in his sleep. He had already acquired a nickname, Jeannot, in a French class.

They lived in a wing of the Palace. Their rooms were situated along the corridor next to each other, each containing an identical bureau (or 'desk' as the usher Matvey called it), wardrobe and iron bed with a pair of bedroom slippers under it. The semi-dark passages, the vaulted ceilings, the supervisor with piercing eyes and monkish look stealing past their doors – all this reminded him of the Jesuit monastery to which he had been going to apply.

Their three daily walks were considered more important than lectures. Malinovsky and his ailing wife believed the Tsarskoye Selo air to have miraculous health-giving properties, and the boys' regime was to be outside as much as possible: rooms were for study and sleep. The tutors took them out in a file of twos, making them all keep step, but the order would easily be disrupted. Gradually he got used to the gardens, having known nothing more beautiful in his life. He learned to distinguish the large, tranquil old Elizabethan garden from the newer, elaborate Catherinean one, with its pavilions, monuments and English follies. The Elizabethan garden between the Palace and the Hermitage had a trimmed Versailles-style hedge and pruned trees, and when they passed by the spinney he seemed to recognise these places, perhaps associating them with Yusupov's garden which he had known as a child.

Weird, idle, fleeting thoughts crossed his mind but he never remembered or went back to them. Sometimes he would smile to himself. Pushchin, who was paired with him, had got used to this, and chatted endlessly, not caring if he was overheard.

They were taken to the Champ des Roses. Through the bushes they could see the airy and transparent Turkish Pavilion. Ancient, foreign-looking stones were embedded in one of its arbours; the tutor Chirikov told them that these were from ancient Greece. The Turks, on whom Kaydanov lectured to them, always referring to them as 'savage', did not seem at all savage here. There were small crescent-shaped ponds, reminiscent of the Turkish moon.

Once on a walk, when Chirikov was as usual busy with his thoughts, Aleksandr lagged behind and peeped through a narrow window of the Turkish Pavilion. In the empty, semi-dark interior he saw carpets and sofas, looking as if the owner of a seraglio, some Turkish magnate, had just left for a moment and would be back soon to smoke the hookah that stood in the corner. Nobody had ever lived in this pavilion; only occasionally, perhaps, the Empress Catherine, with her love of artifice, would have spent time there.

Above the ponds, in specially built huts, the swans wintered – a pair in every hut. An old swan, his beak buried in his lady's feathers, lay on the dry reed mat of one of the huts, and sensing human presence, muttered indistinctly in his sleep, like a dirty sleepy Zeus who on account of his Leda had to freeze in a hut in winter.

They would pass the huge and desolate Palace. Then Chirikov would frown and ask them to walk quickly and smartly. His pock-marked swarthy face would twitch. Aleksandr cast furtive glances at the heavily curtained windows. Silent sentries guarded the doors. They would pass by, making for the Champ des Roses.

The Champ des Roses was a real meadow. A few rose bushes planted in Catherine's time still grew there, but their days were numbered and nobody took care of them, they were growing wild.

Ignoring the tutor, the boys would turn off the path to play at snowballing. Chirikov, forced out of his reverie, would dart from one boy to another, pressing his hands to his chest and begging them hoarsely to stop. Piletsky had a hearty dislike of this ugly and disorderly game of snowballs, but he allowed 'decent' pastimes: riddles, charades and so on.

To the right were the pink stone gates in honour of Count Orlov who many years ago had put an end to the plague in Russia. The story of the hero was related expansively on the marble. Everything looked as if the hero would enter the gates on horseback at any moment: Chirikov's worried, wary look and repeated hisses for silence seemed to confirm it. The gardens were more populated and alive than the Palace with its drawn curtains, deserted and half-dead.

2

Normally he woke up when it was still dark. The sleepy usher, Foma, would knock on his door, grumbling and grunting:

'Wake up, gentlemen! God have mercy on us!'

Then his voice would be heard at Pushchin's door and so on along the corridor – the same grunting and the invariable addition: 'God have mercy on us!'

He would wake reluctantly and Pushchin would knock on his wall. When they got up at six, the candles would still be burning in the corridors and it was still dark outside the windows – a dim winter morning. Across the yard, in the Ladies-in-Waiting Wing, a faint light appeared in the second window from the corner: Natasha, old Volkonskaya's maid, would be coming to dress her mistress, who woke up early. They would run into Natasha during their walks and he had got used to rising to her light.

Once a soft banging woke him. He opened his eyes and listened. It was dark, the room next door was quiet; Pushchin was asleep. He looked out of the window – Natasha's light was not to be seen.

Meanwhile the knocking was repeated – weak and soft – quite unlike usher

Foma's with his gnarled finger. He jumped up quickly, stuck his feet into his slippers, adjusted his night-cap and cautiously peeped out into the corridor.

At nights the tutor on duty usually sat sleeping in his housecoat in front of the duty-room stove. It would either be Kalinich – a huge man with an enormous face who slept soundly and serenely, stretched out in his chair – or the nimble little Chirikov, curled up and moaning softly. When on occasion boys could not get to sleep, they would shuffle along the corridor in their soft slippers. Sometimes through his sleep he could sense somebody watching him: the upper part of the door was latticed and half-veiled by a muslin curtain. This would make him start and mutter in his slumbers. By and by the tutors stopped peeping into his room, usually retreating to their duty-room where they slept till morning.

But now the chair in the duty-room was empty and the whole gallery was dark. Suddenly the knocking came again – almost upon him. He looked closely and saw a man in black, a long shadow, kneeling by the wall bowed in prayer, touching the stone floor-slabs with his brow, slowly and regularly.

He recalled that Inspector Piletsky had volunteered to be on duty that night, and he stood there for a while without moving. Having spread his handkerchief on the floor, Martin Piletsky was kneeling on the stones pressing his hands to his heart, stooped, his whole body demonstrating abject humility. Only his huge feet in black slippers preserved a human look: they reminded him of the feet of a corpse.

It was cold in the corridor, and the Jesuit's prayer seemed to be cold as well in spite of all his zeal; his forehead struck the stone floor like a pendulum.

Aleksandr stood outside his door for a while. At last the cold got the better of him and he returned to his room. A feeling of inexplicable disgust kept him awake. Then the banging stopped, no more sound of footsteps. Perhaps Piletsky had fallen asleep on the floor.

He tossed in bed for some time, angry at this interference with his rest – and suddenly fell asleep. He dreamt that he was at the Jesuit College where his uncle had intended to send him, and in his serene morning sleep this did not surprise him at all.

Soon the church bell chimed six and he heard the familiar gnarled finger knocking on his door. Usher Foma peered through the lattice and said:

'Wake up, gentlemen! God have mercy on us!'

He looked out of the window; Natasha's light was flickering. The night incident suddenly seemed weirdly comic to him. The big feet of the Jesuit prostrated on the floor amused him. Suddenly he remembered an old French narrative poem his uncle Vasily Lvovich was fond of, about a lectern. In it the posterior of a novice bent in prayer served as a lectern for an abbot reading his prayer-book placed on it; most probably the novice's shoes were described as sticking out in the same way as Piletsky's. The monk was the devil, 'the great pretender' as Arina used to call him, the very mention of whose name his grandmother Marya Alekseyevna strictly forbade. Now no one could forbid him to think what he wanted. A shepherd of souls with a cross, a Jesuit, a monk who sat astride the devil and journeyed about the country at dead of night – this was what Inspector Piletsky was.

3

He had grown up in loneliness and found it difficult to get used to company. Gorchakov pretended to be an old man:

'Ah! My old ailments again!' he would sigh, affecting to limp.

'We old fellows …' he would say comically.

Things were easy for him. He was proud of it. He already had followers: Lomonosov and Korsakov tried to imitate him. The masters were well disposed towards him, he was at the top of the class. He had a memory which effortlessly, though without understanding, reflected everything he read, as if in a mirror. He studied diligently. But he was very forgetful in everything else, especially as far as names were concerned, and even seemed to be pleased with this.

'This … what's his name? … oh, yes – Foma … can never remember his name.' This is how he would speak, snapping his fingers like an old man, perhaps like his uncle, the Governor of Nizhny Novgorod.

Aleksandr envied and feared him.

Valkhovsky slept little at night: he studied hard, eager to be the top scholar.

Broglio was the best at tripping everybody up. Twice Aleksandr had nearly been brought down by his foot. Broglio and Danzas were known as 'the Incorrigibles'– so Piletsky had labelled them.

They competed with each other in punishments. Danzas made a point of grinning when Piletsky reprimanded him. The monk's countenance changed when he saw that impertinent grin on the face of this Incorrigible. Having found the Inspector's Achilles' heel, Danzas would attack it with absolute audacity. Ordinary punishments had no effect on him, and new ones had to be thought of: he was made to dress for a day in the childish old frock-coat he had worn on arrival at the Lycée. It was so tight, cheap and poorly tailored that it made everybody laugh, which had an instant effect on him. School uniforms concealed poverty and removed the juvenile shame of home-made clothes. Aleksandr took one look at Danzas and burst into hoots of delight, but when he remembered his own clothes he quietened down; for nothing in the world would he wish to put on his old frock-coat again.

The students did their homework at their desks in the classroom. In the middle of the room was a black table. The tutor Ilya made Danzas and Broglio sit there as a punishment for their outrageous behaviour and the stupid, indecent and absurd faces they pulled. Recently he had started to place them there even if they did not commit any misdemeanours. They had got used to the table and Danzas even had the nerve to assert that he found it more comfortable than his desk. Gauenschield denied Delvig breakfast for not preparing his German conversation, and on another occasion, for not doing his homework, instead of tea he was given a glass of water with a plain slice of brown bread. Delvig especially was punished for his laziness.

Pushkin was also made to sit at the black table as a punishment for his loud laughter which annoyed Kalinich during a calligraphy lesson, and for making drawings of Gauenschield during a German lesson. But he was not particularly friendly with the Incorrigibles. He was awkward and unsociable, and so far had no other friends but Pushchin.

He did not have an aristocratic title like Gorchakov, or the physical strength of Broglio or Danzas, but he spoke French like a Frenchman. He had books he had brought from home – very entertaining ones. In the evenings the others asked him to read something. He refused at first, then read them a few poems by Voltaire, one of them a prohibited poem but great fun, the others not funny at all but apparently remarkable – he read them all with pleasure, in a somewhat doleful tone and for some reason smiling. When someone gave a snort, he slammed the book shut and scowled at him. Gorchakov said that Pushkin had taste.

Soon other boys noticed him gnawing his quills at lessons – he was drawing and writing something. They thought he was taking notes on the lectures, and would pester him afterwards, whereupon he would fly into a temper and, totally forgetting himself, be ready for a fight on the spot. The tutor who was present at the lectures reprimanded him twice, each time very sternly, and gradually Pushkin won the Incorrigibles' respect. He seemed preoccupied with some other matter and was totally oblivious of everything that was said at lectures. Once Gauenschield asked him to repeat a phrase but Pushkin could not and would not. The German became angry, but he did not seem to be afraid, he obviously didn't mind being at the bottom of the class and had some other preoccupation of his own. The Incorrigibles started to watch him closely. Perhaps he was writing poems? Illichevsky – tall but feeble – was upset; he was also a poet but was never angry when he was interrupted. He would toss his poems aside and go out for a walk, romp about or do his homework like everybody else, and only afterwards, in free time when the others walked along the corridor or read books and painted, did he return to his verses. There was nothing strange or peculiar about his activity. Yakovlev impersonated all the masters, Korsakov tried his hand at singing, Delvig made things up, while Illichevsky wrote verses. They were straightforward pastimes – entertaining and even useful in a way. When Illichevsky was made to read a poem, it went down well: it was a fable very similar to one of Dmitriyev's that Koshansky had read to them earlier that day. When Pushkin was asked to read a poem he refused; he flushed as if he had been lashed with a whip and grew confused. So that was why he had been gnawing his quills – it was clear to everyone that his poems were inferior; they didn't work out.

Later it was discovered that Küchelbecker, who spoke very poor Russian, wrote poems too.

Number fourteen was too proud – so the Incorrigibles decided to lay hands on him. But when Broglio thrust him against the wall, he suddenly went pale, started gasping, and cursed in such foul language that even Broglio was shocked. Pushkin had clearly learned some lessons before coming to the Lycée. No one realised that this was the way his uncle Vasily Lvovich had often sworn. He was left in peace.

The others were afraid of his knowledge – he was an eccentric and a madcap, though in quite a different way from Danzas or Broglio. In the evenings the boys wrote home, some of them every day. He never wrote letters.

One night during tea, Inspector Piletsky entered the room with his brisk step and announced that the students wouldn't be allowed to go home at all, but that their relatives might visit them on Sundays and holidays.

At first they didn't understand. Korsakov and Steven asked when they would be allowed to go home. Piletsky answered:

'When your Lycée days are over.'

There was silence. Korff burst into tears; all sat staring at each other in dismay. Their tea grew cold. Küchelbecker pouted, trying to restrain his tears, but the drops continued to fall from his eyes into his glass. Aleksandr looked at them curiously. He recalled the bare walls of the nursery at home, the coals in the stove, his father – then frowned and drank his glass in a gulp. That night, before going to bed, he took out the little volume of Voltaire that Arina had put into his luggage, read the brief poem about the critic Fréron who was bitten by a snake, causing not Fréron's death but the snake's, smiled with pleasure and pressed the book to his cheek. It was in a decrepit leather binding; the leather was warm like an old woman's cheek. He smiled again and fell asleep.

4

The boys often walked along the ponds to the lake: the dam connecting the first and the second pond was called the Devil's Bridge; the piles of marble and granite stones seemed to have been there for ages imitating wilderness. Below them the falling water seethed and foamed. A bizarre but simple monument rose here like a grey rock; the prows of ships projected from it on all sides. Only when the lake froze were they able to come up close to the monument and read the inscription on the brass plate. It was long, as old inscriptions cast in bronze or cut in stone tend to be, verbose and repetitive like the prattling of grandfathers. It was in commemoration of the naval victory that Count Fyodor Orlov had won at Morey many years earlier. Together with the Morey peninsula Port Vitullo and Modona were mentioned, and the names of Captain Barkov who conquered Passau, Berdoni and Sparta, Captain Dolgoruky who conquered Arcadia, and last on the list, Brigadier Hannibal: 'The Navarin Fortress surrendered to Brigadier Hannibal.'

He did not tell anyone about it; he heard the stupid Myasoyedov reading the inscription and saying some nonsensical rhyme to Tyrkov:

'Brigadier – Hannibal – Cannonball.'

And Tyrkov replied:

'Hannibal … isn't that somebody from ancient history?'

Aleksandr did not know for sure which Hannibal it was. They had not talked much about the Hannibals at home. Was this Hannibal his grandfather whose memory had always caused his grandmother Marya Alekseyevna to shed her tight little tears? Or was it the grandfather who had wanted to take his father's estate from them? They had both been in the Navy. He wanted to share his confusion with Pushchin, but put it off. But every time when he passed the lake, he looked at the stark dark-blue veined stone, the dark, verdigrised-bronze prows of ships sticking out from the monument rising from the Devil's Bridge like a solitary pillar. His grandfather.

Secretly, making sure no one saw, he would pull his cap forward over his forehead. The steward took away their cocked hats for ceremonial occasions and locked them in the wardrobe.

It was a salutation to his grandfather.

5

His uncle Vasily Lvovich had never given him the money that his sister Anna Lvovna had asked him to keep safe for him. Aleksandr did write to his parents. Soon he got a letter full of parental love from Sergey Lvovich, who reproached him gently for hardly writing at all: just two letters in all this time! His mother wanted to pass on to him that she was in despair at the thought of her boy having to get up so early – six in the morning was beyond her comprehension. His aunt Anna Lvovna, as always, spoke and thought only of him. Remembering all this, in his safe haven, looked after by his kind-hearted Principal, Aleksandr should try to be diligent and not to exasperate those currently looking after him. Sergey Lvovich felt that the separation would soon become unbearable and – he had made up his mind! – he was going to visit his son. But not a word had he to say of money.

Meanwhile the boys indulged themselves in certain liberties – Korff sent the nimble usher, the black-moustached Leonty, to the German confectioner's to buy some spice cakes. In his boxroom under the staircase Leonty had even set up a sort of coffee-shop: he had a little table there covered with a clean table-cloth, and on request there appeared in no time a cup of coffee and some toasted bread. Their imagination carried them away. They breakfasted at Leonty's like their fathers did at some Palais-Royal café. Once Gorchakov had a little wine-glass of liqueur there and for two days afterwards he staggered about whenever the supervisors were out of sight, imagining he was drunk. They rummaged decorously in their waistcoat pockets and tipped Leonty in great style. Only Aleksandr, Valkhovsky and Küchelbecker lacked money – Aleksandr and Valkhovsky were without a kopeck, while Küchelbecker had sworn to keep his two roubles until the end of the first year.

On Piletsky's orders, the books they had brought from their homes were to be taken away from them. The tutor Chirikov checked their rooms. Aleksandr had decided not to hand in the books Arina had packed for him, not conceiving how he would get by without Voltaire and the illustrated Piron. When the tutor came to remove the books he met him with such an expression that Chirikov recoiled at once. Frail and feeble, his swarthy face marked by smallpox, he always treated the boys patiently and politely. He sighed, looked at Aleksandr askance and shrugged his shoulders helplessly. And Aleksandr gave him the books.

At breakfast they were told that the books would be returned when they had grown up and that there was hope that soon His Majesty would grant them the library of his youth, and in that event the collection would be placed in the gallery known as 'the arch', situated between the Lycée and the Ladies-in-Waiting Wing.

Now he had nothing left from home.

6

Sergey Lvovich did visit the Lycée.

It was not so easy. Having learned that he was going to St Petersburg, Nadezhda Osipovna silently started to pack her things. Sergey Lvovich was dismayed. He had hoped to go to St Petersburg alone and now the journey was losing much of its attraction. At last they came to an agreement: Nadezhda Osipovna would have a new fur-coat made for the journey – it was out of the question that she should travel in the old one – and would join her spouse later in St Petersburg. This was Sergey Lvovich's idea, though he felt that it would ruin him. The journey also had a professional object. To be a Commissioner of the 7th class in the Moscow Quartermaster Service was, no matter what they said, humiliating for him and earned him next to nothing. He was going to St Petersburg to see Aleksandr and at the same time to find out if it was possible for him to be transferred to the capital, and, if this was impossible, then to any other, worthier post. The current uncertainty afforded him some hope: the threat of war was obvious to everyone, reshuffles and new appointments were being made all the time. The post of Quartermaster was a military one. He no longer hoped for a real career because he had spent too long without one, but as an experienced gambler he could not forget that it was chance that decided everything. Nothing could keep him in Moscow any longer. Gone were the days of frequenting the renowned Pankratyevna; God knew if she was still alive. He could barely satisfy his passion for gambling, playing faro without money and now and then with his former fellow Guards officers who now served in the same department and had fallen into obscurity. He had even taken to patience – a solitary and hopeless game without losses or gains, the rules of which his sister Anna Lvovna knew well, always saying that 'gambling is a sin but life is boring without cards.' His long-standing dream of going to Paris, which had originated from pure envy of his brother, had finally been forgotten. It was the wrong time. Now he found it difficult even to make a journey to St Petersburg.

Meanwhile, on the eve of his departure, gritting his teeth, he suddenly announced to Nadezhda Osipovna that he had no money for her fur-coat and they would have to wait for the quit-rent to be paid. Nadezhda Osipovna realised that once again she had been outwitted, and slapped him across the face. She pouted and glared at him, but to her surprise Sergey Lvovich endured it cheerfully enough, hastily kissed the children – and went off.

He had an excellent journey. At the first post-stage he was drawn into a discussion of the political news with a travelling official, to whom he observed that though he thoroughly disapproved of Napoleon, the latest news that he had ordered his wife's dress-maker to be arrested in order to put an end to her squandering deserved a certain respect. The official, apparently frightened by Sergey Lvovich's free-thinking, replied monosyllabically: 'Hm …'

In Valday he witnessed the carousals of a travelling hussar for whom local peasant-girls, famous for their free behaviour, were rounded up and sent to the post-station. The hussar paid not the slightest attention to Sergey Lvovich and did not invite him to take part in the outrageous fun. Sergey Lvovich looked in the big distorting mirror hanging in the wooden house and understood why: he looked too respectable, his face had grown rounder and heavier – he was the father of a family. He shrugged his shoulders and decided to reward himself on his way back. Everything went well in St Petersburg, though Sergey Lvovich was in no hurry to discuss his service and nobody asked him about it. He visited Ivan Ivanovich Dmitriyev and passed on Karamzin's best regards to him.

The servants at Demouth's were renowned for their politeness and Sergey Lvovich at last felt like a dignified person there.

He had been hoping to go to Tsarskoye Selo with Turgenev, but he was busy. This was even more annoying since cabmen refused to drive to Tsarskoye Selo for less than twenty roubles.

According to the strictly observed rules, he could see Aleksandr only on Sundays, and on the earliest Sunday Sergey Lvovich went to Tsarskoye Selo.

He enjoyed the novelty of the road he had never travelled along before. Encountering passers-by driving past him, he assumed an aloof appearance. He ordered his cabman to stop by the entrance to the park.

Approaching the Palace, Sergey Lvovich took himself in hand, adjusted his clothes and walked with small, hurried steps. He was struck by the thought that he might run into the Emperor, and this fired his imagination. He saw himself, with dignified candour, informing His Majesty of the disadvantages of his post, asking his help in settling his affairs, and suddenly receiving an honourable and quite important appointment, and so on. When he reached the Palace he had met no one but sentries. His confidence suddenly vanished and he felt weak in the knees.

In the Lycée he was met by a most unpleasant-looking person with a piercing eye and hostile expression. He told Sergey Lvovich that the meeting was to be postponed because the morning hour specially designated for it had already passed and now the students were about to go for a walk. So he would have to wait till evening, or better, the following Sunday. Sergey Lvovich started bellowing. There were several other parents talking with their sons in the room. Sergey Lvovich knew none of them. They stared at him in amazement. The unpleasant person, who turned out to be the Inspector, chuckled to himself instead of replying and sent for Aleksandr.

On the stairs Aleksandr ran into Piletsky, who looked at him with the fleeting grin that he couldn't bear, with no laughter in the eyes. Piletsky always smiled like this when looking at him.

He came downstairs to find his father in considerable agitation, pacing to and fro across the room with his little steps.

Sergey Lvovich was wearing a grey flecked tail-coat. He was dressed with a degree of care inappropriate to his age: his starched collar propped up his wrinkled cheeks.

Aleksandr had almost forgotten what his father looked like. He noticed Modest Korff's father who was also in the hall – standing immobile, his head curly as a ram's – casting curious glances at Sergey Lvovich. Suddenly he felt pity for his father, and at the same time was ashamed of his fatness and the excessive fastidiousness of his clothes; an old key-ring, a signet, dangled against his paunch. He embraced his son with sufficient decorum. Realisation that they were in the Palace prevented him from pressing his son to his chest, shedding a tear or two and so forth. Then he said to him loudly and with obvious bitterness:

'Your great-grandfather, my son, was received here in quite a different way.'

Sergey Lvovich restrained himself from saying 'grandfather' because the likelihood of his father having been received in the Palace was dubious in the extreme. Generally, it was clear that Sergey Lvovich could not distinguish between the Lycée and the Palace, the school authorities and those of the Court. Accounts of the opening of the Lycée, where the Court had been present, were deeply engraved on his memory.

He soon calmed down. Casting glances at the Korffs, he asked his son what his achievements had been, expressed the wish to speak to the Principal and, raising his voice a little, enquired if Turgenev had visited his son as, according to Karamzin, he had promised.

Sergey Lvovich had not heard about this from Karamzin: his brother Vasily Lvovich, who had asked Turgenev not to forget his nephew, had told him about it; Sergey Lvovich had, however, visited Karamzin before his departure. But the names produced an effect: Korff livened up and they started a conversation. They berated Inspector Piletsky. Korff strongly disapproved of such treatment of the students' parents.

'My son belongs to me,' he said, 'therefore I have a right to him as my own property. Not to allow a man to enjoy his rightful property is criminal.'

Korff was a lawyer.

Aleksandr asked about his mother and sister. His mother complained that his letters were so short. He asked about Arina: where was she?

Sergey Lvovich considered the question inappropriate.

'*Cette bégueule d'Arina* and all the servants are well,' he said with a chuckle. 'What can happen to them? You did not ask after your brother, my son.'

However, Sergey Lvovich asked if he needed anything

Unexpectedly Aleksandr replied that he needed money.

This had an unpleasant effect on Sergey Lvovich.

'But I seem to recall your aunt, Anna Lvovna, giving you a hundred roubles,' he said sombrely. 'It isn't a petty sum. By the way, she asked, my dear chap, not for an account – since the money is yours – but some idea of how you've been spending it.'

Learning that Aleksandr had got from his uncle three roubles which he had spent on nuts, Sergey Lvovich was stupefied.

'Are you sure you've remembering it right?' he asked, gasping.

Then, convinced, he looked to one side and muttered quickly:

'I'll send you some money at the earliest opportunity and remind your uncle of it. Do write to your mother, dear boy, will you?'

They had nothing else to talk about. Korff's father had long since left. The unpleasant person had appeared again and told Aleksandr to get ready for his walk. Sergey Lvovich knitted his brows and turned white. Aleksandr ran off to put on his warm clothes. The bell rang. Sergey Lvovich remained standing in the same place. The visit was actually over and he had nothing to talk to his son about, but nobody – inspector, courtier or generalissimo – had the right to interrupt the meeting of a respectable man with his son before the bell had gone. A group of youths passed by him, on their way to take their walk. Sergey Lvovich raced downstairs, threw on his greatcoat and ran headlong after his son. The Lycéeists were plodding across the park under the supervision of some unprepossessing person. Aleksandr was in the last pair. Getting entangled in the flaps of his greatcoat, his father caught up with him. The pathetic-looking man, whom Sergey Lvovich inwardly decided was 'a corporal', had drawn up his charges loosely in twos and did not make them keep in step.

'I can see at once, *mon cher*, that you have not served in the Guards,' thought Vasily Lvovich with displeasure as he looked at Chirikov. 'Everything slipshod. What a disgrace!'

The path was narrow and he had to take small hurried steps alongside it, finding his way among the trees, in order not to lag behind. The youths looked at him in bewilderment. He realised that having caught up with Aleksandr, he was not actually saying anything to him, and so spoke with exaggerated formality:

'Aleksandr Ivanovich Turgenev will soon be here. He'll let you know how things are going. Goodbye, my son!'

And having cast a glance at the worthless 'corporal', the disgruntled Sergey

Lvovich shuffled towards his cab, looking furtively at the Palace. The encounter with its inhabitants and the turn in his career that he had imagined so vividly had not taken place. His son was at the Lycée – and that was all. The rude and arrogant teaching staff of the Lycée – *tous ces inspecteurs, instructeurs,* etc. – had not appealed to him one bit.

Five

MARTIN Piletsky took pains to pay no attention to him. He always passed him by with his brisk impetuous step, almost brushing against him as if he were empty space. He had the constant craving for power characteristic of Jesuits, the humble pride of one who confessed only to God. He was feared.

He had obtained his brother Ilya's appointment as one of the tutors at the Lycée. His brother worshipped him and in the presence of everyone bowed to Martin with the humility of a subordinate. Martin Piletsky drifted along the corridors like a shadow; unheard and unseen, he sat in the corner during classes, not listening to the lectures but eavesdropping on whispers and rustlings. He always had about him a long narrow notebook with a black binding, which he filled in with his observations minute by minute.

Martin Piletsky had long talks with his favourites. He seemed worried about the fresh-cheeked and scarlet-lipped Modest Korff. In his eyes Lomonosov was discerning, courteous and dependable; Yudin had good manners and a quick wit; Korsakov was eager to please. The Inspector had drawn all these closer to him. He had long conversations with Korff, retiring with him into the niche by the window or into the long secluded gallery that led to the Ladies-in-Waiting Wing. He advised Modest to be careful: the boy was nice-looking and his friends might have a bad influence on him, or could even harm him. He should confide in Piletsky as his spiritual father and forget his father in the flesh. The monk stroked his head and let him go. His classmates spotted this and Modest was embarrassed by the confidence he enjoyed, especially when Danzas mockingly called him 'a lass'. Modest sobbed and Piletsky comforted him, stroking his head.

When Guryev was expelled from the Lycée for indecent behaviour no one was sad. Guryev was stupid and had no friends. Modest Korff had reported him.

Korsakov received permission to issue a school magazine. He circulated a brief proposal to bring out an anthology of contributions by all Lycéeists of literary abilities. Each of them was to write at least one piece every fortnight, otherwise he would be ostracised. To write for anything outside this publication was strictly forbidden. Ilya informed his brother that at lectures Pushkin made endless notes that bore no relevance to the subject in hand. Once he had crumpled up what he had written and thrown it on the floor. It turned out to contain the words: *I am not the owner of a seraglio ...* thickly crossed out, which convinced Ilya that it must have been a poem by Pushkin himself. Ilya said that the prohibition against writing poetry had resulted in nothing but embitterment, and that it would be pointless to deprive Pushkin of paper: he was mischievous and there might be surprises in store. Ilya asked for instructions.

Martin Piletsky knew that Illichevsky, Delvig and Pushkin wrote poems. He believed that poetry could serve evil ends, as had been proved by Voltaire and Piron, whose books had been removed from Pushkin. In one of the books were extracts from a poem called *The Will*, written by a common gallows-bird, a blasphemous Parisian rake and drunken reprobate, François Villon. He told the boys what this Villon was really like.

Piletsky was tolerant but never indulgent with his favourites. He had decided to tame the boys one by one, leaving Danzas, Broglio and Pushkin to the last, although he knew that he really ought to succeed with Pushkin first because of his potentially pernicious influence.

Piletsky suggested that Korsakov's magazine should be called simply *The Tsarskoye Selo Gazette*. Korsakov had beautiful handwriting – the reason for his appointment as editor. Koshansky would check the magazine to assess the literary value of the contributions and Piletsky would censor it from the moral point of view.

Piletsky demanded his favourites' confidence: they had to report to him everything they and their classmates did or even intended to do. He didn't promise forgiveness but guaranteed – as their spiritual father – justice, and they had to be willing to accept his fatherly authority. It began to appeal to Korff and Korsakov that they had a protector always ready to defend and, on occasion, to honour them.

2

Korsakov was a meticulous editor, as well as having a fine, clear hand, inferior only to Danzas's.

They liked the calligraphy lessons. The huge, expressionless, solemn-faced, Kalinich was a connoisseur and devotee of his subject.

He was another personal failure. A tall, strapping figure as a young man, he had moved from the south to serve in Catherine the Great's Court choir, the example of the choirboy Razumovsky, Empress Elizabeth's favourite, being fresh in everybody's memory. The young Kalinich had had the misfortune to lose his voice, and had found no further opportunity; he had become a living monument to the fickleness of court fortune of the past. Having an excellent hand, he had been employed in the end to copy out scores.

He demanded firm lines from his students and was the enemy of excessive pressure and thickenings, and particularly disliked the lingering of the quill at the beginnings and ends of letters that produced unnecessary flecks. This he considered to be the common feature of the vulgar calligraphy of clerks and scribes. He equally loathed 'curls' – broad, spreading letters, which was how Korff and Küchelbecker wrote, taught by Germans at home.

'You won't manage the paraph,' he warned them.

He considered the paraph, the flourish under a signature, to be the summit of the course.

'If your writing is unclear, your thinking is confused,' he would say, though he made no effort to prove his theory.

Aleksandr's handwriting struck him as faintly ridiculous:

'The latest French school. Fluent enough, but poorly joined up. Illichevsky is clearer but he has a tendency to flourishes.'

Nowadays they put their signatures everywhere – whenever and wherever they could, on every scrap of paper. Aleksandr was obsessed with his own signature. He was no longer the son of a Mr Pushkin of the seventh class or the nephew of the famous poet Pushkin – he himself *was* Pushkin, and a poet.

Aleksandr loved his signature. He practised its official variant, with a paraph, a brief one; with the consonants of his surname in reverse: *NKSP*; with the number *14* (his Lycée room); with the numbers *1 … 14 … 16 …* according to the order of the letters in the Russian alphabet; the first letter of his given name with the last and the first letters of his surname: *ANP*. Once, looking at a final copy of one of his poems, he recalled his grandfather's rough monument and signed himself Hannibal. The variety of possible names and signatures was amazing; with each one not just his name but he himself seemed to assume a new identity.

He liked the mysterious and obviously false signatures in the notebooks in his father's bureau. The authors hid themselves behind letters, numbers and anagrams. They had to be guessed at and teased out.

Kalinich approved of Danzas's handwriting most of all.

'Round and fine and springy. He is a natural writer of edicts and orders.'

And he added thoughtfully:

'He's full of mischief and just about bottom of the class in every subject, everybody complains about him, but my God! what a divine hand! With handwriting like his he'll go far!'

Kalinich taught them two types of handwriting.

'If you write for yourself, the only thing you should bear in mind is clarity – to be able to understand what you have written. But if you write for others, try to please the eye. The paraph, used in the proper places, can achieve more than argument. You can tell at once what class of person the writer is: if the letters are a mixture of square and semi-uncial – he's a clerk; if they're springy and black – a soldier. But if the writing is even, without curls or excessive pressure or connectives, the writer will go far. This is public, or, if you like, official handwriting.'

Korsakov had a natural hand. He was quick, evasive, reserved and felt flattered by his post as editor. When asked what Piletsky had talked to him about, he never answered directly. It was obvious that he valued the trust placed in him. He often told unnecessary lies and imitated Gorchakov in everything he did, and since the latter imitated the Emperor, Korsakov was a double dissembler.

Piletsky approved of the first issue of the *Gazette* but noted that they needed more poems, for example Pushkin's. Aleksandr had not contributed to the magazine.

Pouting and scowling, a fleeting, vacant expression on his face, he would bite his nails in corners, furtively and fiercely. Tutor Ilya often reprimanded him at lessons, but if he was spoken to or touched he would give a start and glare at whoever it was with a look of disgust and alarm. Soon everyone learned to leave him alone. When he was writing, everything others said seemed to him pathetic, irrelevant, false and unworthy of the speaker. Once when Lomonosov tried to pull him by the sleeve he burst into a string of terrible curses.

3

Principal Malinovsky had an even step – he had brought this walk with him from England but these days he walked with a hurried lurch.

One morning he left his house that was across the road from the Lycée and crossed the street as usual. Two of the Lycéeists saw him from the window. Then they noticed the Principal cast a blank look at the skies and bury his face in his hands. It lasted just a moment. They were embarrassed and said nothing to anyone.

That day Kunitsyn was pale too. His lips were compressed in the firm expression that he wore when not being listened to in class – he hated being interrupted. That day he didn't answer the questions that, as always, were eagerly put to him. They thought he was angry with them, but he just didn't hear them.

The tutors were silent. It was the day Piletsky took away the books they had brought from home. The mathematics teacher Kartsov, who liked black humour, was silent too and in his sour mood screeched his chalk across the blackboard so that it crumbled under his heavy hand. Gauenschield chewed his liquorice quickly and noisily, in apparent oblivion, and forgot to read Opitz's poems to them, which they were only too pleased about.

It was the day of Speransky's fall. They learned about it a week later: Myasoyedov's high-placed father, as portly as his son, told him about it during his visit.

Only the ushers continued to kindle the stoves as if nothing had happened, tearing birch-bark off the logs and grumbling because of the smoke. Usher Matvey was in charge of the heating and had been waging a war with the steward over the stoves. The steward would claim that it was warm enough without heating but usher Matvey objected:

'It doesn't matter to me if it's warm or cold. But look at your stove – it's red-hot. They're growing, they need warmth. Order more logs, will you?'

Tsarskoye Selo became deserted: Emperor Alexander was away; he had gone off to the Army. Rumours went round, incomprehensible to the Lycéeists: Speransky had suddenly fallen – either he had been executed or imprisoned, as he had turned out to be a traitor. The Martinist conspiracy had been uncovered in Moscow. They did not know for sure what the word 'Martinist' meant. Piletsky gave an explanation. Looking impassively at Pushkin, he said that Martinists were French and devoted to everything French, scoffers and philosophers, irreverent and ready for anything. The spirit of irreverence and wilfulness – this was Martinism; now it would be ended. The main sources of the rot were the Moscow and St Petersburg fashion shops – and French books, which were to be destroyed. They needed to know nothing more about Martinism.

At the end of Boudri's class Pushkin asked him what Martinism was. Boudri sat back in his chair, studying his student sternly.

'Where have you heard this word?' he asked.

He glared at them, suddenly pulled his wig off his head and threw it onto his desk. No one laughed. They looked at his closely shaved skull, his square brow, his glistening coal-black eyes. He spoke hoarsely and abruptly in a rough voice as if he were not in the classroom but in the street or a square.

'Martinism is a harmful superstition,' he said, 'like Illuminism. Martinists are mystics. Abusing the notion of deity, bigots of every age have always tried to obscure reason. Human sacrifices – how many were put to the stake by the Inquisition alone! Aren't modern bigots just like the old ones with their meaningless sacraments and fateful superstitions! Molière gives us a superb picture of the power and pointlessness of superstitions like that in *Tartuffe*.

That is what Martinism is!'

Then he calmly pulled the wig down on his head, adjusted it and told Pushchin to conjugate the irregular verb *coudre* in all its tenses and moods. Pushchin made a mistake and Boudri grumbled:

'More diligence, more attention, or you'll never learn how to speak rather than merely babble!'

He was a good-humoured old fellow but a stern teacher.

So, Martinists were false saints. Piletsky's name was also Martin. From now on therefore, everything about him was Martinism. His informers, Korff, Lomonosov and Yudin, were Martinists.

Immediately after the class Aleksandr called Korff a Martinist and roared with laughter. Korff did not understand but took offence. His lips twitched and his blue eyes dimmed. He was thin-skinned, a sniveller.

4

It was a kind of disease; he was tormented, tried to catch a word, rhymes came to him. Then he would read what he'd written, and be devastated: these were the wrong words. He would cross out word after word, leaving only the rhymes. He became accustomed to words that were wrong, and excessive in number; nevertheless, however imperfect they were, these were his poems. He had no choice but to write them, and then in frustration he would rip them to pieces.

Sometimes he dreamt of poems during the night but forgot them in the morning. Once he dreamt of Natasha. The delirium lasted all through the night, passionate and painful. He woke up in the morning frightened and bewildered – something had happened, something he could not explain, something had changed for ever, he remembered one line, half a line: ... *dear heart, Natasha*, and a kiss instead of a rhyme. He kept wondering what the dream had been really about – Natasha or poetry? But he wrote down: ... *dear heart, Natasha* on a scrap of paper.

He never read his verses to anybody else. He found it difficult to confess them, as if his poems were some sort of crime.

Apart from Korsakov, Illichevsky and Gorchakov contributed to the magazine too. Gorchakov looked on the new venture favourably and even made it up with some of the 'softies' whom he had always treated arrogantly. They were angry with Pushkin for not contributing to the magazine and decided to boycott him. When he learned about it, he laughed but then became furious.

He found a favourite place in the Lycée, where he could hide himself from Piletsky or go to when he suddenly needed to be alone. It was the gallery that connected the Lycée with the Ladies-in-Waiting Wing, an arch over the road. A library had at last been set up there from which they could borrow books, most of them boring: histories of the crusades, journeys along the Nile, a volume of Voltaire – but only his history of Charles XII. But he learned to like boring books. He liked their unhurried precision even when rapid or obscure events were described. He was particularly fond of philosophy books or dictionaries of quotations – these brief truths, in some cases weirdly obvious, could rival poetry.

What Kunitsyn told them about reason, the passions and citizenship was more poetic for Aleksandr than Koshansky's lectures on the art of poetry. There was nothing superfluous in Kunitsyn's definitions, the very words 'freedom', 'reason', 'passion' seemed created for poetry – the rhymes occurred by themselves and proved the truth of the concepts. He was captivated by the young Anacharsis' visit to Athens.

He began to read Barthélemy's novel about Anarcharsis, enjoying the leisurely descriptions of the young Scythian's encounters and impressions. The Scythian was from practically the same region as Malinovsky: the ancient lake Meotica, on whose shores the Scythian had lived, was the Sea of Azov. His untamed and shy heart and mind made him, alongside the Athenian philosophers, a friend of Solon; but listening carefully to the Athenian Sophists' speeches he found he did not share their ideas.

Piletsky watched Aleksandr. He saw him playing ball during a break; his movements were quick, he had a good eye and was very keen. He was completely absorbed in the game but still noticed everything that was going on around him. He did not see Piletsky, however, for true to his system of invisible moral presence, he was hiding himself behind either a column or a door. On another occasion he saw Pushkin talking to Yakovlev so vibrantly and rapidly that he couldn't take in the words. Yakovlev was all ears and listened open-mouthed. Pushkin was talking quickly, eagerly, even gasping slightly. Then he stopped and didn't add another word.

Once he saw an encounter between Pushkin and Delvig, who was in everybody's bad books for his laziness. Pushkin was walking as always, 'wild and guarded' as the tutor Chirikov described him. Suddenly he caught sight of Delvig ambling idly towards him. His face changed, a smile appeared, his eyes shone, he gave a laugh for no apparent reason, then the two embraced and walked in step. Pushkin, normally taciturn and reluctant to answer his classmates' questions, Pushkin, who laughed rarely, abruptly and harshly, was now laughing and jabbering, chattering like a bird; he seemed very fond of Delvig. Piletsky watched them, dismayed, keeping himself hidden. Pushkin seemed genuinely good-natured. The contradictions in his character were inexplicable.

Sometimes the bookcases in the library were left unlocked, and having ensconced himself by the window, he lost himself in books, turning away from those on mathematics and those in German. He could not bring himself to learn German words – they sounded too ugly. Chewing his liquorice, Gauenschield would read Opitz, grimacing, shouting some words and hissing the rest; the poems sounded like vituperation, not like poetry at all.

Piletsky hunted him down. Aleksandr hid himself in the deep doorway of the Ladies-in-Waiting premises, but was triumphantly extracted. Piletsky waved his finger at him but did not say a word. That day Kunitsyn gave a lecture on the Golden Age of man's innocence, nowadays preserved only in primitive societies.

Having walked past him, Piletsky suddenly turned round, smiled and took Pushkin by the shoulders, which signalled confidentiality and a desire to have a face-to-face talk. Aleksandr made an awkward attempt to avoid him. He was ticklish and didn't like to be touched. Piletsky kept smiling. He asked him why he had refused to give his poems to Korsakov. Perhaps he needed some books and would like to have them. If they were acceptable texts, he should simply let Martin know and they would be delivered to him.

Ignoring his question about his poems, Aleksandr named one after another in quick succession the books that Arina had put into his bag and which Chirikov had taken away from him on Piletsky's orders. These were the books he wanted.

'Do you know, my fine fellow,' Piletsky asked him, 'what kind of books they are?'

Without waiting for a reply, he said in the same even tone, smiling:

'You have three days to forget these. Afterwards come to see me, will you? I'll be waiting.'

He took a few steps, then turned back and asked him how he had come to have these books in the first place.

When he learned that the books were from his father's library, Piletsky chuckled:

'Your parent hasn't got much to offer, has he?' he said, still smiling, and shook his head.

Then he looked at Aleksandr with obvious regret and asked him quietly if he had read *The Journeys to Jerusalem*. He could lend him the book if he was interested and he would not regret the time he spent on it. And Piletsky quickly strode off, energetic as ever, finding his way to all souls, directing everyone's destinies.

Aleksandr looked after him and remembered the huge protruding feet that night when the monk had been striking his brow against the flagstones of the floor in prayer.

He had never read *The Journeys to Jerusalem*. Instead, with a surge of pleasure, he recalled his father's copybooks. If he could only get them and hide them away!

His last meeting with his father had been distinctly frosty; he hardly thought about him. He was ashamed of Sergey Lvovich – his tail-coat, his starched collar, the bloated look, the stately bearing, the hurried speech – and the quick little steps. But the sidelong glance that Piletsky had thrown at him on the stairs, together with this insult, now decided everything.

Piletsky had obviously been making fun of Sergey Lvovich in referring to him as 'your parent'. Aleksandr suddenly shuddered, imagining Piletsky calling his mother 'a parent' too. The more worthless his parents were, the more precious they became. He recalled his corner by the stove where he had often hid himself, Arina's earthy hands poking the logs – he remembered them less and less often, usually just when he was falling asleep, but hardly at any other time. Suddenly his hackles rose: nobody had the right to sneer at his father – nobody but he. His father, Sergey Lvovich, this solid short little man who had seemed so tall at home, had stood so nervously and looked so helpless in the Lycée reception hall – and Piletsky had sneered at him.

From now on he hated Piletsky.

Later that day, when the curly-haired, ruddy-faced Gorchakov was walking along the corridor with the Martinist Korsakov, with a springy, rather perky step in imitation of the Tsar's observed gait at the opening of the Lycée, coughing a little as he limped along with his weight on his right leg – he was complaining of his old gout – Aleksandr called him 'a Polish tart'.

He didn't take offence, but just looked at Pushkin with screwed-up eyes and half-open mouth and quickly walked off. His limp was gone. Aleksandr roared with laughter after his retreating figure. Martin Piletsky's brother Ilya witnessed this.

On the same day he overheard Pushkin laughing at Myasoyedov's father, generally disapproved of for his arrogance; Malinovsky often mentioned the fact that he was a Senator. But Pushkin had laughed not at Myasoyedov's father as such but at the Senate in general, which was indecent. He heard Pushkin's snorts of laughter as he quoted some wildly illicit satirical verse about the Senate. He couldn't hear the words of the verse, only the vulgar rhyme. When asked about it, Myasoyedov testified that Pushkin really had quoted the lines:

> *The Senate lay still, as if in the hearse:*
> *'Rise,' said the Tsar, and up went its arse.*

Praising Myasoyedov's good memory, tutor Ilya ordered him to forget the poem. He wondered where Pushkin could have got hold of and learned this poem about the restoration of the Senate's power.

In general, that week, Pushkin was lazy and slovenly, dropping his hand-kerchiefs, refusing to button the top button of his frock-coat, saying that it was too tight, and moodily gnawing in huge quantity the quills so expertly sharpened by Kalinich.

Martin Piletsky's brother asked for precise and immediate instructions on how to deal with Pushkin. Reprimands would only embitter him: first, he would recklessly ignore them, and be likely to react in some outrageous way; and secondly, they might have to reprimand him too often. The black desk was also ineffectual in his case, as with Broglio and Danzas, who boasted that they had got used to it.

5

Koshansky was hurt. His appetite for insults was limitless. Frowning, he stalked about the hall trying to hear if they were talking about him. There was something lugubrious even in his dress: he wore a firm collar and his black bow slapped about like a crow's wings when he walked. He was a new-fangled fop – a sad one. Zhukovsky was the first to have made this gloominess fash-ionable, with an unbuttoned collar, a forelock drooping down over the brow and distractedly rolling eyes. Koshansky's forelock disguised his hairpiece; his hair was thinning. Having found no pleasure in the company of women, the melancholy poets decided that love was not for them. Koshansky had originally been merely striking a pose but had gradually grown gloomy in reality.

Poetry and fair ladies, to which subjects he had intended to devote his life, had turned away from him. His poems were flops, women found him ridiculous, something to do, perhaps, with the extreme self-consciousness of his attire and the carefully cultivated disorder of his appearance. Women and the Muse were the most ungrateful companions. He wooed them both but with no reward. He began to write in the most melancholy of genres – on the deaths of fair ladies. One such poem, on the death of Princess Kasatkina-Rostovskaya, was published in *New Literature*. The level of grief suggested he had been much closer to the dead beauty than had really been the case. In time women came to shun him, and once one of them had curled her lip at him and whispered, if he hadn't actually imagined it:

'Undertaker!'

Wine, the glorification of which he believed to be a sign of dissipation, was his little luxury. He was determined to prohibit the ignorant youths from composing poetry, but to no avail – they went on writing. He began to suggest topics and texts for translations, and so on. Criticising these became his passion. His knowledge was deep and extensive and the Lycéeists were afraid of his criticisms. He felt his immeasurable superiority over them and occasionally favoured them with a gracious response. He called his criticism 'a saving rod'.

Recently some absurd verses had been composed and sung within the Lycée walls. As Deputy-Principal and Senior Master, he hoped to replace Malinovsky as soon as he resigned. After Speransky's fall he considered Malinovsky's resignation inevitable, and so in order to familiarise himself with the life of the Lycée more closely, he often stayed on night duty as a substitute for Piletsky.

He was about to retreat to his room for a rest when he heard the sound of muted singing. He listened to it not without enjoyment at first; the young students had no idea that they could be overheard, and next day he might surprise them with this. Besides, a couplet about Gauenschield was very much to the point – for some reason the boys believed that he aspired to be Principal. But soon his pleasure evaporated: nothing seemed to be sacred for them – anything and everything could come in for ridicule. And indeed, after the singing, the impersonations began. Clowns had appeared in the Lycée some time ago. The idiotic Tyrkov, for example, tried to attract his classmates' attention with his faces. But it was Yakovlev who was the real plague. He could impersonate anybody and with such lethal accuracy that it had to be forbidden. The future Principal heard his own name. Then he heard Yakovlev's voice:

'A tie! A tie!'

It was apparently a request to give him a tie for his performance. The Senior Master felt about for the tie on his chest.

The performance began. He could tell that it had begun, from the way the spectators caught their breaths. He could have interrupted them but his curiosity got the better of him.

Meanwhile Yakovlev whispered in a throaty nasal voice that was nothing like his teacher's:

'*Crowned with corn-ears, the Volga delivered bread* – Its product! Delivered through the canals! From a great distance! Golden corn-ears! – *Ripheus stooped* – It's no large matter for him, a mere trifle! Just leaned over – *and poured mead into the goblets!*' … and so on.

It was gibberish, a senseless set of phrases, but this was exactly what he had told them when explaining Derzhavin's poem. When talking about poetry, he would make a point of emphasising its difference from normality, and would deliberately lower his voice during his readings with inspirational commentaries and allusions in order to make the boys understand and savour the full flavour of the poems – an experience, however, accessible only to the select few. In this way he tried to bring them to a state of intoxication with the elevated meaning of the words, a state of ecstasy essential, in his view, for comprehending poetry. He never allowed them to hear Derzhavin's poems, for example, without the benefit of his commentaries. What could they understand in them? The other day he had read them a couple of lines.

> *In a wreath made of corn-ears the Volga delivered bread,*
> *Ripheus leaned from his slopes and poured mead into the goblets.*

The reaction had been as usual: gaping mouths and all sorts of other things in their heads. Complete indifference. Pushkin was gloomily biting his nails, Danzas was trying to reflect the sun with a piece of glass. Koshansky pointed these two out to tutor Ilya, who was sitting in the class. When order had been restored, he rose from his seat, overturning his chair, began his explanations in a quick whisper – and a complete change came over all faces.

The youths obviously thought his presentation had cost him no effort. Far from it. He wiped the sweat from his forehead with a cambric handkerchief. This was his way of instilling poetry into their hearts and minds, and his efforts seemed to have achieved their goal – his prize was general attention.

And now the boys – just like those unfaithful ladies – were laughing at him, classing him not so much as a poet and teacher but as an actor! This satirical attitude now prevalent in the Lycée was the curse of modern education. He had no doubts as to the instigator of this mood, a hereditary culprit, from a family of scoffers, Pushkin. He heard his laughter, abrupt and indecent, rising above the others who had the courtesy to tone down their reactions. Just like his uncle, who had flooded Parnassus with his obscene and shallow verses, the nephew infected everyone around him. His uncle produced such trivial stuff – you only had to blow on it and it disappeared like a dandelion clock.

He had not heard any verses about himself. But who could guarantee that tomorrow this little devil who made such dubious use of his ability would not dash off some epigram, some couplet or charade, in a genre he had sucked in with his mother's milk? Accustomed to scoffing and associating with poets published in periodicals, where you never came across anything of any worth – he might well be the author of the obscenities now being sung in the Lycée. The teacher had no doubt about it – he trusted his instinct. He imagined the verses about himself. They would certainly be horrible: sloppy and scathing. Mentally he was already underlining the metric blunders in them. Yes, he relied on his instinct; an author can be recognised by his style, even if he is only a boy, just as the character of his crime gives a criminal away. Style is an author's face. In these incoherent lines he could sense the nonchalant reck- lessness of Pushkin, the prankster. Pushkin was the author of these satirical songs; no one else had that sharp, derisive eye that spied out the weaknesses of others: he was a real scourge! He decided to teach him a lesson. Strangely enough he didn't even given a thought to Yakovlev – he was just a poseur, that was all, and nobody ever got angry with him. But Pushkin and Danzas were full of themselves. How did he know this? – Because of their pride: they wrote away, they gnawed their quills, but they never asked him for a single piece of advice. They were ready to imitate anybody but chose no one to imitate in particular. Yet, imitation was the basis of creativity. There was only one student who really promised well – Illichevsky. He kept quiet, took no part in singing songs, knew his place and asked for help and advice when he needed it. The purity of his verse, its meticulous polish and control denoted a poetic talent that would flourish, given time. Even now his poems were easily superior to those of the others. Correcting one small fault after another, following his elders' advice, he was approaching perfection.

Next day he began his lecture by talking about the value of style. He used the thoughts about his own fate that had gone through his head on those sleepless nights when he recited to himself his favourite poems, Derzhavin's and his own; above all, he had contemplated the question of what constituted a good style. *A simple style meant the ability to write as one spoke.* It was wrong to call it a low style just because it was not elevated. On the contrary, expressing common words and thoughts like this was *not low* at all, but noble.

He had managed to engage their interest: Küchelbecker's quill was screeching as he scribbled notes. Even the normally inattentive Pushkin, whose fleeting and elusive glances revealed his absent-mindedness, was gazing at him thoughtfully and apparently committing what he heard to memory.

They could find simplicity of thought, emotion and style in letters, conversations, stories, novels, essays, fables, folk-tales, comedies, satires, pastorals and light poetry. But how could they learn to write simply?

He revelled in their studious attention and their eagerness to hear him answer that question. Illichevsky wrote fables, Pushkin seemed to concentrate on comedies and satires. Simplicity was the most difficult thing to achieve, and these youths already felt this; that was why they tore their manuscripts to shreds in dark corners, not knowing what they needed, what they lacked. They could take no satisfaction in the second-hand thoughts, the borrowed sounds that filled their heads – it was simplicity that was wanting.

He paused.

'You shouldn't look for simplicity in public places where you can learn only vulgar language, but in the conversation of people of the highest society.'

Most of them had never got anywhere near the highest society. Koshansky had been to Razumovsky's reception and had seen the spluttering poet Vasily Lvovich, who, unlike Dmitriyev, did not belong to the higher circles. Koshansky made the boys write down the rules of clarity of style: knowledge of the subject, logical connection of thought, and precision of language. These rules were absolute, but he liked to enliven prosaic theory with poetic images and told them to note down that clarity of style could be likened to daylight, moonlight or sunlight. Generally, his ideas made sense and his observations were reasonable, until either his passion for poetry or his literary ambitions ran away with him. It upset him that some of the boys did not consider it necessary to write his words down – Pushkin among them.

He turned his attention to flaws of style.

Pulling Küchelbecker's translation of Saint-Lambert's *Thunderstorm* out of his pocket, he read it slowly and with relish:

> *At the sound of brass*
> *Fear makes crowds of frightened people*
> *Stampede to the holy temple.*
> *Look, great God, at the number*
> *Of the despondent beseeching you …*

Everyone smiled, Pushkin and Yakovlev roared with laughter, but the teacher wished to keep things calm.

'This is sublime nonsense,' he said. 'It would be hard to achieve anything comparable, however hard you tried. The lines have no connection with each other.'

Without naming the author, he explained why it did not make sense.

'Nothing captivates the imagination of the young more than elevated style. They try to imitate it and what comes out is darkness, verbiage and gibberish. Their style is heavy, clumsy, savage, jangling, uneven, cold, inflated, forced, crude and clumping!'

Mesmerised by his own words, he threw caution to the winds. Küchelbecker sat sulking and bewildered, then stared at his teacher with a wild look in his eyes. All eyes turned to him: only he was capable of such higher nonsense. He deserved the saving rod. Not knowing how to put two words together, he claimed to be a poet. Look before you leap – you've been warned. Obstinacy was going to be punished. But they shouldn't be too ready to mock – their glee was inappropriate. Yakovlev was given to laughter, but Pushkin, Delvig and Malinovsky too made no effort to conceal their delight. Illichevsky behaved more decently: he giggled quietly. It was time to switch their attention to another subject, to give their thoughts a different direction, so he passed on to the definition of *bad style*.

Carelessness was bad; gallicisms, incoherence, a mixture of high and low styles, humorous and serious words – these were all bad. Wine and voluptuousness – fashionable vices of the new-fangled poetry – were bad subjects. The style of these new poets was nebulous, empty, banal, their thoughts were incoherent, they possessed neither fluency nor shape. They made fun of everything; there was no good nature left – just brevity and bitterness, ditties and profanity.

It was not a lecture, it was a *cri de coeur* – he could not bear the type of poetry that captivated everyone nowadays – mocking, superficial, caustic, capricious, singsong and colloquial. The poet Pushkin wrote in this way and apparently his nephew was following in his uncle's footsteps. Gravity, even sombreness – these were the essential attributes of poetry. Young Pushkin was well aware of his target and started fidgeting behind his desk. The lecturer, however, would never refuse him guidance. He had particularly thoroughly studied the art of consonance and harmony between the parts, a vital part of poetry.

And having finished his appraisal, the lecturer returned to the subject of good style. Few had a gift for it, but he wished to see it among the callow, immature talents that had not yet left their nests.

'The style that is smooth and gentle, harmonious, pleasant and fresh, at times witty and amusing, always alive and natural, the style of high quality – grand and solid, with true fire!'

He shut his eyes, and with the smile that he always used in the presence of ladies, said softly but distinctly:

'The style that is silky, velvety ... jewelled!'

None of these youths possessed it.

6

Koshansky was on duty. Darkness was descending upon the Tsar's palace and he had his dinner in the pleasant atmosphere of twilight. The usher Matvey served him a dinner which was not up to standard, and he decided to dismiss the steward as soon as he became Principal. The steward was an out-and-out thief, and the boys were right when they ridiculed him in their reckless verses. But Koshansky did not complain: he was soothed by the wine he had brought with him from town in his huge bag together with Blair's *Rhetoric* and his lecture notebooks. He had seemed to detect tutor Ilya cocking up his ears as the teacher walked by to his post of duty – he had heard the wine swilling about in the bottle. But Koshansky had remained composed. He finished his dinner and relaxed in the gathering gloom without recourse to lamps. The smooth sobriety that he felt after dinner was very pleasant. Good humour was gradually returning to him. His learning was extensive and well acknowledged; the position he occupied and especially the one that he was soon to occupy was an honourable one. He was strict but fair. Still wearing his dark smile, he proceeded unhurriedly into the hall where his charges were gathered. Pushkin was discussing something with Delvig, it must be about the lecture they had recently heard, or perhaps Koshansky's special message to him that it had contained. Koshansky felt like cheering him up. Wine always made him more tolerant. The youngster should not be held responsible for his uncle's or anyone else's sins. They began to talk. Malinovsky, Korsakov and some others came up to listen to the conversation with their teacher. Koshansky had had no intention of hurting the boy's feelings, he had simply wished to direct him. The 'saving rod' was the one salutary remedy for these young scribblers craving for fame. He asked Pushkin what he was currently reading and what he would like to read.

It turned out that Pushkin had just read Dmitriyev's *Fashionable Wife*. Koshansky gave a reluctant smile. Dmitriyev was an exemplary poet, but his *Fashionable Wife* was a seductive poem of doubtful value. It was a slight stain on the poet's otherwise immaculate reputation: a seduced wife, a deceived husband, with all the features of vaudeville. No doubt Pushkin had brought the book from home and had hidden it, or obtained it against the school regulations. Perhaps high society life interested Pushkin as a subject for a comedy of his own: he was crazy about comedies. It also turned out that he was familiar with Krylov's play about fashion shops. What next! He told him that the common language in that play was often vulgar, and that there was much in the exposition and dénouement that was indecent.

Pushkin replied laughingly that real life was even more indecent, that the author very realistically described the backrooms in the shops of the St Petersburg and Moscow *marchandes de mode*, but agreed that the plebeian language could be tiresome.

Tutor Ilya hurried towards them from a far corner. Pushkin was in his black books and needed strict supervision, so he had been taking good care to keep him in sight every second and was following hard on his heels. He remembered his brother's instructions: to watch their faces and mimicking, to pick up the whisperings and scraps of conversations. With Pushkin all this was superfluous – he was rotten to the core, a born mischief-maker – they had to keep a physical and not just a moral eye and ear on him. Hearing the boys laughing, seeing the master shrugging his shoulders in indignation, he approached them and, craning his neck, listened. Pushkin's talk was outrageous. He was speaking about the things that happened in the fashion shops which were the reason for their owners' expulsion from the capitals; what exactly those things were the tutor could not hear and was afraid to hear, trembling for the students' sake. Koshansky was turning more and more crimson and saying indignantly:

'I am older than you and a lot more experienced, but I couldn't have made up all this nonsense, it couldn't have entered anyone's mind!'

Martin Piletsky's brother, not trusting to memory, opened his black notebook and surreptitiously started to note down the words.

Koshansky paused for thought, then he noticed the tutor making notes of his words and waved his finger at him.

'Wh-wha-at?' from tutor Ilya.

But Koshansky turned abruptly on his heels. He staggered on his sharp turn and the tutor supported him.

Koshansky's pleasant mood of a few minutes before was gone. This scape-grace, so precociously knowledgeable about loose living in all its detail, had shocked him. He had intended to cheer up the prankster whom he had indirectly subjected to devastating criticism. But the prankster had turned out not to be embarrassed in the least. Tutor Ilya had seen him staggering. '*Wh-wha-at* indeed!' muttered Koshansky. If tutors were boors, how could they expect their students to be well-behaved? A sudden suspicion sprang up in his mind; had Pushkin touched upon the subject of fashion shops because he considered Koshansky (like many others in the Lycée, he knew this rumour but thought it beyond his dignity to refute it) to be a fop and wanted to show it? Koshansky's face became even darker. As a diligent and conscientious educator and a future Principal, he had wanted to speak to the other students too today, but now he changed his mind. He went to his room, untied his tie and collapsed into bed, not even taking time to reread his poem *On the Death of Princess Kasatkina-Rostovskaya* which had been published in *New Literature,* but at once falling asleep. Educating these raw youths was a wearisome business.

7

Koshansky's criticism had its effect. Everything about Küchelbecker incited the other boys, even the most inoffensive, to mock him: his walk, his height and his deafness. He was hard-working, obstinate, proud and easily hurt. His Russian was poor although he spent days on end at his bureau reading and writing. Sometimes he even jumped up in the middle of the night and wrote in the dark. Illichevsky had taught him to write poetry. He advised him to write in a lighter style, secretly composing epigrams about him. Küchelbecker had many projects on the stocks – outlines of novels, dramas, poems, odes and elegies, all waiting to be written.

Now, after Koshansky's criticism, lines from his poems became catchphrases.

In the morning, hearing the Lycée chapel bell chiming, the class would quote: *At the sound of brass fear makes crowds of frightened people …*

Lining up to go on a walk, they would say: *Look, great God, at the number …*

A sheet of paper was passed from hand to hand on which, in a description of a summer evening, 'twilight' was spelt *twilicht*. Yakovlev swore it belonged to Küchelbecker.

But the others were afraid to mock him openly: he had a fiery temper. It seemed he wanted to kill the offender on the spot: to pierce him with a fork if it was at dinner, throw an ink-pot at him if it was in class, or knock him down if it was during a walk. It was a kind of conspiracy: they laughed up their sleeves and wrote poems about him in secret. They nicknamed him Don Quixote or Willie, Willinka or Wilmushka. They were genuinely fond of him. Every evening they whispered epigrams about him into each other's ears. He was the victim sacrificed to the god of ridicule, Momus. His trousers, his nose, his mulishness, his poems – everything was mocked. The names of his characters, taken from old German books, were truly astonishing: Zami, Zulma, Telasko. Everything about him was bizarre.

Apart from Aleksandr, Illichevsky and Misha Yakovlev wrote epigrams too. Though not with much skill. The genre seemed so unyielding. Yakovlev's were the best: he wrote epigrams on everything that happened in Küchelbecker's life. Willie tore his trousers – an epigram; Willie studied English conversation from the books that he had got from home – another one. Everything provoked merriment:

> *Oh, my God! What a freak!*
> *What a huge mouth! What a huge beak!*

Even the kind-hearted Matyushkin and Komovsky copied them down.

Küchelbecker suspected that he was being ridiculed, but the more he was mocked, the more persistently he hammered out his poems. He had read somewhere that all poets had been ridiculed. Copying out Chapelain's long narrative poem about Joan of Arc, he read in the introduction how the unfortunate poet had been sneered at almost literally to death by Boileau. Küchelbecker disapproved of satirical literature. Boileau had written of Corneille's tragedy *Agésilas*:

> *J'ai vu l'Agésilas –*
> *Hélas!*

In Küchelbecker's view, satire was easy. And indeed, even Broglio – the most careless, useless student, always lounging about the Lycée whistling songs, caring nothing for Boileau or for Chapelain – had hit off a short verse about Delvig:

> *Ha-ha-ha! Hay-hay-hay!*
> *Delvig wrote a poem today!*

Once the satirists slyly slipped an epigram on Küchelbecker into his manu-script pages, and holding their breath, settled down to wait for the effect it would produce. Küchelbecker read it twice, twitched, his nostrils flared, he turned white, but said courageously that the epigram was poor: the language was vulgar and unsubtle and the rhyme was bad.

The offended Yakovlev suggested that Küchelbecker should try to write an epigram too. At once an epigram appeared on 'the new La Harpe'. Küchelbecker was at his funniest when he was angry.

Though Pushkin, like the rest of the boys, continued writing epigrams about poor Willie, he soon concluded that they were thin gruel.

He started to read La Harpe.

La Harpe claimed that every caustic witticism in a conversation could be called an epigram. But the subject of a genuine epigram was a thought that was both witty and simple. Anybody could compose an epigram, but the real gift lay in the precise and sharp use of every word.

The epigrams on Küchlya lacked brevity and simplicity.

Aleksandr did not let Koshansky read his poems. The profound gloom the unacknowledged poet fell into when reading the poems of others, the dispassionate voice in which he delivered his comments, almost always on some practical point, his words of praise and affected smiles, all repelled him. Spotting a fault, Koshansky would swoop like a hawk on the sheet of paper in the young poet's hand, joyfully cross out the unnecessary or meaningless words and immediately produce his own version. A striking feature of his criticism emerged: all errors were the same to him, whether they were simple spelling errors or stylistic shortcomings. His students' fast-blooming juvenilia seemed to offend his self-esteem. They were encroaching upon a sacred art destined for the educated, the sophisticated and the mature; when one of the boys did manage to produce a felicitous poem he considered it a fluke which made him doubt his own talent.

8

In his father's house Aleksandr had grown accustomed to conversations about poetry. Every time his uncle, his father and their friends had spoken about poems, the theatre, women or good luck in gambling, their eyes would sparkle in a special way. A successful poem would make them laugh and fill them with admiration and envy, as if it were a young beauty snatched from under the noses of her parents by a young rake, or a stack of cards that had made a gambler a fortune. If the fine verse was sad, they would screw up their eyes and give each other a serious, conspiratorial look. If a poem was obscene, they would fall silent when his mother, his aunt or some female guest approached the table. Furtively, greatly pleased with themselves, they would tickle each other's curiosity. Koshansky read poetry evenly, raising his voice at the right points, lowering it at others, interrupting the poem and pausing to give an explanation. He knew much more than Vasily Lvovich, but it was a different kind of knowledge. Aleksandr had watched his uncle writing poems. He had seen pages with the ink still wet. He knew that poets praised themselves when a poem came out well, but Koshansky scoffed at all immodesty and pride. Vasily Lvovich castigated Derzhavin and grumbled at Dmitriyev. Koshansky castigated only the dreary Trediakovsky; for him the famous were above criticism. Aleksandr found Koshansky's criticism of his poems unconvincing. His teacher never saw a poem as a whole: each individual line was wrong, the rhymes were poor, there was a lack of smoothness. As a matter of fact he was right and wrong at the same time. He rolled his eyes when he spoke of elevated poetry or of women. He was full of affectation.

Aleksandr had his own critic – the tutor Ikonnikov. The pale and gloomy lover of truth, with his wild stare and his shaky alcoholic hands, was an unhappy lunatic. He truly loved poetry, his own and others', but he rarely spoke about it and almost never made any sensible remarks. He would lift his finger to his pale lips, listen to the verses, and turn even paler. Twice he had told Aleksandr that his poems were poor and it had never even occurred to the boy to take offence. He had suddenly realised that the poems had been poor indeed. On a third occasion he had read him a poem he had considered rubbish, and Ikonnikov had rushed to embrace him. He was a poor madman, a Don Quixote, but he seemed to know some secret. Perhaps the nonsense he had read to him really did have some worth after all.

Soon they learned that Ikonnikov was to be dismissed from the Lycée because of his bad habits and his bad influence on the boys. They blamed both Koshansky and Piletsky. Pale and with shaking fingers, the lover of truth pocketed the only possession he had – the poems of Horace in a leather binding – and came to say goodbye to them.

First he said goodbye to Chirikov. Always good-mannered, little Chirikov fell on his neck and roared huskily:

'Farewell, dear friend!'

The others gathered around them, watching to see if Piletsky was coming. The lover of truth addressed them:

'I flatter myself with the hope, dear sirs,' he said, 'that our relationship won't be ended. The fables of Messrs Yakovlev and Delvig, the ditties of Mr Pushkin will remain in my memory forever. I shall retain a profound respect for your work and hope to enjoy your continued good will.'

Ikonnikov had always made a point of talking to them with no informality. For him they were not raw youths. He embraced little Komovsky and pressed him to his chest.

'Farewell, my dear boy,' he said, 'may our friendship be strengthened by separation!'

He shook Pushkin's and Delvig's hands firmly, bowed stiffly to everyone and left with measured military steps.

Aleksandr had seen friendship, madness, honesty, pride, destitution – but he had never seen such an unhappy person.

9

Delvig, Myasoyedov and others hated Piletsky for one more reason. Their parents brought the chaos of their homes to the Lycée. They were poor and could not afford to go out, but on festive or ceremonial or special days they crowded proudly, if somewhat timidly, into the Lycée reception hall, a throng of ghosts from some outdated world. Mrs Küchelbecker's long German shawl, more suited to Tsar Paul's reign, dragged on the floor. Valkhovsky's father was as poor as a church mouse. These families had long lost the aim of their existence or had never achieved it.

Delvig's grandfather, a Holsteinean, had been loyal to Tsar Peter III, like Aleksandr's grandfather, but later the family had lost its prestige and its fortune. Küchelbecker's father, a German scholar and a poet, had been elevated by Emperor Paul in the last days of his reign, and might even have become Count Küchelbecker, but the Emperor died and so he never did. Valkhovsky's father had always been in the middle ranks and was well acquainted with poverty. They all did their best to neaten up their frock-coats, overcoats and shawls. The Lycéeists knew this better than Piletsky, who tried to eliminate parental influence.

On the rare occasions when parents visited, the Jesuit had always appeared in the hall with his uncertain smile, slinking and sidling like a cat. He didn't join in the conversations but listened in on everything that was being said, making no secret of it. Sometimes, if a mother held her son too long in her arms, he would give a pale smile and, as if sharing parental authority with mother and father, embrace him and take him away. He spoke of the boys' parents with good humour and even gave them jocular nicknames, showing them that he was no remote figure.

'That, er … Bramarbas* of yours!' he said to Myasoyedov of his baggily dressed father, smiling ingratiatingly as he said it.

Myasoyedov later declared that if his father wished, the Lycée would cease

---

*The name of a comic character from Danish/German theatre which entered the German language in the eighteenth century as a word signifying 'braggart'.

to exist. Simple-minded, stupid and mulish, he cursed loudly and everybody knew whom the curses referred to. Young Malinovsky told him to shut up.

'You don't want to listen, do you?' Myasoyedov said in a pathetic voice. 'And do you know what he calls your father?'

'I beg your pardon?' Malinovsky was curious.

'Nothing,' replied Myasoyedov.

'What does he call him?' insisted Malinovsky, looming over him.

'Nothing really,' replied a somewhat scared Myasoyedov.

And he told Malinovsky that the Inspector hoped to 'catch the Principal out', 'unseat him' and take his place, and that he had heard Piletsky mocking the Principal in conversation with his brother Ilya.

'The Principal, he said, is like a woman – he's weak!'

This was what he had said.

Malinovsky clenched his fists; Myasoyedov shut his eyes.

'Very well,' Malinovsky said and tears welled up in his eyes.

Some people were luckier.

Gorchakov's mother, for example, never visited her son, because she was almost always abroad where her younger son was having medical treatment. His uncle and guardian wrote to his nephew occasionally. His letters were written in black round letters – in the hand of a soldier, as Kalinich would say. His aunt wrote to him in French. Gorchakov wrote to her in broad daylight, complaining that his poor eyelids were heavy with sleep.

'For auntie for her curling-papers,' he would say of these letters.

'Mother doesn't like Vienna,' he said. 'It's windy there and she's caught a cold.'

It was nothing to him to get letters from Vienna, Baden or Paris. Piletsky never asked him about his parents, showing at least some attempt at sensitivity.

'My uncle, Peshchurov,' Gorchakov would say to Pushkin with a smile, 'asks me to send him some Lycée poems. I'd like to, but I never get round to it. Have you got anything new? I've got an epigram on the three deputies – it's hilarious!'

Another boy Piletsky spared was Bakunin.

His mother and sister visited him. Then the boys would run past the reception hall, despite the prohibition, peeping in as they did so. Bakunin would stop them and introduce them to his sister, a slender big-eyed girl. His mother was portly and garrulous. She was a famous Court gossip, and if she visited it meant that the Court was in Tsarskoye Selo. Piletsky seemed pleased with the Bakunins' visits. He would catch the boys as they ran past and enquire in surprise why they were there. His face would become animated. Perhaps he was preparing to eradicate their sins, or perhaps he had taken a fancy to

Bakunin's young sister – Pushkin and Delvig's theory.

When Piletsky caught Pushkin on one of these occasions, the Jesuit asked him:

'And what about your poet? Will he come to see us soon?'

Aleksandr turned white. Since the opening of the Lycée his uncle had never come to see him. But the Jesuit meant not him but Sergey Lvovich. He called him 'a poet' in the same tone as a month earlier he had called Myasoyedov's father a 'Bramarbas'.

Aleksandr looked at Piletsky and his nostrils flared. His face suddenly turned dark and ugly. He didn't say a word, only gritted his teeth, turned on his heel and walked away.

'Oho!' Piletsky said after him.

10

Piletsky understood the complex science of physiognomy: it was impossible to deceive him. The impassive faces, evasive glances and coldly laconic replies he had encountered recently suggested a lack of frankness. Their behaviour had changed – the salutary fear had disappeared. In their letters parents complained that they did not hear from their sons because apparently their letters were held up in the post. Pushkin, who almost never wrote home and who had to be reminded to do so, stated loudly that the Inspector took their letters from the post-box and read them; that was why they disappeared. Acting as their spiritual father, Piletsky had indeed offered to help his favourites check their letters, at least as far as grammar was concerned – but only those who had merited his confidence, and it was by their own request. Ilya Piletsky informed his brother that Pushkin had loudly denounced the Inspector on two occasions. These days Ilya had no peace, day or night. Something was brewing in the Lycée. They gathered in groups in the hall or in the corridor. When they caught sight of Ilya they broke up. Korff and Lomonosov, conscientious as usual, revealed that some verses about the Inspector and a petition were being composed. Once, when Ilya was performing his pedagogical duties, eavesdropping from behind a door, Pushkin, Delvig and Malinovsky spotted him.

They approached him menacingly. For some reason Malinovsky began to roll up his sleeves and Delvig, with his usual affected composure, which didn't bode well, asked the tutor how they could help him – maybe he was looking for something? Ilya was a simple-minded man. Seeing his charges' unfriendly expressions, he muttered:

'Wh-wha-at?'

And was amazed. Their anger had disappeared. Pushkin laughed good-naturedly; Delvig chuckled softly. Ilya cheered up, and in his turn asked them if they needed any books, because if they did, he could get them in no time.

They did not need any books, and they all calmly went away. Left alone, Ilya Piletsky whispered in a low voice, looking at their backs:

'Criminals!'

When angry, Pushkin reminded Ilya of a criminal. He went to inform his brother about what had happened.

II

Korff tried to be correct and avoided the trouble-makers. Having learned that the Inspector had allegedly called his parent 'a little bull', he started his usual panting antics, could not make up his mind what to do, and at last, in floods of tears, went to him. The Inspector comforted him and assured him that nothing rude had been said. He found out from Korff who the principal originators of the petition and verses were. Gorchakov was relaxed about everything and never answered anything in detail; looking into his innocent eyes and seeing his nonchalantly raised eyebrows and yawning mouth, nobody could be angry with him. His eyes were grey and cold as ice. Lomonosov imitated Gorchakov. They tried to be men of the world in everything, and especially in the way they walked and talked. They were evidently familiar with high society and its rules: detachment, indifference and no inappropriate excitement. Gorchakov just shrugged his shoulders. Lomonosov did the same.

'Inspectors will be Inspectors!' Gorchakov would say confidently. He believed it to be a *bon mot*, in the mould of those fashionable at Court, something more significant-sounding than it actually was. He and Lomonosov held aloof and pretended not to care.

It wasn't their behaviour that surprised Aleksandr, but the equanimity of his old friend Pushchin, not to mention Valkhovsky's calm and Illichevsky's circumspection. Pushchin just knitted his brows when the Inspector was criticised in his presence, and listened disapprovingly to what Aleksandr had to say. Valkhovsky and Matyushkin continued with their work as normal. They disliked Piletsky, shunned him as much as Pushkin did, and sought no favours from him. Once Pushchin called Lomonosov an informer. But they were the good ones and Pushkin was an Incorrigible; they were the sensible ones and he was out of his mind. He was hurt and infuriated by their calm expressions and rational manner of talking. They behaved exactly as the Principal told them to; perhaps he had been encouraging this composure in order to avoid trouble and disorder – Pushkin didn't care. Only Delvig entirely agreed with him. He listened to him gleefully, hating Piletsky no less than did Aleksandr, the stupid Myasoyedov or the strapping Malinovsky. Broglio and Danzas, bottom of the class, were ready for anything.

Piletsky skulked about the Lycée and managed to have a word with everybody, at the same time giving them a wide berth. Aleksandr noticed Piletsky having a long talk with Valkhovsky and Pushchin, in the course of which he seemed to be spurring them on, and he observed that they parted on friendly terms. He heard the Jesuit's last words to Valkhovsky:

'Your good name is its own guarantee.'

At dinner Aleksandr asked him loudly, with a sneer, making sure that not only his classmates but tutor Ilya could hear as well:

'Are you worried about your good name?'

Valkhovsky looked at him sadly and did not reply, as had recently become his habit. His former friend Ivan Malinovsky no longer listened to him and had gone over wholeheartedly to Pushkin's side.

'Piletsky supports you,' said Aleksandr, 'but we Incorrigibles laugh at the encouragement he gives you!'

Broglio and Danzas snorted, confirming this.

Aleksandr seemed to derive enormous pleasure from provoking the 'sensible' ones. The fact that Piletsky shunned him like the plague flattered him for the time being, as everybody knew. Once when he gave the stupid Myasoyedov, the Inspector's current henchman, a shove, Myasoyedov flared up, ready to start a fight. Aleksandr shoved him again. Pushchin stood nearby, and Aleksandr shoved him too. Pushchin flushed but did not respond – out of either prudence or pride. Provocatively, Pushkin said to Myasoyedov and his old friend:

'If you complain, all the worse for you. And I'll get away with it.'

12

Martin Piletsky, who normally paid no attention to his clothes and despised empty fashionability, appeared all dressed up in a new wardrobe; his starched collar was snow-white, an inconspicuous little decoration shone on his chest. Usher Foma bowed to the waist to him as if to a master. Piletsky was mild and subdued all through the day and talked a lot with the boys in his flat voice. At first he addressed Korff, Lomonosov and the docile Yesakov – he understood their meekness, knew that they were despised as bootlickers and even worse but that they endured it stoically. Then he addressed Valkhovsky, Illichevsky and Pushchin. He told them that he was aware of their sterling qualities, for which they would be rewarded. He decided not to interrupt Küchelbecker's activities – the industrious student was busy copying a lengthy poem by Chapelain. He did not say a word to Pushkin, Malinovsky, Broglio or Danzas.

He passed them by, gazing ahead intently as if they did not exist.

Rumour had it that Piletsky was going to the Minister Razumovsky, that Malinovsky was being dismissed and that Piletsky would be Principal. His favourites went about looking quietly smug; the pranksters, in disgrace, went to see Malinovsky to make a complaint about Piletsky.

13

Having taken up his office as Principal with frenetic activity, appearing everywhere and being involved in everything, Malinovsky had soon burnt out. Still recalling his brilliant beginning and his talks with Speransky, he tried to fulfil at least a pale shadow of the Lycée's original aims.

From the very beginning he encountered a difficulty he could not have foreseen – his superiors' hatred. By the end of the first year he had decided to distinguish the best students with the reward of their names written in gold on a white plaque, which had been hung on the wall, the names of Gorchakov and Valkhovsky engraved on it, as an incentive to the rest of the boys to expand the list. It seemed to work, but Razumovsky had issued a special order to abolish the plate and to refrain from giving premature rewards. The Minister started to investigate everything that concerned the Lycée and soon nearly all the masters began to go over the disgraced Principal's head, reporting personally to the Minister. Speransky's fall had changed things fundamentally: Malinovsky walked about the Lycée like a ghost and everybody around him, except the ushers, treated him like one. The steward Zolotaryov thieved so mercilessly that it became impossible to ignore the students' complaints. The German teacher Gauenschield made no secret of the fact that he gave his reports to the Minister in person. So far he had not been successful, but gradually all the teaching staff except de Boudri and Kunitsyn talked openly about taking over the post of Principal. Koshansky too went to introduce himself to the Minister. Piletsky was expected to fill the post of Principal very shortly and did as he pleased.

The Lycée itself had fallen out of favour; the purpose for which Malinovsky had intended to prepare the students had now receded. The only influential supporter who remained loyal to the Lycée was old Samborsky who had not entirely lost his standing at Court. For the time being the Lycée was forgotten; there were more important things to see to.

Speransky had fallen, war was imminent. The liberal Minister's plans had been interrupted at the very outset. The Lycée continued to educate its students, but the original aim had been lost sight of. Locking himself in at home, the Principal took to that secret weakness that he had earlier pointed to so emphatically as one of the main reasons for Russia's misfortunes – quiet, solitary and hopeless drinking. Now he was rarely to be seen in his orderly shelved office, its papers and numbered files locked in the bureau – he kept another kind of order now: his very weakness was measured. With exceptional precision he poured a certain amount of wine into a glass, drank the amount he ought to and poured the rest back into the bottle. In this degradation he found the order he had been striving for all his life and about which he had written since he was a young man.

The sluggishness and deliberateness of secret drunks appeared in his movements. He had acquired a peace of mind he had never experienced before. Only two masters would come to see him as before, Kunitsyn and Boudri. Kunitsyn was young, intelligent, eager and still full of ambitions; the Principal felt ashamed in his presence. He listened and agreed with everything the youthful teacher said without even listening to him, though previously he would have debated many a point. Kunitsyn reminded him of his own youth. Boudri disapproved of the Principal, frequently frowned and once told him to his face that love of drink was a vice that was an evil, but more harmful than other evils in the end. Malinovsky enjoyed listening to him. It was the voice of virtue, which he had not always been able to follow. Having mellowed and lost his zest, even his interest in life, Malinovsky had finally gained the confidence of his students. His son Ivan would often bring his friend Valkhovsky home with him and soon the boy became a member of the family, a sort of second son. The slightly deaf and quirky Küchelbecker; the quiet and hard-working Matyushkin; the clever and mischievous Pushchin came to talk to him. But sometimes the Principal grew weary of Tsarskoye Selo with its statues and artistically planned gardens. Far away, on the River Donets in the Ukraine, seven miles from Izyum, he had an estate, Kamenka, his wife's dowry. He had very rarely been to it, so preoccupied had he been with important work. All he wanted now was a small cottage, a kitchen garden and a couple of poplars. He would be a farmer – and a teacher to his poor and ignorant neighbours. But he knew that the realisation of this alluring dream would be just another ordeal for him. Kamenka was an old village; it had reverted by escheat before passing into Samborsky's possession and before that had become established as a place of exile for rebellious peasants. Sometimes he thought that they were easier to educate than the boys in Tsarskoye Selo – no public spirit had been created, and no communication was necessary with the hated Minister, which had become more and more irksome to him. Besides, he had been familiar with the business of correction of criminals ever since he had worked at the Reformatory.

His father-in-law, old Samborsky, patron of the exiled Speransky, would come to see him. His mind was as clear as ever. His position at Court had not been shaken by the disgrace and exile of his powerful protégé. The old man still spoke of the benefits of farming and persistently advised Malinovsky to try out the plough that he had ordered from England. The Moscow Governor Rostopchin's advocacy in print of the old Russian wooden plough made the old man indignant. In his opinion, after Speransky's fall, farming was the only occupation for a person who wanted to be useful to his Fatherland. Other employments had once again become unpredictable and insecure, as in Emperor Paul's reign.

On one occasion the old man had fallen peacefully asleep in his friend's huge English easy-chair. Malinovsky, who had been listening to him attentively, got up quietly, took a bottle out of the cupboard, poured a little wine, measuring it precisely, and glancing covertly at the sleeping old man, sighed and hurriedly drank it off to the dregs, turning the glass up in one movement. The old man heard nothing and didn't wake up.

Malinovsky was suddenly appalled by his own decline. He looked guiltily at the sleeping old man who was oblivious of his weakness. All his irreproachable former life and his achievements of the future had been wiped out by that one signature on the police warrant that had destroyed Speransky. Now everything would be as it had been before: no dignity for the Russian people; and the Tsar, who at first had stirred such great hopes, did not now wish to let go the ancient power of the Russian monarchs – to banish people to Siberia, to flog, behead and hang both guilty and innocent – and the humiliation of the Russian people would go on; they would drink themselves to death. What if just once, in their drunkenness, they were to rise and break the shackles of their slavery! But everything had reverted to how it had been, and new humiliations were now being added to the old ones. No more was heard of the convening of a parliament – Malinovsky had been educating his pupils in vain.

Just eight years before, he had drawn up a plan of eternal peace, and now war was looming, an awful war.

Samborsky woke up.

'Bonaparte has saddled a wild horse,' Malinovsky told him slowly, looking at him with inflamed eyes. 'They will soon be lamenting, the sons of Russia, torn from their mothers and wives – hundreds of thousands of young recruits! O Lord, do not forsake your poor in spirit!'

And he collapsed onto his knees, clasped his hands and burst into tears: his Englishness had vanished without trace.

14

Having succumbed to weakness, he admired virtue even more, although it looked as if virtue was impossible at the Palace, in the Ministries or on the streets of St Petersburg. He grew convinced that virtue was a private and a rural property. He disapproved of the passions; only peaceful things were good. He tried to read the new poetry and threw it aside indignantly – it was all about passion. He hated high society: Russian women had forgotten the old Russian clothes, modest and decorous; not only their necks and shoulders were bare, the dresses were so flimsy the entire figure was on show through them. A gust of wind – and not a trace of modesty was left. And as for the men of fashion – they might as well have nothing on at all: a short narrow tail on the coat, their whole torso encased in trousers and a jabot on the chest; they looked like frogs – or eels. One of these short-tailed bards had been present at the opening of the Lycée: Pushkin, the uncle of his student. A feather-brained, peacock-feathered fellow in a frock-coat. The new poets extolled woman as a deity. What a delusion! His poor wife was lying next door. Women were like children – sinning one moment and repenting the next. He liked Derzhavin's philosophical odes, without excessive emotion, fashionable sighs or extremes of love; he would often put on his spectacles and peruse them with great pleasure.

Passion ruled everywhere: in the palace nearby was the unfaithful Empress, abandoned by her husband. The faithless Emperor was no better. And the Lycée itself, with all its turbulence! The Piletskys had tried to get rid of him. Koshansky had taken to the bottle. Only two decent people were left – Kunitsyn and Marat's brother.

Malinovsky had got to know that the Jesuit had in fact been to the Minister and denounced him. When he learned this he had turned white, cracked his knuckles, and said not a word.

Martin Piletsky came to see him. The Principal dreaded him – his pale smile, burning eyes and those sinuous movements made him feel frightened and confused. Confident and calm about the decisions he had taken on his own, in the Jesuit's presence he grew weak and allowed him to take control, to a degree that suprised even himself. Piletsky was perfectly at ease in the Principal's study, where he was inclined to display his arrogance and to assume the air of the next incumbent.

Piletsky insisted that drastic measures should be taken. Dangerous habits had taken root among the students. If the Incorrigibles were not expelled, the whole Lycée would be threatened by the plague. Dissipation among the students was rife. Danzas was reckless, Broglio irresponsible, Pushkin a rake.

The expulsion of these three would be of great benefit to all.

Malinovsky asked him what exactly they had done. There had been appalling incidents. One of them had yelled at the inoffensive Yesakov: 'I'll punch your mug!' just because he had picked up a ball when he wasn't actually playing in the game.

'That was extremely rude,' Malinovsky said, wincing. 'What else?'

'What else?' the Inspector said. 'In Gauenschield's class everyone did their homework except your son.'

'You should have told me at once,' Malinovsky said, frowning. He loathed both Piletsky and Gauenschield.

The Inspector calmed down. His voice became softer and his gestures more polite – the Principal was showing some resistance. Piletsky had understated their faults: Broglio was a troublemaker, Danzas and Delvig were lazy slugs and what they got up to was quite indecent. Pushkin had a passion for mocking absolutely everybody, though he was actually a bright and talkative sort of boy, who sometimes showed sparks of genuine good-nature.

'Why should we expel them then? Wouldn't it be better to have a serious talk with them?' asked the Principal.

Piletsky didn't insist on the expulsion of the first two, though both Broglio and Danzas were not only troublemakers but also poor students; they learned nothing and promised little. But Pushkin – Pushkin should be expelled without delay. He had a filthy temper and undermined authority.

'Mocking verses have been written about all the teachers, and Pushkin is at the heart of all this obscenity.'

'He is not the only one,' the Principal said with a sigh.

They stood in silence for a moment. Then the Jesuit looked at him with some pity and said softly and reluctantly:

'Pushkin should be expelled for his lack of faith.'

Malinovsky turned white. The Inspector looked at him in quiet delight.

In the same low voice Piletsky said that, possessed by his passion for poetic composition, the boy knew all the godless and obscene poems of the eighteenth century and it was impossible to drive them out of his head. This caustic, arrogant and violent-tempered boy was quite unaware of the abyss that had opened up at his feet. Talking had had absolutely no effect on him, for, as the Inspector had noticed, all extremes, including complete shamelessness and lack of faith, apparently delighted him, which made him utterly incorrigible. All these faults, and especially his unbelief, were infectious. Delvig seemed to be under Pushkin's influence, though his laziness made him much less of a danger.

Malinovsky turned even paler. He had no doubts now that the Jesuit was right. Piletsky had brought along the tutors' notes on the students and he informed the Principal that the attempts to correct the students' behaviour had recently caused much resentment. Repeating his view that strict measures had to be taken urgently, he put down the notes and left.

Malinovsky read tutor Ilya's notes attentively. He was amazed at the number of spelling mistakes, automatically underlining some of them as if it were an exercise – and lapsed into thought. He glanced out of the French windows that overlooked the balcony and through the bare gardens saw Chirikov taking the boys for a walk. They were all different, with different ways of walking, and they were all absorbed in their own thoughts and chatter. Pushkin, whom Piletsky considered to be diabolically vicious, was small and agile. It was true that his family were famous for their debauchery and mockery. He looked happy; the fresh air seemed to have a wholesome effect and to lift the boys' spirits. The Principal had always believed that Tsarskoye Selo air was good for them. Suddenly Pushkin burst out laughing and pointed out something to Pushchin who was walking next to him. Malinovsky looked in the direction Pushkin was pointing but saw nothing. The boy's smile was good-natured, his expression honest and open. The Principal chuckled. Küchelbecker had a weird walk with a springy step, his head jerking, his hands dangling.

'Ah – that's what he's like!'

The Principal stood in amazement, as if he were seeing him for the first time. He looked at them all just as a hen looks at the ducklings she has hatched – with anxiety.

And he locked Ilya's notes in the cupboard, next to the empty bottle.

15

When Pushkin and some others came to him at an unusual hour and demanded urgently that the Inspector be dismissed, Malinovsky seemed not entirely displeased. He looked at his son who was among the petitioners: Ivan had grown up. In his father's presence he conducted himself without any familiarity, just like anyone else, and Malinovsky liked that.

He took his time to explain that dismissals and appointments were the Minister's business, not the pupils', and gave a grin while saying so. Then he remarked icily that this was nothing other than outright disobedience, and as such would not please the Minister, and therefore they should do what they were told to do, return to their classroom and carry on with their studies. He relied on their good behaviour from now on, with no further disobedience, and he for his part would not inform anybody either about their actions or their impossible demand for the Inspector's dismissal.

'Go in peace,' he said pensively.

And suddenly he smiled broadly and quoted a Russian proverb, making them wonder whom it referred to:

'Don't boast when going to a feast, boast when you return.'

Malinovsky was very fond of folksongs and proverbs, but it was unclear whether he was referring to the Lycéeists who had risen against the Inspector or to the Inspector himself.

From that day on, the Principal's weakness ended. He appeared once more in the mornings, with all his buttons done up and with that upright bearing he had brought with him from England; during the period of his addiction he had become shrunken and sickly, as if terminally ill.

16

Everything went on as usual. Malinovsky did not take any decisive steps, neither did Piletsky who after his visit to the Minister appeared among the students less frequently.

Every evening the Agitated group gathered together to sing and chant their secret compositions.

Finally, after a lecture by Gauenschield, tutor Ilya succeeded in locating one of the poems; it was Delvig's. With his usual nonchalance he had not even bothered to hide it from the tutor.

Delvig had long been under observation, a cool customer from whom little good could be expected. His politeness was overdone, as if it were pure mockery. For example, he never did his homework but would approach the teachers on Friday afternoons eagerly demonstrating his readiness to revise or study, for which he was praised and did nothing.

The tutor, however, did not manage to get possession of the poem. He demanded that Delvig should give it to him but received a direct refusal. He responded by trying to grab the sheet and felt himself being pushed.

He claimed that Pushkin had rushed at him with a look of utter ferocity, eyes on fire and nostrils flared, had kicked him and yelled at him:

'How dare you take our papers?'

The tutor looked bewildered:

'Wh-wha-at?'

But this did not have its usual effect. So he had to explain that he was just going to check the piece and would give it back later. But Pushkin shouted again:

'And you take our letters from the box as well?'

What struck the tutor most of all was that Valkhovsky, who had always been quiet, sensible and correct, told the other boys to stand their ground and to make their claims. He looked unmoved, but it was obvious that his soundness of character had at last been undermined.

He told the others softly but distinctly:

'Don't be afraid and don't give in!'

Küchelbecker's behaviour was the most bizarre. All that week, when the boys had gathered together in the evenings to compose their irreverent poems, Küchelbecker had behaved more than decently – he detested the Lycéeists' satirical literature because most of it was about him and so he couldn't take any part in its composition. Moreover, though he was ridiculed for his good intentions, he had been busy copying out, with great effort, Chapelain's huge poem about Joan of Arc – the subject of much mockery but perfectly innocent. Being slightly deaf, he had taken no part in his classmates' whisperings and at lectures had usually been plunged deep in thought. But at the end of the week tutor Ilya noticed some changes even in his behaviour. Küchelbecker was particularly indignant that the Inspector had read his letters and he was even overheard using a foul word.

On the day of the incident he was calm and quiet. Suddenly he heard Pushkin's shouting and the voices of the boys crowding round the tutor. Küchelbecker rushed into the very thick of the crowd, waving his arms, reached the tutor and demanded that either the tutor or the Inspector should be sacked immediately. 'Out with him!' he screamed. Then he turned to Korff and Lomonosov who were passing by and abused them for withholding their support.

Not content with this, he shoved forward the more timid boys who were clustering behind, as if he meant to knock them and the tutor together. He looked absolutely furious and yelled at them with real bitterness:

'Don't give in!'

It was obvious that he was an extremist, like Pushkin. It was Küchelbecker's unexpected behaviour that scared the tutor most of all. Now that he found himself surrounded on all sides, he gave up trying to get hold of the poem, the goal of his long search, slipped between Myasoyedov and Delvig, and was off. They turned round but he was already out of sight. Instead, calm and motionless and with a pale smile on his face, just two paces away from them, stood the Jesuit himself, the monk, the shepherd of souls – Inspector Martin Piletsky.

17

He stood calmly, with his hands behind his back, and when they moved away in surprise, he smiled. He said nothing, nor did they. They stood by the window in the corridor. The sun was shining and out of the window they could see the beautiful Tsarskoye Selo highway lined with trees. There was no one on it. It was desolate at that hour. The whole place was completely undisturbed.

They hated him and were ready for whatever might happen. But they were intrigued by his composure and his aloof smile. For the first time they saw how thin his neck was with its huge Adam's apple, how carefully his black silk tie had been wrapped around it. He kept staring at them, biding his time. They grew bolder.

Myasoyedov broke the silence, unexpectedly loudly:

'Why did you call my father a Bramarbas? I didn't like that at all!'

Piletsky looked at him curiously as if the boy were an animal or an insect. And the icy, inhuman stare had a decisive effect. Fear of this chilly remoteness made them more audacious. The timid Korsakov, who had joined the Agitated group, cried out:

'It was your doing Ikonnikov left, it was your doing he was dismissed!'

And he burst into tears.

Slowly and sullenly, not looking at the Inspector directly, Ivan Malinovsky said quietly that their requests were: firstly, that he should restrain himself from making remarks about their parents; secondly, he should stop reading their letters; and thirdly, Ikonnikov should be reinstated at the Lycée.

Piletsky still kept silent.

Then Delvig, the coolest of all, said that if he did not agree, all of them would leave the Lycée at once.

But still Piletsky kept silent, continuing to stare with detached curiosity at these unruly students, this motley crowd. He saw a brawler who thought he was already a poet – a button was dangling loose on his frock coat; a sluggard, Delvig; and the Principal's well-built but clumsy son, in whom the impact of frequent contact with his high-minded father was clearly to be seen (though he was not supposed to be excluded from the general rule of limited meetings with parents).

Suddenly the Jesuit gave a smile. They were waiting sullenly for an answer. Pushkin was glaring narrowly at him, like a wolf-cub. His eyes were burning, his face was very pale. Küchelbecker's long arms were dangling.

Piletsky remained silent, deep in thought. He looked not at them but at their feet and at the stone floor, with an alienated, withdrawn air. Perhaps the profession of teacher suddenly seemed pathetic to him; perhaps he was dreaming of another vocation and a different audience: a trembling flock, with many elegant ladies prostrated in the dust at his feet.

Piletsky smiled.

'Remain in the Lycée, gentlemen,' he said abruptly and made for the way out.

They heard him going down the stairs. Silently they waited for what would happen next.

Stunned, they stood still for some time, not understanding what had happened, and began to discuss in loud voices what the monk would do next. Then they looked out of the window: a carriage was driving slowly along the road. It was carrying Piletsky and his pile of books. There was no doubt about it: the monk was going away; he was leaving the Lycée.

Suddenly Pushkin laughed, in the way that all the Hannibals laughed: showing his teeth. This was his first victory.

He immediately retreated into his favourite bolt-hole in the library. He looked out of the window: the road was empty, Piletsky had disappeared without a trace. As if nothing had happened he opened a bookcase, took out *The Journey of Young Anacharsis*, perched himself by the window and, biting his nails, resumed reading from the page where he had been interrupted by the Inspector.

For a long time the Lycéeists thought it might be one of his tricks and that the Jesuit would soon come back. They debated the matter. Korff, Lomonosov and Yudin were struck by the suddenness of his behaviour. But he had disappeared without question, without saying good-bye to either the staff or the students; he had simply vanished like a shadow or a mirage. The only images that remained in their minds were the broad highway and the slowly receding carriage in which, hunched beside his pile of books, gazing straight ahead with unseeing eyes, sat the Jesuit.

18

For the first time in his life he had friends. Previously they had called him the Frenchman because no one, not even Gorchakov, could speak and write in French as well as he did. Gorchakov would say to his cronies from time to time that Pushkin spoke not French but Parisian, and added once, without meaning anything in particular by it: 'They all speak like that in the streets of Paris.' His other nickname was the Monkey. It was Yakovlev who coined this nickname, as he had many others at the Lycée. His nickname was the Clown. He had a fine voice and with Korsakov sang in the Lycée church choir. Païssy the priest said that Yakovlev would go far with a voice like his, if only he could come onto higher notes less hastily – he had a special gift and passion for music. He could memorise new songs after hearing them once. But his real talent was for impersonation. If such an art were to be acknowledged, Yakovlev promised in due course to be the first master of it, despite the long-standing fame of one St Petersburg guardsman who had been able most convincingly to represent lightning during a thunderstorm.

He could catch the essence of people from their walk and from almost imperceptible gestures. At lessons when others chatted or drew caricatures, he was secretly studying his classmates, the teacher, the tutor, like an artist examining a model, memorising the essential details.

He said that it was not Pushkin who looked like a monkey but the monkey that looked like Pushkin. He gave an impersonation of him: bouncing about the classroom all by himself, gnawing his quills, deep in thought and suddenly becoming aware of the teacher. Yakovlev gave an impression of the teacher too – Koshansky staring gravely at Pushkin, his hands crossed on his chest.

He was a great success at imitating Pushkin's laughter – sudden, brief, abrupt and so ecstatic that everybody laughed.

Following Piletsky's forced resignation, Yakovlev called Pushkin 'the Tiger', perhaps because when he grew angry his walk became a prowl and he lengthened his stride.

Aleksandr now began to attract disciples. Little Komovsky with his tiny fox-like face, flighty, sly but well-intentioned, who at first had seriously disapproved of him, now paid him particular attention and even lent him his copybooks because Pushkin's were in a terrible state. But the only person he was really fond of was Delvig. He was lazy and reminded him of Diogenes: at lessons he would stare at the teacher without listening, but not chattering to his classmates either. What was he thinking about? His eyes were dimmed one moment and full of mischief the next. He devised complicated japes and composed melancholy verses that were almost always pleasant to hear. He enjoyed reading them but attached no importance either to them or to anything else.

Malinovsky was physically redoubtable, sensible and given to laughter. Yakovlev played the fool. Küchelbecker was a scholarly eccentric and madcap. He doted on the poetry of Chapelain, ridiculed by everyone else. Matyushkin was kind-hearted. Pushchin would quarrel with Pushkin and then suddenly stretch out his hand and look at him with his bright eyes and Pushkin would embrace him. He avoided the others. Valkhovsky was a Spartan, imposing a strict regime on himself, and a Stoic, intent on maintaining his composure. He turned pale in a quarrel but did not raise his voice. Pushkin was afraid of him; Valkhovsky was too virtuous for him. Gorchakov was proud but fun-loving, of a different species; Korsakov and Lomonosov did their best to imitate him. The blond 'Swede' Steven, the simpleton Myasoyedov, the red-haired Tyrkov, the business-like Kostensky, the silent, fair-haired Grevenits and a number of others did not interest him at all and he would hardly exchange a word with them. They did not seem to exist for him and they knew it.

Six

Sᴇʀɢᴇʏ Lvovich, who had brought Karamzin kind regards from Dmitriyev, had once again drawn close to him.

With each day that passed, the times were becoming more and more troubled. Speransky had fallen, vigorously condemned, and the suddenness of his fall was frightening. The older generation of Moscow, partly out of hatred, partly out of the delight of inveterate idlers, did not conceal their astonishment and indignation: why hadn't the betrayer been executed earlier? Why had he been merely exiled, and only now? Karamzin was expected to get an important appointment. Sergey Lvovich was thrilled to see that the long-awaited climax of his own career had come; a true statesman, Nikolay Mikhaylovich would not forget those who revered him. A month after Speransky's fall old Shishkov was charged to draw up a recruitment plan and appointed Secretary of State. Those whom the Friends of the Refined considered conservatives and reactionaries cheered up. Sergey Lvovich's career had come to a halt again. Times had drastically changed, and both Sergey and Vasily Lvovich keenly felt the shifting sands beneath them. Count Rostopchin was appointed Governor-General of Moscow, and shortly after this the Martinists' conspiracy was uncovered. Previously Speransky and those close to him had been branded Martinists; now it turned out that the Martinists were the Moscow Masons, the friends of Karamzin's youth. The Martinists were also free-thinkers and Jacobins. It seemed to Sergey Lvovich that all adherents of things foreign were called Martinists.

He understood nothing. He started to panic and to see more of his brother Vasily Lvovich, and the brothers grew closer once again. Vasily Lvovich was also on the decline and needing support; Shishkov, now at the peak of his renown, had defamed him as a godless person. Vasily Lvovich had given Shishkov a fair rebuff and in an epistle addressed to a friend even threatened to take him to court.

He wrote in reply to the old Secretary's charges that he was a man of the Enlightenment and

Sang his country's praises when
He promenaded by the Seine.

He called to witness Saint-Pierre, Delille and Fontanes who had met him there and could certify that he was Russian through and through and proud to be so.

But no matter what he said, the witnesses were in Paris and Shishkov was in St Petersburg and was Secretary of State.

Vasily Lvovich resigned himself to his lot.

His major claims to fame – his visit to Paris, celebrated in the verse of none other than Dmitriyev, his friendship with the charming Récamier; the encounter with no less a person than Napoleon, and finally, his subtle taste, his free-thinking and his light verse – it had all not merely lost its appeal, but become distinctly suspicious. Once praised as the author of *The Dangerous Neighbour*, he now sternly declined the honour and even surmised that the poem had been written by the late Barkov. When his bewildered interlocutor replied that Barkov had died half a century ago whereas the poem mocked Shishkov, Vasily Lvovich indignantly objected:

'Not Shishkov – Shakhovskoy!'

And he stuck to his opinion.

He took the opportunity to dismiss as an absurd fable the rumour that he had been introduced to Napoleon when he had been First Consul, though he had previously enjoyed recounting this anecdote.

'Why would I have been introduced to him?' he said with obvious contempt.

He found it necessary not to declare his former gastronomical tastes, and once, in the Club of the Nobility, when a friend of his, from force of habit, addressed him as a connoisseur of French cuisine, Vasily Lvovich rounded on him, declaring that he disliked all French dishes and preferred buckwheat kasha to all of them. As a matter of fact, this was absolutely true, but it took the imminence of war to make him confess as much. Nowadays Vasily Lvovich spent his days visiting friends and finding out the most reliable news. He did not at all understand the war that was beginning. The rumours wearied him. He talked passionately, however, about the latest troop movements, read the army communiqués aloud at home, and when it came to the Martinists, maintained that he had always been against philosophers, and that there was a difference between logic and delusion. He was to be seen everywhere, in good spirits and mocking the French, but for some reason he came home one night with a lost expression on his face, looked at Annushka with dimmed eyes and confessed to being mortally bored.

'Why can't those damned frogs stay at home?' he said to the sweet-natured

Annushka, who burst into tears.

His renown, which had burst forth so suddenly, had faded in the same way. He was on the wane.

Now the brothers often visited Nikolay Mikhaylovich, but it seemed to them that he found their company wearisome.

2

Karamzin really had been oppressed by his friends. Terrible times were ahead, and he looked at the preoccupations of the Friends of the Refined, his admirers, with horror and bewilderment. They seemed to live only for the day and to have no understanding whatsoever of the meaning and significance of forthcoming events. He had long been observing them. They seemed to be wallowing hopelessly in trifles, and he was astonished to discover that he had been growing more and more irked by the things that had appealed to him five years before. Their exaggerated refinement made him nauseous. Witnessing Sergey Lvovich's affected gestures or reading Vasily Lvovich's light-hearted verse, he recalled the scoffs of the conservatives with unease. Vasily Lvovich's attempts to tune his lyre to a serious tone were mostly laughable. He was acknowledged as leader of the babblers. His flippancy in matters of religion and morals was distinctly irritating. He was irreverent and most probably godless – who knew, perhaps Shishkov was right. Now when that fanatical enemy of the nobility and Karamzin's personal foe, the priest's son Speransky, had been sent into exile, everybody expected Karamzin to get an important post. The Pushkin brothers had even come to congratulate him, and so inopportunely, on the eve of the day when their common literary enemy, Shishkov, had been favoured.

Karamzin was crushed by bitterness: he had won victories but others had reaped the rewards. Rostopchin, newly appointed Governor-General of Moscow, had once been his friend, but the revelations about the Martinist conspiracy – which meant not only Speransky's adherents but Karamzin's friends as well – had put the historian in a dubious position. Everything had changed, but he, the chronicler of the vicissitudes of history, had been pushed aside.

He knew that the literary conservatives against whom he had been waging such a quiet war now occupied the important posts and had been denouncing him, claiming that his works were full of free-thinking and Jacobin poison and that he himself aspired to be First Consul. It was exactly what he himself had once been accustomed to say about Speransky – that he was godless, an admirer of Rousseau and Voltaire, and should be removed from office. So far Karamzin had been left in peace, but Vasily Lvovich was shunned and no longer acceptable in many homes.

Karamzin did not know how to rid himself of his credulous friends' craving for advice, the Pushkin brothers prominent among them. They were particularly gullible and more uncertain about things than anyone else. One feature the two brothers had in common amazed him: in spite of their impressionability and nervousness in the face of events, their 'sensibility', the Pushkins would adjust to any situation within minutes, no matter how unfortunate or shattering it might be, recalling a joke or starting up a passionate argument about the comparative merits of two famous dancers, one slender and one plump. This vitality the brothers shared was a mystery to the portrayer of manners.

When Russia joined the Coalition, Sergey Lvovich grew excited, and was in ecstasies at the threat of war. He read the communiqués aloud, lowering his voice when he came to the names of those who had distinguished themselves. He was annoyed with servants who interrupted him by making the door creak, just as he had been when interrupted in his recitations of Molière.

Nowadays he spent his days visiting his acquaintances all over Moscow and scaring Nadezhda Osipovna with exclamations:

'The scoundrel is retreating!'

At first Nadezhda Osipovna could not understand whom Sergey Lvovich was talking about, Napoleon or the Russian Commander-in-Chief, Barclay de Tolly, whom he, like many others, would condemn for his strategy of constant retreat.

Once he arrived home panting, and casting suspicious glances at Nikita and the maid, sent them out of the room. Then he looked at Nadezhda Osipovna and beckoned her closer. Nadezhda Osipovna couldn't bear his exaggerated gestures, but nevertheless went up to him.

'Nikita and Arina should not be trusted in anything, *rien de rien*,' Sergey Lvovich told her meaningfully. 'Servants are our worst enemies.'

This was important news. Nadezhda Osipovna recalled some injustice she had recently committed in the maids' hall and turned white. Sergey Lvovich paced the room, hastily outlining his plan of action to her. It was unclear whether the enemy would head for St Petersburg or Moscow. If it turned out to be St Petersburg, they should wait, but if Moscow, they should start packing immediately. However, the house was in such a mess, so much old dust lay thick on the shelves, Nadezhda Osipovna had so many little possessions – phials and caskets and so forth – that it was clear that to start packing without an actual emergency was out of the question. Nadezhda Osipovna did not want to part with her big mirror. Sergey Lvovich altered his decision: they would leave Moscow only in the case of absolute necessity and leave everything as it was under the supervision of the villainous servants. He calmed down now that they had a simple plan.

'The children must be sent away,' he said suddenly, in a desperate whisper, suddenly remembering the children.

'Where to?' asked Nadezhda Osipovna in the same whisper.

It was clear there was nowhere to send the children.

But Sergey Lvovich was quick to remonstrate with her.

'Oh, I don't know, my dear!' he said. 'Everyone sends their children away. Maybe to Mikhaylovskoye? Even a crow couldn't get there.'

'I won't part with Lyovushka,' muttered Nadezhda Osipovna.

It made no sense to send away only Olinka, and it was just too much trouble.

Sergey Lvovich suddenly felt tired of all this fuss. There was nothing more awkward and inconvenient in the world than a family in dangerous times – all these preparations and departures.

'Perhaps we should wait, my dear,' he said to Nadezhda Osipovna more quietly. 'They might make for St Petersburg. I promised to be at Nikolay Mikhaylovich's today, so I'll find out. But I beg you: not a word in the presence of that scatterbrain Arina or that Nikita, *pas un mot!* Nikita has been behaving very suspiciously this last week. Don't let them out of the house, will you? They meet all the riffraff in the streets, *toute cette canaille,* and get ideas. Rostopchin himself' (he raised his finger) '– the Governor-General of Moscow – is issuing leaflets to calm and direct *tous ces Nikichka et Irichka!* … Nikita, my clothes!'

He was going out to see Karamzin.

They did not speak of what might happen if the enemy made for St Petersburg. St Petersburg was far away. They forgot about Sashka. Aleksandr Turgenev was there; and, my God! – the boy was in the Palace, in the Palace itself, and could share its destiny with those who dwelt there; and besides, he was not alone, there was a crowd of other boys, teachers, all those *Lycéens,* tutors and ushers …

3

They were taken for walks three times a day as usual. The snow that had fallen on the day the Lycée opened, when they had thrown snowballs, had not yet thawed. They often came across the nimble Natasha, maid to the shrewish old lady-in-waiting Volkonskaya, always walking with downcast eyes. She was dark-eyed and broad-faced. Sometimes the boys would have fights. For bad behaviour at lectures the stern old Boudri made them stand next to him. For being rude or not prepared for mathematics classes they were left without tea, placed at the black desk or made to dress in their old clothes for an hour or two.

They had been at the Lycée for only six months, but their homes had been left forever: they stayed at the Palace and learned things earlier and better than their parents had done, and they had a better sense of the present danger, which signified important changes to come.

One night Aleksandr heard the ringing clatter of a horse's hoofs. It suddenly rang out, passed, and died. Perhaps it was a special messenger. If they had returned to their homes, many parents would not have recognised them. The parental power that the jurist Korff had talked about had been imperceptibly undermined.

4

In March, during Boudri's lecture, they heard the faint sound of a distant trumpet. At first they couldn't understand what it was. Boudri had suddenly fallen into a reverie. He drew himself up and sat, in the full splendour of his wig, listening, not looking at them, his stubborn lips gloomily compressed. Yakovlev was reciting an extract from *Young Grandison*, from which Boudri made those who had not spoken French before entering the Lycée learn extracts by heart. Yakovlev had long finished, but Boudri was still listening to something. Finally he came to, gave Yakovlev a nod, and said, referring either to *Young Grandison* or to something else:

'So it's over.'

Next day, on a walk, ignoring Chirikov's objections, they turned off into the highway.

All the way along it, as far as the eye could see, troops were moving – heavy cavalry. Neither their uniforms nor the pace of the horses, nothing reminded Aleksandr of that slow solemn movement that he had seen in St Petersburg watching a parade. The horses skidded in the mud. There were no resplendent shakos; all the soldiers wore greatcoats and peaked caps with warm ear-flaps. Brass pots clanked from the saddles. It was very cold, with blasts of wind.

'This regiment must be in particular favour,' said Chirikov, who knew some cavalrymen. 'They're all in greatcoats. Oh, no, here are a few who aren't. They must have been disciplined.'

'Why?' asked Valkhovsky.

'Who knows? Look, you see, the saddle of the second on the right has slipped down. At the first halt he'll be another one to be stripped of his coat.'

The officers wore warm tailored coats, which made them look like coachmen. A band struck up ahead, and the squadron passed on.

A few town carriages rattled behind the squadron, slowly and hopelessly – some of the mothers seeing their men off could not bring themselves to stop. They sat in their dark burnouses looking from side to side, weary of staring straight ahead and seeing nothing but the same measured movement of the horses, the same rounded greatcoated backs, in which they could discern not the faintest traces of their husbands or their sons; but still they followed the squadron, daring neither to stop nor to turn back.

On their daily walks now, the boys regularly saw the troops off. They found out their routes: Gatchina, Luga, Porkhov and eventually Opochka. Aleksandr knew that his mother's estate, Mikhaylovskoye, was somewhere near there. Gorchakov's uncle's estate was not far away either.

War had not yet been declared but troops moved through Tsarskoye Selo every day. Soon their appearance changed – the Guardsmen had passed, now came the Cossack regiments. Bearded Cossacks, with their waxed moustaches sticking up, sat in the saddles as if challenging the rest, more firmly and tightly than most people sat in their armchairs, hands on hips and a reckless nonchalance in their pose. They sang a slow measured song with whoops and whistles. Their faces were impassive and they seemed to pay no attention to the Lycéeists. When two of the vanguard noticed them, they exchanged winks, still maintaining their aloof indifference, and in one swift movement tore themselves out of their saddles, exchanged horses and carried on riding as calmly as if they had never left their seats, with the same immobile and dispassionate faces. Only the Cossack on the right had one eye screwed up: he was laughing.

Kalinich continued to stare after them. It was as if he were nailed to the spot, oblivious of everything. When he addressed the boys, they could hardly recognise him – delight and enormous pride shone in his face; one eye was puckered.

'With a musket in our hands and a bullet in our teeth,' he said, and gave them a wink, like the Cossack in the vanguard a few minutes before. 'Oh, my little rascals, my dear little birds.'

Malinovsky revealed that he too was a Cossack – his village was in the Ukraine. Kalinich stared at him with mingled admiration and distrust, and laughed:

'Of course you are. You have a horseman's spirit. All Cossacks are leaders!'

And so Malinovsky was initiated into the Cossacks. Immediately his gait changed – he started to roll in a special way, assumed a challenging stance and often screwed up his eye as he thought befitted a true Cossack. He told his father about the Cossack Regiment that had passed by, and grew even more cheerful. The Principal liked the bold nickname 'Cossack' given to his son. He told him that their free spirit, their cunning and daring, and often their sheer recklessness, were their best features. At the beginning of this war he was placing all his hopes on the qualities of the Russian troops that would be unfamiliar to the enemy. His son had always been robust and shrewd. Now the boy developed a relish for dash and fire. The usher Matvey was from old Cossack stock too, and only when his eyesight had grown worse had he taken up work as a civilian. The young Malinovsky had many a long talk with him and soon picked up a number of bold Cossack sayings.

Reprimanded by Gauenschield for complete failure in German conversation, noted by the tutor in the black book, he winked and said:

'Cossacks in trouble never cry!'

The steward fed them very poorly these days, and at dinner Malinovsky would declaim:

'We'll drink from our fist and eat from our palm.'

Kalinich was delighted. After the Cossacks' passage through Tsarskoye Selo, Kalinich had grown depressed. While on duty he had taken to whistling and humming tunes into his beard. When tutors or teachers were nearby he would fall as silent as the tomb, but in the presence of 'his own', as he called some of the Lycéeists, he was not in the least embarrassed. Once Aleksandr heard him humming sadly:

> *White bloom falls*
> *From the buckwheat, O:*
> *When the Cossack loves,*
> *Alas, he must go.*

He had a deep voice, but so as not to be too obtrusive, he sang at a higher pitch.

It took three days for the militia to pass through. They were wearing grey clothes that reminded the Lycéeists of the bread the miserly steward fed them on. They were quite different from the Guardsmen; they draggled along despondently, covered in dust, quite without the style and fine posture of the Guardsmen – they were peasants.

Looking straight ahead, with sallow faces, they marched past for half an hour, a full hour at a time, and the earth groaned under their heavy tread with a muted sound. They shuffled along, with the faces not of soldiers but of bumpkins. They were endlessly singing *The snow was not white*. Aleksandr recalled the song of the coachman who had driven him and his uncle to St Petersburg – that had also been a long-drawn-out song, soft and slow, in time with the jolting carriage, with breaks from time to time – a protracted, leisurely coachman's travelling song. But the song the peasant-soldiers were singing, strong but indistinct, was more like a cry or a sigh than a song.

'The destitute have taken up arms,' was Kalinich's muttered comment as he tried to draw up his students in a line. 'Oh, my little birds, my poor rascals!'

They saw the horse militia on the move: a very young officer dashed at full gallop along the very edge of the road and nearly trampled them. He slashed the wet twigs of the trees with his sabre; the branches lashed him across his face and he closed his eyes and laughed. Then he turned back his horse, rode up to the Lycéeists and asked the way to Kunitsyn's house. A green twig was stuck behind the cross on his chest, water and tears rolled down his face. He chewed a green leaf in his white teeth and seemed to be drunk. His face was like a child's. He was smiling.

Ignoring Kalinich's exhortations, a few boys went to show the officer the house Kunitsyn lived in. He realised that order was now impossible to maintain and gave it up, saying:

'Go, little birds, go, rascals, just make sure not to be caught, I beg you!'

The militiaman dismounted and they went into the house.

He embraced Kunitsyn. This was the Göttingenian Kaverin. Five minutes later he was acquainted with everyone, and constantly mixing up the names, he talked to the Lycéeists, not listening to what they were telling him. He liked Pushkin and hugged him.

'Pushkin, you're great, old fellow, shall we go to war together? Don't want to? Stay here then.'

He told Pushchin:

'You, old fellow, are too fat, you'll never make it on horseback. Try the artillery!'

He seemed sure that everyone was going to the war as he was. Kunitsyn looked at him with a smile, though he was not normally inclined to be so good-humoured.

'Don't you have wine? Give me a drink of water then, you philistine!' said Kaverin.

Slowly he drank a big jug of water and nodded at Pushkin:

'Pushchin, are you ready?'

He put his arms around Kunitsyn and said to him:

'Come on, don't be such a slug. You're a lazy scoundrel, a philistine!'

Then he embraced Pushkin:

'Off we go, Sasha!'

Normally he called only Kunitsyn Sasha and had addressed Pushkin correctly purely by accident.

Back in their rooms, everyone had a feeling that his elder brother had gone off to the war. That night Pushkin suddenly felt a craving to catch up with him – he looked at the road wondering where he could get a horse. Then, reluctantly, he went back to sleep.

5

When they saw the Guardsmen off they wore their jackboots. The militiamen they saw off in grey uniforms: their navy-blue semi-military frock-coats with red collars had been taken away and they had been issued with grey trousers and short, tight frock-coats of the same colour. This changed their appearance and they could hardly recognise each other. Once they came across old Volkonskaya, walking slowly, leaning on Natasha's hand and breathing heavily. Her nose was purple. Seeing the schoolboys, Natasha lowered her mischievous eyes as usual. Broad-faced, dark-eyed and high-bosomed, she had the look, walking next to the old woman, of the beloved Psyche being led by Proserpina. The old lady, as usual, stopped to give way to them. Natasha stood with her eyes cast down but seemed to be watching them.

'Why didn't you tell me, Natasha, there was a mass today?' the old woman asked her in a deep, rasping voice. 'You see, the choirboys!'

They heard her. They looked at each other and realised that indeed their uniforms were similar to those of the choirboys who often passed by the Lycée on their way to the Court chapel. Gorchakov and all the others felt deeply stung. They conceived a hatred for old Volkonskaya.

They were no longer the favourites of fortune, schoolboys or students, they were not even eremites or monks, as they liked to picture themselves, in their cells, but simply 'the choirboys' from the Court.

The sight of the militiamen consoled them: nowadays everyone was in grey uniform, they were on campaign. Such was war. They were fed meagrely. Previously when the steward had fed them on cabbage soup or given them weak tea, they had sought him out all around the Lycée, and he had hidden from them. Nowadays he didn't hide from them but on the contrary, was eager to show his face. When they complained that there was no meat in the soup, he would just shrug his shoulders and say gravely:

'Orders!'

His ginger sideburns were neatly brushed.

Military frugality was observed in everything.

Tsarskoye Selo, which at the opening of the Lycée Malinovsky had called a peaceful abode, seemed to have changed. They had never noticed before that the place was filled with the fierce memories of wars and its victories: the Turkish Pavilion, the Kagul marble, the Chesme column and the Orlov Gate, all of them with their inscriptions. The palace was empty and silent. The normally uninhabited pavilions seemed actually abandoned and the artificial ruins looked like real ones. The stones of the Greek arbour turned out to be the real ancient stones that had been wrested from the Turks. Greek names – Daphne, Chloë and Phyllis – had long been used in poetry; only old Derzhavin gave his heroines everyday names, Natasha or Parasha. Nowadays Greek and Roman names meant military glory: Bagration was Epaminondas; Kulnev was Decius; Rayevsky and Konovnitsyn were Spartan generals.

The troops were told that the Niemen would become another Styx for the French – an infernal river which could be crossed only once.

Seven

I

WAR began on the night of the twenty-second to the twenty-third of June. Napoleon with four hundred thousand troops crossed the Niemen near Kovno. His troops entered Russia. Half of them were French, the other half Germans and his new subjects of various nationalities. On the march were Prussians, Saxons, Bavarians, Württembergers, Badeners, Hessians, Westphalians, Mecklenburgers; Austrians, Poles, Spaniards, Italians; Dutchmen, Belgians from the banks of the Rhine, Piedmontese, Swiss, Genoese, Tuscans, Bremeners, Hamburgers. They moved day and night, stopping only briefly to rest their horses. They found the way ahead open: it was an unfamiliar war for Napoleon, with abandoned villages, empty towns, without people or fodder, with imaginary victories; a war that in its first stages provoked the strong indignation of the French commander, who had expected a conventional affair – big, sweeping battles with the enemy, a final decisive conflict, occupation of the capital and a quick peace on his terms. The older generation of Moscow were also indignant at the absence of heroic engagements.

The enemy advanced impetuously, its huge forces heading towards either St Petersburg or Moscow. Nothing was certain.

2

Malinovsky and Kunitsyn locked themselves in the Principal's room. The candles were lit, the windows facing the garden were open. All around them was quietness and fresh green foliage, the flames of the candles were stirred by a light breeze – everything as in time of peace. In the Lycée across the road the students were already asleep.

'It is a great grief to me,' Malinovsky said, cracking his knuckles and wringing his hands, 'to contemplate our circumstances in the midst of all this beauty on a night like this.'

Seeing how despondent he was, deploring his weakness and angered by his continued depression, Kunitsyn was impatiently awaiting his complaints and ready to riposte. It was almost criminal to be dispirited at such a time. If Malinovsky gave way to despair, the Lycée would plunge into disorder, as it had in the days of Piletsky. Everyone – the students, staff, the enemies within like Gauenschield – would be affected at once. Kunitsyn had made up his mind to leave the Lycée, this fragile and unstable establishment. He was going to join up. He had enjoyed his duties at the Lycée and was fond of some of the students – not the individuals personally but their craving for knowledge and their steady improvement towards perfection; he had even grown fond of the building itself. He did not want Gauenschield to take hold of the Lycée as Piletsky had once done. But all around him there was profound confusion, and it was easy to weaken and infect others with weakness. He hated these pale faces, the dismay in people's eyes, their disordered thoughts – the symptoms of fear and horror. He believed in reason and its laws, and fear was opposed to reason, it was a primitive thing. The future he had been so actively preparing for now seemed impossible, and another future became clear to him. Now he was preparing himself for war. The Motherland and devotion to her, patriotic duty – all the ideas he had gravely talked about to the Lycéeists had become passions to which he now unhesitatingly abandoned himself.

'The enemy is upon us,' said the pale Malinovsky, 'they're all upon us. I've heard they're marching without stopping. At this rate, in a month we'll have to leave for Reval. For the moment we'll keep this secret. But you should prepare yourselves.'

He said he was unwilling to transfer the whole Lycée to Reval. Some might not want to leave – it was their choice! Gauenschield, for instance, could not leave St Petersburg, and so much the better. He could foresee that most of the masters would not go. In which case some teachers would have to be taken on there. In general the only person to whom he could entrust the school, which had been so unlucky from the very beginning, was Kunitsyn, and only him. It sounded as if Malinovsky was not going to go with them.

Malinovsky confirmed this:

'I'm not going. It's too late for me, I'm tired.'

'The students will get out of hand in exile, without you there. I won't be able to cope with them.'

Malinovsky paced the room.

'Have you had any news from your brother? What does Turgenev intend to do?'

Kunitsyn's brother had joined up about a month before and had sent no news. The Göttingenian Nikolay Turgenev had visited Moscow the previous winter and was now staying in St Petersburg; he was in anguish, his mood constantly fluctuating between terror and hope, and he had no idea what to do with himself. Kunitsyn saw him frequently. He complained of the servile mentality of the lower classes, their coarseness and drunkenness, the ignorance of the upper classes, the severe winters and hot summers that made life in his native land impossible – but he had no idea how to escape from it. Recently he had cheered up: General Wittgenstein's victory had rekindled his hopes.

Malinovsky smiled.

'All the ushers will go with you wherever you go, Reval or Åbo,' he said. 'The students began their course at the Lycée with them and that is how it should continue. I have already given instructions to Chirikov to register all cases of rude behaviour towards the staff in the discipline book. The other day Danzas was insolent to Matvey and chased the steward, he meant to beat him up. I ask you to pay particular attention to this. Snobbery, quick temper, contempt for inferiors – these are the results of their upbringing, their parents' lifestyle and treatment of their serfs. They look for victims for their anger and they've got used to such a state of things. Nobody dares say to a foreign subordinate what he can say to his own people who are his slaves, because that foreigner will have a brother or fellow-countryman in a government post. And this is how Russian dignity is being destroyed. I'm telling you all this not because you can't see it or are unaware of it, quite the reverse; very soon you'll have to put all this into practice, as I have to do now.'

Though in general prone to weakness, on this occasion the Principal had spoken firmly.

'Have you ever seen fire in war-time?' he asked Kunitsyn. 'Fire spread by the wind when cities are burning? I've seen it. It's like a prehistoric landscape, blackened chimneys showing here and there, the remains of what were once houses, families. And now it's the chimneys of our Russian houses sticking up from the ground! In exile, make sure to preserve these young fellows' memories of home, make sure they're kept occupied – writing journals, songs, even verses – anything. It's not good for them to lose their homes at such an early age.'

It was the first time Kunitsyn had seen the Principal in such a mood.

'I've been keeping my eye on them,' said Malinovsky. 'Some of them don't come from very sound homes, and even those they're going to be deprived of.'

They glanced at the Lycée with its dark windows. The building would have seemed uninhabited had it not been for the entrance-lamp, casting its yellow light.

Suddenly Kunitsyn spoke with determination:

'We mustn't leave without you, and anyway, you have nowhere to stay.'

'I'm not so strong as I used to be, and I've used up a lot of energy in vain,' said the Principal softly. 'I am in need of consolation, but I can't find it. All the hidden ulcers have suddenly burst in our country – embezzlement of public funds, looting, as if this were the enemy's camp. There's wholesale pillage everywhere. A friend of mine from Smolensk wrote to me that their Governor, Baron H., accepts bribes by the cartload, and they're blocking the town square! Who can fight two enemies at once? Not our Emperor. The flattery of the great and his own adultery have eclipsed his mind.'

The night was pitch-dark, it was as if the wilderness began just beyond the Principal's garden. He cracked his knuckles and stared at Kunitsyn enquiringly.

'The government seems to fear the new recruits most,' he said, spreading his hands helplessly. 'It's reluctant to trust in the Russian spirit and thinks that recruits are motivated by fear.'

Kunitsyn, turning pale, was silent, and the Principal suddenly paused.

'I believe,' he said with a certain indignation, 'not only in Wittgenstein, who is an excellent general indeed. I trust a peasant or a Cossack most of all, I trust their courage and their zeal ... We know their spirit, even corrupting servility has failed to destroy it, and this is what our enemy doesn't know!'

He paused for breath.

'Nobody knows what might happen,' he said, more quietly, 'but a Russian will show his spirit and prove it in the end to both the enemy and his own rulers. I must believe this, otherwise my life would be without meaning. When our rulers see this spirit, slavery will be abolished, it will fall off like a scab, and then within three years the Russian land will change beyond recognition. My vocation is agriculture and manufacture, not teaching and being the principal of a college.'

And he chuckled.

'However, all this is just idle dreaming, especially when the enemy is already near Smolensk. But for me, to abandon hope means to abandon life. I take a pride in preserving the full powers of my reason. The trouble is that Razumovsky's order to move the Lycée is premature, and I am afraid it might leak to the students. I'm sick to death of all this!'

They parted.

'I'm not insisting on your final answer now,' the Principal told Kunitsyn, 'but I'd ask you not to abandon the young fellows, and gradually to learn to take my place. Most important of all is that we do our best not to let the students guess that things are so bad.'

3

On the map that had been nailed to the wall in the hall, Kalinich, with his calligraphic hand, slowly and precisely marked the movements of the French and Russian troops, and a thick red line slid speedily upwards. He stood for a long time in front of the map.

Corpulent and calm, with a blank expression on his face, he had been marking troop movements daily, and this time was struck by what he saw. He carefully examined the entire map. Pushchin, Malinovsky and Pushkin came up to have a look.

Kalinich whispered the names of the towns, gave a start and said:

'They've gone through us like a knife!'

They stood silent in front of the red line. Ivan Malinovsky looked at each of his friends and said softly:

'Time for Koshansky's class!'

And with their arms around each other's shoulders, still saying not a word, their pranks forgotten, they made their unhurried way to the lesson.

No one could keep silent like Malinovsky. He had the silence of a true Cossack. The boys understood each other well.

Next day the map was removed.

Aleksandr remembered well the highway from Moscow to St Petersburg that he and his uncle Vasily Lvovich had travelled along: the low post-stage buildings, grey with rain, with cracked or blistered wooden posts and sparrows clustered up under the eaves; the old post-master who avoided looking directly into one's eyes; the coachman keeping up an endless song; the rhythmical ringing of harness-bells; the oncoming carts with screeching wheels and the smell of tar. Now the enemy's cavalry was galloping along those same roads, the post-stages were being occupied by the French moving at full tilt, unimpeded, and the thought filled him with gloom. These days geography could be learned from the French advance. Russia, it turned out, was full of towns, villages and hamlets whose names the Lycéeists were now learning with amazement from bulletins. The enemy was approaching Smolensk.

4

The Lycée journalists eagerly adopted the style of Rostopchin, Governor-General of Moscow. The hero of Misha Yakovlev's prose at present was a landowner from Nizhny Novgorod who had supposedly served as a captain under Suvorov, Sila Silovich Userdov, who expressed himself in the abrupt Suvorov manner. Misha Yakovlev painstakingly imitated Rostopchin. 'The

French,' he wrote, 'trample the commandments with their boots. They ruffle their hair, bare their teeth, babble nonsense, but nothing meaningful ever comes out of it. All of them deserve a good whipping!'

Aleksandr read the articles and kept his counsel. Nothing in all this prose reflected the enemy's swiftness, their quiet, rapid movements, the fall of some, the elevation of others, separations, deaths, cities in flames, post-stages raided by the enemy's mounted patrols. The writers' witticisms were ponderous, the vulgar language flabby and overblown like an old man's mumblings. Misha Yakovlev took offence at Pushkin's obvious pride in his own taste. He started to impersonate Pushkin as an arrogant young man. As a genuine artist, he liked to observe Pushkin more than anyone else. This was the most demanding of his performances. It was not easy to be flighty, fidgety and graceful at the same time. This item in his programme required particular inspiration. Before portraying Pushkin he had to rehearse and warm up – jumping over chairs, twisting his head round and round and flaring his nostrils. He could not impersonate him seated, as he did others, without careful practice. Aleksandr enjoyed Yakovlev's performances. And the clown seemed to understand him perfectly. In Misha's abrupt gestures he sometimes recognised not himself but his father. The only mood Misha disliked and failed to understood in Pushkin was the one in which he composed his poems: a morose, half-mad self-oblivion. Misha was a poet too and knew that it was easy to write. He would hum and whistle while writing, and one line followed another.

Valkhovsky's hero was Suvorov, whom he aspired to be like: he ate stale rusks and slept on bare bed-boards, taking off his mattress every night. He was a Stoic, confided only in his friend Malinovsky about the goals he set himself and achieved, and sharply disapproved of pranks.

Gorchakov's hero was the Emperor: he strove to imitate him in everything – he curled his hair in front of a mirror, rolling his natural curls on a comb, walked with a lurching step, screwed up his eyes. The day of the opening of the Lycée was engraved on his memory.

5

Malinovsky's hero was at present the hetman of the Don Cossacks, Platov. He had announced that he would give his daughter in marriage with a dowry of fifty thousand *chervontsy** to the Cossack who brought him Napoleon dead or alive. The Principal told his son about Platov and his astonishing openheartedness and courage.

Küchelbecker's hero was Barclay de Tolly, Commander-in-Chief of the

---

* *Chervonets*: a gold coin worth ten roubles.

Russian army. He was related to him. Küchelbecker had nailed Barclay's portrait to the bureau in his room: a high brow, clean-shaven face and sombre eyes were his hero's features. The one-eyed Kutuzov had a strong, aquiline nose, and in general looked like a tough old bird which had had an eye clawed out in a fight on the wing. General Bagration had the intense ardent eyes of a warrior. Hetman Platov was thick-necked and frank-faced. Only Barclay lacked distinctive heroic features.

Küchelbecker's friends asked him about Barclay, and he spoke in praise of him.

'He's tall,' he would say.

This was not enough for them. Küchelbecker was tall himself, and so was Illichevsky.

'He's a man of few words,' said Küchelbecker. 'He just stroked my head without saying a thing and then went away, that's all.'

The Commander-in-Chief, who kept his counsel and was at this moment retreating swiftly from the enemy, did not engage their sympathy. Quoting his father, Myasoyedov informed his classmates that the Commander-in-Chief was mockingly called 'Babble-and-Only'.

'But he still doesn't talk,' said the disconcerted Küchelbecker.

6

Aleksandr remembered the portrait of Napoleon hanging on the wall in his uncle Vasily Lvovich's study: empty eyes, like those of the statues in the gardens, no smile, extraordinary regularity of features and a simple uniform. At that time these features had seemed classically beautiful.

When he recalled that cold indifferent face now, it seemed to him the face of a corpse. Kunitsyn said that the tyrant who had broken the international treaty with such contempt had to die and that there would be justice for nations and for ordinary people. Kaydanov maintained that by comparison with a consummate killer like Sulla, Napoleon was nothing more than a cold-blooded, indiscriminate bloodsucker and that the world was tired of his massacres.

They asked Boudri about Bonaparte, and crowding around him waited intently for his reply.

The old Frenchman looked at them gloomily and did not seem to be in a hurry to answer. There was grave sadness in his face and his dim little eyes were half-closed. Then he jabbed the pulpit with his short stumpy finger and growled hoarsely:

'He will be punished! There is not a single sufficient or sensible reason for his victory and many for his defeat. He is the heir of revolution and at the same time its murderer!'

And as if unwilling to talk or think about him any longer, the old man snarled at them fiercely:

'Take your seats. You've been neglecting the *Dialogues* and you haven't learned *Young Grandison*. You ought to do more exercises or you'll never learn the French language. Syntax and recurring decimals seem to be beyond your comprehension – and you haven't mastered your spelling yet. In order to train your memory we'll read Rousseau today.* Broglio hates work and is bottom of the class due to his negligence. Danzas is lazy. Delvig is willing to learn but has a poor vocabulary. Gorchakov is top of the class, but suffers from vanity! Korsakov is confident he knows a lot – very sure of himself! Pushkin gets by entirely on his memory, he has stopped learning altogether – he couldn't care less!'

7

The heat was unbearable. The normally taciturn Kalinich, who took them for walks, wiped his face with a bright handkerchief and muttered:

'Winter, my little birds; the frost, my dear rascals, this is what will finish off the enemy!'

Everyone laughed. Malinovsky looked at him:

'What do you mean? It's summer!'

But with a fixed expression on his broad face Kalinich chuckled and said:

'The hotter the summer, the colder the winter.'

It was an old truth, proven by folk wisdom long before their time. They fell silent.

8

Rumours abounded – that three Bavarian regiments had gone over to the Russian side, that the Germans and the Spanish had mutinied, that Napoleon had fled back to France. Crucial encounters were imminent. 'The best way to protect yourself from the enemy is to defeat him,' General Rayevsky was rumoured to have said.

In July the Lycéeists learned the astonishing news. The *Northern Post* was passed from hand to hand: due to the impressive tactics of General Rayevsky who had been in charge of Bagration's vanguard, Bagration's and Barclay's armies had united. On the eleventh of July Bagration had ordered Rayevsky

---

* The odes of Jean-Baptiste Rousseau (1671–1741) were admired stylistic models in Russia during the Classical era.

to attack Marshal Davout's army so as to hold up the enemy, which was essential if the two armies were to be united. Rayevsky had ten thousand soldiers against sixty thousand French. The battle took place around a lake. In the last stage of it the Smolensk regiment marched to the dam under enemy fire with fixed bayonets without firing a single shot themselves. But reaching the dam, the Russians ran against a well-armed enemy convoy. When leaving to take up his command, in the general chaos Rayevsky had taken his two sons with him, Aleksandr, just sixteen, and Nikolay, scarcely eleven, and enrolled them in one of his regiments. During the battle Rayevsky marched at the head of the column with his sons, holding the younger one by the hand. When the standard-bearer was killed, Aleksandr picked the standard up from the ground next to the dead man. The Russian troops threw themselves at the French and defeated them. Bagration had achieved his aim: now the enemy could not prevent the two Russian armies from joining forces at Smolensk.

When their father asked them whether his sons knew why he had taken them to the battle, the younger one had replied: 'So that we can die together.'

9

Smolensk had been abandoned. Word spread that the Commander-in-Chief had personally ordered it to be set on fire and that now the town was just a heap of debris. The fire had raged for more than a day and a night and the French compared the terrible sight to an eruption of Vesuvius. The townsfolk had fled into the woods; only old women and the sick stayed in town. The town of Vyazma was burning too, set on fire on all sides.

The Smolensk peasants hid in the forest. If the enemy found them, they would rob them of their last possessions so as to provide their soldiers with food. The landowners also kept their heads down, and the French returned their rights over the peasants, which had been shaken by mass exodus and the circumstances of war, and promised them security and defence against marauders on condition that they supplied them with flour, vodka, corn, cattle, oats and hay. There was no fodder; diseases more frightening than war itself started to break out. Smolensk had been burnt to the ground on the seventeenth of August and Vyazma soon afterwards. The same was in store for Moscow in the not too distant future. Barclay's retreat before the enemy and his refusal to engage in combat was incomprehensible and even frightening.

10

Mrs Bakunina, a stout, imposing woman with lively, roving eyes, who resided in Tsarskoye Selo, often came to see her son, whom she distrusted, suspecting he was up to no good. Under Piletsky's regime she had habitually conversed with the Jesuit in whispers; her curiosity was uncontrollable. On one of her visits she told her son that Barclay was a traitor, it was common knowledge and soon he would be dismissed.

Everyone was on edge. The pale Küchelbecker had at first opposed the general opinion, but then gave in, tore Barclay's portrait off the wall, ripped it to pieces and stamped on them furiously. Then he looked despairingly at the trampled pieces, picked them up carefully and put them in the drawer of his bureau.

There were whisperings in the Lycée about Barclay's fall. Pushkin kept quiet and listened. He was now showing a quality nobody had believed him capable of, knowing his hot temper – caution. He did not seem to approve of Myasoyedov, who openly referred to the Russian Commander-in-Chief as 'Babble-and-Only'. He listened quietly as the crazed Küchelbecker said that his former idol deserved to be executed. Platov's Cossacks had forced a French corps to retreat near Smolensk – the French had suffered serious casualties, and so the continuing retreat of the Russian troops seemed inexplicable. But Pushkin did not pour scorn on the leader as even the most docile boys had taken to doing, and he listened to the sneers with apparent disgust. The inexorable advance of the enemy, which seemed impossible to prevent or to halt, the gloomy faces of the masters, the ever-pale Malinovsky and the weird silence pervading the streets, the silence of a place they would soon be leaving – everything had changed around him.

They walked quietly about the Lycée, taking care not to make any noise, as though it were a house of mourning. Kartsov, the mathematics teacher who used to cough and splutter, blow his nose and deafen everybody with his loud laugh, was silent as the grave. Geography, as taught to them by Kaydanov, had suddenly changed its character – the enemy was now in the very heart of the country.

Some students – Korff, Korsakov and Komovsky – lost heart and begged to be allowed home, and from time to time the ushers had to comfort them. They longed for their mothers and cried over their letters. Kalinich noticed Danzas grinning at the sight of the tearful boys. Some of the pranksters called Korsakov a coward. To his tutor's amazement Pushkin kept his bad temper under control for a whole week. He couldn't understand this weeping. It made him subdued; he scrutinised the weeping students curiously and said not a word. These days he and Delvig were inseparable.

He was fond of him. He liked Delvig's dash and daring underneath the nonchalance and laziness: Chirikov called him 'a desperado', in spite of the fact that Delvig never picked quarrels or bullied anybody. He made no academic headway and actually seemed to revel in his laziness. He could keep nothing in his head.

'I've lots of time to learn both *Young Grandison* and the Dialogues,' he would say, 'I have the whole day ahead of me.'

There was a method in his indolence.

In the afternoon he would say:

'How time crawls! I have the whole evening in front of me. But I won't waste my time, I'll learn the Dialogues in the evening.'

In the evening he would say:

'Boudri won't come tomorrow. I'm sure of it. The Dialogues can wait.'

Although he never teased anyone, Kalinich would still insist on calling him 'a scoffer and a trouble-maker'.

Once after one of Kartsov's tedious classes, the fearful Korsakov confessed with tears in his eyes that he was homesick – if the war dragged on, he was afraid he might be cut off from his family.

Looking at him hazily and squinting slightly, Delvig said:

'Never mind! I lost both my parents in a battle and was nearly taken prisoner, but then I found them again.'

Everyone stared at him in astonishment. He seemed to be serious. Korsakov wiped his tears and gaped. Pushkin was intrigued.

Then calmly, unhurriedly throwing sidelong hazy glances at them with his blue eyes, Delvig told them that during the 1807 campaign he and his mother had followed his father at the rear of the regiment. It had been getting dark when his mother had remembered that she had forgotten to give her husband an amulet which she believed could save him from being wounded.

She had been in despair, and leaving her son in the charge of the batman, had gone off together with her maid and a sergeant-major in search of her husband. Meanwhile Delvig had taken a nap. In his sleep he had seemed to hear a roaring sound all around him, horses neighing and himself either sailing in a ship or being jolted about in a cart.

But since he had already had this dream once before, he thought it best to stay asleep, and every time the roaring started, he had buried his head in the coarse camp pillow. When he woke up once the batman simply said: 'Go to sleep, your Honour!' and he had fallen asleep again. In the morning he had woken up under the cart, in the woods. Next to him lay the batman with blood-stained hand. It turned out that during the night the enemy had captured a part of the column but the batman, remembering the order not to leave young Delvig and not to stray too far away, had thought it better to drive the cart together with a few others to the nearest woods. There he had taken the sleeping Delvig off the cart and had hidden them both underneath it, where they had waited for the battle to end.

'Did you sleep all through the battle?' asked Valkhovsky, astounded.

'I did,' said Delvig, with a shrug.

And indeed, Delvig would sleep extraordinarily soundly. Even Foma's desperate yelling, 'Get up, gentlemen! Lord, have mercy upon us!' could hardly raise him. He would sleep during lectures too but still be able to repeat the teacher's last words with absolute precision, though without a grain of understanding. He told the others his adventure undramatically and without any embellishment. They were struck dumb. Valkhovsky asked him to tell them about the campaign in detail. Delvig told them about his batman, his dexterity, daring, courage, love of drink and his favourite sayings: 'To fight is no plight', 'Serve a hundred years, you'll never earn a hundred pears' and so forth. After that Korsakov and the other boys lost most of their fear. They drifted to their rooms, discussing Delvig's amazing adventures. Pushkin caught up with him and said to him softly:

'You made it all up, didn't you?'

'No, really and truly!' said Delvig. 'Word of honour – or the devil take me!'

That night, going to bed, Aleksandr heard the usher Matvey who served Delvig grumbling in the corridor at the steward, with whom he was at odds:

'Serve here a hundred years, you'll earn a hundred pears.'

He burst out laughing. His friend was not a liar – he was a poet of the most pleasant and easy-going kind.

II

In the evenings the Principal frequently invited the Lycéeists to his home. Not all of them, only the chosen few, and most frequently Valkhovsky, Pushchin and Matyushkin. They were his favourites.

The soft-spoken Valkhovsky, small, slim, narrow-shouldered and fair-minded, looked on lessons, meals and sleep as duties to be performed, unpleasant or not. He was ready to sacrifice himself, with total composure. The Lycéeists called him a Spartan. During the campaign for Piletsky's expulsion, Valkhovsky had endured his friends' jibes for not taking part in it. Like a Stoic of ancient Rome, he always stood for order. The Principal treated him like an adopted son. Pushchin was the essence of common sense; he put everything to the test and took nothing on trust. He had a good mind and his own sense of mischief. Matyushkin, unassuming and hard-working,

was keen on travel. The Principal, who had spent a long time in Turkey and
in England, enjoyed reminiscing about these countries he knew he'd never
see again, and enjoyed Matyushkin's eagerness to listen. Küchelbecker too
would often be invited to the Principal's evening gatherings. Fiery, foolhardy
and flamboyant, he swung from one extreme to another and his poetry was
confused; but he was good-natured and had a passionate sense of justice.
The Principal's son Ivan had promised to follow in his father's footsteps.
Malinovsky's wife was dying; his amiable daughter Anna offered the young
students tea and (sometimes stale) bread. For Valkhovsky these evenings were
part of the bivouac life he imagined as now the norm at the Lycée, and he
delighted in its rough and ready simplicity. Not for the Lycéeists the *beau
monde* – they were not fortune-seekers or even fortune's favourites. As for
Gorchakov, the headmaster quietly acknowledged his talents and praised him
to the full, but showed no desire to spend any time with him.

'With his brilliant abilities he has nothing to learn from talking to me,' he
would say.

Not surprisingly, the pranksters, Broglio and Danzas, were also deprived of
the headmaster's company. They were irrepressible and capricious.

'There is some hope that Broglio will change with time. But he needs
plenty of it,' he said.

Of the poets, only Illichevsky was invited. His industry, purity of taste,
common sense and modesty appealed to Malinovsky.

'He knows what he is capable of and does not over-reach himself,' he would
say.

He did not avoid Delvig and Pushkin and was pleased to speak to them
in the Lycée, but did not normally invite them to his house, afraid of their
ridicule. Pushkin was as sharp as the devil and always seemed to see the funny
side of things. The Principal did not know how to react to him. He knew
that poetry could affect Pushkin profoundly; he had once seen him turning
pale when reading a Batyushkov poem. But still, the imp of derision lurked
within him. Malinovsky understood Yakovlev better – the boy was musical,
always whistling and humming away to himself, was quick at rhymes, had a
good memory, enjoyed a joke – and above all did not turn pale when reading
poetry.

These days most of the boys were anxious and upset, but Pushkin and
Delvig were coping well.

In the week when Smolensk was abandoned, on the day after the gossip
Bakunina had openly called Barclay a traitor, Delvig and Pushkin, with
Valkhovsky, Küchelbecker and Pushchin, were invited to visit the Principal.

The burning candles, his young daughter serving at the table standing in
for her sick mother, the students at the meagre table – everything reminded

the Principal of the college he had known in England, and he could not believe that at this very moment the French were ravaging Russian villages and urging their horses over Russian highways.

'At present the public is indignant that there are no big battles, and demand immediate victories. But soldiers and citizens must learn the art of patience. This is not a military game – and the whole nation is involved.'

He asked Delvig to tell them about his childhood adventures. Delvig had not expected this but repeated his tale unperturbed, even bringing in extra details to change the course of events. So now he said that he had woken up to find himself all alone under the cart, and had been absolutely terrified. It was only later that the batman appeared, holding a thick slice of bread and a pinch of salt in a hand bandaged in a blood-stained rag. It turned out that having felt hungry, he had gone to the nearest village to find some bread and had been wounded there by a stray bullet. They had had their breakfast under the cart.

'What was the batman's name? What sort of a chap was he?' the Principal asked, smiling and evidently entertained by the tale.

'His name was Ivan,' said Delvig quickly and grew pensive. His eyes became dim. 'He used to sing …' he said, and whispered the words in a quiet patter:

> *I got a letter from my dear,*
> *I read it and let fall a tear.*
> *My beauty wrote to me, she said:*
> *'Oh come, dear sir, I'm sick in bed …'*

Aleksandr looked at him: Delvig had copied out this song the day before and shown it to him. Now Delvig was sitting there quietly, amazed by his own lies.

'He died,' he said softly, 'in hospital.'

His mouth twitched – out of sheer sorrow for Ivan.

When they returned to the Lycée, Delvig told Pushkin that while rubbing his father's weapons with chalk, Ivan used to sing *The snow was not white*.

'Anything else?' asked Pushkin, looking at him.

'He used to sing one more song, about Cossacks,' said Delvig eagerly.

> *White bloom falls*
> *From the buckwheat, O:*
> *When the Cossack loves,*
> *Alas, he must go.*

'He sang that before he died.'

They strolled arm in arm up and down the corridor before lights out, recalling the people dear to them – Delvig his sister, Pushkin Arina, and both of them Ivan the batman.

12

The enemy advanced on Moscow – to universal anger and horror. Kutuzov, everybody's favourite, was appointed Commander-in-Chief, replacing Barclay.

Ten days later they read the communiqué about the victory at Borodino. Nobody dared believe it. A pale Malinovsky, with the buttons of his frock-coat all done up, ascended the platform, read the communiqué and in a hoarse voice expressed general congratulations on the victory. Then he paused for a moment on the platform as if to add something, moving his pale lips abstractedly; and stepped down. In the evening he summoned Chirikov and told him that they ought to celebrate the victory. The students should be made to feel something of this long-awaited joy. He suggested that a play or a performance of some sort should be staged under Chirikov's direction in two or three days' time. The tutor started to object that they had no suitable play. Malinovsky cut him off sharply and forcefully. He said that the students could write a play themselves in a couple of days and that the performance must take place. Chirikov objected that the students were forbidden to write anything and that they had been asking repeatedly for the prohibition to be lifted. In Chirikov's presence Malinovsky immediately wrote a petition to the Minister asking that the students be granted complete freedom to write a play, and referring to their formal request delivered to him by Chirikov.

'I ask you to start at once,' he instructed Chirikov. 'The prohibition is pointless and not worth worrying about.'

He was breathing rapidly, his hands were shaking and he would hear of no objections.

Chirikov gave in. He was about to suggest that his own long poem *The Hero of the North* should be staged, but put this intention aside – two days were not enough, and there was no one suitable to act in it. Boudri had once mentioned that he used to write short plays for his students. And indeed among them a play *L'Abbé de l'Epée* was found: simple and appropriate. It was about a famous abbot, a teacher of the deaf and dumb, but the main character was a deaf mute. They could learn such a play in no time and Yakovlev could play the deaf mute. Poor old Ikonnikov came to see his friend Chirikov with a play of his own composition. It was called *A Kind-Hearted Gentleman* and turned out to be even more suitable. In it a kind landowner, Mr Dobrov, rescued his brother and his valet from an unforeseen and undeserved fate. Magnanimity triumphed in this play. The cast consisted of the squire, Mr Dobrov; his kind but deluded brother, Albert; a non-commissioned army officer, and two local government characters. The parts were distributed. Pushchin had the voice and the energy for the role of Albert Dobrov. Illichevsky played the NCO, because of his height, and Yakovlev played the more important comic local government official part – he was so good at pulling faces. The Principal, pale, gloomy and dead-eyed, oversaw preparations. With glum determination Chirikov busied himself with making and painting the sets. With a huge key the usher Matvey unlocked the door to the main hall, which had not been used since the opening of the Lycée. The chairs were brought in and a curtain was fixed to the ceiling. The whole Lycée was in a flurry, the ushers scurrying up and down the stairs.

Kunitsyn did not take part in any of this festive bustle. He was pale as a sheet and did not even attend the event.

13

The evening was coming to an end. It was hot and the windows were open. The women were wearing summer dresses. The war with the French had been going on for six months but the fashion had not yet changed, it had stuck with the same French styles – grey Neapolitan bonnets with ribbons tied under the chin, lace bodices, Marseilles silk dresses, Lyons dresses with appliqué flowers. The 'Love and the Seasons' quadrille, a favourite of Napoleon's sisters the previous year, set the tone for dancing, which had not altered since that time.

Anonymous old ladies sat about in chairs, sharp-elbowed creatures with ancient shoulders sprinkled with powder and black beauty spots on their cerused cheeks. They scrutinised the Lycéeists, ignoring the stage. From time to time their lorgnettes hung down on their chains as they conversed in loud voices. They looked at the students disapprovingly: they had been imposed on their abode by some whim of the Emperor. They had neither good manners nor proper upbringing, not even a hint of charm that might have merited some attention – they were just a bunch of clumsy schoolboys. Everyone had grown accustomed to these whims and was sure that all this would soon be over and that these schoolboys would be forgotten. With the war on they would soon be transferred elsewhere. They beckoned to Gorchakov and had a chat with him. Count Tolstoy knew Vasily Lvovich. He noticed Aleksandr and nodded to him. Aleksandr could not overcome his shyness: this was high society, the *monde* his mother had talked about with a secret envy and distinct joy. Her dark eyes would glow, her cheeks would flush and she would give a low chuckle. He remembered that chuckle. During the interval Tolstoy introduced him to society.

Tolstoy's face was melancholy-looking, with thick lips, but it expressed some pleasure as he looked at Aleksandr. The boy amused him, like all the

Pushkins. An old lady with an ashen face examined him curiously. She was as old as the hills. Aleksandr bowed and looked shy when he was introduced.

'How awkward they all are these days!' the old lady said.

Two of the other ladies looked at him. The daughter of one of them was still a child. He had run into her a couple of times when walking; she had a small head and was as slim as a willow. They were the Kochubeys and lived nearby. They spoke to him and asked about his uncle, Vasily Lvovich, but hardly listened to his reply and a second later had forgotten about his existence.

He ran from the hall, hid himself in a corner and observed the young beauty from there. Just as when Roussleau had been his teacher, he wanted to be on his own. The usher Foma, passing by, nearly stumbled over him.

The guests were leaving. He ran downstairs and waited. She walked by and seemed to be looking for somebody: she was looking for him. He touched her hand, knowing that everyone would see. Nobody noticed and she said good-bye to him, nodding her small head.

He could not forgive himself his sudden shyness when she was about to depart, and he could not sleep that night. He left his room and went into the gallery. In the corridor he passed Kalinich asleep with his mouth open. He walked openly with no attempt at concealment, and nearly brushed against him, afraid of nothing. Kalinich did not stir. Aleksandr went down the stairs and nobody stopped him. The cold stone burnt his feet. Looking for a trace of her, he walked slowly to the front door and pushed it open – in the flurry of things no one had remembered to lock it. He stood by the door gazing in despair at the yellow light of the lamp. The thought of flight crossed his mind. He wanted to say good-bye to her, to embrace her, then to mount a horse and flee – he would catch up with Kaverin on the way.

This was another Natalya.

14

It was late. After the performance, conceived and brought off with such determination by Malinovsky, there was no elation. Kunitsyn was pale and discontented. They should not have celebrated this victory with a social occasion. It had produced nothing but boredom, the depressing aura that all these unfamiliar people of the Court had brought with them. What an absurd idea! He was calling on the Principal to ask him for leave at an unfortunate time. His brother had been wounded at Borodino; a bullet had passed straight through his chest. He wanted to see him, perhaps for the last time, and was leaving next morning. He knocked, no one responded; he peeped in.

Malinovsky was seated at the table hunched up in his dressing-gown, his head in his hands. He raised his head and looked at Kunitsyn with hazy eyes.

Blind tears were rolling down his face.

'So many lives wasted!' he said hoarsely. 'Now the whole world can see what kind of enemy we have to deal with. May your people be covered with glory, O Lord!'

15

The Lycée was shaken up by this unusual and unfortunate celebration. Malinovsky had received a sharp reprimand from the Minister Razumovsky, These days the Minister was in a mood of black and vicious depression. He believed that it was insane to contend with Napoleon. Recently he had received news from his gardener, Steven, a horticultural specialist, whose son the Minister had recommended for the Lycée. Württembergers among Napoleon's forces had raided his estate and pillaged it bare. The gardener was dispirited most of all by the fact that the damage had been done not by the godless French but by Württembergers like himself! Everything in Gorenki had been smashed, destroyed and trampled over, and only the ransom the gardener offered had persuaded the invaders to leave his gardens. Learning of the Lycée performance, Razumovsky found an outlet for his fury. From now on the staging of plays by the Lycéeists in the presence of strangers was strictly forbidden. The Principal was lectured like a raw youth on the inappropriate-ness of the performance given at the Lycée on the thirtieth of August. The students' request for permission to write and perform plays in their leisure time would now be refused even in the case of private performances.

Malinovsky had fallen into glaring public disgrace. Immediately Gauenschield visited the Minister, and it was clear that he came away having been promised a great deal, and would soon enjoy considerable power. He strolled about the Lycée in triumph, chewed his liquorice with even greater zeal and had long talks with Korff, whose good behaviour pleased him. He told him, in his usual abrupt, puffing manner, how gratified he was that the Lycéeists would hardly develop into real actors, then stuck his hands in his pockets and strutted about the hall, humming softly and sticking out his coat-tail. It was a long time since he had been seen so contented.

16

Küchelbecker had received a letter from his mother: the dismissed Barclay, envied and misunderstood by his enemies, and now betrayed, had submitted uncomplainingly to the new Commander-in-Chief and, swallowing his pride, had given a great personal example of a man's genuine love for his fatherland. During the battle at Borodino he had thrown himself like an ordinary soldier into the most dangerous skirmishes under gunfire and cannonfire, looking for death – but had not found it. He had done his utmost at Borodino to save the people he was in charge of, as he had saved them before as Commander-in-Chief. History would be the judge of whether he had been right in retreating without a fight, but his conscience was clear and it was not for the young and inexperienced to judge military tactics without any understanding of them. The word 'treason' should not be allowed to darken their minds and they should await the verdict of the high command and of posterity.

Küchelbecker immediately read all this to Pushchin, Pushkin and Valkhovsky. Previously Valkhovsky had eagerly joined in the general condemnation of Barclay. His hero was Suvorov, and he stood for the bayonet and the bullet, for the hot old-fashioned fight and the rapid advance. But Barclay's recent behaviour had drastically changed his opinion of him. The boy put himself through exhausting gymnastics before going to sleep and trained himself to be fair, like Suvorov. Pushchin agreed completely with the letter's acquittal of the General. Pushkin was silent: the unlucky, slandered commander had sought death at Borodino. Suddenly he bit his lip, flushed, mumbled something and in confusion ran out of the room: the usual sign that he was deeply moved.

17

The autumn was warm, fine and clear. There were heaps of fallen leaves in the Lycée garden and it gave him a secret joy to wander about stepping on the piles swept up by the usher Matvey who was in charge of the garden. The silence was complete, without breeze or drizzle. Kalinich who had predicted severe frosts was put to shame, but he just shrugged his shoulders.

'I wasn't talking about autumn,' he said obstinately, 'I meant winter frosts.'

The foliage fell to the ground; a few yellow skeletal leaves stirred slightly in the warm wind.

Kalinich pointed out an oak tree to Yakovlev, silently indicating the few remaining leaves that would not fall. Yakovlev did not understand.

'Not all the leaves are shed at the same time,' said Kalinich meaningfully, 'consequently, the winter will be severe.'

He was sure of his folk truths and was reluctant to expand on the topic. And indeed, next day the wind blew, a storm sprang up, the trees in the garden bent and groaned.

It was on a day like this that the Russian troops abandoned Moscow to the enemy.

18

They heard of the fires ravaging Moscow: it was burning on all sides. The conflagration had started by the Yauza Bridge and on the opposite side of the city and soon become widespread. The Moscow gardens had not been spared, the trees had been charred, their leaves blackened and curled.

The magnificent palaces of the Moscow grandees were burning too, the Market Arcades had been turned into ashes, the Foundling Hospital had burnt and crumbled to the ground; the streets across the River Moskva were in flames, fanned by strong winds that blew just at this time.

Turgenev told Kunitsyn the news when he was in town and he passed it on to Aleksandr. His parents, his uncle and aunt were safe and sound in Nizhny Novgorod. His father was cheerful and soon Aleksandr received a detailed letter from him.

Next day Malinovsky asked Chirikov how the students had taken the news the previous night. Chirikov reported how some of the boys had lain tossing in bed unable to sleep, sighing and muttering fearfully, but keeping quiet when he spoke to them and pretending to be asleep. He made no comment on the rest of the night because he had been asleep. When asked who had been worst affected, Chirikov named Pushchin and Pushkin.

And indeed, Pushkin had not slept. He had learned from the communiqué of the horrific devastation of Moscow, but couldn't imagine it at first.

There was no nest in Kharitonyev Lane any more. How beautiful it seemed to him now! Even the threadbare rug by the stove. *Everything* had been burnt and destroyed – the streets he used to stroll along did not exist any more. Most of Moscow had gone up in flames.

In his imagination he walked along the familiar route – along the boulevard, and failed to comprehend that everything about him was in smoking ruins. *Even the gardens were charred and blackened*, Kalinich had said. He listened to the monotonous ticking of the clock in the corridor and shuddered. He had grown accustomed to fear nothing; he did not cry like Korsakov. He thought neither of his parents who had fled to the Volga nor even of Arina – he thought about Moscow, the blackened ruins where he had been born, where he had grown up, where one day he would return. Now he had no place to return to. He was all alone, and with his eyes wide open he lay staring into the darkness that surrounded him on all sides. He recalled the familiar houses, one after another, doubtful whether they still existed. There was nobody he could even ask. Tsarskoye Selo was deserted at that hour. He knocked gently on the wall and immediately a faint knocking came in reply: Pushchin was not asleep. He calmed down. Moscow could not really have been destroyed, and he intended to see it again at any cost. He told Pushchin and Pushchin approved. Aleksandr dreamt of flight, a long journey, Moscow, enemies, revenge. Pushchin knocked again to say good-night.

Foma, come to wake them up in the morning, looked through the latticed window and refrained from knocking: neither the curly-haired one nor the chubby one was asleep. He just said, as always: 'Lord, have mercy on us!' and retreated.

The Principal summoned Pushkin. He asked him if he had heard from home recently, and quietly corrected himself:

'… from your parents?'

Home did not exist any more.

Malinovsky looked at him attentively.

'It will be over soon,' he said calmly. 'People believe it is the French who are burning Moscow. They are mistaken. The French are not insane. It's the Russians who are burning Moscow. Cut to the quick, infuriated, wounded, mocked, they're burning their own city and ready to perish in the flames. But our guests will not survive either.'

Aleksandr stared at him open-mouthed. It was a strange new idea for him and he could not grasp it yet. Malinovsky fell deadly quiet and smiled strangely:

'Do you remember Prince Igor's death and his wife Olga's revenge?' he asked. 'So far you've been taught classical history, but at the end of the year you'll be told Princess Olga's tale because it happened later, in the Middle Ages. Read Glinka's version. After Olga's husband, Prince Igor, was murdered, she heated up a bathhouse for the messengers of the Drevlyans who were responsible for his death and asked the guests if they were all right. And the guests replied: 'Even better than when we killed Igor.' Then she went to the Drevlyans and ordered mead to be brewed, and as a punishment for their crime she took a small tribute from them – three sparrows and a pigeon from every household. The Drevlyans were delighted to be given such a light penalty. Olga ordered a tinder with burning sulphur to be tied to each bird's tail and then let them free: they flew back to their houses to their nests and set them on fire. That's how it was. Brag not when you're going to the feast but when you return. Off you go, and don't be sad. You're doing well.'

The Director spoke the last words spontaneously, forgetting the report in front of him: all the teachers had assured him that Pushkin did no homework and got by on his excellent memory. He was supposed to give him a severe reprimand. He gave him a hug.

19

Sergey Lvovich and Vasily Lvovich, together with others of the gentry, had fled from Moscow to Nizhny Novgorod. Vasily Lvovich was destitute – at the moment of flight he had been penniless and had had no chance to take his belongings with him. Nobody had come to his aid. He had left Moscow in a peasant's cart. All the things he had amassed in his lifetime, everything that had had either sentimental or monetary value, had been left to the mercy of the enemy. He remembered the droshki he had driven in the days when he had been a *brigand* and together with his friends paid visits to the Moscow madams. His droshki had been left in the barn and probably stolen. He recalled the recently repaired carriage that used to convey the charms of the cruel Circe – God knows where it was now! And the pieces of furniture he had grown to love like friends; the sofa exactly like the one on which David had portrayed Mme Récamier who used to smile at him. By now this sofa must have passed to her compatriots. He was no longer young, and having grown used to all these things, he could not imagine himself setting up anew. Besides, he had no money.

He had also had to abandon his library, full of precious books and famous all over Moscow. The strange thing was that for some reason Vasily Lvovich at first regretted this less than his carriage. His library had been extensive and rare, and the loss was too great to recall it too often. Only later, remembering Aretino's book with its illustrations, unique in their way, he clasped his hands and froze. Most of all Vasily Lvovich was tormented by the thought that he had left Moscow in a light coat, and that his entire wardrobe – the fur-coat and other garments he had grown accustomed to as to his own skin – had been lost.

At the same time he nourished a small secret hope that all these things would somehow return to him – it was impossible that they should all have been lost! But he did not share this thought with anybody. He complained to Annushka loudly about the absence of his favourite things, each of them separately: at one moment he missed his pipe, at another his dressing-gown.

'Prince Shalikov asked me to give him that pipe but I refused!'

Or:

'Oh! How much property the villains will pillage! I'll never see my dressing-gown again!'

He avoided talking about his losses among the Moscow refugees. It was hard to surprise them; a contest of distress even sprang up among them. At first they gathered at the Bibikovs' or Arkharovs', who were allotted big houses to stay in and squabbled about who had lost most. On the first evening Vasily

Lvovich said with a sigh that he had lost all his personal property, but the news was received drily. Some there had lost much more.

'What exactly did you lose?' old Arkharov asked him resentfully.

Hearing of the precious library, he said gravely:

'A library? Ha! You can buy another one in any shop. I've lost my parquet floors!'

From then on Vasily Lvovich spoke about his losses only to the Nizhny Novgorod ladies. They treated him compassionately. Their very pronunciation seemed to Vasily Lvovich extremely pleasant and amusing: they drew out their words, pronouncing the unstressed *o* as stressed. Soon he started to woo the beautiful Yeliza Salamanova. The fair ladies of Nizhny Novgorod were less polished than those of Moscow, but Vasily Lvovich found that fresh and exciting.

He settled into an *izba*;* the autumn was cold and he had no fur-coat. But his days gradually started to fill up: he resumed old, long-forgotten connections. His cousin, Aleksey Mikhaylovich – 'the other Pushkin' – turned up in Nizhny Novgorod. He had become even more sloppy and spiteful in his bevaviour; he treated Vasily Lvovich disrespectfully, kissed him too loudly and repeatedly in greeting him, and so on. In the presence of strangers he asked him about the health of his servants, especially emphasising the last word and obviously implying Annushka. Nowadays Vasily Lvovich called him a namesake, denying their kinship point-blank. The namesake gambled all day, and constantly smoked tobacco, coughed and raised his voice. Once he shouted to Vasily Lvovich, passing by with the beautiful Yeliza, out of the window of the house where he had been playing cards for two days on end:

'*Mon cousin*! Have you found my pipe?'

Such impertinence made Vasily Lvovich go rigid. He shrugged his shoulders and walked on. Indeed, many years ago Aleksey had given the pipe to Vasily Lvovich as a birthday present. Soon the squabbles between the cousins preoccupied Nizhny Novgorod society. Karamzin said with some amusement and a sigh:

'Everything on earth changes, only the Pushkins stay the same.'

Meanwhile the displaced Moscow society grew accustomed to its situation and even started to enjoy the nomadic existence. Entertainments were arranged – balls and masquerades. Vasily Lvovich, entirely bewitched by Yeliza Salamanova, decided to come out into the open as a poet. He composed a fine patriotic address to the inhabitants of Nizhny Novgorod, in which he lamented the burning of Moscow. There were no inflated exclamations or comparisons of Russian military leaders with Roman heroes. There was a

---

* A peasant house constructed of wood.

purity, a neatness of style and a certain pathos about his poem. After each stanza came a refrain:

> *Succour us and give us shelter,*
> *Sons and daughters of the Volga!*

The poem was a success. A famous amateur musician, Professor Fischer who had fled from Moscow together with everyone else, set it to music with the stanzas sung by a soloist and the refrain by a choir. At the Governor's ball Vasily Lvovich's song was ecstatically received. The poet's fame impressed the previously cold Yeliza. News of the ball was reported in St Petersburg and Vasily Lvovich was in raptures. The Nizhny Novgorod ladies nudged each other discreetly in the street, their eyes indicating the poet strolling by in unseasonable summer clothes. Vasily Lvovich squinted and passed on sedately.

He soon found himself the object of his namesake's envy. Aleksey Pushkin had grown embittered, and said that Vasily Lvovich's stanzas with their refrain reminded him of a convict in irons begging under windows and turning with curses on street urchins ridiculing him. The strongly worded but appropriate stanzas about the enemy were taken by the poet's namesake as 'curses'. Vasily Lvovich ignored the insult – not for the first time – and pretended to be unaware of it. It was said that even Karamzin smiled at the debauchee's comment. Vasily Lvovich told Annushka:

'Even an *izba* is no shelter from slander.'

Annushka immediately started to rustle up a fur-coat for Vasily Lvovich. She got hold of a merchant's tight-fitting coat, but he declined it – absolutely and indignantly. Annushka and a Nizhny Novgorod tailor spent much time altering it. Vasily Lvovich pulled on the fur-coat, looked at himself in the mirror and recalled the Byzantine general Belisarius as he had seen him on the Parisian stage. He managed to drape himself in such a way that the fur-coat finally lost its ignoble look. He gave in – the frosts were coming on apace. He was penniless and particularly annoyed by the fact that his namesake enjoyed everybody's hospitality and had also won some eight thousand roubles.

However, Vasily Lvovich had no time to fret. At one soirée he got involved in an argument about French literature, of which Ivan Muravyov-Apostol, a respectable but quirky man, spoke disapprovingly. In Moscow Vasily Lvovich had vowed not to speak too heatedly or too sharply, afraid he might be accused of Martinism. But Nizhny Novgorod seemed far removed from Moscow and Rostopchin, and Vasily Lvovich wavered and became deeply engaged in the argument. It was no secret to Vasily Lvovich that Muravyov was an important figure in the Symposium and close to Shishkov. But Nizhny Novgorod, this friendly republic of refugees, ignored hierarchical differences and allowed everyone freedom of opinion. Vasily Lvovich announced that he would always prefer Voltaire as a master of style to any doggerel with Church-Slavonicisms, and that logic was an essential feature of refinement. In his opinion Gresset was a poet and Shihkmatov wasn't.

An argument began on this topic. Everyone was absorbed by the fashionable dispute and by Vasily Lvovich's ardour. Having found himself the object of general curiosity he shut his eyes for a second, like a person throwing himself into an abyss, and recited by heart two pages from Gresset, explaining firmly that military matters were one thing and poetic taste was another. Returning home, he woke up Annushka and commanded her to be ready for anything. Annushka glanced at his sombre expression and gave a soft sob. Vasily Lvovich was trembling either from fear or because Belisarius's cloak, as he called his fur-coat, was too light. Annushka warmed him up and he fell asleep.

Next day, sitting in his *izba*, he received three invitations: for a soirée, a masquerade and a play at Bibikov's. Vasily Lvovich cheered up and his fear vanished without trace. Now he was in full vogue and welcome everywhere – invited to a constant stream of lunches, dinners, balls and masquerades, he had no time for worries. He hardly had time to read the communiqués.

Even the Volga cuisine seemed pleasant to him. Eel liver and sterlet soup, which Ivan Ivanovich Dmitriyev had once told him about, had finally ousted Parisian matelote from his heart. He regained his composure, his self-confidence and a sense of his significance. Yes, he was now languishing in the region where the Oka flowed into the Volga, the region that enriched the whole of Russia with fish and flour. Such was the will of Providence! What could one do? Yes, he used to give dinners – and what dinners! Yes, he used to extol the famous graces of Petropol. He used to flaunt his costly, dashing four-in-hand. He, like all his friends, used to have parquet floors, day-beds and – not that he was bragging about them – oil lamps and bronzes! Sweet Lord, how good he used to be at squandering! Life was different here. He was languishing like a fugitive. But still, he was not like some others – he disdained the ace of diamonds that brought certain people eight thousand roubles, especially if the game was light-fingered. An *izba*, a simple bed, two chairs, a quill and paper – these were his possessions. A kind-hearted maid, of the kind so dear to Piron, was the guardian of his peace. He was a poet, he wrote verses. His namesakes basked in his glory and claimed to be his relatives. Famous writers laughed listening to these clowns. What could one do? He kept silent. Patience and pure taste, poverty and a clear conscience – these were his possessions, the possessions of a poet. And the enemy could not deprive him of this property as they had deprived him of his new droshki, his furniture and his precious library.

In these or similar terms he would talk to the charming Yeliza and certain other beauties, failing, however, to mention his maid. Yeliza wagged her little finger at him as she had seen the Moscow ladies doing. Once again he was a *brigand*, a poet, a blade, ageing but ready for action – of the literary kind!

20

Things had gone differently with his brother.

Sergey Lvovich had had to rescue his wife's dresses first. Then he had put on his Sunday best, thrown his fur-coat over the shoulders of a peasant whom he hired on the way, seized a chest of drawers in passing and, holding a cambric handkerchief in his hands, left Moscow with his wife in a peasant cart. He had thrust the bundle of dresses bitterly into the corner of the cart and then, on the pretext of keeping it secure, sat down on it. Nadezhda Osipovna had not done this herself because she had been afraid to crumple her wardrobe. She had considerably quietened down. The only thing she had taken with her was her own portrait, painted by the famous Vigée-Lebrun in the year when a Guardsman had told her that the two most beautiful women were *les deux belles Créoles* – herself and Bonaparte's spouse Josephine. Now Bonaparte was torching Moscow and she was being jolted in a peasant cart. Lyovushka and Olinka had jumped up on the front and Arina was sitting on the side of the cart with her legs dangling. They had left Nikita behind in Moscow to safeguard their possessions.

No sooner had they left Moscow than a piece of insubordination by Arina unexpectedly took place. Indeed, Sergey Lvovich could call it nothing else but mutiny. Earlier, when she had sensed that they were going to leave for God knew where, Arina had knitted her brows, winced and secretly taken to her phial, which Nadezhda Osipovna had been aware of but pretended not to notice – sometimes she felt wary of her. On the eve of their departure Arina had quarrelled with Nikita.

'We should go to St Petersburg!' she said to him in a low voice. 'Not to God knows where!'

'And who's waiting for you there, Arina Rodionovna, in St Petersburg?' asked Nikita politely, raising his brows.

'Who are they leaving him with? The boy's parents are alive and he lives like an orphan!' Arina paid no attention to Nikita and added in a hiss, 'Out of sight, out of mind, eh?'

'It's like that with everybody,' Nikita said.

'And what about him? What will *he* do, you shameless rascal?' hissed Arina, and sniffed.

'Well then,' Nikita snapped at her, 'what's to be done? Are *you* going to bring him here? These are just words!'

'Perhaps I will!' said Arina.

Though she had packed uncomplainingly, when they were about twenty versts from Moscow she started to rub her eyes and wail in a low voice.

Nadezhda Osipovna was on the point of wailing herself, she was biting her handkerchief. Sergey Lvovich, who could not bear female tears, fidgeted in the vehicle like a cat on hot bricks. At the first stop Arina vanished. They noticed her absence and then saw her walking along the road with a sackful of rusks. They fetched her back. Sergey Lvovich was distraught:

'This is mutiny and desertion!' he said to Nadezhda Osipovna in a low voice.

'What are you up to?' Nadezhda Osipovna asked her calmly.

'I'm going to St Petersburg,' replied Arina, 'to see Aleksandr Sergeyevich. He might be lost there, alone.'

'Irina, are you mad?' asked Sergey Lvovich, beside himself.

Without realising it, he had started to call her Irina and address her formally. Arina gave a sigh, seated herself in the cart, and they set off again.

Sergey Lvovich, accustomed to travelling, suddenly felt joyful – he was sick and tired of Moscow life. He enjoyed the general bustle and uncertainty, the possibility of complete change and a certain stature that he had acquired in his wife's eyes in their terrible circumstances. He who had grown pale at the sight of a smashed glass felt mere surprise now that he had lost everything. Running into other refugees on the road cheered him up. The Muscovites were a motley crew, fleeing in whatever they happened to be wearing at the time. The caravan of carts stretched out for a long distance.

In Nizhny Novgorod he was plunged into blunt reality: the dirty *izba* that they had managed to rent here offended his pride.

'*C'est une* cattle-stall, *mon ange*!' he would say to Nadezhda Osipovna.

He in his best outfit and she in evening clothes would pour boiling water over the bugs that scurried about the walls.

However, just as in Moscow, he was anxious to sneak away from home. He wandered along the bank of the Volga at the confluence with the Oka, met his Moscow friends and got acquainted with a few Nizhny Novgorod people.

He was a person not without significance and overall of independent station. His son was at the Tsarskoye Selo Lycée, in a Court educational institution situated in the Palace itself. His son often wrote to him. Tsarskoye Selo, with the two Empresses and the Court, was in great turmoil nowadays. Of course, only God knew if the enemy would head for St Petersburg, and in such a case, straight for Tsarskoye Selo. But one thought comforted the parents – Minister Dmitriyev was looking after Aleksandr and was like a father to him. The boy was in Dmitriyev's care, in the Palace, and he would share the fate of his Sovereign. *Que la volonté de Dieu soit faite!*

In short, he was one of the three Pushkins, either poets or gamblers, who were the focus of Nizhny Novgorod's attention. A strange coldness, however, had developed between the brothers. Vasily Lvovich seemed to care only about himself and his success. Some time ago he had dedicated an affectionate poem to his brother which Sergey Lvovich remembered as a symbol of faith.

> *In our family household*
> *Where love reigned full and free,*
> *We used to play as children*
> *In the innocence of our hearts.*
> *Do not be sad, dear brother,*
> *Dear tender-hearted brother!*
> *We won't be apart for ever,*
> *Our grief won't last for ever!*

Now the fugitive brothers had joined one another again but past affection had vanished. Moreover, at the very beginning of their exile, Vasily Lvovich had taken pains to get their sister Anna Lvovna off his hands and onto his brother's under the pretext that he had neither money nor possessions and his house was too crowded. Sergey Lvovich had been most indignant: he was penniless too and his shack was even worse. However, the ladies had exchanged glances, making Sergey Lvovich understand that the problem was a delicate one – the impropriety of Anna Lvovna's staying under the same roof with Annushka. So now Anna Lvovna shared her brother Sergey's *izba*. The second circumstance that had contributed to the coldness between the Pushkin brothers was their life-long literary competitiveness. Sergey Lvovich had always, since childhood, felt that he was a poet. His French poems were definitely good stuff, better than his brother's. There was a time when Vasily Lvovich had not been ashamed to consider his brother his equal, recalling how in their youth

> *To the lyre we sang a hymn*
> *To the Creator of the Universe.*

'Sacred poetry!' Vasily Lvovich used to exclaim.

> *From our earliest years,*
> *To You we devoted ourselves,*
> *In You we found delight!*

Sergey Lvovich, who felt revived and rejuvenated in his new surroundings, as he had not felt for a long time, once again felt inspired. The ladies of Nizhny Novgorod confused him with his brother at first and took him for a poet, which deep in his heart he was. He was the first to make Yeliza's acquaintance and when she asked him to write a few lines in her album, he did not refuse. In his brief light verses in French he compared her to a brook that gave an exile a chance to quench his thirst. When later Vasily Lvovich composed a short impromptu too and at Yeliza's request was about to enter it in her album, he was unpleasantly surprised by the proximity of his brother's verses, and grew sullen. In society the brothers behaved like strangers. It was an unlucky moment when Sergey Lvovich took it into his head to play cards with his cousin and lost. His sister Anna Lvovna lent him some money and wondered how her nephew Sashka in Tsarskoye Selo was managing his. Sashka was so young, giddy and inexperienced that he had probably long ago squandered it on some nonsense or other.

Sergey Lvovich replied icily that Sashka had been unable to squander it since his dear uncle Vasily had thought it better to keep the money in his own pocket.

Anna Lvovna made no comment and from then on started to treat all Nizhny Novgorodians suspiciously and hide her *Reader for the Fair Sex*, the pages of which were interlaid with banknotes, under her pillow.

Soon Sergey Lvovich, pretending to be unaware of the fate of Aleksandr's hundred roubles, asked his brother to lend him the same sum, counting on not giving it back and in this way settling accounts with him. Vasily Lvovich refused point-blank, clasped his hands and announced that first, he would never lend money for his brother's ruin and let their namesake put it into his pocket, and secondly, he did not have any.

Sergey Lvovich had once been fond of Karamzin's lines:

> *Care, tenderness and love*
> *Together reward loyalty.*

Nothing of the kind! Not a word about care, not a single word about tenderness from his brother, who had not passed on the money, about love, which did not seem to concern his brother any more; and whenever Karamzin, the author of these lines, met Sergey Lvovich he hardly paid him any attention either.

Sergey Lvovich, received so well at first, soon realised with a shock that he was not taken seriously – as a consequence of his quarrel with his brother and Vasily Lvovich's quarrel with their cousin, whose sharp tongue Sergey Lvovich very much feared. Having been so incautious in the beginning as to have posed as a poet, he now felt unmasked. Yeliza and her female friends stopped inviting him to their houses.

One evening he came back to his *izba* to find Nadezhda Osipovna dressed up and powdered, with a beauty spot on her cheek, in her evening dress with a low neck-line, holding her miniature portrait by Vigée-Lebrun. They had not received a single invitation for that evening. Tears were rolling down her faded cheeks. Sergey Lvovich suddenly shuddered and felt that he would never go back to Moscow; even if the Muscovites humbly implored him, he would never return to the city that had failed to appreciate him. He had no rank but was quite independent, he was neither a borrower nor a debtor. The war threatened all of them equally and his situation was no worse than his brother's, Karamzin's or anybody else's. Fate had made them all refugees. At least his children's destinies were settled: Aleksandr was at the Tsarskoye Selo Lycée, in the Palace, and if the Palace escaped destruction, Sashka would be safe too. He was in the public eye. It was time to put an end to this backbiting. To the ends of the earth, but away from Moscow! There was *no* Moscow. Away, at least, from Nizhny Novgorod!

21

Autumn struck suddenly, the wind howled, wet snow stuck to the branches of the trees, which slashed their faces like whips when they went out for walks. Deserted gardens surrounded them on all sides, the skies were dim. The Great Caprice showed up black like a grave mound in the distance. The bows of ships stuck out from the old grey granite Chesme rostral column. A crimson moon rose, the colour of blood. He found the book by Parny where all these things were named. The gardens were Morven's Forest, the cave was Fingal's Cave. The bard Ossian had sung about it all some time ago.

One day, the thick-bearded, taciturn, homespun man in a blue coat whom they had seen a year before turned up at the Lycée. It was the Court tailor who had made their uniforms. Once again he measured them quickly and nimbly and wrote down the figures, holding a folding measuring-stick in his teeth and ignoring their questions. Then he looked at them, grinned and replied to everyone at once:

'Don't get excited for nothing, Your Honours! There'll be no new uniforms. I'm to make you hareskin coats for the cold season and a long journey. They'll last you a hundred years.'

There were no doubts: they were leaving.

Pushchin, the most practical of them all, started to put everything in order and even to pack. Korff burst into tears.

Moscow had been burnt down. Kharitonyev Lane did not exist any longer. Tsarskoye Selo was no longer 'beautiful gardens' but 'deserted forests' again; their nomadic life was just beginning. His classmates would probably disperse and go home. As for him, he had no home, his father and his uncle were God knows where, in Nizhny Novgorod, and the servants must have run wild and had probably wandered into the woods. He had been left to his own devices and could no longer depend on them. He decided not to give way to fear, clenched his teeth, and with a fierce joy prepared himself for whatever might come. The only person he was really sorry for here was Natasha, Volkonskaya's maid. Now he would wake up to the light in her window.

Out walking he found a knotty, ice-covered stick, and damaging his mittens and breaking the order of the procession, started to knock down frozen branches. He was saying good-bye to this place. Next day they met Natasha at the Lycée and he found a chance to whisper a couple of words to her.

That evening he stole into the arcade. All the other boys were in their rooms. Walking by Korsakov's room he heard a delicate throbbing sound: the music teacher had discovered that Korsakov had a talent for music and his parents had sent him a guitar. He was trying it tentatively before going to bed; too loud a sound could attract the tutor's attention. Chirikov was either busy in the duty room or might have gone to sleep in his own room. The usual routine had been disrupted – soon they were to move to another place, and as if by tacit agreement the old order had been dissolved.

He walked through the arcade and peered out through the dim window. It was pitch-dark; the street-lamps lining the road were blinking; sometimes the wind rushed by and shook the windows. It was cold in the arcade; it had long since stopped being heated.

The door to the Lycée wing was unlocked; only Chirikov who occupied the adjacent room had the right to use that entrance. Recently he had become entirely absorbed in the composition of his narrative poem *Hero of the North* and had grown absent-minded – now and again he forgot to lock the door.

He set the door ajar and looked inside. The hundred-year-old door creaked and he froze. He stood motionless for a moment. It was so cold he started to shiver. He did not really believe that Natasha would come. He heard from the Lycée the sound of Foma's grumbling at somebody, the steward perhaps, and sighing: 'Lord, have mercy on us!' Then it became quiet again. He remembered saying to Natasha simply: 'The arcade, tonight' – and she might have come already and found no one. Then he thought that Foma might lock him in from the other side, as this door was supposed to be locked. He stood still, listening to the mice scurrying in a corner. The wind clinked the glass panes in the windows. It was hard to believe that Pushchin, Küchelbecker, Korsakov and Gorchakov were asleep nearby – as he was supposed to be.

The door opened a little. He could not believe it, his heart started to hammer. Natasha's face appeared in the doorway. She looked around open-mouthed and it was obvious she was terrified. As soon as she saw him she gave a frightened little moan, though it was him she had come to meet. Then she stepped inside hesitantly, looked down, and breathing heavily, started to fumble with the lace of her apron. He embraced her; she stood still with her hands down and said only:

'Oh, sir, they'll punish us!'

She looked different from how he had seen her on walks – her face was broader, more of a peasant face, and her body was larger. He had never heard her voice before. Then he took her in his arms and suddenly felt that he wouldn't let her go for all the riches of the world. He felt the heaviness of her body in his hands, so different from the feel of his classmates Broglio and Malinovsky, with whom he had wrestled earlier that day.

In the corner next to them the mice started to scrabble. Suddenly she pressed him to her chest so tightly that he could feel the beating of her heart. Gasping for breath, she said:

'Oh, master, little master, my dear! They'll punish us. What are you doing? We shouldn't!'

She pressed her lips to his eyes – obviously inexperienced in the art of kissing – and he heard her heart thumping. Suddenly she pushed him aside, broke loose from his grip with an unexpected force and darted through the door like lightning, as only maids can do. He rushed after her, but she had vanished without trace. He groped his way along a bare corridor till he came to a door and without thinking burst in. His head was burning, his heart was thumping. He crossed a room and felt his feet come up against a staircase. He stood leaning against the wall and craning his neck, ready for whatever might happen next. It did not occur to him that if he were found he would be expelled from the Lycée in disgrace like that idiot Guryev. He had to find Natasha at once, but he was lost.

Clenching his teeth, he pushed ahead, ran up the stairs and in no time found himself at the entrance to the Lycée. He was astonished to find that he had been only a few steps away from it. He was dismayed and bewildered. Only Broglio and Malinovsky among his classmates could get the better of him in wrestling; he was more agile than Pushchin and almost as strong as Danzas. He had the reputation of being a tough one, but the fact that Natasha had broken loose from his grip and he had failed to catch her was shameful to him.

He had intended to say good-bye to her, and had prepared a few initial words: 'My dear love Natasha', 'Dear heart Natasha', 'God knows if we shall ever see each other again', 'Is your Argus asleep?' and so forth, but had gone numb when he embraced her, and so failed to catch her when she ran away. He came up to his window trying to understand where Natasha could have hidden herself so quickly – she must have had some hiding-place. Her light was nowhere to be seen, everything looked dim and dead. There on the other side of the wall old Volkonskaya slept, with her blue-grey nose and ashen face, and not far from her was his beautiful, buxom and yet nimble Natasha. He scowled at the window behind which, so near yet so far, lay the chamber of Proserpina and his Psyche.

He was leaving next day.

Meanwhile, Chirikov was not asleep; he ambled along the corridor in his thick felt shoes and with a little cough peeped down into his room through the door lattice. The night was dark, the candle was dim, he could not see a thing, and thinking that Aleksandr Pushkin was asleep, walked on.

22

They were told they were to wait till the anniversary of the opening of the Lycée, which, however, would not be celebrated, because any festivities or even simple entertainments organised by Principal Malinovsky would provoke harsh reprimands from the Minister; they would then prepare for the journey. They would go not to Reval as expected, but to the Finnish town of Åbo.* The present staff would not accompany them. Their teachers and supervisors would be staff from Åbo University. Gauenschield was delighted.

'It will be a sort of Göttingen,' he said.

Malinovsky noticed Gauenschield's satisfaction. One day the Principal left, and came back with a short, shaven old man. The Cossack immediately told the boys in strict confidence that old Samborsky had expressed the wish to accompany and look after them in Åbo. He had travelled a lot, had lived abroad, and had eagerly agreed to undertake one last journey. Malinovsky would stay in Tsarskoye Selo for the time being; the captain should be the last to leave the sinking ship, said Matyushkin.

The nineteenth of October had passed. Since morning Gorchakov had started to limp, saying with a slight lisp:

'A year already! A year since we've been here! We're old men now. Oh, my old gout!'

The day, the nineteenth of October, so dazzling a year before, had passed insignificantly this time round. Next day everything went according to routine. They had a glass of hot honey and spice, which the stingy steward gave them instead of tea – pleading wartime, but in their opinion shamelessly profiting from it. They grumbled – honey and spice definitely put them on a level with the Court choirboys.

Nobody told them to pack and another delay made many of them frown: almost everyone had reconciled himself to the thought of departure. Tsarskoye

---

* Now Turku.

Selo had become alien to them; they had already said good-bye to it in their hearts.

No one liked the history teacher, Kaydanov. His whole being, squat and thickset, was totally unpleasant. He walked with a waddle and carried the imprint of the seminary in Pereyaslavl, where he had taught before coming to the Lycée. He was sly, with little rogue's eyes. A bitter man, he made no effort to conceal his seminary habits in front of his students; he perhaps adhered to them on purpose, out of spite. He read out his lectures from copybooks in an exaggerated, sing-song tone, in involuntary imitation of the rector of his seminary. Misha Yakovlev thought he looked like their priest Païssy. He was the slave of his own secret laziness and indifference. Crafty and uncouth, he derived the greatest pleasure from throwing people into confusion. But his students listened to him, perhaps fascinated by the lofty indifference of his voice and his striking analogies.

That day he was lecturing to them on Fabius Cunctator. Fabius, who had been appointed Dictator, intending to wear out Hannibal, that fearful enemy of peace, carried out constant manoeuvres but never engaged in a decisive battle. The Carthaginian military leader used all his military skills to try to make him fight; but despite the insults, unjust suspicions, complaints and sneers of his fellow-citizens, Fabius did not change his tactics. He was mockingly nicknamed 'Cunctator'.

The former seminarist explained:

'*Cunctator* means "a procrastinator". I ask you to remember this nickname. I'll explain why later.'

Obviously pleased with himself, Kaydanov stared at the Lycéeists with his bloated little eyes.

All the boys were listening to him. Sneering at a commander who had avoided battle was a very familiar practice to them. Even Myasoyedov was curious, and Danzas, who had just rolled a paper ball with the obvious purpose of throwing it at somebody, was also listening, the ball motionless in his hand. Kaydanov had been anticipating such behaviour from Danzas, and was ready to say to him, as he usually did: 'Danzas, you are a real brute', but this time he didn't need to.

The Senate appointed Minucius as military assistant to the cautious Cunctator. Minucius was an experienced commander and a great enemy of Fabius Cunctator.

The new military leader had decided to give battle to the enemy. Hannibal had been looking forward to it – he suddenly surrounded Minucius on all sides. In that decisive moment the insulted Fabius rescued Minucius and so revealed his greatness of heart. He forgot all the opprobrium that had been heaped on him and putting the welfare of his country above everything else in the world, charged down a hillside to engage with Hannibal and defeat him. Then without saying a word to Minucius, he returned to his camp.

At this point Küchelbecker gave a start. He remembered reading his mother's letter about Barclay at the battle of Borodino to Pushkin, Pushchin and Valkhovsky. Bewilderment and horror showed in his face.

Kaydanov looked in his direction, pleased.

Nothing, however could protect Fabius from the suspicions and indignation of his fellow citizens. Varro, the army commander newly appointed at their request, decided to fight Hannibal at Cannes, where the Romans suffered a defeat. The African demon was exultant.

Enjoying their attention and the fact that the faces of the most hardened pranksters seemed confused, Kaydanov paused. He blew his nose unhurriedly. Pushkin's face, the face of a reckless scoffer, was concentrated, his eyes were glittering. He said something quickly and briefly to Pushchin. Kaydanov frowned. He drummed his fingers against the lectern and warned the impatient boy:

'Hush, Mr Pushkin! Silence!'

Kaydanov never called Pushkin or Gorchakov or Valkhovsky brutes. He rose to his feet, his belly protruding grossly, and assumed a dignified air. He noticed the brute Danzas starting to draw a caricature of him, staring at him with dispassionate attention. He did not reprimand him.

'A nation's character,' he said, 'becomes known under dangerous circumstances, and at that time the Romans justly deserved the name of a great nation. Among the general horror and confusion, Rome looked like our Fatherland does now, in the nineteenth century: every Roman offered his possessions and himself as a sacrifice to his native land; a sense of honour and a desire for revenge burned in every citizen. The Carthaginians wanted to make peace but the Romans would have none of it. The Carthaginian commander, for all his great strategic brain, now committed a gross error: he entered Campania and decided to spend the cold season in Capua. And soon Marcellus with the glorious Scipio forced the terrible warrior to leave Italy ...'

Grinning and crossing his arms on his chest, like a hero himself, Kaydanov looked at Pushkin, the clever, mischievous imp, at the brute Danzas, and with a dispassionate air, as if he himself were the Cunctator and had outwitted everybody, said slowly:

'After the lecture is over, proceed to the assembly hall where the latest communiqué will be read to you. On the anniversary of the foundation of the Lycée, yesterday, the nineteenth of October, Napoleon Bonaparte retreated from Moscow.'

They would not be leaving after all.

Eight

Exploding the shells and powder-boxes so as not to let them fall into Russian hands, burying their cannon in the ground, abandoning them on the open roads, Napoleon's army was fleeing. Out of four hundred thousand men, forty thousand remained. The cavalry fled on foot because all the horses had died.

Soldiers let fall their ice-shackled rifles. Guardsmen dragged themselves along in tatters; Grenadiers hobbled in women's torn, sleeveless padded jackets, in skirts of all colours, wrapped up in bast mats, animal skins, sacks. Uniforms taken from dead comrades were tied around their heads; swollen blue from the terrible cold, frost-bitten feet were muffled in coarse cloths and old fur hats. The Grande Armée shuffled along the highways, looting and dying as it went. Already defeated by the Russian troops, the French were being finished off by the frosts. The darkened villages met them with pitchforks. This was another war, a peasants' war. The French had known about the Russian frosts but had hoped for victory before their arrival. And Napoleon had told his soldiers that Moscow was warmer than Fontainbleau and that tales about the Russian winter were travellers' fabrications. They had known even less about Russian villages and had taken no account of them.

Kunitsyn told the Lycéeists all this and his eyes were sparkling. He had no doubt at all that within two or three months serfdom would be abolished.

Nine

I

KOSHANSKY read them the communiqué: Paris had been taken by Russian troops. All day long cavalry squadrons rode from St Petersburg to Tsarskoye Selo, to Pavlovsk and back. Spring had not yet come but the days and the sunsets were becoming longer.

Everything had changed – the enemy that had seemed invincible had fled, the fate of the whole world was being decided. The boys had grown older than their years. Reality, it seemed, was here, right under their noses.

Reveille was sounded from the guardhouse. He stood by a window in the arcade. He listened attentively to the familiar sound – lively and distant. He had long ago given up reading his book, a volume of La Harpe's history of literature.

He went to Korsakov's room. Misha Yakovlev had set his poems to music and Korsakov sang them to the guitar. Yakovlev had turned out to be a fine musician and Korsakov a good singer. Their childish brawls had ended, they were now formed, and everyone had shown talent in one field or another. Yakovlev was such an extraordinary impersonator that he promised to become a famous actor.

Even Danzas revealed a talent – his handwriting. In this respect he put even Korsakov in the shade. Always ready for all sorts of tricks and escapades, Danzas, who appeared shallow and obtuse, nonetheless wrote in such a neat, fine and beautiful hand that Kalinich would look admiringly at his sheets and say with a smile:

'Remarkable!'

Now he single-handedly copied out the *Lycée Sage* and Kalinich, who had scarcely given the magazine any attention before, leafed it through closely and said:

'Better than print!'

Once he drew a picture of Myasoyedov as a donkey and of Küchelbecker tormented by the Muse, and it became clear that Danzas was also an artist.

These days he drew a lot – and portrayed himself as a bear, making the similarity obvious.

The Lycée had its own artists, editors and poets.

Everyone was absorbed in the competition between Gorchakov and Valkhovsky. Gorchakov's memory was extraordinary. He would glance at a page, like Kalinich, as if not interested in its contents, and remember it all precisely. He would repeat what he had read in a flat absent-minded voice, as if reading off the invisible page. His French was perfect. He was diligent but liked to feign laziness and always complained that he had no time to do things.

'My old gout has got the better of me, I haven't read a single line!'

His answers were so correct, detailed and effortless that some of the masters considered him a genius, others a featherbrain, but in general they did not trust his 'knowledge'. He was the top student. Valkhovsky achieved everything with effort and persistence, like a Spartan. Failure did not discourage him and he spent his nights bent over his books. Study was his passion. Many felt that he was quietly but dangerously ambitious. He too was an excellent student. Gorchakov smiled whenever he caught sight of his pale proud rival, who was always calm and serene. The contest between the favourite of fortune and the poor obstinate Spartan delighted their classmates. Gorchakov tried to make it clear to Aleksandr that he distinguished him from the rest. He could not resist Gorchakov's smile and they became friends. Aleksandr was also fond of Delvig; they embraced whenever they met. Delvig was the only person he cared to read his poems to. The expression in his friend's pale eyes revealed the quality of the poems he had just heard. Then Delvig would shake himself as if getting rid of raindrops and say, imitating Koshansky:

'An unmistakable gift!'

Gorchakov patiently copied everything Pushkin wrote. Seeing this, the handsome Korff, who hated Aleksandr, afraid of his scoffs, started to do the same.

He had become famous.

The contributors to the Lycée magazine, known as the Sages after the title of the magazine, begged him for poems as they believed real journalists did. Korsakov sang his poem *Betrayals*, set to music by Yakovlev.

Once a poem would not come out. He wrote the first stanza, crossed out a few words, then crossed out everything, lost patience, flew into a rage, crumpled up his unsuccessful attempt and threw it into a corner. This took place in the assembly hall. Illichevsky, also a poet, picked it up, smoothed out the page and finished the poem.

Koshansky asked Pushkin to recite any poem of his choice. Aleksandr had little wish to recite to him. He had found the name for his stern critic

– Aristarchus. He hated reading his poems to him. Nevertheless, he read him *Betrayals*. As he did so he imagined Korsakov singing it, and Koshansky stared at him in bewilderment. He read with little whoops and without any logical emphasis, and without raising or lowering his voice at the caesuras. Perhaps this was the only way to read these brief, bouncing or *dancing* lines that consisted almost exclusively of rhymes, thought Aristarchus. The poem was about women's unfaithfulness and was a kind of love song or popular dance – a waltz. It had neither Derzhavin's gravity nor simplicity, nor the elegance perfected by Karamzin, only a catching lightness. Everybody had started to sing and whoop, thousands of such poets had sprung up, and their verses were as easily accessible as the fashionable waltz. This liveliness was inappropriate. And what could this boy know about women's infidelity?

Aristarchus looked at him with curiosity. Everything in the poem was in somebody else's voice; the passion itself was borrowed. He asked him to repeat it and listened to the youthful poem, propping up his brow with his hands, closing his slightly swollen eyes and wearing an expression of pouting concentration. He had asked him to read the poem as he would have asked Illichevsky or Yakovlev – in order to say something constructively illuminating. But he couldn't think what to say. He squinted, scrutinised his student and for the first time really saw his features: the eyes were bright and keen, the face intelligent and somewhat secretive. Koshansky was about to say that the iambic trimeter shouldn't have been chosen because it jingled like the bridle-bells of horses being whipped along by a coachman – he had had this comparison ready for a long time but suddenly decided not to come out with it. He adjusted his stiff collar and again looked at the boy, and his look seemed sad to Aleksandr. Aristarchus seemed to turn pale and hang his head. He didn't say a word to the reader, but sighed deeply and walked away across the hall, sombre and sullen, dragging his feet. This was the new school of poetry that he didn't recognise, and that he called 'erotico-musical-shallow'. They all wrote songs, and he couldn't help admitting that compared with these all other poems seemed stiff and clumsy. Their words were immediately set to music and sung; and fame, whose mysteries he could never fathom, was theirs. Batyushkov baffled him: to throw a poem or two, far from perfect, to an audience, to make a stir and amaze everyone, then to hide oneself away for a year or two – such was the fame he reaped effortlessly, en passant. These poets had 'taste'– a word that embittered Aristarchus. At first he compared this mysterious taste to having a musical ear, and made a note of it. Once he heard that ass Kalinich, a guitar-player, saying to Chirikov that the first stage of having a musical ear was to hear when others played out of tune, and the second, not to play out of tune yourself, and that the second stage was much more difficult than criticising others – there were too many critics. The attack on critics by this simpleton for some reason annoyed him and he crossed out his definition. Here, it seemed, was the new proportion or harmony, much talked about nowadays, as if poems were buildings.

> *Oh, memories of the heart! You have more strength*
> *Than recollections of sad reason.*

Batyushkov's lines puzzled him; their syntactical meaning was obscure: what was it that 'had more strength'? Heart, memory or reason? What was it here that produced such an effect on women! This is what taste must be, this is what fame meant. And what about the iambic trimeter that reminded him of the jaunty new way of walking? One could write thousands of them – they would all appeal to the reader. Some of Batyushkov's poems even had three rhymed lines instead of the usual two. So why not four? It all sounded just like chatter, though this poet could produce a powerful line.

He tried to explain the effect of these lines to Pushkin, who was obviously fond of poetry and had a gift for it, but was unable to. Pushkin didn't listen; perhaps he had understood them without his teacher's assistance. The sudden fame of this inexperienced youth was offensive and undeserved. Women flew like moths round the candles of these fashionable poets, even if they were just boys. Bakunina had asked him about Pushkin and Illichevsky. These novices already enjoyed the attention of the weaker sex. Count Tolstoy had told him at their meeting that he would like to listen to the song that the Lycéeists had composed. A lady to whom Koshansky had secretly been writing a short ode had been looking forward to some family celebration to use it as a pretext for inviting 'the poets' and had been asking him about the Lycée writers. It was intolerable.

Fame was now won not by those who had mastered the strict rules of composition and acquired skill through experience, but like a faithless beauty, welcomed any boy who happened to be passing by. Moreover, fame seemed to seek out a particular person in order to give him the title of poet. Why not Illichevsky, who expressed his thoughts and emotions so correctly and fluently? It was a matter of chance: somebody would put a poem to music, someone else would sing it – and the author of *Betrayals* stepped forward. His behaviour was arrogant, he judged others condescendingly and scoffed at Derzhavin; and all this by virtue of *taste*, as if he had been granted this taste as a kind of power. Rumours had reached him that the youth had been composing some infernal satirical poem, but he forced himself not to think about it. It might produce an uproar, the youth might be expelled and the shadow of suspicion would fall on the whole Lycée. This was insulting to him as a poet and a literary man.

Martynov, Director of the Department of Education, had enquired as to whether the boy was capable of writing serious poems. Naturally Koshansky replied with a shrug of the shoulders. The Director himself disapproved of superficiality. But now he too had fallen under the spell of the new fashion. And Koshansky realised with amazement that he himself was beginning to be affected by the free-and-easy lightness of the new poetry, its technical agility, its fresh air and closeness to everyday life, its sheer chatter. He liked it and was angry with himself for liking it.

He went to the Principal, who was ill and did not have long to live. He was consumed by a secret ambition he did not dare confess to himself: he wanted to become Principal.

2

Principal Malinovsky wouldn't admit that he was ill. The French had been conquered and a new era was beginning. He wanted to hold a celebration in the Lycée.

He put on his formal dress and went out. He walked the short distance from his house to the college, step by step, covering it with the persistence with which he had formerly attacked his studies. Usher Leonty had been waiting for him at the entrance stairway and accompanied him to the hall. Breathless, pale and thin, with burning eyes, the Principal stalked the building like a ghost and the Lycéeists scattered when they saw him coming. He noted that it was chilly in the building and gave the order to heat up the stoves. He was feverish. He also signed an order to redecorate the school.

Frequently humiliated by the Minister, who used every opportunity to reprimand him, he nowadays focused his attention on maintenance tasks. Having signed the order he felt tired and was accompanied home. He had forgotten that he had come to make arrangements for a special day, a celebration for which he had high expectations. He intended to change the whole life of the Lycée, and was preparing a major speech to students, staff and guests at the impending event. He wanted to speak about the Russian victory. Everybody was talking about it now, but he wanted to take a different view of it.

'Our enemies believe that the Russian's main incentive is his fear,' he was going to say, 'but his fearless deeds prove otherwise.' He was then going to talk about the sterling qualities of the Russian people, which Europe, in its egocentricity and pettiness, obstinately refused to acknowledge, and he intended to say that in future the students would have to show these qualities, each in his own field, just as the Russian troops had done on the battlefields. He had no doubt that after Russia had covered itself in glory, serfdom would be abolished. Walking across the hall, he noticed the students looking at him apprehensively, and the initial preparations he intended to see to went completely out of his head.

As soon as he was home he busied himself in ordering his affairs. The new era would find them in impeccable order. He remembered his speech at the opening of the Lycée with shame. At that time the public mood had been one of humiliation and fear. Now victory had given the Russian nation a new meaning. Speransky's unfortunate regime had been a bad beginning, and soon a new parliamentary era would open in Russia. If it did not, he would leave this futile business and shut himself away in the Bashkir steppes to devote himself to the more austere task which had long been in his mind. The Lycée celebration would have great significance, and combined with the examinations it would demonstrate the students' progress to the guests. About that progress he had doubts but one thing was beyond all question – the spirit of the Lycée.

Order was his passion. For ten years he had been thinking about the political order in Russia and had drawn up a detailed plan for two chambers of parliament, the public spirit, the creation of good citizens and the securing of lasting peace, and he had compiled an index of the major issues he had been pondering throughout his life, from A to Z.

Now he sat at his desk putting everything in perfect order, as if he were leaving the Lycée. He took a ribbon and tied up his various plans, notes and extracts copied from Turkish and Hebrew books. His hand lingered for a moment. He carefully reread his article *On the Qualities of the Russian People*. He had expected that the eradication of that cringing and servile spirit would start with the emancipation of the serfs. He had pointed out that a foreign servant was treated differently from a Russian one because the Russian servant was a slave. The education of her citizens would create the public spirit that Russia lacked.

He paused in his reading, exhausted. His son Ivan was at the Lycée, his daughter Masha at her aunt's, there was nobody to disturb him. He glanced through the index and glowed with pleasure at the impression of order. Personal characteristics were described systematically from 'Atheism' to 'Zeal', and on the verso of each page he had prescribed the means of developing them if they were virtuous or curbing them if they were evil. He shook his head. He had allowed his project to distract him. Growing uneasy, he got down to Lycée matters. He had long been preparing an alphabetical table on the students and their individual characters and talents. Perhaps this table would be useful for the celebration? Some of its content could be made public without naming individuals.

About Broglio he had written that he was frank, extremely stubborn, sensitive, hot-tempered and appreciative; about Delvig that he was slow to show improvement and quick to get into trouble; that he was sarcastic, indiscreet but good-natured. The striking contradictions in these students suddenly made him anxious; it seemed impossible to bring any kind of order to the table. Had he succeeded in creating a new breed of people as he had intended three years before? At least there seemed to be no servility among them. He crossed out the 'characters' section, leaving only 'talents', and sighed with relief. Gorchakov had exceptional abilities and an exceptional memory; Valkhovsky was very capable; the cautious Pushchin was making good progress; Korff was as meek as a child, very diligent but ingratiating; Danzas's only talent was for drawing. About his son the Principal had written: 'Rare frankness and indiscretion'. Küchelbecker – under the heading *Nota bene*: 'Passionate, insatiably ambitious and tireless in his writing'. Pushkin – under a similar heading: 'Cold analytical mind, considerable shrewdness allied with a habit of mockery, obsessive love for literature and a secret desire for fame.' The words 'cold' and 'mockery' had been written soon after Piletsky had come to see Malinovsky about Pushkin, and the Principal recalled what the monk had said about his atheism. He became agitated, paced up and down his study and sat down to write two speeches: one addressed to the teachers and the other to the students. To the first he sought to point out that the grave public events that had taken place in the first stages of the course had involved many trials for their institution, but in the end, thanks to judicious management, these had been turned to advantage. Diverting their students' attention from petty self-interest, the staff had made them understand the significance of state and military affairs and had prepared them for their future vocation. The rest – concerning the Court's indifference to virtue – he decided to tell Kunitsyn personally and privately. In the speech he could delicately make the point that there was no servile spirit among the students. He was entrusting Kunitsyn with the organisation of the celebration and the drawing up of a guest-list. He experienced an old, long-forgotten feeling of contentment. His head was burning, the paper was swimming before his eyes, but he kept writing, forgetting to dip the quill in the ink-pot so that the quill screeched; he was breathing heavily. Finally he put a full stop, signed the paper, sprinkled the page with sand and collapsed.

He came to late in the evening, summoned his son Ivan and Valkhovsky, made an inconsequential remark, and looked at them in anguish.

He told Kunitsyn, who had just arrived back at the Lycée, that with the happy outcome of the war in which the Russian people had proved its worth, a chamber of deputies would soon be convened, and though it was a shame that the Lycée fledglings were not yet ready, they would be before long. The voice of the people was the voice of God. He asked Kunitsyn to make the necessary preparations for the day of national celebration. It seemed to

Kunitsyn that the Principal had again succumbed to his unfortunate weakness, and he frowned. Malinovsky gave a sigh and looked out of the window: it was already March.

He found it more and more difficult to breathe, his thoughts were getting confused. Speaking with great effort and stuttering, he told Kunitsyn about his children, Masha and Ivan, and his son's friendship with Valkhovsky. 'He's like a godson to me.'

In spite of all the difficulties, Speransky's plan, in his opinion, had been realised. The boys' separation from their families had helped to create a communal feeling that bound them together in a strong spirit of friendship. Only Pushkin and Yakovlev worried him – they were both subject to extremes, and Pushkin could be especially irreverent.

He paused for breath – then spoke about his enemies, Razumovsky and Arakcheyev, from whom he expected strong opposition, and about the Russian parliament again. After becoming agitated, he lapsed into unconsciousness. Kunitsyn ordered everyone to leave the sick man's room.

He was delirious and spoke rapidly and fluently in some unfamiliar language, apparently Turkish; regaining some possession of himself, he asked Kunitsyn about the Bashkir bailiff. He told him firmly that his luggage had already been forwarded and he was going to the province of Ufa where from now on he would devote himself to farming and the enlightenment of the local inhabitants. It was spring, the roads would soon be passable, everything was prepared. He asked Kunitsyn not to leave the Lycée and to be its guardian after his departure. He was tormented with sorrow, wrung his thin hands and sobbed. Suddenly he pressed his hands to his chest and, looking at Kunitsyn with his pewter eyes and apparently taking him for somebody else, said:

'Your Excellency! In this institution of learning of which I am in charge, there is no spirit of slavery.'

Soon Samborsky arrived. His head shook, he was led by his arms. At the door he asked automatically:

'Is he conscious?'

At once he straightened up and walked with firm steps towards the dying man. That night all the masters gathered in the room adjoining the Principal's study. Only Gauenschield was absent.

3

It was quieter than usual. They cast occasional glances out of the window at the Principal's house. At six in the evening Chirikov paired them and they went to Malinovsky's study where he had talked to them just a few days before. A detachment of dragoons stood at the front door. The Principal lay in his uniform. His face wore an expression of complete contentment; his high forehead was smooth and untroubled. Koshansky, Kunitsyn, Kartsov and little Boudri carried out the coffin and set it on the hearse.

The dragoons rode at the head of the procession, the Lycée porter, in mourning, following them. The choirboys preceded the coffin. Two men carried the Principal's only decoration on a cushion. The ushers led the horses and held the coffin steady.

The Lycéeists saw the coffin off as far as the town boundary. There they said good-bye to him. Five had been selected to see him off to St Petersburg: his son Ivan, Valkhovsky, Pushchin, Matyushkin and Küchelbecker – the Virtuous.

4

They wandered about the hall, along the corridors and the arcade, and into their rooms. Nobody stopped them. Pushkin and Danzas discussed what would happen to them now and whether Koshansky would be appointed Principal. They both agreed that he wouldn't because neither of them wanted it. Walking silently along the warm corridor they looked in an entirely new way at these walls, the vaulted ceilings and the candles that had just been lit by usher Matvey: this was their home.

It was no longer a monastery patrolled by the Jesuit, nor was it the miniature academy that the Minister Razumovsky had wanted it to be – it was a home whose master had just died.

Arm in arm, Pushkin and Delvig looked at the Principal's empty windows. This year things had changed at frightening speed. But this building with its staircase, and Aleksandr's room where everything was old and familiar and he could knock on Pushchin's wall, was his own, his home from home.

Valkhovsky, Küchelbecker and Matyushkin were sitting in the corner next to the Cossack who was grieving in all the simplicity of his heart.

It seemed only yesterday that the Principal had walked with his heavy step along this corridor. Efficient and full of virtue, he had behaved as if he had intended to live for ever – his conversations had been well considered, his work sound. He had been strict but fair. Pushkin had heard him reprimanding his son and calling him by his surname, Malinovsky. Like a plebeian in ancient Greece, he had striven for equality in the Republic of the Lycée. He had hated social vanities, and frowned at their escapades. He had reprimanded Aleksandr twice, each time seriously. Only once, during the war, had he smiled at him – a wide, open smile – and hugged him. Now the Principal's house stood empty and dead, and probably soon either Koshansky or Gauenschield, like a greedy creditor or an eager heir, would take possession of it.

5

Life at the Lycée suddenly changed. After Malinovsky's death all the teaching staff, eager for advancement, sought an audience with the Minister, sharing with him their views of the way the institution should be run. Only Boudri and Kunitsyn took no part in this. The Minister knitted his brow, polishing his nails. He dismissed them with a nod of the head or a feeble wave of the hand. He was in a quandary: he had long been waiting for an opportunity to dismiss Malinovsky, but now when he had died it turned out that there was nobody to replace him. What was this Lycée? What was its purpose? Nobody knew. It was an oddity, something like a hot-house where scholarly gardeners grew strange new fruit. He could not have replaced Malinovsky when the fate of Tsarskoye Selo had hung in the balance; he had been necessary to the protection and supervision of the boys. But now that the French had been conquered, it was inappropriate to trouble the Tsar who was still abroad, and besides, it was uncertain what the Lycée was actually supposed to be, what status it was to acquire. It might become an institution that was European in spirit, but this seemed less likely now that Arakcheyev, who never thought of Europe, was gaining power.

The Minister liked Koshansky's dandyish persona and appointed him – not, to his chagrin, as Principal but as Acting Principal. Kunitsyn and the newly appointed Supervisor Frolov were included in the board of directors. Koshansky's pride was wounded beyond measure by the last appointment especially. Just as in the literary world, where he was respected but never published, so it was now, in his profession: not Principal but Acting Principal – and the devil only knew what that meant! He walked pompously across the hall, returned the bows as courteously as he could, and a week later took to the bottle.

Kunitsyn found him in a wretched state.

'I appreciate what you have done for the Lycée,' Koshansky wheezed, staring at him hazily. 'I admit *you* as an equal, but what kind of *figure* is this Frolov?'

Frolov, who had served in the army, often used the word 'figure', which he would pronounce in a special way.

The Lycée had no Principal, and everyone was left to his own devices. A new *figure* had arrived, and everyone seemed to be enthusiastic about him.

The Supervisor of Discipline and Morals came to the Lycée straight from the army. He walked with his chest stuck out and immediately reprimanded Leonty about whom he had apparently been warned – the usher who indulged the boys in their weaknesses.

Glaring at him, Frolov advanced on him:

'What are you up to?'

Had it not been for Koshansky's protection, Leonty Kemersky would have been sacked. Frolov nevertheless demanded that a new usher be hired: Konstantin Sazonov – a young, morose-looking man, almost a boy, with pale rolling eyes and huge hands. He stood to attention so conscientiously when Frolov passed by that the new Supervisor would tell him quietly to stand at ease.

Frolov introduced military discipline to the Lycée: in the mornings Sazonov rang the bell vigorously three times; then the Colonel himself appeared. As a matter of fact, he had been a Lieutenant-Colonel in an artillery regiment, but Sazonov and all the other ushers referred to him as a full Colonel. The Colonel drew them up in three files, and saying: 'May God be with us!' as if it were a command, led them to prayers in regimental order.

He immediately revealed himself as a very energetic man. Honey-spiced drinks were abolished, to be replaced by tea and rolls for breakfast and kvas at lunch-time.

'This is regular practice in the army and military schools,' he growled to the steward, who didn't dare argue.

Previously they had been allowed to go to their rooms at any time and do as they pleased. Now Frolov permitted this only when he issued special forms which he signed personally.

He had a soldier's signature – thick and rounded. He extolled military service and held up cadets as an example to the Lycéeists.

'In my military school there was real order!' he would say. 'Here it's just a veneer!'

He disapproved of and thoroughly despised the freedoms of the Lycée.

In the mornings Sazonov brought him newspapers and edicts. Frolov read them and cut out all the unnecessary bits with scissors.

'As the Prophet said,' he growled, 'remove everything superfluous.'

He referred frequently to Muhammad and the Koran.

Deferring to the social spirit of their education, he entered into conversation with the students when he had the chance. He liked Rousseau. He told Küchelbecker:

'*Emily* is superb! The fellows in my school knew *Emily* by heart!'

This was how he referred to *Emile,* convinced that the main character was female.

Frolov was strict with the ushers: he found them lacking in discipline. He dismissed Matvey and now Aleksandr's servant was Sazonov. There he would stand with his pale-eyed stare and long arms, always deep in thought, and looking sleepy in the mornings. He smiled like a child.

'Konstantin is a reliable fellow,' Frolov would say. 'Not too bright but reliable.'

Frolov thought of introducing riding.

'Equestrian discipline!' he would say meditatively. 'The manège isn't far away, why not use it? Riding improves posture and agility like nothing else.'

And soon they were having equestrian exercises: they rode in the manège, and Frolov was pleased with Pushkin, Valkhovsky and Broglio:

'Look, they bend right over the pommel, they're not afraid of their horses, and the horses obey them.'

Of Gorchakov's performance he spoke contemptuously:

'Not a bad rider, but like a woman. Stirrup's under his toe.'

Küchelbecker, who had taken pains to find spurs, made him indignant:

'Only the Prophet could say who's more scared: the horse of Küchelbecker or Küchelbecker of the horse!'

6

Nowadays on the Champ des Roses they didn't obey Chirikov.

They wrestled and fooled about so recklessly that Chirikov would simply give up, retreat into the arbour and become completely absorbed in drafting poems. Without saying a word they struggled, fell down, rolled on the ground, wriggled like snakes – until one of them put his knee on a fallen opponent. Then loud shouts were heard. Aleksandr would take on any opponent, but often without success. Broglio was strong, his hands were made of steel. Once he suggested a fight and Aleksandr did not refuse, but was immediately seized in a bear-hug, in which he found it impossible to move a finger, and was defeated. He turned white, flew into a fury and never wrestled with Broglio again. He was ashamed of his small stature: he was shorter than Broglio, Malinovsky and Danzas, and envied them their height.

Komovsky was even shorter. Once Komovsky had a fight with Broglio. They rolled about the field like a ball. The main object was to free the right arm – one could then put it around the opponent's neck, draw aside his hand, open his grip without warning and jump up on one's feet. The small and feeble Komovsky wriggled about in Broglio's strong hands like an eel till the mighty Broglio suddenly loosened his grip, and in a flash Komovsky was sitting astride him.

Aleksandr shouted:

'Bravo!'

At that moment he really loved Komovsky – cunning, small and nimble, so inconspicuous that Yakovlev, who had impersonated two hundred people, had never done him.

Aleksandr enjoyed fencing. Wire masks, foils, heavy gloves – in this sport Broglio could not compete with him. Tall, strong and broad-shouldered, he was too static, and retreated before the mosquito sting of Aleksandr's foil.

Valville, an old Frenchman with thin dyed moustaches, was delighted with him.

'*En tierce, couvrez-vous!*'

'*Marchez!*'

'*En quarte!*'

The foils bent, rang, clashed and heels stamped. Aleksandr hadn't the patience to wait for an opponent's lunge and Valville had to hold him back.

Broglio often came away defeated.

'The devil is also of small stature, gentlemen,' the gratified Valville would say. 'Height is of no importance here. Why does Pushkin fence so well?' he asked. 'Does anybody know? Let me tell you: he takes it seriously, like a real duel. Once in the year 1779, I was challenged to a duel ...'

Frolov attended Valville's lessons. Carried away with enthusiasm, he would murmur:

'Not there! To the right!'

Pushkin unexpectedly won his favour.

'Aggressive, cunning, fast and hard to anticipate,' he said of him respectfully.

Having learned that Pushkin was a poet and a satirical one, he frowned but then brightened and said calmly:

'Let him laugh, but only outside the Lycée walls. Derzhavin used to be a dashing blade, a fine swordsman and if he had not become a Minister, he would have been a general. He used to write satires too. But now he has resigned and is no longer capable of service. Pushkin is extremely skilful: his lunges are very good. He has imagination and the dash of the devil!'

But the same imagination made Aleksandr almost last in dancing. Bottom of the class was Küchelbecker. Stout old Gouare taught them, but he could not find the suppleness in them necessary for graceful movement. Küchelbecker stepped out of rhythm, his arms dangled, hearing a command he swayed ponderously to the right or to the left. He tried hard but failed; he made his classmates laugh and broke formation. Gouare asked for Küchelbecker to be excused from dancing.

'As some are born dumb,' he said, 'and can't be made to sing, so some are dumb in dancing and Küchelbecker is one of them.'

Aleksandr, who laughed at Küchelbecker, was no better. Watching his friend lumbering about, he was so amused that he didn't listen to the old man's commands and went rushing on in his own sweet way.

7

Frolov's interest flattered him. Frolov would smoke his long pipe for days on end when on duty, puffing out skeins of smoke.

'Sazonov, flint!' he would yell.

And if Sazonov did not respond at once he would shout:

'What sort of figure are you, now?'

They had one thing in common: both the Colonel and his minion disappeared at nights and came back early in the mornings before the bell. Sometimes in the morning the Colonel would be sulky and would wheeze as if he were being strangled, but sometimes he'd be in a good mood. His secret was soon explained. Once when he was scolding usher Matvey for his slack discipline, he put his finger behind his waistcoat and some grimy cards suddenly slipped down from behind it. The Colonel was a gambler. He went crimson, ordered Sazonov to pick up the cards, stuck them into his pocket, turned on his heel and stumped off. Sazonov was always sober and dull; his expressionless face rarely showed any sign of life. Once when Aleksandr asked him a question, Sazonov simply stood there with a fixed stare, oblivious of everything, and Aleksandr noticed that his hands were trembling. Seeing the boy's amazement, Sazonov smiled at him with his child's smile.

Frolov amused him with his hoarse army voice and his constant references to the Koran and *Emily*. Aware of the boy's capacity for lethal mockery, he turned a blind eye to his gross misdemeanours: the undone buttons, lost handkerchiefs and walks at forbidden hours. The gruff old boy was actually good-natured. He liked to talk to Valkhovsky about military matters:

'Of all the subjects that you study, only mathematics is of any use – for taking aim. I used to be a good mathematician.'

He clearly thought their civilian education inadequate.

Sometimes he gathered the weaker pupils around him – Myasoyedov, Tyrkov, Kostensky, and told them stories about his experiences in the war with Napoleon.

' … And then I get a report, gentlemen, that the French vanguard has shown up. I give orders and what do you think? It turns out to be ours! Too bad, but as the Koran says: to err is human.'

Chirikov, who hated Frolov, claimed that at the first rumour of Napoleon's approach the Colonel had fled from his tiny estate near Smolensk just as he was, without packing any luggage.

But Frolov had appealed to Arakcheyev as an artillerist – this was why he had been appointed as Supervisor at the Lycée.

8

Strict, energetic and high-minded, Malinovsky was gone, but had left a long memory of himself: Valkhovsky, Malinovsky, Matyushkin and Pushchin felt orphaned. The pompous dandy Koshansky had hit the bottle and fallen ill as a result. He was absent for two months. One day a fat, sluggish man, his complete opposite, came in his place; his name was Galich.

They looked forward to his first lecture. They were used to Koshansky's distrustful glances, to the way he would drum his fingers against the rostrum waiting for silence, to his crafty questions and his laughter, to that wailing and hissing of his that he took to be poetic recitation. They were ready for anything.

Slowly the new master made himself comfortable in the chair, looked at them through his glasses without a shade of suspicion, and calmly opened Koshansky's textbook. Koshansky had never diverged from the timetable and the syllabus. The new teacher leafed through the textbook, without paying any attention to his audience, then chuckled and slammed it shut. He put it aside and never used it again.

In the same unhurried way he asked them to read to him from another book, which he had happened to bring from home. It was a play by Kotzebue. Yakovlev read the first scene. The teacher stopped him and asked him in a relaxed tone:

'What's bad about this scene?'

And they realised that he was a gentle, lazy sort with a sly sense of humour, that he was not looking for quick success or the post of Principal, and did not expect a lot from them. A discussion started up.

Aleksandr looked at the new master with astonishment: Galich had taste.

Then the new master opened a tattered book that they immediately recognised: it was by Cornelius Nepos, and Koshansky had been in the habit of reading it to them. But he had been too busy admiring every phrase to take the time to concentrate on the translation.

'All right, let's pull the old man about a bit,' said the new teacher.

They fell in love with him at first sight.

9

Frolov's strictness contradicted his own inclinations and habits. The boys had learned to ignore his army manner and censoriousness and now nobody interfered with them. They were allowed to go for walks with their parents; things were very different from the days of Piletsky when family meetings were virtually like prison visits.

Sergey Lvovich and Nadezhda Osipovna had not returned to Moscow. A vacancy had turned up in Warsaw and Sergey Lvovich was going to take it. The experience of the journey, the remoteness of the place from the capitals that had failed to appreciate him, Warsaw itself with its great number of charming Polish women – all aspects of his new appointment appealed to him. Although his rank remained the same, the move to such a remote province was an attractive enough prospect in itself. He was in no hurry, however, to go off to the outskirts of the Empire and had been finding pleasant uses for his travelling expenses.

His letters to his son became less frequent, none of the family visited him. The boys went out for quiet walks at the forbidden hours. They sneaked into the confectioner's and Gorchakov nonchalantly remarked:

'We lead the lives of rakes!'

They made friends. Gorchakov could talk on any subject, quickly grasped the point and was hard to surprise. His ambition was boundless; he adored fame and went after it effortlessly. All the staff, even the gloomy Kaydanov, were sure of his brilliant future. He listened to Pushkin's poems with pleasure and sometimes made highly apposite remarks. He could tell without fail who would like this or that particular poem and why it would be a success. The brilliant Gorchakov did not treat many like this; he was usually aloof, and the favour he showed the poet was flattering.

They had a lot of free time since they were preparing for the public examination, and were not expected to cover any new material. The late Malinovsky had intended it to be a festive occasion. Now, in the general confusion, this forthcoming examination was the only obstacle and threat capable of exercising any restraining influence on the Lycéeists.

'The main thing is not to lose control of them altogether,' Kaydanov said. 'The curriculum can wait.'

10

His poem about a monk was almost finished. It was in satirical diabolical mode, featuring the mischief of demons who tempted monks, a white skirt luring a monk, and a monk flying astride a devil. He drew a monkey-like, old-womanish head wearing a band – Voltaire. It was as good as his *Maid*. He remembered the babbling old man of Ferney whose glorious verses had forever deprived the Maid of Orleans of her innocence; he recalled the strong tavern notes of the poet Barkov from his father's cache of forbidden books. He would have drawn pictures of Barkov and Villon between the lines but he had never seen portraits of these two gallows-birds. He imagined Barkov as a tall hefty fellow with heavy fists.

He was spellbound by the example of his uncle, Vasily Lvovich. He recalled his laughter, all that hissing and whistling, truly diabolical. Yes, he too was born for secret fame and furtive reading, and his poems would also be stored in carefully locked drawers. Dangerous, dubious fame lured him on.

He could afford to be utterly unbridled. He was sure that his poem would never see print. He remembered the pictures hanging in Dmitriyev's apartment: the riveted smiles and sidelong voluptuous glances, twilight and suggestive shadow, white skirts in oily black gloom. He liked Ossian's opaque poems that remained mysterious even in Parny's translations, with their caves, lightning-flashes and grey waves.

Zhukovsky had glorified the victories of 1812 in his long poem *A Bard in the Russian Camp*, a poem of a new kind, on an exceptional level even for him. Its sharply drawn lines were reminiscent of Derzhavin, it was picturesque as a ballad, and it had the lilt of a popular song. Its lines were instantly memorable and many poets tried to imitate its style. Following Vasily Lvovich's example, Batyushkov satirised the Symposium in a poem that imitated Zhukovsky's glorious *Bard*: entitled *A Bard in the Varangian Camp*, it was a mild swipe not only at Shishkov's madhouse but at the whole idea of the melodious poem.

It was enough to read Zhukovsky's famous first four lines:

> *The noise of battle dies:*
> *Firelight round the camp,*
> *Above us, open skies,*
> *The light of heaven's lamp ...*

The rhymes came immediately, as if suggesting themselves. It was a kind of modern magic. The poet himself could not resist the music of his poems. In the same manner he wrote *A Bard in the Kremlin* and then *The Tula Ballad* about the marriage of his beautiful niece:

> *The Tula tavern is silent,*
> *There are candles on the table ...*

Then a song about Gauenschield came out of the Lycée:

> *Silence in the Lycée hall.*
> *And now – a miracle:*
> *Satan approaches, by my faith,*
> *With liquorice in his teeth.*

Even Koshansky in his fever muttered the obsessive words. Countless nameless poets had composed countless similar *Bard* poems extolling the heroes unsung by Zhukovsky. Such was the extraordinary triumph of the new melodious poetry.

Pushkin could not get Zhukovsky's lines out of his mind; the first two lines tormented him. Zhukovsky's resounding fame, due to these two lines and to *The Bard in the Varangian Camp,* had suddenly become almost *too* loud, and even slightly ridiculous.

He was restless at night. The blood pounded in his temples; he dreamt of exaggerated, tempestuous, ungovernable verses. He composed his *Bard* in a week. His bard was tall and well-built, with prominent cheek-bones and powerful fists. The monastery was being turned into a tavern, a Sodom. Love and fighting in this poem were truly bestial. No one was spared, not even the grey-haired mother superior. Now he was an outcast poet. Zhukovsky's innocent composition would now look pathetic in comparison with these abominably powerful verses. He read the poem to no one; he hid it under his mattress, and his heart beat faster when he checked from time to time that it was still there.

He fell ill and in his brain poetic fever mingled with real fever. He lay in the bare-walled sanatorium, attended by the Lycée doctor, Peshel, who cracked jokes and prescribed random medicines. His face clouded when he examined the patient. He gave him a long puzzled stare and prescribed medicines from the Lycée dispensary that could do no harm: liquorice and cherry-and-laurel water. He gave loud instructions to usher Sazonov who replied: 'Yes, Sir!' and promptly forgot them. Doctor Peshel had his own concerns and preoccupations: in the evenings he stuck a flower in his buttonhole and with a jaunty air drove to St Petersburg. Everybody knew that the doctor was a devotee of Bacchus and Venus and went to St Petersburg to visit its wicked charmers.

Usher Sazonov moved into the sanatorium with Aleksandr to take care of the patient. Their beds were close to one another so that the usher could attend him and keep an eye on his progress.

In his delirium Aleksandr spoke about the infernal poem and groped about the bed as if he were searching for it. Sometimes he opened his eyes and saw the usher giving him a glass of water and spilling it on his chest. Sazonov's face was absolutely wooden, his mouth gaping; he shoved the rim of the glass into the patient's teeth and paid no attention to where the water was going. He was engrossed in his own world.

II

This was the day Nadezhda Osipovna and Sergey Lvovich arrived in St Petersburg on their way to Warsaw.

Their son was seriously ill. Once he opened his eyes, saw his mother's face above his own and shut them again, thinking he was dreaming. Nadezhda Osipovna sat by his bed – aged, pale, in an old-fashioned dress. A tear crawled down her wrinkled cheek. For the first time during his illness he fell asleep: soundly, without dreams, fears or visions, and next morning woke up feeling almost normal. Usher Sazonov was still asleep. His mouth was open and he was snoring loudly.

This time Sergey Lvovich treated the boy in a different way. He told him about Zhukovsky's success and that his uncle Vasily Lvovich had asked his nephew to send him everything he had written. Zhukovsky was at the height of his fame and power; and Batyushkov and his uncle also had a following, though to a lesser degree.

'The reason is, my boy, their rivals' jealousy,' he said pompously. 'They're not like Zhukovsky, who is pleasantly tolerant.'

His father looked at him with a certain respect and even told him about his intentions – something he had never done before. All that was left of Kharitonyev Lane in Moscow were a few smouldering pieces of wood. It no longer existed.

'The furniture – do you remember, my boy, the chairs by the fire-place? Now just ashes and dust. We are homeless refugees, wanderers without possessions, *des vagabonds* in all the senses of the word. I am destitute and bare. But wait, my friend! Now it is everyone for himself and only God for all. There's a wide field of opportunity in Warsaw. That's where we're going! Your mother will soon follow me. The cost will be unbelievable!'

Nadezhda Osipovna pulled him by the sleeve.

His parents hastily took their leave: they were in a hurry, as always. Nadezhda Osipovna looked at Sashka in amazement: there was fluff over his upper lip. Three years ago, leaving for the Lycée, he had been a wild one, but still a child. Now she looked at her son with a feeling of awkwardness and estrangement. Before long this boy would be talking in a gruff voice like all those Guardsmen. How suddenly her youth had ended! She was an old woman now. She kissed her son on the forehead and told Sergey Lvovich to hurry up. He always enjoyed long embraces, sighs, and wiping his dry eyes with his scented handkerchief.

Aleksandr was recovering slowly – from his illness and from the infernal poem. He could see the tops of the trees out of the sanatorium window. He furtively read Batyushkov:

> *The retribution of the skies …*
> *A sea of evil I have seen;*
> *Mothers pale and full of sighs*
> *At the cross-roads I have seen …*

This poem about Moscow, its echoing phrases, touched him inexplicably, he could not understand why, and he lay for a long time with his face buried in the pillow and tears rolling down his cheeks – inexplicably, because there was nothing emotional about the poem. It was a rather precise picture of burnt-down Moscow as seen by Batyushkov.

His friends visited him. Delvig came and kissed his forehead. He had a passion for 'reminiscences'; where he got them – God only knew. He was forever a witness to events that he would later recount. This time he told Aleksandr about an invalid whom he had met the previous day out walking. The soldier, having spent a long time in hospital after being wounded in battle, had been walking the long distance home. He had told Delvig how he'd spent a night in open country near Kursk. Delvig described the singing of the Kursk nightingales in such detail that he left Pushkin in no doubt that he too had heard them.

Delvig was an oral poet. By the time he reached the end of his stories he had begun to believe what he was talking about. Asked whether he had slept well, he would immediately describe his dreams, which he would make up on the spot. He was not the garrulous sort; his greatest pleasure was to sit down by the stove in the corner, listen to others and drop in an occasional word. He would insert whole lines into the stanzas the boys wrote together. He was fond of Pushkin's poems and had a good ear, pointing out what was superfluous. He composed songs and claimed that they were folksongs he had heard in his childhood. He seemed to enjoy food most of all, but poetry gave him the same kind of delight. He would eat ice-cream at usher Leonty's 'café' slowly and in silence, and the same appreciation came into his eyes as when he listened to poetry.

He was the best in Koshansky's Latin classes. He read Latin verses ecstatically and his eyes dimmed. But if he was asked to translate, he was evasive – either his vocabulary was poor or he did not want to deprive the poems of their enchantment. He never finished books that he really liked; instead he enjoyed imagining the characters' destinies. Paper, quills and their scratching repelled him: any kind of work was an abomination to him. He would watch Aleksandr with amazement and a secret enjoyment for hours from some dark corner when he was writing his poems, observing how he crossed them out, clenched his teeth, looked around with a lost expression and finally tossed his quill aside in indignation.

Delvig smiled as he said good-bye to him and kissed his forehead before going off to tell Yudin the story he had just made up. Yudin made fun of him, but Delvig answered his sceptical questions with a composure that took the joker aback and pleased the narrator. Delvig led a full life.

Gorchakov came to see him too. He brought him news of social events.

There was to be a performance at Tolstoy's and the Count wanted to invite all the Lycéeists to see it. Gorchakov's sister Yelena would soon visit him. She was very pretty and would get married soon, but she was so lazy that to his knowledge she had not covered as much as a single sheet of paper in her lifetime. He spoke eagerly of his sister. She was not only lazy but mischievous as well. His uncle Peshchurov had a weakness not often seen – he sniffed tobacco. And – imagine! – Yelena had also taken to tobacco. She had been punished for this, but she was of marrying age and punishments had no effect on her. Well, well, well! By the way, were there any new poems?

Aleksandr, still pale and feeling unwell, listening to what Gorchakov was saying, suddenly turned even whiter: he had just remembered that he had left two of his poems in his room – hidden, of course. He asked his friend to rescue them and keep them safe.

In the evening, before going to bed, Gorchakov managed to sneak back to him. Usher Sazonov had gone for the night and Aleksandr was alone in the ward. Both poems were in Gorchakov's hands. He had read them – they were outrageous, dangerous and might cause trouble, and not only for Pushkin. He couldn't understand many of the words in one of them, *In Barkov's Shade*. If such a poem were found here, in the Palace, under the Emperor's nose, Pushkin would be sent off to the army.

Aleksandr, in confusion, asked his friend whether both poems had really seemed so awful to him. He himself considered *In Barkov's Shade* too obscene, but he was going to send *The Monk* to be printed after he had polished it. Involuntarily he had divulged his secret ambition to Gorchakov: he hoped to see the poem published under the secret signature: *1.14.16.*

Gorchakov shook his head. He was surprised by his friend's recklessness. Both poems were scandalous. He watched Aleksandr's expression with secret pleasure: his words had a profound effect on the young poet. Perhaps they would not send him to the army, but they would surely exile him to some remote monastery. His treatment of grey-haired mother superiors and monks was criminal. He would end up in a monastery himself and sleep on its stone floor. The Lycée would be shut down and everybody would damn his name. Gorchakov got carried away. Aleksandr's crime was serious; a terrible abyss now opened up before him. He, Gorchakov, was going to save him – for the last time.

He suggested that both poems should be burnt without delay: he would stuff them into the stove as soon as an usher had lit it up.

Aleksandr agreed unhesitatingly, affected by the semi-darkness and by loneliness and the whispered pictures Gorchakov had outlined for him. He was a criminal. Not because he ridiculed monks – he couldn't tolerate them, served them right! – and not because he satirised women, but because he had laughed at poems which were excellent in themselves, if a little obsessive. The very memory of his own confused poems pained him. Gorchakov was right: he would be exiled; he would become another Villon; his name would be mud, like Barkov's. This was where his curiosity, ambition and unbridled imagination had led him!

Pleased with himself, Gorchakov quietly took his leave, unnoticed; Sazonov had not yet returned.

It was a wakeful night for him. It was pitch-dark outside and he was surrounded by silence. An ancient candle was guttering. The old clock hoarsely chimed midnight. He was not afraid either of prison or the monastery: he would escape from either. But this silence around him was too deep and his friends were too far away – he was alone in the world. He started to read a French book that Delvig had secretly brought him, *Literary Anecdotes, a Compilation of the Most Amusing Occurrences, Historic Events and Verses,* and the innocent book comforted him.

He woke up early. His servant Sazonov sat nearby, on his bed, and not seeing that he had woken up, quietly started cleaning his clothes. They were dirty and soiled; he stared at them closely with a blank expression, taking off specks of dust and bits of fluff with his long fingers. Still not noticing that Aleksandr was awake, he felt about his sleeves and examined his hands closely, drawing his finger along his palm as if erasing the traces of his night escapade. Aleksandr closed his eyes. Sazonov cast a sudden glance at him and lay down carefully. A minute later he was asleep.

12

Next day the poems were destroyed. Gorchakov showed up fresh and pink, nonchalant and happy, and solemnly told his friend that he could now sleep peacefully. Both poems had been burnt. Gorchakov was the only person who knew about them and he was as silent as the tomb. Being fond of complicated and secret affairs, Gorchakov had done the following: the poem *In Barkov's Shade* he had indeed thrown into the stove, but realising that he was entrusted with an important secret that would lose its fascination if no one except Pushkin and he himself knew about it before burning it, he had shown the poem in strict confidence to the clown Misha Yakovlev. The clown's eager look, his bewilderment, delight and horror when reading it had been ample reward for Gorchakov. Yakovlev had a wonderful memory, but Gorchakov made him swear that he would forget the poem, the name of its author and the name of its temporary possessor. In this way the poem had been killed off.

He had wrapped the more innocent *Monk* in thick paper and sealed the parcel with his signet. It was forbidden to wear rings in the Lycée, so he kept his, a gift from his aunt, in his bureau. He was waiting for his sister to visit him. He was going to pass the poem over to her disguised as his secret notes. She was to give him her word of honour that she would not open the parcel and would keep it in her room until his return from the Lycée or until his death. He loved secrets. Everything had been well thought through. If the secret came out, the danger would not be so great; the second poem was much more innocent than the first. The impression that the threats of imprisonment, monastic confinement and the fate of the Lycée had produced on Pushkin had flattered him. To be the guardian of his friend's secrets was useful to him; it gave him a certain influence and power over him, which he enjoyed to the full.

Ten

HE woke up happy and laughed ecstatically. Everything seemed beautiful to him – the bare walls of the Lycée sanatorium with the sunlight
dancing on them and the window letting in the sounds of the footsteps of
passers-by – the advantage of the ground floor. Everyone he saw amused him:
Doctor Peshel sprinkled with scent and going to town with a rose in his
buttonhole to pay tribute to Bacchus and Venus; usher Sazonov who had
been looking for a quarter coin for the past day. Sazonov was distressed.

'A quarter,' he muttered, 'the whole thing was a waste of time.'

His night fears had passed. Gorchakov, and the burning of the iniquitous
poem, the whole night that had been in the dreadful mode of the new balladry
– it all made him smile. He immediately conceived a new poem – a light piece
without a shade of anger, in which he would bid farewell to Zhukovsky. Like
Zhukovsky who went through his characters and devoted a stanza to each, he
reviewed his classmates and friends. He drew up a list of them: the poets – the
lazy Delvig, the decent Illichevsky, the brilliant rake Gorchakov; Broglio; his
old friend Pushchin; the clown Yakovlev; the dashing blade and Cossack
Malinovsky; Korsakov who had sung his *Betrayals*; and finally, Wilhelm. He
imagined a feast in a bare room, a feast of the Lycéeists, and two stanzas came
out by themselves. They had completely ousted the ill-fated, outcast, insane
satire from his memory as if he had never written it.

In the evening Pushchin and Küchelbecker came to see him.

The Lycée privileges stayed as they were and Frolov had to put up with
them. After all, this was a civilian establishment, not a military one, and it
was unclear what the youths were being prepared for. Many of them had
good qualities: Pushkin was good at fencing, Valkhovsky at drill, Matyushkin
was well-disciplined. In Frolov's opinion they might yet achieve something,
given time. Gorchakov was bad at drill, he was a born civilian, *un chenapan*, a
rascal, but as clever as the Koran. The only person Frolov did not think much
of was Küchelbecker.

'For pity's sake!' he growled, 'He can't even march! He's nothing!'

Taking advantage of their freedom, his friends saw him in hospital without any interference.

Pushchin was still the same as when they had first met at the entrance interviews. The strict Boudri was very fond of him and called him 'Jeannot'. Jeannot was a fat, ruddy, grey-eyed clodhopper; he was born for the life of pleasure. He hated distress, quandaries and extremes. Common sense, a good laugh and a witty word were the things he treasured above all. When declaiming, Koshansky had always fallen silent meeting his gaze. Gorchakov stopped limping when he caught sight of Jeannot. The boys turned to him in their quarrels and he was glad to settle their differences.

Often he and Aleksandr talked quietly through the partition: he was surprised by his friend's unusually sharp remarks, his strange shyness and sudden bursts of anger. But Aleksandr always accepted the other's decisions, though he never responded to his rebukes.

Pushkin was friends with Küchelbecker too, but in a different way. He patiently tolerated his friend's eccentricities and bouts of madness. They quarrelled endlessly in the evenings and met as friends in the mornings.

Küchelbecker endured scoffs and persecutions with the patience of Mucius Scaevola, who burnt his right hand in fire. Korff was afraid of him, claiming that a person like him would stab with a knife and pierce with a fork at table over a trifle. Küchlya was aware that the secret epigram anthology *A Sacrifice to Momus* had been written by his friends about him but he took comfort from his growing belief that poets had always been unhappy. He had compiled a list of unfortunate poets: Camões and Kostrov had starved; Jean-Baptiste Rousseau, his idol, had been exiled and died in destitution. Old Boudri admired Rousseau's odes and often recited his glorious *To Happiness*, rolling his eyes and raising his voice at particular places. Boudri was friendly with Küchelbecker's mother and kept an eye on her son. They both hated Voltaire, a mocker who had hastened the renowned Rousseau's misfortune. Aleksandr had secretly acquired a volume of Rousseau's forbidden epigrams (Arina had included it with his luggage when he had left home, and it had been confiscated by Piletsky) and he had shown it to Wilhelm. The poet had been transported: the epigrams of this martyr were of the most daring kind. In general, poets that got into Pushkin's and Küchelbecker's hands seemed to split in half. They had shared Boileau, for example: Pushkin had borrowed the first volume from the library and Küchlya took out the second. The first volume contained the satires and *Art Poétique*; the second included the translation of Longinus' treatise *On the Sublime*. Küchlya became a disciple of Longinus. He copied out the chapters on ecstasy, on how elevated poetry needs flaws, weaknesses and low points, not simply neat perfection, because the quickened spirit finds elevation in low points. Pushchin remarked that in his own verse Küchlya had so far been keeping to the low points. After listening to all the mockery of the Slavophiles in the Shishkov affair, Wilhelm became a Slavophile himself. He argued that Prince Shikhmatov, the object of the spluttering Vasily Lvovich's vehemence, was a genius, and included him in his list of victims.

Shikhmatov's poem *Peter the Great* was lengthy, resonant and crammed with tenuously linked ideas, but Chirikov liked it too; his own creation *The Northern Hero* was of the same kind. Küchlya copied it out – no small labour – and read it eagerly to those willing to listen. When they saw Shikhmatov's poem in their friend's hands, Delvig and Alexander would beat a hasty retreat.

They all copied out Batyushkov's epigram:

> *Call your barbarous poem*
> *Anything – Peter the Lanky,*
> *Peter of Great Weight –*
> *But for God's sake, do not call it*
> *Peter the Great!*

Chirikov, whose poem was as long as Shikhmatov's, repudiated the epigram; Küchlya in general disapproved of epigrams on principle.

On the previous night Küchlya had learnt from Gorchakov that 'Pushkin was in a bad way', and in spite of their disagreements, felt fonder of him than ever, forgave him certain things, and together with Pushchin had gone to see him. They embraced.

Küchlya carried a thick notebook about with him everywhere: his famous dictionary. In it he painstakingly wrote out in alphabetical order all the statements and sentiments that appealed to him. At first Aleksandr laughed at it, like everybody else, but then stopped laughing and started to note down this and that for him and eventually Küchlya's dictionary became his favourite reading. The industrious lexicographer had copied down Jean-Jacques Rousseau, Sallust, Schiller, Bernardin de Saint-Pierre and Weisse, and gradually the free-thinkers had become his favourite reading. He had written down Weisse's views on the aristocracy, Rousseau's on virtue, Schiller's on freedom. Nothing was neglected: under D he had put down General Dorokhov's biography; under F, two opinions of friendship – those of Bacon and Vasily Lvovich, Bacon asserting that life would be a tomb without friends, Vasily Lvovich claiming that 'He who dreams of friendship is worthy of a friend.'

'I borrow goodness everywhere I find it,' Küchelbecker would say, repeating Molière.

Valkhovsky taught him to be open-minded.

On his present visit to Aleksandr, Küchlya brought his dictionary and a notebook of his poems, which he enjoyed reading; he would recite them with a great deal of effort, squealing and shouting at certain places – then his voice would drop and he would be breathless.

Lately Küchelbecker had been translating Greek hymns from the German, using hexameters. His father, Goethe's fellow student, had instilled in him a love of elevated poetry. They still debated whether hexameters could be used in Russian poetry. Shishkov's supporters asserted that they could be, and Küchlya had chosen this rare metre. He had brought his *Hymn to Apollo* to read. Küchlya's poems were always heavy-going. He read the hymn, a rather long one. Pushchin could stand neither his poems nor his reading of them, but never said so openly, afraid to sting the poet's pride. But he couldn't help it: he closed his eyes and pretended to be asleep. At the second page he started to yawn. Towards the end of the poem he emitted a light snoring but the ecstatic Küchlya mercifully failed to hear it. Aleksandr was happy and eagerly agreed with Bacon that life would be a tomb without friendship. A new stanza had come into his mind: feasting student friends asking Wilhelm to read his poems to help them get to sleep sooner.

They criticised each other. But Küchlya almost never accepted criticism; he argued it out and stood by his every line until he lost his voice. The only mistakes he corrected were these of spelling and grammar. Aleksandr, by contrast, often agreed with Küchlya's, Jeannot's or Delvig's strictures but strange to say almost never corrected the points in question.

Today he was not in the mood for debates. His friend's powers of endurance and his obstinacy (called mulish at the Lycée) were frightening. Illichevsky was modest; Yakovlev carefree; Delvig had taught himself to appear detached. Anyone else in Küchelbecker's place would have long ceased thinking about writing poetry, but Küchlya seemed to be preparing himself for poetic activity like Hercules for heroic deeds, and he was ready for anything.

After Malinovsky's death they all began to think about the future awaiting them. Officers were prepared at military schools, scholars at universities; the purpose of the Lycée was unclear. They had never thought about it before. None of them counted on their father's estates. Küchelbecker's mother scraped a living. He had had to drop music lessons, although he had intended to be a famous musician, a violinist. A violin had been acquired and sent to him, but the family had no money to hire a music teacher. Küchelbecker was always in debt. Sending him two or three roubles to pay back his creditors, his mother always accompanied the money with a note to remind him how harmful it was in his circumstances to run up debts. Next to Vasily Lvovich's dictum about friendship, Küchlya had written in his dictionary:

DEBTS. The best means of avoiding a large debt is to avoid small ones. Disorder is likened to a snowball, which grows bigger the further it rolls. – Weisse.

This was exactly what happened to him: he borrowed half a rouble at a time and at the end of the year wrote home asking for three.

Gorchakov's handling of debts was simpler – he simply forgot about them. Pushkin didn't count on getting any money whatsoever from home.

Only Valkhovsky and Matyushkin knew their future: Valkhovsky intended to become an army officer and Matyushkin a sailor.

Küchlya, secretly in love with the Commandant's young daughter, Velho, was preparing to marry, and had already written home about it. He had got a reply from his mother demanding that he calm down and pointing out that he was too young, and only after graduation from the Lycée and taking up a post might he start thinking about marriage. But Küchlya was convinced that he was going to be a poet and that this was how, in due course, he would achieve a stable position. The unfortunate fate of the poets he was so interested in did not deter him in the slightest. So on the one hand he had been preparing himself for poetic composition as the only true and sound future; and on the other, he was ready for scorn and humiliation. For the sake of poetry he was ready to go to the stake.

Although he laughed at Küchlya like all the others, Pushkin unconsciously started to give more thought to the future. His friend wrote poems by brute force, with obstinacy and frantic zeal, and behind all his talk of poets' miseries, Aleksandr could discern unlimited ambition. His love for the great and good things in life was an article of faith; the letter G in his dictionary was entirely filled with entries on the great and the good, for which he searched everywhere and which consoled him for his friends' mockery. Longinus was his prayer-book. He copied out Pindar's odes, Camões' epic poems and Lebrun's imitation of Ossian, his *Ode on the Lisbon Earthquake*. Malinovsky had given him a history of Turkish poetry, and Mizic had become a favourite. Oriental poetry enticed him with its expressive and elevated but irregular style. Eventually he became a walking encyclopedia for Delvig and Pushkin.

Once he confessed to Aleksandr that in Longinus' treatise he had come across a phrase he had copied out into his dictionary and marked *NB*. It contradicted the idea that great poets were doomed to be unhappy: 'Only what pleases everyone can be considered truly great.' Aleksandr was no less surprised than Küchlya. The strangest thing was that Küchelbecker revelled in his extraordinary delusions and extreme views; he clung to them avidly and took pleasure in predicting, in his poems, the troubles that threatened his future. He was not afraid to know the truth even if it was unpleasant for him. Aleksandr did not understand his friend's proud espousal of misfortune.

He himself craved for female hands to leaf through his poems and for female eyes to grow dimmed. Küchlya believed that true poets were doomed to be misunderstood, but *he* wanted to be understood by everybody, from the humble to the great. Whenever they talked of fame, his uncle Vasily Lvovich and his father grew wittier, while Kunitsyn became pensive.

The *Hymn to Apollo* came to an end.

Aleksandr was silent. Pushchin roused himself and stretched as if waking up from sleep. Küchelbecker stared at him closely, watching his movements suspiciously. Jeannot was a bland admirer of common sense, in Küchelbecker's opinion, of *bons mots*, delicacy, and so forth. He was one of the scoffers. Why was he stretching? Had he again been pretending to be asleep while he was reading?

Küchelbecker felt the familiar fury rising up in him and gritted his teeth, but then Pushkin asked him if there were any new entries in his dictionary. This flattered the unfortunate poet. Küchlya said that he would amend the *Hymn* a little for publication, of the prospects for which he had no doubts. He opened the dictionary.

There were new entries under the letters D and F: Detachment, Dependency, Dissipation; Feelings, Force and Freedom. Pushchin cocked his ears. The strongest feelings were those that depended on the human body – love, for example, which stirred the blood and overpowered the senses; or laziness, which weakened the willpower.

There were in all six principal incentives to the awakening of feelings, and which were responsible for most of the great forces for change: love, fear, hatred, self-will, avarice and fanaticism.

Aleksandr listened to him diligently. Suddenly he remembered how he had looked for Natasha in the dark passages and nearly lost his way; they should show Delvig this definition of laziness as a passion.

Küchlya borrowed goodness everywhere he came across it. The charming Ninon de Lenclos had experienced better than anyone, in his opinion, the meaning of love. She had met Voltaire when he had just graduated from college; already an ageing woman, she had had much to teach him. The other day he had come across a volume of Voltaire in Aleksandr's room and discovered Ninon's philosophy: *After all obstacles to love have been overcome, the greatest difficulty of all remains the absence of obstacles.*

'I don't understand,' said Jeannot all of a sudden, wide-eyed.

Küchlya repeated the precept ecstatically.

'Love needs obstacles,' he said, 'otherwise satiety takes over.'

'How do you know this?' asked the startled Pushchin.

'From Weisse,' replied Küchlya.

They had expected wonders. This beauty who had bloomed in the seventeenth century had had many lovers; she was unfaithful and inconstant in love and steadfast in friendship; Molière had come to visit her and read her *Tartuffe*, she knew frightening things, things about love they had never dreamed of. Küchelbecker read them the article about Detachment. He had recently written down Jean-Jacques Rousseau's dictum: *Philosophical detachment is similar to the calmness of a state under despotic rule: it is nothing else but the calmness of death; it is even more harmful than war.*

All three of them agreed with this. Pushchin doubted the truth of what was said about Feelings – whether it was right to say that only the passions caused great changes. In his opinion they were caused by the intellect.

Küchlya smiled with an air of superiority.

'But poetry,' he said, 'is born of passion, madness and delight, not reason. All are agreed on this – including Batteux and Longinus.'

'No, reason,' said Aleksandr quickly.

He was interested in everything that Küchlya read him about the passions. He seated himself on the sanatorium bed, his leg bent under him, biting his lip.

Love and satiety, greed and self-will were the passions he was afraid of. Delight wasn't a passion, and writing poems did not seem to come from delight. Oblivion, detachment, rhymes that proved the truth of the thought behind them, the instantaneous joy of knowledge, discontent – it could be any of these, only not delight.

Küchlya opened his dictionary and started a debate. Aleksandr made some feeble objection and they fell quiet, each of them thinking excitedly about his future.

His friends left, he would be going to classes next day – Doctor Peshel had said that the treatment had been a success and he was cured.

The inconstant lover and constant friend prophesied to him a future of inconstant pleasure. This passion was more powerful than all the others. Küchlya's poetic obstinacy was nothing in comparison with it. He wanted to dissuade his friend from his unfortunate passion for poems. Wilhelm was deluding himself. His poems were ludicrous; he deserved a better lot.

On his bedside table, instead of medicines there now lay a volume of Boileau and two books by Parny.

2

Now he often wandered about the park, deep into the lime tree alley. He had come to love this place, where he could walk unseen.

He had finished his epistle to Küchelbecker. He condemned the poet's trade to his friend, like Boileau in his second satire. Küchlya should be expecting neither wealth, nor honour, nor fame from his poems. For a few days he had been hiding the epistle from Küchlya. In it he attacked old Shishkov and his Symposium who were responsible for Küchlya's amazing delusions. Delvig admired the poem. At last Aleksandr read his epistle to its hero. Küchlya did not fly into a rage as they had expected, though the piece referred to his poems with no respect.

Now he too wandered about the park, leafing through his dictionary or some other book. Before long his response was ready. Küchlya believed it to be particularly effective because it came from the very Piron whose pranks were well known and so delighted Aleksandr. Küchlya's riposte came under the letter P.

POET. The audacity or foolishness of poets who live in poverty makes them say to their Muse exactly what Agrippina said about her son when it had been foretold that she would die by his hand: 'Moriar, modo regnet!' *– 'Let me die, let him reign.'*

PIRON. Once Piron was about to enter the room of a nobleman when the host opened the door to see another grandee in. The guest stopped out of politeness, to let Piron come in first.

'Don't stop, sir,' the host said, 'this gentleman is only a poet.'

'Now they know who I am,' said Piron, 'and I shall come in first, according to my rank.'

Küchlya would compare poets, even those living in poverty, only to kings and could not be swayed. Despite their disagreements, their friendship remained unbroken.

3

Nowadays he woke up early, with a joy he was unable to understand, female charms filling his mind.

All day long he wandered about the park and waited impatiently for miracles to happen. This was happiness he had never known before. He had never come across the lovely Natasha again. A different maid was seen accompanying old Volkonskaya. Usher Foma told him that Natasha 'had not behaved herself' and had been dismissed. He felt an ache in his heart and asked the usher in the evening what had really happened to the girl. Foma looked at him closely, frowned and shrugged his shoulders.

'I don't know.'

Gorchakov's sister Yelena, whom he had so promptly reproached for laziness, came to visit him. He showed her Pushkin's poem *Betrayals* that everybody liked so much. Pushkin saw the beautiful girl reading his poem. It was these fingers he wanted to touch his pages, these lips to smile, these eyes to grow dim. Fame with women was sweeter and more fearful than Küchlya's pride. He felt embarrassed and ran off. In order to take revenge on the beauty for his embarrassment he wrote an epistle to her, not for publication: in it she was described taking tobacco from a small gold snuff-box. He followed the charms over which the tobacco might spill.

His friends read the epistle. Küchlya rejected it out of hand:

'Tobacco gets up the nose!' he cried triumphantly. 'And it's horrible up there! The poem is worthless!'

4

But happiness was all around him. Both the Palace and the gardens seemed to have revived. These were not Kunitsyn's 'solitary forests'. Russian troops occupied Paris and thoughts of glory filled everyone's mind. In the park he often came across Galich who had come from St Petersburg; he was staying at the steward's, and felt at home in the park. He differed from the other Lycée masters. The Lycéeists knew all about Jesuits and were no strangers to Jacobins, who had influenced their knowledge and behaviour; some of these wanted to turn them into monks, others to make them virtuous. But Galich wanted nothing of the kind – he was just a temporary substitute for Koshansky. He was not interested in Lycée politics and treated the boys not as a teacher would, but as a friend. In his lessons they talked about poetry and art, they didn't have their heads stuck in textbooks. Kunitsyn's eyes betrayed anxiety – a trace of hidden passions and perhaps of unfulfilled ambition. Galich's bright short-sighted eyes had no sadness in them. Koshansky was a cold and peevish Aristarchus, whereas Galich was Aristippus, the teacher of Epicurus, the devotee of pleasure. He was able to enjoy life. Koshansky taught them that the most important thing that poetry concerned itself with was feelings and nothing else. Küchlya copied into his dictionary a passage about the rapture and blindness of poets. Galich claimed that the main subject of poetry was truth.

They walked together and Galich took a huge pleasure in everything, the gardens, the monuments, the Palace. He had been born in Oryol, the son of a country priest. He had studied at Göttingen, travelled about France, Austria and England, spoke French, German, English, Spanish and Italian and knew their literatures. He admired the gardens as a provincial Russian and the monuments as a European.

The lime trees were coming into bud and oak leaves were unfurling. Swans swam about the lake, their down floating on the water. The statues looked different in the sun.

'The charm of this park,' he said, 'is that it is neglected, the trees provide such splendid shade. The park at Versailles is different – it looks as if Euclid planned it.'

He compared the Palace with the buildings of Louis XIV's times. The roofs, cornices and statues had once been gilded but Catherine the Great had ordered the roofs to be painted green; now traces of the former splendour, the old luxury showed through in the sun. Resting after his victories, Peter the Great might have wandered about the woods where there was now a lime tree alley, a favourite place for both the new teacher and the Emperor. Galich would stop by the Kagul marble, put on his spectacles and read at leisure the memorial to the Moldavian victory. He inveighed against the descriptive poems of Delille, in which he found that the description obscured the subject. Man was the central subject of literature, and truth was the most important thing in poetry. He liked elegies and frankly admitted to enjoying Aleksandr's *Betrayals*, but found the poem too fast-moving. He had an unhurried gait; he was starting to put on weight, and maybe that was why he liked elegies – for their gravity and deliberation. Not the gravity of the poems Koshansky had told them about, lowering his voice as a sign of respect – of Milton and Camões, so avidly copied out by Küchlya, trying to discover the secret of these great poets' genius; but rather the gravity of melancholy, reminiscence and evening promenades.

They often lapsed into long silences as they walked, not disturbing one another, and Aleksandr restrained his step, adjusting it to Aristippus' elephantine progress.

One evening, after one such silence, Galich told him that he couldn't think of a better subject for poetry than history and that Tsarskoye Selo and the memories it evoked was a good subject for an elegy. The park, the monuments and the bridges combined the memories of all major Russian victories – from Peter the Great, resting here after his victory over the Swedes, to Catherine the Great. Now these old memories aroused a new awareness – of 1812 and the defeat of the 'world conqueror' in Moscow. Galich told him frankly and kindly that *Betrayals* was fine in its way but a good solid elegy would be better. Soon, some time in autumn, there would be examinations with public recitations, followed by dinner – everybody nowadays was looking for a pretext for celebration, and so why shouldn't he write an elegy for the occasion and read it?

'It's time for you to try yourself in a serious genre.'

And with lowered voice he asked Pushkin not to tell anybody that Razumovsky was going to invite Derzhavin to the examinations.

Galich enjoyed his own idea and simple-heartedly praised himself a few times for it.

'Always think of what is closest to you, what is near at hand – and that's most difficult of all.'

They separated but Galich caught up with him again.

'I meant to tell you that if you wanted to take in the whole park, and then choose the best monuments, you'll need to look at them from different viewpoints and under different conditions to ensure they don't always look the same; the best time for this is in the dark. Walk round here at night and you'll see their main features more clearly. Just make sure you're not missed and they don't start searching for you as if you'd run away. Night is the best time for thinking, and morning for checking things.'

The eyes of the philosopher shone as if he were observing an intricate laboratory experiment.

'This is the discipline of poetry.'

Galich was a gentle and easy-going man, but about truth and imagination he would speak with unshakeable conviction.

Aleksandr had sneaked away from the Lycée before and had had furtive walks in the evenings, but he had never gone too far. Nowadays Frolov paid little attention to discipline – he was engrossed in his cards. Usher Sazonov disappeared at nights as usual, unnoticed. Instead of Frolov's brand of discipline Pushkin was undergoing Galich's, 'the discipline of poetry'.

And so, late at night, not afraid of Frolov, strictly against the Lycée regulations, he strolled about the park. The monuments to Russian victories rose in the half-darkness like Ossianic shadows. These were no graceful gardens, but gloomy forests, deep and dark as in the times of Peter the Great.

5

Delvig made a confession: he had sent his poem to be printed in the *European Messenger*. It was called *The Fall of Paris* and signed with a pseudonym – Ruskoy. The Minister's prohibition of composition and publication had not been abolished. Everyone was mad about serious poetry nowadays. Delvig had become a great admirer of Derzhavin and claimed that no one had ever extolled victories as he had done. He could no longer bear mockery of Derzhavin. To celebrate victories in brief, fast rhymed lines was like dancing on an altar. Pindar and his neo-classical Russian heir, Derzhavin, were the models of this new high seriousness. He had written his ode in the secret hope that old Derzhavin would read it. He addressed him in blank verse:

> *O Pindar of great Rus, O great Derzhavin!*
> *Lend me the rapture of your soaring flight!*
> *Let it be mine, to win me fame for ever,*
> *To make my lyre resound throughout the world!*

Aleksandr reflected. In Moscow, at his parents' home, both his father and his uncle had laughed at Derzhavin's solemnity and lack of polish. His language had become obsolete, his boldness had come to seem too much like gruffness. Yes, it was so, Derzhavin's verse was barbaric, his uncle Vasily Lvovich was right; but *fame* was quite another matter. The monuments at Tsarskoye Selo all seemed to remind him of Derzhavin's poems – the pink and blue stones, the artificial rocks and the columns sticking up out of the water. He remembered Malinovsky. The Principal had never discussed his own poems with him – perhaps he disliked them or had not wanted to award him special praise. The vanity of poets was a worldly disease that he despised. But he had talked to him once about Russian 'literature', as he called poetry, and mentioning Derzhavin, had smiled broadly.

'Derzhavin,' he had said slowly and tenderly and drawing out the main vowel as if admiring the poet's simple name. Aleksandr had been surprised to see somebody so fond of a poet – especially this old poet who had fallen so low in the esteem of the periodicals and was mocked by his uncle and Karamzin.

Now the old poet was remembered like former glory, only recently forgotten. Today, walking past his favourite monument, the Chesme Column, he had thought of the glory of these gardens; neither Karamzin's nor Batyushkov's nor his uncle's glory, but the heavy, reverberating, old-fashioned glory of Derzhavin.

Delvig's rhymeless canticle, however, did not appeal to him. The two decided that Aleksandr should send something to the *European Messenger* too, to the biggest, most important magazine. They chose his poem written for Küchlya, the epistle *To my Friend, a Poet*. Pushkin copied it out in the handwriting of which Kalinich approved – without curls, pressure, or superfluous flourishes, what he called the public, that was to say, official hand. He signed the poem 'Aleksandr NKSP' and posted it. The current editor of the journal was Izmaylov, Karamzin's admirer and a patron of the young. Delvig doubted whether his own poem would be published, but Aleksandr's would surely be. He enjoyed picturing how the journalists would receive, read and criticise their poems.

They laughed softly – but both were apprehensive.

6

Nowadays the Lycée was a republic where disorder reigned. The disagreements of the patricians, as they called the teaching staff, their feuds and intensive intriguing for the Minister's favour and their denunciations of one another had not ceased. Only old Boudri, Kunitsyn and the free citizen of the outside world, Galich, took no part in it all. There was no Principal, Koshansky was ill; Doctor Peshel smartened himself up, shut down the sanatorium and drove to town to conquer its beauties. Frolov would invite the boys for dinner, and Galich and some others started to do the same. They gathered in the steward's room where Galich was staying, and raised their glasses of lemonade to the health of their host whom they had unanimously elected President of their Republic, and the good-natured man accepted the title proudly. They had no classes since they were preparing for the forthcoming public examination.

Even Küchelbecker submitted to the general law of freedom and had twice been seen furtively visiting the German confectioner's.

The inhabitants of Tsarskoye Selo started to pay attention to the Lycéeists.

7

Count Varfolomey Tolstoy was a lover and patron of the theatre. He was an amateur cello player as well, believing the main feature of good playing to consist in a strong bow stroke. He had his own theatre where he was impresario, stage-manager, director, dictator, master and sultan. His serf orchestra, a rather good one, played in the Tsarskoye Selo gardens in the evenings.

The Lycéeists duly received an invitation from him to attend a performance of the opera *Caliph for an Hour*. Till then Aleksandr's knowledge of the theatre had been mainly confined to his father's accounts; he remembered the peculiar expression on his face, the downcast eyes of his aunt Anna Lvovna, and Vasily Lvovich spluttering in all directions when talking about actresses. His aunt had been highly disapproving of the theatre and had shuddered at the very mention of actresses. This alone was enough for him to have fallen in love with the theatre without ever actually going there.

Tolstoy's theatre was small but luxurious. The seats were in a semi-circle, imitating the Hermitage.* The curtain was heavy and embroidered with gold thread. Serf ushers in liveried tail-coats with variegated collars stood in the aisles. The orchestral players too had special uniforms with braided epaulettes. Tolstoy spared no expense over his theatre and his main ambition was to have it resemble the big theatres in every detail. The Count's box was close to the stage, and he seated the Lycéeists nearby as a sign of his favour. Ladies did not go to his theatre and so there were many vacant seats.

Among those invited were all the Lycée poets, Gorchakov, whose uncle had written the opera, and Korsakov, who played the guitar and sang well. As an amateur of the theatre, Count Tolstoy felt that another generation of

---

* The private theatre built for Catherine the Great next to the Palace in St Petersburg by Quarenghi in Ancient Roman style.

theatre-lovers was growing up at the Lycée. He knew better than anybody else that the most important part of a theatre audience consisted of theatre-lovers: laughter, accidental applause, even a whistle, were far better than silence. As the director of the theatre he enjoyed it when somebody was late, squabbled with an usher, stepped on people's feet in the darkness, and so on.

Such was his theatre. The lamps gave off their smoke and the oil hissed. The impresario sat in his box with a blank notebook open in front of him and a pencil in his hands. He clapped his hands and the orchestra struck up. Up swished the curtain. Everybody settled down.

The scene was a Baghdad street at night; from an awning on the front of a house shone little red and green lanterns. All the sets had been painted by serfs. Tolstoy boasted that everything in his theatre was his own, no one and nothing was borrowed; even the curtain was sewn by his maids. The bridegroom, Hussein, wearing a turban with a bugled plume, was on the stage. When his bride, Roxanne, made her entrance Pushkin realised why his aunt had knitted her brow and spat with disgust when talking about actresses. Involuntarily he closed his eyes. Fresh and full-bosomed, with huge immobile eyes and luxurious wide trousers that did not match her slanting shoulders and white face, she breathed heavily and moved helplessly about the stage looking fearfully in the direction of the Count's box. She paid no attention to her bridegroom, who was stretching his arms towards her.

Tolstoy made a quick note in his book. Roxanne was wrapped in a shawl embroidered with golden crescents. Next to her walked her nurse Fatima, a feeble, mercilessly made-up figure. With a forced look on her face Roxanne halted and burst into song. Her small voice was cracked, her head bent down. Not knowing what to do with her hands she eventually folded them up on her breasts as if in embarrassment. Then she remembered her part, lowered her right hand and tried to put her left one on her hip, but her hand slipped down her waist and she pressed both hands to her bosom again. Without looking at Hussein she walked past him almost brushing against him, looking scared, with her head inclined on her shoulder, singing expressionlessly in her cracked voice:

> *Everything frightens my heart,*
> *All of me suffers hurt*
> *When I'm in love.*
> *It seems that in passion*
> *Constant affliction*
> *Hastens to ruin my darling dove.*

Involuntarily, Aleksander applauded. She sang badly, held herself clumsily on-stage, was ashamed of her half-naked breasts, and was utterly helpless. Yet her very awkwardness was touching. She was a beauty.

Somebody hissed for silence, Tolstoy became animated and knocked with his pencil against the paper. Roxanne looked at him and then, at the sight of a creeping stranger who had suddenly appeared, fell into a brocaded chair that stood in the street outside the house, taking care, before falling, to lift her shawl, which she seemed to treasure.

Tolstoy made another note in his book.

She had not finished singing when the Caliph showed up earlier than he was supposed to. He wore a golden gown and a turban and said too quickly: 'What beautiful voices!'

He was shy, fidgety and breathed heavily. There was giggling from the audience and Tolstoy, crimson-faced, said something to the usher, who disappeared.

The first act came to an end. The Lycéeists burst into applause and the audience behind them called for silence; the actors were coming to take a bow. Roxanne bowed low. Only now had she mastered her part, that of an actress. But her bows were hurried, she seemed anxious and tense and was gasping for breath.

Aleksandr clapped his hands, shouting:

'*Bravo! Bravo!*'

She bowed to him too. Her name was Natalya, she was Tolstoy's prima donna and previously his wife's maid.

Tolstoy offered to let the Lycéeists have a look behind the scenes. He wanted everything at his theatre to be just as at the big theatres.

The theatre was luxurious but the wings were small and crowded; the actors' changing-rooms looked like horses' stalls. Tolstoy looked morose. The Caliph in his sumptuous gown skulked by the wall. Tolstoy slapped his face.

'I'll teach you how to make an entrance!' he said. 'You are the Caliph! Why do you conduct yourself without dignity? Remember, you dunce, that you are the Caliph and everybody's superior!'

He waved his finger at Natalya and she lowered her eyes.

8

Tolstoy, undeterred by expense, would take his plays off after three or four performances: then he would grow bored with them and immediately get down to staging another. He produced three plays every three months and Aleksandr had not missed a single performance. He had become a regular visitor at Tolstoy's 'Vauxhall entertainments', as the impresario called his theatre. He went to all the operas and ballets: *The Tunisian Pasha, The Abduction from the Seraglio, The Captive of the Sultan, The Barber of Seville*, he knew all the intrigues and secrets of the Tolstoy theatre, and almost every night he was behind the scenes. Natalya was the leading lady, soubrette, dancer, singer and the master's mistress. She was eternally bustling, anxious and afraid. She had grown accustomed to him and made herself up in his presence. She confessed that she liked his visits – they calmed her down. She said this in a whisper, looking around to make sure that the sultan did not hear her. Her face was constantly strained – she was either trying to remember her part or pretending in front of her master. Performance was the last thing on her mind.

Once, after the second act of *The Captive,* the interval went on too long and he went behind the scenes. He found Natalya in tears: she had just been flogged for a mistake in an entrechat. Tears were rolling down her cheeks but she did not wipe them, afraid that her eyes might become red, and bent her head in order not to smudge her make-up. She pressed herself to Aleksandr and sobbed. Five minutes later she was whirling in a dance with negroes in black and white costumes. She was playing the part of Zemyulba, the Sultan's favourite slave, while the real owner of the seraglio looked at her from his box, with his terrible book, like an accountant's ledger, spread in front of him. Fear and solemnity stood out in her face; the most difficult thing for her was to remember at which points to smile. This time she made no mistake.

Recently Tolstoy had grown colder towards him and no longer distinguished him from the others. Aleksandr had a premonition of imminent separation; this theatre was to be short-lived – Tolstoy had spent too much money on his 'entertainments'. Now he kept a closer watch on Natalya. Aleksandr had written her an epistle, which soon became well known. He had chosen an epigraph from a French poet who had dared to write to a king's favourite. He knew that poets had their own rights and liberties. This was a challenge to Natalya's sultan and Tolstoy was furious with the boy. Natalya was a slave but her charms had their effect on her master. No matter how amusing it might have seemed to him, he was jealous, and at the same time flattered – poets writing madrigals to *his* actresses! His 'entertainments' gave rise to more and more rumours.

He decided to give a lesson to the boy poet who frequented his theatre, to teach him how to behave as a grown-up. Once when Aleksandr applauded Natalya too loudly Tolstoy hissed to him, but unexpectedly the audience, which Tolstoy had almost forgotten about, took the boy's side and started to shout:

'Bravo!'

The indignant Tolstoy was about to give the order to extinguish the lamps and send the audience out, but changed his mind. It was *his* actress, *his* property. He satisfied himself during the interval when he spotted Aleksandr behind the scenes. He immediately had the bell rung and gave an order, loud enough for everybody to hear, not to let latecomers into the auditorium.

'Too much noise!' he said.

Aleksandr burst into rude laughter and left the wings at once.

Returning to the Lycée, he went to Küchlya's room and made him repeat the story about Piron from his dictionary.

'*This gentleman is only a poet,*' Küchlya read in a sleepy voice. '*Now they know who I am,*' *said Piron,* '*and I shall come in first, according to my rank.*'

Aleksandr gave Küchlya a kiss.

'That man does not know who I am,' he said blissfully.

Küchlya offered to read a new entry about virtue, but Aleksandr had already run off.

9

When the next issue of the *European Messenger* arrived, slightly late, Aleksandr pretended to be indifferent. He bit his lip, pale-faced, and watched Gorchakov and Korsakov turning the pages. He expected their amazement and exclamations – but nothing followed. They leafed through the magazine and Gorchakov asked him if he wanted to take a look: nowadays magazines were pretty boring. Still feigning indifference, he looked through the issue; his heart was pounding. Not believing his eyes, he looked at the poets' names and the titles of the poems – there was not a sign of his. He bit his lip and looked the journal through again – nothing. His poem had sunk into oblivion; it did not exist. He tossed the magazine aside and skulked in the corner, biting his nails. They left him alone thinking that he was writing. He wasn't, he was in turmoil. After all, Küchlya seemed to be right about the lot of poets. The absence of his poem was insulting. Were the editors making fun of it? He suddenly hated the magazine: the cover was tasteless, the paper was cheap, and it was altogether boring. Delvig's poem wasn't published either but he was not distressed, on the contrary, he was cheerful.

He thrust the journal into Aleksandr's hands.

At the very end of the issue there was an editor's note in small type: 'We should like to ask the author of the piece "To My Friend, a Poet" recently sent to the *European Messenger,* as well as the anonymous authors of other pieces submitted to us, to reveal their true identity, since we make it a rule not to publish work without knowing the author's name and address. We should like to assure you that we shall not abuse our rights as a publisher by disclosing any names to the public if authors would prefer to remain anonymous.'

They wrote to the magazine at once, looking forward to the reply. The editor's promise to keep names and addresses secret had a soothing effect on Delvig: they had not forgotten the Minister's strict prohibition; to think of having anything printed with their true names was out of the question. Delvig wished he could sign with his real name. Aleksandr was bolder, his initials *NKSP* seemed to him very easy to decipher.

From now on they looked through every issue of the *European Messenger* slowly and carelessly, feigning composure. Finally, in issue twelve, Delvig's poem was published. The issue passed from hand to hand. Aleksandr bit his lip – again he had been left out. It was as if he were in an unknown country with its own laws, where people were easily forgotten.

Now that he had some first-hand experience of publishing procedures, he began to sympathise with Koshansky, who had gone to seed with drink – these periodicals, with their petty rules and policies, were enough to drive anybody mad.

His pride was deeply stung by the delays, and he stopped talking about the poems and the *European Messenger*. Delvig was happy with the happiness that was so close but still unavailable to Pushkin. It didn't matter that 'Ruskoy' was not Delvig's name and that the signature *Aleksandr NKSP* was much more transparent, but Pushkin's *Epistle* was still unpublished, though he might have taken the editor's note as a promise. He gave his poem up for lost and became absorbed in the theatre instead.

10

He was coming back to the Lycée from the Champ des Roses at the forbidden hour, almost running in order not to be late for dinner. He couldn't recognise the familiar road, everything seemed different – the crescents of the ponds, the deep skies – everything seemed closer.

The previous night he had arranged to see Natalya at the Champ des Roses, in the arbour, but even as he went in he did not believe she would come. She had managed to slip away only with great difficulty; her sultan and the guards were now searching for her. At first she was afraid of any noise, the slightest rustle – it might be her master. He was embarrassed to be so inexperienced a lover. He had long known everything inside-out from the allegories in his father's cache; he had read Ovid's *Art of Love* twice and as a faithful disciple he tried to follow it, but instead forgot everything Ovid had said; he did not know that women's faces grew numb from kisses. Ovid had not mentioned this. He had expected endless ecstasy and overwhelming sensations. But what he experienced was nothing like Piron or Barkov, or anything that had been in his father's cache or on his uncle's shelves – and then it started to look like death.

He remembered what Parny had told his Eleanor, but his situation was different – Natalya was always in a hurry. She left – she was late for rehearsal, and he returned to the Lycée. He ran into Valkhovsky, Korsakov and Myasoyedov going to dinner. They looked at him, they exchanged a few words and went to the dining-hall all together. He was amazed – they had noticed nothing different about him. The dinner too was as usual. His head was spinning, he didn't want to leave his friends, he laughed and prattled merrily as he walked with Pushchin, Malinovsky, Delvig and Gorchakov. Everything seemed better than usual. Even Küchlya seemed beautiful. He loved them for their unawareness, for spotting nothing new in him. His former life was over and they were as before. He talked, told stories and laughed endlessly. Life was going on as usual and their close friendship and brotherhood, which he had previously taken for granted, remained the same. They went to their rooms without any disturbance of the normal routine.

Usher Sazonov had made his bed and gone off.

He walked about the room and leant out over the window-sill. He looked up over the roof of the Ladies-in-Waiting Wing but could not see Tolstoy's theatre. A few hours ago he had not been in love with her; he had not been enticed by that night's performance; he had simply been attracted to her for her awkwardness. But now he imagined how she must be looking as she came on stage, and he wished he could have gone to the theatre with her. He clapped his hands and wished her luck. Then he pictured the haughty Tolstoy sitting majestically in his box, looking at the stage and making notes in his thick book – and burst out laughing.

'What's so funny?' asked the sleepy Pushchin from behind the partition.

'I remembered Molière's cuckold,' he replied.

No comment issued from behind the wall, but he felt that Pushchin was shrugging his shoulders – and he laughed again until Pushchin laughed too, not knowing why. The window was still open.

Next day, after the morning lectures, Küchlya showed him his dictionary: he wanted to read him Bernardin de Saint-Pierre's conception of happiness that he had managed to find.

He took Küchlya's dictionary and opened it.

Stages of love: desire, attempts to fulfil it, schemes, coolness, disgust, quarrels, hatred, contempt, oblivion.

He read some other gibberish too, from Weisse: *We should try to act so that all our fellow beings, even cats and dogs, favour us.*

Apparently Küchlya knew nothing of love.

And from Sterne: *Our greatest pleasures end in a shudder, almost of morbidity.*

Only yesterday he, like Küchlya, had not understood this. They both now liked this bizarre thought; but now he was amazed to think that he was not the only one who had had the experience; how, though, could they observe, talk and write about it?

In the evening Boudri brought from town issue thirteen of the *European Messenger*. Delvig was the first to take hold of it and called Aleksandr. He was pale and laughing. He pointed at the opened issue. On page nine was *To My Friend, a Poet*.

Aleksandr looked at the poem; the colour drained from his face and he ran off.

That night Tolstoy was putting on an opera, *The Americans*, and Natalya was singing the part of some gruff American's bride. He did not want to be late.

II

A police lieutenant and three soldiers had turned up at the Lycée. The officer saluted Frolov and whispered a few words to him. Frolov started back and gasped. The doors were shut and the pale-faced usher Matvey walked along the gallery. The boys rushed to the window and saw the soldiers with bare sabres leading a tall man with tied hands. He was walking with his head hung, but hearing their voices, raised his head and shouted in a high-pitched voice:

'Forgive me, fellow Christians!'

A soldier prodded his back with a sabre, the procession passed by and turned to the right. The man with tied hands was the usher who waited upon Aleksandr, who had shared a room with him in the sanatorium – Konstantin Sazonov.

A week later they learned that during his night absences from the Lycée Sazonov had committed burglaries and murders. Altogether he had stabbed nine people. The quarter coin he had searched for unsuccessfully in the sanatorium had been stolen from a cabman whom Sazonov had hired for half a rouble. He had stabbed and robbed the cabman to avoid paying him; the quarter was all his victim had had on him at the time.

Sazonov had enjoyed listening to poems and on one occasion had argued with Delvig. He didn't look like a robber as Aleksandr imagined them to be from reading novels. He was fair-haired, simple-minded and sullen. If Aleksandr had had money, Sazonov would certainly have stabbed him. They had slept next to each other, with no one else near. He recalled how Sazonov had given him tea from a saucer – and couldn't sleep the whole night through.

12

Everything seemed different. Their voices were breaking, their chins had become covered with fluff which they proudly cut off with scissors; but their friendships remained the same. Aleksandr's friends were Delvig, Küchlya and the poets. Illichevsky continued to write fables, giving them a finer and more detailed polish, and Aleksandr had nothing to talk to him about. His other friends were Pushchin and Malinovsky. The virtuous Valkhovsky regarded him with stern disapproval. He honoured the memory of his adopted father, Principal Malinovsky, and had sworn to keep his morals pure all his life. He would lament the decline of morals to Küchelbecker. If Malinovsky had been alive, he would have found a way to reach even the most wayward students, and Pushkin wouldn't have become an idler. Küchelbecker was completely under his influence, though he believed his friend's behaviour was to be explained by passions he was unable to suppress.

Now Aleksandr spent long hours in the park. It was autumn and he wandered along the lime tree alleys. His friends suspected he had secret trysts. 'He has got out of hand and turned aside from the path of goodness,' Valkhovsky would say of him, and Küchlya listened to him in despair.

Aleksandr's theatrical passions passed unnoticed by Frolov but aroused the disapproval of the rigidly righteous. The virtuous shunned him and looked at him in sorrow, at which he merely laughed.

Once Boudri, looking straight at Aleksandr, told them how his brother, a doctor and a very clever man, had wished to protect him from dissipation in his young years. At that time his brother had been writing a treatise about the victims of Venus. He had shown him the agonies and exposed ulcers of the half-dead idlers who had lost their minds and their mobility.

Aleksandr listened to him with curiosity. Boudri talked colourfully and hoarsely. He made Parisian hospitals of that time sound horrible. All this had nothing to do with his rendezvous with Natalya, with her charms or with that joy which, according to Sterne's testimony, for some reason always ended in a shudder, almost of pain. But now these trysts were over – the theatre stood empty, its windows barred. He was no longer seeing Natalya and his friends were mistaken; he had been busy writing.

Eleven

SLOWLY he had climbed the little steps up to his huge sofa and almost collapsed on it, feet and all. The little white dog that was asleep in his lap did not wake up. A wintry sun was glittering in yellow, pink and blue on the carpets, the window-panes were covered with hoar-frost, the yard was snowed up, but it was warm on the sofa and he dozed there, only his lips moving. His night-cap had slipped from his head, bare and yellow like a billiard ball, but with baby-down showing here and there. His sofa was his realm; there he kept everything that he had written, and slept there too. He had got himself onto it with a particular intention. The copy of his tragedy *Atabalibo* that he had promised to Razumovsky was lying in the little bookcase to the left of the sofa, the place where the previous day he had deliberately left his slate. He looked at it askance, almost superstitiously. He would take a slate-pencil – and poems would pour forth as they had done all his life. He closed his eyes and took the pencil, looked at the fluffy snow over the Fontanka river, wrote a word and erased it, then another and erased that too. He put the slate back on the bookcase. His little dog, which he had named Gornostayka,* and affectionately called Tayka, was curled up peacefully against his chest and warmed his heart.

While the horses were being harnessed and before dressing, he intended to correct a couple of lines in his tragedy. But he changed his mind and decided to do no corrections and not to spoil the perfect copy. He was actually reluctant to part with it, and suddenly he decided not to. He considered this latest work his best: the death of the Peruvian emperor and the eclipse of the sun had come out very well. Everything that he had written during his lifetime, all those numerous odes, were just trifles, mere knicknacks in comparison with this tragedy, and as far as he remembered they had come out effortlessly. Sometimes he felt as if his writing career were just beginning. He was slightly apprehensive about today's journey. He had had to do much

* Little Ermine.

travelling in his life: he had sailed along the Volga, he had ridden about the steppes, to Orenburg, to Petrozavodsk and back, to Mogilyov and back, to Kaluga. But this journey to Tsarskoye Selo was going to be the most difficult of all: he would have to put on his Senator's uniform and ribbon; thrust his feet into *valenki** and his hands into mittens; put on his fur-coat, pull up the collar, and speed over the snow in a sleigh – and his day would be completely disrupted. But he couldn't avoid it: everybody was waiting for him to appear and speak words of encouragement. Watch would be kept on the road far into the distance to see whether he was coming. Before his retirement he had never neglected his duty, he would arrive early, stay on and go carefully into the details, and he had always been indignant with those flighty and frivolous people who knew everything and succeeded in everything while lounging at home.

He had always attended examinations in the provincial gymnasium, so he couldn't ignore the Lycée, the new establishment that was the talk of the city. He had known its Principal well – Malinovsky, who had just died so suddenly. He had no idea who was in charge there now. The great number of deaths around him had long since ceased to upset him, they were simply an irritation. Unfortunately, all the people of his age had already died, then the younger ones had died – and many projects had begun and been left unfinished. He had grown accustomed to this confusion of the times. He couldn't agree that new things were best. He had no wish to encounter the poet Zhukovsky at these examinations. A most respectful correspondent and a pleasant personality in his poems, he had enticed the old poet: he had asked him for a few poems to include in his *Almanac* and had published his best work in it. Now people didn't buy Derzhavin's editions, they preferred Zhukovsky's anthology, and with very little labour the young man had managed to peck up the golden grains. His *1812* poem was of doubtful value; everything in it was *romanced*, and even its heroes waltzed! But one had to admit that the man was gifted.

Throughout his life he had always had troubles with people. The young now seemed to revere him, but in reality were two-faced; they also seemed to laugh at him. Such was life! Nowadays he was worried not only about his works that he kept in the little bookcases that marked the two ends of the sofa, he was worried about people too. He never had a single spare moment, seeing to his publications and finding good artists to make engravings for them, to say nothing of worries about his houses, his estate and heirs – he had much expenditure and distress.

The trouble was that he had no children. By no means did he want the

---

* Felt boots.

family line of Derzhavin to cease; so he had chosen his youngest nephew, had written a petition for His Imperial Majesty's permission to add his name to his nephew's – who, however, had refused the honour, saying he was unworthy and would not be able to bear the weight of it on his shoulders. This had not discouraged the old man: he had found a relative from his home province of Kazan, a Horse Guards Colonel. Derzhavin had arranged to get him married to his niece and to hand them on the family name – but the niece had refused it. What could be done, with women and their whims? He had offered his name to another relative living in Kazan, a worthy person – but that had not come off either. When a young, cunning and intelligent fellow called Bludov, from a wealthy family, started to frequent Derzhavin's the poet decided to make him his heir – but his wife, Darya Alekseyevna (whom he had immortalised by the name of Milena), hounded Bludov out of the house.

His old age was irksome and sad. Under no circumstances could he endure two things: first, to do without women, and secondly, to die, in the sense of complete extinction. As recently as two years before, Milena had thrown jealous scenes: his heart started to beat faster every time he saw the blood colouring the little blue veins on female temples. He was ready to do whatever the beauties desired: they had supreme rights. And if they gave him a lingering look, his heart was fired; and if they happened to play Bach or Cramer on the harp or piano he immediately started to write on his slate at the little table by the window. When other guests left he was oblivious, but he always asked a beauty to stay – just to be there, to sit quietly near him. The most precious members of his household were his young nieces. The thought that his family name would cease to exist was unbearable. That was why he liked to go out, to watch people and try out his surname on them. He had made arrangements in his will concerning his estate and since nothing he did came out as desired the first time, he kept rewriting it.

He was burdened by the thought that his poems would cease to exist too, that death would put an end to them. Recently he had been writing major tragedies. Poetry for him was like the gambling that had nearly ruined him in his youth. Now his wife allowed him small sums for small losses, and he indeed incurred small losses. But he couldn't bear the idea that either his estate or his fame would be lost.

His sofa would fall apart, the manuscripts and copies would fall out of the side-bookcases and be scattered around. While his heirs were alive at least something would survive, but what would happen when they died? He needed somebody to whom he could hand over his poems and his genius, not just his manuscripts. That was why he was angry with Zhukovsky, who might have been his successor. Some young men came to see him and brought him their compositions to listen to; sometimes his hopes rose, but quickly subsided.

There was much translation these days (an occupation for the elderly, for those who did not dare write what came into their own heads). Generally speaking, writers seemed to be less ambitious, more delicately sensitive and wealthier than in his day. He had nearly chosen a suitable person but had given him up; then he had chosen someone else and given him up as well. He did not want to pin his hopes on a mature poet. Mature poets had already shown what they were capable of; they did not promise immortality, and just like his heirs, did not want his name and would not accept and did not even understand his fame.

He had been searching earnestly for those who would; he listened to them desperately – and continued his search.

A programme was attached to Razumovsky's invitation. The examinations at the new establishment were substantial, the youths were passing from a junior to a senior year. The first examination had taken place four days before – Derzhavin had not attended it: Scripture, Logic, Geography, History, German and Moral Philosophy did not arouse his curiosity – they were the same the world over. He wouldn't go to the second examination since it concerned only Latin, French, Mathematics and Physics, of which he had little knowledge. But the last one was in Russian, and the visitors were explicitly invited to ask the students questions. He was going to exercise this right. He had already commented on the programme but was generally pleased with it: styles, figures of speech – and in conclusion, recitation of original compositions.

He liked those shy, stumbling, squeaky young voices, shouting out their lines. A long time ago he too had got confused and shouted his words. He decided to miss the beginning and arrive in time for the last part. He would stay until the very end, when the students would exhibit their skills in painting, calligraphy, fencing and dancing.

It always took his coachman, Kondraty, a long time to harness the horses. Derzhavin had always wanted to have strawberry roan or light bay ones, but had never managed to obtain them and now had a team of greys.

He took a nap. Then his wife came in and said:

'Ganyushka, Ganyushka, it's time to go!'

They took off his warm dressing-gown lined with squirrel fur, though he was reluctant to part with it. They put him into velveteen knee-high boots and a Senator's uniform with a ribbon – he stood still. His valet pulled a grey fluffed-up wig onto his head – he swayed. Then he was wrapped in a fur-coat, its collar was pulled up, he was taken downstairs, sat down in a closed sleigh, tucked in on all sides – and driven to Tsarskoye Selo.

2

Sergey Lvovich did not like to talk about Warsaw. Now he and his family stayed on the Fontanka, the same street where Derzhavin lived, though at its very end, in the district of Kolomna. Just as in Moscow, in German Street, here in St Petersburg he found himself among tradesmen; craftsmen's widows and the poor were all around him. Sergey Lvovich told everyone that he had settled here because of the air, and because of the garden, which was a rarity for houses in St Petersburg. He had let himself go – all because of his ambition. If he had not pursued his career, he would have nothing to regret now. Having lost his friends, he grew proud of his children. Who could have thought that Olga would become pretty! He became convinced of this when he took her to see Aleksandr. Previously he had not noticed either her or her beauty. But Aleksandr was surprised and delighted to see her; his friends – Gorchakov and others whom Sergey Lvovich did not know – looked at Olga with the expression he knew so well, the one that he had worn when young. Sergey Lvovich looked at Olga and for the first time saw that she had indeed grown pretty.

He looked at everything through a stranger's eyes. Sashka's poem had been published in the *European Messenger*, a thing that had never happened to Sergey Lvovich. He was delighted, showed his friends the magazine and complained about the Lycée's strict rules:

'Instead of signing it "Pushkin", poor Sashka – just imagine! – had to have it signed with an assumed name, an anagram, a riddle, a rebus!'

Having looked through Sashka's poem, he minced into his study and sat down in front of a sheet of paper; he wanted to recall a short elegy he had recently composed but had lost while moving from place to place. Generally both his library and his cache had thinned out; almost everything had been lost in the moves.

Soon he got a letter full of exclamations from Vasily Lvovich: in his opinion Sashka's epistle was a brilliant beginning. Sergey Lvovich reread the poem and he too was convinced – it was brilliant indeed, perhaps the beginning of a literary career, and not just a little poem published by the editor as an encouragement.

Like all other parents he had received an invitation to attend the examination. Without bargaining with the robber of a cabman, he hired him for twenty-five roubles and promised to give some more for vodka. Important figures had been invited to the examination and under the circumstances Sergey Lvovich considered it petty stinginess to bargain with a cabman.

3

Kondraty jumped off the footboard, opened the door of the carriage and helped him out. The trip had rocked Derzhavin to sleep. He told Kondraty to stay where he was and took a short walk to stretch his legs. Without thinking, he went further along the familiar road and was surprised when he reached the palace so soon. He was chewing away at his lips.

He stopped at the marble steps. Huge statues of Hercules and Flora stood by the entrance. They were covered with snow.

'You see, she's snowed-up too,' he muttered, looking at Flora.

Apprehensively he climbed the steps, still grumbling.

It was getting dark, and the lighting was poor. Suddenly he wanted to brush the snow off the goddess's steep hip, but did not manage to reach even her little finger. Besides, the snow was too hard. He banged the stick a few times against the frozen crust, gingerly went down the steps onto the path and, shielding his eyes with his hand, looked at the colonnade. He couldn't see anything through the snowed-up poplars but felt a strong yearning for the old days. There stood his idols, Greek and Roman thinkers in bronze, all looking alike. The Russian poet Lomonosov shared their company. After he had first seen him here, Derzhavin hadn't been able to sleep at night for two months, tormented with the craving to see his own statue next to these figures. Hoping that one day his dream would come true, he had commissioned likenesses of himself and of his then wife, Plenira, at an exorbitant price. But his statue had never reached the colonnade and now stood beside Darya Alekseyevna's linen-covered sofa. As for Plenira, his second wife had hidden her under the sofa. The same destiny, it seemed to him, lay in store for his own statue when he came to die.

First he had felt a pang of envy but then realised that it was not worth it. Such indifference all around! He was sure that not all the statues in the colonnade were still intact, and the same would have happened with his – they would have looked at it, kicked it down the steps and he would have counted them with his head! He had wept once, many years ago, on this very step where he was now standing: the secretary had made a mistake; it had ended well, but how dearly he had paid for it! Now, thinking about it, he felt nothing.

He forgot about the examination and that he was expected. He wanted to succeed at least in something in these gardens, in his fight against time, which he had always been afraid of, and which now besieged him on all sides. He did not want to look at the monuments, the arbours or the Chinese Village, which was still unfinished; he did not want any reminiscences. He knew these gardens as well as his own. Just here he had encountered Bezborodko, striding past in fury; over there the Empress's favourite Orlov would take walks and had once boasted how he had managed to stop a cart running downhill – everything that he had believed to be the essence of his life had suddenly vanished. Oriental luxury and coolness were no more in the bare and rational Alexandrine epoch. Even the military victories were different nowadays, and he did not understand them as he used to understand Suvorov's triumphs. His *Lyric-Epic Hymn on the Downfall of the French* had been uninspired, and had passed unnoticed beside Zhukovsky's *Bard*. He had always written about time and death, about the frailty of things, but he had not expected it to come to him, and so soon. If it were not for his aching legs he would have gone at once to the lake where he had rowed in a boat with Plenira; the lake was frozen, but he would have hammered it with his stick.

He walked towards the Lycée; the new inhabitants were now in the Ladies-in-Waiting Wing.

He was very tired and felt that he shouldn't have come to Tsarskoye Selo. But Principal Malinovsky might have taken offence if he hadn't.

He entered the building, and handing the porter his marten coat looked at him thoughtfully and started to wonder if Principal Malinovsky were still alive. Figures in uniforms were already hurrying downstairs to see him in and to support him by his arms. Irritated, he broke free. He hesitated for a moment and started to climb the stairs with an effort. In the hall he remembered that the Principal had died.

He was helped to sit down. His head shaking, he looked about him and seemed to grow younger: many young eyes looked at him as if at a miracle. He dozed off a little, but heard everything distinctly, as if through a haze, paying no attention to anything in particular. At last the recitations were announced. He thought for a moment that he wouldn't stay for the fencing and dancing but would taste the lunch.

Suddenly he heard his name and his poems. He turned in his chair and started to listen, nodding. They were reading his old poems which had been recited countless times over the years. But he forgot that they were his own, and they touched him like somebody else's work.

Then he heard a clear, reverberating voice. He looked closer. The voice, resonant and agile, came in bursts – like a bird's notes borne on the wind. He started to feel about anxiously for his lorgnette, but couldn't find it. And this voice spoke suddenly to him alone and to no one else:

'*Recollections in Tsarskoye Selo.*'

He started to shake, mouthing these words with his coarse, sagging, soldier's lips – voicelessly, soundlessly. He was looking at the schoolboy and the schoolboy seemed to be looking at him. His eyesight had long since started to betray him but nevertheless he saw as if in a mist: the schoolboy's eyes were bright and burning. Nobody read poems like this: with little swellings and lingerings at the ends of lines, as in song. And as if listening to Bach, he raised his old and sinewy index finger and, oblivious of everyone, just perceptibly started to point the metre. He was listening to the recollections of this young novice who had nothing to remember, but who had recalled for him everything in these gardens – both the old victories and the new ones.

The reader mentioned his name in his poem. Forgetting himself, he reached out for his slate but his hand froze in mid-air: he wasn't at home, it was a public occasion. There was no slate and he no longer needed it. He wanted to write things down:

> *The cover of the sullen night hangs heavy …*
>
> *… This is Elysium at the midnight hour,*
> *The enchanted park of Tsarskoye Selo.*

By the time Aleksandr finished, only a few were looking at him; most of the audience were looking at Derzhavin.

The scrawny, shrunken old man had drawn himself up to his full height and now stood with his head held back: his face expressed, meaninglessly, the former rapture that, of all those present, only old Saltykov remembered. Tears were rolling down his wrinkled worn face. Suddenly, with unexpected agility, he pushed the chair aside and hurried towards the reader to embrace him.

But no one was there. Aleksandr had run off.

Not giving in to the torpor that usually overcame him at this time of day, Derzhavin talked animatedly to Razumovsky.

Razumovsky hadn't understood a thing. He said that he would like to see Pushkin as a prose-writer.

'Let him be a poet,' Derzhavin said and waved him away impatiently.

Still managing to hold himself together, only his head visibly trembling, he sat down to a long dinner and on this occasion ate abundantly and avidly, taking advantage of his wife's absence – following the physicians' advice she normally deprived him of the most delicious things at table. He sipped wine, listened to Sergey Lvovich's prattling and even answered him. Leaving Tsarskoye Selo, he fell almost asleep onto the cushions of his sleigh and muttered, barely audibly, to the old coachman whose name was the same as his valet's:

'Kondraty – full speed!'

PART THREE

Youth

I

W HEN usher Foma told him that Mr Karamzin and some other gentle-men were waiting to see him, his heart started to pound; he rushed downstairs so impetuously as to make the usher, dumbfounded, exclaim: "Esu Christ!'

He could never get accustomed to the mercurial features and unpredictable behaviour of Mr Pushkin, Number 14.

They were waiting for him in the library. The meetings with parents took place in the big hall.

Karamzin had been staying in St Petersburg for more than a month and had been much spoken about; he had come to St Petersburg to petition the Tsar for the publication of his *History*. The fat Bakunina had passed on the rumour that the Tsar had welcomed him heartily and that publication had been arranged; however, on another occasion she told her son and his friends that nothing had been settled yet and that nothing was known. She was reluctant to say anything more about Karamzin.

When Kunitsyn returned to Tsarskoye Selo he told them of Karamzin's success; he had been made such a fuss of that the court had *had* to agree to publication of the *History*. Rumour had it that there had been a celebration in his honour. And now he was in Tsarskoye Selo, at the Lycée.

He was not alone. Aleksandr's uncle, Vasily Lvovich, stood in the middle of the gallery, his hands folded behind his back, next to a third person – tall, baggy, with hunched shoulders, wearing spectacles – it was the first time Aleksandr had seen him and he guessed at once who it was: Vyazemsky. Vasily Lvovich embraced his nephew as he always did in the presence of strangers, not looking at him and casting sidelong glances at his friends.

Vyazemsky watched them narrowly and exchanged glances with Aleksandr.

'Your Excellency.'

He spoke to Vasily Lvovich, alluding to the customs of the Arzamas Society. His uncle hesitated.

' "Here"!' Vyazemsky said.

'I do remember, Your Excellency,' replied Vasily Lvovich, with a flourish in his voice. Vyazemsky's soft reddish hair was dishevelled and a jaunty little tuft stood on end at the back of his head. He looked like a cockerel spoiling for a fight.

They burst out laughing, and Karamzin shook his head.

But his uncle had never been called 'Your Excellency', and nor had Vyazemsky. This fooling was quite new to him. He was breathless.

His uncle drew a handkerchief from his pocket, cleared his throat and adjusted his waistcoat, as he always did before reading his impromptus.

But no, this was not a poem. Stumbling on every word and spluttering, his uncle read, with great seriousness, something resembling either a document in Church Slavonic or some mumbo-jumbo written by a clerk:

In the month of February, on its twelfth day, in the second year after the Lipetsk Flood, the meeting of the Arzamas Society took place at the Old Lady's. Those present were Their Excellencies Thunderer, Svetlana and Here. Armed against the insanity of the Symposium with a red hood and a quill – 'you'll read all about Shakhovskoy later' – *it was voted that Cricket should join the Society. His Excellency Hark …*

'In other words,' his uncle suddenly concluded, 'you are a member of the Society. Cricket, that's you, my boy. And "Their Excellencies" – that's their titles – are Their Excellencies, the genii of Arzamas.'

The Arzamas Society of Unknown Literati was the talk of the city. In his comedy *The Lipetsk Waters*, Shakhovskoy had portrayed a pathetic young poet called Violet, in whom he had satirised Zhukovsky. The comedy was good fun and a great success, but all the Friends of Taste had taken up arms against Shakhovskoy. He was peppered with epigrams; now he was called nothing else but Jestovskoy and his comedy was nicknamed *The Lipetsk Flood*. Long, meaningless prayers were written in Church Slavonic in honour of the insane Symposium of Amateurs of the Russian Word, all those tongue-tied clerks who happened to have such a powerful, witty ally as Shakhovskoy. Vasily Lvovich strutted about the two capitals ranting and babbling.

Gradually the Friends of Taste had refined this mockery, thoroughly enjoying the conspiracy against their opponents.

One day Count Dmitry Nikolayevich Bludov, passing through the provincial town of Arzamas, had got so bored waiting at the coach-station that he had decided to portray Shakhovskoy and the recent events in an elaborate composition in the style of the Slavophiles, entitled *A Vision in a Certain Town*. From this moment all those waging war against Shakhovskoy and the Symposium had become Arzamasians, the anonymous inhabitants of Arzamas. They had set up the Arzamas Society, its emblem a goose, since Arzamas was famous for its fat geese.

Zhukovsky had taken an active part in all this. The members of Arzamas held meetings at each other's homes and in the most unexpected places; even chance encounters of two or three members in carriages or theatre stalls were also considered meetings. They gave themselves airs and posed as old grandees

– like members of the Symposium. They called each other 'Your Excellency'. They wore red hoods at their evening meetings – when any of them published a translation from French, members of the Symposium called them Jacobins. Minutes of their meetings were interminably long and hilarious. The secretary of Arzamas was none other than Zhukovsky. The minutes were written in strict clerical style. Even months were named in the Slavonic manner; they had reinvented the calendar. After that their own names struck them as much too banal, so they looked through Zhukovsky's ballads and named themselves after his characters and even after random words: *Rhine, Black Raven, Smoky Stove* – anything was acceptable. And now with Aleksandr. He was nicknamed Cricket, a certified member of Arzamas.

Karamzin looked closely at Aleksandr. He greatly respected and valued this time of youth, when a whole being brims over and lips twitch before breaking into laughter. And yet the smile of this young man was sad.

Vyazemsky raised his finger like a provincial secretary reading an article of law and quoted the text:

> *The fire blazed and crackled,*
> *The cricket's cheerless chirp*
> *Announced the midnight hour.*

He pronounced the word 'chirp' with a special Arzamas-like intonation.

'All of us, my boy, have these names,' Vasily Lvovich said quickly. 'For instance, Vyazemsky is called "Asmodeus", Batyushkov is "Achilles" – because of his height: you've seen him, haven't you? – he's tiny. As for me, they call me simply "Here".'

Aleksandr asked him to repeat his name. It seemed extraordinary.

'*Here*,' his uncle repeated reluctantly, 'as in *Here you are.*'

'No, not *Here you are*, just *Here*,' Vyazemsky corrected him.

'That's what I'm saying: *Here*,' said his uncle irritably.

Of course, all the names were funny: Achilles and Cricket, but 'Here' was something altogether different.

'It's from Zhukovsky, my boy,' explained his uncle, suddenly becoming gloomy: '*Here is a pretty girl ... here lightly snaps the lock ...* and so on. What does it matter! *Here*, well?'

He was obviously displeased with his name.

'I am *Here* but Dashkov is *Hark*,' he said later, cheering up. 'And Turgenev is *Two Huge Hands.*'

His uncle was completely engrossed in the matter of his name.

Vyazemsky spoke to Aleksandr in a more serious tone.

'The Members of the Symposium are like horses in their stables – in teams. Why should only fools be together? So we decided to become brothers too

– to live in harmony, arm-in-arm. When do you finish at the Lycée? Our meetings are on Thursdays.'

Then he asked him seriously – and the tuft rose on the back of his head – if he had read Zhukovsky's new ballad and Bludov's review of it, which was extremely perceptive.

Karamzin asked Aleksandr how damp Tsarskoye Selo was and in particular the Chinese Village where he was going to take his family this summer. It was a recent decision, made the previous day, and now on his way to Moscow he was joining his friends in order to look at the little house where he intended to stay.

The nimble-footed Lomonosov looked in, and Vasily Lvovich recalled the golden days when, in a fit of inspiration, he had written *The Dangerous Neighbour* and Lomonosov and Pushchin had been at hand at Demouth's. He now introduced the boy to Karamzin and Vyazemsky.

Karamzin invited him to come and see him.

The visitors were about to leave when the breathless new Principal arrived just in time to meet them. Wiping the sweat off his brow with a handkerchief, he explained that he had come here as soon as he could. Oh, if only he had young legs! His exuberance was excessive. And everything changed at once: Vyazemsky looked through narrowed eyes at Aleksandr and saw his dismayed expression and flared nostrils. The Principal was podgy, pale-faced and broad-bottomed, with the blue eyes of a Baltic German, constantly rolling. Heavenly kindness was written all over his face, and flattery and compliance in his gestures. He was delighted to see such guests, and so on.

The jokes stopped at once; Arzamas vanished without a trace. Karamzin turned out to be in a hurry, and asked the Principal to let Pushkin and Lomonosov accompany him to the Chinese village, which was just a stone's throw from the Lycée.

They went up to the little wooden chalets, which looked so cold and desolate it was hard to imagine anybody actually living there. With a sinking feeling the historian looked at the Chinese Village where he was doomed to stay that summer. He had taken the monastic vows of a historian, Pyotr Vyazemsky had said – but even monks didn't inhabit such cold and damp dwellings, however elegant. Vasily Lvovich was perplexed.

'It's quite a distance from here to the kitchen – if it's in that tent, the food will get cold.'

He referred to the chalets in military parlance – as 'tents'.

A weird figure suddenly loomed up in front of them: a breathless, preposterously fat old general stood at the entrance to the Chinese Village as if barring their way. Aleksandr recognised him: it was Zakharzhevsky, the

Commandant of Tsarskoye Selo, who had appeared to greet the guests. No greeting followed, however.

The general introduced himself and muttered that the Chinese Village was not completely ready, and he asked them to postpone their survey.

He was pale and his eyes glared as if the huts were his personal property and about to be taken away from him.

'Would you have the doors opened?' Karamzin said calmly, also turning pale. 'We'll wait here.'

The general hesitated, and in the hoarse tight voice of a military leader forced to retreat, gave the order to open the doors.

Then he departed.

They saw the mouldy walls of the chalets. Vasily Lvovich assured Karamzin that they would be fine in summer. Aleksandr looked first at Karamzin and then at Vyazemsky: it was clear that the Palace retainers, who hated outsiders and guarded the darkest corners of Tsarskoye Selo from the invasion of the Lycéeists, had been thrown into panic at the sight of the great man. He bit his lip, his nostrils flared and he snorted quietly. Vyazemsky looked at him above his spectacles.

'Look how angry the Cricket is,' said Karamzin, smiling.

The Commandant had retreated before Karamzin's troops.

Then Pushkin and Vyazemsky, in brotherly Lycéeist manner, strolled around arm-in-arm examining all corners of the new domain. Vasily Lvovich attached himself to them and made some apt practical comments. He had found a suitable place for a wine-store.

'What one has to bear in mind, my friends, is that in the heat the wine might go sour.'

Karamzin was not a wine-drinker.

Vyazemsky had just enough time to tell Aleksandr that there was a serious literary war on: that the Symposium was very powerful, Shishkov was close to Arakcheyev and kept him informed about the Lycéeists' progress, that Karamzin's enemies had nearly destroyed him in St Petersburg, however great the respect in which he was held by those with taste; that Jestovskoy's comedy was enjoying huge success; and that Zhukovsky was being laughed at. 'But let's wait and see: taste, intellect and Arzamas will win the day!'

He would send Aleksandr an Arzamasian triumphal anthem called *The Coronation of Jestovskoy*.

2

Now he lived for these brief encounters.

The previous summer the retired Lieutenant Batyushkov had come to the Lycée and asked to see Pushkin, and he had still not forgotten that meeting. The retired Lieutenant was of small height, 'tiny', as Foma had described him. He told Aleksandr in a soft voice that he had called upon him to thank him for his epistle. He was poorly dressed, in a grey military jacket and peaked cap. He looked at Aleksandr with his sad, absent-minded eyes and nothing about him bore any likeness to the indolent sage and lover of women whom Aleksandr knew from the poems that he liked so much. He had addressed this languorous man in his *Epistle* as

> *Playful philosopher and bard,*
> *The happy idler of Parnassus . . .*

Now Batyushkov rarely appeared in the periodicals. In his epistle Aleksandr had mentioned this:

> *Have you too, young dreamer,*
> *Parted at last with Phoebus?*

Now he wished he hadn't. Pensive and distracted, his visitor seemed to have lost his way here in Tsarskoye Selo and to be unsure how to get home. Aleksandr recalled his poem about Moscow burning:

> *Only cinders, rubble, and dust-filled air . . .*
> *Only pale hosts of paupers*
> *Caught my eye everywhere . . .*

In the same soft voice he commented on the building of the Palace and the flaws in the proportions of the wing that had been added later, and then he suddenly asked Aleksandr why he had called him 'the Russian Parny' in his poem?

He had once written about the same subjects as the French poet, but that was all over now.

Recollections in Tsarskoye Selo which Aleksandr had read at the examination in the presence of Derzhavin was in Batyushkov's opinion Pushkin's best poem. Why couldn't he write a poem about all these great deeds? Quite enough epistles had been written already.

No, he was no Epicurean, nor a dreamer.

Aleksandr, slightly stung, replied that he had been writing a poem – a humorous fairytale – in a colloquial style. The poem was about a hero called Bova, a cunning king and the ghost of Bova's feeble-minded father.

Batyushkov told him quietly that he himself had been thinking about writing a fairy-tale of the sort and suddenly asked Aleksandr:

'Leave Bova to me, will you?'

He smiled, and Aleksandr was immediately reminded of his poems about indolence and sages of leisure. Then he looked sad again, shook the Lycéeist's hand and left without a backward glance, small, slight and upright.

Afterwards Aleksandr wandered along the school corridors and passages for a long time, fretting. Then he shook his head and came to his senses.

When Delvig asked him what Batyushkov had talked to him about, he was reluctant to say. And then Delvig asked him if Batyushkov had liked his epistle. He replied:

'*Chacun à son goût.*'

He didn't want to think about it all any more.

In the evening he reread everything he had written that year. Many lines seemed superfluous and he crossed them out.

Later Zhukovsky gave him a book of his poems. Zhukovsky was tall, his long hair covered his forehead; he was given to laughter and talk. Batyushkov, by contrast, seemed oblivious of people and saw only buildings and their proportions. Zhukovsky, first looking around him, remarked that the Principal had something feline about him and it was true; he was sleek and satisfied, therefore good-natured.

Karamzin, Vyazemsky and his uncle Vasily Lvovich, on their way to Moscow together, came to see him again. Karamzin was going to spend the coming summer in Tsarskoye Selo, and rumour had it that the great historian would be an adviser to the Tsar. Such was the fruit of enlightenment; everything was possible!

His Arzamasian uncle was at the height of his fame – he was the oldest Arzamasian, his skirmishes with the Symposium and the 'Philistines forgotten by taste' were still remembered. Aleksandr was in rapture when he accompanied the visitors to the Chinese Village where Karamzin would choose the home he was to live in for the summer. The houses, it was true – part of a monarch's uncompleted whimsical scheme – were damp and looked more like uninhabited summerhouses than human dwellings. Knitting his brows, Karamzin examined them. The ceilings were low, the structures were excessively small. He chose a larger one for his family; the adjoining one, connected to the first by a roofed passage, for his study; and a third one for kitchen and servants. Aleksandr thought he heard him sigh. He would have been surprised to be told that his visitors needed him more than he needed them.

Karamzin was unsettled and depressed. He had come to St Petersburg from a Moscow that had been rebuilt with such speed that a stranger's eye might have failed to notice the traces of the great fire, a Moscow where everybody revered him. Eight volumes of *The History of The Russian State*, the result of twelve years' labour, were practically finished. He needed the Emperor's permission to publish the book – and money. He had composed a foreword as eloquent and passionate as he could possibly manage. He had been apprehensive about his journey to St Petersburg. What if his project were to fall through? The Tsar's beloved sister, Yekaterina Pavlovna, had not replied to the historian's letter. He had resigned himself to bad news, to the inevitable humiliation; but reality had proved to be beyond his worst expectations. He had pined in St Petersburg for six weeks – the Tsar had shown no desire to see him. The tension had worn him down to a shadow of his former self; the only people he was pleased to see were these clever young Arzamasians, and with gloomy satisfaction he embraced their indignation at the Tsar's treatment of him, this cat-and-mouse play. Meanwhile he had had to cringe before the authorities, and – what could have been more humiliating? – had even had to visit his greatest literary enemies, the humourless old idiots of the Symposium, and to be deprecated by them. He had petitioned not only the Master of Ceremonies but also the Deputy Master of Ceremonies at the Palace for an audience with His Majesty, only to suffer an icy refusal.

He had nearly reconciled himself to going cap in hand to see Arakcheyev, the Tsar's friend and favourite, but he couldn't go through with it in the end. A friend of Arakcheyev, a general, said that having heard that publication of the *History* would cost sixty thousand roubles, the Tsar had allegedly exclaimed: 'What nonsense! I'll never allow such a sum!' Eventually Karamzin had had to dine with a despicable individual, the secretary Pukalov, whose wife was Arakcheyev's mistress. And then, reluctantly and almost groaning with humiliation, he had had an audience after all with Arakcheyev himself, and shortly afterwards the Tsar had agreed to see him. His Majesty had intended to read the foreword and had started it twice, but couldn't go further with it, assigning, however, sixty thousand for the publication and giving Karamzin permission to stay in Tsarskoye Selo if he wished.

Jaded, humiliated and made to feel like a scoundrel, Karamzin had arrived at Tsarskoye Selo to choose his home and had called at the Lycée together with Vasily Lvovich to remember his youth. He admired Aleksandr. Seventeen! How tender and immature this age was! Oh, how impossible at this age to grovel and debase oneself! What dreams, what poetry, what future!

His uncle Vasily Lvovich, 'Here', was even more in need of Aleksandr.

He was the gloomiest of them all. He liked everything in moderation and believed that whatever they said his Arzamasian name sounded indecent. He had come to see Aleksandr with conflicting feelings. On their journey in the carriage he had boasted a lot to his friends about his nephew.

'His latest epigrams are much better than anything he's ever written,' he said indiscriminately to Vyazemsky, a connoisseur of satire who needed no reminder that the Pushkins had always written epigrams and that his nephew had grown up as his uncle's disciple and follower. Vasily Lvovich felt envious of his nephew, who had joined Arzamas and been given a decent name – Cricket, *without the initiation rituals he himself had had to go through*, and which he couldn't recall without profound regret. It had happened at Uvarov's house. At first everything was jolly and theatrical. He was clothed in a tunic embroidered with sea-shells; a wide-brimmed hat was put on his head and a staff placed in his hands.

He was a pilgrim, and Vasily Lvovich found the ritual quite appropriate – *The Pilgrim* and *The Dawn of Midnight* parodied Slavophile mysticism. Then he was blindfolded, which was all right too. But when he was taken to a cellar, he started to dislike what was being done to him, and from then on it became even worse. He was covered with a few fur-coats – which he was told had been purloined from Shakhovskoy – and nearly suffocated. All this was accompanied by chanting of verses in Church Slavonic. They shouted:

'*Courage! Courage!* Vasily Lvovich!'

He always had courage for anything that made any sense. But he saw no sense in this ritual, which was supposed to echo the nonsensical character of the Symposium. Then they made him shoot at a scarecrow and the scarecrow suddenly shot at him. His friends told him later that it had just been a cracker, but he fell down – not out of fear, of course, but from shock. Then he was baptised in a tub – and it was not amusing in the least, but potentially lethal. On behalf of the Symposium it was announced that Arzamas was a brothel, a gang of robbers and monsters – with which Vasily Lvovich was in almost full agreement.

By way of reward they elected him an Elder of Arzamas. Before the admission of the Cricket, the Elder, 'Here', the Cricket's uncle, had thought that every member had to go through these tiresome rituals. But no, the Cricket had joined *in absentia*! So much for rituals!

Though his own initiation had been an honour, it was somehow immature, disrespectful of his age, and had smacked of buffoonery. But deep in his heart Vasily Lvovich gloated that Karamzin, who of course knew nothing of his own initiation – or perhaps did know – had treated his nephew favourably and was interested in him; the boy promised well and as this at times excessively boisterous Arzamas had sprung from his *Dangerous Neighbour* and his battles with the Slavophiles, so this boy was the fruit of his upbringing – a fact that should not be forgotten.

3

He had visitors; Batyushkov and Vyazemsky had been to see him, but his room was still the same, Number 14 – a bureau, an iron bed and a latticed window above the door. In his poems he called it 'a cell' and himself 'an anchorite' or 'an invalid'; a decanter with cold water became 'an earthenware pitcher'. He was a young thinker; he wrote about languor, death, which was a kind of languor, and a girl in a transparent flimsy shawl. He knew the window across the road, where the fleeting shadow of Natasha used to appear, better than his own. He wrote poems about that window, in which it separated pining lovers, or was opened furtively by a shy hand. One could see the crescent moon from that window, and he nearly wore his eyes out looking at it, but all he could see out of his own was the wing with old witches in it, not a girl in a shawl. Natasha had long been banished. His friends would probably write on his tombstone:

> *Here sleeps a young sage undefiled,*
> *Of languor and Apollo the foster-child.*

He gnawed his quills, struck out lines, roamed about the Lycée, and sometimes sprang out of bed in the middle of the night to scribble down a poem – about indolence.

In the mornings the bewildered Foma picked up the remainders of the quills, grumbling:

'The geese are on the wing again!'

The young thinker lived, enjoyed himself, and died with equal readiness, almost with detachment; he played a simple reed-pipe about which he had once had an argument with Küchlya. They argued about what a reed-pipe actually was. In the end they were amazed to realise that none of them had any idea what it looked like. Küchlya refused point-blank to consider it an ordinary shepherd's pipe.

The young sage was in love and his love and torments would probably end in death, easy death that did not differ from sleep.

One day, in the hall he saw a very young, very slim and tightly corseted young Bakunina, who had come to see her brother, and realised at once that he was in love.

This was a world far removed from his experience in pursuing the maid Natasha or seeing an opera in which that other Natalya sang in her cracked voice. This was a deep, passionate love, though felt from afar. He had called the maid Natasha by this name in his poems, and Natalya – Natalya. But Bakunina he called Eveline, like Parny's beautiful beloved whose name was

Eleanor. To Eveline he could write only elegies.

The need to see her became a ritual for him – if not all of her, at least to catch a glimpse of the hem of her dress behind trees. Once he saw her clothed in black as she walked past the Lycée, talking to somebody. He was happy for three minutes – until she turned the corner. The black dress became her. At night he could not bear to go to bed, looking instead at the trees from behind which she had appeared. He wrote a poem about death which had sat down at his doorway, dressed in black. When he read the poem, its anguish frightened him – he knew that it was an imaginary anguish and an imaginary death but it made his poem even more melancholy. Little did he realise that he simply wanted to see her, not even to talk to her. What could he have said to her? And as time went on, a meeting became more and more impossible and even unnecessary. At nights he pined and sighed.

Once, giving a groan, he froze. He heard exactly the same sigh behind the wall. Pushchin was awake.

They talked. Jeannot reluctantly confessed that he had been in love for the last two weeks, and that it had made him sleepless. Two minutes later Aleksandr found out with amazement that his friend was in love with the very same Eveline – Yekaterina Bakunina.

But strangely enough he was not angry, and it did not cross his mind to be jealous. He listened curiously to Jeannot, who complained that Bakunina rarely came to the Lycée. Next day Pushchin, blushing, thrust a sheet of paper into his hand and demanded that he should read it. He read the page. It was an epistle, written in a light style. For the first time in the poet's life, it ran, a poem had been written by command – the command of a beauty. The author was obviously not Küchlya – he wrote only about friendship and autumn storms; nor by Delvig, who referred to himself in his poems as an old man or a medieval scribe, a Nestor. Pushchin was convinced that it belonged to the beanpole Illichevsky. The first lines troubled Pushchin: written by command – did it mean that they had actually had a tryst?

Aleksandr looked at him and felt pleasure. All three of them were in love with the same girl at the same time. It was amazing. He did not say anything to Illichevsky but when his despondent shadow stalked the corridor, he observed him closely.

When they finally converged, all three of them, face to face – he, Pushchin and Illichevsky, Illichevsky froze, and his jaw dropped when he realised that his secret had been discovered.

The two others' long roars of laughter upset him deeply.

Aleksandr was still glad to catch sight of Bakunina and still kept watch for her, but his nocturnal sighs became less frequent and he slept soundly and calmly till morning. Once he grew genuinely sad when he had not seen her for a few days. But the truth was that he no longer wanted to come into contact with her and was even afraid of an actual encounter: perhaps he had never really been in love with her? He put his poems to her aside and tried to banish her from his mind.

4

He knew that his poems were better than his uncle's – Vasily Lvovich was incapable of poems like these; and even Batyushkov wouldn't spurn the image of death sitting at the poet's doorway. An imaginary earthenware pitcher with clear water – a decanter standing on a simple bureau, a window, a girl; such were love and death to the young thinker, hermit and idler – such were his dreams. He was no longer an invalid with a balalaika, or a monk. He was a sage.

Adults craved a life like this. Gorchakov admired this indolent sage. Diligently, sticking out the tip of his pink tongue, he copied out all his poems, and his eyes dimmed slightly; these poems flattered him. This sage, Apollo's favourite, seemed to enjoy a balance of contentedness and control, his feet on the ground and yet his head in the clouds, very like Gorchakov himself. He did not like to see Gorchakov copying out his poems or to hear his praise.

Once the new Principal gave him a sheet of paper with some poems he had accidentally come across: they were his own.

The Principal approved of them. He gave him the dreamy, slightly melancholy smile of an accomplice, his pale blue eyes hazy, his wide mouth curled in a grin.

The Principal had long been waiting for an occasion to praise his work, and rattled off one quatrain and then another. He had memorised the work of the Lycée poet.

Pushkin gritted his teeth, turned round and walked away. The Principal looked at his receding back; the wide mouth shut, the beatific expression vanished. He put an arm behind his back and slowly returned to his office.

But no, he was neither a sage nor an idler.

After Karamzin, Vasily Lvovich and Vyazemsky had left, he had wandered about the whole evening in a strange state of resolve and self-oblivion, nostrils flared. Danzas held his breath with a pencil in his hand as he watched him, then began a quick sketch but was unable to finish it. When Misha Yakovlev came up to him, he explained that he had tried to draw Pushkin as a monkey composing verse but it hadn't come out: his sketch looked more like Voltaire – with no resemblance to Pushkin. But since Pushkin was a cross between a monkey and a tiger, Danzas then decided to draw him as a tiger preparing to spring; this time the likeness was indeed there, but unfortunately it came out as a real tiger – ready to spring, but strangely preoccupied, laughing abruptly, with blank-looking eyes. Arzamas was waiting for him. He avidly anticipated the moment when his uncle, the Elder of Arzamas, would call upon him to speak. He did not know yet what he would say but he had a good idea how he would be answered.

That night he woke up with his heart thumping – he felt doomed. Karamzin and Vyazemsky had laid their hopes in him. He was in the heat of war, war against the enemies of taste, of poetry, of the intellect, of Karamzin and Zhukovsky. Some elders speaking an outlandish language and behaving like old men from folk-tales, a multitude of scribes and clerks of the Symposium were fussing and scheming.

He wasn't acquainted with them personally. The Symposium had crowned the most dangerous of their gang, Shakhovskoy, with a laurel wreath for his ridicule of Zhukovsky in his play. Dashkov had written an ode, *Jestovskoy's Crowning*, and Vyazemsky had sent it to Aleksandr, who had copied it all down. This Jestovskoy was of a rather different stamp from those of his Symposium colleagues whose surnames also started with S – Shikhmatov and Shishkov. He was witty and Vyazemsky said that the hated play which mocked Zhukovsky was funny and had been a great success with the audience up in the gods. So much the better! He had been blamed for the death of Ozerov,* a decent playwright: making use of his position as a theatre-manager Shakhovskoy had declined Ozerov's play, killing it, and the author had gone mad and died. Here was a crime that cried out for revenge. These enemies laughed at Zhukovsky's elegies, Karamzin's subtleties and Vasily Lvovich's levity. The bearded old fossils scoffed at common sense. He hadn't read and never would read their antediluvian poems, their schismatic prayers, their shrill ancient Russian scribbles that they called odes. He was a hereditary enemy of those fanatical, nasal-sounding, Orthodox scribes and barbarians. This was war! It was unfair to keep him, with his passionate heart, in seclusion and not allow him to enjoy the innocent delight of burying 'the destroyers of Russian literature' (the Amateurs of the Russian Word had long been nicknamed 'the Destroyers'†) – and all those members of the Symposium with their decorations, ribbons and stars!

War!

But here in Tsarskoye Selo he could not attend Arzamas meetings and taste the renowned Arzamasian goose. Instead he saw the slanting shadow of an unprepossessingly dressed general strolling despondently towards the Palace

---

* See footnote on page 469.
† Amateurs … 'Destroyers' – *Lyubiteli* … '*Gubiteli*'.

accompanied by a corpulent Commandant.

The general had a meaty nose and the pendulous parted lips of an HQ clerk. He halted and said something to the Commandant in a nasal voice, and seeing how the portly Commandant stood to attention and cowered in front of him, Aleksandr realised it was Arakcheyev. The general looked around with dim eyes, put an arm behind his back, and apparently oblivious of all these statues, columns and the whole place with all its old glory, stuck out his chest and proceeded into the Palace.

Aleksandr had been gnawing his quill writing a poem about an unknown beauty. When he looked around he felt that the general and the Commandant had filled this garden with a frightful banality which left no room either for women or for poetry. He stuck the sheet of paper with the poem into his pocket.

War!

Flaring his nostrils, he was writing now about 'The Symposium of Destroyers of the Russian Word'. Though he did not know those barbarians personally, and had never met either the grey-haired old Shishkov or the monk-like Shikhmatov, he had the feeling that he had.

It was they who secretly sneaked round the Lycée. Their names did not matter – all things old hindered progress. The poet Sumarokov whom Shishkov had promoted to genius was just an envious dwarf; Jestovskoy was a villain.

Galich had unwittingly helped him. The fat and gracious apostle of languor, or simply indolence, had no inhibitions and had given them a talk about satire.

Satire could be personal (libel), private or general. Libel pinpointed the particular way of thinking and acting of an individual and sacrificed his dubious honour for the sake of the general welfare, chastising those mad or depraved persons whose harmful influence on society's morals could not be checked by any other means. Personal satire targeted the follies, eccentricities, vices and even physical defects of mainly contemporary compatriots.

Holding his breath, with a fixed smile, without taking notes, Aleksandr listened to this podgy intellectual.

So poetry was not to be found only in the music of elegiac complaint, in his love for the girl he called Eveline, not only in generalised satire in mockery of monks and grey-haired mothers superior – in close proximity to the Palace as he was – but in personal and private as well as general satire. He was looking forward to engaging with his enemies. It was for good reason that his uncle had been received into Arzamas wearing a Jacobin hood.

War!

5

Pushkin, Pushchin and Lomonosov had received invitations to a ball at the Bakunins'.

Aleksandr had been nervous the whole day: it was his first experience of 'society'. Eveline was waiting for him. He had no idea what the encounter with Katerina Bakunina would be like.

Lomonosov asked Foma to give his uniform buttons a good rub with a piece of chalk and admired the way they now gleamed. Jeannot tried to stretch out his trousers – he had grown out of them – but finally gave up the attempt.

Off they went to the ball. Aleksandr was sombre and awkward; he had written too many poems to Eveline to relish seeing her in reality or even to harbour any expectations.

The Bakunins' windows were brightly lit; female shadows flitted behind them and he suddenly became breathless, burst out laughing, took Jeannot by the arm and said he would dance tonight.

Jeannot, also in love, was going to dance too.

Hundreds of candles were lit; the musicians tuned their violins.

Pale, with sloping shoulders, an uneven flush on her cheeks, Bakunina met them with the smile he had feared. Perhaps she wasn't so beautiful after all? He noticed for the first time that she took after her mother. A group of pale young men looking strangely alike surrounded the mother. These were the ladies' men, the gossip-mongers whom Pushchin hated so much. The elder Bakunina adored them. Two hussars with pelisses slung from their shoulders came up to them: Solomirsky and Chaadayev, both of them renowned dandies, rumours of whose foppishness and rivalry had kept Tsarskoye Selo society entertained. They liked to turn up at balls together, almost never talking or looking at one another, followed by gazing female eyes. The fans swayed, the belles exchanged remarks.

Eveline's female friends burst out laughing, and both hussars, as if by a command, headed towards them.

The dancing started. Young Bakunina and Solomirsky opened the ball.

Wherever Chaadayev went, he became the man of the moment; others were of no consequence – the elder Bakunina was aware of this, and the news of his new appointment had already reached her.

Chaadayev was dancing the mazurka, and as usual the ladies wondered what his secret was – he was neither handsome nor ardent as befitted the dance; he danced without dash or fire. Eveline remarked that he looked like a statue. Everyone agreed. He danced neither quickly nor slowly, and when he gave a reluctant, slow smile, it looked like a reward to all the ladies and they smiled back. Aleksandr gazed at him spellbound.

They were coming back together. Chaadayev walked with careful tread, never brushing against the twigs of the trees or swinging his arms. You couldn't have found a smarter uniform; you couldn't have found a more upright person. Approaching the barracks, Aleksandr felt that his companion was a very clever man. He was not the slave of chance.

6

In the Principal's opinion Pushkin was a most difficult and incomprehensible example of a young man who always acted contrary to his own interests.

When put in charge of this weird and controversial institution, the new Principal had first of all tried to understand its goals and to ensure that everyone understood his position. He was ready to tame – with kind-heartedness.

Principal Yegor Antonovich Engelhardt strove for correctness in everything. Brought up in a large but modest Lithuanian town, from the very beginning of his career in state service he had made a point of not seeking a complete understanding of everything that happened but of thoroughly thinking through each step – his own and other people's. The unpredictable Emperor Paul had made him Secretary of the Maltese Order. Having only a vague idea of why the Emperor needed this order, Engelhardt had immediately learnt by heart all the articles of its statute, and he could recite any of them without hesitation. This had impressed the Emperor. Tsar Aleksandr Pavlovich, his successor, was not so good at memorising statutes and Engelhardt had volunteered to be his tutor, coming to his rescue on more than one occasion. In this way he had discovered the major objectives of the pedagogical profession – namely, to teach a young man how to avoid trouble and how to discipline himself in such a way that order becomes second nature to him.

In 1812 he had become the Director of the Pedagogical Institute. He was well-educated, good-natured and tolerant. He read selected extracts from the best philosophers – both classical and modern; and always derived some benefit even from the most obscure and worthless ones. Nor did he refuse to read and to derive benefit from the free-thinkers, who were coming into fashion again. Engelhardt had become used to changing trends and always followed the latest vogue. In theory he approved of free-thinking.

Count Arakcheyev took a liking to him, despite his learning. Engelhardt, incapable of passing over a lucky chance, had bought land in Tsarskoye Selo, some way off from the Palace. Encounters with the Emperor, infrequent and insignificant, but all the more pleasant for that, had soon brought him to His Majesty's attention.

When Engelhardt was summoned by Count Arakcheyev to be told about his appointment as the Lycée Principal, he wrote a memorandum on the Lycée on the spot, in Arakcheyev's office. Arakcheyev was accustomed to introducing order wherever it was needed, as he had done with the Emperor's youthful indiscretions. The school was in utter chaos, the students were out of control, the institution itself had a dubious reputation. The memorandum was written with dignity and intelligence. He insisted that the Principal should be liberated from any petty and distracting dependency on the authorities that would be constantly obstructing his actions: 'The Principal of an institution should be like the father of a family and run it accordingly.'

This was exactly what was needed.

Arakcheyev repeated:

'The father of a family ...'

And Engelhardt, bowing his head, quietly agreed with his own idea:

' ... of a family.'

Slowly and imperceptibly the Principal started to look about him, searching for ways into hearts and minds. He realised that only the junior students of the future would be, so to speak, the children of his heart; as far as the seniors were concerned, he was sure of one thing: they had to stay at the Lycée for another year and a half and they would benefit from any improvement, however trifling.

Gradually he learned their tastes, inclinations and little weaknesses. Major faults were considered a breach of good manners and had to be firmly dealt with; but he turned a blind eye to minor misdemeanours. He was struck by one thing: despite the students' secret or passionately displayed ambitions, which had been encouraged by the first Principal Malinovsky and his friend Kunitsyn, despite their undoubted confidence that they were destined for greatness, nevertheless, it was quite unclear what career awaited them and what they would do after their graduation.

He began by wiping out the pernicious tendency towards passion which had formed under the first Principal, eager to erase his memory from their hearts. Then he tried to convert this objectless and therefore dangerous orientation of their minds to more modest everyday ambition. He had long talks with Korff and praised him for his understanding. Not serving the motherland but rather a successful career was the only thing that could make a young man truly happy. Gorchakov, Lomonosov and Korsakov had the style, manners and inclinations that would make them suitable for the diplomatic service. He remembered how in his youth he had started his career as a diplomatic courier, and he decided to teach them how to make diplomatic envelopes, not an easy matter because an envelope for diplomatic documents had to be made without scissors. He taught them the forms of correspondence and how to write dispatches and keep a diary. He enjoyed recalling these things, and his charges were glad to pick up these details before taking up their appointments.

Sitting down with them, he good-humouredly recalled amusing incidents and anecdotes about kings and diplomats. He had been attending the Aachen Congress and had seen almost all the sovereigns of Europe. Gorchakov listened to him avidly. In this way the Principal began to prepare them for the adroitness and sophistication necessary for that precarious but brilliant walk of life.

Other Lycéeists were even simpler to deal with: Valkhovsky and Matyushkin, for example, had enrolled in a civilian and not a military school by mere chance. Early experiences had made Engelhardt wary of military drill, and he was unwilling to introduce it at the Lycée in case Arakcheyev started meddling in the Lycée's affairs. His task was much more complex. It was easy to prepare an army officer: not so easy to educate a Minister.

He hadn't turned his back on Speransky's plan which he had heard so much about, but he wanted to give it a more modest and practical shape. In short, he wished his students to be successful, and the rays of their success would also illuminate him, their Principal and father.

But the third kind of boy was the most difficult and dangerous: Pushkin, Delvig and Küchelbecker – the poets. Küchelbecker was quite uncomplicated and despite his quirks he was kind and did not bear grudges. Delvig was a supercilious mocker. But Pushkin …

Engelhardt had his own ideas as to how to build the success of this student who had earned Derzhavin's approval so quickly and effortlessly at the examination and enjoyed the favour of Karamzin and others without any particular right to it. But while he was at the Lycée he had to be made to remember his place.

Engelhardt approved of poetry, very much so, but he approved of it as an educative means, as entertainment, as something women were fond of, and last of all as a pleasant and sober occupation. He disapproved of it as a *passion*. Those goose quills gnawed to the quick, those sharp, fleeting or blank stares, that wild smile – it was all passion. He had tried to appeal to Pushkin's better nature but when he heard his cruel laughter at some sad and innocent passage from an outmoded poet, he shuddered. He realised that Pushkin was arrogant and cold and lacked good nature. Too early an acquaintance with and encouragement from all these writers visiting him at the Lycée had inflated his ego and corrupted his pride. Frankly speaking, his poems were frigid too, and in Engelhardt's opinion poetry should have warmth above all else.

Deep in his heart, though he would never have confessed it, Engelhardt would have been delighted to be close to Karamzin, whereas it was this schoolboy Karamzin had come to see. And when the Principal had talked to Pushkin about his poems, the response to his compliments – silence, detachment, disregard for his praise and even obvious disdain for it – had shocked him.

Engelhardt was neither a ladies' man nor a hypocrite. Devotions took up a strictly limited amount of his time. But he believed contempt for the church to be something black and nefarious, redolent of inquests and prosecution. Recalling his previous work in the Maltese Order, he was well aware of the significance of religion, in all its aspects, for one's career and a stable and respectable life. Rumour had reached him about Pushkin's scribbling, near-criminal stuff about monks, *nuns* and so forth. He was no prig, however, and he did not want to go into it.

The only other way to the heart of this young man was *women*. Engelhardt was an experienced man and knew what weight – sometimes crucial – a woman's smile or word of approval might have. He wasn't old – a man of pleasantly middle age, forty. He was still an accomplished dancer. It was hard to remember what he had been like at the age of twenty, and almost impossible to imagine what he would be like at sixty. He was determined that his students should acquire polite manners and polish in female company. He realised why Pushkin was so cold, abrupt and impertinent with him – it was the influence of the hussars' barracks that he had taken to frequenting. But he couldn't put an end to these visits. So he decided to organise evenings at his own home and to invite the Lycéeists and the ladies of his family circle. This might draw Pushkin closer to him, and even tame him. He had had occasion to observe that even cut-throats could become *chevaliers servants* and *cavaliers gallants*, soft as wax, in female society.

7

The Principal had decisively erased the traces of the previous inhabitant of his house. There were flowers everywhere, and an artist had painted floral murals. The evening would have been a success had it not been for Pushkin.

He was impossible during the dancing. First, he was a poor dancer – but that was no great matter; apart from Gorchakov all the Lycéeists danced badly and it merely made people smile. The trouble was that a distant relative of Engelhardt, Marie Smith, was paying a visit to his family. This young lady's lot was a touching one – she was a widow. And so Pushkin began to demonstrate as zealously as he could that he was touched – but it would have been better if it had been by the young widow's circumstances, not by her charms.

He held her close and became quite breathless during the dancing. To his amazement Engelhardt noticed that the cultivated young Mrs Smith (née

Charon-Larose, a relative of his wife) was not left indifferent by the scapegrace's advances; her face glowed. With a slight gesture of his hand the Principal stopped the music. Yet another initiative had produced the opposite effect on Pushkin from that intended – and moreover, a scandalous effect. This youth had reduced his light-hearted social occasion with young ladies and gentlemen to the level of the Schuster Club* ... Engelhardt had been envious of the Bakunins' ball and had wanted to emulate it – Marie was in no way inferior to Bakunina! He had planned that she would be his modest queen of the ball. And now ... But even more alarmingly, the boy and Marie suddenly disappeared, and the Principal had to search for them in the garden *personally*. Fortunately he discovered them. He would never invite Pushkin to his house again, but who could guarantee that the reprobate would not arrange a tryst – tomorrow or in a week's time, in his garden, or somewhere in the vicinity?

8

The Karamzins took up residence on the twenty-fourth of May. Nikolay Mikhaylovich had left the Moscow he was so fond of on a single friendly, casual word from the Tsar, for which he had waited five years. Appointed His Majesty's historiographer and adviser, he was going to live in a damp, cramped and uncomfortable chalet in the 'Village in Chinese Taste' in the Catherine Park at Tsarskoye Selo. The Village, consisting of a handful of tiny houses with narrow windows and decoratively painted eaves and walls, situated not far from the Small Caprice, was unfinished. In four of the chalets porcelain stoves, fire-places and wall-tiles had been put in, but the rest had been abandoned and become homes for bats.

The chalets were intended for bachelor courtiers. Pleasant-looking little gardens surrounded them. Karamzin looked at the three dainty dwellings he had picked for himself and his household with a secret bitterness, afraid to confess either to himself or to anyone else that these structures were playhouses, pretty and pleasant to look at, but most inconvenient to live in. Turgenev, who had petitioned for him to the Tsar and had had the chalets prepared, would have been highly offended. Before his wife, Katerina Andreyevna, Karamzin always showed complete composure. His Majesty had recently taken to walking by the Village and had already presented his wife with a bunch of flowers that he had plucked himself. The hidden bitterness never left Karamzin. The Tsar came to see his historiographer and adviser, but never once did they actually talk. Karamzin turned white when he saw the expression on the Emperor's pale, seductive face as he gave the flowers to his

* A club in St Petersburg whose membership consisted mostly of shopkeepers and artisans.

beautiful wife. But he had to publish his *History of the Russian State*, and so he resigned himself to his lot and prepared to wait.

In the mornings, in his study-chalet, he looked through the manuscripts written in his large and distinct handwriting and corrected tiny flaws. At three in the afternoon he would put on his black English riding coat and a grey Arab would be saddled for him. He would ride and his servant would walk before him. Sometimes Karamzin pointed out mushrooms and the servant picked them.

He never met the Emperor on these rides, perhaps he never would, and was almost glad of that.

Then followed dinner and evening tea.

How idle and free his life had become after the completion of his work; how affectionately he was treated at Court; how little notice was taken of him by the enigmatic Tsar!

He endured the artificiality of his current dwelling, the artificiality of the position he found himself in, like an ancient Stoic – with a smile. That was why, hearing the quick quiet strides of Pushkin, who had no idea what Karamzin's inner life was really like, he slammed his diary shut. That was why he forgave him the expression with which he looked at Katerina Andreyevna, a silently imploring expression, the meaning of which the ageing historiographer knew only too well.

9

Pushkin saw this beautiful composure, these attentive grey eyes, for the first time. Lomonosov, who accompanied him, barely recognised him. He had grown used to Pushkin's silence, he knew that Pushkin was shy and prepared to shine next to the sombre, unsociable poet. It wasn't difficult for Lomonosov to be witty.

But Pushkin didn't even allow him to open his mouth: he had been transformed.

It was as if he had found himself, as if he had only now understood what he was. In three minutes he achieved his aim. He heard Katerina Andreyevna's clear laughter and saw how surprised Karamzin was – he hadn't heard laughter like this for years.

Next day, after classes, he quickly had dinner and ran to the Karamzins. It was the hour when Karamzin was in the habit of going out for a walk. She was in her chalet, at her embroidery frame, and was surprised and startled to see him.

'Anyone walking by this isolated hut can easily peep through these windows,' she explained uneasily.

Then she made him unfold the silk threads and, kneeling before her, he gazed intently at the long fingers that picked the silk from his hands so calmly and adroitly. Soon she dismissed him, saying that they would be looking for him and he would be punished. He shouldn't hide from his Principal. He left in despair: he was nothing more than a schoolboy to her.

Now he even forgot the way to the hussars whom he had grown so used to, and who had grown so used to him; his fate was sealed. Instead he visited the Chinese Village every day.

And what of the young widow whom he had named Lila?

But she had nothing to do with the Chinese Village. It would be an offence even to think about her here. In his hostess's presence, he could think of no other woman, even though he was nothing more than a schoolboy to her.

10

And a schoolboy was exactly what he was – in his Principal's opinion a schoolboy capable of anything.

Every evening the Principal looked down from his balcony and twice spotted Pushkin making off as fast as he could. If it had been anybody else he would have had a heart-to-heart talk with him. Engelhardt could not prevent the senior students from having late walks, but he decided not to allow juniors to have them in future. He frowned. He knew about Pushkin's visits to the hussars' barracks. What might he have learned there, next to the stables! He also knew that these visits had now ceased and that every evening Pushkin was at the Karamzins', which was quite a different matter. But still the Principal watched to see if the young widow was about – just in case. And often, to his disappointment, he found she wasn't. Then he began his solitary walks about the Tsarskoye Selo gardens, secretly afraid of what he might find. He did not trust the young widow: she had sobbed a little on the first day of her arrival – for decency's sake. She was young and given to laughter.

She was bored – Engelhardt wasn't particularly entertaining company. And though this schoolboy lacked good looks, she had immediately singled him out – probably out of her very boredom. Hence her blushing and breathlessness while dancing, signs the Principal had spotted at once and knew to be inspired by Pushkin.

Bakunina was his Eveline. The young widow had become his Lila. The very name sounded like a kiss.*

The Principal was right to be afraid of what he might come across in the gardens – perhaps he might find them kissing? They were indeed having

---

* *Potseluy* or *lobzaniye* in Russian.

trysts, and she was helpless, submissive and eager – her guilty kisses were hungry. For the first time in his life he learned what power over a woman was; she gave herself to him unconditionally. Yes, he was a mere schoolboy, and perhaps he particularly relished the fact that she was a young widow: at their trysts he imagined the shade of her jealous husband appearing from the cold realm of the dead to take revenge on the lovers. It was not only the late husband, however, who might have appeared to him, but another shadow – the Principal, who had a nose for such things, now prowled about the gardens on the watch for the lovers.

II

Another of Engelhardt's aims and hopes was to encounter the Emperor. An accidental meeting, the monarch's careless nod, would guarantee the Lycée's and his own welfare for years. During his walks the Principal often thought about the future. He wished his charges success, which would be his too, as their 'father', and this success depended on the Palace. As for his achievements, which seemed so effortless to strangers, they had been hard-won.

Friendship, together with the prospects for the future of his wards, his 'sons', was blossoming. It was not only the 'diplomats' – Gorchakov, Lomonosov, Korsakov – who were friendly with him, both at his evenings and in the realm of ideas. He had made friends with Pushchin too, having won his goodwill by the justice and benevolence with which he had resolved the quarrel between Küchelbecker and Malinovsky.

Only the Spartan Valkhovsky, minion of the first Principal, met his favours politely but unsmilingly. He was extremely, excessively virtuous and honest. Ah, young man, don't get carried away!

Les extrémités se touchent – he was disliked by the most virtuous, Valkhovsky, and the most wanton, Pushkin.

He thought of the likely future of each of them: Valkhovsky, with his straightforward passionate nature, would choose the military – state service would be too subtle for him (God bless him!). It was no longer necessary to think about what kind of success he might meet with.

But Pushkin was a different matter.

The Principal hated him for his arrogance and callousness, and begrudged him any future success at all. But after all, he was responsible for him, and if the Lycée could bring up diplomats, why couldn't it produce successful poets? And it should never be forgotten that the Palace was nearby. Searching for the all-too passionate young widow, the Principal was fearful of the Palace's proximity and at the same time wished for nothing else.

12

Now every morning Pushkin woke up with a new objective: he had to be certain that in the evening he would sit at the round table, see and hear her slow French speech, so different from the burring guttural speech of his mother and the babbling of all the young women he had ever met. Everything was tranquil and reliable in that house, at that table, in her presence. An occasional softly voiced question from Karamzin, this great man with the sadly curved mouth, the silence of this museum-like sanctum, the occasional pranks of their children who ran in from next door – and she would be there, she would always be there, with her grey intelligent eyes. He couldn't imagine this room without her. He forgot the hussars, his Lycée time was running short. Although it was difficult and she had forbidden him to do so, he would appear at untimely hours – he hated seeing them together. The Chinese Village was a stone's throw from the Lycée. Once he came when she was out. It was a dull and rainy summer. He found Karamzin alone. Muffled up in a rug, he was sitting by the fire made up for him by his servant. He did not look like an adviser to the Tsar; he was just an old man of letters, alone in his cold beautiful study.

He was cold himself, he had cooled. Nothing disturbed or could disturb his peace here. Vyazemsky had said that Karamzin treated his post as if he had taken monastic vows – indeed, he was a dedicated monk. He had cultivated his equanimity and was certain that if they followed his advice, the whole country and its turbulent history would achieve the longed-for peace, would find it in the existing order – the only possible if not particularly comforting cure. Peace in Russia depended on the wise system of serfdom and it was silly and useless to argue with this natural law, central to the Russian way of life. And his own peace rested on reconciliation with the existing order, even though it might be unpleasant at times; he put up with it for the certain and sound rewards it would bring. He believed in it in spite of the fact that his pride was stung and he sometimes felt a void around him.

At long last, success came. Just as the Tsar had once received him immediately after he had had an interview with Arakcheyev, now next day, after he had given flowers to Katerina Andreyevna, His Majesty suddenly gave permission for the publication of the *History*. But Karamzin was torn by doubts, his troubles were not over yet. It was a bitter blow to him that for some reason his work was to be printed by the military printing house, more suited to producing orders than historical books. The director of the printing house, General Zakharzhevsky, had today returned the manuscript with the request that it be submitted for censorship. He thought the State Historiographer was above censorship! The only censorship he was subject to was that of the Tsar – and no one else! This odious general, envious of his position in Tsarskoye Selo, appeared to be overstepping the limits of his power. But then – he might not be ... Karamzin had to keep silent! Suddenly he felt a burning and barely suppressible desire to complain to Pushkin, this Cricket, and could barely contain himself. He knew that this young man, the amusing Pushkin's nephew, who followed women with his passionate stares, wrote ardent poems and fretted at the Lycée, would soon calm down. Karamzin was interested in the education of the young: how impetuous and precipitate Speransky had been in setting up these educational institutions everywhere without any system or plan. What seeds for the future!

But it seemed the only people he could really relax with in the world were the Arzamasians and the Lycéeists with their eagerness, their nonsense and spontaneity, their ceaseless laughter and debates. He asked Pushkin to read something new to him and prepared to listen. Pushkin pulled a sheet of paper out of his pocket, flushed and hid it again. Karamzin, with a shrug of his shoulders, gently asked him to read. He knew that his gentle requests were never refused. Pushkin started to read and became flustered, but gradually his voice grew firmer.

Listening to the Lycée poet reading his latest poem, Karamzin suddenly realised that Pushkin had brought it here, to his house, in order to read it to Katerina Andreyevna.

My uneventful days drag slowly by ...

... Let me die, but let me die in love!

How he had read that last line!
To whom had he written it?
The poem itself was marvellous. Karamzin smiled silently, nodded without a word of comment, and said goodbye to him with warmth.

Yes, he was afraid to confess it here, but in Tsarskoye Selo he would have been completely alone had it not been for these youths. The other day he had finished the foreword to his cherished work – and there was no one to show it to. Turgenev was busy and he hadn't seen him for some time. When the diplomat Lomonosov and the poet Pushkin were sitting with him in his house, he seized a moment of silence and, with the manuscript of the foreword to hand, read it to them, the first to hear it, his credo. And from the very first phrase, as he read it he noticed that some corrections were required, something he hadn't realised before. *For a nation, history is like the Bible for Christians*, he began to read – and stopped, looking at his listeners. Oh, the bright eyes of youth! All lofty and obscure words acquired here, in Tsarskoye Selo, their true meaning. 'The Bible', 'Christians' – Lord have mercy! These were words that Prince Golitsyn* might have used. He could be nearby in the Palace talking at this very moment about the Bible and Christians. And without ceremony, on the spot, in these young men's presence, he made an amendment: *History is the holy book of the people.*

He went on reading, casting glances at Pushkin.

All of us are citizens – Europeans, Indians, Mexicans or Abyssinians. The personality of every individual is tightly bound up with his fatherland – we love it because we love ourselves. It is not Greeks or Romans who captivate our imagination: they belong to the human race and are not strangers to us by virtue of their virtues and weaknesses, triumphs and calamities. But for a Russian ear a Russian name has a particular charm. My heart beats faster when I read about Pozharsky rather than Themistocles or Scipio.

… It ought to be appreciated that from time immemorial, stormy passions have stirred up civil society …

Pushkin sat quietly and only his eyes, like those of his mother, the beautiful Creole whom the historiographer had recalled a number of times, lit up or dimmed expressively. It was so quiet that the listeners seemed to be holding their breath. They were his real listeners, for whose sake he was imprisoned in this bird's cage, in this beautiful Chinese chalet. When he had finished and turned back to the first page, Pushkin recited it to him – by heart. And for the first moment in all this time when he had had to wait humbly for the imperial audience, had had to conceal from his wife his anguish, his emptiness, his old age, when he had had to smile and smile – the ageing writer felt happy.

He stood up and touched Pushkin's hand as he walked past him. He left the room and wiped his tears away behind the door.

He also read to this young poet a page that lay on his knees for checking against his notes – a passage about the carefree Golden Age, about Prince Vladimir called 'Vladimir the Red Sun' by his subjects, and how Vladimir ordered three hundred pots of mead to be brewed and feasted for a week with the boyars in Vasilev and revelled in the strong brew. *And from then on,* Karamzin read to Pushkin, *in the Palace hall, the Prince entertained the boyars, sword-bearers and distinguished and specially invited persons with weekly feasts.*

Pushkin's gaze flitted distractedly about the room; he was looking for a

---

* President of the Bible Society in Russia and (1805–1817) Minister for Religious Affairs. He was a close friend of Alexander I from childhood; his pietistic conservatism had a strong influence on the Tsar, and especially when he was Minister of Education (1816–24) made a most retrograde impact on Russia's development.

pencil and paper. Catching sight of both on the table he picked them up, started to gnaw the pencil – his bad habit – suddenly asked the meaning of some obsolete words, wrote down the answers and bit his lip (so much for the manners Sergey Lvovich had taught his son!). Karamzin was amused, and after these questions inserted some explanations into his text to satisfy readers who might think of the same questions.

'Why don't you write a nice little poem, in the old tradition – something humorous, decorous and subtle?'

But Pushkin seemed to gaze through him and wrinkled his nose at this advice. His wilfulness was amazing – Sergey Lvovich exactly. Maybe he didn't like the words 'nice little poem'? But Karamzin himself wrote such poems, *Ilya Muromets*, for example, and never considered them unworthy. What was needed for this genre was humour, decorum, grace, and these were anything but trifling. Pushkin's eyes wandered; he was not listening, but sat gnawing the pencil. At length Karamzin reached out and took the pencil from him. Pushkin did not take offence; his thoughts were wandering until he was ready to talk again. No, he was not Sergey Lvovich. In this mental wandering he was more like his mother, *la belle Créole*. And he definitely took after her in his facial features too.

13

That year their walks meant more to them than their lessons. The teachers did not demand silence in class; discipline had long been forgotten and the masters cared only about the examinations that loomed over both pupils and staff alike. Only Myasoyedov occasionally found himself at the black table, not because of his ignorance but because of his rudeness. Kunitsyn had grown quieter, and was stooped and stern. He listened indifferently to Korff's regurgitation of his previous lecture from which he had dutifully taken notes, and corrected any omissons. He never questioned Pushkin – he knew that he almost never took notes. But Kunitsyn was the only master Pushkin listened to; they seemed to understand each other well. Such partiality made Korff grit his teeth.

Only once, when explaining to them the concept of the social contract, did Kunitsyn become roused as he had in previous times.

'Tyrants violate the social contract,' he said, 'but since supreme power belongs to the people, the contract is then annulled on both sides once and for all.'

He paused, his cheeks flushed. Küchlya screeched with his quill, scattering ink.

Kunitsyn calmed down, and in a low voice asked them to note that he was referring to the past.

Küchlya put his quill aside.

Now their walks were regulated: the Court was in Tsarskoye Selo. They were supposed to make no noise and to walk in a file in orderly fashion: the Emperor liked orderly formation and flew into a temper when he noticed people walking out of step, even if they were civilians.

Pushkin, Delvig and Küchelbecker had made a pact to walk separately from the others. They strolled behind the rest of the file, arm in arm, debating Horace, Parny, Rousseau, Schiller, Shikhmatov, old Shishkov, and female inconstancy.

These days they read all the periodicals as they were published – even Küchlya's mother in Moscow subscribed to an old-fashioned magazine called *Amphion*; she paid fifteen roubles for it and had to skip a visit to the Lycée. Lomonosov even had his own bookcase with two or three hundred books of his own. Boudri brought books for Küchlya. Küchlya shed copious tears over *The Vicar of Wakefield*; a volume of Gresset was pounced upon by Pushkin.

Küchelbecker was a vehement debater. Delvig almost always disagreed with him. Pushkin enjoyed their debates; they all stuck to their own opinions, which were often at opposite extremes. Once Küchlya called Horace a self-satisfied society fop, a pedant like Koshansky; at this, the other two stopped in their tracks. Another time, taking against Küchelbecker, who always carried Homer about with him in Greek and made efforts to recite the text in a doleful voice, Pushkin called Homer a babbler, and he and Delvig were delighted with the expression of horror on Küchlya's face. Now that Pushkin was an Arzamasian, he listened impatiently to Küchlya's praise of Shikhmatov-the-Rhymer and his ode to Peter the Great.

Once Gorchakov, who enjoyed light verse and copied it out from whatever sources he could find, showed him a French Revolutionary poem in which three surnames were scorned in alternating couplets:

> *Vit-on jamais rien de si sot*
> *Que Merlin, Basire et Chabot?*
> *A t'-on jamais rien vu de pire*
> *Que Chabot, Merlin et Basire?*
> *Et vit-on rien de plus coquin*
> *Que Chabot, Basire et Merlin?*

An hour later Pushkin read Küchelbecker a couplet in the same metre ridiculing the three Princes of the Slavophiles whose surnames started with *Sh*.

> *Shishkov, Shikhmatov, Shakhovskoy.*
> *Shikhmatov, Shakhovskoy, Shishkov.*

The very names of the members of the Symposium sounded as if they had been created for epigrams and could be metrically arranged with ease. Küchlya demanded to know who was the author of that scribble which, like all epigrams, he did not consider a poem.

Kunitsyn's lecture on ancient tribes plunged them deep in thought. They had got used to seeing historical reminders on their walks. They had been walking past them for five years – every day; the Chesme rostral column in the lake and the Kagul monument had their own special significance for all of them. Here was the Classical Antiquity Delvig was so fond of in his poems. Passing by the Kagul cast-iron monument, Pushkin always touched it and the chill under his fingers never failed to surprise him.

After the final victory over Napoleon the Tsar came back to his Palace – and everyone expected miracles. Nowadays either he or the Empress came for short stays – just three or four days, when they were free between European congresses. The Lycéeists had got used to the peculiarly brisk and unsteady gait of the ladies-in-waiting, who always passed them in a hurry.

Later they saw him a few times – plump and fair-haired, walking along the alley with his chest stuck out, in small measured steps. They were aware that he was going to Babolovo, that he had again arranged a tryst with the Commandant's young daughter. Gorchakov told them about it, gasping. From some sources or other he knew absolutely everything about the Tsar: when he got up, when he prayed, whom he had dinner with, whether he talked much to the officer on duty. He considered this kind of news a political matter and shared it only with a chosen few. He knew all the new regimental uniforms designed by the Tsar and Arakcheyev. Once he told Pushkin that the Tsar had visited Karamzin but hadn't appointed him to a high academic post and was not in a hurry to start publishing his *History* in order not to elevate him excessively in others' eyes. Karamzin had made a mistake – he shouldn't have been in so much of a hurry.

But the Palace stayed silent, with the curtains in almost all the windows half-drawn. Who was staying there? A demi-god, the conqueror of Napoleon? The ruler of half the world? Or the flabby-thighed friend of Arakcheyev and Golitsyn? The sentinels at the main staircase stood like statues.

Soon they learned that they wouldn't be staying at the Lycée much longer: Count Razumovsky had issued an order bringing their graduation forward by three months. By June 1817 'there will be no trace of us here', Malinovsky said in his Cossack-like manner. They tried to guess who was hounding them out. Gorchakov suddenly made a subtle suggestion.

'It must be our dear and highly respectable Principal who is trying to drive us out as soon as possible,' he said, 'since he can't claim the whole credit for our class if it's successful.'

Matyushkin indignantly objected to this and so did Pushchin, who trusted the Principal and immediately gave his opinion:

'It's the Tsar.'

And to the quiet question 'why?', Jeannot replied meaningfully:

'We make too much noise ... And we stare too much.'

14

She was the wife of a famous husband. Her life was serene, apart from the inconvenience caused by the uncertainty of their current situation at Court, where she would be making her appearance in the winter. Soon her husband's renowned scholarly work, the fruit of many years' labour, would be published. The first proofs were to arrive soon. He was eager to see them and she, as always and without question, would help him to read them with that care and attentiveness of hers which she was well aware was her most appealing characteristic. They would spend every day working at this table, reading the proofs and checking the notes – in their Chinese chalet, among the flowers. There were many flowers here, too many – they were sent to her every day from the Palace. She knew perfectly well why her husband had received the long-awaited permission to publish his *History*. He did not seem to realise the reason. Well, she would have to use the abilities she knew she had, in her walk, her eyes, her voice, and to remain – not for the first time! – unavailable. Tsarskoye Selo was no fun. In the evenings the Lycéeists would come; she loved their laughter and arguments. Pushkin, wild, restless and twitchy, would become shy when she approached him, his eyes would grow dim, and every time she would have to encourage him with a smile or a word. And what anecdotes about the Symposium – her husband's ludicrous opponents – escaped his lips when she looked at him! He was seventeen, sometimes it was frightening to think how young they all were. And she was thirty-six.

She had been serenely happy.

And now she was unhappy.

Nobody could guess what had cost her that serenity. She had lost control over herself a few times recently, which had never happened before, and quarrelled with her poor stepdaughter, then she had cried and bitten her handkerchief, and now in the mornings she could hardly wait to get out of the hothouse she lived in, to leave her wise and celebrated husband and the children – to be alone. Sometimes she pictured her whole life as a failure, from childhood. Her spinster aunt, Obolenskaya, had brought her up. On holidays she would be taken to the huge house of the Vyazemskys, and would kiss the old Prince's fleshy cheek, and he would stroke her head. She had known that this was her father and guessed vaguely at some irremediable tragedy. Her surname was not Vyazemskaya but Kolyvanova, and she was not a princess. She had asked her aunt many times where her surname had come from, and her aunt had explained to her that it had been given to her after the Estonian town, Reval, where she had been born: Reval was Kolyvan in Russian, and therefore her name was Kolyvanova. Once, out on a walk, her aunt had pointed out a pale, strikingly beautiful lady and had told her it was her mother. That was the beginning and the end of her acquaintance with her mother. She was of humble origin – she heard her governess saying quietly that she was an illegitimate daughter. That was when she started to bite her handkerchief. At twenty-two she had fallen in love with a poor ensign with a similarly unprepossessing surname, Strukov. So deeply had she fallen in love with him that she had to be very quickly married off. The old Prince had given her a highly substantial dowry, so that she was a lucrative prospect. Consequently she had been married off well – to an intelligent, refined and famous person: a widower and fourteen years older than herself.

And then she had become more settled, the faithful wife of a famous husband, a virtuous mother for their children and a kind-hearted stepmother to his daughter.

But no, she was not a kind-hearted stepmother. In the same way that she had grown up without a mother and father and her own place had been occupied by her half-brothers and sisters – for instance, the red-haired, clever and amusing Pyotr Vyazemsky – she found that her rightful place in her new family was already occupied too. The presence of her husband's first wife, Liza, still lingered about the house. Liza's portrait hung above her daughter Sonya's bed, and Katerina Andreyevna came to understand a certain rare sigh that would escape her husband: he was sighing for *her*. Still serene, enchanting and slender, Katerina Andreyevna was just beginning to grow slightly heavier: a graceful walk, alert bright grey eyes, a high bosom, and now this incipient fullness. She had no wrinkles yet. She led a comfortable life. Every day she read the foreign news to her husband. Once she read about the reckless courage of Ensign Strukov, who had defended himself, with a fellow soldier in a besieged fortress, from a detachment of hostile mountain tribesmen and had been seriously wounded. The article was about unsung heroes in remote places. Ensign Strukov was then promoted to the rank of Colonel. Katerina Andreyevna was suddenly taken ill.

Pyotr Vyazemsky was scared to death of her. He told his friends quietly that she was of an awful disposition. She had noticed that people had started to feel sorry for her stepdaughter. And indeed her reproaches to her were intolerable, she knew it. She felt sorry for Sonya too – and made her life impossible.

Katerina Andreyevna's life was full: she had a stepdaughter, her own seven-year-old daughter and two sons. In the mornings she and her husband read proofs. But still she gave a deep sigh of relief when he went out for a canter on his grey Arab. She was not at all cross at Pushkin for having frightened her. He was a shy youth, with an abrupt laugh and an expression in his small brown eyes that made her laugh so as not to be angry with him.

But still this expression of his was flattering – as if her thirty-six years did not exist for this daring youth. The look on his face was more precious to her than the familiar pale and languorous stare of the Emperor. Her first impulse when she had noticed the Emperor looking at her like this was to leave the place at once. But her husband and his work, this book, and the children …? She stayed put, having determined not to give in.

When she was to be introduced to the Empress and the dress had already been brought from St Petersburg, she had suddenly been taken ill and had spent the night in tears. Next day the Emperor had sent a servant to enquire about her health, and flowers were brought to her. And when the Karamzins, invited to the court ball, had been making their way through the crowd, the Emperor, to the great confusion of the Court, had got up and asked her to take his seat – her, the illegitimate daughter of Vyazemsky! She knew what they had been whispering about her and how deeply despised she was. Zakharzhevsky, Commandant of Tsarskoye Selo, went pale with hatred whenever he saw her. And he was in charge of the army printing office where her husband's work was to be printed. But she decided not to give in.

And strangely enough, she felt she had acquired an ally. Not her husband, of course; he did not suspect and was unable even to imagine all these perils. This historian – who had written so much about tsars and rulers, about the dark events of history and its victims, and had just finished a chapter on Ivan the Terrible – was in an agony of suspense because the Tsar would not grant him an audience. And she realised that he did not understand the Tsar. Whereas she, as a woman, had understood him at once: had understood his cunning and his cruelty, his womanish weaknesses and masculine anger.

They were having breakfast. On the previous day her husband had been informed of the forthcoming audience in the Palace with His Majesty. Now a servant reported that a messenger had arrived from the Palace. Karamzin had already put on the ribbon of his order, but it had turned inside out, and he started to rearrange it in front of the mirror. Pushkin was there. Katerina Andreyevna was struck by the sidelong glance her husband cast at the schoolboy; it was the familiar discreet sneer of the literary man, expressing his derision for all these ribbons, crosses, audiences and so forth. Pushkin returned his quick glance and both burst out laughing. She flushed with pleasure: for some reason it appealed to her that her husband – a celebrity, a historiographer – was exchanging glances with this schoolboy as though they were equals.

However, the messenger had not come to ask the historiographer to the Palace, but instead brought a basket of flowers for his wife. Karamzin told him drily to thank the sender and fell silent. Perhaps it had not been intended as an insult, but the audience, to all intents and purposes definite, had been cancelled.

Pushkin suddenly turned pale and, without saying a word, hastily took his leave and ran off. When he had left, Karamzin looked after him and sadly shook his head.

Katerina Andreyevna ordered the flowers to be placed as near the door as possible – it was too stuffy for them in the main room – and started to chew her handkerchief.

15

The Lycée began to have its secrets. Now Pushkin was apparently hiding something from Pushchin. But Jeannot was shrewd. Finally the truth was out: Jeannot had come to know that Aleksandr had secret trysts; for some time he had noticed a difference in him. Their shared love for Bakunina had not changed their relationship – Pushkin was always cheerful, laughing eagerly at Misha Yakovlev's jokes or Danzas's cheeky pranks. Only when he gnawed quills, retreated into secluded places and stared blankly into space, the signs that he was busy composing poems, did Jeannot leave him alone. He had grown used to it. But it was different now: Pushkin was abstracted and unrecognisable. When Jeannot caught sight of him and the young widow in the garden, he cheered up: he had found the explanation – Pushkin was in love again. He was surprised that Pushkin did not hide it – he spoke eagerly about this love and its object just as the hussars did. It seemed unlikely, however, that the young widow was the reason for his protracted gloom or for making his friend's character, in the Principal's opinion, so impossible. Jeannot shared this opinion.

Previously when Pushkin had frequented the hussars he had been livelier. Now he threw up everything to visit the Karamzins.

Pushchin too kept things back from his friend, and Aleksandr had already noticed that Jeannot, Valkhovsky and Küchlya disappeared from the Lycée together, at the same time, as if by a command. Once Delvig joined them too. Aleksandr was tormented by curiosity – perhaps it was some secret that he didn't share?

Soon, however, Küchlya told him what it was all about: he was a Stoic but couldn't hide things for long. It turned out that while Aleksandr had visited the hussars, the boys had made friends with the Guardsmen who stayed at Tsarskoye Selo. The Guardsmen realised, said Küchlya, that without

knowledge man was on a level with cattle, and they had formed a group with
Burtsov as their leader; Küchlya confessed that he thought highly of his intellect. Aleksandr had met Burtsov with the hussars. Studiously polite, he had
spoken only to Chaadayev and taken a hasty leave when the hussars started
to sing. He was a staff officer and the hussars didn't like this breed. When he
had gone, somebody called him a dried-up stick.

Küchlya told Aleksandr, swearing him to secrecy, that Burtsov was a friend
of Kunitsyn's and that over tea Kunitsyn gave him lectures on political systems
and Adam Smith. Aleksandr was surprised that the Guardsman appeared to
be behaving like a Lycéeist.

Lowering his voice, Küchlya said that no one had any doubts: Arakcheyev
and Golitsyn had violated and betrayed the social contract – despite the
victories of 1812 serfdom had not yet been abolished. They would have to
wait for a couple of years and if it hadn't been abolished by that time – they
would have been deceived. While mankind, as everything indicated, had been
continuously perfecting itself, the aristocracy had been using its power for its
own purposes, and as Burtsov had so convincingly proved, here lay the root of
all ills. Valkhovsky too could support this. The main thing for the time being
was not to give way to despair or become detached, otherwise the crowd (that
is, the Court) would swallow a person up. Success in society poisoned the
soul. Küchlya would speak long and passionately. How he delivered the words
'for the time being!'

Aleksandr was silent. So this was what it was about!

His friends knew more than he did. How much time he had missed! He
braced himself but feared that tears might spurt from his eyes. Just think of
it! They kept things back from him as if he were an immature youth or even
a little boy, or an incorrigible and reckless joker! And this despite the fact
that the emblem of Arzamas was the red hood of the Jacobins! His uncle had
joined the society wearing it! In less than a year he would break free from this
Lycée – and then, on the first day of his freedom, he would put it on. He was
an Arzamasian! He was a friend of Chaadayev, who had more knowledge in
his little finger than all these friends, these pedants and know-alls. But Delvig,
how could *he* have done this to him – have hidden things from him? He wept
without realising it. Tonight he would go to the hussars – it was time to see
Chaadayev, who wanted to talk to him tête-à-tête. He knew that the silence of
the Court was a betrayal, and so were the Tsar's predatory walks in the Park, a
betrayal not of the social contract that had been concluded a long time before
by anonymous parties but of the tacit agreement over constitutional reform
that had been reached in 1812. He left Küchlya without saying a word and
made for the door. In half an hour Engelhardt would retreat into his rooms
and Pushkin would go to the hussars. It was too early to wait for the evening.

How much time he had lost already! Tomorrow, no, tonight he would speak to Chaadayev. Why not now?

Suddenly he ran into the Principal.

Engelhardt had been following him. His face wore a beatific smile, his head was held high, he looked satisfied. Raising his eyebrows, he told Aleksandr in a low voice that he was free from lectures and classes that day (as if he weren't already!) and that he was to go to the Karamzins at once: Prince Neledinsky-Meletsky had come to visit them, and wished to talk to Pushkin about a matter that could not be postponed.

16

A dinner table was laid in the Chinese chalet. The guest of honour was sitting at the head of the table and Aleksandr was offered a seat next to him. The guest was a congenial stocky little old man with turquoise eyes, wearing a wig with a short ribboned pigtail, though pigtails had been out of fashion for some sixteen years. The old courtier greeted the young man in a soft, slightly jingling voice. His paunch, clothed in a thick white waistcoat, wobbled with pleasure: he was relishing the meal. He bantered with Katerina Andreyevna, much to her amusement, while he ate; old Prince Neledinsky-Meletsky was a distant relative on her father's side, and this renowned admirer of women had not avoided her in her youth.

'My angel, my dear hostess!' the courtier said, 'how marvellous these peaches are in their own juice! This juice is like a mist or a haze, while the pear juice is as clear as sunlight.'

Karamzin was smiling as he must have smiled thirty years before in the presence of his elders.

'Young man,' said the courtier to Aleksandr, 'learn from this household how to enjoy fruit. You won't find such taste and understanding in every house. Yesterday, for example, I dined at a certain general's. First we had my favourite buckwheat kasha in earthenware pots. I will admit I was touched. Then followed pike, which I also like, and goose with mushrooms – very good. But then … then … ah! pickled pears, pickled melon, pickled peaches! Isn't it a sacrilege against nature? To reduce these fruits to the state of cucumbers or cabbage!'

His small turquoise eyes were shining, his white satin belly jerked.

The little old man was a glutton.

After dinner, not to hold things up, Katerina Andreyevna left them to their business. They sat down on the sofa. Neledinsky-Meletsky was in no hurry to get down to business. He looked at Pushkin. He had already managed to observe the gloominess and nervousness of this young poet recommended by

Karamzin, had spotted the fleeting, mischievous smile about his lips and eyes and had decided that he should flatter him first and make him feel something of the spirit of the old court ... He was director of entertainments and senior court poet at Pavlovsk Palace.

In the absence of ladies, he told them an anecdote.

'Last week,' he began, addressing both listeners, 'we were told that a man, some rogue, had turned up at the Palace with a mare that was supposed to understand everything and answer questions by signs. The Empress was told and it was decided to organise a private performance. The rogue brought his horse into the drawing-room and the performance began. Either the horse was indeed very clever or the man really was a rogue, but everything went superbly until the middle of the performance, when the actress felt the call of nature. Can you imagine? A boy rushed to find a hat to put it under the mare, but meanwhile the owner, the rogue, without turning a hair, dashed up to her and started to shove it all back inside the animal with his fist. The ladies burst out laughing – I was disgraced. The servant rushed around the horse with the hat; the man took fright, bowed and started to back towards the door. The Dowager Empress's lady-in-waiting Katinka Nelidova was pointing her lorgnette here and there but couldn't see anything and pestered me with questions: "Why are they laughing, Yushinka? What's wrong?"

'And I answered: "Nature, my angel, simply nature!"'

The narrator smiled beatifically with his juicy lips. Karamzin, somewhat bewildered by the simple-mindedness of the old courtier, eventually burst into hearty laughter.

He felt as if this Chaulieu figure of the previous century,[*] this poet, singer and clown, had lifted a burden from his shoulders.

It was the first time Aleksandr had heard the voice of the previous century.

'And now, my dear chap,' the old man addressed Pushkin in the same engagingly frank manner, 'I'll take some fresh air in the garden before having a nap. Would you like to accompany me?'

In the garden, leaning on his walking stick, he took a seat on the bench and in a totally different voice, looking unsmilingly straight into Aleksandr's eyes, began to speak softly and slowly, not anticipating objections.

No doubt they had heard here in Tsarskoye Selo that on the sixth of June there would be a celebration in Pavlovsk for the wedding of Grand Duchess Anne[†] and the Prince of Orange. Six thousand wax candles would be lit in the

[*] The Anacreontic verse of Guillaume Amfrye, abbé de Chaulieu (1639–1720), was imitated by a number of Russian poets of the late eighteenth and early nineteenth centuries.
[†] A sister of Tsar Alexander.

Palace. Five hundred ladies would be invited for the masque, which would be enacted to Batyushkov's script. Both courts, the Emperor and the two Empresses, would attend. The celebration was being organised by Neledinsky. Bonfires would be lit all around the Palace, and peasants would sing and dance round them. During dinner a choir was to sing verses which had been commissioned from him, Neledinsky. The Prince was a pleasant, unassuming, intelligent and sensitive person. He had fought Napoleon under the command of Wellington and had been wounded. It was no shame to write verses for such a Prince. Neledinsky would have written them with great pleasure and considered it a great honour, but the young poet must have noticed that the old man had grown withered; he now lacked fire and the passion of youth.

The little old man sat fluffed up like an old sparrow, and his pigtail twitched. Nikolay Mikhaylovich had recommended Pushkin, and Neledinsky could recognise the bird by its flight. He wanted him to write the verses about the Prince, but the Prince himself could serve simply as a pretext. He had fought for the lilies of the Bourbons – so Pushkin would have to mention the peace and also Napoleon, who had risen and fallen again, this time for ever.

'If Gavrilo Romanovich* were alive, he would have hugged me with delight for this,' said the little old man.

Everything about him – the sudden switch from a court incident to an important matter; the old-fashioned, grave, abrupt tone; Derzhavin's name – it was like some old court anecdote that Pushkin seemed to have heard from his uncle in Moscow.

'You stand recommended by Nikolay Mikhaylovich, and my old eyes don't betray me,' said the old courtier. 'Take a fresh quill, a sheet of paper – and when I've taken my nap, the poems will be finished. All important things are done in an hour, no longer. I'll take them with me. It will be as I say, or I've learned nothing in my life.'

17

He found neither Chaadayev nor Rayevsky in; only Kaverin was at home, and extremely glad to see him.

'My dear chap, I laid a bet that you wouldn't come. Now I'm bankrupt. I was sure you'd fled the Lycée for St Petersburg and that they were searching for you on the roads. But Molostov told me you were too busy wooing and had been seen in the woods running wild with love. I'd better start writing a letter to my bailiff and tell him to cut down the oaks – I have to pay up to Molostov on my bet. I'll ask my bailiff to send you some berries from my

---

* The poet Gavriil Derzhavin, who had died the previous year.

grove. Molostov will be here in a minute; he's catching up on sleep after duty
... Let me take a look at you, my friend.'

He gave a low whistle.

'Oh, you are unwell indeed. I envy you. You look like a suffering lover, you
torment beauties with your eyes, none of them can resist you. And look at me
– no matter what I do: apply mustard plaster, drink vinegar, suffer – I look as
ruddy as a country wench. Nobody believes me. You're lucky to catch me. I'm
running a high fever, but I have to ride my Whirlwind to Pavlovsk tomorrow.
Orders. Levashov's stables are to greet the Prince of Orange.'

Nobody liked Levashov, Commander of the Regiment. When one of its
squadrons had been billeted in Sofia, Levashov had stayed in a house beside
the stables and the hussars had called the house itself the stables. Orders had
been issued from the stables.

Kaverin was irritated by all the fuss of the Court, the tiring business of
guarding it, the Commander's sycophancy, the Prince of Orange – and did
seem to be ill. He drank glass after glass of chilled champagne, saying that if
it did not help the fever then at least it would cure him of the French pox.
He called the Prince of Orange's bride the Maid of Orleans, and said in his
mock-Latin that the Prince was finally leaving:

'*Deinde post currens*, meaning "A turkey travels by post-chaise",' so he
explained.

Kaverin's Latin was notorious throughout St Petersburg. He intimidated
police officers with it ...

He sat looking at Aleksandr and became more and more angry.

'Do you want me to help you to abduct your beauty? Did I fight Napoleon
to take messages to the Prince of Orange's escort, to the Maid of Orleans's
chambermaids? Do you know, my friend, as soon as I repay my debts I'll go
to Levashov and hand in my resignation. It's all too much!'

He took some paper from the table, perhaps an order, and lit his meerschaum pipe.

Aleksandr sat stunned, biting his lips. What would Kaverin call his verses:
'Message to the Prince of Orange'? He almost hated the great Karamzin, who
had passed him over to the old courtier. His heart was beating fast.

> '*My child, you are crying because of a lass?*
> *For shame!' he told me, 'oh, alas!'*

'No, this is what *I* am telling *you*!'

Kaverin tried to make him speak.

He had an amazing ability to surmise Pushkin's thoughts by just glancing
at his expression.

'Your face is cloudy. Would you like me to show you thunder and lightning?'

And he imitated thunder and lightning: his nose and mouth became zigzag-shaped. He squinted and made his eyes glare. Aleksandr burst out laughing.

'A very close resemblance.'

'Give me a poem, my friend,' he asked. 'But please, not an elegy, I'm not in that frame of mind today.'

Kaverin asked for an epigram. Nobody could listen to epigrams as he could. Pushkin seemed to write them with the sole purpose of reading them to Kaverin. He wasn't in the mood for epigrams but Kaverin insisted.

Pushkin recited the first one he could remember:

> *'My dear uncle, have you been sick?*
> *I've asked about you everywhere –*
> *Three whole nights without a wink!'*
> *'I know, I know ... Chemin de fer.'*

Kaverin screwed up his eyes, bared his white teeth and clasped his hand to heart. He sat like that for a moment and then burst out laughing.

'Well, my friend, it seems to be about me,' he said in a thin voice.

He embraced Aleksandr.

'Clever boy. That's the conversation I'm going to have with my uncle. Yes, of course, he must be ill – how did you know?'

Aleksandr stared at him in bewilderment. He knew nothing of Kaverin's uncle. It was a habit with Kaverin: he immediately applied epigrams to his own life. And when Pushkin recited an epigram to him he always felt that it was understood, that it wouldn't have to be copied out and would be learned by everyone at once. He regretted that he hadn't written an epigram about the Prince of Orange and sighed.

'Consider the charmer yours. I'll help,' promised Kaverin. 'Chase those clouds from your face, will you?'

Molostov and Saburov came in, in their uniforms and pelisses, busily jingling their spurs.

'Molostov,' Kaverin addressed him, 'you've won – Pushkin hasn't fled – it's as you said. He wandered, wild with love. I'm staking my light bay stallion, I want to win back my oak grove.'

Cards appeared.

'Tonight, Pushkin, you'll be lucky at cards as all unlucky lovers are. Sit down here. You'll rake it in. The oaks shall be ours! *I know, I know ... Chemin de fer!*'

Saburov, a cold-blooded gambler, was keeping a close eye on the other players' fortunes. When they were winning, he matched their stakes.

Kaverin wouldn't tolerate this.

Kaverin won. Molostov's face darkened.

Saburov put down his stake. A moment later Kaverin lost everything.

The game continued. The pale and sullen Molostov was indifferent as he played, but he played recklessly. His pockmarked face was flabby, his eyes were lacklustre and slightly swollen.

He was either frightened or embittered.

Kaverin was raging too.

'Molostov, your fate is being decided,' he said. 'I'm staking the bay stallion, three thousand of my debt and I'll sell your new harness by auction. Your saddlecloth is excellent. The game is almost over.'

Molostov was in a new hussar uniform, with close-fitting blue trousers – all spick and span. Flaring his nostrils, Aleksandr watched the cards.

'Jack!' Kaverin said. But it was Two of Hearts.

Kaverin lost again and was upset.

'Your fate is clear,' he told Aleksandr. 'The charmer has surrendered. You can't bring luck to gambling any longer.'

Breathing heavily through his nose, he sipped the cold champagne – his medicine – and stayed sober. He took a breath and started his favourite sad song that he always sang when he was distressed. It was a lament.

> *I sit in company*
> *And nothing do I see*
> *But a girl with red hair:*
> *How I wish she weren't there.*

Kaverin's song was already familiar to Aleksandr.

'No, not *a girl with red hair*,' Molostov said all of a sudden. 'You've made that up. *And nothing do I see but a mug of cold stewed tea* – we used to sing it at school. Nothing to do with *a girl with red hair*.'

He was suspicious that he was being teased on account of the beauty, red-haired indeed, who would come to visit him from town – for 'billeting' as they would say.

'No. *A girl with red hair: How I wish she weren't there*,' said Kaverin with a smile.

'I shall soon be saying goodbye to you,' Molostov said. Everyone looked at him.

Pale and angry, he spoke reluctantly, unsmiling.

'I'm off.'

'Where to? Wait till you're on duty,' said Saburov.

They were joking. Kaverin was smoking his pipe. No one laughed.

Molostov lowered his voice and said huskily:

'I can't stay here with you. I'll be leaving this pleasant abode. I've asked for a transfer.'

And with a quick gesture of his hand, in a low voice, he told them a story. The guardhouse where he had been on duty looked out onto the Tsar's study. Normally there were curtains on the windows but that night they had not been drawn. The lit interior was visible through the window. Molostov could see Prince Golitsyn, the Minister for Religious Affairs, leaving the study while the Tsar sat at his desk reading. Suddenly he had risen, come up to the window and looked out of it.

Molostov said:

'His gaze was fixed. All expression, politeness or a smile, had left his face – completely washed off. He stood gazing, without blinking. Then he went up to the desk, leaned against it with his clenched hand and started to pray, softly at first and then louder and louder – "From the most humble ... Aleksandr Pavlovich ..." and so on to the very end, to "Amen". I realised it was Amen for me too. Sleep, sound sleep was needed, I thought – not for him but for me. I decided to go to bed. But I couldn't sleep. When I went home I was wide awake all night.'

Everyone was silent.

'Perhaps I'll get some sleep on the road. Amen to my duties!'

Turning white, Kaverin said:

'It's Golitsyn, this is his doing. His song.'

He looked into Pushkin's eyes, clasped his hand and repeated the poem, speaking the last line distinctly: '*How I wish she weren't there.*' Then he paused.

'I'll see you off.'

And he saw Pushkin back to the Lycée, singing softly all the while:

'... *a girl with red hair ... wish she weren't there.*'

18

No, Kaverin was right, he shouldn't have played with Molostov. Now the oaks would be cut down in vain – the Tsarskoye Selo hermit hadn't been born to eulogise the Prince of Orange; Pushkin did not crave Palace wisdom. That night he wrote a note to the young widow, and Foma, who had become his factotum, made sure it was unobtrusively delivered.

Next day, after dark, they met. The young widow had a tender name, Marie. She gave herself unreservedly, trembling with fear and desire. He didn't want to call her Marie and gave her another name – Lila or Lida, and to this too she submitted. Of the two lovers, she was the more reckless. Together, without any definite arrangement, they now deceived the Principal, the shade of the jealous husband, and everyone else.

Within a month she had learned with this boy what she had never believed to be possible, what she had been able to guess at only vaguely and what, echoing her aunts, she used to call *hell* and *vice*. In the mornings she looked in the mirror with a secret fear that anyone could tell it all just by looking at her.

The only thing she didn't agree to was to let him into her bedroom at night. She was staying in a spare corner room facing the garden, separated from all the other rooms in the Principal's house. She trembled with the madness that passed from him to herself and back from herself to him. No, it had to be the nearby grove or the old garden, the lake shore or the shadows of the abandoned theatre – all those places that she left in her crumpled clothes with leaves stuck to them, under the permanent threat of being caught like a wench by the night-watchman. But not her room, not the white bed-covers above which the Principal had hung her husband's portrait, which he had framed himself with rare skill.

They had arranged to exchange regular notes through Foma, brief ones, and no poems – beware of the Principal!

She would hide her answers about the time and place of the next tryst in the Principal's garden, in a knothole in an old oak.

He would forget her as soon as they had parted.

He hadn't been at the Karamzins' for a week.

One night he woke up and realised that he couldn't live like this any longer; tomorrow he would slip away first thing in the morning or during the walk, just to see her window or a corner of her chalet. Every poem he wrote now was written in the secret hope that it would somehow get into her hands. Otherwise he wouldn't be able to write or rewrite a single line. He had finally understood that he couldn't live a single day without this woman who was old enough to be his mother, that he must see her no matter what, and that the torment he had written about in his poems to Bakunina had been a mere surmise of the real torture that he was experiencing now and that was only just beginning.

She was the wife of a great man, a sage and a teacher, and she was unreachable, untouchable. He felt a surge of hatred for any kind of calm, any kind of cautious wisdom. The very sound of her name should be kept secret. He bit his lip when he talked to Pushchin about his visits to the Karamzins', afraid to say 'at Karamzina's'.

She was the only person who understood him.

Only at her feet, next to the Tsar's flowers that she did not water, letting them wither and be thrown away – only at her feet could he talk, chatter and joke, while she laughed.

The Tsar had offered her a seat when she entered the ballroom, and – bravo! – had not been successful.

Without her he couldn't carry on a conversation, he didn't hear Delvig or Küchlya asking him questions; he was afraid of the fate that was in store for him – to be silent all his life, till the very end; to be unable ever to call her by her name to anyone, even to Pushchin, to be afraid of himself and of others who might guess.

He drew a monogram in the sand – *N. N.*, her monogram. He would go to meet Lila, frighten her with his abruptness, rudeness, insatiability, his choking, guttural laughter and that soft bird-like scream of his, uttered at those moments when nobody else laughed. He was enjoying the newness of it all. Returning to the Lycée at nights, he longed to see a narrow footprint on the ground and to kiss it, that footprint of the woman whom from now on and throughout his life he would call *N. N.*

19

It was coming to an end – the time of innuendoes, insulting refusals to see him, and dubious deliveries to his wife of flowers from the Tsar's conservatory. A Palace footman had come the day before to inform him that His Majesty would give him an audience. This had taken place and though not a word had been said about business matters, and on the host's side the conversation had been quite pointless, what mattered was that the audience had taken place. He had finally commenced his long-awaited career as adviser to the Tsar, though he no longer wanted the post, so hurt had he been by the Court's indifference. At their next meeting he was going to tell the Tsar simply and clearly that it was time to overcome the delusions of his youth and to be a proper ruler. Now ... autocracy. Now ... serfdom and slavery. Avoid congresses, and deal with two important state questions – concerning the Guards and the Tsar's harmful advisers. And though at this last meeting the Tsar, with the usual smile about lips and eyes, had strung him along with some pleasant and meaningless platitude and knitted his white brow, Karamzin no longer doubted that the invitation to stay in the Chinese Village actually meant something. He was the Tsar's adviser; this was no longer in doubt.

If only he could make up for wasted time, if only ... He enjoyed receiving the young men: one was a dancer, another ... another upset him. God bless them, the young scapegraces of the Lycée! Katerina Andreyevna took the boy too seriously – she laughed both with and at the young braggart. He was raw and immature – but what sadness, based on nothing really, what cutting mockery of his literary rivals, and what devotion to Arzamas. Nikolay Mikhaylovich liked Arzamasians who worshipped him, they were the only people in St Petersburg worthy of friendship; the only thing he insisted upon was decorum.

Katerina's brother – the sweet-natured Pierre Vyazemsky – was a natural journalist, a little too fervent perhaps. Karamzin had already had a talk with Bludov about bringing Arzamas into decent shape, without any excesses and doing what it was supposed to do – fight for the reform of refined taste. Jokes were all very well, as long as they were appropriate and decent. The practical joke played on Vasily Lvovich may have been appropriate, but it had hardly been decent, it had been growing more and more absurd, and there was no knowing where it might end. It smacked of hussars' revelry, of their debaucheries and bravado – anything but defending writers like himself and Zhukovsky. Of course it was right for young people to jest, but surely they could combine pleasure with serious business. Bludov intended to start a satirical magazine – full of jokes, but tasteful ones.

Karamzin liked Chaadayev, though he had heard contradictory rumours about him. Avdotya Golitsyna had said he was a marvellous dancer, at which Pushkin had assumed a mysterious air and kept silent. They were in fact a noisy pair – but this was youth. Today Pushkin had asked him if he could bring Chaadayev to see him, and the invitation had been gladly extended. Youth stood in need of his instruction, but he too needed these young people – their talk wasn't entirely meaningless. General Vasilchikov valued Chaadayev, and it was obvious he would make a brilliant career.

Oh, how many brilliant careers he had seen budding but unfulfilled; how many laurels that had never been wrought into wreaths! How strange! His elders respected Chaadayev and women took to him for some reason. Avdotya Golitsyna always talked about him wistfully, and the last time she had discussed mathematics she had first quoted a phrase of Chaadayev's, with a significant look. Oh, Avdotya! Mathematics and beauty! Chaadayev was a hussar and an intellectual. How amazing the new era was. He disapproved of the arrogance of the young; it was groundless. They seemed to consider themselves judges of everyone – even of him. Why was his right eyebrow raised? It looked very like arrogance. Avdotya called him an intellectual, and he wore a cold expression, as of a person who held power.

Looking at this beautifully buttoned hussar, immaculate as an hour-glass, with his youthful shock of curly hair and his small eager nose, Karamzin felt he understood this youth; he was clever without awkwardness, his gestures and words were spontaneous but few, he was not too familiar. Pushkin adored him: he studied Karamzin and the impression the hussar produced on him. He was found amusing, like a child; overall, he made a good impression.

Chaadayev looked around smiling with his plump bitten lips, but there was no smile in his wide eyes. Karamzin was displeased to see that these eyes had noticed everything: the withered flowers of the Tsar's bouquet that the host had been ashamed to throw away; the proofs on the two little tables – the second one was Katerina Andreyevna's. He looked around the Chinese chalet without saying a word, and Nikolay Mikhaylovich had to explain that it was by chance they had come to be staying here, and in spite of Vyazemsky's efforts things simply weren't up to standard, like the plaster, which had already started to peel. Only today the Tsar had reprimanded Zakharzhevsky for that and rightly so. But Chaadayev was not surprised and asked no questions. It turned out that he knew the Chinese Village and how it had come to be built. He took an interest in the most mundane things in the same way that women did. Maybe that was why Avdotya thought he was so clever!

Chaadayev had become transformed in talking about the unnecessary construction of this unreal village in the Chinese style (there was in fact nothing else to do in the Chinese Village but talk about it). The hussar spoke of the egregiousness and scrappiness of all the buildings in the gardens of Tsarskoye Selo, all ephemeral and incomplete – such had been the point of their creation. He looked out of the window and examined a fresco of a dragon. Cameron's depiction bore little resemblance to a Chinese dragon. These imitations of Oriental culture taken from Europe were amusing in the extreme.

Karamzin answered drily that as a matter of fact it was the climate that had forced him to take advantage of the Tsar's invitation. St Petersburg was Peter the Great's brilliant mistake – calculated to make one flee to any other place, but Karamzin couldn't live far away from it at the moment because he had been awaiting delivery of the proofs of his book. It was more convenient to stay at Tsarskoye Selo than at his estate near Moscow or at the other one on the Volga near Simbirsk, with its temperate climate, salubrious air and the river, where people lived longer. Warming to his theme, he added that Simbirsk was also easily accessible to foreigners, and that on the Neva it would have been wiser to have founded simply a small merchant town for the export and import of merchandise – that would have been more than sufficient; without St Petersburg there would have been no tears and no corpses.

Katerina Andreyevna busied herself and did not join the guests. She could have, but was unwilling to do so. She wanted to see and hear them when they were alone, without her. She looked at them and listened to them through the slightly open door. Pushkin fidgeted and involuntarily looked around as if searching for her, as he usually did when she was not present. She smiled. She was curious about something else. Although she had got used to the stifling greatness of her husband, and he was certainly the cleverest and the best contemporary writer of all she knew, nevertheless his inviolable status frightened her, as well as the indifferent, polite expressions on the faces of the footmen who brought flowers to her. That was why she was listening to the conversation so avidly.

It seemed to her that Nikolay Mikhaylovich knew everything. These men were young and couldn't imagine how many books and manuscripts lay behind his every word. But Chaadayev also frightened her. What gave him the right to question him so calmly, patiently and formally, and what made her famous husband answer him so painstakingly?

She looked at them more closely.

She had known some renowned men of fashion, she had grown used to the hussars' dandyism, no one saluted more elegantly than Kaverin and she smiled at the dedicated courtesy, ease and elegance with which he touched his shako.

But *this* was dandyism she knew nothing of. What perfection – this pelisse, these gloves – and yet without looking ridiculous!

Kaverin had the air of being ready at any moment to tear off his cartridge-pouch and lay it at a woman's feet out of sheer courtesy. Katerina Andreyevna recognised the strict and merciless religion of courtesy in his polish, composure and calm. The hussars that she saw in Tsarskoye Selo were so energetic and impetuous that their clothes seemed to restrain their movements, but with Chaadayev clothes, words and deeds seemed to be in perfect harmony. What was he really like, this quiet hussar? Pierre Vyazemsky said that he had defended the regimental banner at Borodino for the whole day when still an ensign; that he had taken part in the battles at Leipzig and Kulm, that he had been in the Emperor's guard on the day when Russian troops had entered Paris. She was fascinated to observe them together, her husband and this friend of Pushkin's.

Chaadayev looked around the rooms that had been brought into order with such difficulty by Pierre and Turgenev and asked Nikolay Mikhaylovich whether the walls were damp – they were badly built. Nikolay Mikhaylovich couldn't tell him anything about the walls – they didn't interest him. Chaadayev pointed out that the roof was too high and that it was therefore impossible to warm the house up. Nikolay Mikhaylovich expressed surprise that Chaadayev knew about such matters. Chaadayev explained that he had learned this in Langenbilau in Silesia where his regiment had once been quartered, and that the experience had taught him how to live. He had realised that the peasants' faces and the houses there had something in common – the absence of indifference. This building, on the contrary, bore the signs of indifference, probably because it had been built by slaves.

Both Nikolay Mikhaylovich and the hussar were taciturn by nature.

Russia had been waiting for her history – Nikolay Mikhaylovich's great work. Would he soon be writing about Peter the Great and his time? Katerina knew that Tsar Peter would not play any significant role in her husband's history because his books were designed to be instructive, and therefore the greatest Tsar, Ivan III, would be given pride of place and be the one most substantially described. The hussar argued that under Peter the Great Russia had become a part of Europe. Aleksandr fastened his eyes upon him. Nikolay Mikhaylovich was rather too loquacious today. Of course Chaadayev was right to talk of advances in mathematics, and so on. But history was more than a geometrical problem.

It was time for her to join them. She went out into the garden, cut some lilac that reminded her of her native town and came back. The hussar was speaking of slavery with an authoritative expression that Katerina Andreyevna found irritating. Slavery was everywhere – the very bread they ate was produced by slaves. Chaadayev spoke serenely, but Nikolay Mikhaylovich seemed bored and replied carelessly that he was exaggerating. She peeped through the open door and was amazed. The hussar was pale, even his lips had turned white. He spoke of slavery as other hussars spoke of their rivals in love, with whom they would fight a duel tomorrow; the white lips bore not a trace of a smile. What strange passion! Perhaps she should go in and interrupt them? But the hussar went on. Slavery was his *idée fixe*; in his opinion, slavery was the reason why Russia could never be the most powerful country in Europe, and it was autocracy that stood in the way of the abolition of slavery. There were degrees of slavery, the difference being purely quantitative. But as soon as slavery in all its forms – serfdom, and so on – was abolished, Russia would become a great country. He maintained this with absolute conviction, as if it were soon to come about.

This was too much for Nikolay Mikhaylovich. 'Fashionable modern exaggeration,' he said to the hussar in a dead voice; in the idea of 'degrees of slavery' he could see only confusion. It depended on how the word *slave* was to be understood. Chaadayev had spoken of bread produced by slaves. Wasn't it the case that slavery was a law of nature you couldn't argue with and which it would be naive even to discuss? It had been tried and tested by life a long time ago. Slavery fed us and the statute of slavery was the basis of existence and therefore inviolable. The task was to make slavery more humane and sensible. *Slavery would always exist* and those who rebelled against it should be subdued like children. He could have wished they had learned the lessons of ancient and recent history: from France, for example.

Absolute power – or better stated, autocracy – was essential, and had been proven by history, even though one could certainly argue about much that was unnecessary and excessive in it. Suddenly Pushkin erupted in that undignified laughter of his – those strange little barks – and fell silent. It was nervous laughter. Karamzin took from his desk a sheet of paper on which

Prince Vladimir Monomakh's admonitions on women and children had been copied out and read a paragraph from it. *Never cease to beat your children ...* and so on. This text had just been sent to him, and contained crucial variant readings by Malinovsky and other scholars ... He was making it clear that he was busy. Was he really?

Katerina Andreyevna peeped through the door. Chaadayev was smiling broadly, Pushkin was enjoying himself. It would have been better if they had taken offence, like children. Chaadayev's spurs gave a little jingle, and Pushkin and his tutor (as Katerina Andreyevna called the hussar) at last left the house.

Nikolay Mikhaylovich gave a thin short laugh; he was clearly put out.

20

That night she lay awake for hours listening to her husband's feigned and soundless sleep. She knew that he was lying still as a corpse, unable to sleep, recalling Chaadayev's every word. Half an hour later she heard his soft subdued sigh. Pretending to be asleep, he did not believe she was either.

Next morning she woke up early.

She looked askance at her famous husband, her educator and friend, and a sudden thought terrified her: perhaps the youths were right, perhaps all these twenty years she had believed in him in vain, allured by his wisdom? And if he sought some sort of monasticism why did he need her here, next to him? Why did she go on living, restraining her feelings and growing older? She was still a beautiful woman.

She slipped out of bed and looked at herself in the mirror. She recalled the expression on the face of Pushkin, her amusing *admirateur*, who was just a child. Was he indeed? Her husband had taught her patience and self-possession, but these crazy youths had unanimously called it slavery and Nikolay Mikhaylovich had picked up their challenge courageously, head on, yes, it was slavery. But the conversation had had nothing to do with her.

She felt rather sorry for her husband. Yesterday he had talked with his usual, entirely characteristic wisdom, but the young men had not accepted his remarks. His self-delusion was amazing: he had spoken to them as if they were juniors, in the voice of a past era. Grandeur was out of fashion, it ought to be disguised – the only condition under which it could be forgiven. She had asked Chaadayev what had made him transfer to the Akhtyrsky Regiment, and Chaadayev had replied that they had a smarter uniform. To her husband he talked about hundreds of more important things. The Akhtyrsky uniform really was smarter: it was fur-trimmed, and not of that abominable pale-green colour, but dark blue. He was, simply, a hussar, and his answer was a hussar's.

He danced the mazurka better than anyone else. Rayevsky was a long way from his perfection; Pushkin could not dance at all – he snorted and gasped for breath during a waltz. He simply could not cope with being so close to a woman. She ought to make him keep his distance on his future visits. What trivial nonsense was she thinking about!

She looked at herself in the mirror and stepped barefoot and noiselessly onto the chilly floor, not the carpet, but the stone-cold floor about which her husband had warned her for many years. She felt once more the cold she had been fond of in her childhood, the cold that had nearly killed her once.

What was wrong with her? Was it fond memories of her youth, things she had long lost the habit of? Still barefoot, she walked about the drawing-room where Chaadayev had sat the day before – he was amusing too – she knew these great dancers who always strutted the floor as if it were the last mazurka in their life. The maid peeped at her out of her room and drew back in fright. She again seemed to be losing her composure. 'Slavery …' – she remembered Chaadayev's words. Here she was, walking undressed in the morning, frightening the maids. What nonsense – she was no longer young! She was just lonely; she should ask Avdotya Golitsyna to come to stay. When Avdotya was here she felt neither nervous nor frightened by her husband's mistakes.

Avdotya's melodious voice had such power that if she had been here when the argument had taken place, they would have spoken differently and the unpleasant conversation would never have occurred. Chaadayev would not have behaved so haughtily and Pushkin would have had no doubts. She knew it. It had not just been a conversation about autocracy and slavery, it had also been a conversation about the Emperor, her husband and herself. It was strange, but it had indeed been about her. Nikolay Mikhaylovich had not understood this. Avdotya would have understood. The maid brought a soft shawl and wrapped up her feet. She smiled silently; her husband was still asleep. The girl gave her a letter, and at once she forgot everything.

The night-watchman had brought the letter. The maid always confused things, never knowing to whom messages were addressed or from whom they came. Katerina Andreyevna looked at the coarse envelope without an inscription – no, it was not from the Palace. She surreptitiously made the sign of the cross. Thank God!

Then she ordered a paper-knife to be brought and tore the envelope open. Having read its contents, she glanced at the maid and flushed all over her face, shoulders and bosom. She threw the note down on the table and calmly told the girl not to take any letters from anyone unless told to. Then she wrung her hands and proffered it to Nikolay Mikhaylovich who was just entering the room, calm and ready for his work and his walk. He looked at her in astonishment and perused the message. He hesitated for no more than a moment, then burst out laughing with that dry, shallow laughter that went no deeper than his throat. Then he smiled, perplexed. The note was a hasty scribble – time and place: six in the afternoon, at the theatre. This was how trysts were arranged. This was the 'letter' the girl had handed on. They were laughing longer than they needed to at this stupid message, which by mistake had been passed on by the stupid night-watchman to the stupid maid.

Then Nikolay Mikhaylovich pondered: who had actually written the note? And suddenly he said: Pushkin. Then, very precisely, with regained cheerfulness and like the historian he was, he explained all the circumstances of this silly occurrence: the boy had simply written to some girl of his about a date, and the night-watchman had either misheard or got muddled and brought it to the wrong address. She had so often heard her husband explaining historical misunderstandings, and been surprised at their simplicity, that everything became clear to her at once. He was right. It was a plausible explanation. But presently, raising her head, she said calmly: 'We should teach him a lesson.' Nikolay Mikhaylovich agreed: yes, the boy should be taught a lesson, and he gave a sigh. He had called him a 'boy' as he had never done before, and this surprised her somewhat. Then they had a good long laugh and went to their rooms, and she forgot about the letter and about Pushkin, whom Nikolay Mikhaylovich now called 'a boy'. But in the evening she suddenly wondered whom the letter had been meant for. To whom had he written? She grew angry with herself for her curiosity and breathed heavily.

She felt hurt and stopped believing in his future, in his poetry, and trusting his shyness. And it was unpleasant to her that her husband had called him a boy, though perhaps it was just as well.

And Nikolay Mikhaylovich?

For him, as if by magic, everything had vanished, taking away his concerns about his cherished and immortal work which, completed and published, would live on when he himself had long rotted away, and the bitter truth about the old and the new Russia would moulder away unadmitted, in this very place or not far away, in the Palace, in Tver, without the response that he awaited no longer, but without which, he knew, Russia would find neither peace nor happiness*. Just as he himself now lived here in Tsarskoye Selo which was neither the old nor the new Russia. And something else that had begun to oppress him and that he was unwilling to think about was

---

* In 1811 Karamzin had been invited to meet the Tsar at Tver and had submitted his 'Memorandum on Ancient and Modern Russia' to him with the aim of counteracting Speransky's reformist influence. Although Karamzin's conservative ideas lay close to the heart of Alexander's policies, the Tsar gave no response to the memorandum and did not appoint him to the leading post he had been hoping for.

his wife's sudden late blooming, her disturbed breathing, their whole life in Tsarskoye Selo, humourless and unsettled, away from their old and trusted friends, in the company of these restless Lycéeists instead – these likable but exhausting youths. And, then – the argument with Chaadayev, not even an argument, just a quiet hostile silence on his part. He had grown used to having friends and enemies, but this was different: his young admirers were worse than Arakcheyev, whose coarse and vulgar mind he had managed to put up with, because at least it was better than the serpentine flattery of the Jacobin Speransky, son of a priest. Dear God! The people he had to get along with! Yes, the Lycéeists were friends, but so remote from him that he was afraid of where they would lead Russia, if they were to lead her at all. This urchin, Sergey Lvovich's frivolous son, a poet – and a dancing hussar. Leaders! It was all too much. And like no one else he knew that the Tsar's courtesy to these boys meant nothing and was thoroughly false.

And now, as if by magic, everything had vanished.

It was a trifling event not worth discussing: the boy had made a mistake in the address and had sent some billet-doux to Katerina Andreyevna. But the trifle troubled him. Things normally started with trifles. How she had flushed! They would finally have to show the boy his place and it would serve him right. The only thing that frustrated him was the unsettled state of his own household. It was a far cry from the routine on his Makatelema estate, the simple, solitary, northern life, but he had to attain more order here too: he should have hired a chambermaid with more sense. What ridiculous trivia one had to deal with at the end of a life that was turning to ashes and only occasionally, and pointlessly, bursting into flame. He knew it himself – yes, the other day he felt he had spoken absurdly in front of those youths who had sat here in his study like judges. He had spoken at such length and so passionately simply because he had not talked to anybody for a long time; he had had no one to talk to since those three days in Tver, after which his hopes and dreams had been shattered. He was revered and everyone fell silent before him, so it was strange that he now seemed to talk as if before judges – first in his audience with the Tsar and then in conversation with these youths. The Tsar had listened to him as if he had cared not a jot either about the old Russia or the new one. With these young fellows it was even worse. They behaved as if they knew both.

The fact that Katerina Andreyevna had suddenly lost confidence in the boy was, however, amusing, and even entertaining.

His young friend, mercurial and effusive, was hardly more than a child, and he had taken him perhaps too much into his confidence.

The world was becoming petty. Such was the new Russia.

Meanwhile Katerina Andreyevna neither smiled nor laughed. She was waiting for him as she had once waited only once before in her life – for the inconspicuous Ensign Strukov whom she had suddenly recalled this year, after reading about his valour in a newspaper. Her youth had flown. Or, as she had twice told herself that summer with voiceless lips, looking into the desolate night – life itself had flown.

She had forgotten the ensign again: she had commanded herself to forget him. And indeed, all thought of that unfortunate circumstance of her youth had disappeared; it had no connection with this boy and his silly billet-doux. But still, combing up her hair and breathing heavily, she remembered it.

Pushkin had come. He was sitting in their small round Chinese hall that seemed suddenly alien. Let him wait. She was calm and composed. She was listening. Nikolay Mikhaylovich was not in a hurry either. Pushkin frantically paced the room, stopping momentarily every now and again. At last she heard her husband entering the room. She would not let him talk to Pushkin face-to-face – his icy detachment would ruin everything. Karamzin stretched out his hand to give the letter back to Pushkin.

She came into the room at the moment when Pushkin, pale-faced, had just been handed his letter. Seeing her, he turned even paler. He did not look at them. Nikolay Mikhaylovich supported him by the elbow and led him to the settee. How tamed, how pathetic he had become! He was still holding his billet-doux and had not even put it into his pocket. She suddenly found him ridiculous. Nikolay Mikhaylovich talked to him directly, without coolness or malice, like a father, gave a laugh, and took the letter back, to reread it and analyse it in detail, as a kind of puzzle. Its brevity was astounding, and suggested that it had not been the first one to be written. But if it were not, how could he have been so careless, setting so little value on his passion? What was one to think about the person this anonymous and reckless note was meant for? Or maybe it had been meant for no one, and all this ferment of emotions was futile, like most poetry?

Pushkin was listening to him apparently unconcerned; listlessly he raised his eyes to her.

His self-possession had left him; he had even forgotten to greet her.

How clever, how wise her husband was! He simply made fun of him. He said that it was due to his protection that Pushkin was now sitting on the settee and had not been made to stand in a corner. He started to speak more heatedly of the pity Pushkin aroused in him. He also reminded him that only Aleksandr Turgenev was interested in his poems. Yes, they had been welcomed here in this chalet, welcomed optimistically in hopes that even better ones would follow. The Karamzins had encouraged him, but from now on they would be careful. The most absurd thing about this episode was his age.

Aleksandr, open-mouthed, stared into a corner. Then Nikolay Mikhaylovich reminded him of his recent conversation with Chaadayev. He called the Lycée 'the German Quarter',* where young people led a life of dissolution, imagining themselves Europeans. Yes, the Lycée really was the German Quarter, like that in Peter the Great's time, where the corruption of Russia had begun. Prince Vladimir Monomakh's dictum was great indeed: *Beat your child tirelessly*. That pathetic son of a priest Speransky was incapable of producing any comparable educational precepts – he was a laughing-stock. What was to be done with a passionate sixteen- or seventeen-year-old Don Juan? A Lovelace who forgot his friends and was still clutching the manuscript apparently so dear to him?

He was indeed still clutching the letter absurdly in his fingers, as if he had gone numb and lost all awareness. At this point Katerina Andreyevna burst out laughing – it was really very funny. He came to his senses, looked at the sheet of paper, crumpled it and looked up at her in astonishment.

Her laughter was growing louder and louder.

And he realised that his love, his hopes, his dreams, his poetry, his life and all he thought about it, his future – everything had been scorned, there was nothing left and there would always be nothing. She was laughing louder and louder at him. Completely unexpectedly, still holding the folded note in his hand, he burst into silent, unrestrained tears. He had never cried like this even as a child. His tears were not just rolling or streaming, they were bouncing down his cheeks, and after a minute the dark-green arm of the settee glistened as if washed with rain.

Nikolay Mikhaylovich left the room quietly. It was not what he had wished or expected. Pushkin rose, dropped his note at last and ran from the room, not looking where he was going, ran with the long blind light strides of someone running away for ever. He had not given her a last glance. But she was looking at him, and if he had seen the look in her eyes, he would not have cried like a child but would have stayed.

21

These were epigrams – iniquitous, malicious.

Karamzin clutched them in his hand convulsively. He read the first one. At least it had some geniality about it, however mischievous. The opening line was how old peasantwomen talked, coming back from the market. And this was the luminary of the new poetry! A new Voltaire! He did not reread the second epigram. He recognised his conversation with Chaadayev, distorted, maimed, shamelessly misinterpreted. He had no doubt who the author was

---

* A part of St Petersburg where foreign specialists settled under Peter the Great; subsequently the fashionable young flocked there to mingle with foreigners.

– and lost interest. To have escaped from all these tiresome visits, to live here in the Tsar's lonely estate, between friends and enemies, and to be betrayed by … a boy, Vasily Lvovich's nephew, a Lycéeist! Katerina Andreyevna had spoilt them all. Wasn't it strange that she had been acting younger than her years?

And he felt that he would not let her see these poems. He was afraid not that she would not share his anger – that was out of the question – he was afraid that she would be upset. He had noticed the expression on her face after his conversation with the hussar – an expression that was altogether too tender, too affectionate. Then she had taken her husband's hand in hers and kissed it suddenly. She had kissed his hand when he had signed the first proofs of *The History of the Russian State*. But why now?

And he said nothing to her about the poems.

When he saw Pushkin out of the window, on a Wednesday evening, he beckoned to him, confronted him with the epigrams and secretly enjoyed the impression this produced. How pale the poet grew! It was the childishness of it all that enabled him in large part to accept what had happened. He had flirted with Katerina Andreyevna, imagining, perhaps, that he was a hussar, and had written her an epistle, probably as a joke – the Lycée Principal ought to have been informed about it … to think how young men were being educated in Speransky's foundation! He had listened, confused, to the well-deserved reprimand and burst into tears like a child – amazing! The arm of the settee looked as if it had been soaked by rain through the window. He had then decided to take his revenge – and now here was the result.

He was not crying now, though he turned almost as white as before and, as on that previous occasion, did not say a word. Without the light, condescending chuckle he had permitted himself the first time, but drily and tersely, Nikolay Mikhaylovich told him not to visit him again until he had thought it all over, until he had learned to understand Russian history – or at least the distance between himself and the crucial events and themes of Russian history. And in order to get used to this distance, which was essential both for himself and for Russian history, he should for the time being keep his distance from the Chinese chalet …

22

He had not seen her for a week. No, not a week – eight days. He sneaked into their garden and saw her handing Nikolay Mikhaylovich proof sheets of his *History*, with the acrid smell of print on them. She was busy reading them. No matter what had happened with Pushkin, the *History* was sacred. However well he knew her, he did not know her sense of humour; probably only Karamzin did. The fact was, he had not seen her for eight days.

He had forgotten his tears, forgotten them forever. If he had not, he would not have been able to live, and would not have deserved to live. Now, after those shameful tears, he had learned to control himself – he wept no more, but sought consolation in leisurely, laconic conversation with Chaadayev. He had noted down certain phrases from the discussion between Chaadayev and Karamzin as accurately he could, and he shared Chaadayev's opinion of the elegance, simplicity and impartiality of Karamzin's great work. He started to write, and the rhymes came to him unbidden, impartially. Karamzin had spoken objectively of the necessity of autocracy, its inevitability.

> *In his History, elegance and simplicity*
> *Prove to us with complete impartiality*
> *The necessity of rule absolute*
> *And the overwhelming appeal of the knout.*

No dreamy in-betweens. The whole point of epigrams was their precision.

He had not seen her for a week. After going to the hussars and meeting Shishkov there, he woke up in the middle of the night and, spending the next day talking of precision, looked at his own life with precision – and was astonished and terrified. He thought with horror that the only truth he knew would have to disappear from his existence – he would have to hide her from everybody, first of all from himself, and would be unable to talk about her or even mention her name. This was what came through to him most of all. He was sentenced to silence. He could not even mention her in verse. What should he do? This love could not pass, and it was impossible to forget. But he was forbidden to confess it. He had already started to lie to himself. Spontaneously he spread his arms wide – he was afraid even to think about it. So he didn't. Only precision remained possible for him. He went on writing poems, the usual ones. Batyushkov might have liked them, yes, Batyushkov would have praised him for them! To hell with him!

And then on the eighth day it became clear to him: he was unhappy, and happiness was impossible. Supposing he wrote about this?

> *Happy he who in his passion*
> *Dares look at himself without fear.*

In his passion. At once he felt better. This was his nature. This was no Lycéeist's love. It was passion, which he had dared not confess to himself. Now the Lycée, with its exercises, fears and secrets, was over. Passion, and the fear of passion, had taken hold of him.

She could not understand herself. She was displeased with herself, dissatisfied with the deity to whom she had sacrificed her life and her youth. Alas, where was it, youth? She was ageing, and only her great husband's care and diligent patience gave her brief moments when she felt young again. She was growing old before her time. Today she remembered Avdotya's simple, expressionless glance, which had shown that she was interested in the boy. She remembered Pushkin giving Avdotya a quick look of dismay, almost in the same way as when he had cried. She simply felt sorry for him, as if he were a child. But the boy was astonishingly ardent, and sudden reckless passions fired him up all at once. And she felt that she would not give him up to Avdotya and, having realised that, she grew angry with herself. Pushkin had behaved with complete propriety recently, and had even attempted more than one clumsy joke. She was simply being too self-critical, and she noticed that this contributed to her discontent.

Every day Nikolay Mikhaylovich went for a ride in the woods to pick mushrooms, and she observed the way he sat in the saddle. If only he relaxed a little more one could say he rode like a young man, like a Guardsman. Impossible! He rode as befitted an intelligent and great man no longer accustomed to riding, and his excellent posture was a little comic. When he had gone out, she would take a walk. The Palace seemed to enclose her on all sides. She would leave her picturesque but bare Chinese chalet to go and look at the monuments in the park.

After those unrestrained tears, which now put him to shame, Pushkin did not dare appear at the Karamzins'. He wandered about until on the seventh day he felt he was suffocating.

While Engelhardt was away, he roamed the gardens, consumed by his one and only passion, and with forced interest examined the monuments of Tsarskoye Selo.

And this is how they accidentally ran into one another. He saw her at once. She was looking at a black plate with embossed letters commemorating the glorious battle of Kagul; the plate gave an account of the battle like a concise historical note of the sort she had read and corrected many times in *The History of the Russian State*. She read it from beginning to end and leaned against the cast iron. It was a hot day but the metal was chilly; she touched it and drew her finger along a name. It was at that moment that Pushkin spotted her and rushed up to her like a spurred horse.

She was more pleased to see him than she ought to have been, than she had expected herself to be.

He embraced her waist and suddenly, breathless, sank down at her feet and pressed his lips to her slender foot. She closed her eyes.

He did not say a word; he was lying at her feet and she was at a loss for what to say and how to say it. His mind completely out of control, he rose to his feet, still gasping, unable to tear himself from her. Instead of embracing her he had dropped at her feet as if cut down, mortally wounded.

He started to come to the monument several times each day – in the afternoon and in the evening. On the first day he studied the whole detailed list of the victorious deeds of the heroes of Kagul. He was proud to see the name of Ivan Abramovich Hannibal among them. Next day he reread the list. His black mood had disappeared, and coming back from the Kagul monument he suddenly burst out laughing. He had not died, he had not gone mad. He laughed out of sheer happiness. Back at the Lycée he wrote all night.

She said nothing to her great husband – his peace of mind was the most precious thing. Pushkin was just a mad boy; she felt sorry for him.

She tried to forget about what had happened at the Kagul monument. She realised that as usual she had done the right thing when she had decided not to give him up to Avdotya. That look he had given her – how promptly he had submitted to her! And then – he had fallen at her feet as if mortally wounded. But he had not died. And she laughed as she had not laughed for a long time – flushing, with open lips.

He had fallen at her feet! As if mortally wounded! But he had not died, he was alive and his poems were alive. So alive that when she read them she cast her eyes down as if they were his personal letters to her. He had not died – he was a survivor!

She flushed with joy.

Nobody could have said that Pushkin had not been affected by Karamzin. Would his poems really have been the same if he had never met him? But now, with each day that passed, his writing was becoming different.

Once Karamzin asked him how his 'little poem' was going, if it was finished yet.

This first-rate and famous writer, already tasting the bitter dregs of the poetical life, was asking about a new verse tale that had only just been begun and that he had sampled, keenly interested.

Step by step, patiently and persistently, Pushkin was following Karamzin and writing a clever 'little poem' with the light clever chuckle characteristic of Karamzin, a poem that bade fair to compare with Karamzin's best verse. The subtle chuckle was personified in the heroine, who was called Zoya. Zoya was a perfectly sensible girl who was not going to ruin her life out of gratitude to the hero,

To go to jail to please the Tsar.

The poet cleverly avoided conclusions, and the result was charming and ironic, showing a subtle awareness of Karamzin. He avoided rhymes so as to achieve the honesty of prose. He continued this witty tale to a turning-point and then dropped it, refusing to read or think about it any more.

He had learnt to discard. Rhyme had previously proved the truth of a thought. Those who wrote without rhymes were afraid of truth. Rhyme used to be a goddess. Now the highest proof of truth, the sharpest edge of reason, of the mind, was love. It was not love, however, but unhappiness that lay in store for him. Still ... Long live the Muses, long live reason! He had been writing his new poem for five days and two nights. Rhyme, love – absolute, not half-hearted – and reason! Russian history for him was the creation of the Karamzins.

Rhyme. And love was as true as rhyme. Not half-hearted, not a caprice of the mind – long live reason and the Muse!

Russian history, the ancient Russian Motherland! Rhyme was the proof that the idea was right. His love was proof of the truth of events, the events of Russian history, of his motherland. He learned from the Karamzins – from Katerina Andreyevna Karamzina. How often he had grumbled at his motherland when official quills had screeched about it. His 'little poem' was to be a true epic. The history of the Russian land was the creation of Katerina Andreyevna Karamzina.

When he had suddenly dropped at her feet, when he had wept wildly at the Karamzins', he had suddenly known and felt that there was only one cure for it all. He had risen to his feet, gone for a long walk, thought deeply – and suddenly burst out laughing.

23

Archimandrite Photius was full of joy. He had been threatened with Gehenna but no, he wouldn't have it! He knew human nature. People swallowed his bait, got caught in their sins and he promised them a cure. He could sniff sin as a dog sniffs game. He had recently been put in charge of the Yuryevetsky Monastery, in the poorest of parishes.

It was a sign of appreciation and elevation and all on account of his shrewdness.

It had just been reported to him that the Herod Golitsyn had fallen from favour.* Rejoice, Isaiah! Golitsyn was the epitome of all sins.

He visited Countess Anna Orlova-Chesmenskaya. A serious person! She held power over half the world.

---

*As a result of the campaign against him by Photius and others for alleged 'lack of piety', Golitsyn was dismissed from his post as Procurator of the Holy Synod at this time (1816), remaining, however, Minister of Education and in October of the same year becoming head of a merged Ministry of Education and Religious Affairs.

He was exultant.

Anna Orlova, daughter of Aleksey Orlov, who had made his fortune overnight when he had rushed Catherine over from Peterhof and murdered her husband Peter III at the dinner table, and all his life, like a child, like a schoolboy, had been fond of fun and fist-fights. Now the rest of the family refused to see Anna Orlova because of him, Photius. What wealth she had inherited! The Yuryevetsky Monastery would be no longer just a monastery, a fraternity or a patrimony – it would be a state in itself, and all due to him, Photius! He had become Anna Orlova's spiritual father and personal confessor, but was in no hurry to absolve her sins – let her come to him a few more times.

Now he had achieved the removal of Golitsyn from power – a voluptuary and a slippery sodomite. And how devilishly wealthy Anna was! A roomful of Ancient Roman gold statues: now they were his. He would have them melted. And Anna would make sure her uncles did not interfere.

Photius had arrived at Tsarskoye Selo to see Anna. Here sin was rampant, on show! Here events took place that only he, Photius, had the power to influence. The deceased Emperor Paul still disturbed some people's peace. But Photius had a surprise in store for His Majesty – he had a wound on his chest which he didn't allow to heal. At any moment he could present the Tsar with the sight, would rip his shirt open – and he would prevail!

He slept in a coffin, which Anna had made warm and comfortable. He woke up early and was in ecstasy all day. The time had come for the Yuryevetsky Monastery to take control of Russia. Time to dance!

He took Countess Anna Alekseyevna Orlova-Chesmenskaya, submissive, by the hand and, as always nowadays, began to sing and hum, swaying from side to side before her.

'O Anna! O beautiful girl! Anna!'

He sang and hummed in his thin voice, exhilarated at what lay ahead, swaying from side to side, and clasped her in his arms.

'Anna! You beautiful girl!'

But at this moment Annushka – so he called her when he was happy – at this moment Annushka, so thrifty when she had to pay her spiritual father his due (which she did with promissory notes and money orders), slipped a sheet of paper into his hand.

Still humming and rejoicing – 'O beautiful girl! O Anna!' – he glanced down at the sheet.

He continued his singing and swaying. The sheet of paper must concern some secular matter.

Singing and swaying, he noticed that it was a poem.

A Devout Wife … !

He was aware that poets devoted poems to her. Prince Nikita Shikhmatov, for example, had extolled her.

'O Anna! O beautiful girl!'

He danced, holding his beautiful Anna by the hand, and suddenly recited in a resonant voice:

> *A devout wife's soul*
> *Belongs to the Lord of all,*
> *But her sinful body*
> *To Archimandrite Photy.*

And unable to cease his dance, which seemed to be inspired from above, he chanted in the same thin tones:

'Satan!'

And, still swaying, he continued to sing of the poet who had written these lines. He sang the order:

'Away with him – to the Sol-ov-ki Monastery!'

24

He had caught them!

He had caught this couple – and where? – in his own house, in his very own – God help us! – unassuming Principal's house where he lived, he, the guardian of this place and of these Lycéeists! He, the real founder of the Lycée, who took care of everyone and created friendly relations with all, he who had joined this gathering of those seeking guidance, he alone had achieved all this with his labours! But he had always been modest. When Korff had tried to say that the marble plaque the Principal had had put up – *Genio loci* – was the recognition of *his* deserts – hadn't he stopped him? The Lycée plaque had been put up in honour of the Emperor and of the Lycée, not of himself. Anyway, his efforts had been rewarded.

Outsiders always caused misfortunes. He had caught this couple in the most indecent circumstances! He had been entrusted with the education and welfare of these youths, he had been watching them and taking good care of them, asking only one thing – that there should be no interference from outside. But this Pushkin, who simply fell on women, had brought dissipation! He had taken urgent measures. The young widow, Marie Smith, had packed her things and Foma had immediately been ordered to take her to the station. Today. Now. She had already left. The Principal had been honouring the memory of her husband whom he had never known. But did it matter? He had hung up his portrait as a reminder to the young widow, to encourage her to conduct herself properly. And he had caught them! He was not going to allow a word to be said about what had happened, and he himself would not breathe a word about it to anyone. It was too shameful. He had to conceal it.

He decided not to take action at once; he postponed it for a day, unwisely. He, Principal Engelhardt, the real *genius loci*, had caught Pushkin with the young widow. Quietly he told the policeman:

'He … He must be … I want to see neither hide nor hair of him here any more!'

And so it would have been – but the next day was the day old Neledinsky-Meletsky arrived with an inscribed watch from the Dowager Empress. Engelhardt felt relieved he hadn't expelled the urchin the day before. What a piece of good luck! He made a note about Pushkin in the discipline book: 'Both his heart and his mind are empty.' Pushkin was exultant but restrained himself. He made a note in the Principal's album too – shorter than the others and appropriately evasive: There were no ungrateful ones at the Lycée. No word about the Principal directly. Being a good-natured person the Principal was truly upset by Pushkin's callousness – he didn't seem to be moved by the gift of the Empress's watch; he hadn't said a word, though he seemed pleased enough. He would have to be more careful with him. He placed his real hopes in others. Korff had said that Pushkin was cold and empty and had only two passions – women and poetry.

How could Engelhardt have imagined that this watch, this gift from the old Empress, would be given to the dissipated, heartless and empty-headed Pushkin! How to explain that! Korff, intelligent, sincere, hard-working and making good progress in his studies, had been right about Pushkin. And as for the widow – not a word had been or would be said about the whole affair.

Who could have thought that his poems could have such power! He was a scoffer and a wit, God knew where he could have read all these French authors; he had long been familiar with Voltaire's every verse but his knowledge of literature was superficial, and he showed no interest whatsoever in German literature. The Principal wanted to educate his charges as polished citizens, but instead – what devilish mockery!

Now the Principal had had to survive this further humiliation of the Empress's gift. Never mind! At least it was a recognition of the Lycée – except that the scoundrel did not even value the honour of the gift and even seemed to have just lost it. Yet another thing to worry about!

He gave a sigh. He would have to talk to Pushkin.

What he had had to put up with that year at the Lycée because of him! Küchlya was eccentric, but from a respectable family, and all his eccentricities were to be ignored. And now Küchlya, despite his respectable father's acquaintance with Engelhardt, had suddenly had his say (no doubt under Pushkin's influence).

He had said that the Principal favoured only those who could easily change their opinions. The Principal had done his best to make Arakcheyev look favourably on the Lycée. And this urchin had infected all the students! And what if something terrible happened? Even Küchlya had had his say. Pushkin would alienate everyone from the Principal. He had to find out if this rogue had really lost the watch.

Foma, keep an eye on it! – On what? – On the watch, Foma. Oh, oh!

25

No one knew him, no one knew where he lived. Who was this Arakcheyev? How and why had he appeared on the scene? Why, before getting an audience with the Tsar, had Karamzin had to see *him?*

There was some mystery about it. Women in particular became heated on the subject. Rumour had it that he had rescued the Emperor when he had been drowning. Others said it wasn't true, that the accident had never taken place. How then had their friendship started? Simply because he had been 'loyal without flattery' as his motto said? The Tsar was showered with flattery from every side.

It was whispered that he was illiterate, and he was pleased to confirm the rumour, although as a matter of fact he was a reasonably educated man.

He had been in the artillery in his younger days. It was said that he had got rid of Speransky in 1812 but that wasn't true either: he had got on well with Speransky, though they hadn't seen much of each other.

What was the secret of his power then? Nobody knew. Perhaps it was his love of military discipline and drill, which he knew better than anybody else.

The Tsar personally supervised the mounting of the guard. He had to have something to believe in, and he believed in military discipline. Military discipline would solve all problems! If the peasants were organised in military settlements, there would be bread and all would be well. Only Arakcheyev could match the Tsar's love of drill. He trusted him from the moment he first saw 'loyalty without flattery' in the flesh. Drill made conscience unnecessary. The perfection in drill now achieved had been unparalleled even in the reign of Emperor Paul. Somebody had said that it wasn't drill that inspired the Russians to victory over Napoleon. This was just the idle talk of the younger generation; they would have talked differently if they had spent twenty years drilling. Many new-fangled methods of education had appeared from abroad. The Lancasterian system from England, for example – one pupil teaching another: under this system, learning was said to be very rapid. But the trouble with this was that you'd no sooner look round than learning would have taken place. Suppose the whole army learned to read!

It wasn't going to be allowed. And it wasn't just reading – let them read! – what if they started writing too?

Blasphemous leaflets had begun circulating. Here, read them. He issued an order to check all written and printed matter in the barracks, to collect it and bring it to him for checking. He took a bundle of handwritten and printed paper brought for him to read. It was tied with a piece of cord in accordance with his usual demand. He quickly looked through the sheets to see if anything caught his eye. Nothing. Thank God for that! Nothing. He was expecting to see some responses to military settlements.* Everything seemed strangely tranquil. He disliked flattery but he liked order. People wrote to other departments, so why didn't they write to this one too?

No, no critical attitudes here.

But these inflammatory verses were now in circulation:

> *No mind, no feeling, no honour at all,*
> *Who's this, 'no flatterer – but loyal'?*
> *– A common, well-disciplined corporal.*

The verses were anonymous, apparently from ill-wishers. Who are they, Lavrov? It's your job to find out. *A common, well-disciplined corporal,* he read bitterly more than once. Spend twenty-five years in the artillery first and then teach. Keep an eye on them, secret agent Lavrov, find out who they are. Teach them. Just drill. Fall in! Right dress! Present arms! Atten-tion!

26

Suddenly, like everything that happened in his life, Pushkin had acquired a friend and follower – a mad cavalryman. He had galloped his horse like a rider seeking a quick death, the quicker the better. Pushkin had first seen him in the hussars' quarters, galloping towards him at full tilt. A small, tightly buttoned figure in a new uniform, with enormously wide trousers instead of the old narrow ones, a smart new pelisse on his shoulder and a dagger in his belt, hurtling towards him. A policeman was already yelling to him to stop and warning pedestrians of the danger when he suddenly halted as if rooted to the ground. The small, wiry grey mare was breathing heavily, all in a lather

---

*What Alexander I conceived as a humanitarian project – the establishment of a part of the peacetime Russian army in settlements combining military service with farming and 'normal' family life – proved intensely unpopular and eventually unworkable owing to the harsh regimentation with which the scheme was implemented by Arakcheyev.

and throwing her narrow head upwards. Foam dripped from the bit. The cavalryman explained:

'She bolted.'

And he proceeded at a walk towards Pushkin.

It was clear that he had deliberately spurred on his horse, but no one pointed this out. It was known that he was quick-tempered and had fought two duels. When he dismounted, he turned out to be an extraordinarily handsome and quiet youth. He had come to see Molostov and Kaverin on a business matter – a duel; Yuryev had challenged him. He didn't mention the reason. When he saw Pushkin, his face lit up and he fell upon him.

It was Shishkov, a poet, who for a long time had wanted to make friends with him.

Aleksandr Shishkov wrote spontaneous, witty elegies similar to Pushkin's. Lately he had started to write epigrams. He imitated Pushkin so closely that Pushkin had begun to disapprove. But Shishkov didn't bother to conceal the fact. Their first meeting was as passionate as their immediate friendship. Shishkov smoked his pipe and choked on its smoke, but having the reputation of recklessness he had to smoke, he couldn't help it. He was frank with Pushkin.

Perhaps too frank. At first Pushkin was struck dumb. Shishkov was the nephew of the famous old 'Land Admiral', head of the frightful Symposium which had been waging war against Karamzin and who had been annoying and inspiring his uncle Vasily Lvovich. *The Dangerous Neighbour* wouldn't have been written had it not been for the Land Admiral and his stooges.

After 1812 times and expectations had changed – things couldn't stay as they were. A new breed had appeared, and the Land Admiral happened to have a flighty nephew. The famous uncle who kept an eye on him wearied him. The nephew didn't agree with being called 'Shishkov the Second'. 'It's my uncle who's second, not me.'

Shishkov took a card from the table and thrust another into Pushkin's hand. But Pushkin did not want to play tonight. Shishkov watched him with a card in his hand and said in resonant tones:

'Uncle for uncle!' And he pulled two portrait cards out of his cuff and threw them on the table.

Everyone fell silent. Aleksandr stared at Shishkov in disbelief. His uncle Vasily Lvovich against Admiral Shishkov! Just recently some people had cursed his uncle while others had sworn loyalty to him, and today it was 'uncle for uncle'! The enemies' rivalry had become ridiculous: surely this was going too far? He threw his cards onto the table. His uncle was amusing indeed, but he did not like this laughter. Shishkov the Second tended to end things either in laughter or with a pistol-shot.

Kaverin shuffled the cards with the two portraits.

'Desperate,' he said.

Meanwhile the desperate youth was reciting his epigram. That was why he had come, on his grey mare, in his splendid new uniform.

The epigram was concise. It was obvious he had read all Pushkin's – this one might well have been his. He recited in a calm, even tone:

> *You wanted freedoms – take the tide:*
> *Trousers have changed from narrow to wide.*

Then he looked at the hussars in their wide trousers, pressed his hand to his chest as his gaze fell upon Pushkin, tossed away the indispensable pipe he had grown tired of, brought his slender, wide-trousered legs together and dashed away.

27

He knew that every day he would roam about near the Chinese chalets, not actually reaching hers but sometimes passing nearby. Once he heard her voice – she was talking to her children. 'My little ones,' he heard her say, and froze. When she said her next words in French he thought that perhaps the Tsar was paying her a visit again. He stood still, holding his breath almost to suffocation, then heard Neledinsky's gently pompous voice and burst into soft laughter. She always spoke Russian to her children. He stood there listening to her talking to them; her quaint, singsong tones and grammatical mistakes always disarmed him in spite of Koshansky's advice to beware of the latter. Standing there for the third day in a row and listening to her wonderful speech, with sudden understanding he said out loud:

'Indeed!'

He realised that he had learned all of Russian history, from Vladimir the Red Sun onwards, here at the Karamzins', and not from Nikolay Mikhaylovich but from Katerina Andreyevna. A Vyazemsky on her father's side, she was a princess from head to toe, but spoke to her children tenderly and in the quaintly rustic manner that Arina had done. By what luck had he met her? Here, so close to the Lycée, just a stone's throw from it, in a Chinese chalet in this phantasmagorical Chinese Village.

Passion took greater and greater hold of him.

He truly couldn't breathe. He took deep breaths, gasping as he did during his fights with Malinovsky but not giving up and afraid that somebody might notice. How touching were her conversations with her children, how melodious her laughter, how lively her expression! She listened to his poems in her own particular way, without comment, and then a week later would recall and recite them line by line, softly and slowly, with growing conviction and confidence in him. Her attentiveness made it clear that his poems were both appealing and precious to her, and he heard them, and saw himself, in a different way. Once she said a line wrongly; he was about to correct her, but then decided to let it stand exactly as she had said it. He couldn't help it; it was final, beyond his and certainly beyond her power to change, for ever. He couldn't foresee what was in store for him; he just knew that he had to keep silent. Not a word even to himself, he had to bury his passion and his transport deep inside himself, from the very beginning. It was forbidden; it was a crime against the great writer Karamzin, against his uncle Vasily Lvovich, against her half-brother Vyazemsky (Petya as she called him), against his father and mother. He shuddered at the thought that his fate was sealed forever. He didn't dare visit the Karamzins; it was an open wound. Where and how would he see her in the coming year? Would it be like this all his life?

His uncle's family life had been a mess and he had had to flee to Paris to recover from the scandal; his grandfather's life had been a disaster, and so had his great-grandfather's, but none of them could have even imagined the love that had struck him and pierced him like a bullet. The secrecy in this love was agonising – and it was never-ending, irrevocable, never letting him free even for a moment.

And so it began.

But he was ready for it – from the very first.

Her wise husband was the genius of this place, the God of the Chinese Village. He saw and knew and endured it. The only thing he couldn't reconcile himself to was that she loved this ageing man so profoundly. She refused to have her portraits painted and didn't want her beauty talked about. Karamzin was getting older. But it wasn't his work, his talent or his *History* that lured her. No, she loved *him*, this infinitely subtle intellectual and teacher, she loved *him*, as beautiful young girls did, and it was incomprehensible to him. Such modesty and self-oblivion – was it some black magic? He imagined the two heads together – that of the cunning, ageing enchanter and that of the beautiful, eternally young woman. Not a word about this love. But if a word or a line ever did escape his lips, he would conceal it among other loves and tell lies if he had to. And keep silent. To the end.

This was just the beginning.

28

This permanent passion, bottled like wine, would lose its strength at times. He sighed and took a different look at her, at himself and his life. But he still suffered the deep wounds of love and the memory of them.

The passion retreated. He forgot his epigrams.

Chaadayev was in a similar position: obsessed with just one thought and one secret. Pushkin did not know what it was but could guess. Only at Chaadayev's did he feel at ease.

Love was absent in the intellectual's abode; for him love was either sad or ridiculous. But here there was no sadness or mockery either. The very thought of love, like the thought of disease, disappeared here.

Love had never crossed the threshold of this room. Chaadayev's secret was of a different kind. He had designed a precise means of achieving happiness; not for himself but for everyone, for the whole of Russia.

Nobody could call him a dandy or a fop. So perfectly conceived was his appearance that his hussar's uniform lay as if sculpted on him. But it was not dandyism. There was nothing superfluous about him. No partiality.

Molostov lost a ring to him at cards. Chaadayev looked at it closely and brushed it off the table.

'When they sold a slave in ancient Rome,' he said, looking at the surprised Pushkin, 'instead of shackles they drew a line around his leg, below the knee.'

And since Pushkin's bewilderment hadn't been dispelled but was growing, he said gravely:

'I don't wear rings. They remind me of slavery.'

Now Chaadayev sniffed a slice of bread brought by a servant with his tea as connoisseurs smell wine to distinguish between Lafite and Chablis and looked at him with his clear expert eyes, calm and unhurried.

'We and the slaves who wait on us,' he said, looking at the departing servant (he had no batman), 'don't we breathe the same air? And bread? And the furrows that were ploughed by slaves in the sweat of their brows,' he said, 'isn't that the soil that supports us all?'

He pushed the ring aside with his foot. And without raising his voice he said:

'This is a vicious circle which strangles us all. My dear friend, you won't be able to recognise yourself or your poetry when we break free – and it will be soon. You better than anybody else feel the times we live in and the time that is at hand. The main thing is to recognise the crucial moment. My dear friend, everything we are waiting for will come true because time itself is working for us. You haven't been to Switzerland, have you? I've seen free peasants there. They walk with a different step. Slavery is infectious. There isn't a single village left any more with all these military settlements. By God, how infectious it is. You can't imagine how high it reaches, how it rules everything and is crawling up to the throne to take a seat next to the Tsar. When the Tsar finally sees it, slavery will disappear, it will vanish as if it never existed.'

Pushkin was listening to Chaadayev, as usual, with all his being. It was the only proper way to listen to Chaadayev – economical with his words, even more so with gesture, and unsmiling. Suddenly Pushkin threw himself back in his chair.

'What we need is Brutus, then?' he said, inspired.

Chaadayev was silent.

'You seem unsettled today. My dear friend, soon you'll taste what freedom is,' he said calmly. 'What poems you'll write then! Slavery will vanish. This will come about. It will be so!'

He asked Pushkin politely if he had seen the Karamzins recently. The things he appreciated about Karamzin's *History* were the sheer sound of its language, its simplicity and the impartiality of the narrative. But Ivan III, though of course a good monarch, could by no means be considered the greatest of all. The historian hadn't paid enough attention to Peter the Great: this was the time when the flags of all nations had visited Russia, when real international communications had started. What did Pushkin think about that?

The values of Karamzin's household, however, could scarcely be overestimated. The wonderful tone, the very atmosphere of the house, the rare beauty of the hostess – her astonishing conversation, with her level-headedness, breadth of knowledge and confidence in the truth. She was charming.

'What's the matter, my dear chap?' the hussar asked anxiously.

Pushkin turned first white as a sheet and then crimson. He searched for words and got confused. He looked pathetic. Chaadayev watched him closely. He believed in Pushkin. Inaccessible to love, he yet understood its anxieties and reverses. Seeing and guessing almost everything, he carefully and calmly prepared and poured his young friend a cup of the black fragrant coffee he had received from England, distracting him from his thoughts by these orderly actions. He asked no questions. Had his friend acted otherwise, Pushkin would have burst into tears like a baby. His life was a misery. But now he calmed down.

Chaadayev embraced Pushkin when he left.

29

Reveille.

It had just begun to dawn, the day had not yet broken. Everything was as usual; behind the wall Pushchin was still asleep.

Reveille. The first sound was the trumpet – doleful but vibrant, and immediately followed by the high-pitched, precise, loud clear sound of the signal drum.

Reveille.

A dilapidated volume of Dante that he had been leafing through that night fell from his hand.

The final year at the Lycée passed as if it had never had been.

Reveille.

The high-pitched, loud and precise sounds took away his shallow sleep, his delusive, mouldering dreams. His love was as exact as time, like a military step, like a march, like the future. Most of all, more precisely than anything else, the future was foretold by what had passed. The history of Russia according to Katerina Karamzina was in his heart and mind.

Reveille. Rapid and precise.

They graduated from the Lycée, whose walls had proved unable to contain them any longer, three months earlier than had been planned. On the ninth of June 1817 the Tsar and Prince Golitsyn appeared in the assembly hall of the Lycée and next day the first Lycéeists left the Lycée forever.

Reveille.

Three years later, in a hurry from some European Congress, the Tsar sent an order to fence off the Lycée from the Palace. Immediately! Precisely, clearly, loudly.

Reveille. The Lycée march to Delvig's verse.

Reveille.

Everyone had come. They were seeking appointments. How different they looked now; at the Lycée everyone seemed to look the same. Only after leaving the Lycée did they seem to acquire their individual walks, each his own, an extraordinary one in Küchelbecker's case. What appointment was suitable for *him*?

But he too signed his name.

They signed a statement that they would not join any secret societies. All of them signed the document with a light heart.

Pushchin was the first to arrive, followed by other Lycéeists and guests.

All had signed the statement with a feeling of satisfaction; they were applying for appointments; life was beginning.

Pushkin made up his mind that he would go to his ancestral estate – Mikhaylovskoye.

They agreed to meet on Lycée anniversaries. Where? When? In this building with columns. Everyone said good-bye. Pushkin and Delvig embraced.

Pushkin too signed the undertaking and gave a sudden laugh. What about the Lycée anniversary meetings? It had been agreed that all the Lycéeists would meet every year on the date of the opening of the Lycée, the nineteenth of October. Misha Yakovlev was elected anniversary secretary. But these were his own people, 'fellow beasts', as they called themselves, not a secret society.

And what about Arzamas? He even had the Arzamasian nickname of Cricket from one of Zhukovsky's ballads. He was indeed like a cricket, keeping the rest of them awake with his chirruping. He would hardly succeed in a career. Would he be able to work every day of the week except Sundays and holidays? Unlikely.

The Lycée was not yet over. The lectures, the routine at Tsarskoye Selo, the dawn awakenings, the strolling about in compositional obsession all day long – all these were over, but not the Lycée itself. The Lycée could never end.

His family? He had none: his father lived an imaginary life; his mother was a creature of temperament who quickly grew excited and lost interest without rhyme or reason. His only family was Arina.

All he had were Arina and the Lycée which would never end – that was all. Such was his life. Nothing changed. And who did he have at the Lycée? Pushchin, Delvig – and Küchlya, his brother in the Muse and in destiny: these few were his real kin.

It wasn't the authorities or Engelhardt who had produced this kin. As far as he was concerned, Malinovsky remained their only Principal and Tsarskoye Selo was their native land.

A thinker might ask how exactly this fraternity had come about. Why had Tsarskoye Selo been so dear to them? Was it because they had got up at the same time each day, had the same food, had walks together and been taught by the same teachers? Was it these facts that had produced the extreme closeness that they would preserve till the end of their lives? The thinker might so conclude – and be wrong. First of all, not everyone had dinner. The Incorrigibles were sometimes not given it. Life is a matter of routine, but unity is also needed, and those who create it are never forgotten. Engelhardt was unable to do it no matter how hard he tried. First there had been Malinovsky, then the interregnum, and only towards the end Engelhardt. Could it have been Pushkin who created this Lycée unity, the serious thinker might ask? But he couldn't even remember half the Lycéeists. Was it Yakovlev, then, who impersonated two hundred people including the policeman?

It could have been either.

Each of these two remembered his real friends.

There was Gorchakov with his incredible memory, which surprised himself no less than others. That memory later became renowned throughout the diplomatic world. Once he met Pushkin on the road – their estates lay near each other. As soon as they saw each other they embraced like brothers. They were Lycéeists. Engelhardt could have had absolutely no understanding of this. Who could have understood it?

Perhaps Misha Yakovlev indeed, impersonator of those two hundred people: acquaintances, passers-by, that policeman. It was not for nothing that he had been elected anniversaries secretary.

Long live the Lycée!

No matter where they were to be or where their destinies were to bring them. Küchlya was to spend ten years in a fortress in solitary confinement. And every year he would mark the sacred first day of the Lycée – the nineteenth of October.

30

Next night he was at Avdotya's.

Her Old Russian beauty and her Old Russian eccentricities struck him as extraordinarily novel. It was she who had started to call herself Avdotya in the Old Russian fashion when nobody else would have thought of doing so. She had been previously known as *Eudoxie* or, to her elders, Yevdokiya. A gypsy told her she would die at night in her sleep.

The next day she stopped accepting daytime visitors, but at night her house by the Neva would be brightly lit. Rows of carriages with cabmen holding torches would arrive at the house by the river – the street would ring with the sound of horses' hooves. The guests would come and go till morning and the last to go would leave at dawn. Wags nicknamed her the *princesse nocturne*. She had turned day into night and night into day.

When she was young she had fallen madly in love and had soon been married off to old Golitsyn. Her elderly husband had little interest in what she did and never interfered with her activities. She did her best to escape fate and death with rare composure, recklessness and even courage.

She wrote a book on mathematics and had it published. When the Princess of Night started talking about arcs and tangents, Vyazemsky surreptitiously made the sign of the cross. Avdotya was a friend of Katerina Karamzina. She dressed herself in a light blue sarafan, which suited her nicely.

When Pushkin was working on his new fairy-tale poem,* he wanted to see no one else but Avdotya. He couldn't write his poem without her, he couldn't help it; without her his life lacked fullness. Katerina Andreyevna was always with her.

He would come to see her in the small hours.

Cabmen were a torture he had known nothing of at Tsarskoye Selo. His father, who counted money grudgingly and always bargained with cabmen, now became a model for him: it was no easy business to bargain with a cabman when he went to see the Night Princess.

He would stare for a long time into the deep black Neva.

---

* *Ruslan and Lyudmila.*

A porter with a heavy mace saw him into the hall – the Princess was accepting visitors tonight.

He entered. Some cavalrymen had just left. Avdotya had on her usual evening dress for visiting nights: covering her famous shoulders was a heavy gold-brocade sarafan embroidered with expensive precious stones. Her beauty threw him into instant confusion.

In her silvery musical voice she was talking about the new trends which were not to her liking – and which could not even be named in Russian. Who could remember all the prodigies of the present time, such as Katenin, now a very influential figure in the theatre.

Pushkin looked down, embarrassed.

Indeed, Katenin had become renowned for both his poetry and his plays, but was not always talked about favourably. It seemed no accident that Katenin disliked love poems. His poems were well-written, complex and powerful, but his opinions were quite different from those of Zhukovsky and Karamzin. Avdotya was not interested in such distractions. He took no lessons either from the wise, knowledgeable Karamzin or from the admirable, hard-working Zhukovsky. Was he no good at folk-heroes? On the contrary! Well might he sing the bitter soldier's song to himself:

> *Home came the soldier*
> *From his school of slaughter –*
> *Tired – tired.*

And here he was coming from his school – to Avdotya. *His* folk-heroes would be all right! And his poetry! He would go to see Katenin the very next day. He recalled his 'little poem' and gnashed his teeth.

In her silvery musical voice Avdotya remarked to him that men seemed to excel both in the arts and in the sciences. However, when her mathematical book had been published in Paris, men had failed to understand it.

The porter came in and reported:

'The Prince is asking to see you.'

Avdotya's aged husband had come to see her!

'It's night-time. I'm in bed. He's welcome in the morning.'

The porter reported back:

'Her Excellency is in bed. She asks you to wait until tomorrow morning.'

This was a wicked mockery. The old Prince always laughed at her whims and only extreme necessity would have made him appear before dawn.

But she allowed Pushkin to stay.

She threw off her heavy sarafan, with its precious stones, as ancient warriors must have taken off their armour. Her Old Russian speech was resonant, her

Old Russian shoulders were magnificent and eternal. Avdotya's charms filled the room.

'Blow out the candle,' she said.

31

Freedom! Freedom alone was what he valued, freedom alone was what he lived for, but he couldn't find it anywhere – in love, in friendship, in youth.

He loved and felt like a prisoner in shackles: he could speak not a word of truth, not a line. He did not dare approach her, all he could do was make sure that no one guessed or imagined or could imagine his secret. He was doomed for life – until death.

As Cricket, the elect member of the freedom-loving Arzamas, he joined Vyazemsky in laying blame on Shakhovskoy. He wrote in response to Ozerov's death:

Ozerov's spirit calls out to us: 'Avenge me, friends!'

Ozerov died of mental illness.* Vyazemsky called him a genius and claimed that it was Shakhovskoy's envy that had killed him.

At the Karamzins' Chinese chalet people walked on tiptoe as if at the bed of a gravely ill patient. He had to learn to hate and to revere.

Freedom!

Chaadayev was the first to talk to him about it.

He heartily disliked the Arzamasian Bludov. There were many courtiers more important than he was, and his jokes were elaborate and not even funny. Now he was on a diplomatic mission. Oh well, good luck to him.

Karamzin's achievements were sacred. Chaadayev had to be praised. Freedom and reason!

At home he found victims. Sergey Lvovich, seeing his son was an adult who had written an undertaking not to join any societies, complained that neither his brother Vasily Lvovich nor even his wife could understand them, the Pushkins, that is, him, Sergey Lvovich. He was putting his servant Nikita at his son's disposal. He had been turning a blind eye to his son's peccadilloes … and so on and so forth.

He himself used to … And even now sometimes … His son's poems … were quite felicitous. He himself used to …

The previous year the traveller Anseleau had written that the name Pushkin was propitious for poetry. His uncle Vasily Lvovich was growing older …

---

* See page 409. The tragedian V. A. Ozerov was celebrated for the sensibility he infused into the French classical model – especially as performed by the great actress Yekaterina Semyonova.

Would Aleksandr like to have a look at their ancestral estate, Mikhaylovskoye? He wouldn't mind at all. He was granting him Nikita forever. Such was his will …

So this was the nest of his ancestors!

His grandfather used to live in this oblong house, where he had left a long memory of himself. If, however, one learned the history of a past epoch from family history, the whole history of the Russian state would be one continuous story of passions and madness. Anyway … Arina managed this house of his grandfather's well, and it seemed better-looking and more convenient, and had better food, than his father's shack in St Petersburg.

Early next morning he hurried to the window, darted past Arina who was busy laying the table for tea, and ran to the lakes.

They were at the bottom of the hill. Lake Malenets was quite small and of irregular shape. He threw himself into the water from the steep bank while his horse waited for him. Then he decided to ride to nearby Trigorskoye 'Castle' – so he called the neighbouring house – which throughout his life, as it had been before his arrival, was the home of the sturdy oakling called Praskovya Aleksandrovna Osipova. She took a great interest in Pushkin. She had read and admired the poems that everyone was trying to obtain copies of and had known his parents well and long enough to realise that his mother was unable to appreciate her son's talent. She knew her far too well. Praskovya Aleksandrovna didn't mind that he wrote so openly about love, but she didn't want her daughters to be in his company. They were too young for that! She was afraid they might come to understand what she herself understood better than anyone.

That day a boat had sailed across the lake. A square patched sail billowing in the wind had moved slowly in the direction of Petrovskoye. Perhaps vessels had sailed here too in the times he was now writing about.

But this wasn't a fairy-tale. Looming on the hill like an ancient fortress or a castle, he could see Trigorskoye, which didn't look like a peaceful estate. Here, he knew, Ivan IV had razed a Polish fortress to the ground. He had come here immediately after leaving the Lycée because it was a place where he could breathe freely. He had come here to complete a long poem he had begun while still at the Lycée. It was known that he had been writing it, that it was almost finished and that soon it would be read … but no one had any idea what it would be like. Nobody expected anything serious, however, from any of the Pushkins.

He sharpened his long light quills thinking about Russian antiquity and freedom. The Trigorskoye hills were inspiring. Ivan IV, personification of crowned wrath, had defeated his enemies here. This place was a site of early Russian history; not the peaceful Russian world of Prince Vladimir, no, this belonged to the history of war. He had come here with Tsarskoye Selo undiminished in his mind. No, war, not peace.

Such was the theme of his first narrative poem. He was thinking about ancient Rus, about Vladimir's fabled reign, about the Russia that still lived in the glow of recent victory.

For Vladimir's Rus lived to this day, and the same heroes rode about it, amongst whom he distinguished some who were different. One of these, a figure with a name similar to that of Shakespeare's Falstaff – Farlaf, a fat betrayer – interested him most of all.

Ancient Rus and its heroes were alive and fighting for it still, for beauty, for Lyudmila. Rus was the same, beauty was the same.

His native places hadn't changed.

And now he was here. He was going to ride to Trigorskoye.

32

He had arrived home two days before. He had spent the previous night out. Fickle women stirred his imagination. He could tell them at first sight, at half a glance, but today he had suffered a failure. He had noticed her graceful walk, her slender foot and freely moving figure, very close to him; he had followed her, but found the door shut.

How had she managed to escape so quickly? It was impossible. She had such a short stride. All right then! He decided to wait in the yard and paced it to and fro, unable to understand how he could have been outstripped so easily, like a boy. The slender foot inflamed his mind. He walked faster and faster, breathing heavily and gasping. He was ready for anything. Soon patience came to an end. He climbed the stairs and knocked loudly and rapidly on the door. He found himself hammering with his whole fist, suddenly aware that he might smash the door down. Her slender little foot had decided everything. The night would be impossible without her. How had it happened? Why had she slipped away from him? The fickle flirt! In silent rage at the locked door and the fickle female, he paced up and down like a pendulum in front of it. He was alone in the yard. He walked for an hour, two hours. He was determined not to give up, he couldn't calm down, he felt humiliated, his blood was raging, he would go mad if he didn't see that little slender foot. Very well! Then he felt calmer as he paced, prepared to wait till night. She would have to come into the yard at some time.

He walked about the yard with controlled rage. She was nowhere to be seen. Never mind! He strode around till dark cursing all lightskirts and himself.

He found out her name. It didn't sound Russian: Liza Steingel. Lots of them were flocking to St Petersburg these days. What the charmers wanted was money.

He was no stranger to the mysteries of the night and the tricks of fickle beauties, but he couldn't understand this one. Where had she gone?

Love was a secret quiet war. He despised these women and scoffed at them, but couldn't live without them.

What was the pull of love – the unexpected? Love was dangerous, threatening disease. Available to everyone like a loving-cup, the young charmers spread the disease of love. On that particular day the unknown female whom Pushkin had been cursing as he waited for her outside all day hadn't let him in because she was infected.

Love was blind, mad; otherwise he wouldn't have suffered such defeat.

He ridiculed these loose women, felt contempt for them, forgot them for a while. When he thought how he could have loved, when he thought of the creatures he was wasting his life on, his blood boiled. But he did not hate them. On the contrary, he hated and scorned those who hated women, those absurd pathetic men who had never known love or youth but had reached the peak of success in everything else.

33

He went to the theatre every night without fail. The glorious Semyonova was performing, and he listened in rapture to her famous voice.

He could also see two men in the audience waiting for her every night, motionless and unblinking. One was Prince Gagarin – her common law husband who dared not admit to it. The second was a one-eyed eagle, rapacious but loyal, the poet and publisher Gnedich. Semyonova was from peasant stock, born a serf, but she could play tsarinas like the real thing. Pushkin was absorbed not only by the tragedy on the stage but also by this unparalleled theatrical passion – this real-life drama. He had heard a lot about Gnedich and Semyonova. There were two Semyonov sisters, Yekaterina and Nimfodora, who stirred everybody's curiosity and amazement. Nimfodora was a singer – voluptuous, majestic, serene. Everyone who saw her on stage found her voice and her figure utterly transporting. What a gift from the gods to have such a voice and to be able to sing like that!

Yekaterina, her great actress sister, was pursued by bad fortune, as befitted the muse of heroic tragedy. In those memorable days when Napoleon had been defeated by the concentrated efforts of a nation of such terrifying power, Ozerov's patriotic play *Dmitry Donskoy* had been staged, and the young and not yet famous Semyonova had starred in it. It was an unprecedented night. A liberated national audience did not hide its emotions and greeted Semyonova with tumultuous applause and tears of joy.

On one and the same night she had been crowned a great Russian actress and national idol. The whole country had heard that applause. Yekaterina Semyonova's voice had become the voice of Russian victory.

And so it had remained ever since.

But fame didn't stand still and waited for nobody.

Yekaterina's fame became too great for her roles. Let Nimfodora enjoy the fame of a singer; Yekaterina wanted to achieve more. And her popularity kept growing.

At that time the most famous actress in France was George. Her acting had enthralled Europe. She had transformed tragedy from bare passion and memorable speeches, giving passion a melodious voice.

Eventually George had come to St Petersburg. Semyonova saw her on the stage and her destiny was set: her acting changed, making full use of her remarkable melodious voice. An extraordinary contest began between the empress of the Russian stage and the queen of the French, and eventually Yekaterina prevailed. The tears of the audience and the soldiers' ovation for *Dmitry Donskoy* were still in everyone's memory, and when theatregoers again heard Yekaterina Semyonova's voice, they were instantly won over to the new melodious tragedy.

She made the first and the final speeches of the heroine the essential features of tragedy. In her hands tragedy took hold of the audience's mind with individual lines and key words, and her ecstatic worshippers pronounced these like an oath or an exorcism. She was the soul of tragedy – plot and meaning were no longer essential. Her very gestures – opening, breaking off, concluding – became famous. Her version of melodious tragedy was all-conquering. Sober sense was routed, however much the tragic impact of word and gesture might depend on it.

And then help arrived for the great artist.

Gnedich, the one-eyed eagle, his physical stature surpassing everyone else's, did not live on petty poetic fare. The primary source of all epic, the great *Iliad,* had attracted his attention and he had decided to write a Russian version. Gnedich knew Russian poetry and had great faith in it as the most unconstrained and resonant of all poetries, and most able to absorb the poetry of other nations and show them to their advantage. Only Homeric challenges interested Gnedich. He decided that Russian poetry could not live without Homer. He studied and translated *The Iliad* and carried on his work day after day, year after year, volume after volume – the diligent labour of a monk and bibliophile.

Russian poetry could rest assured – there would be a Russian *Iliad.* Precision was Gnedich's religion. He did nothing by halves. When the one-eyed eagle had seen and heard Semyonova for the first time, his fate was decided: the love of a bibliophile and monk! Could anything on earth be more torment-ing? But he bore his love like an ascetic's fetters and could not accept life without them.

When they had learned about the Parisian George, and when his Aphrodite had begun her unprecedented contest with her, he had become a labourer in the service of love. During rehearsals he crawled about the stage on his knees, raising his hand when she had to start, showing the height of the pitch, lower-ing his hand when she had to lower her voice, stretching to indicate a pause. And hearing the voice of the woman he loved, he was vigilant and persistent, just as when he was translating Homer. During the performance the one-eyed eagle silently mouthed the words along with her.

Pushkin looked and listened without taking his eyes off her. Did the great actress understand entirely what she was playing? Sometimes she seemed to perform as if spellbound. During the interval he would rush behind the scenes, seized with passion and the desire to clutch her hands – her beautiful, inanimate hands – and shake her to rid her of the sorcery of tragedy. This was how great actors changed the course of acting. In this way the era of classical tragedy had come to an end.

Once he failed to restrain himself: he threw himself at her feet and said something in a hoarse whisper. She looked at him closely, without a smile and without understanding.

He took her hands into his and kissed them – for the first and last time.

She was unforgettable – like fame, like life and pride.

Passions were all around him.

Semyonova's voice beckoned and bewitched. It wasn't the meaning of what she was saying, but her power and truth of expression. Audiences burst into applause after a single word from her, or her briefest remark.

Passions were all around him.

He went to see Semyonova no matter what she played. In the first row sat the one-eyed eagle, and Pushkin involuntarily looked to see whether there were worn-out places on the poet's knees from his crawling about the stage during rehearsals teaching her the beginnings, pauses and endings of the lines that she pronounced in her famous voice.

Passions were everywhere, amorous passion, political passion.

In Paris the heir to the throne, the duc de Berry, was assassinated.

He went to the theatre to see, one more time – and for how many more? – a Russian tragedy, Yekaterina Semyonova, to hear her voice, without which the next day could never come, a tragedy that would stay in his mind for a whole night, an unresolved exclamation, until morning, a tragedy that each evening brought the one-eyed Gnedich into the theatre.

Yet strangely enough, though Semyonova was a genuine passion for him, it was not one of love but of artistic admiration.

He listened to her, ready at any minute to burst into applause. On this particular night, after the first act he pulled a miniature portrait out of his chest pocket and without looking at it, with a generous gesture, gave it to the person sitting next to him who was staring straight ahead of him, but who immediately looked round and passed the portrait to his neighbour: it was a likeness of Louvel, assassin of the duc de Berry, with the inscription: *A Lesson to Tsars*. The stalls stirred.

And he burst into wild applause for Semyonova.

34

Life was simple for the Minister. His libertine past had taught him that wisdom consisted in learning how to get what one wanted.

The Minister's haunches were growing flabbier thanks to his special partialities, and his smile more sophisticated and secretive.

He had achieved great power since dealing with issues of faith and had found very subtle solutions. Photius was his enemy but for the moment he wasn't afraid of him.

He preached subtlety, in both education and religion, and grew fatter and more bloated in the process.

His power expanded and extended. He cherished those, no matter how lowly, who were particularly indebted to him. They were his supporters and defenders. The Academy of Sciences was the asylum for his creatures. He feared nobody, but some time previously a rumour had reached him concerning certain irreverent youths. Once von Fock from the Special Department sent him a copy of a rhymed lampoon about him produced in a beautiful hand. Von Fock was a Baltic German and had done him this favour with some pleasure. Let the Prince read the poem! Golitsyn read it, and his haunches shook with rage. He ordered the culprit to be found. Pushkin. There were many Pushkins, but only one of them – the ambassador Musin-Pushkin – deserved, in Golitsyn's opinion, any attention. Later Prince Golitsyn received a report that Pushkin was a minor and had just graduated from the Tsarskoye Selo Lycée.

Prince Golitsyn read the lampoon once more. A devil must have written it – it was in the most infernal style:

> *You can press him for answers*
> *On various fronts!*

Whom did this Pushkin address? The anonymous company of tramps? Keep an eye on him, Special Department! Watch him, von Fock! The conclusion was shockingly crude:

> *Why not try from the rear —*
> *Best spot for the old dear!*

Involuntarily the Prince clasped the button on his uniform and thrust his chest out. Damned if he wouldn't resolve this issue immediately! What was to be done? Where was this rascal to be sent? He was being sharp, was he? Let him try *his,* Golitsyn's sharpness! He wrote in the spirit of the frivolous mob, did he? He smiled. Golitsyn was accepting the challenge. Here you are, Pushkin. Here is your freedom. You want it? Take it!

Where were the rebels today? Where was the struggle for freedom taking place? In Spain. There the mob had risen against the lawful power — the Spanish against the Austrian king who had come to rule over them.

Next day it became known that Pushkin was to be exiled to Spain.

The Prince rubbed his hands: no one returned from such journeys, from the country of shooting and stabbing, where the king waged war against a foreign nation, or rather, the nation against a foreign king. This little wit would never return! A lesson for tsars might turn into a lesson for poets!

Next day some students came to see Pushkin and told him about this plan. Pushkin had a look at their flushed boyish faces, shook the hands stretched to him and suddenly burst out laughing; his laughter was happy and hoarse.

'The Spanish will win,' he said, 'and I'll be back for a celebration. Golitsyn will be the one to look stupid!'

> *Why not try from the rear —*
> *Best spot for the old dear!*

Who were these boys? In strict confidence, in whispers and splutters, they told him they were pupils of the Nobles' boarding-school of the Pedagogical Institute. They were second to none in climbing over walls, that was how they had got here. They would have to go soon.

God knew how they had come to know Golitsyn's secrets.

Pushkin had his supporters. Küchlya was their teacher at the boarding-school. The boys worshipped him.

35

One day a police officer knocked on his door and took him away. The simplicity of the event surprised Pushkin. The policeman brought him to the police headquarters, to the Head of the Department, Lavrov.

It wasn't so simple, however, it was just the beginning. Von Fock himself had summoned Pushkin to the Special Department and this German was no simpleton. He had summoned Griboyedov once, and on returning home the playwright had burnt everything he had ever written. By the evening his house had become like an oven – the stove was red-hot. Lavrov was just a rank-and-file policeman, and to him the matter seemed straightforward.

Lavrov made Pushkin wait for three hours. Pushkin paced about the reception hall, then went up to the window, but the curtains were drawn. Finally Lavrov came out of his office. He looked at Pushkin and shrugged his shoulders.

'Not tall, are you?' he murmured, surprised.

Pushkin restrained himself.

Lavrov was amazingly simple. Without ceremony he pointed to the big bookcase and said:

'This is all yours, catalogued.'

The bookcase was filled with Pushkin's epigrams and files denouncing him. The police had long been taking an interest in him. Eventually Lavrov explained why Pushkin had been brought here – because he must know better than anybody what illicit things were being said and by whom.

'I want you to report this information to us,' Lavrov said.

Pushkin laughed. How clever! Golitsyn was far behind him. He should learn from him.

Lavrov left him alone in the office to give him an opportunity to have a think.

He was locked in.

After some time he suddenly grew sad, though he was not afraid, least of all of a policeman. But still …

It was getting dark when he arrived home.

Lavrov was famous for sticking to old-fashioned police practice. He had looked meditatively at his hairy fist, then at the figure under arrest. And his glance had been understood. Lavrov had the peculiar respect of the policeman for famous thieves and serious killers. Pushkin he considered a serious criminal, but whose guilt had not yet been proved. Let him think things over.

36

Fickle women, the essence of whose lives was unfaithfulness, were supposed to be the most ardent in their betrayals and their passions, they were supposed to be reckless, untamed, and devote themselves tirelessly to love.

Nothing of the kind! They were cold and sober. How bizarre this restraint was. Love was their trade, yet they considered it boring and inappropriate to show any enthusiasm for it. They knocked up their prices, treating caresses carelessly and casually; their passions didn't warm them.

They were arrogant and calculating. Their jealousy was cold too – it was just a business rivalry; their pride was astonishing.

Once he found himself with one who knew poetry, read the most fashionable journals and was generally well-educated. She followed the vogue in everything.

'Nobody reads Voltaire nowadays. How can one be interested in him?'

He listened to her closely.

'Who is interesting then?'

'Bassompierre.'

There was some such writer. What hadn't she read? She yawned in his arms. Then she flicked her pretty little foot twice and said indifferently: 'Come on, again.'

Her detachment was remarkable.

He asked her name. It was foreign and sounded made-up: Olga Masson. All sin with her was calculated and joyless. Both Olinka Masson and Liza Steingel had come to St Petersburg with a clear aim. They had come from those far-flung provinces beloved of Romantics, not for passion – passion was a tiring business – but for material profit and accompanied by their avid aunts, who knew the art of inconspicuousness and didn't interfere with their nieces. Gradually they accumulated a hoard of possessions, and eventually they left the city to enjoy family happiness, leaving behind only boredom and careless remorse. Perhaps poverty had been a means of avoiding ruin. All the same, roaming about on one occasion hoping to find a bed for the night and finding his pockets empty, he recalled the song *A Soldier is a Poor Man*, felt his own poverty to the depths, and murmured:

> *Pushkin is a poor man,*
> *Nowhere to lay his head,*
> *Because of his hopeless idleness*
> *Knows neither home nor bed.*

37

The calmness of Fyodor Tolstoy could match any amount of passion, as his juniors had to admit. Those who didn't were soon convinced of it whether they wanted to be or not. He was not eager to fight duels, but he didn't avoid them either. Up to a hundred lives were said to have been lost in his duels.

He heard that Griboyedov had mentioned him in his comedy *Woe from Wit*.

> *Sent to Kamchatka, he returned an Aleutian*
> *And now he's light-fingered beyond absolution.*

The first line was quite true. When he met Griboyedov, Fyodor Tolstoy asked him to make the second line refer specifically to card-sharping, otherwise the public might think that he stole silver from dinner-tables. His impassiveness was even more impressive than his duelling.

Fyodor Tolstoy couldn't bear evasiveness. He liked quick and definite solutions. He took an interest in Pushkin who was the talk of the city.

Having heard that Pushkin had been taken to Lavrov and had spent the whole day there, and the various stories about what had happened to him and what the police had done to him, Fyodor Tolstoy commented briefly and simply:

'They must have flogged him.'

The jaws of all the St Petersburg dandies dropped. How had they failed to guess it before!

An hour later an elderly lady was gossiping about it in detail:

'There's just a desk and nothing else in the cell. It's just big enough to stand in. Suddenly – imagine – the trapdoor in the floor opens and he sees a few people with canes – that's it. The victim doesn't even know who's in charge of his case!'

By evening everyone knew about it. People gossiped, argued and drew their conclusions; new details emerged. In the evening, walking along the street, Pushkin came across some acquaintances who cast a quick glance at him and backed away. Or did he just imagine it?

Von Fock's day in the Special Department was coming to an end.

In his notoriety, Pushkin longed for a day when he wouldn't be mentioned by anyone, anywhere. Rumour had it that the police had flogged him. A flogged poet would no longer write seriously, he would no longer be dangerous. He hadn't been sent into exile yet, only flogged. His exile was a major problem but von Fock was in no hurry; he was taking his time.

Another reason for postponing his exile was that there was more than one possible place available for him.

But his case was not only about exile.

Photius knew only one place suitable for Pushkin, the author of those disastrously alluring poems: the Solovetsky Monastery. There he wouldn't dream about fatal maidens, he would be bridled once and for all. After ten years spent there he would learn humility. He was good for nothing anyway. He would forget his literary tricks forever.

Arakcheyev wanted him to be thrown into the Peter and Paul Fortress or to be made a soldier for life.

Prince Golitsyn had suggested that the freedom-lover should be sent to Spain. Although it was easy to get rid of Pushkin, there was no unanimity as to how this should be done. No agreement was reached. Besides, there was no written instruction yet. What, then, was to be done?

Chaadayev galloped on.

Although he had to be in the capital as soon as possible, although his horse was the fastest on the road, its pace was measured.

Chaadayev galloped on.

Even if he were not fast enough, even if he had to curb his steed to avoid an accident, he had to have completed his journey by nightfall. He would find Karamzin at home and speak to him. He had no time to lose. He rode with no superfluous or accidental movements. The horse breathed regularly and galloped evenly. He would return the same night. In a soldier's life night and day are the same. He would tell Karamzin about the danger that threatened Pushkin. The poet was hated by the champions of slavery and blind despotism. The defendants of slavery had risen in arms against him. They hated the poet. His hour had come. But without this poet there could be no future. Special care was needed!

Chaadayev galloped on.

The narrow nostrils of his steed breathed and moved regularly; it would not fall or stumble.

Without literature the country would be wordless and the nation's memory dumb. Slaves would not destroy Pushkin.

Chaadayev arrived at Tsarskoye Selo, dismounted, and looked into the horse's wise eyes. It was a proud horse and it threw its head back as if in reply to this human scrutiny.

Everyone had already started to get used to Pushkin's bad luck, to his forthcoming exile and the growing rumours about him. Chaadayev's visit changed this attitude. Pushkin was in real trouble. Time was precious. Whatever sentence threatened him, one thing was clear. The time had come to save him. The hussars fell into discussion.

Katerina Andreyevna was silent. Chaadayev was calm and attentive and Nikolay Mikhaylovich was his usual discreet and shrewd self. Katerina knew that a serious discussion would take place tomorrow and decided that she would be truthful with him: he was the only person who could rescue Pushkin. Chaadayev was right: one word from him to the Tsar could decide Pushkin's future. It wouldn't be easy. She would just have to use her wits again and pretend to be calm.

Soon Nikolay Mikhaylovich would see the Tsar. It wouldn't be easy to talk about it, but Pushkin could not be left to perish. Of course, he was a madman, but his epigrams were the more lethal because they were funny. Each of them revealed his personality and his voice. It was the fact that they were funny that made them lethal.

The most important question turned out to be the simplest: if not the Fortress or Spain, where?

Suddenly the Emperor smiled with the corners of his lips. He wasn't in a mood for harsh decisions today. Besides, Karamzin had a charming wife. So when Karamzin suggested southern Russia, he suddenly said:

'Inzov? Splendid!'

This strange name belonged to the Chief Trustee for the Welfare of Foreign Settlers in the Southern Territories, stationed in Yekaterinoslav. This wouldn't even be exile – more a kind of career transfer.

Catherine the Great had been fond of name-games. She had once written a play about an adventurist whom she named by compressing the names of a few famous adventurists into one: Caglifalkjerston. She had also invented Inzov's strange name.

Grand Duke Constantine had had an illegitimate son, whose name had to be such that it didn't betray his origin. So he had been given a foreign name – Konstantins. Then a Russian surname ending had been added to it and the rest of the name struck out, producing Inzov.

Katerina Andreyevna trembled as she waited for her husband. She was worrying about Pushkin. She felt guilty, blaming herself for what had happened. She even burst into tears. When Pushkin came to have a talk with Nikolay Mikhaylovich, she met him calmly and silently.

Nikolay Mikhaylovich talked neither about Pushkin's future nor about his poem (he still called it 'a nice little poem'). He had little to say and simply asked Pushkin to promise to reform. Could he promise? Could he give such a promise?

Pushkin was on a bed of nails. He said abruptly:

'I promise ...'

Katerina Andreyevna gave a sigh of relief. A burden was lifted off her shoulders. Pushkin added quietly:

'For two years.'

Two years! Katerina Andreyevna burst out laughing. What precision! Thank God for that! Pushkin would be Pushkin, and how boring life would be if he were different!

But where was he going?

He was going to the Crimea. She knew nothing about the Crimea: where was it? what sort of place was it?

Looking through Nikolay Mikhaylovich's new books, sent to him from the bookshop, she leafed through them one after the other with a practised hand. She wanted Pushkin to know where he was going.

One of the books was a description of the Black Sea and the surrounding area, published in Paris by order of Napoleon. Apparently he had had a great fondness for the sights of the Crimea. The book wasn't new, but it was a sumptuous edition with depictions of magnificent landscapes on huge pages. In one of them a girl in a long dress was shown descending from a steep crag carrying a tall pitcher on her shoulder, and a mountain tribesman was watching her from above.

Katerina Andreyevna read the name of the place: Erzurum.

She looked at Pushkin. He was examining the picture, and suddenly said: 'I won't forget this place.'

Katerina Andreyevna was happy in the knowledge that Pushkin wouldn't forget it and that her geography lessons with him had proved no less important than her husband's history lessons.

38

His brother Lyovushka had eventually appeared. Pushkin said that he would write to him, only to him. They were rather close. He would write to him about himself and his life and Lev would keep him informed about their family – where they were, what they thought and talked about.

Pushkin had indeed decided to write to his brother about everything. There was no more certain way to make his letters known to all. But now when he was leaving, he regretted that there was no time to spend with his brother. The flighty Lyovushka was frustrated, considering he had such an elder brother, by the fact that he couldn't write poetry. So Pushkin would address his letters to him and everybody would know what he wrote about.

In the last two days he packed and made final arrangements. His long poem *Ruslan and Lyudmila* was to be published; he had been to the theatre to see Semyonova and had a word with Gnedich about his poem and his exile. And Gnedich, who believed in Pushkin and his destiny and appreciated him as a theatregoer, bent his thin neck and promised to take care of the poem which was going out into the world as an orphan. They both listened to Semyonova, Pushkin for the last time.

He looked with pleasure through the thick manuscript of the finished poem with his flowing handwriting. He had arranged his affairs. He had not much time left of that spring day to say good-bye to all his friends.

Two evenings before his departure he went to see Nikita Vsevolozhsky. It was impossible to leave without bidding farewell to the hussars and his present life, which was to change so profoundly even if only for a couple of years.

He wanted it to be a proper farewell. Nikita Vsevolozhsky was a man who knew how to do things on the right scale. It was necessary to say good-bye to Pushkin with style and panache, without thrift or sparing.

So open your arms wider, all you hussars!

By the morning shtoss* was in full swing. Vsevolozhsky was as strong as a young oak.

He was an outstanding gambler.

'Vingt-et-un†?' he suggested.

The game was rapid, the stakes big.

'No, vingt-et-un is no good, let's return to shtoss, shall we?'

He tossed the money and the coins jingled. Soon he had raked up the whole pile in one go.

'Drink to my health, Kalmuck!' he said.

A little hussar standing by the table poured the wine. The cork flew and they raised their glasses.

Pushkin was biting his lip. All his money was gone.

He picked up the bound manuscript, ready for the press, of his new poem.

Eventually the amount of his debt became clear.

'How much?' he asked.

'We'll reckon up later,' Nikita said. 'It's your call.'

He took his bound manuscript and put it on the table.

'The old losses and a fresh stake, all together.'

Nikita dealt the cards.

'Don't count on the queen of hearts,' he advised Pushkin, 'She isn't your queen.'

Pushkin was fascinated.

'Which is mine then?' he asked Nikita. 'It's not the queen of diamonds, is it?'

'Impossible to say,' said Vsevolozhsky. 'Might be her.'

Pushkin was unable to smile.

Vsevolozhsky was superstitious and flamboyant. He called a jack a slave.

'I'm not reckoning on the slave.'

He didn't count the jack, but still won. By the morning he was winning all the games.

---

* A German variation of faro, the fashionable gambling game in Pushkin's day.

† Familiarly known in Britain as 'pontoon' and in America as 'blackjack'.

He set Pushkin's bound manuscript aside with a certain respect.

Pushkin went home on foot.

The night was lighter than day. He heard his footsteps ringing.

He took off his hat and made a low bow. To whom? There was nobody in sight.

To St Petersburg. Tomorrow he was leaving for the South.

The Neva was rolling slowly and majestically, as always, as it had in Peter's time, as it would roll in his grandchildren's time.

He had bowed to St Petersburg as if to a person. He stood for a while with his hat in his hand, looking thoughtfully at the city, and then returned home.

39

Next day he was at General Rayevsky's.

Not an old man, he was strict but considerate.

He told Pushkin:

'I know that my son is a friend of yours. We'll be in the Crimea together with my young daughters. We'll meet in Yekaterinoslav.'

The General knew that Pushkin was going into exile, but thought of it as if it were a demotion of a captain or lieutenant.

He added suddenly: 'We must go. It's time,' and gave Pushkin a nod.

Pushkin perceived that the General, the hero of 1812, could not for a single day cease to be a loving father. He couldn't go to the Crimea without his young daughters.

His son Nikolay was a hussar and lived in Tsarskoye Selo, where he had seen a lot of Pushkin and eagerly looked forward to reading his poems.

And Pushkin? No military man, he was to be exiled. He might have been expected to be defenceless. But no – nothing of the sort! Though he was just a poet, he was a warrior too. He was the commander of an infantry regiment of iambuses, a cavalry squadron of trochees, Cossacks' pickets of epigrams which always hit their targets with lethal accuracy – and the shorter they were, the more frightening they sounded, like bullets. General Rayevsky, the war hero, talked to him tersely and simply as if he were a junior officer in another part of the army.

Pushkin had survived the war without leaving Tsarskoye Selo but he knew what war was like, he knew the strength of the enemy. In his first long poem about ancient heroes and the enemies of Russia he imagined a different war – for glory and beauty – for Lyudmila – a war like the ancient wars but which turned out to be a war of the future, in which the flying Chernomor, tiny and feeble, whisked off the fair Lyudmila.

It seemed to him that such a war was quite possible, and the victory too. He thought about the dark force of war – betrayal, the cowards Rogday and the fat Farlaf.

Katerina Andreyevna noted that he had portrayed Lyudmila as if she were a real person and that he seemed to be in love with her. He was afraid he would fall at her feet and confess that when he was writing the poem he had been thinking of her as Lyudmila.

When he thought about Katerina he tried to imagine what she had been like in her youth. It was for this reason that he portrayed Lyudmila with a certain playfulness.

He saw Arina for the last time, embraced her and said good-bye.

'Goodbye, mother,' he told her.

Arina froze. She looked at him closely to see if he was joking, but he was serious. She looked around. Thank God, they were alone.

'What do you mean, sir, Aleksandr Sergeyevich?' she said, astounded. 'You've got a mother.'

'Yes, I have,' he said gravely, 'you!'

Tears, silent and restrained, rolled down Arina's cheeks, her usual tears.

He was leaving in a post-chaise. Everyone he expected to come was seeing him off.

Pushchin examined the horses and the harnesses and was not impressed.

'Well, they're not relay horses, they're post-chaise!' the cabman said.

Malinovsky came too. He was indispensable at departures, arrivals and all sorts of occasions of change. His nickname, The Cossack, was still fresh in everybody's mind, while the memories of the beginning of the Lycée, of his father the Principal, of the Minister Speransky, were already blurred. He was still The Cossack, and ever since Pushkin had so named him in his verses, Malinovsky had been fond of him and his poems.

Pushkin was going far away, in some sort of service. Their farewell was deeply felt, and Pushkin was dearer to him than ever.

'*And now they mount their mettled horses*,' said Malinovsky, quoting apropos from Pushkin's new poem.

Everyone smiled. Malinovsky said it with a wry expression on his face.

Küchlya spoke breathlessly, screwing up his eyes:

'Malinovsky knows the poem by heart!'

Everyone fell silent. The poem that had not yet been published was already being quoted. His fame had already begun, among the Lycéeists.

He was being exiled … and his exile was to be within Russia. He hadn't seen much of Russia yet: now he would see and get to know more of it, starting not with the slow northern plains but the South, the region of passions and crimes. There were no fewer passions in his native land than in Spain, where

Golitsyn had wanted him sent. It wouldn't be too bad an exile! It was as if they wanted to turn him into a criminal. Very well ... ! Would he return? And find anyone he knew? Or would history have turned things upside-down? It could happen so quickly.

He was calm. The cabman was waiting.

40

He was getting to know his country, in all its vastness and strength, from the highways – and wasn't this the best way to learn it? The coachman sang all the time.

This was what Russian song was like – long-drawn-out, pensive, melancholy! He listened avidly, for hours on end. He started to understand why this sadness was so majestic, so unhurried, so overwhelming. It was sung by coachmen on the roads, long, endless roads. Sleep shut out the song. A new life was beginning – fast but not in haste.

The post-chaise bell fell silent. The coachmen had left the carriage. He was alone at the arranged place, Yekaterinoslav. He stretched himself and adjusted his clothes.

His legs were numb after the jolting of the carriage. His exile was exile indeed – nobody was waiting for him, nobody met him, he had nowhere to stay. He went through the only open door, which turned out to be the entrance to a tavern. He cursed it; its low ceilings reminded him of a coffin.

He could bathe! There was a flood in the town. The Dnieper roared continuously, then groaned, then grew quiet. The tavern was flooded, the water rose above floor level. Without hesitation he rushed downhill to the swollen, sighing river. It seemed to be taking a breath before the next onslaught. A boatman scrutinised him carefully, but when he heard that he didn't wish to go anywhere in particular, just to take a trip out on the water, he let him into the boat.

Pushkin observed his stare, his narrowed mistrustful eyes and his silence. The boatman rowed slowly and deliberately, plying the oars only at the end of the movement and leaving them to the will of the waves, as if he had ceased to row. Pushkin asked him whether he could sing. The boatman at once began to sing in slow, measured tones. Pushkin listened to the beautiful old song. It wasn't by chance that the boatman was screwing up his eyes: the song was about an abduction by a Cossack chieftain with a gun. Pushkin burst out into hoarse laughter. So this was the place where he had been sent to reform! It was a robbers' song. He took a long trip down the Dnieper, then told the boatman to wait and plunged into the river.

His body seemed to have been fettered by the long journey. Only now while swimming did it start to feel like his own body and he like himself again. His legs began to forget their weariness. At last the boatman, apparently tired of waiting for him, rose to his feet – but not from impatience: shouting could suddenly be heard from the Dnieper.

'Catch them! Those two in shackles!'

The boatman brought Pushkin back to the tavern. It turned out that two prisoners had escaped and managed to swim off. He had heard the shouting of their pursuers.

This was no longer a game or imagination. This was not yet poetry, but what he had seen and heard himself, people's bodies, hands splashing in the water, shackled legs paddling. This was how his exile had begun.

In the evening he started to shiver feverishly and violently in the tavern. In his delirium he was fleeing from his pursuers; breathing heavily, he asked for ice-cold water in the desert, seeing and hearing nothing, bewildered. Eventually his hand grasped an ice-cold mug of water brought by a terrified servant girl.

He was lying on somebody's coarse cloak – where had it come from? – and expecting nothing. His limbs remembered the jolting road. He remembered the boatman with his intent eyes, and hearing the shout: 'Catch them!'

There had been two of them. Chained together, shoulder to shoulder, they had been fleeing captivity over the water. Freedom! The only thing it was possible to swim for in shackles, chained to another human being.

He spent the next day in bed, in complete darkness. It was like the Solovetsky Monastery as Photius had recommended, or being made to stand to attention as Arakcheyev had wanted. After all, they had prevailed.

'Bring a light!' A stern, authoritative voice was suddenly heard. 'Why is there no light here?'

Still not expecting or remembering anything, he realised that it was necessary to have light. He came to his senses.

General Rayevsky stood in front of him.

Old Rayevsky, who was angrily giving an order not to leave Pushkin in the dark and demanding a light, was like a caring relative for him at that moment. He felt protected and at once started to breathe deeply and evenly. He wouldn't be lost with such a companion.

His son Nikolay hadn't changed either, he never changed or concealed his opinions. Pushkin, used to protecting his poems as a soldier makes sure his heart is protected in battle, read them to Nikolay without any reserve, and if he thought the verse too strained Nikolay would respond with straightforward, robust laughter. Pushkin had always respected the hussar's frankness, and could never forget Nikolay's disapproval of his ardent, impulsive wish to talk to the Tsar about Sophie Velho, with whom His Majesty was conducting an affair.

'Forget it,' the hussar had said to him bluntly.

Now after the insanity of this cursed tavern, he wasn't sure if the episode of the two prisoners had really happened or if it was just his delirium. A new poem was tormenting him and he was raving about it. The vision of the two prisoners shackled together and swimming to freedom didn't leave him. He needed the loud clear laughter and common sense of Nikolay Rayevsky, the one person whose judgement he could trust.

Nikolay told him that nobody would believe the story:

'It's too unreal.'

It was indeed hard to believe what had really happened, what was in the prison report. It was hard to believe verse to be more exact than prose.

The date of departure was decided – they would go to the Caucasus first and then to the Crimea.

41

Every day from early morning, a silent, sullen, bad-tempered queue of barely alive people, whose hands, legs or patience had failed them, crowded around the pit filled with curative water, expecting miracles.

Feigning scepticism, they in fact believed everything. The least likely eventuality was that their youth and strength would come back to them. But this was what they were hoping for.

Was there no hope, then? None at all? It was all clear. Nobody had any hope. And youth, and strength? They might well return, anything could happen. But everything stayed the same as ever. Keeping calm was the thing. There was nothing else.

Obediently he climbed down into the pit full of lukewarm water. The despondent, sullen queue crowded behind him, the prematurely old, silent and grim, who had come hoping for good luck and a miracle – the return of their life and strength that only the baths could bring. He didn't believe in the waters but under the supervision of a calm doctor he tried various baths, and once coming back from the waters alone he suddenly burst out laughing – at nothing in particular, and smiled at his own unexpected laughter. It was the hot waters that had made him laugh. General Rayevsky's distinguished doctor saw to the procedures with military precision. He certainly avoided monotony.

'Hot sulphur bath!'

A week later he ordered:

'Today, warm acid and sulphur.'

Another week passed and he suggested:

'Now ferrous. Iron is essential.'

It was after the ferrous bath that Pushkin had burst out laughing.

The general's favourite doctor was extremely experienced and had a profound understanding of illnesses. He was aware first of all that in general diseases were little understood; secondly, that so was the action of the waters; and thirdly, that the waters were actually curative. He had his own method, not derived from medical textbooks: it consisted of a gradual transition from hot waters to cold. For two months Pushkin took baths, under the doctor's strict supervision, first in hot sulphurous, then in lukewarm acidic-sulphurous, then in ferrous, and finally in cold acidic waters. The General was very pleased with his doctor. 'Iron is essential,' he would say of the ferrous bath.

He kept his own kind of company now, a society of immobility. He realised that the bizarre clouds – variegated, grey, ruddy, purple – weren't clouds at all but ice-covered mountain peaks glistening in the sun. He recognised them: Beshtau, a five-peaked mountain looking like a domed cathedral, Mashuk, the Iron and the Stone mountains, and the one that reminded him of a viper – the Snake.

When he had carried out the doctor's instructions, bending over a spring and seeing the reflection of his face, he felt completely normal and realised it was time to move. On their rides together he and Nikolay Rayevsky had talked a lot. Nikolay took after his father and remembered everything he said. He and Aleksandr held similar views on everything. Nikolay had recalled Napoleon's chimerical plan dating back to his sudden friendship with Emperor Paul, which ended equally suddenly with the Emperor's death, a plan resembling the cloud-like peaks of the Caucasus: the plan for a joint military campaign to create a Russian India. Pushkin had said that these Caucasian mountains not only offered a scene of unbelievable beauty but could provide Russia with a friendly trade link with Persia.

Sixty Kuban Cossacks of the coast watch saw them off. Pushkin admired their free posture and their gallop. He said ecstatically to Nikolay Rayevsky:

'Always in the saddle, always ready to fight, always on the alert!'

42

His journey into exile was undertaken with urgency, by special command.

The cunning plan of the impulsive and dishonourable Golitsyn had failed – he remained in Russia and not in Spain. He was fascinated by far-flung places, as Russians are. But face-to-face with his motherland he encountered the most unbelievable and wonderful things, unknown to almost anyone, here in his home country.

As his travelling companion he was lucky to have not a poet but a famous general who did not keep military matters from his family, from his countrymen – or from his country's future. These were no mute places, all of them spoke, and their speech was precise, similar to his own, for which he was being exiled. An almost mathematical precision was the hallmark of his verses, and this was the trouble with them: the more precise his poetry was, the more authentic its subject-matter, the more unbelievable it seemed. His writing was unbelievable. But the entire country was beyond belief. It was a waste of time to try to prove otherwise. The scrupulous precision of a police report did not help either. He had to conform. And he was conforming. But he felt he had to take advantage of this convention, he had to take advantage of his genuine wound, to write about *her*, about such things and in such a way as if these were the last words one would write before one died. For him, the censor did not exist – police censorship, the power of which he knew only too well, for it had driven him from the capital. The only censorship he recognised was the awesome censorship of his own heart and his dear friends. His life was taking its inevitable course: Nikolay Rayevsky, a hussar and a connoisseur of poetry, was his only genuine friend here.

They reached the Crimea – an important but forbidden part of his homeland. From noisy and bustling Kerch they made for Kaffa, which had proudly renamed itself Theodosia. Night fell early here, the darkness and the heat heavy and visible. They sailed round the Crimean coast to Gurzuf where General Rayevsky and his young daughters were waiting for them. At night, on the frigate *Rusalka*, a light and nimble vessel, he began to write an elegy.

He watched the Crimean shore. Poplars, vineyards, bushy laurels and cypresses – a more graceful sight than anything else in the world – accompanied them.

The shore was close and he remembered the book on the Crimea from Napoleon's time, how he and Katerina Andreyevna had looked through it together, and he could not escape from the thought that he would meet her in this region.

He recalled everything about her, not vaguely and from a distance, but saw her here, in the cabin of this frigate, looking out at the laurels and cypresses keeping pace with them on the shore. He remembered his desire to fall at her feet, the desire that had never left him. Here, under the large and tangible stars, unable to shut out this vision which would be his doom forever, he fell on his knees in front of her.

No one would insult the name of Katerina Andreyevna; even if this mad love were one day to be discovered, it wouldn't be taken seriously once it was learned that she was twice his age. Particularly if it were discovered by a woman, for women were merciless in the matter of age. Her beauty would remain unknown as she herself wanted it to be, in the modesty of her heart – there were no portraits of her.

So began his exile.

He was doomed to this love, this insanity. He knew that – God help him! – he would never breathe a word about her. But his first outburst – crazy, schoolboyish, ending in ridiculous failure – that outburst of childish tears that he had been incapable of holding back and that would be remembered by all sensible people, that naive and childish outburst – what did it have to do with these wounds, these deep wounds of love?

For this was what she was to him.

His poems appealed to her dear intelligent eyes, she knew them and loved them. She understood what inspired them, all his unfulfilled and forgotten intentions. And she laughed at his duels as if they were childish pranks.

He was writing this elegy as if it were the last words he had to say.

He wouldn't add anything else. About anyone or anything. And the fact that these would be his last words made every one of them true. The poem was an exorcism. Now he could write the truth boldly, Katerina's peace would not be disturbed. He would write to Lev and ask him to send the poem to be printed anonymously. In poetry, as in battle, a name had no importance.

He knew that when he wrote of her, darkness or the sullen sea would always be the only witness. And this love of his, which it was impossible to cure, which he would bear for ever, was like a wound, a wound such as old Rayevsky knew better than anything, and so valued his doctor for not deceiving him with false hopes of recovery; old Rayevsky's wound that ached every time the weather changed.

Head high, breathe deeply! Life, like poetry, would go on.

> *... But love's old wounds,*
> *The old deep wounds of love – nothing can heal ...*

His exile to the South was no accident, it was like a continuation of the Lycée. For the Lycée had been conceived here, not in the capital. Many years before, when he himself had been a babe in arms, Malinovsky had been on diplomatic service in this region, protecting Russian interests; and while watching prisoners and exiles, he had begun to write his treatise on the abolition of slavery.

And now he, Pushkin, was exiled here, to witness in this place that thirst for freedom that could make fugitives shackled together swim with unbelievable speed to their destiny!

Long live the Lycée!

And here he was too, writing an elegy about an impossible love which life had denied him. And like an accursed being, not daring to name her, he sped on, full of strength, as if intoxicated with images of forbidden things that never could come true.

Notes

The text

The first part of Yury Tynyanov's novel *Pushkin* was first published in serial form in the journal *Literaturnyy sovremennik* ('Contemporary Literature'), nos 1–4, Leningrad, 1935; the second part in the same journal, nos 10–12, 1936 and nos 1–2, 1937; and the third part in *Znamya* ('Banner'), nos 7–8, Moscow, 1943.

For first, journal publication, the first two parts of the novel were seen through the press by the author. The third part, however, was written and first published when the author was gravely ill and able neither to revise and prepare his manuscript for publication nor correct proofs. The text as published by *Znamya* was highly unsatisfactory, with omissions of words illegible in Tynyanov's manuscript or overlooked by the editors, 'contextual' insertions, and additional errors unconnected with the original. In 1956, in the first complete volume edition of *Pushkin*, a new text of the third part edited by B. Kostelyanets was included in a selected edition of Tynyanov's works published by Goslitizdat, Moscow, reissued in a complete edition from the same publishers in 1959.

The text used in the present translation is that published by Izdatel'stvo 'Pravda', Moscow in 1981. The text of the first two parts is the last published during the author's lifetime (the first part within a collected edition of Tynyanov's works from Goslitizdat in Leningrad, 1941, the second in a separate edition from GIKhL, Leningrad in 1938). The text of the third part is that edited by V. Kaverin and Ye. Toddes (first published in 1976 in a separate edition of *Pushkin* by Khudozhestvennaya literatura, Leningrad), which differs considerably from both the first journal publication and the first complete volume editions of 1956 and 1959; Kaverin and Toddes studied Tynyanov's original manuscript and consulted relevant archive material to arrive at new readings and some textual rearrangement towards a version closer to what would seem to have been the author's intentions.

In translating the third part of this novel we have preserved the author's terse style and sentence and paragraph structure as in the first two parts, but where the provisional nature of the text seemed particularly noticeable, in blatant repetitions and contradictions, for example, we have adjusted the text accordingly. We have occasionally combined a succession of very short sentences or run paragraphs together when it appeared advantageous to do so, but overall have done our best to respect both the often scenario-like nature of this part and our feeling that had Tynyanov seen his work through himself he would certainly have revised and corrected the text he left.

Part One: Childhood

Page

13   *Nikolay Mikhaylovich Karamzin* (1766–1826), prose-writer, linguistic reformer, critic, editor, poet and historian, dominated the Russian literary scene from 1791 to 1803, providing the bridge between the eighteenth century and the nineteenth. The tale *Poor Liza* (1792) and other narratives and *Letters of a Russian Traveller* (1790s) created a reading public in Russia. He created a literary language and style that broke away from the dominant Church Slavonic tradition, coining and using new words that he modelled on the French, such as *interesnyy*, 'interesting', *vliyaniye*, 'influence', *trogatel'nyy*, touching. *ottenok*, nuance. Such words expressing everyday emotions and shades of meaning had not existed before in Russian; modern Russians find it difficult to believe that they are not of Russian origin.

15   *the war with the Sansculottes.* The campaign against France that began in 1799, waged by the coalition of Russia, Britain and Turkey, to be joined by Austria.

16   *His heart had been broken by a beautiful woman.* Karamzin had been close to the wife of Aleksey Pleshcheyev, Nastasya, renowned for her intellect, but had married her younger sister Yelizaveta, who died in 1802. He had addressed his *Letters of a Russian Traveller, 1789–90* to the whole family.

     Letters of a Russian Traveller. One of the most influential Russian prose works of the eighteenth century, written under the influence of Sterne, Ossian, Thomson and Rousseau when Karamzin was making a tour of Germany, Switzerland, France and England (first published in serial form in the 1790s).

     'Aglaya'. The nickname given by Karamzin to Nastasya Pleshcheyeva; the name of one of the three Graces. *Aglaia* means 'splendour' in Greek.

18   *The words of the song were highly evocative for him.* The poem is ascribed to Karamzin.

19   *the Red Gate.* A triumphal arch built in 1753–57, a rare example of Elizabethan baroque. Despite its name, it was demolished by the Bolsheviks in 1928.

     Philemon [...] Baucis. Couple symbolising marital happiness in Greek mythology (and Ovid's *Metamorphoses*).

     'Horace glorified Tivoli [...]'. In a letter to Ivan Dmitriyev of 4 April 1799 Karamzin wrote: 'Horace extolled Tivoli [the farm given him by Maecenas, freeing him from salaried work], we can turn the Samara Hill into a Russian Helicon [place of poetic inspiration].'

     the refuge of the great Jean-Jacques. Rousseau's villa 'Hermitage'.

     Derzhavin's ode on Betsky. Derzhavin's poem *On the Demise of the Patron* (1795), to the memory of the Catherinean grandee I. I. Betsky, who had been in charge of charitable organisations. A reference to the literary war between the innovators (followers of Karamzin) and the literary archaists with their love of odes, solemnity, pomposity and Church Slavonicisms.

Page

23 *Aleksandr Vasilyevich Suvorov.* Suvorov (1729–1800) was one of the most celebrated of Russian military commanders. First seeing action in the Seven Years' War (1756–63), he played a distinguished part in the Russo-Turkish Wars of 1768–74 and 1787–91 and subsequently against the French in Italy and in the Swiss expedition of 1799.

24 *I would like to find father's principality.* Recent research has suggested Cameroon and the Lake Chad region beside Ethiopia, Nigeria and Timbuktu as possible places of origin of Abram Petrovich; Tynyanov believed that he came from Eritrea.

34 *three young pine trees on a hillock.* Affectionately remembered by Pushkin in a piece of late autobiographical blank verse ('... I have revisited that corner of the earth [...]', 1835) in which he recalls his exile at Mikhaylovskoye and describes seeing these three trees ten years later (i.e. three and a half decades later than Pushkin's father is depicted as seeing them at this moment in the narrative), still marking the boundary of the estate, now noticeably older and surrounded by (translated literally) 'a green family ... of young pines, clustering in their shade like children'.

35 *The brass hat with the Maltese cross [...] Preobrazhensky Regiment.* In 1797 Paul I took Malta, seat of the Knights of St John, under his protection and was declared Grand Master of the Order. The Maltese cross subsequently appeared on the headgear of the soldiers of the Preobrazhensky, Semyonovsky and Izmaylovsky regiments.

38 *Vigée-Lebrun.* Elisabeth Vigée-Lebrun (1755–1842), court portraitist of Marie-Antoinette, emigrated from France in 1789 and in 1795 found refuge in Russia.
the nobles' resumption of their privileges. Emperor Paul had little sympathy for the nobles' privileges or liberties, pressing young noblemen into state service, levying a tax on landed estates and insisting on much tighter discipline in the army. Some nobles mistakenly believed that his death in January 1802 marked the cancellation of these measures.

41 *Peter III.* Tsar of Russia for six months, Peter III (1728–62), son of Charles Frederick, Duke of Holstein and grandson of Peter the Great, was a great admirer of Frederick the Great. He withdrew Russia's forces from the Seven Years' War and restored East Prussia to Frederick. This enraged the army and the aristocracy, and in June 1762 Peter was deposed by a group of nobles inspired by his wife Catherine and led by her lover, Count Orlov.
Kochubey. Count and later Prince Viktor Pavlovich Kochubey (1768–1834), Minister of Internal Affairs, personal adviser and confidant of Alexander I; from 1827 Chairman of the Council of Ministers.
Prince Adam Czartoryski. Polish statesman (1770–1861) who fought against Russia in the Insurrection of 1794, but, sent to St Petersburg as a hostage, gained the confidence of Emperor Paul and the friendship of Grand Duke Alexander, who as Tsar appointed him Minister of Foreign Affairs, 1803–04.

Page

50 *the rank of chamberlain.* A senior court title, equivalent to third and fourth class in the Table of Ranks (Privy Councillor or Active Civil Councillor in the Civil Service, Lieutenant-General or Major-General in the Army).

51 *Grécourt.* In the poetry of Jean-Baptiste Grécourt (1693–1743) eroticism mingled with religious free-thinking.

57 *Piron.* Alexis Piron (1689–1773), playwright and author of witty fables, satires and epigrams.

    Dorat. Claude-Joseph Dorat (1734–80), author of erotic and sentimental poems, epigrams and tragedies.

58 *Barkov.* Ivan Barkov (1732–68) was famed for his pornographic poems.

59 *'To a Fire-place'.* Vasily Pushkin's first published poem (in Ivan Krylov's *St Petersburg Mercury*, 1793).

    Karamzin was publishing his letters [...] in his journal. In 1802 Karamzin started a historical and political journal *The Messenger of Europe*. He gave up the editorship when appointed imperial historiographer in 1803.

60 *Elmire.* Heroine of Molière's comedy *Tartuffe*.

63 *Talma.* The tragic actor François-Joseph Talma (1763–1826) was famous for the realism of his performances. Among the myths circulated by Napoleon's Royalist opponents was one about Napoleon taking lessons from Talma in order to acquire the conduct and manner of speech befitting a monarch.

79 *the fat Aristippus.* The Greek philosopher and hedonist Aristippus, a pupil of Socrates, lived in Corinth with the famous courtesan Lais.

80 *He ridiculed King Frederick.* Frederick the Great (1712–86), wishing to earn the reputation of an enlightened monarch, invited Voltaire to Prussia. In his memoirs Voltaire later lampooned Frederick and the Prussian regime.

    Mme Deshoulières. Mme Antoinette Deshoulières (1638–94), author of sentimental pastoral verse.

85 *Praskovya Aleksandrovna.* In exile at Mikhaylovskoye Pushkin was to be a close friend of Praskovya (1781–1859), by then remarried as Osipova-Vulf, and her four children – two daughters, a step-daughter and son Aleksey Vulf.

92 *marquis de Dangeau.* Philippe, marquis de Dangeau (1638–1720), a favourite of Louis XIV and author of memoirs in which he described the life of the French royal family and court in intimate detail.

93 *Lebrun.* The odes of Ponce-Denis Ecouchard Lebrun (1729–1807) enjoyed huge contemporary popularity and earned him the sobriquet 'Pindar'.

96 *Scarron's poem about the life hereafter.* Paul Scarron (1610–60), perhaps the most gifted of French pre-Classical writers, invented the genre of the burlesque, mocking existing literary forms, one of his most celebrated works being *Virgile Travesti*, in seven books, a parody of the *Aeneid*.

101 *'The Nightingale'.* A free translation, ascribed to the satirical poet Dmitry Gorchakov (1758–1824), of a fable by La Fontaine; circulated in handwritten copies.

104 *dared to refer to Napoleon as 'Buonaparte'.* A hint at Napoleon's humble Corsican

origins; the family name was thus spelt until 1768. Use of the spelling expressed contempt towards him as a usurper of the throne.

the boarding-schools of St Petersburg Jesuits [...] Novosiltsev. The Jesuits established colleges in a number of Russian towns, attended by pupils from the oldest and most time-honoured Russian families.

117 *Khitrovo.* Elise (Yelizaveta) Khitrovo (1783–1839), favourite daughter of Field-Marshal Kutuzov. An eccentric figure well-known in St Petersburg society, fond of displaying her ample proportions at balls in middle age. One society wit, surveying her near-naked state, remarked: 'It is time to draw a veil over the past.' She was to meet Pushkin after his return from exile and, to his acute embarrassment, fall deeply in love with him. This, however, did not prevent what grew into one of the closest of Pushkin's friendships with older women.

118 *the Minister Speransky.* Mikhail Speransky (1772–1839), son of a priest and educated in a provincial seminary, was the outstanding statesman of the first half of Alexander I's reign. In 1809 he produced a plan for the reorganisation of the Russian structure of government on the Napoleonic model, but was dismissed when Napoleon invaded Russia in 1812. Restored to power under Nicholas I, he was responsible for the trial and conviction of the Decembrist conspirators of 1825. He codified Russian law.

121 *he said that all the present troubles had started with the Orlovs.* The Orlov family rose to eminence when Grigory Orlov (1734–83) became Catherine the Great's lover. He planned the murder of her husband Peter III, and his brother Aleksey committed the deed (1762).

122 *Bonnets.* Among the ideas and scientific discoveries of the Swiss naturalist and philosopher Charles-Etienne Bonnet (1720–93) was the thesis that the non-existence of the soul can never be proved.

126 *The famous Duport.* Louis Duport (1782–1853), Parisian dancer and choreographer who lived in St Petersburg from 1803 to 1812.

'*Göttingenians*'. Young Russians educated at Göttingen University (opened in 1737), at the time the most important centre for the study of political economy in Europe. They held firm views on the advantages of free labour and competition and were free-thinkers.

127 '*Turgenev's litter*'. Ivan Petrovich Turgenev (1752–1807; unrelated to the writer Ivan Sergeyevich Turgenev) was a prominent Mason of the late eighteenth century and Principal of Moscow University. His sons who survived to adulthood were Aleksey (1781–1803), whose promising career in diplomatic service was cut short by his early death; Aleksandr (1784–1845), writer, historian and a Cabinet Minister, 1810–24, a close friend of the Pushkin family; and Nikolay (1789–1871), pardoned by Nicholas I for his part in the Decembrist Uprising, who was to become well-known as a liberal economist and author of books on the emancipation of the serfs.

Uvarov. Sergey Uvarov (1786–1856), man of letters, a Hellenist, in his youth a member of the Arzamas Society, was President of the Academy of Sciences before becoming an extremely reactionary Minister for Education and chairman of the Central Censorship Board.

127 *Stein.* Heinrich, Baron von Stein (1757–1831), who liberalised the Prussian state but at the same time fostered the dangerous myth of German destiny and aggressive nationalism. When Napoleon insisted upon his dismissal in 1808 he withdrew to Austria. In 1812 he went to St Petersburg and built up the coalition against Napoleon. He became the guiding spirit of the opposition to French imperialism.

Le Moniteur. Paris newspaper published from 1789 as an organ of the Revolutionary government.

128 *war with the Turks.* The Russo-Turkish war of 1806–12, one of the many that took place during the eighteenth and nineteenth centuries.

Zhukovsky. Vasily Zhukovsky (1783–1852), an influential poet and translator, who launched the Romantic movement in Russia with his translation of Gray's *Elegy Written in a Country Church-Yard* (1802), edited the journal *Messenger of Europe*, and was tutor to the future Alexander II. He was to be one of Pushkin's closest friends and his de facto literary executor.

137 *Vestris the Elder.* Gaetano Vestris (1729–1808), famous ballet-dancer and choreographer from Florence.

159 *Empress Catherine I who had sacrificed all her jewellery.* When Peter the Great, at war with the Turks in 1711, found himself surrounded by the enemy, his mistress Catherine (who was of lowly, probably Lithuanian, birth), accompanying him, is supposed to have given up all her jewellery and persuaded other Russians to contribute theirs in order to bribe the Turkish vizier to make peace. This legend helped Peter, who wished to marry her – which he did in 1712 – to present her as the saviour of the motherland.

PART TWO: The Lycée

166 *Prince Potyomkin.* Prince Grigory Potyomkin (1739–91), Catherine the Great's lover and partner in ruling the Russian Empire. In charge of the new lands in the south acquired by conquest, he achieved the annexation of the Crimea.

170 *his lifelong friend Stroganov.* Count Pavel Stroganov was a member of the liberal four-man committee that advised Alexander I in the early years of his reign.

the edict for increased taxation of the nobility. Stipulating a tax for one year only (1810) of 50 kopecks on each registered soul in a landowner's possession.

The Tilsit peace had angered the nobility. Napoleon designed the peace treaty signed at Tilsit in 1807 to cause Russia's international isolation and the reduction of obstacles to French interests. This aim was not achieved, but many Russians

Page

took the Tilsit treaty as a capitulation by Alexander and openly expressed their dissatisfaction with his policy.

178 *Minister Martynov.* Ivan Martynov (1771–1844), translator and journalist, head of the Department of Education.

184 *the young Grand Dukes.* Younger brothers of Alexander I: Nicholas, born in 1796 (nineteen years younger than Alexander) and Michael, born in 1798.

   Marmontel [...] La Harpe [...] Condorcet. Leading idealistic and educational French writers of the pre-Revolutionary period. The epic novelist and historian Jean-François Marmontel (1723–99) was a contributor to the *Encyclopédie.* The poet and critic Jean-François de La Harpe (1739–1803) was the author of a widely read history of literature. The marquis de Condorcet (1743–94), a mathematician and economist, believed in the infinite perfectibility of man.

189 *The Dowager Empress.* Mariya Fyodorovna, widow of Paul I, mother of Alexander I and his brothers and sisters.

193 *Demouth's Hotel.* The oldest and most fashionable hotel in St Petersburg at this time.

195 *Shishkov's Slavonic dictionary.* Admiral Shishkov compiled a number of dictionaries in order to substantiate his theories of the etymology of Russian words from Church Slavonic, in which he linked words of quite different meanings by their forms.

197 *the new-born king of Rome.* François-Charles-Joseph Bonaparte, Napoleon I's son by Marie-Louise. He was proclaimed king of Rome on his birth in 1811 and Emperor Napoleon II on his father's second abdication on 23 June 1815, being formally deposed five days later. He lived throughout his life at Schönbrunn with his grandfather, Emperor Francis II of Austria.

199 *Colencourt's recall.* As a result of his failure to reconcile the disagreements between Napoleon and Alexander I.

217 *Shakhovskoy was ruling the theatre like a tyrant.* Aleksandr Shakhovskoy (1777–1846), dramatist, manager of the Russian theatre in St Petersburg and since 1802 in charge of its repertoire, was a powerful member of the Symposium of Amateurs of the Russian Word and ally of Shishkov.

   an acclaimed opera-singer. Nimfodora Semyonova (1787–1876). Her elder sister was the celebrated tragic actress Yekaterina (1787–1849).

   Bobrov. Yelisey Bobrov (1778–1830) played unsuitable heroic roles before discovering his true talents as a comedian.

221 *Turgenev.* Nikolay Turgenev (1789–1871), brother of the Pushkins' friend Aleksandr Turgenev. Economist: author of a work on taxation theory in which he vehemently put the case against serfdom, he was an ideologist of and participant in the Decembrist movement; abroad during the uprising, he was given the death penalty in absentia.

230 *soon after his arrival in Paris Romme became President of the Convention.* De Boudri seems unaware of the facts. Gilbert (or Charles) Romme (1750–95) did,

Page

however, become a member of the Convention and played a part in the creation
of the Republican calendar. He committed suicide when condemned to death in
the Terror.

240 *Nobody knows for sure if war has started or not.* By the beginning of 1812 war
with France seemed imminent. In February and March Russian army regiments
began to pass through Tsarskoye Selo but it was not until June that Napoleon's
army crossed the Niemen.

241 *Speransky was arrested last night.* On 17 March 1812 Speransky was exiled to
Nizhny Novgorod, and then to Perm, in Eastern Siberia.

243 *he has burnt his paper on the 'Convocation of Deputies'.* In time of war or the
imminence of war Malinovsky's paper on turning Russia into a parliamentary
monarchy might have been considered unpatriotic or treasonous.

263 *The Martinist conspiracy.* 'Martinism', a system of ascetic thought deriving its
name from Saint Martin (c. 316–97), the first great leader of the Western monastic movement, was one of the newly emerged religious and ethical teachings seen
by the rulers of Russia in the wake of the French Revolution as threats to both
the social and the political fabric of the nation. Speransky's fall may have been
connected with his suspected sympathies with and even engagement in Masonry
and mysticism.

267 *'The Senate lay still [...]'.* At the beginning of his reign Alexander I addressed
the issue of the Senate, which had lost all real significance under Paul I. His first
edict concerning the rights of the Senate and the establishment of ministries did
not essentially change the working of the state machine. The status of the Senate
remained the same: its members were appointed or dismissed according to the
Tsar's personal will and lacked the power to control the ministries.

293 *'The journey of Young Anacharsis'.* The abbé Jean-Jacques Barthélemy's *Voyage du
jeune Anacharsis en Grèce* (1788), a recreation of public and private life in Greece
in the sixth century BC.

294 *Diogenes.* Diogenes of Sinope (c.412–323 BC), founder of the Cynic sect, preach-
ing an austere asceticism and self-sufficiency. He became legendary for his
ostentatious disregard of domestic comforts and social niceties. He was said to
have lived in a tub ('like a dog' – the origin of the name 'Cynic') and to have
wandered through Athens by daytime with a lamp 'looking for an honest man'.

296 *Saint-Pierre, Delille and Fontanes.* Three great literary names of the day. Jacques-
Henri Bernardin de Saint-Pierre (1737–1814) was the author of the Rousseauesque
novel *Paul et Virginie* (1787), a story of love untainted by civilisation; the abbé
Jacques Delille (1738–1813), poet and translator, was regarded as the equal of
Virgil and Homer; the eminent university figure Louis de Fontanes (1757–1821)
was a friend of Chateaubriand.

298 *Barclay de Tolly.* Prince Mikhail Barclay de Tolly (1761–1818), Russian military
commander, served throughout the Napoleonic Wars, with an interrupted period
as commander-in-chief of the Russian forces. He has been described as the real

Page

architect of Napoleon's defeat in Russia.

300 *'Young Grandison'*. Title of an abridged French translation of Samuel Richardson's epistolary novel *Sir Charles Grandison* (1754), portraying the perfect gentleman. All Europe was enchanted by the novel.

308 *General Wittgenstein's victory*. Pyotr Wittgenstein (1768–1842) was the general who commanded the victorious Russian First Corps in the early battle at Klyastitsy near Polotsk in Belorussia.

326 *Do you remember Prince Igor's death [...]?* Igor (877–945), grand prince of Kiev and reputedly the son of Ryurik, prince of Novgorod – considered the founder of the dynasty that ruled the lands of Rus until 1598 – was killed by an East Slavic tribe while attempting to extract more than the customary amount of tribute from them.

327 *Aretino's book*. Clearly one of the works of Pietro Aretino (1492–1556) that offended Milton (who called Aretino 'that notorious ribald of Arezzo') as well as those who placed him on the list of forbidden literature in Russia.

329 *Ivan Muravyov-Apostol*. Diplomat and writer (1768–1851), father of the Decembrists Sergey (executed in 1826), Ippolit and Matvey.

330 *Belisarius's cloak*. The legend of the Byzantine general Belisarius (505–65) becoming a blind tramp begging for alms was popular in Russia.

345 *'Oh, memories of the heart! [...]'*. Opening lines of Batyushkov's poem *My Genius* (1815).

356 *Cornelius Nepos*. Roman historian (c.100–c.25 BC), a contemporary of Cicero, Atticus and Catullus. His *Lives of Famous Men* is untrustworthy but written in a clear and elegant style.

357 *His poem about a monk*. A narrative poem of some 400 lines thought to have been written in June or July 1813 when Pushkin was in his fifteenth year. It was published (from the manuscript in the Gorchakov family archives) only in 1928. At the beginning of the poem Pushkin refers to Voltaire and his satirical poem about Joan of Arc.

360 *'The retribution of the skies [...]'*. From *To Dashkov* (1813).

365 *'Betrayals'*. Written between November 1814 and March 1815. Pushkin extols the charms of 'proud Yelena', 'enchanting Yelena' whom he can't forget despite his flings with the young Chloe, Lila and Temira.

366 *Kostrov*. The poet and translator Yermil Kostrov (c. 1750–96) first translated the *Iliad* into Russian, in a version that has stood the test of time.

376 *'To my Friend, a Poet'*. Written at the beginning of 1814. Making playful use of the solemn hexameter, Pushkin tries to persuade his stubborn friend to forsake the vain quest for literary glory and enjoy life.

380 *Aleksandr had written her an epistle [...] He had chosen an epigraph from a French poet*. Written in mid-1813, *To Natalya* is the earliest extant poem of Pushkin's. The epigraph is taken from a satire by Pierre Choderlos de Laclos, author of *Les Liaisons dangereuses*, on Louis XV's love for Mme du Barry.

Page

392 *Bezborodko*. Prince Aleksandr Bezborodko, Catherine the Great's last chief
minister, appointed in 1781.

'Reminiscences in Tsarskoye Selo'. Written in good time for the examination of
8 January 1815, in October–November 1814. In his ode Pushkin refers to the
memorials to Catherine's military victories in the Tsarsoye Selo park, describes
the 1812 campaign, pays tribute to Tsar Alexander as peacemeaker, and calls upon
Zhukovsky, the leading modern (Romantic) poet of the day, to write a sequel to
his patriotic poem *A Bard in the Russian Camp*, written immediately after the
battle of Borodino (1812).

PART THREE: Youth

397 *Karamzin [...] had come to St Petersburg to petition the Tsar for the publication
of his 'History'*. Karamzin had been working on his *History of the Russian State*,
planned in twelve volumes, since 1803. Early in 1816 he arrived in St Petersburg to
show Tsar Alexander the manuscript of the first eight volumes and to seek their
publication.

398 *The Arzamas Society of Unknown Literati*. Founded in 1815 for the purpose of
opposing the Russian Academy and the Symposium of Amateurs of the Russian
Word, the Arzamas Society united the literary reformers led by Karamzin. Its
style parodied the bureaucratic solemnity of the sessions of the Symposium. Its
members included Zhukovsky, Batyushkov, Vyazemsky and Vasily Pushkin; the
future Decembrists Nikolay Turgenev, Nikita Muravyov and General Mikhail
Orlov; and the future reactionary statesmen Uvarov and Bludov. In 1818 the
Society ceased to exist as a result of literary and ideological disagreements.

400 *the Chinese Village*. One of the examples of Catherine the Great's *chinoiserie* built
by the Scottish architect Charles Cameron in the park at Tsarskoye Selo: a score
of chalet-like little houses surrounding a pagoda.

402 *Batyushkov had come [...] to thank him for his epistle*. Batyushkov had seen
Pushkin's poem addressed to him published in a journal. Batyushkov had not
written or published poems during the period of his service as a lieutenant in the
campaigns of 1813 and 1814; in *To Batyushkov* (October 1814) his young admirer
begged him to return to literary activity.

'Only cinders, rubble, and dust-filled air [...]'. From Batyushkov's poem *To
Dashkov* (1813).

404 *the humourless old idiots of the Symposium*. Admiral Shishkov was President of the
Russian Academy, concerned with the preservation of standards in the use of the
Russian language. The Symposium was an informal branch of the Academy. It
was in the satirical tradition of the Arzamas Society that every new member had
to make an inaugural speech in the style of either the Symposium or the Academy.

Page

406 *'Here sleeps a young sage undefiled [...]'.* From Pushkin's poem *Testament to My Friends* (1815).

414 *He had been attending the Aachen Congress.* The congress of the Allied powers on their withdrawal from France, which restored French independence in 1818, had already begun in Aix-la-Chapelle, now renamed Aachen.

421 *'My uneventful days drag slowly by [...]'.* The original first line and the concluding line of Pushkin's poem *Desire* (1816), one of a score of poems written in 1815 and 1816 inspired by Yekaterina Bakunina, sister of a fellow Lycéeist.

422 *Pozharsky.* Dmitry Pozharsky: a militia commander during the Polish-Lithuanian and Swedish invasion of Russia during the Time of Troubles; one of those who drove out the invaders and set up the election of Mikhail Romanov as the new Tsar in 1613.

    'Vladimir the Red Sun'. Vladimir I, the Great (c.956–1015), the first Christian sovereign of Russia, who consolidated the Russian realm from the Baltic to the Ukraine, with Kiev as his capital.

443 *the greatest Tsar, Ivan III.* Ivan III ('the Great'; 1440–1505) shook off the Tatar yoke and was the first to become 'Ruler of all Russia', adopting the two-headed eagle of the Byzantine Empire.

444 *Prince Vladimir Monomakh.* Grand Prince of Kiev, 1113–25. A popular, powerful and enlightened ruler who colonised new territories and founded new towns, including Vladimir, which replaced Kiev as capital of Rus towards the end of the twelfth century.

451 *'Happy he who in his passion [...]'.* Opening of an elegy written in 1816.

453 *Zoya.* Heroine of Pushkin's poem *Bova* discussed with Batyushkov.

454 *Archimandrite Photius.* Pyotr Spassky (1792–1838), fanatical antagonist of the mystically inclined Prince Golitsyn for control of policy within the Russian Orthodox Church.

456 *'A devout wife's soul [...]'.* This epigram, circulated in handwritten copies, is attributed to Pushkin during his exile in the South.

459 *'No mind, no feeling [...]'.* The last three lines of an eight-line epigram by Pushkin on Arakcheyev, written in St Petersburg some time after he left the Lycée and before his exile; its first line reads: *Oppressor of all Russia [...]'.* Arakcheyev's motto on his personal seal is quoted: *'no flatterer – but loyal'.*

467 *Küchlya was to spend ten years in a fortress in solitary confinement.* For his participation in the Decembrist uprising Küchelbecker was sentenced to twenty years in prison, later reduced. He spent two years in solitary confinement in the fortress at Schlüsselburg, and in 1827 was transferred to another fortress in what is now Latvia. He remained in solitary confinement until 1835, when he was exiled to Siberia for the remaining eleven years of his life.

470 *Ivan IV.* 'Ivan the Terrible', Tsar of Russia effectively from 1547 to 1584.

472 *Dmitry Donskoy.* Dmitry Ivanovich (1350–89), Grand Prince of Moscow, who won a major victory over the Mongols at Kulikovo, near the Don, in 1380.

Page

473 *An extraordinary contest began.* Semyonova played the same parts as George, who made her St Petersburg debut in 1808, and in 1809 triumphed in George's presence in one of the French actress's favourite parts. The poet and publisher Gnedich did much to promote the rivalry between the two.

475 *The Minister.* Prince Golitsyn was now Minister of Education.

477 *Griboyedov.* Aleksandr Griboyedov (1795–1829), author of the celebrated verse comedy *Woe from Wit* and a diplomat who was killed by a crowd in Teheran; the subject of Tynyanov's second novel, *The Death of Vazir Mukhtar* (1928).

479 *the Solovetsky Monastery.* Monastery complex on one of the Solovetsky group of islands in the White Sea to the north of Archangel which served as a prison. The Solovetsky monks, faithful servants of the tsar, served as jailers of his political opponents from the sixteenth century. Solitariness, high walls and the harsh climate made imprisonment here unbearable.

the Peter and Paul Fortress. The first building raised in St Petersburg. Originally a fort to protect the town from attack by the Swedes, from 1721 onwards it began to serve as a high security political jail. Among the first prisoners was Peter's own rebellious son Aleksey. Later the list of famous inmates included Dostoyevsky, Gorky, Trotsky and Lenin's elder brother Aleksandr.

481 *Yekaterinoslav.* Today Dnepropetrovsk on the Dnieper. The town was founded by Prince Potyomkin in 1783.

482 *'Ruslan and Lyudmila'.* The work that made Pushkin a national figure, a satirically fantastic verse fairy-tale set in the tenth century in the reign of Prince Vladimir. It was published in August 1820, at the beginning of Pushkin's exile. The famous and enchanting prologue ('Beside the sea a green oak stands') was written later.

484 *Chernomor.* Character inspired by the Russian fairy-tale about a nail-sized dwarf with an arm-length beard, developed under the influence of other Russian and French eighteenth-century fairy-tales.

485 *'And now they mount their mettled horses'.* A quotation from Canto I of *Ruslan and Lyudmila*. Ruslan sets off with three other knights to find the heroine after she has been snatched from the wedding chamber by the evil Chernomor. Her father, Prince Vladimir, offers Lyudmila's hand and half of his domain to the one who brings her home.

487 *Sophie Velho.* Alexander I paid visits to the house of the Court banker, Joseph Velho, in Tsarskoye Selo in order to see his daughter Sophie. On one occasion Pushkin met the Emperor there.

488 *the Caucasus.* Annexed to the Russian Empire in 1793 and in Pushkin's time a volatile area highly hostile to Russian occupation.

the Crimea. Annexed to Russia in 1783; formerly ruled by the Tatar khanate centred in the town of Bakhchisaray.

490 *Theodosia.* The name means 'gift of the gods' in Greek.

he began to write an elegy. In his essay *Nameless Love* (1939) Tynyanov analysed a number of Pushkin's works he thought connected with his 'secret love' for

Katerina Karamzina: the narrative poem *The Fountain of Bakhchisaray* (1822), the dedication to the narrative poem *Poltava* (1828), the lyric poem *On the hills of Georgia* (1829), *Fragments from Onegin's Journey* (1825–30), and others. Tynyanov interpreted numerous mysterious hints and references in Pushkin's poetry in this light, and pointed to certain well-attested moments in the poet's relations with the Karamzins, including the mortally wounded Pushkin's last request to see Katerina. Tynyanov came to a conclusion regarding his life-long fidelity to her that diverged from the prevailing view of Pushkin as an inconstant and unfaithful person, incapable of strong emotions.

491 *'But love's old wounds [...]'*. From the elegy *The light of day has faded* (1820).

Some Early Poems by Pushkin

This selection includes some of the poems that feature in or are concerned with characters in Tynyanov's novel, most of them belonging to the Lycée years. Pushkin's lyric poems are always in regular metre and always rhyme. In translation it is not always possible or desirable to preserve these forms of an original to any degree of closeness, though most of the following translations broadly do.

To My Friend, a Poet is translated by John Dewey; *To a Young Actress* by David and Lyudmila Matthews. These two translations are reprinted (the first slightly revised) from *The Complete Works of Alexander Pushkin*, Volume One: *Lyric Poems: 1813–1820*, Milner and Company, Downham Market, 2001 (www.pushkininenglish.com), by permission of the publisher. *On a Portrait of Chaadayev* is translated by Anna and Christopher Rush. The rest of the following translations are by Antony Wood (© Antony Wood 2007).

All verse included in the novel is translated by Anna and Christopher Rush and Antony Wood.

To a Young Beauty who Took Snuff

How can this be? Not roses, Cupid's flower,
      Tulips at their proud best,
Fragrant jasmine, or lily of the valley,
      The flowers you loved, wore daily
        Upon your marble breast –
Oh my Lucile, how changeable you are . . .
You used to sniff the morning bloom's aroma –
      Now it's that dire green weed
      Which fashion's restless need
Has artfully transformed to fine grey powder!
Let some Marburg professor with snowy hair,
      Hunched in his high old chair,
His awesome mind applied to Latin prose,
Take, in a coughing fit, his panacea
And stuff it up his venerable nose;
Let some young mustachioed dragoon
      Viewing the crimson dawn,
      Still dreaming, fill his room
With thick grey smoke from his beloved meerschaum;
Let some old beauty who has lost her bloom,
Retired from love, forsaken by the graces,
Her body quite without unwrinkled places –
All she has left propped up with stays and trusses –
      Let her pray, and yawn, and huff
And find, in one good pinch, unfailing respite; –
But if, my beauty! . . . *you* are so fond of it . . .
If I – the power of fancy! – *were* the stuff,
      And your snuffbox closed on me . . .
      And you took a pinch of me
In those soft fingers – rapture! Down I'd spill
      Inside your silken dress,
      Over your smooth white breast,
      I'd spill and spill until . . .
But no, an empty dream. That happiness
Isn't for me. Fate is unkind. Enough!
      . . . Oh if only I *could* be that snuff!

April 1814

From To My Friend, a Poet

[...]
Trust me, Ariste, forswear the scribe's impedimenta,
Forget those streams and woods, drear tombs that none would enter,
And do not burn with love in unimpassioned song;
Descend from dizzy heights, before you fall headlong!
Already poets are, without you, ten a penny;
Once published, they are soon forgotten by the many.
For even now, perhaps, far from the crowd's hulloos,
And swearing vows eternal to his witless muse,
A second father of a new *Telemakhida*,
Ensconced beneath Minerva's shield, awaits a reader.
Beware the fate of bards whose verses, all hot air,
By their sheer bulk are sure to drive us to despair!
[...]

But what? You knit your brow, preparing a riposte;
'It's pointless,' you will say; 'on me your words are lost.
When once my mind is set, I hold to my position;
Know that the die is cast: the lyre's my firm ambition.
Let all the world find fault or judge me as it will;
Be angry, shout or curse – a poet I am still.'
Ariste, he is no poet who can rhyme by number,
Whose scratching quills of ream on ream make ink-stained lumber.
To write good verse is hard; far easier, no doubt,
It was for Wittgenstein to put the French to rout.
Derzhavin, Lomonosov, Dmitriyev – summation
Of genius immortal, honour of our nation –
Engender common sense and teach us wisdom's lore;
And yet how many books, once born, are seen no more!
Rifmatov's, Grafov's works – all sounding brass and rumble –
On Glazunov's top shelves with weighty Bibrus crumble;
None will remember them, none read such futile verse,
And on them is impressed the stamp of Phoebus' curse.

But let's assume that you climb Pindus without falling
And justly earn your title to the poet's calling;
Then all will read your works with pleasure most profound.
But do you think that countless riches will abound
Because you are a poet? That you'll sup the nectar
Of constant revenue as freelance tax-collector?
That you'll have iron chests with golden coins replete

And like a sybarite do naught but sleep and eat?
No writers are as rich, dear friend, as you conjecture;
Fate grants to them no pile of marbled architecture,
Nor coffers fit to burst with coins of purest gold;
Earth hovels, garrets high: these are, if truth be told,
The stately halls and palaces in which they've flourished.
While all praise poets, only journals keep them nourished,
And Fortune's rolling wheel will always pass them by;
Born naked, a Rousseau must also naked die *[. . .]*

Early 1814

From Reminiscences in Tsarskoye Selo

[...]

Where are you, Moscow of a hundred cupolas,
            Jewel of our fatherland?
        The vista of a majestic city
            Is now replaced by ruins.
How cruel to Russian eyes, your stricken face, O Moscow!
        The palaces of tsars and the great have vanished,
        Fire has swallowed all. The towers are blackened,
            The mansions of the rich laid low.

            In the homes of opulence,
            The shady groves and gardens
    Once thick with fragrant myrtles and the trembling lime,
            Now all is cinders, ash and dust.
    In the quiet hours of a lovely summer evening
            No murmur of merriment is heard,
No lamps are seen along the river, no lighted groves,
            All is silent, dead.

    But, mother of Russian cities, take comfort now,
            Observe the invader's fate.
        The hand of God the Avenger
        Has seized him by the arrogant neck.
    Behold him flee, he dares not look behind him;
        His blood a ceaseless river in the snow,
            Cut from the rear by the Russian sword,
He flees, and in the dark of night meets hunger and death.

[...]

October–December 1814

To a Young Actress

You're no successor to Cléronne;
The Lord of Pindus did not scroll
His law for you. To tell the truth,
The gods sent you a minor role.
Your voice, the movements of your frame,
Those glances from your staring eyes
Do not deserve, I must be frank,
The praise they shout with loud surprise.
Your fate dealt you a cruel hand
When it allotted you your place –
A third-rate actress, Chloe dear!
But still you have a pretty face.
You always manage peals of laughter,
Lovers long for your caress
And so before you lies the crown.
I can't deny you your success.

You charm the audience with your spell,
Your voice to cadence seems immune.
Immobile, standing on the stage,
You sing – but mostly out of tune.
And we, with eager, zealous hands
Clap loudly as we can. They shout:
'Bravo! Bravissimo! What skill!
You're popular with them, no doubt.
No whistles, jeers or savage wit;
To your sweet charms they all submit.

And when, with awkward gaucherie
Upon your breast you fold your arms
Then raise and fold them back again,
Displaying coy and bashful charms;
When you assure the young Milon
That you're in love, and soothe his fears
Without much feeling, babbling on,
Then automatically shed tears;
And when you fall into your chair
With sighs so awfully anodyne,
Blushing, almost out of breath,
They whisper: 'Ah! My God! How fine!'
We would have hissed another off,
But beauty clouds our sanity.
Dear Chloe! See, the wise men lied:
Not all in life is vanity.

Bewitch us, Chloe, with your looks.
Your lover's blest in heaven above,
Who stands before you tenderly
And boldly sings you songs of love.
In verse or prose upon the stage
He worships you and humbly bows.
What answer would you give him now?
You would not dare to break your vows.
Ah! Blessèd is he who can forget
His role with the actress he caressed!
He'll squeeze her hand, and in the wings
He'll hope to find himself more blessed.

May–September 1815

The Rose

Where is our rose?
Why so forlorn?
Blown is the rose,
Child of the morn …
Do not say:
So youth must pass!
Do not say:
And happiness!
Say to the flower:
*Ah, what a pity
Your time is over …*
And point to the lily.

?1815

To Baroness M. A. Delvig

I am in my seventeenth year, and you are eight.
Some time ago I was eight years old myself;
That time has long since passed. – It is my fate,
For better or worse, to be a poet, God help!
We can't take back what we've already had,
I am already old, and I admit it.

Belief is all we have that can defend us.
Now you're a child, like Cupid, and as pretty:
When you have got to my age, you'll be Venus.
  And if by then I haven't died,
  By the almighty will of Zeus,
  And if I'm able, still, to write –
  I'll write you, my dear baroness,
  A madrigal in Latin taste:
  It will astound, but not by art;
  It won't abound with well-turned praise –
  It will be written from the heart!
  So: – 'For the sake of your bright eyes,
  O baroness, those glittering balls
  When we would gaze at you with sighs –
  One glance, I beg you, of those eyes
  For all my previous madrigals.'
  And when young Cupid and great Hymen
  In my adorable Maria
  Both greet a beautiful young woman –
  Shall I, concluding my career,
  Succeed with an epithalamion?

(?)December 1815

Desire

I weep, and tears are comforting to me;
I do not speak – my tears cannot be heard,
And in the very aching of my heart
I find I have a bitter remedy.
Empty vision of life – I've had enough!
Away, I call on you to disappear!
The torment of my love I hold most dear;
Oh let me die, but let me die in love!

1816

To Chaadayev

The falsities of love and hope,
Of quiet glory, are outworn;
Those fantasies of childish scope
Have vanished as the mist of dawn.
But still we burn with fierce obsession,
Impatience overflows our soul;
Beneath the yoke of dire oppression
We listen for our country's call.
In hope and torment we await
The sacred moment of first freedom,
As lovers, languishing, await
The longed-for moment of first meeting.
And while we thirst for liberty
And live for nobleness of mind,
So let our country's legacy
Be passion of the highest kind!
Believe, my friend: the star of wonder
Shall shine, the star of destiny;
Russia will one day wake from slumber
And grave our names, when she has risen,
Upon the shards of despotism!

1818

On a Portrait of Chaadayev

By one of Heaven's high decrees
Born to the shackles of the Tsar,
In Rome he'd have been a Brutus, in Greece, a Pericles,
But here he's only a hussar.

Between 1818 and 1820

The light of day has faded,
The dark blue sea is swallowed by the mists of night.
    Blow to me, blow to me, willing breeze,
    Move beneath me, darkly brooding ocean.
    I see the far-off shore ahead of me,
    The enchanted regions of the midday lands;
    I yearn towards them, rapt in memories ...
Feelings are roused, and tears; my soul quickens, then cools;
    I am surrounded by familiar dreams,
        And all the mad love of the past,
    And all I suffered, everything dear to me,
    The cruel deceits of my desires and hopes ...
        Blow to me, blow to me, willing breeze,
    Move beneath me, darkly brooding ocean.
    Fly, my good ship, take me to unknown lands,
    Follow the whims of indiscriminate seas,
        But not to those sad shores,
    My country, where first passions flamed,
    Where the gentle muses smiled to me in secret,
        Where my youth was spent and lost in storms,
    Where light-winged joys betrayed my heart to suffering.
        In search of new experiences
    I have fled from you, the country of my birth,
    I have fled from you, the devotees of pleasure,
The momentary friends of momentary youth;
    And you, my confidantes in aberration,
To whom I sacrificed, indifferently, myself,
Peace of mind and glory, life and liberty –
    You are forgotten too, my young betrayers,
    Secret companions of my golden spring,
    You are forgotten too ... But love's old wounds,
    The old deep wounds of love – nothing can heal ...
        Blow to me, blow to me, willing breeze,
    Move beneath me, darkly brooding ocean.

September 1820